NOVELS BY JANE McILVAINE McCLARY
Maggie Royal
A Portion for Foxes

MAGGIE ROYAL

A NOVEL BY

Jane McIlvaine McClary

SIMON AND SCHUSTER · NEW YORK

This novel is a work of fiction. Names, characters, places and incidents are either the product of the author's imagination or used fictitiously. Any resemblance to actual events or locales or persons, living or dead, is entirely coincidental.

10   9   8   7   6   5   4   3   2   1

Library of Congress Cataloging in Publication Data

McClary, Jane McIlvaine.
   Maggie Royal

   I. Title.
PS3563.A2612M3   813'.54   81-5339
ISBN 0-671-24968-1   AACR2

The song "I Look to the Eas'—and I Look to the Wes'," copyright © 1969 by the Atlanta Chamber of Commerce, from The Lost Legacy of Georgia's Golden Isles by Betsy Fancher. Reprinted by permission of Doubleday & Company, Inc.

Excerpt from "the Bear" in Go Down, Moses by William Faulkner appears by courtesy of Random House, Inc.

For My Family—
Nelson, my husband
Steve, my first son
Penelope, my daughter-in-law
Christopher, my second son
And in memory of
my daughter, Mia

God created man and He created the world for him to live in; I reckon He created the kind of world He would have wanted to live in if He had been a man— the ground to walk on, the Big Woods, the trees and the water, and the game to live in it. And maybe He didn't put the desire to hunt and kill game in man, but I reckon He knew it was going to be there, that man was going to teach himself that, since he wasn't quite God yet. So I reckon He foreknew man would follow and kill the game. I believe He said, so be it. I reckon He even foresaw the end. But He said, I will give him his chance, I will give him warning and foreknowledge too, along with the desire to follow and the power to slay. The woods and fields he ravages and the game he devastates will be the consequence and signature of his crime and guilt, and his punishment.

—WILLIAM FAULKNER, "The Bear"

BOOK ONE

WASHINGTON
1950

· I ·

"Outrageous!" Warren snorted. He handed her the morning paper across the breakfast table. "How dare he exhibit your portrait without permission?"

"Warren, what are you talking about?"

"See for yourself. There, on the front page of the second section."

Maggie Royal stared in disbelief. A young girl, wearing a white dress. Long hair, dark as the forest, streamed behind her. Her arms stretched before her, each finger rigid and distinct, with the tension of desire. Her head was flung back and her face was filled with wildness and inner passion.

Live oaks draped in moss served as background. They were half-obscured by a silvery mist that seemed to writhe and float until she could almost feel and taste it, sweeping in from the sea. Cold and flavored with salt, stinging her eyes as she sat there in her Washington dining room so many miles, so many years away.

"Miss Maggie Royal" read the caption. "One of the Stark paintings on display at the Off Beat Gallery in Georgetown. The paintings of Jared Stark of Stark Island, Georgia, are being shown to record crowds. They have been described as haunting, ghostly, impressionistic, and individualistic. *Miss Maggie Royal* is one of the artist's early portraits, painted on his island home. The model was 'a cousin, as wild and shy as one of the island deer. I wanted to show the transition from child to woman,' Stark says, 'that other-world quality, an innocence and a certain impassioned wonder that was always with her. I tried to show it in her hands, reaching out to life.' "

It was suddenly very quiet, the only sound that of Thomas, the butler, moving about in the pantry.

Maggie Royal became aware of her husband's voice.

"Miss Maggie Royal, indeed!" He paused for an instant, holding the paper up in order to study the picture. She couldn't tell whether there was jealousy or disparagement in his voice, but the way he used her childhood name grated on her ear. He knew the name belonged to the years before she had known him, that it was what she had been called on the Georgia island that had been home, and that only those who had known her there used the familiar form.

Warren looked up. "It doesn't do you justice, Magdalena. If it hadn't been for your childhood name, I wouldn't have noticed it. You know I prefer a more stylized form of painting."

She thought of the portrait of Warren that hung over the fireplace in the living room. He had commissioned his old friend Bill Draper to do it. It showed him sitting behind a gleaming mahogany desk, his hands clasped in front of him. It was solid and sincere and unmistakably Warren Chadwick, looking every pinstriped inch a future ambassador.

He had on the same suit now, or maybe it was one of the half-dozen he'd had tailored for him the last time they were in London. Warren's clothes were as restrained as his movements or his speech. His suits were hung in mothproof bags in his closet. Some plain, others with pinstripes, but all either navy blue or oxford gray. He wore them with blue or white shirts from Turnbull & Asser and a folded monogrammed white linen handkerchief in his left-hand breast pocket. Once she bought him a pink shirt from Garfinckel's to take on a Caribbean cruise, but when she asked him to wear it, he said he had given it to Thomas.

His ties were from Sulka, navy with a red stripe predominating. His shoes were from Lobb in London, and Thomas saw that they were always highly polished. And she had trained Mrs. Meadows, the laundress, to wash his close-ribbed navy and black socks by hand and to for God's sake put the ones that matched back together.

Warren's speeches were as carefully thought out as his wardrobe. He never spoke without knowing beforehand what he was going to say, and he hated waste and disorder in words or actions. She had been fortunate in being able to persuade Thomas to come with them when they left London. All her friends said he was a gem, the perfect gentleman's gentleman, straight from the pages of the *Forsyte Saga* or P. G. Wodehouse. And Maria, the Portuguese cook, had finally learned not to fry everything in olive oil. Although she had never mastered the art of Cook Ada's beaten biscuits, her "flaky puffs" were almost as good. Now that the restoration of the house was completed to Warren's satisfaction, back to its eighteenth-century original, but with all modern appliances, it ran smoothly and well. Thomas and Maria were competent to cope with the little dinners for eight Warren called zoo dinners, couples from the various embassies or government agencies who knew how to talk well. That reminded her that cousin Adele was coming from Charlottesville for the night. That meant they'd be up late with much "she-she" talk—the Gullah word for feminine chitchat.

"Magdalena," Warren said sharply. "You're not listening. I asked you how much you think your cousin wants for the painting."

"I wouldn't have the faintest idea." Her voice sounded to her as if it were coming from a great distance. "You know I haven't seen Jared since England. The war . . ."

"But you must know the painting."

She shook her head. "Jared hadn't begun to paint seriously then. He must have done it later . . . when he returned . . ."

"You mean he painted it from memory?"

It was becoming difficult to speak. "Yes," she answered quickly, "from memory, from when we were growing up on the island."

"Would you like to visit the island again?"

"No," she replied vehemently. "I wouldn't."

She heard the car pulling up at the front door. It must be time for him to leave for his nine-o'clock briefing with the Secretary. She wished he would go and not pursue the subject further.

"Come, now," Warren persisted, the way he did when posed with a diplomatic problem, refusing to give up, no matter how hopeless the chance of agreement might seem at the time. "Come, now," he repeated, leaning forward across the table in a conciliatory fashion. "What is the status of your property there? Is it mortgaged? What have you done about taxes?"

"There you go, asking me all those masculine questions." She poured herself another cup of coffee. "You've always said I was hopeless about money. I was brought up to believe it wasn't nice to discuss it. Somehow it was always there, like the Spanish moss and the clouds in the sky. It never occurred to me that it would ever run out." She took a deep breath. "Warren, I've explained all this before. For tax purposes and family reasons, Gramma willed Stark Island to her descendants in a very complicated way. Each of her children inherited a different part of the property, to be passed on to the next of kin, surviving husband or wife, in turn to be passed on to their descendants.

"Jared inherited Great Oak. When Gramma died, we were about to get into the war. The aunts and their husbands all had other places. Great-Aunt Meg and Aunt Amy moved to the nursing home in Starksville. The Long Point Negroes left for war jobs on the mainland. Old Newt stayed on as caretaker, but house and farm were going to ruin." Defiantly she reached for a cigarette.

"You know you shouldn't smoke," Warren said.

"Dammit, Warren; just one with coffee."

"All right, go on."

"The Long Point house had been burned by the Klan in retaliation for Jared's father's pro-Negro activities. Jared's sister, Susan, married Sparrow and moved to Cambridge, and his mother went to live with them." She ground out her cigarette and put her hands in her lap to control their trembling. "We all thought Jared died when his plane went down over France. When I heard he was alive, I didn't, I couldn't, see him." She forced herself to look at Warren. "I was married to you. I went to my lawyer and had him draw up a paper to the effect that Jared could have control of my share of the property as long as he maintained Great Oak and protected the island's natural resources."

13

"That reminds me." Warren took off his reading glasses and began polishing them with his handkerchief. "I invited the senator from Georgia to dinner tonight. His wife's away."

"Warren, he's such a dreadful old bore. And Adele is coming up from Charlottesville."

"I know," Warren said apologetically. "But I thought you might be interested in hearing about your island. I saw him at the Metropolitan Club the other day. He told me several land speculators are fighting over it. He said most of the heirs have agreed to sell out. All but your cousin. The Senator says he shoots at everybody who comes ashore."

"The island is Jared's life," Maggie Royal said.

"Well, I don't see how he can hang on to it," Warren answered emphatically. "Some fifteen hundred acres and fifteen miles of beach as his own private preserve! Not in this day and age. Magdalena, I really think you should go down and see what is happening. Talk some sense into your cousin. You still have the deed to the land you inherited. By selling, you stand to make a lot of money." He glanced at his watch and frowned. "I'll be late for the Secretary." His face suddenly looked tired, almost vulnerable. "Not too much doing this week. After our do tonight, there's only the Hortons' dinner party Friday. You might cancel that. I find her pushy, and him vulgar. All those locker-room stories. We're due for a weekend with the Greenes at Sea Island. I'll fly down and pick you up. Didn't you tell me that the old golf course had been made into an airstrip?"

By his oblique diplomatic method of negotiation, he was forcing a showdown. "Warren, why do you want me to go back to Stark Island?"

"Because this must be settled between us, before we leave the country, go to another post."

"I've tried to be a good wife," she said defensively.

"You have, indeed," Warren agreed. "In everything but . . ." He paused, as if, for once, he did not know quite how to continue. "I keep thinking of Mr. and Mrs. Hanson."

The Hansons! It was such an odd thought for Warren to have, she almost burst out laughing. Yet she knew what he meant. The farmer and his wife, in that crowded, grubby English country cottage, overrun with children, evacuees, and animals, had exuded love and warmth. Here, they had everything except that intangible life-giving quality.

Thomas stood at the door, holding Warren's black homburg and the silver-handled cane the staff had presented to him when he left the Court of St. James's.

"Mr. Ambassador, the car is waiting."

"Thank you, Thomas," Warren answered, beaming. "But I'm not an Ambassador yet! I still have to be confirmed by the Senate." He looked at his watch. "I'm to appear before the Senate Foreign Relations Committee next week. But first . . ."

"All right, Warren," she put in quickly. His persistence always won out in the end. "I'll write. I doubt if there's a telephone on the island. There never used to be. I'll plan to go next week."

Warren rose, came around the table. He bent over and kissed her on the forehead with that absent air that told her his mind was already focused on the seemingly insurmountable problems that he faced as Deputy Assistant Secretary for European Affairs.

"I'll have Miss Welford get you a plane ticket," he said, returning to the present. "To Atlanta. Isn't that where you change for Starksville? You seem tired, my dear. A change will do you good." Pausing, he turned to face her. "Magdalena, the Senator is on the Foreign Relations Committee." The questioning look on his face sent a pang of guilt through her.

"I know, Warren," she answered. "We'll have a good dinner. The Senator is a dreadful racist and a bore, but I promise to do my best."

His face relaxed. "I know, my dear, you won't let me down."

The words seemed to hang between them, fraught with the draining consciousness of irony.

He took his hat and cane and headed for the door. "No," he said, speaking as though to himself. "You don't look anything like that wild and windblown girl in the painting. Still, I understand the fellow is being talked about. The painting might be a good investment." He set his hat at the correct angle, dignified, as befitted a "hot article" about to be named one of the country's youngest ambassadors, yet with a studied, faintly raffish air, as though to make him seem less formidable, and started down the steps to the limousine, where Austin, their driver, waited, holding open the rear door.

"Will you be needing the car this morning, Mrs. Chadwick?" Austin asked, looking up at her standing in the doorway.

She shook her head. "No, thank you, Austin. I have just a few errands on Wisconsin. I'll walk."

"In that case, I'll have the car serviced. It's due for an oil change," Austin said, tipping his cap.

She stood looking after the long black car as it drove slowly away. It was one of those Washington days in early March that, after the long, raw days of winter, extends the hope of eventual spring, giving a sense of light and air and a lift in spirits. Rays of sun caused the polished knockers on the doors along the street to shine. A young man recently appointed a presidential assistant walked past. He was carrying a briefcase, his forehead furrowed in thought. A young girl holding books with a belt tied around them came out of another doorway. She waved good-bye to her mother at a second-floor window and began running to catch the bus at the corner.

Maggie Royal thought of what Warren had said, that Jared's painting would be a good investment. Is that all I am to you, Warren? Well, she told herself, she'd been a good one. The latest "report card," rating her for her performance as a foreign-service wife, had increased

Warren's standing in the State Department, adding to his chances of soon being named an ambasssador. Thanks to Gramma, she had learned to swerve away from dangerous or controversial subjects at dinner parties the way a horse swerved away from a difficult fence. Over the years she had disciplined herself to reserve her own opinion in the face of the most outrageous statements, to steer the conversation to easy, safe channels.

A chill breeze stirred the leaves of the ginkgo tree in front of the house. She reminded herself to have Horace, their yardman, cut down the tree before its mating season released the unpleasant odor that caused Warren to hold his handkerchief at his nose whenever he went in or out of the house.

Slowly she closed the door, shutting out the bright March morning. The sun coming through the arched fanlight caught her reflection in the elaborately carved Chippendale mirror. Her skin, kept soft with weekly facials at Arden's, still carried a hint of tan from their week in Jamaica at the Round Hill Club. She had learned the art of makeup, the eyeliner and shadow to deepen the blue-violet color of her eyes, the touch of rouge to highlight the Stark cheekbones, the right amount of lipstick. The wild, unruly hair, coarse as a horse's mane, was drawn back smoothly into a neat chignon, but no amount of eyeliner and mascara could recapture the mood of expectancy and love of living of the girl in the painting.

She steadied herself against the mahogany drop-leaf table.

You knew someday you'd have to go back, she told herself. You knew, when you heard that Jared was alive, that you would have to face that other self, that long and leggy, silly, trusting *enfant de nature* known as Maggie Royal, and bury her, once and for all.

She went into what Warren called her writing room. "You must have a place to write, Magdalena," he had said when they bought the house and began redoing it.

"But I'm not writing," she had said.

"Never mind; you will again, once we're settled."

He had brought her the modern typewriter resting on the stand beside the Queen Anne desk. She tried it once, but found it too sophisticated. Now, whenever she typed lists for dinner parties or benefits, or wrote letters to Adele, she used the battered old portable that had been through the London blitz.

The room was her favorite. It was the only one in the house that seemed lived in. The rest of the rooms were set pieces, filled with fine antiques and the art treasures that Warren had collected on his travels.

A photograph of Warren shaking hands with President Roosevelt at Yalta stood in a silver frame on her desk. It showed Warren as he had looked when they were married in 1944, tall, distinguished, a controlled man, one of taste and even temperament.

She picked up the porcelain of a warbler in a magnolia bloom which he had given her for Christmas. "A collector's item," he had said then. Like myself, she thought bitterly, another possession. Good for standing in receiving lines or sitting at the head of long, well-appointed dinner tables and making the right conversation, or making sure food is of gourmet caliber, served piping hot, the seating according to protocol.

A photo album and pile of new magazines lay on the George III oval Pembroke table. She opened the album at random. There were the coming-out pictures that Sparrow's friend Mac Malloy had taken on the island for "*Life* Goes to a Party"—Gramma, the aunts, Constance, Adele, and herself, all in one picture, together in the receiving line at the last gala at Great Oak. She turned to others, less professional—of Gramma seated on the veranda in one of her flowing white gowns, pouring tea; of Uncle Oomlot, tall and spare in his perfectly cut jodhpurs and incongruous deerstalker hat; of Newt and Cook Ada by the kitchen doorway; and Sapelo, Jasper, and Jazzbo with the horses. There was a lovely drawing of her mare, Azilia, which Jared had sketched for her, but there were no photographs of Jared—only the empty pages from which she had torn the snapshots taken on the island and in England.

No self-pity, she had told herself. The madness was over, the dream ended, shot down in flames.

That file is closed.

Now Warren was forcing her to reopen it. Re-examine the memories, return to Stark Island and the past; the sense of being torn, first one way, then another, was reasserting itself. As if to reanchor herself in the mainstream of her present life, she picked up her engagement book.

There, she told herself as she looked at the numerous entries, is the reason why I no longer write. Page after page of luncheons, teas, dinners, benefits, and functions for visiting dignitaries. Speeches at the Press Club and Pan American Union. The Dancing Class at the Sulgrave Club, weekends in Middleburg during the foxhunting season, and for the spring race meets.

She glanced at the day's notations: a luncheon meeting to make plans for the Heart Ball, a fitting at Dorcas Hardin, two cocktail parties, and dinner at home. Adele was in town for a Junior League meeting. She was due to arrive in time for tea, and to spend the night. She must cancel the cocktail parties—it would give them more time to talk—and ask Maria to make the "flaky puffs" Adele loved.

Maria was tall and angular, with strong, broad hands from hauling fishnets on the beaches of her native Algarve. The faint lines of a black mustache, characteristic of many Portuguese women, decorated her upper lip. She had come to the residence in Lisbon one day to sell her sardines and collapsed on the doorstep. The embassy doctor had been called and had diagnosed tuberculosis, a disease common in Portugal. Warren had paid for her to remain in a sanatorium until she was pronounced well. She had come to work for Maggie Royal as a waitress, and been only too happy to follow her back to the States. She asked time off only to go to mass, and never minded how many dinner parties she had to cook for. She was "a treasure," Maggie Royal's maidless friends said enviously; devoted to "A senhora," as Maggie Royal was to her.

Now she stood by Maggie Royal's desk waiting for her market list to be checked and for the day's orders.

"*Mas gateous, por favor,*" Maggie Royal said, speaking her mixture of Portuguese and Spanish.

"*Sim,* madam," Maria replied, and they both laughed.

At one of her first dinner parties, when she had just begun to study the difficult language, Maggie Royal had asked for "*Mas gateous,*" thinking she was asking for more cakes. Instead, she had asked Maria in Portuguese for "more cats, please."

Now it was a standing joke between them, and when Maggie Royal said, "*Mas gateous,*" Maria understood she was to bake a cake.

"And flaky puffs," Maggie Royal said. "My cousin, Mrs. Trimble, will be here in time for tea."

They discussed the menu for dinner, and Maggie Royal reminded Maria to order from Magruder's the Canadian bacon that Warren liked for breakfast.

"*Sim, senhora.*" Maria turned to leave. At the door she paused. "Beg pardon, *senhora.* I forget to tell you. Thomas was busy serving breakfast, so I answer. A gentleman called. I know you no like to be disturbed at mealtime."

"Did you get his name?" Maggie Royal asked.

"No. Sorry."

"Really, Maria!" Maggie Royal spoke with a kind of violence that caused the cook to glance at her in startled surprise. "How many times have I told you to write down names and telephone numbers? It could be important."

Maria bowed her head and twisted the folds of her gingham skirt with her large, reddened hands. "I beg pardon, madam," she said stiffly. "Maybe the *senhora* would like me to leave?"

"Oh, Maria." Maggie Royal's icy control collapsed. She reached out her hands helplessly, like a child in a gesture of contrition. "Maria, forgive me. You know Mr. Chadwick and I couldn't get along without you. Maria, you're family."

"Maybe the *senhora* is tired," Maria said, faintly mollified. "A vacation, perhaps?"

Maggie Royal's shoulders sagged. What had possessed her to speak to her beloved Maria in such a manner? "Yes, Maria," she admitted. "I am tired. Doing the house has taken such a long time." She stood up, smiling, and crossed the room. "Maria, don't ever leave me." She put her arms around Maria's sturdy shoulders. "I wouldn't know how to cope without you."

As soon as she entered the gallery, Maggie Royal wished she hadn't come. The moment she saw the paintings on display, she knew that what she had fought against for so long was happening. Jared and the island were being resurrected from that dark place in her subconscious where she thought them buried.

Her painting—she already thought of it as hers—was hung in the most conspicuous place, facing the entrance. Next to it was one of Jared's wife, Cindy Lou. Whoever hung the show couldn't have guessed the irony. There, side by side, were Jared's women. So utterly unlike. Herself, Maggie Royal, long legs and flat boy's body in the plain white Worth dress she'd worn at her coming-out party, reaching eagerly toward the future. Cindy Lou seated on the bench in the gazebo, a Southern belle from the top of her golden head to the tips of the open-toed sandals she always wore, to show off the small, high-arched feet she was so proud of. Her heart-shaped face and half-smile looked deceptively open and innocent until one looked closely and saw the merciless glitter in her round blue eyes.

A striking profile of Jared's mother, sitting at her loom by the hearthside of the Long Point house, her black hair falling in a single braid to her waist.

Jared's father, Lawyer Stark, bent over a book, a pencil tucked behind his ear. There was an ache in her throat as she gazed at the fine, familiar features, the aquiline nose, the hands with long, tapered fingers so like his son's.

There was Newt, the butler in Gramma's day, dark and dignified in his black cloth livery and white cotton gloves. Old Ada, the cook, her head wrapped in a red kerchief, taking her ease outside the basement kitchen, while newcomer Ada, the kitchen maid, sat on the step peeling potatoes. Joe-Ali fishing from his bateau with his cast net. Some of the Long Point Negroes clearing brush in the woods. All were vividly alive, drawn with the same haunting quality, as if the artist had laid bare their innermost yearnings.

In a room to the side were some animal studies. Jared's dogs, Rufus and Ranter; a striking pencil sketch of King, his Appaloosa stallion; island deer behind the dunes; and Old Ugly, the alligator, emerging from his black pool. There were landscapes. The ruins of the mission the Spaniards built; the watchtower guarding the pirates' cove; the family burial ground, with its mossy slanting stones inside the gray wall of tabby, shells held together with cement made from sand and burned oyster shells.

Almost covering a large expanse of wall was Great Oak itself, painted in moonlight. The great gnarled lumpy, low-slung oaks seemed to sway in dancing rhythms in a dreamlike world, their hanging moss like dark feathers. In the painting they were no longer friendly, not the "welcoming trees" loved and remembered from her childhood. Nor was there any candlelight flickering from behind the windows of the great towered and turreted house. The tower and the myriad chimneys rose against a black-purple sky, the color of the grapes in the ancient arbor.

She stood looking at it for so long it seemed that the cloud halfway across the moon moved, darkening the canvas until the house became a ghostly sepulcher. It was only then that she noticed that the roof was gone. Her cousin Jared had painted an empty shell.

"Maggie Royal!"

She whirled around. Sparrow McKinney was planted squarely in front of her, beaming. She stared at him, spellbound. He was a little portlier perhaps, but with the same roundish face and sandy hair that wouldn't stay in place. His suit coat was creased and his tie askew, but behind his thick glasses his brown eyes gleamed with kindness and quick intelligence.

"Sparrow! Oh, Sparrow!" She flung her arms around his neck, greeting him as if they were meeting on the island at the beginning of vacation. "Sparrow, how wonderful to see you!"

"And to see *you,* Maggie Royal. Lovely as ever."

"Why didn't you let me know you were coming?"

"I didn't know until yesterday when I could see the people at the Department of the Interior. I called your house and the maid said you were busy. I thought I might find you here." He glanced past her at the painting of Great Oak. "Susan wanted me to see the exhibition."

"Oh, Sparrow, how is she?"

"The same," he replied softly. "Not beautiful, striking . . . the way you are." He broke off, embarrassed.

"But beautiful inside," she said quickly, "and warm and wonderful and kind . . . so kind . . ."

"Yes." He nodded gratefully. "Fine and brave and uncomplaining."

"She still can't walk?"

He shook his head. "We've tried everything. Every kind of operation and therapy. Nothing's worked. Still . . . we have a good life, Maggie Royal. We're happy."

"I can tell that from looking at you," Maggie Royal said softly. She looked away, at the people starting to fill the gallery.

Two women in fur capes stood before the Great Oak painting.

"I shouldn't say this," one said confidentially. "But I really do prefer Grandma Moses!"

"If you ask me," her friend said, "that's a horrible house. All that's lacking are ravens!"

"Will you have lunch with me?" Sparrow was saying. "I don't have to be at Interior till two."

She glanced at her watch. Noon. She could call and cancel the fitting and postpone lunch.

"Sparrow, I'd love to. Just let me telephone . . ." She hesitated and then smiled. "Sparrow, have dinner with us and stay the night. Adele is coming. It would be such fun. We haven't seen each other for ages. She'll be thrilled when she hears you're here."

"I don't like to be away from Susan overnight, but there are some things about the island we need to discuss. I'll see if Mrs. Weatherell, our housekeeper, can stay till I get back."

They went to an insignificant place on Wisconsin Avenue, where it was possible to get a table without a reservation. At noon the room was almost empty. Sparrow ordered beer for himself and a dry sherry for Maggie Royal.

"Tell me what you thought of the paintings," she asked when the drinks had been served.

"They do bring back the island, don't they? They're the first ones he did when he came back home."

"You mean there are others?"

Sparrow's face became serious. It was a moment or two before he spoke. "Yes, but very different. Much more abstract. More violent. Jared's entire style has changed, just as he has."

"I thought he might be here," Maggie Royal said carefully. "For the opening of the exhibition." She found a package of cigarettes in her Phelps shoulder bag and took out one.

"Both Susan and his mother tried to get him to come up and visit us," Sparrow said, leaning forward to light her cigarette. "He refuses to leave the island. Only goes to the mainland for supplies; I flew down." Sparrow paused and then added slowly, "He wasn't terribly pleased to see me."

"You're his brother-in-law!" Maggie Royal exclaimed, shocked. "Practically his oldest friend."

Susan wrote to him about letting the Park Service have her share of the Long Point land. "You knew about Mr. Stark's and Joe-Ali's deaths? The burning of the Long Point house?"

Maggie Royal nodded. "Adele wrote me. It must have been terrible for Jared when he returned to the island and found out."

"Yes," Sparrow agreed shortly. "He's bitter. It's as if everything— Harvard, the Lincoln Brigade, and Spain, England, the war—had been in vain. His idealism, his flair, his daring, all seem to have gone. I think the tragedy of his father's death, the stupidity of his murder, broke him. His passion, everything that was alive about him, has turned into rage." Sparrow drank some beer and continued carefully, "You knew that Jared volunteered for a unique and dangerous mission. In July 1944 an air unit was formed to attack German V-1 and V-2 launching sites. Jared refused leave to take on this assignment." Sparrow took another swallow of beer. "I'm not sure of the details. All I know is that something went wrong and Jared was forced to bail out over enemy-held territory. One leg was broken. It was never set right. I gather he's in pain most of the time."

Maggie Royal did not realize that her fists in her lap were clenched until Sparrow stopped speaking. She let out her breath and unfolded her left hand, where her diamond engagement ring had left a red mark. For a moment she stared at it, reliving the long wait for Jared, and finally the news . . . the shock and horror and then the curious peace that had come over her when she had thought that at long last the anguish and indecision were past. Now it was as though Sparrow's words were slowly unthawing a part of herself that had long been frozen, leaving her once again young and vulnerable and torn.

"Shall we order?" She heard Sparrow ask, and forced herself back to the present.

They ordered hamburgers. Sparrow looked across the table at Maggie Royal, finding it hard to equate the elegant woman before him with the girl Jared had painted. Her figure beneath the perfectly cut suit was as slender as he remembered it. There were the classic Stark features: the distinctive nose and high arched brows, the long, swanlike Modigliani neck. She is beautiful, he thought objectively, but she had not reached the pinnacle of beauty he had once imagined she would. For the marvelous eyes, the color of the petals of the spring violets the flower vendors were beginning to sell on the street corners, held the sadness of a woman unsatisfied. And her mouth, vivid and red in contrast to her thick dark hair, no longer laughed.

Maggie Royal eyed the hamburger the waitress placed before her. "I cannot comprehend why, in this rich country, food is so tasteless. Look at this. Paper-thin and interred in a coffin of sodden bun!"

Sparrow winced at the sharpness in her voice. "I'm sorry," he said gently. "I should have taken you somewhere else."

For the second time that day Maggie Royal hated herself. She reached out a slim hand and touched his arm. "Dear Sparrow. Forgive me. For some reason I'm terribly edgy. Must be spring coming on. Gramma used to give us a tonic when we were children." She made a face. "One of Nurse Dah's home remedies: blackstrap molasses and castor oil. Tasted awful! Sparrow, I'm so happy to see you, to be here with you after so long."

The affection in her eyes, the warmth in her voice, astonished him, the way sudden kindness always did, catching him unexpectedly and giving him a rush of happiness that was like the flash of a bluebird's wings against a cloud-filled sky. "We could send it back and order something else," he said hesitantly.

"The hamburger could be leather, for all I care." Maggie Royal picked it up and began to eat it. "Tell me about you. What brought you to Washington besides the exhibition?"

Now they were back on safe ground, and Sparrow was eager to tell her about subjects close to his heart. He had come to Washington from Boston, where he was teaching prep school boys conservation and natural history, to attend a meeting at the Department of the Interior. He had been chosen to head a new section devoted to the problems of offshore islands, a position resulting from his Harvard thesis on Stark Island. After leaving his wartime correspondent's job, he had developed it into

A Naturalist's View of the Atlantic Offshore Islands. His friend Mac Malloy, the former *Life* photographer, now free-lancing, was also an ardent conservationist. Mac had illustrated the book with wonderful color photographs. Now they were collaborating on another, entitled *The Natural Treasures of the Golden Isles.*

"I talked to the people at the Carnegie Foundation," Sparrow said. "It's possible they'd be willing to give a grant to a group of us who want to study shore birds. Stark Island is the perfect place for such a study." He continued enthusiastically, "Susan and I have talked about it at length. We feel the island, the marshes, should be preserved at all costs. Do you know, Maggie Royal, I have boys in my classes who've never been out of the city, never seen marsh grass or a bird in its natural habitat. Fortunately, people are starting to realize that our natural resources are in trouble, that something's going to have to be done to protect them."

"Warren says . . ."

She broke off, staring down at the uneaten half of the hamburger on her plate. She wondered if, by speaking Warren's name, she had subconsciously meant to break the spell that discussing Stark Island brought about.

"Yes?" He was waiting.

"Warren says that private islands are out of style. Since the war, there's no longer money or servants to keep them going. The land is too precious. It offers such extraordinary opportunities for resort development and profit that it's the equivalent of an irresistible force."

"True," Sparrow acknowledged. "Great Oak is terribly run-down. The Long Point settlement is deserted. The old Negroes have died. The young ones have gone to work on the mainland at Tarrington's mill or the Army base. But, Maggie Royal, there are so many other possibilities!" Eagerly he ran on: "Imagine a place where children could go to learn about nature, camp out, and study the birds and animals and the plant life. Stark Island is so rich in history. There could be digs for archaeologists, studies by naturalists. Maggie Royal, the possibilities are unlimited."

He paused and then continued: "Right now the island is the scene of a tug-of-war between the Park Service and Tarrington. He's taken over one of the smaller islands, built houses all over it, and lined the beach with hotels and apartment buildings. The state and the Park Service consider Stark Island one of the most beautiful and historic of the Golden Isles, with all the qualifications to become a National Seashore.

"So far, the Park Service appears to be the best bet. They have detailed plans for nature-study groups and maps of the tracts held by the heirs who haven't the money or interest to keep or maintain their property."

"You think the Park Service . . . ?"

Sparrow nodded. "I believe they'd do their best to preserve the island. They've even made a provision that since Susan is handicapped, she can have special permission to drive on the beach, if and when she visits the island." Sparrow waited for her to respond, then hurried on. "Something has to be done. Soon. The horses, pigs, and cattle have gone feral. They've multiplied so rapidly the island can no longer support them. Even the deer are suffering. The animals are starving. You loved the island the way Jared did, the way I did. Maggie Royal, you're the only one who can save it."

His urgency transmitted itself to her. Her eyes filled with distress. Still, she could not bring herself to face what she had put off for so long.

"I don't think you can go back to a place you've loved so much. That's why I haven't. It could never be the same, especially without Gramma."

"Maggie Royal," Sparrow said intensely, "do you remember those days on the island when we thought it would be forever? When we were young and everything was outside of time? You mustn't let it go to a speculator. Resort hotels, boardwalks—who knows what they would do! The woods cut down, the dunes leveled. Old Ugly's pond filled in. Maggie Royal," he implored, "you've got to go down and see Jared."

"No!" Her voice was tight and strained. "He left me. Broke our date." She swallowed and continued with effort. "Married Cindy Lou."

"Jared tried to make a go of it. Even lived on the mainland and worked for his father-in-law when he came back from the war. Was his errand boy."

"You remember how Tarrington snapped his fingers every time he wanted something. 'Boy, bring it here. Boy, do this.'" Maggie Royal shook her head wonderingly. "I can't see Jared in that role."

"It didn't last long. Cindy Lou had begun drinking and playing around while he was overseas. Last I heard she'd been committed to a sanatorium, a drying-out place in the mountains near Asheville."

Maggie Royal took a deep breath to steady herself. "What about his son? Jared's son?"

"When Jared was reported missing, Big Boy Tarrington had himself appointed legal guardian. Tertius—his real name is Jared the Third—goes to the boys' school at Aiken."

"He was born after Jared was in Spain. He'd be twelve now. I wonder if he has green eyes and a way with horses."

Sparrow took her hand from the table. "Maggie Royal, you're the only one who can talk sense to Jared."

"No!" she cried again. Her violet eyes were huge in her face, pale now beneath the tan left from her winter cruise. "Jared died. I married Warren."

"But he came back to life!"

"To me he's dead. Anyway"—she withdrew her hand and fumbled in her bag for another cigarette—"I've changed! I'm not the Maggie Royal you once knew."

"I wonder," Sparrow replied softly.

Neither of them finished their hamburgers. Sparrow hunted for his wallet, going through his suit pockets, finally finding it in an inside pocket.

"*You* haven't changed," Maggie Royal said, remembering his bird-watching equipment, the notebooks, binoculars, and camera he was always mislaying.

Sparrow smiled. "I'm getting worse," he said, putting down a tip for the waitress. "Susan says there are days when she has to remind me who I am." He stood up. "I'd better be off or I'll be late for the meeting. I'll telephone Susan and tell her I'll be away overnight. Mac Malloy will put me up. We need to discuss the new book."

"Come at seven, then." Maggie Royal pulled on her gloves. "We'll have a drink with Adele before the others arrive."

He kissed her on the cheek, and she watched him hurry off, knowing that already he was preoccupied, thinking about his meeting, or a bird, or perhaps Susan, walking with his head thrust forward, giving him that familiar, round-shouldered look.

The March afternoon had turned chilly. She burrowed deeper into the mink jacket Warren had given her for Christmas, and began to walk faster.

Flower vendors peddling their early-spring daffodils and violets were already out on street corners. She paused to buy a bunch of daffodils to put in the guest room. They would not last like florist's flowers, but she felt sorry for the old blind black man who, with his white hair and prominent features, bore a faint resemblance to Newt, her grandmother's butler on Stark Island. She paid him an extra dollar and took the flowers. Then she turned into Q Street and began walking briskly, hoping to escape the memory of that last wartime spring with Jared, sitting under the Spanish chestnut amid the daffodils as the rooks cawed in the high towers and buttresses of Chatfield Castle and the light of the lovely drawn-out English evening changed slowly, fading into dusk.

Maggie Royal had finished fixing the flowers in the guest room and had ordered tea to be served in her writing room when the doorbell rang. She ran to open it.

"Adele!"

"Maggie Royal!"

The cousins fell into each other's arms, both saying at once how wonderful it was to see the other again, how well the other looked.

Adele's eyes sparkled. "Maggie Royal," she cried, flinging her shapeless felt riding hat onto a Sheraton chair, "it's so exciting to be here, away from the children, even for a day, not that I don't love them. But nine, four, two, and another on the way does get to be wearing, especially as Tyger travels with the team when they have games away from home. Tyger," she explained, taking off the tan polo coat she'd worn all through boarding school, "is not only coaching the university football team but running our Charlottesville farm. 'Course, it's just a little old bitty farm and we have only a few old hunters. Jere, our oldest, is already hunting. Missy will be coming along soon. Maggie Royal, you should see little Maggie. She has your hair, Gramma's blue eyes, and Tyger's smile . . ." She broke off, gazing around the gleaming hall, with its oval giltwood mirror and the long walnut-case clock that Warren had bought in London during the war. "Oh, Maggie Royal, your house is just gorgeous. You must show me everything."

"I forgot you hadn't seen it since we finished the renovations. Oh, Thomas . . ." She nodded toward the butler, who was surveying Adele's battered suitcase with a disparaging expression on his long, dour white face. "Please take Mrs. Trimble's bag to the green room. Come, Adele, I'll show you up."

At the sight of the green room, Adele began jumping up and down, clapping her hands. "Maggie Royal, it's just marvelous. Wherever did you get that bed?"

"Dolley Madison is supposed to have slept in it. We picked it up at an auction near Orange. Warren, that is. He's responsible for the good things in the house." She went over to the dressing table and straightened the daffodils in their pale green Wedgwood bowl. "Warren is a perfectionist."

"And you're the perfect wife," Adele said admiringly, sitting down on the bed and rumpling the green silk spread. "And that's a perfect suit." She sighed, gazing enviously at the navy-blue Chanel Maggie Royal had bought in Paris on her way home from Portugal. "What I wouldn't do for your figure. After the children, I just gave up dieting." She patted her ample stomach and surveyed her unfashionably long tweed skirt, baggy brown sweater, and matching cardigan, leftovers from her school years. "I've decided I was just meant to be fat. Anyway, Tyger says he likes me this way, and that's all that matters. Maggie Royal, how *do* you stay so thin?"

"I think my stomach shrank during the war, when we really had very little to eat. Then, too, I work at it. I drive to Middleburg and ride. I hunt two or three times a week during the season." She went to the door and turned. "Come down when you're ready. Tea's in what Warren calls my writing room, at the foot of the stairs, just off the hall."

Adele appeared in the writing room as Thomas was bringing in the tea tray. Her face was flushed with excitement and she had buttoned her cardigan the wrong way. She plunked herself down in a walnut wing chair and exclaimed with delight at the sight of Maria's apple pastries, fresh from the oven. "Flaky puffs! How yummy!" She glanced uneasily at Thomas, who promptly left. "My goodness! Wherever did he come from? He terrifies me."

"Don't mind Thomas," Maggie Royal replied, pouring the pale

China tea. "He drove for Warren in London, and then went to Portugal with us. He's the perfect gentleman's gentleman and butler." She lowered her voice. "I must admit, though, I've never seen his expression change. He views life with that gloomy relish usually associated with nannies and Irish grooms."

They chatted at first with caution, almost as if they were afraid of the closeness and sympathy they'd known as children. But in spite of the separate routes their lives had taken, the old close relationship soon revived.

"Warren's going to be an ambassador," Maggie Royal said. "He's not confirmed yet. It could take from a week to a month from the time the President sends his name up."

"Just think," Adele said, "you'll be an ambassador's wife! Aren't you excited?"

Maggie Royal nodded. "Warren is very young to be named an ambassador. He went to Yalta, you know, as a special assistant. And in Portugal he was our acting ambassador when the ambassador himself was ill. Since then he's gone straight up the FSO ladder. But tell me about you."

Adele reciprocated with an account of Missy's new braces—"They're frightfully expensive, and she has to wear them until she's at least sixteen"—and news of Jere, who could catch a football like his daddy used to at his age. She went on to describe the old farmhouse they'd done over—"There's a big playroom, a yummy kitchen and a pond out back . . ." She broke off, staring at the silver-framed photograph of Warren and President Roosevelt at Yalta on the Chippendale table. "Compared to your life, mine is pretty dull!"

"You have a husband and children who love you," Maggie Royal said quickly, "and you're useful, the way Gramma wanted us to be." She set down her cup and offered Adele another flaky puff.

"I could have married a millionaire," Adele said dreamily, selecting a particularly crispy, flaky pastry from which syrupy apple oozed. "You remember that friend of Taylor's, Piers something-or-other, with the Caddy convertible and the polo ponies?"

"Yes," Maggie Royal said, "I remember. He was crazy about you."

"Well, I didn't love him, so I didn't propose," Adele said, biting into the pastry. Maggie Royal started to laugh.

"That's what I've missed," Adele said, "your laughter." She gazed at her cousin, at the wonderful coloring, the faintly tanned skin molded over fine bones, the dark hair and violet eyes with long lashes. Maggie Royal had everything, she thought; then why the hunger in her eyes, the nervous need to smoke one cigarette after another?

"Have another flaky puff," Maggie Royal urged.

"I might as well," Adele said placidly. "I'm eating for two. Oh, dear." She began unbuttoning her cardigan, and rebuttoning it correctly. "Kattywampus!"

"Kattywampus! I haven't heard that word in years. Gramma used to say we were all kattywampus, do you remember? Darling Adele, kattywampus or not, I'm so happy to see you."

Adele glanced at her quickly, but the light in her face had already gone out, leaving it rigid, without warmth or life. She looked around at the perfectly appointed room. Maggie Royal might have beauty, money, position. But what she had was a house, and a house was not a home without children.

The fire burned lower, and they rambled on, playing "Whatever happened to so-and-so?" and "Do you remember when . . . ?"

"Sparrow's in town," Maggie Royal said finally. "He's coming to dinner. He's worried about the island."

"I know," Adele said. "He wrote to us."

"Well, what are you going to do about your land?"

"I don't know," Adele said. "I was waiting to talk to you. Tyger says the property is valuable, maybe we should hang on to it for the children."

They were both being very careful, Maggie Royal thought, not to mention Jared. The clock in the hall struck six.

"I invited the guests for seven-thirty," Maggie Royal said. "Sparrow said he'd come at seven. He's dying to see you. We can have a drink before the others arrive. You'll have time for a bath and a rest . . ."

"Rest!" Adele burst into laughter. "Imagine me resting! Oh, Maggie Royal." She threw her arms around her cousin's neck. "It's divine to be here with you!"

Maggie Royal went to her bedroom and shut the door. It was a beautiful room, like the rest of the house, in subdued and perfect taste, from the Williamsburg-blue walls to the understated curtains of English chintz which matched the slipcovers on the chairs and chaise longue.

When they had begun redoing the old house in Georgetown, she had asked the architect to make the master bedroom and the room next to it connect. The smaller room had been made into a dressing room for Warren, with built-in closets and drawers for his suits and shirts. Ultimately she had furnished it with a bed.

"You work so hard, darling," she told him. "You need a room to yourself, to come back to after you've been working late."

She remembered the hurt look that had crossed his face. She had determined to compensate for her withdrawal and had done so by being solicitous about his well-being, running the household and entertaining with a talent that filled Warren's colleagues—like Hugh Greene, whose wife could never provide meals that were hot or on time—with envy.

She hadn't known then that the care and attention she lavished was in lieu of a child, a son, to carry on his distinguished New England name.

Their wedding photograph stood in a monogrammed silver frame.

28

She studied it now. Warren looked tall and dignified. "Solid in the right sort of way," Binkie, her British stepfather, had said. There was a fond, indulgent smile on Warren's face, and his right hand was cupped over hers. She wore a lavender copy of a Norman Hartnell gown Miss Jarvis had made, Gramma's pearls, and a little matching turban.

She had been twenty-four, Warren thirty-seven.

Sparrow arrived at 7:15, looking rumpled and flushed. "I'm sorry," he apologized. "I met Mac Malloy for a drink and we got to talking about our book. Then I got caught in traffic. I hope you don't mind my not dressing." He gazed at Maggie Royal's stylish crimson silk dinner dress.

"Of course not," she reassured him. "It's informal. There's just the Senator and the Greenes and ourselves. Ellie inherited great vulgar chunks of California real estate from her father and loves to give lavish parties. Hugh used to be an international lawyer, and is now an adviser on European commerce in the State Department. He's very knowledgeable, particularly on rare manuscripts and modern art." Maggie Royal indicated the drinks tray. "Do fix yourself a drink. Warren just got home. He's washing up and will be down in a moment."

The Senator from Georgia was on the dot. "Fust thing I learned in Washington when I came here twenty-five years ago was to forget Southern People's Time," he said when Maggie Royal complimented him on his promptness. He was in his late sixties, silver-haired with a mustache, and wore a black string tie. He resembled an ad for Kentucky bourbon, to which he was partial. He had known Gramma and Maggie Royal from the time he had come to Stark Island as a young Senator with President Roosevelt. Now, because of seniority, he was one of the most important men in the Senate.

Warren came in. He kissed Adele and told her how well she looked.

"Like the break-up of a long hard winter!" Adele retorted, laughing.

"It's good to hear your laugh again," Warren replied. His smile was warm and friendly and his manner exactly right as he greeted the Senator and Sparrow. Within seconds he established himself as master of the house, seeing that everyone had a full glass and shaking up the fire that had burned down. He looked well, too, Maggie Royal thought, watching him objectively. He was always immaculately turned out. Lately he had taken to playing squash and had lost weight. It made his beautifully tailored suits fit even better.

"Congratulations, sir," Sparrow said. "I understand you're to be Ambassador to Bmunda. I'm not sure where it is, or how to pronounce it, but it sounds exciting."

Maggie Royal saw Warren wince at the "sir," and then quickly recover.

"It's a very small country in what we call the armpit of Africa. Yet it's a challenge. Very unstable politically. They're struggling for their independence. There's a revolution every year or so. But the country's full of minerals that are important to us. Hard on Magdalena, though. Moving again, just when we've finished remodeling the house." He glanced at the Senator. "However, we may not be going anywhere. I haven't been confirmed yet."

"No problem there." The Senator squeezed Maggie Royal's arm. "Not with such a beautiful and talented wife!"

Warren smiled at her approvingly. "If anybody can cope, it's Magdalena. I'll never forget the time . . ." And he proceeded to relate a quick, amusing story about the difficulties of entertaining in foreign countries when one did not speak the language.

Thomas came in silently and passed around a plate of hot hors d'oeuvres.

"Isn't it awful?" Adele said, helping herself to a cheesy morsel. "I'm still hungry. After that scrumptious tea, too." She lifted the jacket of her dress. "I don't know how much longer I'll be able to wear it," she said, indicating the gap at her waist that she had pinned together with a large horse-blanket pin. "I have another four months to go!"

"Miss Maggie Royal," the Senator said, "can't yawl get your cousin Jared to make sense! He won't let nobody come on that island. You and I know it's but a matter of time 'fore those no-'count trees are cut down and li'l ole hardscuffle paths are paved."

"The trouble with the South is that the aristocracy insists on hanging on long after its time is past," Warren said. He glanced at Maggie Royal and went on, speaking slowly, meaningfully. "The ultimate irresponsibility lies in refusing to give up something when you can no longer hold it or afford it."

Maggie Royal bit her lower lip. "I wonder where the Greenes are?" She moved away from him and spoke to Adele. "I told Maria to serve dinner promptly at eight-fifteen. There's chocolate soufflé for dessert. I don't want it to fall."

At that moment the doorbell rang, and Thomas ushered in the Greenes.

Ellie Greene was tall, big-boned, but well-dieted. "Just back from Maine Chance, my dear," she told Maggie Royal as she kissed her, chic in narrow black velvet pants and a satin overblouse. Three strands of pearls that matched the ones in her ears encircled her neck, made longer by her lacquered, upswept hairdo. "My dear, I'm afraid we're terribly late. I barely had time to change into my old pants after cocktails at the Wheelers'. Warren, love, you and Maggie should have been there. Everyone was talking about the Hiss case. Dean Acheson said he would take Hiss's word over that of Chambers any day. There were gaggles of White House people, and—"

"Darling Ellie and Hugh," Maggie Royal interrupted. "Of course you know the Senator. And this is my cousin Adele from Charlottesville, and Sparrow McKinney from Cambridge."

"My dear, you said we'd be just family." Ellie Greene's eyes swept over Adele's expandable basic black that had obviously weathered several pregnancies. She sat down, lit a cigarette, accepted a martini, and began talking about somebody named Tom in the State Department whose name had turned up on a list prepared by one of the committees investigating subversion.

"Really too frightful," Ellie said. "His career is being ruined, just because he belonged to some silly radical group in college."

Hugh Greene gave Adele a friendly handshake and the kind of smile characteristic of people in government, guarded, judging, while its bearer sums up the person being introduced, deciding whether or not he or she is worth wasting time on, exuding that superficial charm and false manner that becomes automatic after years on the cocktail circuit.

"How nice to meet a cousin of Maggie's," he said, releasing Adele's hand. "We think a lot of Maggie." He was a tall man, and, like Warren, well-groomed. Yet, unlike Warren, who always seemed in command of any situation, there was an insecurity in his manner. One sensed immediately that Ellie held the purse strings and the whip hand in their marriage.

The Senator and Sparrow were deep in a discussion about Stark Island. Warren had Hugh cornered by the bookcase and was discussing a rare Blake manuscript advertised by Christie's, when, to Maggie's relief, Thomas announced dinner.

"I hope you'll enjoy Washington," Hugh said to Adele when they were seated. "There are several exciting art exhibitions. One at the Off Beat Gallery by a painter named Stark."

Adele glanced quickly at Maggie Royal. Her face had suddenly become very still, and her spoon clattered against her early-Meissen soup plate as she set it down.

"I met Jared Stark at a Pudding dance," Ellie Greene interrupted. "I thought he was divine." She glanced at her husband. "Naturally, that was before I knew Hughie."

"What do you think of his painting?" Warren asked.

"Striking. Shows a lot of talent," Hugh Greene said.

"If you ask me, Jared Stark's one of them com-mune-ists," the Senator said darkly. "His daddy was always one for stirrin' up trouble. Got the nigras all agitated."

"Will they live?" Warren asked, pretending he had not heard the Senator. "Do you think they'd be a good investment?"

"Oh, Warren," Maggie Royal protested. "Why must you think of art in those terms? A painting is like marriage. You should take it on only when you can't live without it!" The pained look on Warren's face stopped her.

"Just as you say, my dear. Still, I like to know what I bargain for."

"I know, darling," Maggie Royal amended quickly. "Warren, I think we need to open another bottle of wine."

They were smiling at each other. Yet Adele sensed tension between them. "I beg your pardon." Adele turned to Warren on her left. "I was miles away with Maggie Royal on our island when we were children. I was thinking how different our lives are now. Maggie Royal is so beautiful." Impulsively she continued. "Whereas, I'm just me." She gave her sudden irrepressible giggle. "A suburban hausfrau with a good-hearted, football-loving, golf-playing husband and children." Instinctively she put her hand to her waist, wondering if the gap where she had pinned it together showed. What the hell! she decided, I'll diet when I get home, and she reached for another hot biscuit from the silver basket passed by the silent Thomas.

Sparrow was also watching Maggie Royal. She's become like her grandmother, he thought as his hostess sought to steer the conversation away from names and local gossip. Where, he wondered, had the island Maggie Royal gone? The girl with passionate feelings and wildly blowing hair, of flashing eyes blazing with life.

The Senator turned to Maggie Royal. "Yawl got a chance to make a fortune. Big Boy Tarrington wants to build a Tarrington Island Community that would make what he's done on Gwinnett look tacky as all get-out. Great Oak would make a grand clubhouse. 'Course you'd have to get shed of all that old stuff. Put in modern. Set up bars and bridge tables. He showed me his plans last time I was down home. 'Big Boy,' I says to him, 'yawl have everybody in the South flocking to Stark Island!' "

Thomas passed the duck *à l'orange* once again. The Senator waved him away. "No, thank you. I've had gracious plenty.

"Big Boy asked me to talk to Jared," he continued. "Jared didn't want to see me. Fact is, he didn't want me to come ashore. 'Jared,' I told him, 'yawl know puffectly well yawl can't hang on to this hyar island. Not with taxes going up all the time. Before the last war in Europe it was different. There was nigra help aplenty. I mind the time I visited Great Oak with President Roosevelt. There were ten to twenty nigras in the house alone. Eighteen or more shacks with smoke coming out in the settlement." He drank from his wineglass and delicately wiped his lips with one of Maggie Royal's damask napkins. " 'No suh!' I told him. 'Yawl can't keep a place like this without nigras.' "

"Why couldn't it be a wildlife preserve or a National Park?" Warren asked reasonably. "Something all the people could benefit from."

"Yawl got to have a pro-tected community," the Senator declared emphatically. "First thing you know, place'd be overrun with niggers. No suh!" he repeated, his face turning red. "Trouble enough keepin' 'em in their place with all these Yankee notions about lettin' nigras vote and go to school with white children."

Maggie Royal was aware of the same burning shame she had experienced as a child when she heard guests at Gramma's table talk about "the darkies," as if they were no more human than the mahogany sideboard.

32

"And what's wrong with that?" she heard herself saying.

"Why, Miss Maggie Royal," the Senator said, shocked. "Yawl ain't gonna tell me you believe all that Yankee talk 'bout equality. A good ole home girl like you. Why, Miss Maggie Royal, yawl one of we people!"

Maggie Royal was aware of Warren's warning glance. With great effort she fought back the words she longed to cry out, and directed the conversation to the Alger Hiss case, which everyone in Washington was discussing.

The dinner plates were removed and Thomas passed the dessert. Liberal helpings of the soufflé were consumed while Warren held forth, lucidly and well, on what was beginning to be known as the Age of Suspicion. With clarity and his Oxonian choice of words, he explained that for ten years the House Committee on Un-American Activities had been trying to discredit Roosevelt reforms by telling the country they were Communist-inspired. Warren sipped from his wineglass and continued. "To partisans on both sides, Alger Hiss has become a symbol. Liberals see him as a representative of New Deal achievements under attack. To the conservative right he stands for the hated Eastern elite, the university professors, and intellectuals."

"I understand Thorny is being investigated," Adele said when he paused. "Thorny is our Boston cousin," she explained to the Greenes. "His grandfather Lowell Thorndike was our ambassador in London before the war. The FBI has dug up information about those left-wing organizations Thorny belonged to in college."

"That sounds ominous," Sparrow said.

Maggie Royal laughed at his worried expression. "Don't tell me you took part in any left-wing riots?"

Sparrow hesitated. "I did swallow a couple of goldfish on a bet one night," he admitted finally, "and went on a pajama raid at Radcliffe." He paused and then added, "All we got were some dirty socks."

Maggie Royal drank from her wineglass. She felt light-headed and oddly reckless. "I think it's dreadful," she said when the laughter died down. "These investigations remind me of Hitler or the Spanish Inquisition."

"Magdalena tends to exaggerate," Warren said from the other end of the table.

Maggie Royal's color rose as she reached into the silver box before her for a cigarette. "Warren, I merely said that in a free country one shouldn't have to put up with government checks."

"My dear, I've asked you not to smoke at the table," Warren said reprovingly. "It's not fair to Maria's cuisine."

"The American people feel the country is in danger from Communist infiltration," the Senator said to the table at large. "From the State Department pinkos who want to recognize Red China"—he gazed pointedly at Warren—"the subversives that fought in Spain, the Jews, and the nigger-lovers."

33

Maggie Royal took another drink from her wineglass. She realized that Thomas had refilled it five times. Perhaps that was why she had a fatalistic feeling that the situation was spinning out of control.

"There's no value in believing, in having opinions, unless you're willing to fight and die for them," she said. "If the good people of Germany had spoken out, Hitler wouldn't have been able to almost conquer the world."

Although the Senator had lost his Deep South accent that matched his string tie and sideburns, he seemed determined not to lose his temper. He was like a seventeenth-century squire waiting for his opponent to do him physical harm before he could challenge him to a duel. "Miss Maggie Royal, what happened in Germany will never happen here."

"But it already *is* happening here," Maggie Royal cried wildly, caution deserting her.

"Magdalena," Warren interrupted from the other end of the table. "Don't you think we should adjourn for coffee?"

She glanced around the table. No one would meet her eyes. Only Sparrow was smiling, his expression alert, interested. She lit a cigarette and thought: I've broken every rule from bringing up controversial subjects to attacking a guest at my own dinner table, so I might as well smoke.

"Warren." She waved her hand holding her cigarette at him. "Let me finish!" She turned back to the Senator. "Remember what Hitler said in *Mein Kampf*—'the greatness of the lie is always a certain factor in being believed . . . some part of even the boldest lie is sure to stick.' "

"My goodness," Adele said, impressed. "Did you learn that at Miss Mayo's, or was it on one of Gramma's needlepoint pillows?"

Maggie Royal laughed, suddenly enjoying herself. "Actually, from Warren. One of his speeches. Would you like coffee, Senator," she asked courteously, "or perhaps brandy?"

The Senator's face was scarlet. "No, thank you. I've had gracious plenty." He rose and made a courtly bow. "Good night, Miss Maggie Royal, ma'am. Yawl understand if I rush off. Got some homework to do, about those nominations before the committee." His voice was normal, but in his eyes Maggie Royal saw resentment, anger.

Warren showed him to the door.

"Well, my dear, you certainly poured it on him," he said when he returned. "Something tells me we won't be having him to dinner again for a while."

"Oh, God, Warren. I didn't know I was letting go until I got going," Maggie Royal said, suddenly contrite.

"It doesn't matter, Magdalena, I didn't know you read my speeches."

"But it does matter." She was looking up at him. "I was rude, Warren. I'm sorry." She stopped suddenly. Her chin lifted. Her throat tensed. "No, dammit, I'm not sorry. The son of a bitch had it coming."

34

Sparrow grinned. "Atta girl, Maggie Royal. Give 'em hell!"

"Don't forget you're coming to Sea Island next week," Hugh said to Warren as the Greenes went out the door. "After coping with that African trade mission, you'll need some sun and sea air."

Sparrow glanced at his watch. "Time I was leaving, too."

Maggie Royal walked to the door with him.

Sparrow planted his old felt hat squarely on top of his thinning hair and turned the collar of his shabby overcoat up against the chill March air. "You were great. Shades of the old Maggie Royal!"

She reached up and kissed him lightly on the cheek. "I'll speak to Warren about the foundation."

"Speak to Jared, Maggie Royal."

Her face twisted into a wry smile. Her head lifted in that old proud way. "I suppose I've always known that one day I would have to go back."

Sparrow went quickly down the steps. At the bottom he looked back. She was still standing in the doorway, rigidly, very straight. Like a diver about to dive.

Warren turned to Adele in the hall. "She doesn't realize how much I depend on her." With an air of uncertainty Adele found both endearing and totally out of character, he added helplessly, "I try, but somehow I don't please her." Then, as though embarrassed at having disclosed this chink in his emotional armor, he was himself again: composed and correct. "Good night, Adele. Do stay as long as you can."

After Warren went up to bed, Maggie Royal asked Adele if she wanted a nightcap or anything to eat.

Adele said she would just have a bedtime snack. "Remember, I'm eating for two!"

Maggie Royal poured milk into a glass and set it on a tray with a piece of Maria's chocolate cake, and carried it up to the guest room.

"It's all so lovely," Adele said enthusiastically, gazing around the beautifully appointed room. "And, Maggie Royal, all your towels match! Do you remember when your mother opened in that play at the National—what was it called? Anyway, she came to the apartment and had fits because none of your towels matched."

"I remember," Maggie Royal said. "I've changed since then."

"I'll say!" Adele sank down onto the bed. "For one thing, you almost never laugh—not the way you used to, as if you meant it." She picked up the cake and took a bite, dropping crumbs onto the apple-green silk blanket cover that matched the color of the walls. "And you're not writing anymore."

Maggie Royal rose and went to the window. "It's warm in here. Would you like it opened? You must see the garden in daylight. I hate to leave it. In another month the Japanese magnolias will be in bloom. Lilac and dogwood, too."

35

"You haven't answered my question," Adele persisted, brushing crumbs onto the green carpet.

"There's so much to do: luncheons, meetings, cocktail parties. Never time."

"You used to say that one could make time, anytime; that people can do anything they want to. Write, paint, ride horses. And you have Maria and Thomas." She waited for Maggie Royal to finish lighting a cigarette and answer. When she didn't, she continued. "I'll never forget your book *Dancing Wax* and your articles from London. The blitz and buzz bombs. The one about the little boy in the shelter pretending the dice were sugar lumps. I saved them all. And your book that was made from them. I was so proud. I bought copies for everybody."

"It all seems a long time ago," Maggie Royal said. "Adele, you must be exhausted."

Adele went on as if she hadn't heard her. "Your Warren is charming, and, Maggie Royal, he loves you so. He almost never takes his eyes off you. You would never have married anyone like Tyger." She sighed and drank some milk. "Tyger's just Tyger. Old-shoe. He never talks anything but football and horses and his golf game. Sometimes I have the feeling he thinks sex is like golf." She giggled. "The idea is to get to the hole in as few strokes as you can!"

"Adele, you're terrible." Maggie Royal was laughing.

Adele set down her empty milk glass and clasped her hands around her knees. "You should laugh more. But then, you were always the serious one. Repressed but loaded. Like Jared!"

Maggie Royal felt faintly desperate. "Adele, we'll talk tomorrow."

But Adele was not to be put off. "I understand he's gotten very odd. Living at Great Oak and painting weird pictures, with the whole place coming down around his ears. It was rather mean of Gramma to buy all those stocks on borders and not leave any money!"

"You mean margins." Maggie Royal noticed the daffodils in the Wedgwood bowl were already drooping. "Why doesn't Big Boy Tarrington pay the bills? I keep seeing his advertisement for those planned communities in magazines. He must have millions, moving the earth around, putting in harbors where there weren't any before, filling in the ones that were there."

"You know Jared's pride! He would never accept help from anyone." Adele paused and then rattled on disconnectedly. "I know you loved the Island, but I was always glad to leave. Now that Gramma's gone, I have no wish to go back there. Ours was a very involuted family. Gramma said the Black Starks, Jared's side, were tainted. They acquired sorrow, the way some people acquire animals or antiques."

"Adele, darling . . ." Maggie Royal began again.

"We were all a little in love with Jared," Adele continued dreamily. "I saw him in uniform before he went overseas. The handsomest thing, with that dark skin and those green eyes. Maggie Royal, you look so strange. Are you all right?"

36

"Adele, I really must go to bed." She bent over and kissed her cousin good night. "I'll see you in the morning. As Gramma used to say, 'Sleep tight. Cover your head so the bugs won't bite!' "

"I miss Gramma," Adele murmured sleepily. "She gave us confidence and security. She brought us up to believe that if you wore a Brooks sweater and pearls and went tea-dancing in a black dress, you'd marry and live happily ever after."

"Yes," Maggie Royal agreed. "Seems strange now, doesn't it? I remember her telling us once that if you behave as you should, obey the rules, your feelings will flow from right actions. She made it sound so simple."

"Maybe it is."

"Yes," Maggie Royal agreed. "The trick lies in knowing the right action."

Maggie Royal heard Warren's knock and thought: Please, God, not tonight.

Her white low-necked nightgown exposed her shoulders and the shape of her breasts. Without makeup and with her hair lying loose on the pillow, she looked young and lovely and serene.

"Magdalena," Warren whispered.

"Must you call me that,"—her voice was ragged, cold—"when everyone else calls me Maggie or Maggie Royal?"

"It's because nobody else calls you that. It's the only thing of yours I've got."

She turned her face to the pillow. "Warren, it's terribly late."

His face went white. He turned, retracing his steps. At the door he paused. "Magdalena, we can't go on like this."

"I know, Warren. It's just that . . . that I'm so tired. I promise to try—"

He cut her off. "I'll give you a divorce, if that's what you want," he said. His hand was on the doorknob. "Or you can return to me as my wife." He hesitated. "But if you do, you must put him out of your life for good. Is that clear?"

He left as he had come, softly closing the door that separated her room from his.

In all the years they had been married, Warren had never mentioned Jared's name. Yet there had never been a day, an hour, a moment that he had not stood between them. Suddenly everything seemed painfully clear. The glow from the streetlight coming through the window, the moving curtains, the outline of the chairs and dressing table and chaise longue. It was the same light-headed, curiously reckless, fatalistic feeling she had felt that day in London when she learned Jared's plane had crashed.

As if at long last the agony of indecision was to be resolved.

She felt her heart move, lifting with anticipation, like that of a person going home.

STARK ISLAND
1930–1933

*

Maggie Royal used to say she had no desire to go to heaven—only to Stark Island.

It had been a royal grant to her direct ancestor Jeremy Stark, who came to the New World from Stark Island in the Outer Hebrides in 1733 and eventually built the island's splendid manor house, Great Oak. This Stark had been one of the small band who, with James Oglethorpe, persuaded the Indians to surrender their territory peacefully, land which later became the colony of Georgia.

Jeremy Stark became a general in the Revolution, an intimate of George Washington, Nathanael Greene, and "Light Horse Harry" Lee. Jeremy Stark married Magdalena, daughter of the viceroy of Peru, who had been en route to Spain on one of the Plate ships carrying treasure to the Old World in 1715. The ship had been wrecked off the coast. All hands, including Magdalena's father, had been lost. The baby, Magdalena, had somehow floated ashore, tied to a bit of wreckage found amid some of the flotsam, including the crate containing the magnificent silver place plates, that had washed up on the beach. She had been brought up at the Spanish mission on the island. There she had nursed Jeremy back to health when, following an attack of yellow fever, he'd been sent from the mainland to the mission hospital.

When he recovered, Jeremy built Great Oak for his bride, naming it after the immense live oak beneath which they were married.

The first great house was as white as orange blossoms, as perfect in architectural symmetry as the eight Doric columns added later to its facade, as the famous circular staircase down which future generations of Stark brides descended to be married.

In time, Stark Island became one of the great antebellum plantations of the South. The production of sea-island cotton, rice, and sugar, which brought high prices on the English market, made it possible for the Starks of that time to live in luxury befitting royalty.

The gardens were famous. Wide allées led from the house to the sound, past the famed "great oak" and the tomb of the first Jeremy, which dominated the family burial ground inside the high tabby walls.

Thomas Jefferson sent cuttings from his vineyards at Monticello and urged planting the olive grove, pointing out that olives were "fitting additions to any meal" and made "piquant seasoning." Arthur Middleton, a signer of the Declaration of Independence, brought cuttings from the first four camellias André Michaux, the French botanist, planted in the New World, at Middleton Place, near Charleston. Each subsequent generation added its own unique visible touches to the arboretum.

The first Jeremy had many children. The first son was named Jeremy, and the first daughter Magdalena Royal, after his royal wife. It became traditional for the first son and daughter of each subsequent Jeremy to be named Jeremy and Magdalena Royal, known to intimates as Jere and Maggie Royal. Further tradition insisted that Jeremy and Magdalena Royal be painted by the leading artists of their time, the portraits to hang in the dining room.

In spite of the first Jeremy Stark's opposition, and that of James Oglethorpe, Georgia's founder, as well as that of his close friend John Wesley, the great Methodist preacher, the scourge of slavery swept over the new colony. After July 7, 1749, when the prohibitions against rum and slavery were withdrawn, gangs of Negroes were brought from Africa and the West Indies, to be sold on the block in Charleston and Savannah. By the time of secession, the Starks owned hundreds of slaves, who lived in the Long Point community, cultivating tobacco, rice, and cotton.

When the War Between the States began, many slaves absconded to the mainland. The priceless silver place plates saved from the Spanish treasure ship and Stark-crested tea service were buried beneath the great oak, and the horses, pigs, and cattle turned loose. The family, taking little with them other than Jeremy Stark's portrait, painted by Charles Willson Peale, moved to the town house in Starksville.

When the war ended, the plantation lay ruined and devastated. The house had been burned by a detachment of Sherman's men. The once-cultivated fields were eroded and overgrown. The magnificent gardens had reverted to jungle. The animals not caught and killed by Northern troops had become feral, reverting to wildness and roaming the island at will.

Maggie Royal remembered the afternoons when the children gathered on the veranda where her grandmother served tea and told stories of how it was after the War Between the States.

On Stark Island she was known as "Gramma," a shortened version of the Negroes' "Grandmammy." Although all the relatives called her Gramma—and the servants Miss Gramma—she was Maggie Royal's true grandmother.

Gramma had been born in 1860. She was not bothered by her parents' poverty after the war. Everyone in the South was poor then. To be an old family with new money would have been a disgrace.

Although their financial position was precarious, her father made some fortunate deals that enabled him to send her younger brother, Orville, to Harvard. Gramma and her sisters Amy and Meg attended Chatham Academy in Savannah, where the girls had "blue blood but no greenbacks."

The year she was fifteen, Gramma went on the Grand Tour—what she called a "learn-you, dern-you" tour of England, France, and Italy. The family returned to Starksville just as the yellow-fever epidemic of 1876 began.

Three weeks after their return from Europe, Gramma's father was dead. Her mother, who had nursed him, followed within the week.

Instead of accepting proposals from a number of affluent young men, or agreeing to live with the New Orleans relatives or the Virginia cousins, Gramma at sixteen did what in that land of magnolias and migrained women was considered an incredible thing. She moved to Stark Island to live in what had once been the overseer's house.

As was customary, Stark Island had been left to the oldest son. Following the death of Gramma's oldest brother, Jeremy, who died at birth, the property reverted to her brother Orville, known as "Uncle Oomlot" by future generations. In those days it was customary for planters' sons to be sent north to be educated, in order to learn "Yankee cunnin' " before returning to run the plantation. At Harvard Orville met and married the first of his two wives. His interest lay in women and in thoroughbred horses, and he had no desire to return to the ruined plantation. Gramma, on the other hand, had been brought up on stories about the island. Visiting it with her father, she had fallen in love with the wide flat beach and dunes, the thick jungle of palmettos and live oaks, the wildness of the wind and the sea. She persuaded her brother to deed her the land, with the understanding that it would always be his home, as well as hers, and that she would eventually reimburse him.

Possibly, she was inspired by Frances Butler Leigh, the famous Fanny Kemble Butler's daughter, who had returned to Butler Island and was a legend among the defeated island gentry. For Gramma always spoke of the older woman with intense admiration. Following her example, she cared for the few slaves that had remained on the island, and for the others who began straggling home from the promised land of the interior, hungry and homeless.

She paid the Gullah Negroes by shares, dividing the crops, supplying them, meanwhile, with food, clothing, and whatever sums were necessary for their immediate wants. She drove off the carpetbaggers, threatening them with her father's shotgun, accusing them of making promises for "twenty acres, a mule, and an umbrella," which they never fulfilled.

She learned enough medicine to be able to administer to pregnant women, colicky children, the aged and infirm beset with arthritis and "remonia" (pneumonia).

Always a fine horsewoman, she rode Golden Isle, one of the wild horses she had managed to round up and break, training the beautiful chestnut mare to be amenable to her side saddle. Gramma's blue Stark eyes sparkled like the sapphires grandfather gave her as she talked of those enchanted island years, when, freed of the restrictions of town life, she was able to spend days galloping along the sandy trails, learning island lore from the Negroes.

For a time, the plantation prospered. Then the price of cotton dropped drastically. Gramma found it necessary to mortgage the land.

She worked from daybreak to what the Gullahs called "hag hollerin' time," after midnight, toting up the farm books.

Her hands were callused from hoeing her garden, and she became hard and "so thin I couldn't make a shadow!"

"I wore trousers and men's shirts and was burned brown as a field hand," she told the children sitting in an awed circle around her feet. "I always wondered what your grandfather, Mr. McDermott, saw in me!"

Grandfather McDermott sailed his schooner, the *Wild Duck,* from New York, putting in at the island during a storm. He rowed ashore in his dinghy, walked past the ruins of Great Oak to the overseer's house, with its unpainted boards and sagging porch, and knocked on the door.

Gramma used to tell of the unforgettable moment in 1886, when, clutching her shotgun, she opened the door, expecting the usual unctuous, cigar-smoking Yankee carpetbagger. Instead, on that wild night, with lightning flashing behind him, she saw a tall, sunburned, red-bearded sailor standing in the wind and rain, holding a crushed, sodden, knitted watch cap in his hands.

"Coup de foudre," Gramma said. "Bolt of lightning. Something that rarely happens—a moment in time when there is no past or future, only the now. I knew it was fate. God had sent this man with the shy, wonderful smile, even features, and gray eyes to be my love. It didn't matter how poor he was. I would have followed him to the ends of the earth, which, in point of fact, I did.

"Girls in my day did not throw themselves at men as they do now," she continued, her eyes twinkling. "I had to pretend to be hard-to-get!

"I held out for two whole weeks, until your grandfather forced me out onto the end of the bowsprit. He threatened to push me into the sound if I didn't say yes. You know how strong the current is. No one can swim against it. I was afraid he meant what he said—for he was a violent man, a raider—and that I'd be carried out to sea." Her eyes misted. "Instead, he carried me away on his yacht.

"I didn't know until later that it was his. He led me to believe that he was just one of the crew. His fingernails were dirty and his clothes ragged. He wore dungarees and rubber shoes with holes in them.

"Times were very bad then," Gramma continued. "There'd been a blight, and the cotton crop had failed. I was unable to meet the mortgage payments, and the bank foreclosed. The island was taken over by the bank."

It wasn't until they were married that Gramma learned she had wed one of the richest men in the country.

Maggie Royal's grandfather was Diego McDermott, the coal magnate, known as "Spanish Mac." His ancestors had been washed up on Irish soil when ships of the Spanish Armada were wrecked off Galway.

From the old, faded daguerreotypes hanging in Gramma's sitting room, he looked to be as wild and romantic as his Spanish-Irish heritage.

He arrived from Ireland in the hold of an immigration vessel in the wake of the potato famine during which his parents died. The tails of his shirt stuck out from the holes in his only pair of trousers. He migrated to Pennsylvania and went to work in a coal mine. He wasn't long past the age of thirty when he patented improvements on mining machinery that doubled the production of anthracite, and were destined to make him millions. By the time he was forty-six, when he met Gramma, the mine in which he had originally worked was only one of the many mines he owned.

He took Gramma around the world on her wedding trip.

On their first anniversary, she awakened to find the *Wild Duck* anchored off the Stark Island dock. She was about to call out to grandfather, when she reached under her pillow and discovered the deed to Stark Island made out in her name.

"We'll rebuild Great Oak house," Grandfather said, as Gramma wept with joy in his arms. "We'll make it big enough for our children, and our children's children. It will be a place for them always to come back to!"

Maggie Royal wished she had known her grandfather McDermott, but he died of a heart attack in 1910. Old faded photographs showed him wearing white gloves and his gardening coveralls as he welcomed Theodore Roosevelt, who came to the island to hunt deer.

To the end of his life, his biographer wrote, he was unable to get his fingernails clean. In spite of scrubbing them with strong soap, they remained as black as the coal he mined in his youth, forcing him to wear gloves on the golf course and at dinner, never allowing him to forget the earth from which he had wrested the black diamonds that had made him the tenth-richest man of his time in the United States.

He could not have been as black as his nails, or as he was painted by his biographers and the press, for Gramma loved him dearly. She told Maggie Royal, "Mr. McDermott was the gentlest and most amiable of men. He was my life!"

He was twenty years older than Gramma, and they had only twenty-four years together. During that time he devoted himself to rebuilding Great Oak house and the gardens.

Maggie Royal's grandfather belonged to an age that believed anybody could do anything. A time of vast wealth and individualism, of vanity and recklessness, when men were lauded for their daring and could do with impunity things that in later years would signal their downfall.

It was an era of appalling arrogance, of feudal concepts and consummate cruelty, of great style and abysmal taste.

The big house was built on the foundations of the first Great Oak. It was very different from the original mansion, with its facade of columns and perfect Grecian symmetry. Grandfather had never had a house of his own. The *Wild Duck,* bought when he made his first million, had been home. Now he decided to combine everything he had ever wanted under one Spanish-tiled roof.

The house, estimated to be two years in the building, was to take ten. A boardinghouse was erected as quarters for the army of workers employed in the construction, while the materials, including granite from Vermont, were brought by boat or barge. During the decade required to complete the house and gardens, Gramma gave birth to five of her seven children, two of whom were stillborn, leaving Grandfather a free rein with the house.

The result was a turn-of-the-century triumph, a bouillabaisse of architecture reminiscent of the Spain of his ancestors combined with touches of Georgian, Colonial, and French Renaissance, spread over two acres, without thought of saving money or space, larger, grander than any other island mansions, including those the Morgans and Rockefellers built on Jekyll and the Carnegies on Cumberland.

As the adored only son, Jere, Maggie Royal's father, was pampered and dominated. When he entered Harvard at the age of 17, in 1912, two years after his father's death, Gramma bought him a Hispano-Suiza Alfonso XIII. She also provided a string of polo ponies, a Negro valet, and an allowance that in those days was considered exorbitant. Gramma gave him the bachelor quarters in the pool house, where he entertained his classmates from Harvard and his friends from Savannah. Newt, the butler, was instructed to place an unopened bottle of bourbon in each bedroom daily.

"Jere was always in scrapes of some kind," Gramma's sister Meg said. "I mind the time he was arrested for drunkenness and disturbing the peace in Starksville, and put in jail before the newly appointed sheriff knew he was a Stark Islander."

Gramma went to Starksville and swept into the jail, demanding that her son be freed at once. The Starksville jail was a putrid place of peeling paint and lack of plumbing. The jailer sat with his chair propped against the wall and his hat down over his face, dozing. As Gramma swept past, he spat, hitting the hem of her long white skirt.

Gramma wheeled around. Using her parasol, she gave the feet of the chair a push, sending chair and jailer crashing to the floor.

"Stop spitting, you son of a bitch," she told the startled jailer. Prodding him with the point of her parasol as he scrambled to his feet, she added, "Next time stand up in the presence of a lady!"

She found her son in the drunk tank in the midst of a crap game with some sharecroppers who had been in town for Saturday night. He was on his knees, engrossed in throwing the dice, hurling them expertly against the wall and watching them roll back down onto the floor. As he cried out the pleas and exhortations learned from the island Negroes, his cellmates egged him on, betting on whether or not he would make his point.

The stench of vomit, urine, and sweat was almost overpowering. Holding her lavender-scented Irish-linen handkerchief to her nose, Gramma ordered Jere to come with her at once.

"I'm having a winning streak," he answered. "Mother dear, why don't you do your shopping or make your calls. You can pick me up when you're ready to go home!"

Shortly afterward, Gramma had the jail painted from top to bottom, and a special Stark suite built on the second floor. This was furnished with antiques and expensive curtains, a pool table, and a bar that was kept well stocked, in case any further members of the family should mistakenly be—Gramma's word—incarcerated.

Jere McDermott left Harvard his junior year to go to England. War had broken out in Europe and he was determined to fight. He joined the newly formed Royal Flying Corps.

The legendary Rosa Lewis, the Duchess of Jermyn Street, kept open house for the "brave American boys" at her Cavendish Hotel.

It was there that she introduced Jeremy to Mairin (Gaelic for Maureen) O'Connor.

Uncle Oomlot told Maggie Royal how her parents met. "One of Rosa's old Harrovians—there were always languid young lords on the premises drinking 'cherrybums' of champagne, who had gone to Harrow or Eton and on to Cambridge or Oxford—brought Mairin to the Cavendish. Rosa mistakenly showed them into your father's room.

" 'An' 'ere's the loo,' Rosa cried, flinging open the door. Your father was about to take a bath and was stark naked. 'Fourteen shillin's,' Rosa cried, 'young Stark not included!'

"Rosa always claimed your mother decided then and there young Stark *was* to be included. But Mairin wasn't about to capitulate until she found out he owned an island and a Hispano-Suiza Alfonso XIII!"

As the star of a hit comedy, Mairin was the toast of London, pursued and acclaimed by everyone from the Prince of Wales to the fourteenth Marquess of Wickwold, Earl Wickwold de Marr, Baron Marr, Lord of the Five Isles, and Hereditary Grand Falconer to the Kingdom of Galway, known to his friends as "Binkie," and to Rosa Lewis as "Lord Thingummy."

Jere pleaded with Mairin to marry him. She refused, her excuse being that she could not forsake England in wartime.

When the war ended, Jere came home sporting numerous decorations and walking with a limp, which made him even more irresistible to the Southern belles who gravitated to the island. Possibly he might have succumbed and agreed to let any one of a number of ambitious mamas ring out the wedding bells, if Mairin had not suddenly appeared in a revue Ivor Novello brought to New York. She was an overnight sensation, wearing a top hat and tailcoat and doing a tap dance. Jere abandoned the island, and, with Gramma's warnings about adventuresses and loose women ringing in his ears, drove the Hispano to New York and laid siege.

Mairin found New York different from London. Lacking the adulation of the lords and dukes and belted earls, finding only callow collegians hanging out around the stage door, she was more receptive. Possibly she was impressed by the Delmonico dinners and the flowers sent daily by train from the island gardens to decorate her dressing room. For, when the run of the play ended, she eloped with Jere McDermott.

When Mairin returned to England to star in another revue, Jere went with her. Not content to play a minor part in the life of his actress wife, he volunteered for the American relief organization established by Herbert Hoover to relieve Europe's postwar food shortage. He worked hard, spending a large part of his personal fortune and distributing food to starving children and adults. Meanwhile, the marriage began to deteriorate. Within the year they agreed to separate. Soon afterward, Jere was driving a truck, carrying food and supplies, when a child ran onto the street in front of him. He jammed on the brakes.

The truck skidded off the highway and overturned, pinning Jere beneath it and killing him. He died without knowing that Mairin was pregnant.

Maggie Royal grew up to resemble her father, with the straight, high-bridged Stark nose and cheekbones. "Tall and thin," Gramma used to say, "covered with skin." Her only legacy from her mother was her eyes, blue-violet, Irish eyes, "put in with smutty fingers."

For the first few years of her life, Maggie Royal lived in England, cared for by nannies and governesses, while her remarried mother continued to perform. Whenever she went to the theater in later years, the little trills and glissandi on the trumpets and woodwinds and the bangings on the drums evoked memories of squeezing sixpences into slots that released tiny pairs of opera glasses with which you could study the expressions on the faces of the men in the orchestra as they warmed up. There was a sense of safety and plush and gilt and chocolates in silver paper which Miss Speers, her nanny, let her have as a treat. Then the magic moment when the theater went dark and the footlights shone on red velvet curtains, the excited anticipation, and the need to stand in order to see better, which meant being pushed by her nanny back into her overlarge seat.

She remembered waiting anxiously for her mother to return to the flat from rehearsals. She saved up the things that had happened that day to tell her, how the pony she had ridden in the park had shied at a lorry while crossing the street. She had not fallen off, and the riding master had said, "Well done." She thought her mother would be proud of her, but instead, she asked her maid, Naomi, to call Nanny to take her away, as she was absolutely exhausted and must have her rest before the evening performance.

Maggie Royal did not cry, because that annoyed her mother.

"If you must cry," Mairin said once, "consider those who have to look at you."

Maggie Royal tried hard to please her. She hated to sit still. Nonetheless, she learned how to sew and to knit and do crewelwork. She made a cloth for her mother's dressing-room table as a surprise. Later, she found it in the wastebasket. Mairin had used it to wipe off her cold cream, and had thrown it away, the way she did the sketches of horses, and the flowers Maggie Royal left on her pillow. Later, she would find the crumpled papers and dead blossoms in the trash.

Maggie Royal would have preferred anger, overt hostility, physical punishment, anything but indifference. Her mother made her feel as if she were a non-person, as though she did not exist. "Actresses shouldn't have children," her stepfather Swanson, the director, consoled her. "If they do, they shouldn't talk about them!"

Maggie Royal lost herself in the books, the play scripts her mother brought home. She wept over Jane Eyre's schooldays, and tried to understand Oscar Wilde. She delved into the *Forsyte Saga* and finished *Tess of the d'Urbervilles*. But the book she loved most was *Wuthering Heights*.

Following a visit to Devon, where Miss Speers had a sister on a farm near Barnstable, she was Cathy, racing across the wild moor pursued by Heathcliff. She had loved the wind and wildness and wandered for hours before she was found. Miss Speers had been frightened and then furious. "What would your mother say?" she scolded. "Traipsing around like a common Gypsy!"

"I wish I was a Gypsy," Maggie Royal retorted. "Then I could live outdoors. Not be locked in a flat and have to wear dresses."

After this episode, Maggie Royal was sent to the boarding school in Kent, where she identified with Jane Eyre. Night after night she lay huddled beneath the sparse covers, cold and unhappy. In order not to feel afraid and alone, she dreamed of a horse that would be all her own, a golden chestnut with a white star, like Golden Isle, the mare her American grandmother described in her letters.

She pored over the letters signed "Gramma." Reading and rereading the descriptions of the garden, the beach, and the animals, she tried to visualize Stark Island. High palms like those at Cannes, where she had spent a summer in a huge hotel facing the crowded beach. Strange wild creatures, mules with extra-long ears, and enormous pigs, as shown in the puppet shows the hotel put on for children. Indians, as pictured in her book of American history, and black people, with rings in their noses and ears. She dreamed strange dreams, and filled the notebook Miss Speers had given her, "in order to learn penmanship," with stories.

Most of the stories were about Stark Island. There was one in which she became mistress of a great house on a remote island. She lived alone in a tower, writing stories in her notebook. A young chevalier came riding from the wood on a wild stallion. He called to her to run away with him. The tower was guarded by a fierce nanny wearing a gray cap and cloak with a red lining, white cotton stockings and black high-button shoes. Somehow Maggie Royal managed to escape from her. The young chevalier scooped her up onto his white stallion, and they galloped off through a misty wood full of loving, friendly animals.

"You must bring her home," Swanson, who was Mairin's second husband, said, when they visited Maggie Royal in Kent. "The child's miserable and suffering from neglect."

From then on Miss Speers tutored her at home.

Miss Speers was one of a long parade of nannies and mademoiselles, for servants did not last long with Mairin O'Connor. Naomi, who had been with her from the time she began her career in the chorus line on the London stage, was the only exception. Tall, tight-lipped, and dour, she guarded her like the huge Irish wolfhound, Tara. Naomi was aggressively possessive, jealous of Maggie Royal and of Mairin's husbands. Later, when Swanson had the marriage annulled, he complained that, between the "damned bitches, the woman, and the dog," they were never alone long enough to consummate the marriage.

When the C. B. Cochran hit musical, starring Mairin, went on tour, Maggie Royal was finally allowed to go to America.

She was ten when, in the spring of 1930, her mother sent her from England by ocean liner with Miss Speers.

In Washington, Aunt Lucy and her daughter, Adele, who lived in Middleburg, Virginia, saw them off on the Atlantic Coast Line. Aunt Lucy was tall and spare. She wore a tweed suit and a brown felt riding hat, and asked Maggie Royal if she had foxhunted in Leicestershire. Maggie Royal said she hadn't, and Aunt Lucy told her she must come to Dunwoody and hunt, that Virginia was considered the Leicestershire of America. Maggie Royal liked her cousin Adele at once. Adele had short, very curly hair and a wide, guileless smile. She was somewhat plump. Her sweater was buttoned crooked, and there was a gap where a hook was missing from her short plaid skirt.

Maggie Royal never forgot the excitement of being "aboard the cars." The president of the railroad, General Elliot, was a friend of Gramma's, and their compartment was filled with flowers and fruit, courtesy of the Atlantic Coast Line. Even Miss Speers was impressed by Gramma's private railroad car—with the name *Maggie Royal* in full gold leaf on each side, and designs blown in the frosted glass above each window—that waited for them on a siding in Savannah, to be attached to the Starksville short line.

"Comfy quarters," Gramma demanded when Grandfather ordered the car to be built by his friend George M. Pullman. "Not stiffish!"

The train stopped at the small brick Starksville station, in view of the *Great Oak* waiting at the pier.

Captain Ben, who ran the boat, Big Dick, and Hercules and other island Negroes who had been "in town" for the day waited to load the gear aboard for the trip to Stark Island.

Maggie Royal's heart beat faster as the boat rounded the last bend, and the black shape of the island rose before her.

It was long and narrow, wider at the southern end, narrowing to the north, shaped like one of the cloudy green bottles dug up near the sites of the old Indian village and Spanish mission. In the distance the tower and chimneys of Great Oak rose above the tall trees.

At the sound of the boat's whistle, the children already in residence for the summer came running through the park beneath the shrouded oaks, accompanied by barking dogs. The new arrivals poured off the boat and fell into one another's arms, everyone talking at once.

"The cousins!"

In the beginning she was overwhelmed by them. The English children she knew were carefully dressed boys and girls, speaking only when spoken to. This was a raucous, self-assured group, wearing old faded shorts and jodhpurs, who welcomed her with, "So you're Maggie Royal, our English cousin," and gazed at her as if she had dropped in from some planet in outer space.

Gramma saw a thin shabby little girl, small for her age, whose blue-violet eyes were huge in her pinched white face. Her long straight black hair was pulled tautly back into two braids hanging to her waist. She had outgrown her blue coat with the brown fur collar and matching hat, and her leggings were too short. Leggings at ten years old, and in Georgia?

"Miss Speers makes me wear them," Maggie Royal said. "They itch!"

"Well, you won't need them here," Gramma said tartly. "And you've outgrown your coat. It's . . . kattywampus." At sight of Maggie Royal's look ("like a waif," Gramma said later), her heart went out to her. "Come," she said, taking Maggie Royal into her arms. "Come and see Great Oak. Your new home."

The long avenue was bordered by the live oaks originally planted in honor of General Oglethorpe's first visit to the island. The oaks, planted not for a day but for the tomorrows of subsequent generations, formed a cathedral nave, a formal canopy extending to the great house.

As they drove along, smelling the scented air, hearing the creak of the carriage and Sapelo's soft voice urging on Gramma's prizewinning hackneys, fat island pigs turned to glare at their approach. With snorts and indignant grunts, their piglets scattered like buckshot. Sleek wild cattle and horses grazing by the wayside lifted their heads and vanished in the underbrush.

Regal black swans floated on the lake Grandfather built at the bottom of the terraced gardens; wild ducks and geese, the honking calls of which could be heard in early fall and spring, came to set down on the ponds during their annual migrations.

48

Crepe myrtles, rose and white oleanders, and magnolias bloomed amid the oaks, with their dundrearies of gray Spanish moss.

The great oak that stood in front of the house was so old that its limbs, bent by their own weight, reached along the ground, plowing into it, to emerge covered with fine green ferns farther on. For hundreds of years its gnarled branches had extended, like arms, in a gesture of welcome. Its raised roots provided resting places where the small animals that roamed the island could curl up in sleep. Cattle and horses could stand beneath its leafy boughs for protection against the cold wind and squalls that blew in from the sea.

The house her grandfather built was a vast towered, turreted, and chimneyed place, so massive and lacking in proportion its very ugliness held a fascination.

As a final whimsical touch, Grandfather had painted the stuccoed exterior a Bermuda blue, whereas the window frames and sills were painted green to ward off what the Gullah Negroes called the evil spirits or "hants."

Great stone steps led up to the veranda with its white-painted wicker furniture and joggle board on which generations of Great Oak children "joggled." There were huge pots of ferns and rubber plants. The steps were guarded on either side by ferocious openmouthed lions, which Gramma always patted when she went in or out of the house. The huge carved front door bore a heavy brass knocker displaying the Stark coat of arms, a lion tied to a tree with *Keep Tryst* scrolled over it, derived from the clan motto of Stark Island in the Hebrides.

A six-branch brass chandelier lit the front hall. The floors gleamed with wax. A mirror in an ornate gold frame hung over a huge chest. Next to it was a blackboard carrying this warning: "BEWARE OF SNAKES, TIDES, GETTING LOST."

Gramma explained that the trails were deceptive. It was easy to become lost winding between the stands of palmetto, oak, and pine. After a number of guests new to the island failed to return from walks, she had put up the blackboard—on which everyone was to list his destination and estimated time of return. A search party was sent out for those who failed to show up at the appointed time, and the culprits were severely reprimanded.

From the hallway, steps led down into the vast vaulted living room. It was so large that Gramma's concert grand and the heavy mahogany furniture carved with lion's-head arms and feet, looked almost as small as the furniture in the playhouse built in the pool house for the children to play in.

A sixteen-branch Waterford-glass chandelier held candles made from the wax of island apiaries. The candles that Gramma bought by the gross for the wrought-iron and silver candleholders and sconces had been hand-dipped on the nearby island of Ossabaw.

A fireplace large enough to roast one of the island oxen stood at the end of the long room. Mantel and chimneys were made of stone brought in sailing vessels as ballast in the early days of the colony. Glass-fronted cabinets held Gramma's treasures bought on her wedding trip, Canton china, French snuffboxes, and Venetian glass.

At the other end of the long hallway, steps led down to the basement dining room. The long mahogany refectory table built to fit the room's proportions could seat forty "without rubbing elbows." Gramma did not permit electric light during dinner. Family and guests dined by light from the candles in the chandelier overhead and in the holders at the corners of the table.

A great staircase led from the hall to the upper floors. Gramma told Maggie Royal it had been bought out of an Elizabethan monastery that was being demolished. Grandfather McDermott had decided it did not look old or "antique enough." He ordered little holes to resemble worm holes drilled in it. He liked the effect so much that instead of carpeting it, he left it bare, ordering that it be waxed with "dancing wax" from the can in the pantry with the full-skirted lady dancing on it.

Maggie Royal had never had a banister to slide down that, as Gramma said, was "a fanny wide," and her first afternoon at Great Oak, she practiced sliding down it, landing with a thump in the hallway.

Maggie Royal knew she was happy because from the moment she arrived on Stark Island she couldn't wait for each new day to begin.

It was torture to lie in bed waiting for Miss Speers to get up, permit her to dress, and then have to wait for breakfast to be served in the nursery. It seemed to her there would never be enough time to explore the island and discover all its wonders.

· 3 ·

Two days after Maggie Royal's arrival there was a storm. It swept in from the Atlantic, draping the island in fog and sheets of rain. It reminded her of the wild Devon moor.

The morning of the gale, she awakened when it was barely light. Unable to restrain herself any longer, she pulled on her clothes—shirt, shorts, and sneakers handed down from various "cousins." They had been unearthed in the trunk in the nursery in which generations of Great Oak children had grown up, surpervised by Dah, the ancient Gullah nurse, who considered Miss Speers an interloper.

She slid down the wide banister, landing lightly on her feet.

Ignoring the sign on the blackboard, she stepped around the dogs asleep in the hall, cautioning the spaniels and pointers, house dogs belonging to various members of the family, to be quiet, and closed the front door behind her.

She followed the path that led through the dark tunnellike woods. The ground, cushioned by fallen oak leaves, was springy underfoot. The air smelled like ripe bananas, from the wisteria climbing around the trunks of the oaks, mixed with the dampness of rain and sea and salt. The woods opened suddenly, disclosing a round pond shining like a silver dollar in the midst of the greenery surrounding it. The trees were thick with white birds, as if bits of cloud or cotton had caught on them. Sensing her approach, the birds rose from their nests, a chattering mass of wings beating upward toward the gray sky overhead. Beneath them the wild animals drank from the fresh-water pool. Several deer lifted their heads, turned, and vanished into the palmettos. The horses turned to stare. At the sight of them Maggie Royal laughed aloud with joy. Instinctively she searched for the golden horse of her dreams. But the horse was not there. It was merely a bunch of feral tackies, their coats matted with mud, balls of gray clay swinging from their tails. She walked on. The wall of green parted to disclose the beach. She began to run. Her long unbraided hair was soon soaked, her face wet and shining. Breathless, she stopped and glanced around.

The sand pushed up by the wind into high dunes walling the trees and palmettos beyond, the beach all looked the same. She began walking back the way she had come, pausing to watch the pewter-colored waves rolling in, the gulls circling overhead. She climbed the dunes, seeking the path by which she had come, skirting the forest until she was certain she had walked farther than necessary. Still there was no break in the wall of green. She turned toward the beach. Several wild horses stood in a circle, huddled together, heads lowered, tails whipped between their legs by the wind. A red cow and calf approached, and a family of pigs bounded into the forest, their tails curled over their backs.

She was hungry now, wet through, and cold. Finding a dune, she leaned against it, shutting her eyes against the wind and rain.

An instinct that somebody was there caused her to open them.

A boy stood in front of her, tall and lanky. Khaki trousers were rolled up to his knees, and he was barefoot. His face was narrow and bony. Rain sparkled on his hair, silvery against the black. His skin, reddish brown like the color of the American Indians in Miss Speers's American-history book, made her realize how pale she was from the London winter. His eyebrows were dark, almost fierce. But it was his eyes that caught and held her. Dark, green, the color of wildly tossing waves. Beyond him two liver-and-white pointers ran along the beach.

"Are you lost, little girl?" he asked.

Little girl, indeed! She bristled. Who was this island boy to ask her such an impertinent question, she who had crossed the Atlantic, while he probably had never been farther than Starksville, if there. "No, I'm not lost," she lied, sitting very straight and mustering what dignity she could in her tatterdemalion shorts and wet windswept hair.

"Then what are you doing here?" He gazed down at her accusingly, as if she were an intruder.

She forgot her shyness. "I am Maggie Royal McDermott, and I belong here."

"I beg your pardon," he said coldly, making a pretend bow. "I might have known from the funny way you talk. *The* Maggie Royal. All the way from England!" His eyes had changed color. Now they were like bits of green glass. Hostile. "Of course, it's *your* beach. Forgive me for intruding."

She wondered why he had a chip on his shoulder—"chippie," Miss Speers would have said.

"It's really not my beach," she said gently. "It belongs to all the Starks, just as Grandfather said."

Some of the hostility went out of his voice and eyes. "You shouldn't go wandering about alone."

"And why not?" she asked defiantly.

"There are snakes, tides, hants at the boneyard."

"What are hants?"

"Ghosts." He rolled his eyes mysteriously. "Things that go bump in the night."

"But it's daytime."

"The Plateye can get you anytime!"

"Plateye?"

"An evil spirit. The evilest of spirits!"

"And what is the boneyard?"

"That's where the island animals go to die, or when they are dead, they're taken there and buried in the ravine. They say there are people bones, too. Slaves were hung from the hanging tree. Duels were fought in the clearing."

Maggie Royal's small proud head lifted. Her eyes flashed. "Once I was lost on the Devon moor. All kinds of ghostly things happen there. I wasn't scared. Besides, I feel I've always known Stark Island. From Gramma's letters. I used to dream about it. I could shut my eyes and see the tall old trees, the horses and deer and alligators."

"Would you like to see an alligator?" he asked suddenly, unexpectedly.

"Oh, yes," she cried delightedly, forgetting how wet and cold she was.

"All right. Follow me." He called to his dogs, who came bounding up from the water's edge, and plunged into the wall of palmettos behind the dunes.

Light shafted through the greenery. Birds made rustling noises in the oaks and palmettos. The face of a young deer stared at them, framed by palm fronds, then silently vanished.

He walked fast, noiselessly, striding ahead with one foot directly in front of the other. "Perusing," he called it.

"That means to survey, to examine closely," Maggie Royal said, remembering her grammar.

"Maybe that's what it means where you come from." He paused to observe a cardinal perched on a dead branch. "Here it means to walk slowly through the woods. It's a Gullah word. The Gullahs are the island Negroes. They speak a kind of language of their own. For instance, that bird is a 'redbuud.' " He stopped suddenly. Gazing down, he stepped off the path, beckoning her to follow. "I walk around ants," he explained, pointing to a long zigzagging line of tiny creatures carrying matter in their mouths.

The prayer she had noticed on the needlepoint pillow in her Grandmother's room came to mind.

> *Dear Father, Hear and Bless*
> *The Beasts and Singing Birds*
> *And Guard with Tenderness*
> *Small Things That Have No Words*
> *Amen*

He led her to a large dark pool. "I talk to animals," he said when they reached the water's edge.

"Like Dr. Dolittle," she said.

He swung around. His green eyes were turned on her in their full green intensity. "You've read the Dr. Dolittle books?"

"Oh, yes. They're wonderful!"

"Have you been to Puddleby-on-the-Marsh?"

She shook her head."Oh, but I'd like to, and meet Jip and Polynesia and Dab-Dab!"

"So would I." For an instant his green-eyed gaze held hers. Then he looked down into the pool. "Be quiet," he cautioned, squatting down beside it, "while I make my 'gator calls!"

It was a few minutes before his strange hoarse calls were answered. Then the creature with its broad rounded snout, evil red eyes, and awesome jagged teeth swam toward them. "Hi, Ol' Ugly," he called out. The alligator came to the water's edge. Maggie Royal, entranced, did not move.

"You're not afraid?" He sounded surprised. "Girls are usually scared of Old Ugly."

Their glances met and suddenly the boy smiled, a warming grin that came like sudden sunlight after the darkness of the storm-filled morning. It lit his thin face, and his eyes shifted color again, flooding her with their all-green approval.

"Come on," he said, rising. "Let's go for a walk on the beach."

He told her the birds she had seen were American and snowy egrets and that the rookery was one of the most famous in the South. Bird-watchers, he said, came from all over the country to see them during the spring nesting season.

They walked back along the beach. He showed her shells and told her their names: turkey wing and lettered olive, whelks and scallops and sand dollars—some of which he threw back into the ocean, explaining that they were still alive.

It was long past breakfast when the boy left Maggie Royal at Great Oak, but she no longer cared how late it was or how much she might be scolded. She watched him swing down the drive, calling to his dogs. Only then did she realize she did not know his name.

Miss Speers, the governess Mairin had sent from England in order to keep Maggie Royal from becoming *"une petite sauvage,"* did not last long on the island. She missed Green Park and her nanny friends and found the island Negroes and their customs barbaric. Clinging to her fragile gentility, she wore her Green Park outfit—gray cap and cloak with a red lining, white cotton stockings and shoes—whenever she went walking on the island trails. At night she changed into a gray wool dress, black stockings, and black high-button shoes in order to dine alone in her room. She liked to display the crested references she kept in her bureau drawer, and looked down on the black servants.

Miss Speers had eyes like searchlights on prison ramparts, and her voice was as sharp as the shell of a razor clam. At mealtimes she would not let the children speak, and rapped their knuckles with a ruler if they put their hands on the table. Even Gramma found her intimidating and called her Miss Medea.

When Miss Speers complained to Gramma that Cook Ada was slovenly for following the Gullah custom of plastering her head with salt to ease a headache and then using some of it to flavor her famous terrapin stew, Gramma wrote to Mairin that the governess was a troublemaker, had all the servants up in arms, and she would have to go.

She was replaced by Mademoiselle. Mademoiselle was young and pretty and sang French nursery rhymes like *"Sur le Pont d'Avignon"* and *"Au Clair de la Lune"* in a high clear voice that enchanted the Negroes. At night she joined the servants in their quarters, where Jazzbo, one of the stable hands, played his fiddle. Mademoiselle taught Jazzbo some of her French ditties, and the Negroes instructed her in the old plantation chants and the Gullahs' coastal slave songs. The strains of:

> *I'm go' lay down,*
> *I'm go', I'm go'*
> *Lay down my life for the Lord*

would waft through the warm scented night to the closed-in sleeping porch of the children's wing, where Maggie Royal lay looking through the screens at the stars.

Apparently Jazzbo instructed Mademoiselle in other things as well, for one day the governess rushed into the nursery, tears streaming down her cheeks.

"Your gran'mère, she fire me," she choked, "tell me to go home and not come back to thees island." Mademoiselle could not understand what she had done wrong. "Josephine Baker is black, yes?" she protested. "She has white man for husband, yes?"

Following Mademoiselle's departure, Gramma wrote Mairin not to hire anyone else. Although Dah, who had nursed generations of Great Oak children, had been retired, she would find somebody else or Maggie Royal could take care of herself. The outside governesses, she concluded, made trouble in the household. Either they considered the Negroes ignorant and patronized them or, like Mademoiselle, were altogether too familiar.

Mairin had returned to London to get a divorce in order to marry her leading man in her current hit. Her husband-to-be was several years younger than she, and she was glad not to be embarrassed by *"une petite sauvage"* on her honeymoon. To her joy, Maggie Royal was allowed to remain on Stark Island, growing like one of the wild horses, long and leggy and free.

"Jared, it must have been Jared," Gramma said when Maggie Royal told her about the boy she had met on the beach. "Jared Stark, of the Long Point Starks. Jared would be about thirteen now."

55

. .

Whenever Maggie Royal thought of Stark Island she thought of her cousin Jared. In her mind the two were intermingled, one with the other.

He wasn't really a cousin. More a "connection," as they said in England. It was just that everyone found it easier to call one another cousin than to sort out the complexities of generations and their relationships.

Jared was descended from Robert Stark, the black sheep of the family, who escaped from Scotland with a price on his head, imposed for murdering a fellow clansman he said had "ravished" his sister. Once in the newly formed Georgia colony, he had become a buccaneer, robbing the ships that plied the coastal waters. The ruins of the watchtower that had been his stronghold still stood at the south end of the island, and the children spent hours digging near the cove where he anchored his ships, finding rum bottles, pottery, and, once, a Spanish doubloon.

There was an unmistakable air about Jared. His sharp features, the Stark nose, high cheekbones, dark olive complexion, and extraordinary green eyes—the eyes of a young hawk, Gramma said—were inherited from princes and pirates, Indian chiefs, and the Creole beauty one of his forebears had married after the Battle of New Orleans.

That first summer, Maggie Royal and Jared were constantly together. At night she had only to close her eyes to recall the way he moved through the woods, silently, effortlessly, like one of the island deer. There was a quietness, a separateness about him, a sense of mystery that set him apart. He had a deep primitive bond with the island, a closeness to its earth, as if something of the earth's violence and simplicity were a part of his being.

For Maggie Royal, Jared was the key to the island's mysteries. With Jared she came to know the bends and ruts made by wagons, which made horse travel dangerous, and the holes where pigs had rooted. Through him, the oaks became her friends. Their trunks, sprayed with coral-colored lichen resembling splashes of red paint, served as landmarks, blazing the tracks zigzagging through the dark woods. Some of the oaks spread over almost an acre, with trunks ten feet thick. Bromeliads and tree ferns grew from them. Jared told her about the resurrection fern, how its curled, withered fronds remain dry and lifeless until reborn by rain, becoming verdant and alive once again.

On a warm day she and Jared would see alligators sunning on the mud banks, or in the lonely remote swamps of the interior, a dark terrapin head bobbing among the stumps of long-dead trees crowned with osprey nests of sticks and moss.

The cousins sensed that Jared knew secrets they could never know, and this gave him a glamour that made him their natural leader. Gramma hired him to act as a kind of tutor and teach the younger children island things.

Through him, they learned to check the crab pots in the sound and fish for mullet from the bateau; to go clamming in the thick, oozing mud on the point, feeling for shells with their toes; to gather oysters from the tidal creeks and to eat the translucent shrimp, clear as gelatin.

Maggie Royal could not always remember Jared's face, but she never forgot his hands, long, tapering, artist's hands, deft and sure, strong and yet gentle enough to soothe a tiny bird fallen from a nest. On the rare occasions when his arm stole around her, when they were moved by a small fawn drinking or a wild newborn colt struggling to its feet, she felt a melting sensation as he drew her against his shoulder.

At other times he withdrew to some dark inner place where she could not reach him, not speaking for long hours as he filled page after page of his sketchbook with island scenes. Gramma called it the dark side of his nature. "People who grow up on an island, near the wind and sea," she said, "are sometimes wild and strange. The Black Starks have an 'acquired sorrow.'"

Maggie Royal came to recognize his moods, which were like the clouds overhead, on dark days gray and forbidding, on fine days shot through with light, yet always changing. She sensed that he had a curious sexual authority, as tangible and unforgettable as his green eyes, which when he was happy or interested were flecked with yellow lights like those of the sun shafting through the cabbage palms.

In her experience of rejection and paradox, Jared represented a secure island world, a haven where if one did what had to be done, protecting nature and avoiding injury to the birds and animals, one could live with freedom and dignity, as Jared's family did. For Jared lived on the island all year round, leaving only to go to public school in Starksville, commuting daily by the island boat.

"We try to live as the Indians did," Jared's father said one day as Maggie Royal studied his collection of arrowheads and artifacts dug from the Indian mounds. "We eat from the rivers and the land. We are fortunate to live in a place where change comes slowly."

Unlike his buccaneering ancestor, Jared's father was a quiet, thoughtful man who had renounced a promising legal career on the mainland to live in the tabby house he built on the point called Long Point.

Jared's mother, like her forebear Tomochichi, the Indian chief who became General Oglethorpe's friend and whose portrait beside that of his nephew, holding a captive eagle, is familiar to every Georgia school-child, was beautiful—tall and straight and strong. Her hair, which hung in a long braid to her waist, was the color of the tame crow that roosted on her shoulder or sat on the rump of her white pony when she rode through the woods.

She was a silent woman who did not speak unless spoken to. Yet when she looked at her husband or son or daughter, there was a light in her eyes, an expression Maggie Royal had never seen in her own mother's face and that made her throat ache.

Jared's sister, Susan, was Maggie Royal's age. Polio when she was eight had left her crippled from the waist down. Only after the most painful and arduous therapy was she able to graduate to a wheelchair. Never again would she walk.

But although she lost her robust quality, during the long months of illness, she never lost heart. Through her days of pain and suffering she managed to smile and show her concern for those around her. Jared adored her and spent hours reading to her from the books in his father's library, and she was one of the few he would allow to see his rough sketches.

Maggie Royal's visit to Jared's house introduced her to another world. In a way she could not then articulate, it was brought home to her that one should develop a sort of intensified perception about human life, that it is the response people make within themselves to each experience that molds and shapes them. "Each person should take a hard look at himself," Jared's father said once. "Human freedom, achievement, begins with the individual."

Negroes called Jared's father Lawyer Stark and his mother Miss Maria. They came to her for the cough syrup she made from pine needles and to find out which roots were best for medicinal purposes. Without a doctor on the island—only old Dah, who had served as a midwife for generations of Long Point children—Miss Maria's knowledge of medicine and salves was indispensable.

Joe-Ali was practically a member of the family. He was a huge man, at least six feet, four inches tall, and so strong it was said he could catch one of the wild island bulls and throw it down with his bare hands. In his mid-forties, he was lean and lithe, with the passionate eyes of a visionary.

Joe-Ali lived in the cabin of an old fishing boat hauled high up onto the Long Point beach. His living quarters were immaculately neat. The walls were lined with shelves of books which Jared's father had given to him and taught him to read. When not poling his boat along the tidal creeks, Joe-Ali read the classics, Gibbon and Greek plays, Jane Austen and Henry James. Jared's father called him a black Thoreau.

Several tame raccoons kept him company. Aristotle, Plato, and Sophocles. They lived in the big oak beside Joe-Ali's quarters. When Joe-Ali called to them, they came down out of the tree and leaped onto his shoulders, wrapping themselves around his neck like fur pieces.

Joe-Ali refused to work at Great Oak. Proud and independent, he spent his days fishing from his flat-bottom bateau, but whenever Jared's father or mother asked him to plow the kitchen garden or mend the picket fence, he was quick to do so. "Lawyer Stark and Miss Maria are my friends," he said simply.

On Stark Island the seasons were marked by the comings and goings of guests and relatives. During the summer, the fall shooting sea-

58

son, and over the Christmas holidays, the big house was chockablock. The relatives most often in residence were the Howards from Virginia, the Pritchards from Boston, the LeFevres from New Orleans, and the Cromptons from New York, Gramma's daughters, their husbands (Gramma called her sons-in-law the "John Does," for she could never keep them straight) and children. Gramma's younger sisters, the maiden aunts Amy and Meg, helped as hostesses. Both had been sent north to school—Aunt Meg had gone on to Wellesley, where she was pictured in photo albums wearing a long skirt and middy blouse and winning the hoop race. In Gramma's words, both had "overreacted," finding Eastern social cliques and their attitude toward the South arrogant and in-furiating. ("Meg hated the North," Gramma said. "She was convinced white slavers would kidnap her and hold her prisoner.") Now they re-fused to travel farther from the "home place" in Starksville than to the island for holidays and special occasions.

Great-Aunt Meg was Maggie Royal's favorite aunt. She was a spec-tacular horsewoman. She had caused raised eyebrows by becoming one of the first women of her generation to ride astride, wearing breeches, boots, and a divided skirt when she hunted with the Starksville foxhunt.

Gramma believed that genealogy was important. In each genera-tion there was one person designated to feed and nourish the family tree. Aunt Amy was "teacher." "Learning the ancestors," she called it. In the ledger in the "present" room she noted down new births, birthdays, an-niversaries, weddings, deaths, pregnancies, and illnesses. Occasionally she cornered one of the children, demanding to know which Stark fought at the Battle of Bloody Marsh in 1742 or what year Great-Uncle Lowell Pritchard had been ambassador to Great Britain. Or made them recite the names of the people in the portraits in the dining room. (Aunt Meg, who spoke of the War Between the States as "the recent unpleas-antness" as though it were yesterday, always refused to identify the Union uncle, saying, when told he'd been captured and died at Ander-sonville, "Good! I'm glad they got 'im!")

Adele Howard soon became Maggie Royal's favorite cousin. Her father, Uncle Randy Howard, was a master of foxhounds in Virginia, and her mother, Aunt Lucy, was a keen horsewoman. Unlike Constance Crompton, she was fun to be with and always ready to do things.

Constance's mother, Aunt Emily, had married Tom Crompton, a New York advertising executive, and lived in New York and Greenwich. Aunt Emily was known as "the starer" because whenever she entered a house she went about staring at the invitations displayed on mantels or bulletin boards and at other things, often picking them up, turning them over to find out where they were made, as if estimating their value. Maggie Royal sensed at the outset that Aunt Emily did this with people too, deciding who would be of value to her, discarding the rest. Her daughter Constance, two years older than Adele, was cast in the same mold as her mother, and clearly resented having to give up her summer at their house in Greenwich to come to Stark Island. Constance spent most of the time sunning by the swimming pool or playing bridge and Mah-Jongg with the grown-ups.

The boy cousins most often visiting Great Oak were Adele's older brother Jere, Thorny Pritchard, Noble LeFevre, and Constance's little brother, Harry, known as Harry the Horror, initially because of his popping balloons blown up for another child's birthday party and later for similar pranks.

Noble was the son of Aunt Leonie, who had married a New Orleans LeFevre. He was slender and graceful, with the drawn, hollow look of a French aristocrat. Girls adored his Byronesque looks and manner. Although at fifteen he was only a year older than Thorny, he wore a world-weary air along with his overelegant clothes—narrow slacks and silk shirts with broad collars, open at the neck, that displayed the golden hairs on his chest. Aunt Leonie was said to be in reduced circumstances. Her husband had lost a fortune gambling and committed suicide by walking into the Gulf of Mexico. The cousins believed this was the reason why Noble refused to swim in the pool or the ocean.

Thorny, even thinner than Noble and a shade taller, had alert brown eyes and a long aesthetic face. Alongside the impeccable Noble he resembled a scarecrow, his shirt and trousers hanging from his frame as though from a clothesline. He wore glasses, and as Maggie Royal soon discovered, read "deep" books. When not reading, he generally swam. "Forty laps a day," he said. "Life is a balance. Moderation in all things. It's important to balance the body with the brain."

His father, Thorndike Pritchard, was a Boston banker and the son of Lowell Pritchard, a former ambassador to the Court of St. James's. Uncle Thorndike smoked a pipe and was a famous yachtsman. Summers, he sailed his two-masted schooner down from Massachusetts and anchored it in the sound. His wife, Aunt Hope, heavyset and hearty, had bobbed hair and a deep voice and hunted with the Myopia foxhounds. She played tennis every morning, golf every afternoon, and bridge every evening, competitively and with great concentration. The cousins said her strong muscular legs came from her having been captain of the field hockey team at Miss Porter's School, where Gramma had sent all her daughters, believing her children should go away for at least five years to be exposed to the Northern point of view.

Great Uncle Oomlot was Gramma's younger brother. His real name was Orville, but once when one of the children tried to call him by his proper name, it came out Oomlot.

Uncle Oomlot loved fast women and fast horses. He had married two and been fortunate in that all had been able to provide him with thoroughbred horses, a racing stable, foxhunting seasons in Virginia and Leicestershire, sports cars, suits, and Peal shoes. "I've managed for sixty-eight years without doing anything for myself," he announced proudly when he moved into the tower room from London, where he had lived with his last wife before her death. "With luck I'll survive a few more years."

Because of arthritis brought on by his numerous falls from horses, he spent much of his time in his bed in the tower. "I'm at home here with my eccentricities," he said comfortably. The four-poster was piled high with books and papers. His Labrador, Boy Five, lay at his feet. Every dog he had ever owned, beginning with Boy One when he was "but a little shaver," had been called Boy. "Somewhere," he said, "I lost count. Since then, every dog has been Boy Five."

On rainy afternoons, Maggie Royal stole up to the tower room to sit at the foot of his enormous bed and listen to him reminisce.

"Maggie Royal," he commanded whenever she entered his bedroom, "fetch the port. My boy Dick has hidden it again. I think he puts it in with my shirts. Look in the chest of drawers."

Inside Dick hid the bottle in a different place each time. He liked to tipple and occasionally sampled Uncle Oomlot's priceless port. "I've ordered Outside Dick to make me a pine coffin in preparation for my demise," Uncle Oomlot said as she searched. "I'm going to bring it up here and put it under my bed and fill it full of liquor. It'll be safe there. My boy Dick won't dare touch it!"

When she found the bottle, she poured Uncle Oomlot a generous portion. "Umm," he sniffed appreciatively, "nothing like the 1927 Croft. Maggie Royal, let me explain to you about port. 'The Englishman's wine,' it's called. How they love their port. Maggie Royal, pour me another libation."

"Uncle Oomlot, you know you shouldn't. Gramma says—"

"Hang Gramma! I've never done what I should, and I don't intend to start now. Why, in 1862 a wine writer named Charles Tovey reported that one Mr. Vardon drank 36,688 bottles of port in twenty-three years. His usual daily quota was four bottles . . ." and he would be off on a dissertation on the vintage years and the fact that the Croft had more body and sweetness, whereas Fonseca and Graham possessed more finesse. "Maggie Royal, pour yourself a libation. Time you learned to drink like a gentleman, I mean a lady," he said, extending his glass for a refill. "Always remember that a good vintage port is a great wine; all other ports are just good ports."

Then he would take another drink, sigh with gratification, lean back against his pillows, and begin.

"Where were we? Yesterday we were in England, hunting with the Duke of Chatfield. . . ."

Gramma was what Cook Ada called "a grand-ee dame" from the hems of the white floor-length skirts she wore when not riding or playing tennis, to the top of her carefully coiffed silvery-white head. On the island her word was law. She ran the house and plantation as it had been run in antebellum times. Affey was her favorite. Affey's mother had been Joe-Ali's younger sister. She died when Affey was born. (Noble whispered that she was an "outside child," born out of wedlock, with a white father, hence, her "permanent sunburn.") Gramma had brought her up in the big house and sent her to school on the mainland, after which she returned to Great Oak as Gramma's personal maid.

Affey was not like the other servants. There was an air of mystery about her, something different, something special that went beyond her light skin and sensitive features. Nor did she associate with the others. On her days off she stayed in her bedroom in the nursery wing. There she remained reading or bent over her fine sewing, leaving it only for her solitary evening walks.

Maggie Royal once asked Gramma why Affey seemed different, why she sometimes caught her looking at her in the strangest way. It was an unreadable look that really said nothing at all and yet again seemed to speak volumes, but about what, she couldn't decipher.

Whenever Gramma did not want to answer a question or discuss a certain matter, she pursed her lips and looked away, changing the subject. "Maggie Royal, draw the curtains, please. The sun's in my eyes."

After breakfast each day, Gramma put on her riding habit for the customary morning ride to check on the fields in cultivation and discuss the work to be done with Mr. Cullen.

The farm manager was a big beefy man with a full belly that hung out over the top of his work pants. His neck, with rolls of fat bulging from the collar of his blue workshirt, was the color of the red clay of the Georgia interior from which he sprang. He wore his straw sombrero, its sides bent upward, square on his head, and ornate cowboy boots of heavy leather "good for kicking pigs when you got 'em down." He was a Georgia cracker from the back of his red parchment-wrinkled neck to the tip of the long-thonged whip with which he flayed the mules that pulled the farm wagons.

The whip was his symbol of authority. He wore it on his right hip and across his back, level with his left ear. The long plaited lash came across his chest to find the end of the hickory handle at his hip. After passing it around his waist, he returned it to the handle, where it was fastened with a loop or two. He prided himself on his expertise with the long thong, with which he could knock the tip from a cigarette or discipline his ferocious "catch dogs."

His hounds were strange leopardlike dogs with brindled black and brown markings. They had voices like bloodhounds. Their eerie, haunting baying at night, while hunting coons or pigs, reminded Maggie Royal of slaves and escaped convicts being pursued through the dark swamps.

At hog-killing time, the wild pigs were rounded up and put in the holding pens that dotted the island. Cullen called it "doing the hawgs." At the farmer's bidding, the hounds smelled out a large boar, then proceeded to quarter, like sheep dogs, moving in closer and closer, forcing the pig to run in circles and become confused. Finally the boar charged.

At the farmer's command the "git 'im" dog grabbed the pig by its ear. Then Cullen leaped astride the pig as if it were a downed steer and quickly tied its legs. Rising to his feet, he gave the terrified beast a resounding kick with one of his heavy boots and called the dogs to him.

Wherever Bo Cullen went, his dogs went also, crouching at his feet as he stood talking, following him on his rounds, cringing at the sound of his voice and the crack of his whip.

Cullen was one of the "good old boys" at the courthouse, and was said to be an active member of the Ku Klux Klan. The Negroes hated and feared him, whispering that he had been party to a number of cross burnings and a lynching at the clearing, known as the hanging ground, at High Point, on the east side of the island. They called him a "poor buckra," which, translated from Gullah, meant "poor white trash." They feared the dogs as they did his whip, knowing both could hurt and maim. At intervals he walked through the Long Point community cracking the long-thonged whip, flicking it at the Negroes who failed to get out of his way fast enough. "Teaching 'em their place," as he said. "Here comes de big man!" the Negroes warned when they saw him approaching, and it was a signal to the women to call their children indoors.

Gramma argued that farmers who would stay on an island were hard to come by. Mr. Cullen, she said, was honest and hardworking, and it was necessary to understand that there were occasions when firmness was called for.

Maggie Royal loved to ride with Gramma in the back of the green Packard car that had been brought on a barge from the mainland. Jazzbo had been provided with a livery and promoted to chauffeur. He kept the car as polished and gleaming as Sapelo kept the hackneys' harness, and seemed not to mind Gramma's habit of throwing lighted firecrackers past his head in order to warn the island cattle and other animals out of the way of the touring car.

Sometimes they visited the Long Point settlement. When they drove along "the street," people came out of the cabins to wave and call out, "Howdy, missus." Gramma paused, saying a word here, a word there, inquiring about each person's health, offering remedies for those who were ill or infirm.

The island community was virtually self-sufficient. Meat from island pigs, cattle, and deer was butchered and cured. Vegetables and melons came from the garden, and there was always a canning or preserving operation ongoing when they came in season. There was a carpenter, cooper, wheelwright, and a blacksmith to trim the mules' and horses' feet (shoes weren't necessary on the sandy island trails), a head plowman, cow-minder, poultry woman, and as they'd been called in plantation days, plowboys.

There were many others "on the street," the Long Point settlement.

Gramma said she was godmother to so many children she had lost count. Many were descendants of the original plantation slaves. The old people, like Dah and Cook Ada, were Gullahs. They adhered to the customs and superstitions, the sorcery and intricate rituals and brooding ghosts, that their ancestors had brought from Africa to the great antebellum plantations. From Africa too came their ancient burial rites and their belief that dead men's spirits visited the earth in the form of hants or duppies.

Their tabby houses were built of oyster shells, burned in a kiln to form a kind of lime, which, mixed with sand and water, became cement-hard, forming rough, creamy-white shell walls. Windows were rimmed in blue to ward off the hants.

Usually Gramma and Maggie Royal stopped to visit Dah. She had been born in the time of slavery. After the war she had traveled as far as Savannah with her parents to the promised land. There she had almost died of chicken pox during the postwar epidemic brought on by the returning soldiers. She spoke of the dead lying in maggoty heaps; how when she was brought back to her island home the soles of her feet would "pop and pus would stream out" as she walked.

Nobody knew how old Dah was. She had forty "heads" of grandchildren and fifteen great-grandchildren. "You must care for your own," she said positively. "They are the stars in my crown." Whenever a new "grandbaby" or great-grandbaby was expected, Dah announced proudly, "It will be a new star in my crown!"

Dah's world consisted of a fascinating company of mischievous spirits. Her house was papered with newsprint to deter the "spirits dat come at hag-hollerin' time [midnight] and first cock crow [3 or 4 A.M.]." Oyster shells simmered on the stove to ward off the "miseries." Dah showed the children how to sprinkle salt and pepper in the corners of the rooms—Maggie Royal envisioned dozens of sneezing spirits—to keep out whatever witch managed to squeeze past the broom blocking the doorway beneath the upside-down crab and horseshoe hanging over it, or through the blue-rimmed windows. All of them were preventives against the witch that would shed its skin, "sit on your chest and ride you until you feel like you're smudderin'." Gramma said it sounded as if Dah was suffering from insomnia or a chest cold and offered Vicks VapoRub.

When Gramma returned from her morning outing, she consulted with Cook Ada about the day's menu. Together they visited the various storerooms, which Gramma unlocked with keys from a linen bag with a drawstring that she wore tied around her waist.

Cook Ada ruled her basement kitchen with a hand of iron as black as the pots in which she made her famous fish soups and stews and other island delicacies. Nobody, least of all she, could recall how old she was. Every year she threatened to retire because of her miseries, which she tried to ward off by wearing a Gullah asafetida bag around her neck.

Maggie Royal believed Cook Ada remained at Great Oak because she did not think her "darling Miss Maggie Royal Gramma" could manage without her.

On hot summer days the children stopped by the cool basement kitchen, where Cook Ada provided ice-cold lemonade and home-baked cookies. Or they sat on the grass while she "rested," sitting on the steps shelling peas, telling stories of the old days. Dah, her mother, had told her about life in the big house before the war, a time when there were never fewer than twenty house servants to tend the family and the occasional guests who came to the island by boat, as many as a dozen at a time, bringing their children and house servants with them. Ada described "the feets," the great fetes in the fall when the shoots, banquets, and balls took place. And she recalled the war, and the end of plantation life, when many of the slaves ran away to become "free persons of color," going north or following Sherman's army to some hoped-for promised land. Ada's family and a few others had remained on the "street," which they considered home. They had suffered through the burning and devastation and what Ada called "de revelation," the period of reconstruction when "darling Miss Maggie Royal Gramma" sought to rebuild the plantation.

As Cook Ada told it, she had cooked for so many famous visitors that she had lost count of all but the Presidents, of whom there were three, Wilson, Hoover, and the first Roosevelt. President Hoover had complimented her on her "tarry-pin" soup, and Mrs. Hoover had eaten three of the "flaky puffs" she baked for tea. When Gramma and her guests called her into the dining room to compliment her on her food, she made everyone stand up, hold hands, and sing "Precious Lord, take my hand, down by the water's edge." On these occasions she also said a prayer, using a different one every time, and gave her "darling Miss Maggie Royal Gramma" a hug before returning, with a wave and a final "bless you all," below stairs.

Newt, the butler, was Cook Ada's son. Newcomer Ada, the kitchen maid, was Cook Ada's granddaughter, and Uncle Oomlot's valet, known as Inside Dick as opposed to Outside Dick in charge of the mules and farm wagons, was a grandson. In the stable, Ada's husband, Sapelo, held sway over the grooms, his son Jasper and his son Jazzbo, as well as Hercules and Cumsey, and in the gardens Ada's nephew Isaiah ran a staff of ten assorted relatives. Ada's and Sapelo's progeny, in short, embraced almost all of the inhabitants of Long Point.

Although most of the island families moved inland or north during the "pestilential season," the hot summer months, as they had for generations, Gramma remained in residence, refusing, no matter how hot or uncomfortable it became, to leave her beloved Great Oak.

During those depression years when millions were out of jobs, Maggie Royal's only connection with the outside world was what she

65

heard on Uncle Oomlot's radio and occasional random remarks put out by the tutor.

Mr. Crutwell, who was British and Oxford-educated, lived at Great Oak as tutor. During daily sessions in the nursery, Maggie Royal and various cousins in residence learned what Gramma termed the basics of reading, writing, and 'rithmetic. Maggie Royal did not like the tutor, who had a beaky nose, eyes too close together, and bad breath. But she did not complain for fear Gramma would make him leave the island and she would be forced to go to school on the mainland. She had already read the classics recommended by Mr. Crutwell, and the "compositions" that filled her loose-leaf notebooks came as easily as her instinctive knowledge of the woods and wild animals. This freed her for other activities.

The days were timeless rounds of riding, sailing, fishing, and clamming, of playing among the desertlike dunes which separated the stretches of dark woods that rippled in the sun and seemed to have no beginning or end, of exploring the dark brackish pools where the alligators lived, protected by walls of sand pushed inland by wind and sea. The cousins played from "sun to sun," when the sky turned the mauve and rose of island dusk and the air became fragrant with the scent of jessamine and the children returned to the house, sun-warmed, faces burning and lips tasting of salt, to eat chowder, fresh oysters, fried chicken or shrimp, cornbread and black-eyed peas, baked yams, and other island foods.

By the 1930's many of the Sea Islands had been bought by Yankees. Even the most vituperative Yankee haters like Maggie Royal's Great-Aunt Meg were forced to admit that although Sherman's men had destroyed the island plantations during the War Between the States, Northern money had brought them back again.

The marshes and rich acreage that had produced rice, cotton, and indigo in antebellum times had been purchased by wealthy members of the industrial aristocracy for as little as fifty cents an acre, to be used as shooting islands. The abandoned rice fields, their sluice gates no longer guarding the waterways, provided fine duck hunting. The second-growth timber that grew up when the rice fields were no longer flooded made fine cover for all sorts of game.

In late fall and over the Christmas holidays, members of the family and their guests came to shoot.

They spent hours in the blinds built of wood and marsh grass spaced along the old rice canals, waiting for the wild ducks to fly overhead. They rode with Jasper and Jazzbo, the horse handlers, to the fields to shoot dove and to the woods for the wild island deer.

Maggie Royal hated seeing the deer driven from the woods by the dogs handled by mounted drivers. The hunters were placed at intervals, called "stands," along the trails or fire lanes as the dogs drove the deer toward them. In order not to be shot by another hunter, the visitors were asked to stay at their waiting spot until a conch horn was blown signaling the end of the drive.

She wept when she saw her first buck hauled back on the wagon, its great antlered head lolling to one side, its eyes glazed, and blood coming from its mouth. Although Gramma assured her it was necessary to kill the deer that destroyed the crops in order to keep the population in balance, she could not dispel the sight of the dead animal, once so fleet and proud. From then on she unconsciously resented the florid-faced men and self-assured women who came by island boat or in their own yachts with carefully oiled guns from Abercrombie & Fitch in New York or Purdey of London. They went out mornings in the wagons pulled by mules or oxen to shoot rail birds, marsh hens, island quail, or deer and eat Cook Ada's lavish lunch of venison or quail at the long wooden table set in the clearing at Middle Point, the center of the island.

Jared and Joe-Ali, the tall Negro Jared credited with teaching him most of his island lore, taught Maggie Royal to handle guns. She shot skeet and tin cans off a fence post. At Christmastime her Great-Uncle Oomlot gave her his matched pair of D-grade Parker 16-gauge shotguns and told her to go out and "shoot for the pot." She went with Jared and Joe-Ali to get some venison for the holiday season. But when a big buck broke from the palmettos and the men stepped aside to give her the first shot, she looked right down her sights and was unable to pull the trigger. She saw Jared and Joe-Ali gazing at her questioningly and was ashamed.

"It's time to go home," Jared said. He patted her shoulder. "That buck was just about out of range anyway."

He never mentioned the matter again.

The island abounded in wild turkeys. Since early times they had been useful in controlling the leaf-worm caterpillars that destroyed the long staple sea-island cotton.

The rare invitations Gramma issued to friends and relatives to hunt them in the fall and spring were prized above all others. For many hunters believe that the North American wild turkey is the most magnificent game bird in the world. Also that no game demands more skill and knowledge of the hunter.

Calling up a wild turkey is so difficult that few but the most dedicated and knowledgeable turkey enthusiasts are able to master the innumerable variations of yelps, clucks, and gobbles necessary to lure a gobbler to a human "hen" calling to him from a hidden place in the forest.

Joe-Ali was known as the "huntingest man." His turkey talk was famous throughout the state, where he had won numerous turkey-calling contests. Blackbeard, the wise old gobbler identified by the length of his black beard, who patrolled the Middle Point territory, was one of the few island turkeys able to resist the seductive calls from his "caller."

The spring mating season runs about six weeks, Joe-Ali explained. When the weather turns warm, the gobbler sets up his stomping

67

grounds. In the early morning you can hear his thunderous gobble before he leaves his roost and begins to call his girls. Each turkey has a harem of a dozen or more hens to service. The hens arrive one by one. Then they repair to their nests to begin laying eggs. In about two weeks the eggs are fertilized and laid and the gobbler becomes expendable. That, Joe-Ali concluded, is the very best time for turkey hunting.

Every morning during the season, Jared and Joe-Ali went to the woods at first light. (Jared's father said you could tell a dedicated turkey hunter by his eyes, because they were usually red and underlined by dark patches and slightly glazed from sleeplessness.)

It was understandable that Jared should become obsessive about turkey hunting. It appealed to the loner in him, that dark silent place he often retired to when people were about.

His Indian blood made it possible for him to move through the forest as silently as the shy island deer and to sit, as his mother did before her hearth, as motionless as the trunks of the trees he leaned against, sometimes for hours at a time.

His desire was not to kill turkeys. It was to get them "talking and walking," responding to the calls Joe-Ali taught him to make, rendered so skillfully that a wise and wary old gobbler could be persuaded to show himself to the hen he believed to be waiting in the bushes. "Some people have every kind of gizmo" he explained. "But the only way to get the true sound of a lovesick hen is with the mouth call. Most old-timers use calls they make themselves. Joe-Ali showed me how to use a cedar-box caller. It's made from Uncle Oomlot's discarded cigar boxes. There's a cedar paddle attached. You scrape it across the two top beveled lips of the box, but I prefer my wing-bone 'yelper.' " He pulled it from his pocket. "It's the wing bone of a wild-turkey hen. A small tip section of cow's horn is attached with an eighteen-inch piece of rubber tubing to give the call a 'bell-like' tone.

"I practiced calling daily for two years," Jared continued. "Once you learn how to call and listen—that's what makes turkey hunting exciting, that short space of time when you can actually imitate, call the turkeys to you. The way a wing bone works, you suck through it. It's not easy to use. You've got to get that break in the yelp. First second you make a bad note, the turkey is gone! But to get a gobbler working, responding"—Jared's eyes shone with excitement—"that's the ultimate!"

He told Maggie Royal he would take her turkey hunting on her birthday. Adele asked to come too.

Jared shook his head. "Turkey hunting isn't a group sport, like killing doves or quail. It's an individual thing. You need patience, quietness. Sometimes you have to sit like a stone. Absolutely still for hours. Thorny would want to discuss the flawed decadence of the bourgeoisie or the capitalistic aspects of talking turkey. Adele, you'd be sure to giggle, just at that crucial moment when a passionate old tom starts sprinting toward you."

• •

68

Maggie Royal's twelfth birthday, in 1932, came finally, on the last Saturday in April. "The hardest thing about turkey hunting," Jared told her, "is putting your feet on the floor in the morning. I'll meet you under the great oak at four. We should be out at least a half-hour before daybreak."

Maggie Royal worried that the alarm might not go off. At one she awoke and switched on the flashlight and looked at the time. Again at two. At three she arose in the dark, as quietly as possible in order not to awaken the cousins. The floor was cold as she stood on it in her bare feet. Quickly she pulled on the clothes she had laid out the night before. Khaki pants and sweater and floppy felt hat. Jared had warned her not to wear colors. "A red hat and Mr. Tom'll be in the next county. The more camouflaged you are, the better. A turkey's eyesight is so keen he can almost see you blink!"

At a quarter to four she was under the great oak. The air was cold and as fresh as the wind, carrying with it the scents of the marsh, aromatic grasses, salt, and the sea.

Over the tops of the trees rode a thin embroidery of gray light heralding the oncoming daylight. It was her favorite time, that predawn time when one is filled with a sense of renewal and anticipation.

He came so quietly she didn't see him until he whispered, "Follow me."

"Jared," she exclaimed, "what have you done to your face?"

"Shhh, burned cork to dull the shine. Effective camouflage."

In the dim light his teeth shone white against his black face as he smiled.

"Joe-Ali's lucky. He doesn't need a disguise. Let's go." He started ahead. "Be as quiet as you can."

They turned off into the dove field, where what the Negroes called the "moanin'" doves fed on grain following the harvest. They followed the edge of the field to the thicket bordering the swampy ground where, during periods of wet, there was a pond green-glazed with mossy scum. "Blackbeard's territory," Jared said. "With luck we might see him.

"Positioning yourself is important," he explained as they made their way through the underbrush to Middle Point.

"Turkeys seem to prefer to travel uphill to a caller. So you get into position in such terrain that the gobbler will come up to you. Experience teaches you which turkeys won't leave certain places when they can't see where they're going. Blackbeard, for instance, won't cross the stream that feeds into the pond." He pulled his caller from the pocket of his jacket. "I've got to get it in my mouth and start warming up. I can tell on the way if I'll be good today!" He looked up at the tops of the trees, black against the still-dark sky. "It's so early the gobblers are still roosting."

Maggie Royal waited, motionless, as the soft grunting roost yelps came at intervals.

Widening streaks of gray light began to break the forest into component parts of trees and bushes. The birdsong was almost deafening. Crows cawed overhead and a cacophony of sound came from the smaller birds in the trees. A woodpecker hammered at a dead oak, and from somewhere nearby came the hoot of an owl. They moved on silently. Suddenly Jared left the path, plunging into dense underbrush. She followed, stepping on a branch that broke beneath her high-laced riding shoes. Jared turned, frowning, a warning finger against his lips. They continued in silence. Jared pushed aside branches, which sometimes rebounded in her face as she followed in the footsteps of his rubber boots.

He stopped beneath an oak. His blackened face broke into a smile as he cupped his ear with his hand.

From deep in the woods came a distinct gobble.

Maggie Royal felt a growing excitement.

"He sounds close."

"He's not," Jared whispered. "Sound carries on a clear morning. Come on. We've got to move closer."

They hurried on, lured by clearly heard gobbles coming now at intervals.

Jared paused to point out fresh signs, scratches, droppings. Again the gobbler gobbled. Closer now.

They came to a sandy knoll. Jared pointed to a moss-covered log. A clump of violets grew alongside it, and there was a stump to lean against. "Make yourself comfortable," he cautioned. "If you really want to see a tom, you're going to have to sit absolutely still for a long time. Once I start calling, you're not to move."

Maggie Royal sat down on the log. She stretched her legs out in front of her, her back against the rough bark of the stump. Jared leaned against a slanting tree, motionless as a heron eyeing a fish. Patches of light made gold pockets as the first rays of sun filtered through the green overhead. Mist wreathed the green-gold pond below. A doe and her fawn stared at them briefly, framed by the pink haze of maples growing amidst the gray of the bearded oaks.

It seemed to Maggie Royal that they were a part of the life of the forest and all that was around them. She was aware of the white petals of the tiny star-shaped flowers growing by her left foot, of the color of the moss on the log and the green glaze of the water below. A whippoorwill spoke from a nearby tree, and she remembered old Dah saying that the bird's cry meant warm weather, time to go barefoot. She looked at Jared's profile. His face was still and concentrated. He stared at the mottled trees, as if seeing the secret of the universe in their depths.

Jared put his wing-bone caller in his mouth. The nesty, broody "yelp" of a nesting hen penetrated the forest. This was followed by a seductive "cluck." No sound came in response. Jared repeated the call. Suddenly a gobble sounded, coming from the swampy area below. A cardinal called to its mate, and then the gobbling, closer, stronger. Maggie Royal's heart was pounding as Jared's eagerness and anticipation were transmitted by his subtle, seductive calls, little happy, singing sounds. Key-oak, key-oak, key-oak, each succeeding note shorter than the one before it.

Time had ceased, like the individual bird calls now blending into one vast joyous song as the day was launched. She did not know how long they'd been there when she saw the turkey, coming toward them, walking slowly, deliberately, its bearing as regal as that of a peacock, its feathers almost as beautiful.

Jared called very softly. The turkey paused. He gobbled and spread his tail feathers with a vroom sound, as though opening a giant fan. His head glowed with blood and his chest expanded to meet his neck. His wings drummed against the ground as he went into his strut, his male dance of territory and domination.

Maggie Royal found herself trembling. She was almost afraid to breathe for fear the turkey would hear her and end its mating dance. Still he advanced. His magnificent tail feathers fanned out and he was displayed in all his glory, believing Jared to be the mate awaiting him.

On he came, pausing every few steps to glance around and stare in their direction. Just when Maggie Royal was sure that he had seen her, he returned to his strutting display. The loud vrooms caused the birds to fly off and a red squirrel to scuttle up a tree. On he came, prancing, beating his wings against the ground.

He was so close she could see his chest and tail feathers, burnt orange and gorgeous greens, shimmering in the patches of sunlight from the newborn sun. His beard was black and at least fourteen inches long, and when he lifted a foot, she saw its long protective spur.

She could almost have reached out and grabbed his beard when three deer caught their scent and burst from the brush. The turkey, alarmed in the midst of his magnificent strut, made the wild turkey's danger call, an odd *putt* noise. Instantaneously he shrank to a bronze shadow. Like a wisp of fog he vanished into the brush and palmettos. Maggie Royal, relieved of the suspense and excitement, let out her breath.

After a while Jared sighed and moved. "Well, Maggie Royal, happy birthday! You saw the ultimate turkey. The boss man. Blackbeard. You can tell it's him by the length of his beard. He's patrolled this territory for at least four years."

The sun was high now, parting the trees with its gold dust. The mist was gone from the marshes. From the direction of the beach came the ocean's low murmur, rising and falling, yet insistent, like a train among distant hills, always passing, never quite gone.

"There aren't many girls you can be quiet with!" Jared said as they turned toward home. His eyes were the bright shimmering blackish-green color of the short feathers that had fanned out from the turkey's chest. He put his arm around her shoulders, and she was aware of a sudden surge of happiness as he drew her against the clean-smelling hardness of his side.

· 4 ·

Islands provide isolation from all but the changing seasons and daily necessities that are more a condition of the mind than actual geographical separation. Stark Island, swathed in mist and moss, lent itself to desire and unreality, and the Starks behaved accordingly, believing the world to be their oyster, like those from the tidal creeks, that were served on the half-shell.

The first time the outside world broke into Maggie Royal's safe, self-contained island existence was in 1932, when Charles Lindbergh's son was kidnapped and murdered. Gramma forbade any of the children to go to the mainland without Hercules or Jasper, two of the biggest and strongest island Negroes, as bodyguards. On the island, they were restricted to the area around Great Oak, and their whereabouts meticulously recorded on the blackboard at all hours of the day and night.

That summer Gramma took Maggie Royal to Washington, to meet and have dinner with President and Mrs. Hoover. The President planned to give her father a posthumous decoration for his work in the relief and rehabilitation of Europe's children.

The President was, as Jasper said about Gramma's big horse Darien, a good doer. When he visited Great Oak, Gramma always served him six courses of Cook Ada's most treasured recipes, beginning with his favorite terrapin soup. In his thank-you letter, the President complained that he could not get his chef to prepare the dish to taste like Ada's, with her special spices and ingredients.

"It's hard to think of a nice house present for a President," Gramma said. "I have it!" She snapped her fingers. "A few choice cooters for soup. We'll borrow Uncle Oomlot's wicker shirt basket and carry them to Washington!"

So she ordered Jo-Jo, the number-one procurer of turtles on the island, to catch a half-dozen saucer-sized diamond-back terrapins, and wheedled Cook Ada's receipe from her to give to Mrs. Hoover.

It was midsummer, and the only way to ensure the terrapins' freshness on their arrival at the White House was to pack them in the wicker hamper and carry them alive.

The *Maggie Royal* was being overhauled, so it was necessary to take the Atlantic Coast Line Pullman from Savannah. Gramma reserved a compartment for herself and Maggie Royal. Affey had a berth in the sleeping car. When the porter came around to take their tickets, he was shocked to find Affey sitting in the compartment next to Gramma, working on her embroidery. He explained that Negroes were not permitted in the section of the train reserved for whites.

"Rubbish!" snorted Gramma. "Affey is a member of my family, and I intend to have her stay with us."

The porter, obviously agitated, proceeded to explain that if any of the passengers saw Affey in the parlor car, she might be in "bad trouble!"

"In that case, we'll all move into the Negro section," Gramma said. "My good man, be so kind as to move our luggage. Maggie Royal, Affey, come along. It will be a good experience!" She turned back to the porter. "You may be sure that my good friend General Elliot, who is president of this railroad, will hear about this!"

Gramma never walked. She swept. Wearing a smart blue-and-white suit and high, round Queen Mary hat, she strode along the aisle. Affey followed, carrying her Vuitton overnight case. Maggie Royal trailed behind, holding the wicker basket, from which the heads of the terrapin protruded.

Gramma sailed by the long queue of people waiting to get into the dining room. The steward came to meet her and politely told her she must go to the back of the line and wait. Maggie Royal held the basket of terrapins ("They might get stolen," Gramma warned, "and then we'd have nothing to give the President!"), which seemed very heavy, as they stood rocking in the narrow passageway. Gramma talked to the woman in front of her about the problems of raising soybeans, and the woman replied that she once had a cousin raising soybeans on a farm near Montgomery, Alabama, but that he had been bitten by a rattlesnake and died.

She, herself, was from Savannah, on her way to Washington to see her sister, who was married to a dentist in Arlington.

"We're going to the White House," Gramma said, "to see President Hoover." She pointed to the basket. "We have some cooters to give to him."

The woman turned to look at the heads protruding from the basket, and let out a startled exclamation. At that moment, the steward beckoned her to a table in the dining car. She went quickly, without looking back. Maggie Royal saw her sit down next to another woman, and pretty soon both women were laughing as they covertly eyed Gramma.

Finally it was their turn. Maggie Royal was very hungry and the basket seemed very heavy.

"Only two," the steward said, motioning Affey back to the door-way.

Gramma became rigid. "I see three vacant seats at that table," she announced. "Maggie Royal, Affey, come along!"

"But, Ma'am!" The steward trotted along behind them. His hair was slicked back and greased. In his shiny black suit and agitation, he reminded Maggie Royal of a worried crow.

"Ma'am," he said, as Gramma was about to sit down, "I can't permit Negroes in the dining car."

"Well, that's just too bad," Gramma said. "We'll all eat together, or not at all."

"Ma'am," the steward said, "I'm sorry to have to tell you, but you can't be served in here."

Gramma stood up once again. "You may be sure my good friend General Elliot will hear about this. Come, Maggie Royal. Come, Affey."

Maggie Royal's stomach groaned as the mouth-watering aromas emanating from the train's kitchen followed them along the corridor.

They sat alongside one another in the scratchy, plush-upholstered seats in the coach reserved for Negroes, with the basket on the floor between their feet.

The other travelers sprawled in their seats, some with their heads on each other's shoulders, others with their feet in the aisle. Those who were not asleep stared furtively. The children put their fists up to their mouths and giggled, their shoulders shaking. Still others ate lavishly from baskets with checked napkins over the top. Fried chicken and biscuits, cornbread and ham, and pieces of pie. Maggie Royal could hardly control the grumbles coming from her empty stomach.

Gramma maintained her rigid, ramrod-straight posture, reading one of the Mr. Glencannon stories she greatly enjoyed in the *Saturday Evening Post*. Affey, her face impassive, bent over her needlework. Each time a greenish reptilian head emerged, pushing up the top of the basket that had been loosely secured, in order to provide air, Gramma tapped it back with the ivory handle of the Japanese fan she had bought on her around-the-world wedding trip.

The motion of the train, the sandy, piny landscape flashing past, finally put Maggie Royal to sleep. Gramma and Affey dozed off also. Suddenly they were awakened by a commotion across the aisle.

"Get it away from here!" shrieked a large Negro woman. She was wearing a pink hat with roses on it and standing on top of her seat.

"No, ma'am!" the porter replied positively, shaking his head. "Ah ain't gonna touch no cootah loose in de sitting car!"

He left to get the conductor.

The conductor was equally at a loss. "We don't allow terrapins in the coaches," he mumbled helplessly.

"All right, Maggie Royal," Gramma said. "Long as people are making such a fuss about a little old bitty turtle, you get down there under the seat and catch it." She turned to the conductor and observed conversationally, "You see, we're taking the terrapins to President Hoover at the White House."

Maggie Royal had on her best navy-blue dress with the white piqué collar and matching jacket, white knee socks and black patent-leather slippers that buttoned across the instep, in which she was to meet the President of the United States. Gramma had forbidden her—she did not caution, she forbade—to get dirty, and the floor of the car was covered with soot, cigarette butts, and soiled pieces of paper. Maggie Royal had seen what those "little bitty" turtles could do to a finger if they got a chance to nip it. However, Gramma never asked people to do anything, she commanded; and when she used her commanding tone of voice, one didn't disobey her.

The car was in an uproar. Children were standing on seats. Women screamed, and men pretended they had to visit the lavatory.

There was nothing for it but to dive down onto the filthy floor, wriggle under the seat, grab the turtle as it pushed itself up into the corner, and drag it out by its tail.

"Eeek!" screamed the woman, still standing on her seat. The conductor and the porter and the other passengers who had been in transit and had found their way blocked by the chase, backed away as Maggie Royal straightened up, holding the wildly wriggling candidate for the presidential pot.

"Now what shall I do with it?" she asked.

"Put it back in the basket," Gramma answered, lifting up the lid and permitting another terrapin to escape.

"Dear me," Gramma continued. "Aren't they active, though? That means they're good and fresh, and will be all the better to eat." She glanced around at the assembled crowd. "Somebody catch it, please."

"No, ma'am," the porter repeated, rolling his eyes, as all eyes turned toward him. "Ah ain't gonna touch no cootah!"

By now, the second, fleeter than the first, was halfway along the aisle. Maggie Royal thought it odd that so few of the people in the coach seemed to have ever seen a terrapin before. They reacted as if a rattlesnake had been thrust into their midst. There were horrified exclamations of, "Catch it, hurry." Yet not one person offered to do so.

Feeling quite heroic, she pounced on it and returned it to its basket, where Gramma was holding the remaining turtles at bay, tapping their emerging heads with her fan.

"There," she exclaimed when the escaped terrapin was secured. "Nothing to it." She turned to inspect her granddaughter. "Maggie Royal, whatever do you mean getting so dirty? Look at your knees. I told you you must be bandbox-fresh to meet the President of the United States."

It's doubtful if anybody on that train believed a word Gramma said about taking terrapins to the President of the United States. Not until they saw them escorted through Union Station by a gold-braided presidential aide, into whose hands Gramma thrust the basket with the heads emerging from it.

Maggie Royal didn't realize then that they were entering a besieged city where some twenty-five thousand penniless World War I veterans were encamped in parks, empty stores, and abandoned warehouses. These were the Bonus Marchers, who had come to ask the President for relief from the great depression. They had appealed to President Hoover to receive a delegation of their leaders, but the President had sent word he was too busy, and had then locked himself behind the White House gates, which had to be unchained to let Gramma through.

By the time they reached the White House, after almost a whole day and a night without food of any kind, Maggie Royal felt as if she would faint from hunger. But there was no time to do anything other than "freshen up" before going to see the President. They were shown to what the aide explained proudly was one of the most famous rooms in the White House, the Lincoln Bedroom.

Gramma stopped in the doorway as though she had been shot, blocking Maggie Royal's view and causing Affey to almost drop the Vuitton case.

"How incredibly tactless of the President," Gramma said to the aide. "I am a Georgian, you know. I'm afraid we really must have another room."

The aide looked shocked. After conferring with someone in authority, they were shown to a room where Dolley Madison was said to have slept. This was more to Gramma's liking, and Maggie Royal was relieved that Gramma was not going to write any more letters.

They walked from the White House to the State Department building next door, where the President was waiting for them. Outside the gates and the iron fence surrounding the White House, Maggie Royal could see the thin, pinched faces of the Bonus Marchers. They wore shabby suits, and many were without collars. They stared silently through the bars with eyes dulled, deadened with hopelessness. Some carried crudely made signs. "We need bread. Jobs. Our children are starving."

Maggie Royal's stomach turned over and she felt ill with something that had nothing to do with her hunger.

That night Gramma and Maggie Royal dined with President and Mrs. Hoover. While the Bonus Marchers fought the mid-August heat, disease, rats, diminishing food and water supplies, as well as the loss of hope, they entered the dining room decorated with cut flowers, candlelight, and crystal. Although Gramma and Maggie Royal were the only guests, the President and Mrs. Hoover wore evening clothes. Butlers and footmen—all the same height ("They all matched," Maggie Royal told Adele later)—stood at attention, absolutely silent. Marine officers stood by, wearing dress blues, and buglers in glittering uniforms waited to announce the President's departure from the feast.

The President said hardly a word as he ate steadily through seven courses, the first of which was the terrapin soup.

Afterward, Gramma asked Maggie Royal why she had left her dinner untouched.

During the early depression years, weeks passed when the only way Maggie Royal knew it was Saturday was because chipped beef and grits were served for breakfast. This meant that there would be waffles and maple syrup on Sunday. The trip to Washington sparked a dawning awareness. Although island life was not conducive to creating what Jared's father called a concerned and impassioned atmosphere of the mind, she began to realize there was a world beyond the boundaries of Stark Island that was filled with people less fortunate than she.

She found herself following the presidential campaign, reading the newspapers that came to the island twice a week, and listening to Uncle Oomlot's radio. She heard Gramma discussing that boy Franklin. Gramma knew Mrs. Roosevelt, Senior, and had visited her at Hyde Park, and the *Wild Duck* had put in at Campobello the summer Gramma spent cruising in the Bay of Fundy.

Maggie Royal assumed that the newly elected President was a godsend for people who tend to blame things on others. Some of Gramma's friends called him a monster and a tyrant, and considered the Roosevelt revolution second only to reconstruction. Cook Ada, however, always called the period after the War Between the States the revelation. Maggie Royal assumed it was all in one's point of view.

Whereas Gramma believed the New Deal signaled the end of the capitalistic system, Jared's father argued vehemently in favor of Mr. Roosevelt. "Seventeen million unemployed. Hoovervilles and shantytowns everywhere. Sharecroppers dying of starvation in Georgia. People taking paving blocks out of the streets of Chicago to build shelters. Selling apples on street corners. Something must be done. The Bonus Marchers don't care that Hoover saved Europe. They need food. Gramma calls it creeping socialism. I say Roosevelt is introducing social progress."

The Negroes looked to President and Mrs. Roosevelt as their saviors. When they heard that President and Mrs. Roosevelt were coming to the island from Warm Springs, the excitement was intense.

Cook Ada was in what she called a tizzy. She wanted to begin cooking her famous island delicacies immediately for what would obviously be a ceremonious dinner. She ordered newcomer Ada to climb up a ladder and get out the silver place plates, encased in protective flannel, that resided on the top shelf of the butler's pantry.

Aunt Emily was concerned about seating arrangements and called up Ambassador Lowell Pritchard, Uncle Thorny's father, for advice on protocol. Aunt Meg worried for fear the President would bring Fala, who would be set upon by the hunting dogs. Aunt Amy hoped that

Eleanor would let well enough alone and not upset the island darkies with her radical philosophy.

Gramma solved the seating-protocol problem and upset Cook Ada's plans by deciding to have one of the island's famous oyster roasts on the beach.

"But do you consider that proper for a President?" Aunt Emily asked, shocked.

"Sure ain't what de President of the You-nited States is used to," Cook Ada muttered darkly.

"Eleanor will feel more at ease," Grandmother replied crisply. "Anyway, it's more islandy."

On the day that the *Maggie Royal* picked up the presidential party in Savannah, the excitement on the island was as intense as it must have been when the slaves heard of the Emancipation Proclamation.

Cuffee, who was to provide the cold chicken, champagne, and the ingredients for the President's favorite old-fashioneds, was an instant celebrity. He paraded along the settlement street, wearing his starched white linen coat with a fresh rose from the greenhouse pinned in his buttonhole, like Uncle Oomlot when he came downstairs for ceremonial doings.

When the island boat, decorated from stem to stern with red-white-and-blue bunting and streamers, came in sight, a cheer went up from the Negroes assembled on the bank that could be heard back on the mainland. Newspapermen and photographers, who had been forbidden to tie up at the dock or come ashore, attempted to take photographs of President and Mrs. Roosevelt (Fala did not come) from a fishing boat they chartered in Starksville.

Jared, helping to run the island boat that summer, stood proudly by the gangway as the President was helped ashore and into Gramma's Packard touring car. Jazzbo, Jasper's son, was behind the wheel. Gramma had bought him a gray chauffeur's uniform with a black stripe down the sides of his trousers, a matching cap, and black leggings. The arrival of the car had caused so much jealousy and ill feeling on Sapelo's part, who felt the young Negro had usurped his place in the island hierarchy, that Gramma bought the old coachman a new maroon coat and silk hat, and agreed to let him drive Mrs. Roosevelt, the Georgia Senator's wife, and herself in the landau.

"You understand, Sapelo," Gramma said diplomatically, "that the President is crippled, and would not be able to get into the carriage."

Now old Sapelo, his ebony face gleaming with pride, and his silk hat steamed to a high gloss from being held over the spout of a boiling kettle, sat at attention in the driver's seat, holding his long-thonged whip upright in front of him in a kind of salute.

The President did not look like a monster or a tyrant. He looked like a tired, rumpled man with a smile as warm as the summer day. His face, beneath his straw panama hat, was wet with perspiration from the

78

effort of getting into the car, but he graciously thanked the men who helped him, and Jazzbo for holding open the door.

Mrs. Roosevelt hung back, waiting until her husband was settled. She wore an overly long dark skirt and blouse, and her hair in a pompadour. She did not at all fit the picture of the flaming radical Gramma painted. "Poor Franklin," Gramma said. "If only he had married someone with a touch more style."

Maggie Royal had no interest in how she was dressed. What struck her was the way she gazed at the people lining the banks, really seeming to see them, each and every one, and the shy smile and look of honest concern on her face.

Mrs. Roosevelt, Gramma, and the Senator's wife were settled in the landau, with the hood rolled back, behind the hackneys, brasses shining, braided, and rubbed to such a high gloss they even had dapples behind their ears. The Secret Service men climbed into the farm wagon used on deer hunts, behind the mules driven by Outside Dick.

The cavalcade, with President Roosevelt and the young Senator from Georgia in the center, started off, to drive slowly along the avenue to the house.

The President was installed in a fan-backed wicker chair on the veranda, with one of the Indian blankets Jared's mother wove on her loom tucked over his knees to hide his shrunken legs. Newt served him an old-fashioned, which he professed to be just the way he liked it, and lit his cigarette. The President sat smoking it in a very long holder, and reminiscing with Gramma about Campobello.

All the children lined up to be presented to the President of the United States. They wore their best clothes. The boys had on their Buster Brown suits, all but Constance's little brother. Harry the Horror was the image of Little Lord Fauntleroy, in a brown velvet suit with a white scalloped lace collar and cuffs, matching knee pants with three buttons down each side, white knee socks, and patent-leather slippers with bows on them. While Aunt Emily was giving the children final instructions— "Say 'How do you do, Mr. President,' then curtsy or bow"—the Horror had a tantrum. He went out and rolled in the dust on the avenue, screaming that he didn't want to meet any old President, and kicking his mother in the shins when she went to retrieve him. Aunt Emily handed him over to Newt, who picked him up as he did the sofa pillows, and took him out back and beat him the way he beat the carpets, sending up clouds of gray dust.

Maggie Royal wore her white communion dress with a wide blue sash and patent-leather slippers with the strap across the instep that Gramma ordered each year from Slater's in New York. Affey had given up trying to curl her hair into fat finger curls like Adele's, and had simply tied her long straight hair back with a thin blue ribbon. With her flat boy's body and long legs she looked like Alice in Wonderland.

At the last minute, Gramma sent Constance indoors to remove her red nail polish and clanking bracelets, and wash her face.

Maggie Royal thought of the day she had gone with Gramma to the White House to meet President Hoover. The man Gramma insisted had saved Europe had not looked at her as he shook her hand, and his handshake had been cold and dry.

This President did not look cold or austere. His handshake was warm and firm, and he did not gaze at her the way most grown-ups gaze at children with that glazed uninterested expression people wear at cocktail parties; but as if he were really seeing her. After her curtsy, he called her Maggie, and told her he had seen her mother in Noël Coward's new revue.

At mention of Mairin, Maggie Royal saw her grandmother's lips purse into a thin line, the way they did when any of the children were impertinent or vulgar, or brought up a subject she did not care to discuss.

Before Gramma could signal Maggie Royal to move on, she blurted out, "Why, Mr. President, you're nice. You're not a cold fish like Mr. Hoover."

Adele punched her from behind, and Aunt Emily glared; but President Roosevelt threw back his great head, and his chuckle of appreciation was rich and long.

"You have your mother's eyes," he said when he subsided. "When you grow up, you'll be as beautiful as she is."

"He didn't say anything like that to me," Constance pouted. "All he said was, 'Nice to meet you, little girl.' Little girl, indeed!" she exclaimed indignantly. "Why, I already have the curse. I bet you don't get it until you're fourteen."

After the "family" had been presented, the Long Point people and house servants gathered at the foot of the steps. Jared and his parents came first. They lifted Susan up onto the veranda in her folding chair. The President leaned over and kissed her cheek, and Susan's eyes filled with tears. It was a gesture that meant more to the crippled girl than any words he could have said.

Jared's father, in his worn tweed jacket with the chamois patches at the elbows that dated back to his Harvard days, and his mother, with her long black hair and the crimson skirt she had made for herself on her loom, stood out from the crowd of city relatives and guests, dressed in their best as if to go to a diplomatic reception.

President Roosevelt and Jared's father had known each other at Harvard, and the President had heard of some of the cases Lawyer Stark had handled in recent years.

Jared, now sixteen, and growing, as Gramma said, like wild asparagus, wore his one good suit, the pants of which were already too short. There was a quietness, a sudden new maturity about him as he bent to shake hands.

Of all the people on the island, Cullen, the farmer, was the only one to refuse to shake President Roosevelt's hand. His excuse to Gramma was that the dove field needed to be plowed prior to fall planting. "You see how diligent he is," Gramma boasted. The cousins knew better. "I heard him call President Roosevelt and that wife a his a goddam nigger-lovin' son of a bitch," Thorny said.

Gramma had solved the problem of which of the Negroes were to be first in order of importance and social standing, by choosing teams, as in charades. Cook Ada had been designated captain of the in-house women, to decide in what order they would be introduced. Newt was captain of the in-house men. Sapelo of the grooms. Isaiah of the gardeners. Outside Dick, the farmhands. A number of glum faces indicated some felt thcy had been slighted.

While the President remained on the veranda, smoking and talking politics with the Senator from Georgia, Gramma drove Mrs. Roosevelt around the island. "The only thing we have to fear," she told Mrs. Roosevelt, "are snakes!" For some reason, Gramma thought they lived in trees. She explained to Mrs. Roosevelt that she always wore a big hat and drove her surrey, believing that the fringed top would keep the reptiles from dropping onto her head.

The First Lady asked to see where the Negroes lived, and urged Gramma to pause in order that she could speak to those who lined up along the street. Gramma said later, she asked a lot of questions about them, and remarked that she was honored to meet Jared's father, whose articles on human rights she had read in *The Nation* and *New Republic*.

"Surely it would be more useful for Eleanor to devote herself to ridding the country of those odious billboards and Burma-Shave signs," Gramma told Aunt Emily, voicing one of her principal aversions, "rather than stirring up the Negroes."

In the afternoon, everyone moved down to the beach for the oyster roast. A great fire was built. The grown-ups sat in canvas chairs under little awnings to keep the sun off their faces, and drank Newt's special mint juleps served in frosted silver cups that Gramma had won at horse shows.

Jared's father urged the repeal of the poll tax. "The courthouse gang should be investigated," he said. "There's no way a Negro can get a fair trial in our county. Judge Upton, who replaced Judge Cantwell when he retired, should be recalled."

"I'll make a note of it," President Roosevelt replied.

"Well, now, Mr. President," the Senator said, "Ah wouldn't be hasty if I were you. LeRoy Upton is a good ole boy and he sure worked hard to help get you elected!"

Freed of their party clothes, the young people played hopscotch and stickball. Jazzbo and the band he had put together from Long Point played fiddles and guitars and spoons and sang spirituals.

Both President and Mrs. Roosevelt and their party ate mightily of the translucent oysters, so fresh and clear and shining that the President said he could have placed one on top of a prepared speech and still been able to read it. There were fried chicken and country ham, roast corn, yams and salad, and Cook Ada had been given free rein to bake flaky puffs filled with fruit, and one of her famous chocolate cakes.

Gramma was too polite to let young Franklin know what she thought of his New Deal. She did express her opinion that the President's departure from the gold standard was nothing short of lunacy, and that to pay a farmer *not* to farm was madness.

"Maggie," the President told Gramma, "I have no expectation of making a hit every time I come to bat. But something has to be done." He turned to Uncle Thorndike, the Boston banker. "As you know, many banks are failing, and seventeen million unemployed. Surely it's time the workingman had a New Deal." He patted Gramma's hand and gave her the smile that had influenced millions of votes. "I know you think I breakfast every morning on a dish of grilled millionaire. My dear, I assure you I don't. I much prefer scrambled eggs."

Jared never took his eyes from Mrs. Roosevelt, absorbing every word. She was very intense. She spoke of Negro rights and the persecution of the Jews. She said Hitler wanted to rule Europe, and that if fascism were allowed to triumph, it would mean the end of the free world.

Newt, hovering in the background, waiting to take away her plate, listened to her fearsome forecast of the future. Finally the butler mustered his courage to interrupt and ask the First Lady if she would like a second helping. "That is," he added quickly, "Missus First Lady, ma'am, if you think there's time before the world comes to an end."

The President roared, and Mrs. Roosevelt joined in the laughter.

Soon after the picnic supper the presidential visit came to an end. The President and Mrs. Roosevelt were driven to the dock, along the roadway lined with Long Point people, cheering and clapping. The President was helped aboard the island boat. Taking his cigarette holder out of his mouth, he called out good-byes and waved. As she watched the boat vanish into the nighttime mist, Maggie Royal sensed that the day was one she would never forget.

After the Roosevelt visit, life on Stark Island returned to its usual summer routine.

Gramma insisted that the Great Oak children learn to do everything as well as possible—that in life, as in tennis, they follow through and finish what they began. They did not argue with Gramma. They assumed, as everyone else did on the island, that it was up to them to live up to what was demanded of them.

Breakfast was served at 7:30 sharp, and those who did not sit down on time, grown-ups included, did not eat. The children in the nursery were obliged to eat heaping plates of porridge, often decorated with prunes, which, if unfinished, would be served again at the next meal, ice-cold and gluey.

By eight everyone was dispersed, to the stable to ride, to the golf course, or to sail on the sound. Both tennis courts by the shingled pool house would be full, with mixed doubles of grown-ups and children or a class presided over by Miss Hoxie.

Miss Hoxie Frommer, who had once been state champion, came over from the Starksville Country Club once a week to give lessons. She was big-boned, heavyset, and tireless. She wore white tennis dresses and a green eyeshade. She stood at the net, feet spread apart, racket in one hand, a cigarette in the other, firing balls from a bushel basket at her feet, first to Maggie Royal's forehand, then to her backhand, while the child in turn ran from side to side until she was completely out of breath. "Ah declare, it won't do you no good, child, if Ah just keep hitting that li'l ole ball to the same place!" Miss Hoxie would say, placing her hands on her hips. "Now, this time try to run a little." Then, shouting, "Move! Move! Now, swing. Follow through!"

Maggie Royal found golf boring and never got past the first tee, so to speak. Nonetheless, she and the others were forced to have a weekly lesson with the pro Gramma hired from Atlanta. She lost a large number of balls in the swamp that bordered the nine-hole course Grandfather McDermott had built and where Woodrow Wilson had once played before becoming President.

The pro, Frank, was young, and had slick black hair parted in the middle, and very white teeth. He smiled a lot, and it seemed to Maggie Royal he spent more time than needed standing behind the girls, instructing them how to hold their clubs. Maggie Royal did not like his touching her, and his breath against her cheek smelled of tobacco and occasionally of liquor. Adele and Constance, however, thought he was very handsome and rolled their eyes and giggled when he slid his arms around them and whispered in their ears.

Riding was the most important requirement. Gramma herself was a fearless horsewoman. There were pictures of her in the Great Oak scrapbook foxhunting in Virginia and Leicestershire. Old-timers remembered her winning the flat races at the annual Starksville Fair on Golden Isle, one of the wild horses she had broken. In 1928, the year before the stock-market crash, she had rebuilt the stables and kennels for the gun dogs, transforming the crumbling wooden buildings into the picture-book structures they'd been in the great days of the plantation. It was a magic place, where the children never tired of roaming—all, that is, except Constance, who was afraid of horses and hated riding, but was obliged to try anyway.

The stable was Sapelo's domain. Sapelo had white grizzled hair and a face as black and gnarled as a cypress stump. He remembered Grandfather and the great days when Gramma rode at the Starksville Horse Show and brought home blue ribbons and silver cups. Now he saw to it that his son Jasper and grandson Jazzbo kept the stalls mucked out, the tack polished and supple, and the brasses on the harness shining.

There was always laughter in the stable, and although Gramma forbade it, generally a dice game going on afternoons, in which the boy cousins took part. The girls also learned to shoot craps, and a variety of four-letter words that would have astounded Gramma if she could have heard them practicing them.

Although Maggie Royal had had a few riding lessons in England, Gramma started her on old Scampie, a twenty-year-old pony on which numerous cousins learned to ride. While she led, riding Darien, her great seventeen-hand hunter, Maggie Royal trailed along on a lead line. It was a marvelous sight—Gramma, wearing a linen skirt, brown Nardi coat, and felt hat, looking down from her side saddle, occasionally telling Maggie Royal to sit up straight, "like a queen," while Darien's great coarse tail struck the child across the face at each stride, causing her eyes to water. In a short time, Scampie was put out to pasture and Maggie Royal was given her choice of the ponies.

Mornings she rose before the sun burned away the mist that rolled in from the sound. Making sure not to wake the other children, she went to the field where the ponies were turned out, put a halter on whichever one she could catch, vaulted onto its back, grabbed the mane, and headed for the beach. Many times she galloped down the avenue only as the breakfast gong was ringing, turning the pony loose to graze while she went indoors to eat. Gramma caught her once, but didn't mind the early-morning ride or that Maggie Royal was in pajamas—only that she had gone inside to eat before seeing to her pony, rubbing it down and cooling it off. To press home her point, she ordered Maggie Royal to come to her room after breakfast.

Gramma wore white nightgowns, exquisitely hand-sewn by Affey. Her white cashmere shawl was so fine it could be drawn through her wedding ring. It lay around her shoulders while swatches of lace or a velvet ribbon pinned with her diamond heart circled her throat. On her bedside table was a jewel box covered in crimson velvet with a lock and tiny gold key. It overflowed with gems—rubies, sapphires, emeralds, and the Stark pearls. But instead of the diamond-encrusted traveling clock, which she said never kept the correct time, she consulted a cheap pocket-watch, steel-framed, its glass cracked, that Mr. McDermott had bought with his first earnings in the mines of the New World.

"Maggie Royal, you're getting to be a big girl now," Gramma observed as her granddaughter stood before her, digging the ruptured toe of her sneaker into the faded Aubusson carpet. "Time you stopped being kattywampus. Your shorts are torn and your sweater is buttoned all cockeyed."

Maggie Royal gazed apologetically at her exquisite grandmother and began rebuttoning her cardigan.

"Come here, child," Gramma said more kindly. "Sit." She patted the bed beside her. With a quick impulsive gesture she took Maggie Royal's hard brown, faintly grubby fist in her elegant jeweled hand. "I know you think I'm unreasonable, demanding. But, Maggie Royal, it's better to give too much than not enough." Thoughtfully she added, "There is one need we never outgrow. It is the need to feel cherished by someone, to know there is a place we belong." She gave Maggie Royal's hand a quick squeeze. Then the moment was past. She reached for the day's lesson, adjusted her "pinch-knees" on her straight Stark nose, and began to read a passage from Xenophon, addressing a cavalry commander about 300 B.C. " 'The duty will devolve on you of seeing, in the first place, that your horses are well fed and in condition to stand their work, since a horse which cannot endure fatigue will clearly be unable to overhaul the foeman or effect escape; and in the second place you will have to see to it the animals are tractable, since, clearly again, a horse that will not obey is fighting for the enemy and not for his friends.'

"It applies to people as well," Gramma said, shutting the book. "It is your bounden duty to keep well fed and in condition to stand up to your school and your work. Affey," she called to her maid, "I'll get up now. Child, go see to your mount."

The children were subjected to a summer of expert instruction. Gramma had hired the Major, a former cavalry officer from Hungary, where he had been horse master to the royal family. While Gramma sat on the veranda doing her needlepoint and supervising, the Major drilled his charges in the square dressage arena set up under the trees.

As the days passed, they learned to jog without stirrups and with a crop stuck inside the back of their jodhpurs to ensure a straight back. No use of spurs, whips, martingales, or bits other than a plain snaffle was permitted. The Major emphasized that the art of riding finishes when abuse begins. As Gramma put it, "You can't go to a horse and apologize by saying, 'Sorry, I didn't mean it.' "

"Pat-stroke-make-much-of-him!" cried the Major, standing in the center of the arena as his pupils went around and around. "Keep leg on, but do not pennch ze horse!"

At the end of the summer, parents and visitors were invited to a demonstration. The pupils were asked to ride into the arena and go through the movements of the exercises they had memorized and practiced. "Ze first impression is ze most important," the Major instructed as each waited for her turn. "Come into ze ring as though queen—think bosom!"

Maggie Royal tried to "think bosom," hoping she would develop one, like Adele and Constance, but in those days of bosomy Southern belles she was destined to be flat-chested.

The lessons with the Hungarian Major paid off. Her truths were those learned from horses—fearlessness, quickness of thought and action, heightened awareness and sensitivity. To her a horse was like the sea and the air and the island. Horses felt her control, her concentration of will, and reacted accordingly.

Her happiest hours were spent riding along the many sun-dappled trails or racing along the beach.

When she rode at the Starksville Fair, Gramma made her ride side saddle, wearing a proper habit—the uncomfortable derby which she hated and string gloves. Although she won a blue ribbon and a small silver loving cup and Gramma's friends commented on how nice it was to see somebody riding like a lady instead of the new modern way, she longed to be back on the island, riding astride, bareback.

There was nothing ladylike about the wild races through the woods, playing hide and seek, prisoner's base, or Yankees and Confederates. Maggie Royal resented the fact that the boys always played the part of dashing Confederate soldiers, slashing with palm-frond swords at the girl cousins whom they pretended were hated Yankees.

· 3 ·
THE FAIR
Summer 1934

· 5 ·

The summer of 1934, when Maggie Royal was fourteen, was the summer
of Azilia. In the spring she saw the mare running freely along the beach,
a golden chestnut with a star in the center of her sculptured head, small,
curved breedy ears and clean, unblemished legs. The veins that rippled
like tongues of flame beneath her satiny coat; the dark, liquid, intelligent
eyes; and the long, lovely stride bespoke some ancient kingly breed trac-
ing its ancestry to the Darley Arabian and the horses brought by the
early Spaniards when they attempted to settle the Golden Isles. The
horse was the answer to Maggie Royal's dreams, the epitome of all the
horses in all the horse books she'd read.

Cullen, the farm manager, pursued the mare with his dogs, driving
her into the pen with the horses to be sent to the mainland and sold at
auction or to dealers like Horseface Lewis, owner of the Starksville Livery Stable. "Quality of them Sandhill tackies ain't much no more. Too
much inbreeding and not enough feed on the island," Lewis said disparagingly as he eyed the horses in the corral. He was about to leave when
the chestnut caught his eye. "Once in a while something turns up like
that mare." He spat out a wad of tobacco. "Throwback, mebbe, to the
first horses the Spaniards brought or some of the mares and foals the
planters imported from England."

Maggie Royal pleaded with Gramma not to sell the horse.

"We're in a depression," Gramma said, fingering her pearls. "I
can't afford to keep more horses than we already have, and Lewis has
made me a good offer."

"I can break her, Gramma, I know I can. Gramma, please. She'll be
another Golden Isle."

Maybe it was mention of Gramma's all-time favorite, on which she
had won many of the silver julep cups, that persuaded Gramma not to
sell. "She is a dream to look at!" she acknowledged. "Controlling her
will be something else."

The mare was named after the Margravate of Azilia, founded in
1717 to transform the golden isles into a Utopian settlement. Designed

87

to become an earthly paradise, it never came to pass, proving only to be a dream.

Azilia was no dream. She was a biting, kicking, rearing reality that required time and patience. Every morning for a month Maggie Royal crept out of bed and downstairs in order not to awaken the household. She walked out into the morning mist to the corral. There she sat on the top rail and spoke softly to the mare as the horse watched warily from the far side. As the days passed, Azilia began to accept her presence.

Finally Maggie Royal was able to walk up to her and hold out the feed bucket. One morning Azilia approached slowly, cautiously, sticking out her nose until it touched the bucket. For a long time the girl and the horse studied each other. Then the mare took a tentative step, threw back her head, and blew mightily in a gesture of acceptance.

That afternoon Maggie Royal returned to the corral. She walked up to the mare, holding out an apple. Suddenly Azilia extended her long neck and snatched the apple, biting deep into it and dropping half of it. Maggie Royal picked it up and again offered it to her. This time she took it more slowly, and Maggie Royal was able to rub her silky neck as she ate.

Maggie Royal slipped the halter over Azilia's head as she munched on the apple. Still nuzzling and talking to her, the girl adjusted the rope shank and started to lead the mare. Azilia followed haltingly, her eyes wary in her beautiful head.

Azilia suddenly pulled back and then reared, almost jerking Maggie Royal off her feet. Luckily she had thought to bring one of Gramma's hat pins. Quickly she pricked the mare's chest, a trick learned from Aunt Meg, who maintained it surprised and distracted an unruly horse, making it easier to control it.

When Azilia became more tractable, Maggie Royal led her to the small paddock where the harness horses were broken to driving from the ground. The mare flinched and tried to jerk away, but Maggie Royal managed to hold her, keeping her close to the outside fence. After a while Azilia became calmer, more amenable as, using the long harness reins, Maggie Royal drove her in a circle. Soon Azilia's tail began to hang naturally and she no longer fought against the bit as Maggie Royal stopped and started her, rewarding her each time with a piece of apple. Finally the mare began to come to Maggie Royal automatically when Maggie Royal called her name.

When she walked away, Azilia followed without protest. Her ears were pricked, watching. Suddenly the mare stopped. She rested her head against Maggie Royal's shoulder, waiting for her to rub it. Maggie Royal knew then that Azilia was hers.

That night there was an oyster roast on the beach. The long wooden table on which luncheon was served in the woods during the shooting season had been set up. It was laden with roasted corn, potatoes, relishes, biscuits, home-churned butter, jams, and several different cakes and pies.

The boys returned staggering under loads of driftwood for the fire.

When the oysters were crisp and succulent, they heaped their plates and sat down.

"The salad's good," Maggie Royal said. She had on a man's white shirt over her tattered shorts. In the firelight her hair was black against the whiteness of the shirt. Her face and thin brown arms were like the dark polished wood.

"Fodder!" Jared put in lazily. "She thinks she's part horse!"

"Shut up, Jared," Maggie Royal said.

Constance predictably put in her oar. "You're right, Jared. We all know Maggie Royal would rather be horse than human."

Maggie Royal's long black hair whipped around like a horse's mane, inky black in the firelight. "I'd rather be crazy about horses than boy-crazy."

"Just because you're part horse doesn't mean you can ride that un-broken mare," Jared said, grinning at her angry face.

Maggie Royal wheeled like a horse at the sight of the wild pigs in the palmettos. She shook her head and her fists at Jared and vanished into the darkness.

"You shouldn't tease her," Adele said, sitting down beside Jared. "Why are you suddenly so hard on her?"

Jared turned, surprised. "Why, she's just a kid."

Noble belched and stood up. "Far as Maggie Royal is concerned, sex is in a class with splints and colic. Come, Constance, let's take a walk."

When it was time to leave and Maggie Royal still had not returned, Adele asked worriedly where she could be. "You don't suppose she went swimming—that shark . . ."

"Let her be," Jared said. "You know how she is. She likes to be by herself."

Maggie Royal rode into the circle of firelight, coaxing and nudging the mare with her bare heels. The horse walked hesitantly, ears back, nostrils distended with dislike, making soft disdainful snorts, like heavy breathing.

Maggie Royal sat as proudly and regally as a queen on Azilia's sat-iny bare back. As she looked over the mare's curved ears at Jared, there was a triumphant expression on her face.

Within a few days Maggie Royal had a saddle on Azilia's back. By the end of the summer she was racing Jared along the beach. It annoyed Jared that she always won.

The king of the island herd was an Appaloosa that Cullen had bought out of a shipment brought in by a dealer from the West. The farmer wanted what he termed a "shit-and-git" horse, a short-coupled, strong-quartered Western-type horse that would win for him at the Starksville Fair. He had brought the stallion to the island on the boat. Hoping to control the horse, he had put a chain shank through the halter and across the stallion's nose. In order to lead him off the boat, the farmer gave the rope a rough jerk, pinching the horse's nose at its most tender. The stallion's ears went back. It reared, pawing the air with its front hooves. The hot-tempered farmer unleashed his long-thonged whip and began slashing furiously. The terrified stallion reared again, slipping its halter and coming down almost on top of the man.

Freed, the stallion leaped ashore and galloped away, finding sanctuary with the wild horses and mares in the forest. There Jared and Maggie Royal saw him galloping, mane and tail flying, leading the mares to drink at one of the pools or to graze in the park at night. Once, returning from Long Point, they came upon the horse standing in the center of the trail, his aristocratic Arabic-type head held high, listening, an arrogant motionless shape of power and pride. At sight of them he tossed his head, pawed the ground, and snorted. Then he took off like the evening wind, vanishing into the shadows.

"I want him," Jared said determinedly, his green eyes darkening. "I mean to have him."

The annual roundup was held in late June, after the cousins had arrived. Boatloads of people came from the mainland, guests and dealers looking for saddle or plantation horses or ones to race at the Starksville Fair.

Gramma and Great-Aunt Amy came to the corral in the surrey, leading the parade of friends and relatives staying at the big house. Great-Aunt Meg rode the dock-tailed cob she kept on the island.

Most of the crowd set off for the beach, where old and young lined up, holding one another's hands, forming a human wall on either side of the track leading to the open gates of the corrals.

"What'll I do if a horse comes at me?" Constance asked nervously. "That wild stallion Jared's so anxious to catch could kill me."

"Not likely," Adele answered dryly. "He'd probably take one look at you and run in the other direction."

Under the direction of Cullen, the boy cousins and Negroes prepared to round up the animals in the interior and drive them toward the enclosures, which were built with a platform out over the water so the wild horses and cattle could be loaded onto barges and transported to the mainland.

"That Cullen!" Adele exploded as the farm manager rode self-importantly back and forth, issuing loud peremptory instructions to the Negroes by the corral gate. He jerked his quarter horse to a stop with a long-shanked curb, causing the horse to open its mouth and throw up its head in pain. Simultaneously he jabbed it with long-roweled spurs. "I wish Gramma could see what he's really like," Adele added, "but he butters her up so she thinks he's God."

The stallion and his herd were by the green-surfaced pool where the egrets nested. The Appaloosa turned his head and gazed at the intruders, motionless as a statue. In the dimness of the woods his spotted rump gleamed like streaked moonlight.

The roundup crew advanced on the horses, driving them out of the forest onto the beach. Suddenly the stallion became aware of their peril. On he came, kicking and squealing. Snaking out his head, he bared his teeth. Darting around his charges like a sheepdog, he drove them back toward the sheltering woods. When he saw the riders blocking his way, he whirled. The mares and foals followed, an explosion of flying manes and tails as they raced along the beach toward the enclosures.

"For God's sake open the gate!" Cullen shouted at the men sitting on top of the corral gate. The onlookers leaning against the fence leaped aside as the stallion and his charges swept between the human lines bordering their route.

Before he could swerve or slow down, the stallion, driven by the shouting, whooping riders, was through the gate and had crashed to a stop on the far side of the corral. Somebody slammed the heavy gate shut as the mares were shunted into the adjoining corral.

The horse whirled to face its captors, trembling and snorting. Foam and rivulets of water ran from its sides and rump. For an instant all was quiet. Then several dealers converged on Gramma at once.

"I'll give two hundred dollars," one said, pointing at the stallion. Jazzbo identified him as a killer buyer, one who bought horses to sell to manufacturers of dog food.

"I'll make it four hundred," Horseface Lewis said. "That's a good price, Missus McDermott. Depression and all. Ain't many buying pleasure horses these days." He glanced back at the stallion braced against the fence, ears back and teeth bared, daring all comers, and spat onto the ground. "Ain't gonna make no pleasure horse at that, but maybe he'll be good at stud."

"Please don't sell the stallion." Jared stood looking at Gramma, his green eyes pleading. "I know I can ride him and that he'll win at the fair. I'll pay you back with the prize money." His eyes flashed. "I'll prove to you I can ride him!"

Before she could speak or call out to stop him, he had reached the corral fence, shinnied up it, and jumped from the top down into the pen.

"Master Jared," Jazzbo cried out, "don't you all go near that horse!"

Gramma and the aunts leaned forward to get a better view.

"Atta boy, Jared," Aunt Meg called out in her deep mannish voice. "Show 'em what a proper Stark is made of."

"I'll make it five hundred dollars," Lewis, the dealer, said, reaching for his wallet. "That's more than a fair price."

With a gesture of one white-gloved hand Gramma waved the man away.

Jared, holding a hackamore, walked slowly, steadily, toward the horse. The way the boy held himself, the proud tilt of his head and the sparks in his eyes made him seem one with the magnificent animal.

The watching crowd grew silent, tense, as Jared, crooning in the soft voice he used in the woods when approaching an island deer or wading bird, advanced slowly toward the stallion. The horse never took its eyes from Jared. As the boy came toward him, he moved along the fence until he was at the wide heavy gate.

"Throw it back," Jared called tersely to Jazzbo. "Tie it back alongside the horse."

Quickly Jared climbed the fence. The horse found itself pinned between the corral gate and the bars. With a sudden swift gesture, Jared reached down and slipped the hackamore over the unsuspecting stallion's head.

In the sky above, a hawk shrilled as Jared, seizing his chance, dropped lightly from the high fence onto the horse's back.

Jazzbo slammed the gate shut as the stallion shot into the center of the corral, bucking, twisting, and turning. Jared held the hackamore rein firmly, giving and taking, his body moving easily in concert with that of the horse.

Maggie Royal watched mesmerized. Jared, she realized, was the young chevalier she had fantasied about when she was small. Then it didn't matter what the horseman looked like. What mattered was whether or not he had light hands and a secure seat.

Finding his rider wouldn't be dislodged, remained clinging like a bur on its back, the stallion suddenly soared, a mass of spotted fire and muscle, hurling itself against the side of the rotting corral. The onlookers massed there fell away as the fence splintered beneath the horse's volcanic rush, spreading panic amid the mules and other horses. Even patient Job, Gramma's driving horse, started, and Sapelo lunged for his head.

Constance screamed. "Harry, come back!" Maggie Royal whirled and saw that the little boy had run directly into the stallion's path. At the sound of Jared's warning shout, he stopped, uncertain which way to turn.

The thunder of hooves drowned out the shrieks from the sidelines as Maggie Royal grabbed the helpless child and pulled him from the horse's path. She felt the stallion's hot breath and for a flashing instant saw Jared's face poised above her. Exultant, triumphant, complete.

"Cousin Maggie Royal," Harry said calmly, rubbing his wrist. "You hurt my arm!"

An hour later Jared rode the lathered stallion to the stable door, slid off its back, and led it to a stall. There the animal permitted him to sponge off the drying sweat and gently rub a cloth over the spotted gray-black coat.

"However did you do it?" Maggie Royal asked, awed.

Jared gave her one of his rare and wonderful grins. "I steered him to the beach and let him run himself out!"

92

"What will you name him?" she asked. "Assuming Gramma lets you keep him."

"King," Jared replied. "King of Great Oak!"

Jared did not kowtow to Gramma as some of the other cousins did. He maintained his independence and never asked for favors. King was the first thing he had ever asked Gramma for. She knew horses and horsemanship from the moment she had first been lifted into a basket cart atop the fat Shetland pony pictured in the old scrapbooks. Egged on by Aunt Meg, who considered Jared the finest natural rider she had ever seen, she had no choice but to present him with the stallion.

"Mind, now," she told him tartly, "I expect you to pay me back with whatever purses you win at the fair. In spite of young Franklin Roosevelt's giveaway programs, I don't believe in giving anybody something for nothing!"

From then on, to Cullen's annoyance and chagrin, King was Jared's horse. He was as wild and reckless as Jared himself. He had a habit of kicking out at anything or anybody who came near him. Jared's dogs soon learned to steer clear of his heels, and once when Cullen came too close, warning him away from a newly planted field, the Appaloosa, at the sound of the farmer's voice, whirled and lashed out at him with his hooves. In a flash the farmer loosed his long-thonged whip and struck back at the horse. The horse went for him. Jared, furious at the farmer's stupidity, might have let King have his way and savage him if Gramma hadn't driven up at that moment to see the new planting.

Soon Jared could do anything he wanted with the horse. In a week he was riding him under Uncle Oomlot's old Whippy saddle. He put cedar logs across the Long Point path, forming a kind of cavalletti, like that the Hungarian Major had schooled him over. King took to jumping like wild ducks to water. When he heard Jared's whistle, the stallion came at a gallop from wherever he was, to bury his nose in Jared's hands, seeking an apple or a carrot, or to rub his head against the boy's shoulder.

Jared galloped King along the beach, matching the stallion against the other horses. King led all the way, passing even Azilia, Jared in complete control, his long lithe body moving in rhythm with the stallion's giant stride.

"You'll see," Jared cried triumphantly. "He'll beat all the other horses at the fair."

The Starksville County Fair was the big event of each summer. On the morning of opening day, the stable at Great Oak was a bustle of preparation: Jazzbo collecting tack and Uncle Oomlot's old racing saddle for Jared to use on King; Sapelo, the coachman, lugging the harness to the boat and loading the hackneys that would pull the landau in which Gramma and the great-aunts would ride in order to open the fair.

On the island landing the horses tensed, sensing a departure from their usual routine. At Jared's slow, patient urging, King walked on board, to stand quietly, disdainfully, looking out over the sides of the barge. Following his lead, Azilia, who was herd-bound and hated to be parted from the stallion, leaped on deck, resenting the partition between them, to stand fidgeting and gnawing the wooden planks.

The horses were unloaded at the Stark Island pier in Starksville and ridden through the crowded streets to the fairgrounds, where they were stabled in the long unpainted shedrows beneath the live oaks.

During the week of the fair, the Great Oak people stayed with the in-town great-aunts in the big brick Stark house on the main square. It was four stories high, with floor-to-ceiling windows that opened onto wrought-iron balconies from which, in the distance, could be seen the outlines of Stark Island.

A veranda, draped with wisteria, overlooked a brick-walled garden in the rear. Maggie Royal called it a galloping porch. "Veranda," Aunt Amy corrected. "They have porches in the North. Verandas in the South." Porch or veranda, it had been a fine place when she was little to ride her stick horse made from a broom handle with an old sock stuffed with Spanish moss for a head. Potted ferns in scrolled iron pots lined the veranda. A swing hung on chains from the ceiling, flanked by white-painted wicker chairs with wide round fan backs. The grown-ups sat there evenings, sipping their toddies served in tall frosted silver cups.

The great-aunts had both been fine horsewomen in their day. Aunt Meg still rode out daily, riding astride, to Gramma's horror (even as late as the thirties, few "ladies" rode astride), in jodhpurs, tweed jacket, and brown felt hat. When not on a horse, she strode about carrying a hunting whip, which she brandished at the servants when she issued a command, or at the children when she wanted them to stop chasing one another through the house, or to discipline the dogs and cats.

There were dogs everywhere. Hounds the aunts were walking for the Starksville Hunt, gun dogs and strays from the pound. The dogs slept on the floor, on chairs, and in the beds. The guest rooms, used only during the week of the fair, were full of fleas.

Aunt Meg regaled the company with the trials of Maggie Royal's mother when her husband brought her to Starksville on their wedding trip. Mairin, then a famous star, was used to suites at Claridge's and the Ritz. She had never before traveled without Naomi, her personal maid, and the only South she knew was the south of France. She had never met eccentrics like the aunts.

Mairin was given the large front room in which General Nathanael Greene had slept as commander-in-chief of the American Revolutionary Army in the Southern Department in 1783 (according to the plaque the DAR gave the aunts one Garden Week when they opened the house to the public). When Mairin rang for breakfast—it had been years since she had come down for the meal or risen before noon—nothing happened. Finally Aunt Meg climbed the stairs to see what it was she wanted. She found Mairin observing her neck and chest, red with flea bites, in the mirror. Instead of the expected reaction of horrified apology, Aunt Meg burst out laughing. "My dear, what a shame! And on your wedding trip, too. I'm afraid there are fleas in all these rooms. They haven't been aired since the week of the fair."

Along with the anticipated horse races, the star attraction at that year's fair was to be an air show, the first ever held in Starksville. Posters proclaiming the Doug Davis Baby Ruth Flying Circus were tacked on lampposts and billboards. Gramma carried an ax in the trunk of the Packard touring car, transported to the mainland, in order to conduct her antibillboard campaign. Whenever she came on one of the billboards advertising soft drinks or Burma-Shave that were currently springing up around Starksville, she ordered Jazzbo to stop the car and chop down the offending sign. The fair posters suffered the same fate. Nor was there anything the organizers of the fair or the city fathers could do about it. Gramma was a Stark of Stark Island, and the Starks were laws unto themselves. Thus the organizers simply rebuilt the billboards and had more posters printed to tack up on the lampposts and storefronts.

Gramma was a fixture at the fair. Wearing one of her long white dresses, white picture hat, and elbow-length gloves with tiny pearl buttons and carrying a frilly white parasol, she was driven to the grounds on opening day in her shiny landau. The matched pair of hackneys bought from Uncle Oomlot's old friend Ambrose Clark in Cooperstown, New York, were bay with square docks that set off their muscled hindquarters. Their polished coats and well-pulled manes spoke volumes for Sapelo's stable management. The black harness boasted every strap in place, and the brasses had been polished with the coachman's special mixture of ashes, sand, and a pinch of salt.

Sapelo, looking very smart in his maroon livery and high silk hat, had covered the seats with deerskins and folded back the top of the carriage to expose the passengers.

"Heads up! Heads up!" he cried as the arched-neck hackneys pranced through the crowds of calicoed and overalled country people. "Don' you all know better'n for block off Miss Maggie Royal's carriage?"

Mr. Lovewell, the mayor of Starksville, came bustling up to welcome the ladies, helping them down from the carriage, and escorting them to the flag-draped stand overlooking the finish line. The front-row boxes in the rickety wooden stand were assigned to the most prominent citizens and island gentry. Ownership of the boxes was handed down from one generation to the next. Gramma told stories of newcomers, Yankees who had bought hunting islands off the coast in the twenties and thought their money could buy the purple ribbon to pin in their buttonholes, marking the wearer as someone admitted to the members' stand and the front-row line of shabby boxes with their uncomfortable upright, rush-matted chairs, failing to understand that only Georgia gentry sat there. She particularly deplored Big Boy Tarrington, the paper-mill owner, who worked his way into Starksville society by marrying into the old shabby-genteel Cantwell family. When he'd been denied acceptance at the Jekyll Island Club, he had bought a neighboring island, on which he was building a resort and an enormous mansion.

Gramma's box was the most prominent. It had belonged to her Grandfather Stark, who had reviewed the "Sons of Starksville" as they marched past on their way to Savannah to defend the Confederacy.

After descending from her carriage, Gramma swept through the crowd on the mayor's arm, nodding graciously to the local people. They were followed by Fletcher Dornbush, editor of the Starksville weekly *Herald;* Mr. Tavis, her solicitor; "Drop Kick" Keeler, who had kicked the deciding goal at Ole Miss in 1923, and as a bootlegger during Prohibition and now an undertaker, was the richest man in town; Mr. Perrin, the butcher; Mr. Cooper, the baker; and Jenny Carson, the candlemaker, who made candles of wax from island apiaries.

The fair was a combination county fair and carnival. The country people and Negroes saved their best produce for the stands, which also sold watermelon pickle and pineapple upside-down cake, homemade breads, and jams and jellies.

They came driving buckboards and farm wagons and Fords, streaming toward the fairgrounds: young girls, awkward in stiff starched mail-order dresses as shapeless as their bodies, already misshapen by hard labor and too-early childbirth, and unaccustomed high heels; their husbands and brothers, self-conscious in ill-fitting suits, shirts, and cloth caps; the older men in bib overalls and straw hats, their women bright in calico and sunbonnets. Through them all moved the Negroes, talking, laughing, singing softly among themselves.

People spread checked cloths on the ground or over picnic tables in the grove and ate heartily of fried chicken and country ham, potato and macaroni salad, home-baked cakes and watermelon. Afterward the men sat leaning against the shade trees, dozing, their heads resting on their chests, faces hidden by the brims of their straw hats. The women cleaned up and exchanged recipes and gossiped. The children ate apples on sticks and spun-sugar candy and ran up and down the midway, round-eyed, with sticky hands and faces. Then slowly the grown-ups drifted back to the booths, where the men shot tin ducks moving along a track and threw baseballs at cardboard bottles. The women gaped at yard goods and the stuffed animals and dolls they hoped the men would win for them.

Gramma was conscientious about buying the things that sold least well, the butcher's wife's pickle that was too sour, Mrs. Cantwell's peaches that were too sweet, the mayor's wife's pound cake that was too heavy, Aunt Meg's pot holders that unraveled, and Aunt Amy's knitted sweaters with the uneven sleeves. Gramma left an assortment of weird objects, tagged with her name, at each stall for Sapelo, Jasper, or one of the cousins to collect before they went home. Nobody ever found out what she did with them afterward, for no one ever saw them again.

Jared and Maggie Royal vied with each other at the shooting gallery, where Maggie Royal managed to hit all but one of the tin ducks that bobbed up and down on a landscape that showed a river and palm trees. Her reward was a slap on the back from Jared and a large stuffed bear.

Adele led the way to the test-your-strength machine where the mayor, Cullen, and a number of other men were swinging the hammer. The Great Oak farmer whirled the implement around his head and brought it down with a crash on the anvil, causing the weight to fly up its vertical track and fall down again.

"That's easy," Thorny said scornfully. But when he picked up the hammer and brought it down, the hammer glanced off the anvil and he lost his balance.

"Not that way, stupid!" Adele said, grabbing the hammer. She whirled it in the air and brought it down with all the strength of her tennis-playing muscles. The weight bonged against the top and the seam split in the arm of her new green dress.

"You've torn it!" Thorny said delightedly.

"Darn it," Adele exclaimed.

"Darn it yourself!" Thorny laughed.

"I'll get Affey to do it," Adele said.

Hootchy-kootchy dancers emerged from behind a tent with a naked lady painted on it to stand on a platform. They undulated their hips to tinny Eastern music from a scratchy phonograph record while a barker with a young-old face and dead eyes sought frantically to entice the men ogling the girls from below into paying to enter the tent. The young boys blushed and grinned and poked one another in the ribs while their elders winked at the girls and made lewd remarks. They crowded forward, pushing up against the stage as a magnificent Negro woman came out onto the platform and began slowly swaying her hips in time to the tinny vibrations emanating from the Victrola.

Maggie Royal recognized some of the most prominent men in the county—doctors, the fire chief, the Starksville school superintendent, merchants, lawyers, and bankers—Cullen and his courthouse cronies; Matt Harper, the county sheriff; Harold Haskins, the lawyer for the Ku Klux Klan who had played fullback for Georgia Tech and was known as Loudmouth within the "good-ole-boy" fraternity; Judge LeRoy Upton, who replaced Judge Cantwell when he retired; Horseface Lewis, the owner of the Starksville livery stable; and a number of hangers-on. They rolled their eyes and poked one another. Little Willie Rigsby was the butt of many of their jokes. Little Willie was a small cotton farmer. He had the peaked, undernourished look of the sharecropper, and a club foot. In order to augment his meager income and support his aged mother, he acted as bagman for the courthouse gang. He went around the Negro community collecting votes by promising a donation to their church—a donation which somehow never came. "As long as they vote for the 'right' people," Mr. Stark explained, "the Negroes don't have a problem with the poll tax. Their votes are lumped in with those of dogs and long-dead citizens."

Now laughing and talking and spitting tobacco juice, Cullen and his friends bought tickets and started into the dancers' tent for the show. "Where's Little Willie?" Cullen asked, glancing around as the bagman shuffled off in another direction. He jerked his thumb at Horseface Lewis. "Get 'im," he ordered. He winked at the horse dealer. "We's doin' him a favor. Showin' 'im what he's missing!"

Maggie Royal left the boy cousins, who stood to one side of the tent laughing self-consciously and pretending uninterest, and went to the tent where the Gypsy fortune-teller read palms. No one knew if she was a real Gypsy or not, but she had dark skin, strange penetrating black eyes, and big gold-hoop earrings. Her arms were covered from wrist to elbow with cheap clanging bracelets she boasted of buying whenever a horse she bet on won. She lived in a caravan around which ragged children scuttled like the stray mongrels that grabbed at the hot dogs and buns and melting ice cream thrown down onto the ground.

She sat at a table covered with a red satin cloth and peered into a round glass globe.

Maggie Royal crossed her dirty palm with coins, and shivering in anticipation, waited for her to speak.

Every year she told her the same things: "A tall dark man . . . a light-haired woman that means to do you harm. You will make a long journey. There will be sadness, much danger, death. You will have a long life . . . men will love you. . . . Always in your hand there is a dark man." She looked up, started to speak, and then once again bent over her hand. "You whisper horses!" Maggie Royal asked what she meant. "Irish Gypsies say it means having a special way with horses, a means of communication that makes it possible to do things with animals others cannot." Again she paused, then added, "You will be lucky . . . with horses!"

"And love?" Maggie Royal whispered.

"You will have much luck with horses," the woman said, standing up and turning away.

The horses were a motley assortment: plantation horses, "turn-row" horses trained to follow corn or tobacco or cotton, to turn at the end of each row, Western horses, cow ponies and quarter horses, island horses, small tough marsh tackies, and a few thin weedy race horses that had once run at the big tracks before breaking down to be sold, going down-hill from reputable racing establishments to the county fairs, the leaky-roof circuit, rows of gray unpainted shedrows the last resort of the half-milers. They changed hands as fast as the boastful youths from the piny woods and red-necked farmers from the barrens lost their hard-earned crumpled bills to the Negroes' shell games.

Some of the horses had sores and gouges, cuts and abrasions. They did not jog. Those who led them around the paddock took a short hold, forcing them to keep their heads up and not permitting them to bob them. Once on the track, they galloped in order to disguise their lameness.

Each year Gramma complained to the mayor about cruelty to the horses. Each year Mr. Lovewell nodded and agreed. But each year following, it would be the same, the same horses, novocaine deadening the pain in their tired bowed legs, injections of heroin and coffee as stimulants, and the same stunted old-young riders with the buzzers and burs under the saddle.

Year after year one saw the same faces, the bow-legged jockeys in their grimy tattered silks, leaning casually against the shedrows, fingering their whips and smoking endless cigarettes, while the owners in shiny store-bought too-tight suits and trainers in wide-shouldered checked coats and fedoras whispered to the jockeys to "watch number eight" or "get the gray that won last week" or "pull the favorite and let number five, the long shot, win!"

Yet along with every vice and chicanery perpetuated against steeds and stewards, there existed a certain code, honor among the owners and riders who would slit one another's throats for a purse but fight to the death to preserve their nomadic way of life from outsiders.

During the week of the fair, horse racing took place every afternoon. The track was not properly graded or rolled. There were dips and undulations and an occasional rock or hole. Sometimes bottles and cans were tossed out onto it by drunken rooters. When it hadn't rained for a while, the going became as rough and hard as tabby building material. When wet, the surface was as slippery as glass. There were frequent falls, often at the far turn, where it was hard for the judges to see fouls and where horses out of control ran wide, sometimes crashing into the rail. When a horse broke a leg, Dr. Proxmire, the Starksville vet, would be summoned to put the horse down, shoot it in the head where it had fallen.

Gramma argued that the racing was too dangerous for Maggie Royal. She was an amateur, a child competing against toughened professionals. Her competitors could, despite Jazzbo's all-night vigil, find a way to "get at" Azilia, inject her with dope of some kind that would either slow her down or make her crazy, unridable. They could ride Maggie Royal off or try to unseat her, wedging a leg or an arm under hers in the far stretch, or slash her across the face with a whip.

"But you rode, Gramma," Maggie Royal argued. "And won."

Gramma fixed her with her "see-through-you" look, the look with which she sized up Lewis and the dealers who came to the island, deciding whether or not they were trustworthy.

"You're like me, Maggie Royal," Gramma said, "pigheaded, determined. Life won't be easy for you." She sounded like the Gypsy fortune-teller. "But you'll come back, if bloody, I hope unbowed. Function in disaster and finish in style!" She paused. She did not use the same language as the Gypsy woman, but in essence she said the same thing. "The important thing is to love the game beyond the prize." She smiled, and for a moment they were very close. It was one of the few times when she extended her cheek in order to let it be kissed, for she belonged to the school that believed it "wasn't nice" to touch.

Maggie Royal's race on Azilia was on one of those hot humid days of summer that the country people say "seem to lean on you," when energy pours out of one like the sweat the men wiped from their faces with bright-colored bandannas and the women sought to control with their palm fans advertising "Drop Kick" Keeler's Funeral Home.

As the afternoon approached, the heat intensified. The crowd thickened like the dust that settled on counters and food and gave Maggie Royal's mouth a dry, gritty taste. The sound of the Ferris wheel, speeding up and then slowing down; the jangle of the merry-go-round, which she rode with little Harry; and the shouts of the barkers, mingled with the sound of Devil, one of the race horses—his nervous system had been shattered like the broken bottles lying on the ground—trying to kick in the sides of its makeshift stall, made her head ache.

Jazzbo's race came first. He had brought his "travelin'" mule, the one he rode to the settlement. The crowd watched, cheering him on as the mule, its jackrabbit ears flat back and its long yellow teeth bared, refused to budge. Despite aid from Jared, who swatted its rump with a rolled-up newspaper, it refused to walk to the post, bucking every time Jazzbo dug his heels into its sides and kicking out whenever it was hit with his whip.

"Fool mule!" he muttered angrily. "Morning-glory mule! Can't git 'im for stop mornings. Afternoons he won't run a lick!"

Then it was time for Maggie Royal's race. She had not slept well, going over every inch of the uneven track in her mind the previous night. She wondered why she should be nervous when at home neither speed nor terrain bothered her. She attributed the light-headed feeling to not having eaten lunch.

In the area under the trees by the shedrows that served as a paddock, the jockey heroes were surrounded by small boys who gazed at the riders with awe and admiration, dreaming of New Orleans and Hialeah, or the gold at the end of the rainbow, the great New York tracks.

There was hardly room amid the crowd for the horses.

There were five other entries in the ladies' race: a country girl on a lathered plunging gray that required four people to secure the ancient corroded racing saddle on its narrow flea-bitten back; two sisters well-known on the circuit riding former platers that had once run on the big tracks, and a girl from the Starksville Riding School on a small chestnut. The chunky bay quarter horse with Western tack, ridden by a small blond girl with a long ponytail hanging down from beneath a black sombrero and leather chaps, who had won the previous year, was the favorite.

Several young men stood in an admiring circle around the blond girl, laughing and making jokes. She smiled, tossing her ponytail to and fro, teasing them back. She looked and acted as cool as the multicolored soft drinks revolving in their glass containers on the counters of the food stands. Maggie Royal saw her turn and stare. Then she said something to the boys, who in turn looked over at Maggie Royal, snickering.

Maggie Royal decided they were laughing at her jodhpurs and the derby Gramma forced her to wear.

"If it ain't Little Miss Muffet," one of the boys, bolder than his friends, commented loudly. "Come over from her island to show us poah folk how to ride."

"Yaaa," his friends chorused. Slapping their thighs, they began to chant: "Little Miss Muffet, sat on a tuffet, under the WC, so busy thinking how stinking was Lincoln, she forgot about Robert E. Lee."

Maggie Royal's face burned. She wished she could vanish into the dirt beneath her high laced English riding shoes. Then anger replaced the nervous anxiety that held her rigid and faintly nauseated. She turned away, pretending indifference, and thought: I'll show you! Just you wait. . . .

Suddenly Jared was there; Adele, Thorny, and little Harry brought up the rear. "Don't let them bother you," Jared said reassuringly, looking across at the blond girl and her entourage. He looked competent and professional wearing the Great Oak silks and peaked racing cap in preparation for his race on King, which was to follow hers. "Azilia can run rings around those horses."

"We're so excited," Adele said breathlessly. "Thorny and I each bet two dollars on you. Maggie Royal, you've just got to win."

"Be careful," Jared said anxiously. "Watch that blond. She looks as if sugar wouldn't melt in her mouth, but when it comes to racing, she's as hard as a blacksmith's nail."

It was time to mount. Jared and Jasper checked Maggie Royal's saddle girth and then Jared gave her a leg up. She had pulled her stirrups up two holes, and she tried to look nonchalant and professional as she knotted her snaffle rein the way real jockeys do.

The band played "Camptown Races" as they left the saddling area. Maggie Royal glanced down and saw the Gypsy fortune-teller, who pointed confidently to her left wrist to indicate she had bet on Azilia. Maggie Royal smiled and waved to her.

The band switched to "Dixie" as they reached the hard dusty track. Maggie Royal brought up the rear as they rode single-file behind the old man who led the post parade in a faded scarlet coat. He was a former jockey and his face was as dried and cracked as his untended tack. Azilia danced along, staring and shying at the crowds.

There was no starting gate. The horses lined up on the far side of the track. The girl on the frothing gray plunged in front of Maggie Royal. Azilia snaked out her head and bared her teeth. Maggie Royal snatched her back before the mare was able to bite the other horse. She was aware of how dry her mouth was, of the smell of dust and sweat. This was very different from the private bareback races on the island. She felt strange and awkward and insecure with her shortened stirrups and slippery, unfamiliar too-small saddle. She wished the starter would let them go, but the gray kept breaking ahead of the rest of the horses and having to be brought back. Azilia fidgeted and plunged, yearning to be freed to run.

After four false starts the starter dropped his flag. The horses, accompanied by a great cry of "They're off," sprang forward, leaping into a gallop. The wind whipped Maggie Royal's shirt taut against her breasts and blew off the hated derby. Her hair streamed out behind her and she was aware of a roaring in her ears and a sense of utter helplessness as Azilia's stride lengthened and she found herself galloping faster than she ever had before.

Before the rider alongside, the girl on the gray, could shake her bat at Maggie Royal, they were coming into the turn on the back stretch, all of the horses bunched together. Maggie Royal had never before made a turn at such speed. Blinded by her loose hair whipping across her face and the dirt thrown up by the horses ahead, she had no control. She could only crouch on the mare's back, her left hand clutching a handful of mane, her knees drawn up, gripping her sides as tightly as she could. She prayed Azilia wouldn't stumble on the hard clods of clay or strike one of the beer and pop bottles that the exuberant crowd tossed out onto the uneven track.

Suddenly there was a heart-stopping shout as, directly in front of her, a horse went down. Then a sickening, crunching thud as the gray alongside collided with the downed horse. The gray's hind legs aimed at the sky as the horse and its rider somersaulted over the fallen horse lying in its way.

Azilia was almost on top of the melee. Maggie Royal stiffened, waiting for the collision that seemed inevitable. Then somehow they were free. The wild mare, as quick as the lightning that flashed over the island, as surefooted as Tabby, the stable goat, swerved and changed leads, sidestepping the dust, the shouting, and the anguish of fallen horses and riders.

Before Maggie Royal could let out her breath, they were flying down the homestretch.

Seconds now and they would be passing the post and wooden platform where the judges stood. There was only one horse in front, the quarter-horse favorite. Maggie Royal drove Azilia toward the rail. She had a quick flashing impression of the blond girl looking back. Then the horse cut in front, shutting Azilia out. The mare bobbled, thrown off her stride. Maggie Royal saw a triumphant look on the other rider's face and thought how stupid she was to have lost the race.

But Azilia was not beaten. From some ancestor out of her past, perhaps one of the thoroughbreds the planters bred for the match races that took place in the South, the will to win had been bred into her. Without conscious direction from her rider, she made another flying change, swerving outward from the rail. Her ears went back, her stride lengthened, and the little mare ran as though for her life. Just as the winning post flashed by, she extended her head to win by her white-splashed nose.

"Thank you, Azilia," Maggie Royal whispered, burying her face in the mare's mane as they pulled up. Dropping the reins, she put her arms around Azilia's wet white-foamed neck.

Maggie Royal heard wild cheers as she rode back to the grandstand. Gramma and the aunts were standing up, clapping. Jazzbo and Jared ran out onto the track to escort the panting lathered mare to the judges' stand.

Jazzbo did a triumphant buck-and-wing, swooping down in a low bow, clapping his hands as he fetched up again.

Jared ran alongside. "My God, Maggie Royal. Thought you were a goner when that horse fell at the turn."

"Dat girl almost made de mare fall down," Jazzbo muttered darkly, jerking his head in the direction of the blond riding back, grim and unsmiling.

"I'll bet she tries to claim a foul," Jared said.

"Let her," Maggie Royal answered, suddenly confident and wildly happy. "She tried to ride me into the rail. I should be the one to register an objection."

Jared looked up at her and smiled. Reaching for her hand on the reins, he gave it a quick hard squeeze.

From their box Gramma and the aunts gazed down, smiling proudly.

Maggie Royal waved the racing bat she had borrowed from Jared at the judges, and they gave her permission to dismount. Adele and Thorny, and the others, even Constance, crowded around as she accepted the silver loving cup presented by Mayor Lovewell.

Then it was suddenly unbearably hot, and in the midst of her triumph she felt breathless and faint.

"Please, Miss Maggie Royal," Jazzbo said, touching her shoulder. "Affey want to speak to you."

"Surely not this moment, Jazzbo."

"Yessum. Please. She right over there." He pointed to Gramma's maid leaning on the rail. Maggie Royal thought how pretty she looked with her pale café-au-lait skin, and how well dressed, wearing one of

Aunt Emily's hand-me-downs—one of the short dressmaker-type dresses that she bought by the dozen from Best and Company in New York.

Simultaneously she was aware of a wetness between her legs.

"Miss Maggie Royal, you've got to do something!" Affey said positively when she reached her side. "There's blood all over the back of your jodhpurs."

The late-afternoon sun slivering through the oaks that shaded the fairgrounds touched Maggie Royal's face. It was burning in a misery of embarrassment. She realized she had for the first time what Constance called "the curse" and that everybody, including Jared, had seen her win a horse race with the back of her jodhpurs covered with blood. She wanted to run and hide and never show her face again.

Affey had brought along a rubber belt and sanitary pads in her reticule. They went to one of the wooden outhouses, where they stood in line for a long time. Affey stood behind Maggie Royal so the women also waiting there would not notice her stained breeches. Finally they were inside the foul-smelling two-holer, which, by late afternoon, lacked soap or toilet paper. Maggie Royal thought of Uncle Oomlot's advice: "Be sure to take toilet paper with you wherever you travel. Especially fox-hunting and Russia."

Affey showed her how to adjust the belt and attach the pad. Then Maggie Royal waited, trying not to breathe the awful stench, while Affey went to get her white linen riding coat from the tack trunk.

Maggie Royal emerged wearing the jacket to hide the seat of her jodhpurs. She would gladly have given away her silver cup if it had meant avoiding having to face her cousins and the crowd.

There was racing every day for a week. Most of the same horses ran each day. The crowd came to know them and chose favorites as rivalry waxed keener. The morning after her race, Azilia walked out lame. She was carefully examined, and Dr. Proxmire was called to come and look at her. Nobody could find anything wrong. Still, she didn't improve, making it necessary to scratch her from her remaining races. Then on the third morning Jazzbo noticed a tiny festering spot on her tendon, not much larger than a pin-prick. He cut away the hair in order to let the sore place drain. To his astonishment, he noticed a long bay horse hair slowly working its way out like a splinter. He pulled it out and held it up in disbelief.

" 'Tain't Azilia's hair. She's chestnut."

Old Sapelo, who had been around the track in Gramma's day, explained what happened. It was, he said, an old trick. Someone, possibly the blond girl on the bay quarter horse or one of her group, had gotten hold of Azilia, threaded the hair into a needle, and drawn it across the mare's tendon where it would rub and fester and cause lameness. If one of Azilia's chestnut hairs had been inserted instead of that of a different color, they might not have suspected foul play.

It was too late for Azilia to race again that year. The important thing was for her to become sound again, as sound as the silver dollar with which Maggie Royal crossed the fortune-teller's palm.

The next day the cousins yelled themselves hoarse, cheering Jared home. On two consecutive afternoons Maggie Royal saw the powerful mass of spotted power that was King roaring down the homestretch between crowds of waving, yelling people, Jared bent low on the stallion's neck. Then the triumphant white grin that split his dark, dirt-covered face as he rode back to where the judges stood, jauntily gesturing with his bat, then dropping lightly from the horse's back, to find himself surrounded by the Starksville belles—Maggie Royal called them the "sillies"—a silly twittering pack that set Maggie Royal's teeth on edge as they sought to entice him back to their wisteria-shaded verandas and ply him with Coca-Cola and cakes and inconsequential chatter.

The barnstormers, tall, thin, leather-clad men with thin mustaches and a laconic death-defying nonchalance, dropped down onto the field adjoining the fairgrounds. Afternoons they put on thrill shows with wing-walkers and parachute jumpers and whatever they could think of to titillate the public and persuade people to go for rides in the open cockpit of a rickety Army-surplus World War I trainer for as little as three dollars.

Jared bought a chance and won a free ride. When he descended into the rough pasture from this first unforgettable ascent he was never to be the same again. From then on his eyes were raised skyward where clouds with names like cumulus and cirrus vied with frail machines of wire, wood, and fabric.

Maggie Royal joined him to watch the air show that took place each afternoon. They stood against the wire fence separating the field from the public, among thousands of gaping upturned faces, eyes glued on the godlike creatures passing between earth and sun with flimsy transparent wings. They watched, mesmerized, almost afraid to breathe as the figure wing-walking crawled like an ant along the back of a bug.

"Wing-walking . . . requires extreme concentration . . . now he's worked his way out of the cockpit . . . he's waving back from the wing tip . . ." The announcer's voice rose excitedly. "He's hanging on by his heels . . . any lack of concentration on the pilot's part can cause the plane to flip right over . . . causing considerable concern to all aboard."

Laughter from the crowd. The voice resumed: "Now he's got the stick over to the right . . . he's setting up into the wind at ninety miles per hour. It's nice and breezy and cool up there. Now he's working his way back into the cockpit. . . ."

The antlike figure vanished from the wing and a cheer rose from the crowd.

"Fella 'most as good as Omar Locklear," commented a tall man in a greasy coverall with a cigarette hanging from the corner of his mouth.

"Omar Locklear?" Jared asked.

"One of the first wing-walkers," the man explained. "After the war. Stood on his head, he did. Straddled the fuselage with no hands and hung by his feet and did a ladder transfer upside down from one plane to t'other. Died." The man spit the paper from his cigarette that had stuck to his lip. "Some accident had nuthin' to do with wing-walking."

"I'd sure like to learn to fly," Jared said feelingly.

"Ain't too hard to be a flier," the stranger said, squinting hard into the cloud-strewn sky. His white teeth flashed a quick smile. "You just got to wanna be one!" He took a last drag from his dying cigarette and settled his long lanky frame against the fence. "My name's Al Daniels, and I'm thinking of starting a flying school here in Starksville." He jerked his thumb in the direction of the hangar. "I'm rebuilding one of them tin-bucking machines." He reached for his crushed pack of Camels and lit another cigarette. "Be glad to give you some pointers."

"You mean it?" Jared's eyes blazed with excitement the way they had after he won his first race on King.

The big race, the one with the largest purse, the one Jared needed to win in order to pay Gramma back, took place on the last day of the fair.

Jazzbo led King around the saddling area. He wore a green-and-blue-checked jacket, a pink shirt, and green-and-blue-striped necktie. A rub rag stuck out of his back pocket, and Uncle Oomlot's old field boots had been polished to a high gloss. His black face split into a wide white grin as he called out to his friends on the rail, "This hyar hoss belong to Jared Stark. Lawyer Stark's boy. Lawyer Stark done help many a one!"

Jared joined him. "Best watch out," Jazzbo warned as they stood waiting for the race to be called. "I hear talk they's out for you. Somebody slipped a bucket of cold water into King's stall when I turned my back for go and get his tack. Good thing I watching the hoss like a low-flying chicken hawk. For true! He drink that before the race, he not run a lick." Jazzbo rubbed an imaginary speck of dust from the stallion's rump. "Lot of money bet on that Devil horse."

Devil had beaten King in two of the four races, and the rivalry between the two favorites was intense. Devil was a onetime stakes winner from the North. As the result of a pile-up he had damaged a front leg falling, literally, on evil days, winding up on the "frying-pan circuit," so called because of the Gypsy-type outfits who brewed coffee and stew over open fires at the country fairs. His suspicion of humans surfaced in the way he unsociably lashed out at bystanders and reared back, seeking to free himself from the rusted chain his owner-trainer pulled taut across the tender part of his nose.

His jockey, "Bugsy" Malone, had been fined several times for doping horses and riding people off. He had the thin nerve-sick body of the sharecroppers who scrabbled for a living, motivated by a burning hatred for those with more or with less than they had.

A gaunt pitted face peered out from beneath a raveled black cap. Bugsy was not much older than Jared, but the eyes he focused on him with cold dislike seemed as old as the clay hills rising inland where one drove past the shabby farms and homesteads belonging to the pine-landers, who, like the land they sprang from, seemed dead, burned out from years of draining physical erosion.

"Jared, be careful," Maggie Royal warned as the old man in his scarlet coat blew a toot on his trumpet and called, "Riders up."

Jazzbo threw Jared up onto Uncle Oomlot's racing saddle. He checked his girth and his leathers. Jared looked very competent amid the motley assemblage, as, holding his racing bat in his teeth, he carefully knotted the reins of King's snaffle bridle.

Jazzbo turned the horse loose, and then they were following the others out onto the track, the stallion prancing sideways and snatching at the bit in his mouth.

Maggie Royal fought her way to a place on the rail. The stands were jammed, the bleachers behind the boxes packed with farm families eating hot dogs and ice-cream cones, sold by the hawkers, and drinking soft drinks. Balloons floated out over the track, and the carnival sounds of the barkers' cries of rides and games could be heard when the band stopped playing.

The horses broke into a canter as they neared the stands. Gramma and the aunts and their guests waved and called good luck as Jared passed in front of them, standing high in his stirrups like Bugsy Malone and the other pros.

They couldn't see the start on the far side of the course. They heard the spine-tingling "They're off!" Seconds later the thunder of hooves on the concretelike track heralded the horses' approach. Then they burst into view, their jockeys yelling and swearing at one another, "Aaaaaarah, comin' through . . . Goddamn, let me past . . ."

King was in last place, at least five lengths behind the pack.

"Must have been left at the post," Jazzbo said worriedly.

Maggie Royal stood on tiptoe, trying to see around Jazzbo's woolly head.

King's stride lengthened, starting to eat up the distance between himself and the front-runners. Jared sat like a bur, hardly moving in the saddle, his face buried in the stallion's mane.

"Look at that horse run," screamed the crowd. "Go, King, go."

As they came to the final turn, King passed two horses and went on to take the leaders, a gray quarter horse and the leggy black Devil.

Then he was past the gray, and only the black remained in front.

"My God!" Thorny cried, lowering his binoculars and grabbing Maggie Royal's arm.

"What . . . ?" She got no further. Something flashed alongside

King's head. The tandem broke, and King swerved. They heard the sickening sound of the infield rail break as the stallion's legs met it and Jared's body planed over the horse's head.

Maggie Royal ducked under the rail and began running along the track. King was struggling to his feet when she reached him. Sweat and lather ran from the horse's body, mingling with blood from a terrible wound. Handfuls of muscle, gristle, veins, and sinews bulged from his right leg above his knee.

"Please . . ." She hammered on the back of the man blocking her path. "Let me through."

"Don't move him," somebody said. "Looks as if he's bad hurt."

Then the man moved aside and she saw Jared's inert form, surrounded by the crowd, from which the smell of sweat, tobacco, and whiskey was almost overpowering.

Thorny and Jazzbo carried Jared to King's stall, where he regained consciousness lying on bales of hay set out under the trees.

Dr. Bartow, the Starksville doctor, told him he thought he had a minor concussion.

"What about King?" he asked, trying to sit upright.

The doctor pushed him back against a rolled-up horse blanket. "Easy does it. Rest for a bit first."

Jared bent over and retched into the bucket somebody had put beside him.

"You'll be nauseated for a while," the doctor said. "Blow on the head brings it on."

The sillies twittered up, saying how sorry they were, and wasn't it awful what that terrible jockey had done? "Why, Jared could have been killed," Mary Sue Lovewell, the mayor's daughter, shrilled in her high-pitched voice. "I'm certainly going to speak to Daddy and see to it that awful Malone boy never rides here again."

Jared did not seem to hear what the girls said. His eyes were on his horse, standing in the center of the walking ring where Doc Proxmire was slicing away at skin and sinew. Jazzbo and Maggie Royal took turns holding the torn flesh in place.

"Jared," Mary Sue said pleadingly, "you're still coming to the dance tonight. My mother is countin' on you at the house for supper. . . . Jared . . ." She sounded annoyed. "Did you all hyar what I just said?"

"Sorry," Jared managed, "I'm staying here with my horse."

"Well, really," the girl pouted. "You promised . . ."

Jared got up then. Ignoring the girls, he walked over to King.

"Will he be a cripple?" he asked the veterinarian.

"Depends on whether or not the joint is injured," Doc Proxmire replied, speaking around the catgut he held in his teeth. "If it's just muscles, he should recover."

For two hours the vet worked, sewing up the wound. The onlookers who gathered to watch the operation commented that it would take a miracle to make King run again and that he should be destroyed.

"He's living," Jared answered grimly. "He's breathing. The cut is a long way from his heart."

Jared did not lodge a protest against Bugsy Malone.

"Starks don't complain," Gramma said. "All's fair in love and horse racing."

"Yes, but the prize money," Jared replied. "What about the money I owe you?"

"Never mind," Gramma said. "The horse is yours for whatever he's worth now—which isn't much."

Maybe it wasn't nature as much as Jared's care that brought about King's recovery.

He ignored all invitations from the Starksville sillies to the swimming parties and luncheons, the dinners and dances that wound up the festive week.

"You're really missing something," Noble told him. "Cindy Lou Tarrington's back from visiting on Long Island. Her daddy is giving her a dance at the country club." Noble rolled his eyes. "She's hot stuff! Wait until you meet her!"

"Give her my regrets," Jared answered vaguely, concentrating on changing the bandage on King's wound.

At night Jared and Jazzbo took turns attending to the stallion. Maggie Royal and Azilia returned to the island.

Daily, Maggie Royal waited for the afternoon boat to find out about King's progress.

After a week, Jared was able to load King onto the barge and bring him home to the island. To keep the horse's muscles from atrophying, it was necessary to force him to walk. When he hobbled forward, he would stride short and stumble. To make him take longer strides, Jared had Maggie Royal lead him around while he followed, hitting the stallion with the end of a shank. The onlookers thought Jared was being needlessly cruel. Even Gramma commented that if the horse couldn't walk, he'd certainly never be able to run again.

"Maybe not," Jared answered with Stark stubbornness, "but what have we got to lose by trying?"

Each morning Jared and Maggie Royal worked together, long, slow work to rebuild the injured muscles and sinews. It was a terrible thing to see the stallion struggle to keep up with Azilia. Slowly King improved. They took him swimming in the surf. The great wound healed and his torn muscles mended. At sight of Azilia and the other mares his ears pricked and some of the old fire came into his eyes. His steps became longer, less halting. Before summer ended Jared was able to ride King slowly along the beach. But the stallion had lost his powerful, freewheeling gallop. He would not race again. Gramma suggested that as long as Jared was going to college and Maggie Royal was to be sent to boarding school, King be retired and that they breed Azilia to him.

Using money earned working on the farm and giving riding and sailing lessons, Jared was learning to fly at the newly built Starksville airport.

In the beginning, Thorny joined him, but after a few flights he announced he could think of better ways to die, and anyway, he had no time to waste on expensive capitalistic pastimes that would never prove useful to mankind or be anything other than an amusing sport for the idle rich.

"One of these days you may need to land in a barnyard without an engine," Al Daniels told Jared, insisting that he have twice the number of hours granted his other students. "I wanna make sure you can."

Al taught him aerobatics and to visually appreciate the speed of flight by following the contour of the hills, skimming dangerously close to the tops of trees and buildings, and to fly along a deck of clouds, letting the bottom arc of the plane's propellers slice into it.

After eighteen hours of dual instruction, Jared celebrated his first solo flight by doing a series of loops and dives directly over Great Oak while Gramma and her guests were playing croquet. Jared leaned from the cockpit, laughing, as the players waved fists and mallets and ran for cover.

Gramma was very angry, but there was nothing she could do to deter him from his love affair with flight. Daily he flew, regardless of weather. Diving down, he scraped the tall corn with the plane's landing gear, and caused farmers on the mainland to complain that their cows had stopped giving milk and their hens laying eggs.

As summer neared its end, the world that had seemed not to exist beyond the boundaries of the island began to make itself felt.

Maggie Royal felt a new kind of unrest, as though the things heard on the radio that were happening in Europe were building to a climax. Days when the rain slanted across the island, curtaining off the oaks like hanging moss, she wrote in the journal in which, like Fanny Kemble Butler, she was recording life on Stark Island.

Now that Jared was spending so much time on the mainland, she no longer saw him daily, riding King along the beach, singing when he thought himself alone, or sketching island scenes. But when she did, she alternated between breathless excitement and agonizing waves of shyness that made her want to avoid him and at the same time long to be with him.

One night Jared's mother prepared an island dinner—wild-onion soup, crayfish in sour cream, buttered poke sprouts, and dandelion greens. Jared's father talked about the chances of war in Europe. In that warm kitchen, war seemed as remote as Gramma's hope that a Republican would win over "young Franklin" in the next presidential election.

After supper Jared's father read William Faulkner's "The Bear" aloud. Summer was ending and it was chilly at night. A fire had been laid and lit on the hearth. The dogs lay in front of it. Jared's mother sat to one side, in her rocker, darning a red sock, her dark Indian features and long black hair gleaming in the firelight. Susan sat in her chair, motionless, with that quality of serenity that was her gift to those who knew and loved her. Jared was filling in the background of an oil painting of Old Ugly's pool—varying shades of green.

Maggie Royal watched his face as the light from the fire played over it. He already seemed older. His face, in shadow, was dark and withdrawn, as if already he had left childish things and the island behind him.

" 'I will give him warning and foreknowledge too, along with the desire to follow and the power to slay. The woods and fields he ravages and the game he devastates will be the consequence and signature of his crime and guilt, and his punishment.' " Jared's father closed the book and stretched. "Time for a nightcap."

It was past eleven. Maggie Royal should have been at Great Oak by ten. Nonetheless she accepted the small glass of dandelion wine which Jared's father poured from a green glass decanter found on the island.

Gramma would be angry, but the day was dying hard, leaving behind it a record of activity that included riding, two sets of tennis, a game of croquet with obstacles that included "jumping" the lying-down branch of the great oak, a swim, and the discussion at dinner about the possibility of a second world war.

A typical island day in which anything seemed possible and the only problem lay in the fact that there might never be time enough to do all the things one wanted to do.

It looked as if a storm might be coming up, and Jared's father suggested that Jared walk Maggie Royal home.

It was very dark and easy to understand why the Negroes did not go about at night. The huge gnarled trees, their moss-hung branches stirring in the night breeze, took on the grotesque appearance of monsters, a haunted quality that lent credence to the superstitious belief that they harbored the hants that roamed at night.

In the stillness before the oncoming storm came the eerie melancholy cry of an owl.

"Hu hu," Jared said, using the Gullah word for "owl."

The cry came again, sounding lonely, lost in the dark night.

Maggie Royal shivered, remembering Dah's belief that the hoot of an owl presages death.

There was a flash of lightning and a clap of thunder, sounding as if all the ancient rusted cannon that had once been fired from the ruined Spanish fort were being fired at once. The rains came then, in torrents, a solid wall of water.

They could hear the crash of surf against the beach, pounding like the ghostly hooves of the black stallion that, ridden by one of the Spanish invaders of long ago, was said to gallop along the woods trails on storm-filled nights.

Maggie Royal was wet through. Jared held a flashlight in one hand as they walked. He put his other arm around her. She felt his long lean body against hers amid the wild rain and crashing thunder. She clung to him, and his hold tightened. His arm trembled and he drew her closer. Her blood began moving through her body with a slow sweetness, like honey from the island apiaries in the warm sun. Lightning flashed, and in that instant Jared's eyes, wide and dark, searched hers. In them was a look of surprise and recognition.

"I've got to get you home." He pulled away from her so abruptly that she stumbled. "Gramma will be angry," he said, striding ahead.

The storm was as sudden, as violent, and as soon past as passion.

By the time they reached the avenue leading to Great Oak, the moon had risen. They could see the tower and chimneys, like huge blunt fingers pointing skyward. Instinctively she moved toward him, but he did not glance at her. He stood in the center of the avenue staring at the house. In that wild wilderness the vast structure seemed unreal, like a stage set. Jared's face wore the same set, purposeful expression with which he had gazed at King before making the stallion his.

"Someday it will be mine," he said, speaking as if to himself. "I will be master of Great Oak instead of a poor relation. I will come in the front door instead of the back. . . ."

Suddenly it was Labor Day. The gourds on the vines along the fences of the Long Point settlement were dry on the dying brittle vines and the green marsh grass was turning gold. The cry of the waterfowl became shriller and more urgent, as if knowing their peace was soon to be shattered by the guns of the hunters.

The next afternoon Maggie Royal rode Azilia to the clam flats. As she approached, she saw Jared. He stood bent over, his legs apart, khakis rolled up to his knees. He had taken off his shirt, and as she sat on her horse watching, she had a sudden almost irresistible desire to go to him and run her hand the length of his long brown back. She knew it would be warm and soft and at the same time firm, unlike that of Noble, who slept late mornings and lounged around the house drinking beer.

Jared straightened up and saw her. He stood ankle-deep in gray slime, his hands on his hips, looking up at her. There was that strange unfamiliar expression on his face, the same look she had seen the night of the storm.

"Come help me dig," he said. He pointed to the cairnlike pile of clams. "Weekend guests coming. I told Ada I'd get a ton."

Maggie Royal dismounted and turned Azilia loose. She had trained her to come when she whistled, and she knew the mare would not wander far.

She took off her sneakers, rolled up her jeans, and waded out to where Jared was at work. Soon she had almost as many clams as he did, and as she leaned over to drop them into the bucket, their heads collided. She straightened up and jumped aside, laughing.

Jared reached out and gently touched her cheek. "You've got mud there. Is it true you're leaving tomorrow?"

"Mother's getting married again. A belted earl with a castle in Leicestershire. I'm to go to Miss Mayo's school in Virginia. I'll have a chance to foxhunt." She dug her toe into the sand. "Shucks, ah don' wan go nawth to Yankeeland."

Jared smiled. "You'll like it."

"I won't," she said, turning away. "I don't ever want to leave Stark Island."

"Then don't."

"They say I have to."

"They?" Jared's eyes darkened, changing color in that extraordinary way, a kind of sea change such as took place on the sound, clear as jade one moment, changing to dark green, the cypress green of the painting he was working on. "You don't need to always do what 'they' say. All this, the sun and wind and sea." He reached down and scooped up a handful of oozing gray mud. "It should have taught you what you want, what to fight for."

She looked at the wet sand-mud seeping through his fingers, like time running out.

He opened his hand and the last of the mud drained away, leaving a shark's tooth. He started to toss it away.

"Don't throw it away," she said, reaching out for it.

"You want it? Put it on a chain and wear it. It will remind you of . . ." He threw wide his arms and looked upward at the sky. ". . . all this, Maggie Royal, all we've been lucky enough to have." Bending over once again he began slashing at the mud-sand with his knife, making crisscrosses until it struck a clam.

"Go away, Maggie Royal," he murmured, not looking up. "Go away and grow up!"

·4·

SPARROW
CHRISTMAS
1934

·6·

Sparrow McKinney first came to Stark Island over Christmas vacation in 1934. He was seventeen and a freshman at Harvard. He met Jared Stark one morning when he noticed a downy woodpecker doing its ra-ta-tat-tat on the trunk of an elm outside Massachusetts Hall. He had just come from Biology I, where he had argued with the professor about the difference in color between the primaries and secondaries of one of the more obscure Empidonax flycatchers. The professor insisted that the upper tail coverts were the same as secondaries, whereas Sparrow maintained the primaries matched.

He paused on one side of the walkway to look at the woodpecker, when somebody joggled his elbow.

"Sorry," a voice said. "A hairy, isn't it?"

"No, it's a downy. You'll notice its outer tail feathers are barred, whereas a hairy's are not, and its rattle call descends in pitch toward the end."

Sparrow sounded exasperated. He was tired of having birds incorrectly identified. Somehow people tended to confuse the commonest species, when it seemed to him inordinately simple to learn the topography of a bird and make the correct identification.

"I can tell you're an expert."

"Well, I have a life list of four hundred species ..." Sparrow paused, deciding he sounded stuffy. He started to move on, but some instinct, some ESP that something important was about to happen, caused him to remain where he was.

"I'm Jared Stark."

Sparrow drew his eyes down from the woodpecker and looked at Jared. He saw a tall, very dark boy with astonishing eyes, green and iridescent as the neck of a mallard duck.

Several Radcliffe girls pushed past, wearing long tweed skirts and saddle shoes and shapeless sweaters, all talking at once and carrying bulging book bags. They looked back at Jared.

Simultaneously the woodpecker flew off, probably back to the orchards and shade trees where his kind were more at home than in busy Harvard Yard.

"I'm Sparrow McKinney." He took Jared's extended hand, and as he did so the name Stark rang a bell as loud as that in Memorial Hall. Curiously, Sparrow had recently read a biography of Matthew Stark of Stark Island, Georgia, the well-known ornithologist and friend of Audubon who discovered and named several species, including the rare Stark snipe, a bird found only on that particular island. "You're not related to Matthew Stark of Stark Island?" he asked excitedly.

"He was my great-grandfather," Jared said. "You know the island?"

Sparrow answered that he had read about the egret rookery and asked if any Stark snipe had been seen there recently.

"They're very rare, almost as rare as the limpkin. People come from all over the country hoping to spot one." Jared smiled, and it was like the sun's rays splitting a dark cloud. Sparrow had the feeling he only smiled when he meant it, and, like his eyes, the smile could change his appearance, from one of a certain dark melancholy to joyous enthusiasm. "By the way, I was on my way to lunch. Have you eaten?"

Again Sparrow had an odd feeling that this meeting was foreordained. "Why, yes," he answered. "I mean, no, I haven't eaten. I'd like to very much."

Instead of the Freshman Union, with its humdrum food and pandemonium, Jared suggested a small Italian restaurant several blocks away. A small sign to the right of the black-painted doorway said "Giovanni."

Inside, the proprietor greeted Jared with wildly gesticulating arms, asking how he was getting along with his Venetian-art course and launching into an animated discussion of the brushwork of an obscure eighteenth-century landscape painter named Guardi.

Sparrow observed his newfound acquaintance. He had an air about him, a manner that commanded attention. Something inborn that can't be taught, that one has or has not.

Although the restaurant was crowded, the owner immediately set up a small table in a corner for them and asked if they would have an aperitif on the house. The menu was as long and complex as Sparrow's life list of birds.

"Pay no mind to it," Jared said, pushing his aside. "Giovanni has already made up his mind what we're to eat."

The proprietor returned with two Campari sodas on the house. He had a long, sad bloodhound face, a drooping short collar and tie. He smacked his lips and rolled his faintly bloodshot eyes as he told them what they were to eat. "Plain white pasta with a Genovese sauce." The green sauce, rich and very thick, was, he said, made of ground basil, oil, salt, pepper, garlic, and Parmesan cheese.

"How did you know about Matthew Stark?" Jared asked after their order had been decided upon.

"He is one of the little-known great Americans. Reading about him changed my life. Most of us want a good life, but few of us attain it. Matthew Stark was one of those rare men with the talent for finding and living by the correct values. A romantic and a rover, an engineer, mathematician, and naturalist. He managed to cram several careers into a lifetime of joyous achievement."

The food came, and Sparrow kept on talking. Afterward he realized that one of his new friend's most flattering characteristics was the ability to draw people out and to listen.

He stopped, embarrassed. "Forgive me." He started to eat his pasta, now lukewarm. "I didn't mean to talk so much. What I really want to hear about is your island."

"No, please go on. I'm learning things I never knew before."

It might have been the close, secluded corner, the intimacy of the smoky, crowded restaurant, or the wine the proprietor recommended to accompany the meal that led Jared to talk more about himself at that initial meeting than he was ever to do again. It was a strange hour, an electric encounter during which a friendship was founded. It was still early in the academic year, and Sparrow supposed Jared was homesick. But when he knew him better, he realized he was essentially a loner. Although popular, particularly with women, who found his dark good looks, his air of mystery and mastery, fascinating, he was not really gregarious or outgoing, more of a silent, inward person. But at that first meeting he talked about the island as rapidly and hungrily as he devoured the excellent food.

Nonetheless, it was hard for Sparrow to visualize what he was talking about. He had never known people rich enough to own an island. In fact, he had never before known anybody who was rich.

Sparrow's father had been a New England dairy farmer. He had been killed in a freak accident when a tree that had been struck by lightning fell on him. His mother took in sewing. She was a strong, remote woman who worked as hard and as long hours as humanly possible. When Sparrow was at home, they had little to say to one another.

Sparrow was never quite sure why Jared and he became friends. Whereas Jared was tall and athletic and good-looking, Sparrow was heavyset, nearsighted, and inclined toward fat. He preferred reading and bird-watching to more strenuous forms of activity. (His real name was Cyrus, but everyone called him Sparrow. The name derived from his camp days, when the newspaper he worked for as a newsboy had sent him to camp for a week. Whenever he didn't know what species a bird belonged to, he automatically said it was a sparrow.) No girl had ever taken him seriously, whereas Jared was invited to every deb party that season.

But although their worlds were very different, their politics were similar. Sparrow was suffering through the depression and was a hundred percent behind President Roosevelt. Jared was even more radical,

116

rallying to Norman Thomas, the Socialist candidate for President, and an admirer of Walter Gropius and his Bauhaus school of all-inclusive art. They also shared a liking for pasta, walks along the Charles, and Benny Goodman, a twenty-four-year-old clarinetist trying to form his own band.

It was possible, too, that Jared liked Sparrow because he could talk to him about his island. Not having a place of his own to go home to, Sparrow understood more keenly than most how Jared felt about his roots and his heritage.

When Jared invited him to come home with him for Christmas vacation, Sparrow immediately accepted.

The trip south was to Sparrow a revelation.

There was, first, the excitement of traveling from Boston on the New York, New Haven & Hartford's *Merchants' Limited*. It was the luxury train that the "sailing lists"—Choates, Lowells, Searses, Thorndikes, and other well-known Bostonians—traveled on. The bar was stocked with their favorite beverages and cigars. The conductor wore a blue frock coat and a fresh boutonniere and, it was said, a mouse at one time lived in the observation car—protests from passengers saved it from being exterminated, and it was permitted to ride back and forth until, presumably, it died a natural death.

Sparrow was enthralled by the clanking, cindery cars as the train crossed a corner of Rhode Island and raced into Connecticut. He took long, rolling walks through the swinging aisles, pausing now and then to speak to college friends or stopping on the platform between cars to smoke. He and Jared had dinner together in the dining car, with starched napery and white-coated waiters with glistening black faces. Then night, shut off from people passing by, trying to undress, pull off his trousers while doubled up behind heavy green curtains in a nest of white sheets and brown blankets. Lying in his berth, he felt exultant peering through a crack in the raised blinds, seeing towns, farmlands, hills, valleys, and houses full of people sliding past, people who heard the long, drawn-out whistle in the night, saw the lighted train flash past, heard the sound of it die away like their dreams as the knowledge was borne in on them they were destined never to know the freedom of travel.

Then morning, awakening to a snowless sunlit country, the slash pines and cypress swamps of the Carolinas, the flat dry, sandy soil of Georgia.

At Savannah, the Starks' private car *Maggie Royal* was pulled up on a siding. It was painted blue with a horizontal green stripe ("to ward off the hants," Jared said, and Sparrow didn't know if he was joking or not). It was pulled by a shining locomotive that was already getting up steam, and wore a polished black-and-gold iron plaque on its nose designating it as number-24 Baldwin Locomotive Company of Philadelphia.

They came on board to be greeted by the New York relatives, cousins from Virginia and Louisiana, and a clutch of New England relations en route to the island for Christmas. Jared introduced Sparrow to a young white-coated butler named Cuffee whose knobby wrists jutted out from a short white mess jacket. He asked what they would like from the bar and buffet at the end of the car, where cold chicken and Virginia ham, salad, rolls, cakes, and several varieties of wines, both red and white, and an unlabeled bottle of whisky were displayed.

The New York relatives had a daughter named Constance, who rolled her eyes at Jared and asked him to sit beside her. The Louisiana relatives had a tall, romantic-looking son named Noble, who said he was looking forward to seeing Cousin Maggie Royal, Cousin Adele, Cousin Thorny, and so on in a very thick accent that caused the word "cousin" to sound like "cuss-in," with emphasis on the "cuss." The parents all looked much alike: the men—Jared called them the "John Doe" uncles—portly in dark suits, reading *Time, Saturday Evening Post, Fortune,* or *Literary Digest,* the women in expensive tweed suits. The latter discarded their jackets and fur pieces, saying they'd forgotten how hot Georgia could be in December, but then, it was chilly on the island at night. "It rains a lot," Aunt Emily from New York commented. "It really does become too depressing. I sometimes wonder how Gramma stands it all year around." "She loves it," Aunt Lucy from Virginia said. "She has the farm to run, and that big house, and there's always company."

Sparrow heaped a plate full of food from the buffet and ate while Jared conversed about hockey and football and wondered if his horse, King, was all right, if the island boat that had been leaking last summer had been repaired, about the fence in the south field that needed to be replaced, how the fishing and crabbing had been, and a wealth of island topics Sparrow knew nothing about.

He had hardly finished his meal when the train ground to a stop at the Starksville station, a small Spanish pavilion, with arches, wrought iron, and palm trees. It was painted the same blue and green as the private car. Jared explained they were the family racing colors. Sparrow had never heard of a family that could transfer its racing colors to a railroad car and station. On the other hand, he supposed that if you were one of the great feudal families of the country and had an island and a town named after you before the Revolution, anything was possible.

A gate with a sign reading "PRIVATE: STARK ISLAND BOAT" opened onto a wooden pier where the boat, a steam-driven freight boat, waited for them. As they clambered aboard, lugging suitcases and gear—Sparrow had his second-hand binoculars, and a Leica bought with money earned working as a soda jerk—he saw several fishermen lounging at dockside glance at them. One of them muttered an obscenity and spit into the water, strewn with fish parts and refuse.

When all were finally aboard, the captain of the boat, a heavyset

Negro Jared introduced as Captain Ben, backed off from the pier and spun the wheel. The boat straightened itself, chugged off past the public docks, and headed into a channel bordered by spiky spartinas and cord grass. It was a warm, sunny day. The marshes were the brown-gold color of an American woodcock and the water sparkled in the sunlight. Sparrow tried to identify the water birds that flew up as the boat passed. He saw and recorded a stately American egret, three black ducks, a great blue Louisiana heron, and countless shore birds.

Jared grabbed his arm and pointed. "The tower and chimneys of Great Oak!"

Sparrow reluctantly took his eyes away from the marsh and gazed at the dark green smudge of island. Suddenly the trees parted and he saw a vast structure. He counted a dozen chimneys of varying heights and a high round tower.

"Holy Cow!" he gasped. "You call that a house!"

Jared laughed. "Keeps the rain out!"

Jared's parents and his dogs, Rufus and Ranter, waited at the dock to welcome them.

The passengers disembarked. The girl Constance threw Jared a darting look, her eyes fluttering like the silver-spotted wings of the fritillary butterfly that chose to alight on Sparrow's duffel as he set it down to shake hands with Jared's parents.

Suddenly there was the sound of shouted greetings and dogs barking as boys and girls of all ages came running from beneath the oaks. They all looked alike, in ragged pants, sneakers, and baggy sweaters or windbreakers. They flung themselves on Jared, pulling at his sleeves, laughter and insults pouring from them. "How come you let Yale beat you? Where'd you get that keen sports jacket? Jared, when will you take us fishing?"

Sparrow was introduced to dozens more young people, Cousin this and Cousin that. He wondered if he would ever sort out the Southern cousins from the Northern kin. It was like trying to distinguish all the different species of warblers one from the other.

Jared eventually freed himself, promising they would see everybody at the Great Oak Christmas party the following day. While the others clambered into assorted horse-drawn vehicles to go to the great house, Jared and Sparrow stowed their luggage in a wagon pulled by a gaunt gray mule and driven by a giant Negro Jared introduced as Joe-Ali. The wagon, Jared explained, was left over from the days when hundreds of mules once worked in the plantation fields. Then Jared called his dogs, two liver-and-white pointers, and he and his parents and Sparrow set out to walk to Long Point.

Sparrow was excited to be on this island that he had read about, so rich in legend and lore, so closely interwoven in the historic fabric of the country. The forest he was walking through had echoed to Indian war whoops and Spanish mission bells, to the boom of cannon from the ruined fortress, the chants of the slaves, and wild songs of throat-cutting Highlanders, the Black Stark and his piratical band. Rich men, poor men, beggar men and thieves, priests and pirates, planters and plunderers, hermits and Highlanders, soldiers blue and gray and millionaire robber barons had fought and hunted over the verdant beautiful woods and white-sand beach.

Jared's father's eyes were as blue and piercing as Jared's were green and impenetrable. In contrast to the Great Oak men, who wore brass-buttoned blue blazers and flannels, Mr. Stark wore an old blue sweater with a tear at the elbow, faded khakis, and sneakers. Sparrow already knew he had given up a promising legal career in Boston to return to his Southern homeland. As a member of the Lawyers' Guild, he had espoused the cause of the Negro, participating in the defense in the famed Scottsboro case. Currently he was working to eliminate the bloc voting controlled by the plantation owners and the poll tax. Jared boasted proudly that his father had managed to register a number of Negroes who voted for President Roosevelt. When Sparrow mentioned it, Mr. Stark roared with laughter recalling how Isaiah, the ninety-year-old gardener at Great Oak, had replied, when asked how he accounted for his good health and longevity, that he had simply never tried to vote before.

"They say in Starksville that my father's laugh is the only one you can hear in the depression," Jared said with pride. "Even those who hate his guts, like the Great Oak farmer Cullen, say it echoes from one end of Main Street to the other!"

Sparrow thought Jared's mother was beautiful—tall, with hair as black as the head of a black-crowned night heron and the same eyes as Jared's. She had given Sparrow a firm handshake and told him she was happy to have him stay in her house.

There was a sudden roar of wings as a wild turkey, its feathers like polished bronze, whirred from a dense green thicket and flew over their heads. Sparrow heard the faint tinkling note of a horned lark and the low yank-yank of a white-breasted nuthatch in a pine tree as they passed a horse paddock.

Jared paused and let out a shrill whistle. A horse came running across the field and slid to a stop, putting its head over the fence. Jared rubbed its forehead, crooning, "Well, King, old fellow. How goes it?" He vaulted over the fence, bent down, and ran his hand along the horse's legs. "Looks as if you're sound and ready to be ridden again!" The horse pushed against Jared's chest and blew on him.

"Come along, Jared," his father said. "You can ride later. Susan's waiting at home."

The sandy path led beneath towering oaks festooned with Spanish moss. Two does crossed in front of them, and later, a family of wild pigs, looking bumptious, comical as they charged purposefully into the underbrush, their tails tightly coiled over their backs.

"European wild hogs," Jared's father explained. "Brought by the early British."

They walked between walls of green, palmettos and live oaks, glossy magnolias and slash pines. Sunlight slivered through the Spanish moss. A flight of merganser ducks flew overhead.

Jared paused on a shaky plank bridge by a brackish tidal pool and made an odd noise, almost a bellow. "Old Ugly's pool," he said fondly. "Biggest 'gator on the island. Close to fourteen feet long. He's hibernating somewhere there in the mud."

Jared said that poachers came in the night to kill the island alligators for their hides. They stole cattle and wild horses whenever they had the chance, selling them to rodeos or for dog food. They slaughtered the deer and wild pigs and sold their meat to hotels on the mainland, sometimes leaving them wounded and dying in the forest.

For a long time they walked along a causeway spanning golden marshland stretching away from them on either side.

A wall of dunes blocked the beach from view. They clambered up a white-sand hill and stood on top of it. The view was breathtaking. The beach ran on and on, white and dazzling in the late-afternoon light. Ten pelicans flew north, skimming over the breaking waves. Scoter ducks darkened the ocean swells. Three red-and-white island steers stood ankle-deep in the surf. A fishing boat heading out to sea was silhouetted against the falling orange sun.

"Our problem is how to preserve this wilderness," Mr. Stark said quietly, "this virgin seashore, for future generations, how to fight off predators, speculators, and the state. They want to build a bridge and connect it with the mainland."

The beach was hard and packed from the surf. Pieces of shell, all sizes and shapes, lay half-buried at the high-water mark. Ghost crabs darted into their holes behind the embroidery of shells.

Bottles and wooden fish buoys, tin cans and pieces of wood drifted up along the tide line, reminders of human destructiveness and waste.

Halfway to Long Point there was the sound of hooves coming from behind. Sparrow jumped aside just in time. A golden horse, mane and tail flying, tore past. A girl, with long black hair streaming behind her like a banner, crouched on the horse's back. Her legs and arms were bare, and Sparrow had a glimpse of a dark laughing face with flashing eyes. The girl waved and called out and then was gone, a rush of wind and hooves and hair.

"Who on earth was that?" he asked, brushing dust and sand from the good gray flannels he had traveled in.

Jared stood motionless, looking after the galloping horse. Slowly, wonderingly, he shook his head. "That's Cousin Maggie Royal for you! Trying to run us down."

He had never before mentioned a cousin with the name Maggie

Royal, but something about the way he spoke it made Sparrow think it would not be the last time he heard the name.

They came to the Negro settlement. Jared called it "the street." Children played in yards behind vine-covered fences. Strange-looking chickens pecked around doorways. Jared explained that in the Gullah community they were called "frizzled" and were believed to be searching for conjure bags hidden beneath the doorstep by an evil spirit. "Some historians believe the word 'Gullah' is derived from the Golla tribe of present-day Liberia," Mr. Stark said. "Although," he hastened to add, "the first Georgia slaves came from Gambia and the Niger River sections of Africa. Later from the Gold Coast, the Congo, and Portuguese West Africa. Those who know the Gullah people have a healthy respect for them," he concluded. "Many have second sight.

"Without radios in their fishing boats, they somehow always know when one of their own is in trouble. The other day Joe-Ali told me the island boat had lost its rudder and Captain Ben was stranded off Starksville Sound. It was coming on dark and we should go get him and bring him home.

"I got out the bateau and went to the place with Joe-Ali. Sure enough, there was the *Great Oak,* without a rudder."

Jared's house was at the end of the same settlement street, overlooking the sound. A wing of pine logs had been added to the original tabby quarters, framed by live oaks and a towering magnolia.

When Sparrow walked into that house, overlooking the sound, its shelves laden with books, classical records, and island artifacts of all kinds, he felt an instant allegiance, a sense of homecoming, that he had never felt before.

The house exuded warmth and welcome. The combination kitchen and family room was warmed by a fine driftwood fire that was kept burning day and night during the chill winter months. A scrolled sign was propped on the mantel, a quotation from Herman Melville, "Push not off from that isle; thou cans't never return." The ceiling had whitewashed beams; pots and pans were hung from them. Shelves were lined with home-canned fruit and vegetables from the kitchen garden, and herbal medicines. There were glass cases filled with Indian relics and rare bottles and shards found on the island. Jared's easel and painting materials took up one corner, his mother's loom another. The room smelled of baking bread, and there were always people in it.

Susan had not inherited her parents' striking features or her mother's eyes. Her hair was the same in-between color as her father's, and there was a dusting of freckles on her slightly upturned nose. She was rather small and, owing to illness, her body had lost its shape. But her eyes were direct and filled with brave good humor. Her smile was warm and her handshake firm. Sparrow instantly liked her.

Twice a week she went to Savannah for therapy, and at home she exercised with rings and a trapeze bar over her bed, pulling herself up and down. The doctors doubted she would ever walk again, but she insisted it was only a matter of time and effort. Susan's illness had matured her. She had read seriously and thought about what she had read. Sparrow found he could talk to her about things that mattered, without self-consciousness.

On Christmas morning, Sparrow awoke to the croaking call of a night heron passing overhead. For a moment he couldn't remember where he was. Then he realized what it was that was different. The only sounds he heard were natural sounds—the noise of waves against the nearby beach, the wind sighing through the trees, and the scream of gulls.

He lay listening for the island day to begin.

Suddenly, although it had been late by the time they trimmed the tree and went to bed, he couldn't wait to be up and about, along the shore where the sea birds were, or in the woods. Quickly he doused his face with water from the blue-and-white china pitcher on top of the marble washstand; grabbed his binoculars, camera, and notebook; and slipped out of the house.

It was that magic hour when the first reflections of returning sun slowly color the sky and the lingering symphony of night singers yields to the chorus of day singers waiting joyously to salute the dawn.

A layer of pale blue mist hovered over the marsh, becoming a deeper blue as it touched the gray waters of the sound.

The air was so cold and clear, he felt reborn. There was a touch of frost, but the camellias along the street were beginning to bud, and in Jared's yard clumps of pale white narcissus were starting to bloom. There was a sudden scratching noise as he turned onto the trail. He froze, listening, but it was only a wild cow eating jessamine.

He saw a blue heron and a white egret rise as he skirted the marsh. Several brown hens scurried through the tall grass, making loud clacking calls. A flock of red-winged black birds flew off, orange wings flashing.

He turned inland, onto the woods path. It was very still. His feet trod on pine-needle covering as noiselessly as had those of the Indians who had followed the same path centuries before him.

A large angry sow stood in the center of the path glaring at him. As he approached, she snorted and then turned her curling tail and vanished into the woods, her young exploding from the underbrush in all directions and running after her.

Suddenly there was silence. No wind moved, or twig cracked. Then a miracle happened. Sparrow heard a drop of water strike a palmetto frond. The mist had cleared and there was no rain. Another drop slid off a leaf and struck a fern at his feet. Dew dripping!

That instant, he heard a gun go off. He jumped and stumbled over a root, and his glasses fell off.

Before he could reach down and find them, what appeared to be a young boy wearing a knitted cap, jeans, and a buckskin jacket came out of the underbrush. He was leading a horse and carrying a rifle. "What are you doing here?" he demanded. "This is a private island."

"Mind if I find my glasses?" Sparrow answered nervously, gazing at the gun. "I can't see very well without them."

He retrieved them among the pine needles at his feet, put them on, and received a shock. The boy, he saw immediately, was a girl—and as she yanked off her cap, releasing a mane of wild black hair, he saw it was the girl who had galloped past them the previous day, almost running them down.

"Oh!" she said. "You're Jared's friend." Her astonishing black-fringed violet eyes widened. "I thought you were a poacher." She smiled, displaying teeth as white as the pate of a widgeon. She indicated the gun. "I've been shooting mistletoe out of the trees for Christmas decorations."

"I'm Sparrow McKinney," he said, thinking that if he hadn't lost his glasses he couldn't possibly have mistaken her for a male. "Mind putting the gun aside? It makes me nervous."

"I'm Maggie Royal McDermott." She gave him a long, level, measuring look. Her eyes seemed very large in a face that was long and oval-shaped, with high cheekbones, a straight nose, and stubborn chin. She flung her head up. Her neck was long and white, like a western grebe's.

"This is the best time of day," she said conversationally, leaning the gun against the pine tree.

Sparrow heard a sharp metallic "tchip." He put his fingers to his lips as the distinctive call note was heard again.

Frantically he searched the tops of the trees with his binoculars.

"There's a little bird up there," she said, pointing to a branch near the top of a tall pine.

Sparrow looked and saw the bright patch of yellow at the base of the tail that is the myrtle's trademark.

"You have good eyes," he said. "You must be a bird-watcher."

She shook her head. "Sometimes bird-watchers come from the mainland. They stalk through the woods with notebooks and binoculars and cameras. I couldn't ever be that serious. I just like to know the birds are here, all around me, and listen to them sing."

"We're not always watching," Sparrow said, as several more warblers darted in and out of the palmettos at the side of the trail. "Sometimes we listen, too."

"What are they?" she asked, following his gaze.

"Myrtle warblers. They like the berries of the wax myrtle. Hence the name."

"I see now why you and Jared are friends," she said. "You both know so many things."

"You could easily learn. You have a good eye, and this is a wonderful birdy place."

She gave him a long straight glance. "All right." She stood up with a quick motion, like the warblers now darting back and forth amid the green fronds.

"Sit down and don't move," he cautioned. "Look, over there, on that branch. That's something else again!"

"Oh," she gasped, "it's beautiful."

"You're seeing something very special," Sparrow said excitedly. "Something rare and accidental in winter in this area. 'Gorgeous' is the way it's described in bird books! Here, take my glasses."

By the time she had adjusted the glasses, focused for his nearsighted gaze, the brilliantly plumaged bird had moved from its conspicuous perch on the top of a small pine to a magnolia branch. There its purplish-blue head and red underparts contrasted with the dark green background.

"What is it called?" she breathed, handing him back the glasses.

"A painted bunting. In the South it's known as a nonpareil. Usually you only see them in summer."

"Heavens," she said, "it's late. Gramma will be livid if I miss breakfast." She glanced at him hesitantly. "All right if I move now?"

"Of course." He smiled apologetically. "You mustn't mind me. I get carried away."

"I know," she agreed solemnly. "May I come with you some morning? You and Jared?"

"Of course." He was fascinated watching her. She was like her mare, long and leggy, with a slender aristocratic neck and a thoroughbred tilt to her head. She seemed a natural, as much a part of the island as the gulls circling over the beach. She was just on the edge of life. Her face had the innocence and toughness of a child making the transition to adulthood. There was something vulnerable and at the same time untouchable about her that set her apart. She was too tall and too thin, and yet, standing there in her ragged jeans, Keds, and wild black hair, she seemed more feminine than the Radcliffe girls and Boston debs with their sophisticated guile and self-absorption.

She picked up the hackamore rein. The chestnut mare, her coat as glossy as the feathers of a wild turkey, lifted her head.

"She's beautiful," Sparrow said sincerely.

"Yes." Maggie Royal smiled. "Beautiful and bad. But I love her. Nobody else would put up with you, Azilia, now, would they?" She scratched the mare's forehead. She took a deep breath. "Isn't it a glorious day? Merry Christmas!"

Then she put her left hand on the horse's withers and with a sudden quick motion vaulted onto the mare's back. He heard the girl's exultant laugh as the horse leaped into a gallop, racing to meet the sun, reddish orange as a black bird's wing, above the rim of the sea.

Sparrow watched until his eyes blurred in the blazing light.

The moment, as brief and ephemeral as the drop of dew on the fern, was past, leaving him with a lingering sense of beauty and the memory of the girl, Maggie Royal, as she rode wildly, fearlessly to meet the morning.

He saw the little tabby house ahead as a cardinal spoke, singing its salute to Christmas morning, a note as fresh and clear as the rainwater he had washed in.

Susan was setting out feed for a bold blue jay that was sharing her windowsill with a black fox squirrel almost as big as the tomcat in the yard.

"Merry Christmas," she called. "Would you mind chasing that awful tom out of the yard? He frightens off the birds."

Sparrow shooed the cat away, shut the wicket gate, and went in to a breakfast of fresh fish Joe-Ali had caught in his flat-bottom bateau, and homemade bread.

Presents were piled under the tree, and there was an assortment for him. Jared must have written beforehand, for his father had carved a Savannah sparrow from a piece of driftwood for him to remember the island by. His mother had fashioned a pottery ashtray for his pipe. Jared gave him a new fountain pen, which he had thoughtfully filled with ink, and a pocket checklist of island birds. Even Joe-Ali had a gift. He had carved a decoy, a lovely replica of a blue teal, accurately painted.

Susan presented him a handsomely bound collection of Audubon "Birds of America" prints.

Sparrow had been at school or with strangers for the past three Christmases. Now he was under the roof of this warm and unique family. He was hard put to say thank you around the lump in his throat.

They were due at Great Oak for the traditional Christmas festivities at noon. Jared's parents said they intended to remain at home with Susan, who was not up to attending. Sparrow argued he'd be glad to stay home with them; Mr. Stark had some bird books he longed to read, and he looked forward to a game of chess with Susan. But he was told that Christmas at the big house was an occasion he shouldn't miss, bringing the family together, almost literally, from the four corners of the earth.

An animated stickball game was under way on the lawn in front of the house when Sparrow and Jared arrived. All ages seemed to be playing and yelling at once. Maggie Royal handed Sparrow a broomstick and told him he was at bat. He handed it back, saying he had to go indoors and make his manners.

"You're sure?" She grabbed the stick and ran back to the plate. She wore a red sweater that made her hair and eyebrows seem very dark and gave her a merry Gypsy look. The proud carriage of her head, tilted slightly, the eyes flashing with excitement, communicated passion, impatience for life, just as now she waited impatiently for the pitcher to throw, to be unleashed.

She swung at the ball and batted it out into center field. There was a chorus of "Come on, Maggie Royal. Atta girl-yah!" as she flung down the broomstick and ran madly to first base, tripping over it as the baseman caught the ball. She sat on the ground, safe, laughing triumphantly. Sparrow thought that he would never forget her as she was at that moment.

"Come on, Jared," she called out. "Take a turn at bat."

Jared looked suddenly tentative, almost uncertain. The phrase "caught off base" crossed Sparrow's mind.

"Not now," Jared said, continuing toward the house. His voice had a kind of gruffness. "It's almost time for the present opening."

Jared told Sparrow that Gramma—everyone calls her that, he explained—celebrated Christmas as it had been in plantation days. Great fires of fat wood and huge Yule logs blazed in all the fireplaces, while doors stood open as a welcome to all comers. Boughs of holly, magnolia leaves, cherry laurel, and blue-berried cedar; white wax myrtle and red-berried cassina; and green fans of palmetto decorated the house. Smilax encircled a great silver bowl filled with what was described as "Gramma's very heady punch."

Mistletoe was hung over the doorways. Each year the cousins challenged each other to see who could shoot down the clumps of mistletoe in the tall oaks with the fewest shots. The best shot was awarded the first kiss under the mistletoe Christmas day.

Sparrow had difficulty remembering all the people he met that day. It was very Gilbert-and-Sullivan, with sisters and cousins, aunts and uncles clustered in groups, like clumps of wild island asparagus. One of the relatives had just returned from a government mission to Moscow and was discussing the awful famine and purge taking place in Russia. Another uncle-in-law, a Boston banker, insisted that FDR was driving the country into bankruptcy. A cousin that worked for *Time* magazine said Roosevelt was bleeding the country white with his New Deal programs. Someone quoted the Republican national chairman, John D. M. Hamilton, as having said that all working men and women would soon be required to wear steel dog tags around their necks, stamped with numbers.

The great-aunts, Meg and Amy, Jared told him, were the outside aunts who lived in Starksville. Aunt Amy was round and plump like one of the island quail. Aunt Meg was tall and as thin as one of the new fenceposts in the paddock field. She had a deep voice and shingled hair and was said to be a famous horsewoman. She was talking to the Reverend Mr. Johnson of the Starksville church about nesting doves, pointing out that there was a shortage for the shooting season.

The New York aunt who had been complaining about the servant problem in the North broke in: "I think it's shameful for great big men to go out and kill those poor little birds by the bushel."

"Doves are migratory," Aunt Meg shot back. "We don't shoot *our* doves, just Yankee doves passing through!"

There were a number of other superior eccentrics, foremost among them Uncle Oomlot, Gramma's brother, who lived in the tower. He was immaculate from the waist up, in a white shirt, crimson cravat, and velvet smoking jacket. From the waist down he wore vivid red-white-and-blue-striped pajamas and moth-eaten carpet slippers from which most of the fuzz had disappeared. White-haired and bespectacled, he reminded Sparrow of Santa Claus as he handed out forbidden sweets from the pocket of his jacket to the children when Gramma's back was turned.

Many grown-ups and children bore the same name, handed down for generations. Aunt Amy did her best to place Sparrow. When told he was not Howard's son from New York, she insisted he looked like the Boston relatives and must be related to the Pritchards.

Finally they all gave up trying to pigeonhole him and simply, because he was there, assumed he was one of them.

After freeing himself from Aunt Amy's persistent questions about his parents and background, he gazed around the room, hoping to see the dark-haired Maggie Royal. As she was nowhere to be seen, he decided to take temporary refuge in the lavatory. He went upstairs and took the first door he came to. He found himself in one of the most marvelous rooms he had ever been in. It was obviously Gramma's bathroom and he had no business to be there, but he could not resist looking around. After locking the door, he took careful stock.

There was a fireplace with a marble mantel. Family photographs in silver monogrammed frames covered its surface and that of the dressing table. Priceless piles of necklaces and bracelets and earrings lay amid crystal bottles with silver tops and silver-backed brushes.

A gardenia plant filled the room with its scent. A pair of Peal boots with wooden trees stood in a corner. There was a great long bathtub with gold claw feet, gold-mermaid taps. A wicker wooden seat was built over a porcelain bowl decorated with roses. Alongside it stood the *pièce de résistance:* here on this wilderness island was a black porcelain bidet!

An account book with pages of careful figures lay open on a table alongside a satin chaise longue. Books and magazines were piled on an ornate ormolu table.

Sparrow pulled the long chain, but to his embarrassment, the toilet would not flush. He washed his hands, careful not to disturb any of the matching hand towels, combed his hair, and polished his glasses. Again he pulled the chain, and again nothing happened. He took a deep breath and unlocked the door. A handsome light-skinned maid came down the hallway as he peered guiltily from the doorway. He realized she would find the toilet unflushed and wonder what he had been doing in her mistress's bedroom. He had the feeling she would check the jewels as soon as he was out of sight.

He went down the great staircase and started back to the living room. He was wondering whether Maggie Royal was still outside playing stickball when she slid down the wide mahogany banister that led to the upper regions and landed at his feet.

"Mercy!" she exclaimed, turning crimson and picking herself up. "I didn't know anybody was here. I mean, I thought you'd all be in the big drawing room."

"It's been a long time since a pretty girl fell for me," Sparrow told her.

"Oh, you . . ." She gave him her wide, delighted smile. "Come on," she urged, smoothing down the skirt of her red wool dress. "Our people will be coming in for their Christmas presents."

Before the family unwrapped their gifts, the servants were invited in. They filed past Gramma in her lionshead chair. She shook hands with the inside help and the outside help. Gramma called the handsome girl with the light skin and delicate features Sparrow had seen in the hall Affey, and presented her with a bolt of beautiful Japanese silk to make into a dress.

"It's beautiful and I thank you," the girl said formally, "but, Mrs. McDermott, you know I never go anywhere."

Sparrow noticed she did not speak like the other Negroes and was the only one who called Gramma Mrs. McDermott. All the other Negroes called her Missus Gramma or Miss Maggie Royal. One, a huge regal woman with a bandanna tied around her head, whom Gramma called Cook Ada, flung her arms around the mistress of Great Oak, calling her, "My darling little Miss Maggie Royal. Tunka punka!"

The outside Negroes came next. Sapelo and Jazzbo dressed in dark suits, their shoes as polished and glossy as magnolia leaves. Outside Dick, who supervised the Delco generator and farm implements, Isaiah, the head gardener, who had helped lay out the arboretum, and many others whose names Sparrow was never able to remember. Each man, woman, and child was handed a gaily wrapped gift. This ceremony took a long time, and although she was sitting down, it seemed to Sparrow that Gramma must be exhausted and the day hardly begun.

As the last black child, eyes huge with awe and anticipation, left, clutching his present, the in-house children rushed to the piles beneath the tree. For at least an hour the uproar was so loud it was impossible to hear anyone's thank-yous. Somehow everyone seemed to have known Sparrow was coming and to have provided a gift for him. He was embarrassed, as he had brought gifts only for Jared and his family.

Gramma sought to put him at ease. "It's a tradition in our family," she said, putting one of her diamond-studded hands on his arm. "Everyone, all the children and grown-ups, make or buy something with their own hands or money for our people. They come first. You couldn't possibly bring a gift for everyone. It takes me all year to stock my present closet." She gave him a smile as brilliant as her sapphires. "We're just so pleased to have one of Jared's friends with us."

Maggie Royal came up then and shyly handed him a wrapped

package. "It's nothing much," she said deprecatingly, "but I hope you'll like it."

He carefully unwrapped the little box, opened the top, and stared wonderingly at its contents.

A beautiful and fragile wild-turkey egg. It was light buff with numerous small reddish spots, lying on a bed of Spanish moss.

"Why, it's fabulous!" he cried. "Copacetic! Have you any idea how rare a wild-turkey egg is? Wherever did you find it?"

"I didn't know it was rare," Maggie Royal answered. "I found it by a log in the swampy place near Middle Point. I knew you liked birdy things." She stole a glance at Jared, but he was busy examining a book about Augustus John. Uncle Oomlot had given him the biography of the great British painter that mentioned his American tour during which time he visited the island and painted Gramma. "I can't thank you enough," Sparrow said with conviction. "Oh, boy, wait until I add this to my collection. Jared, look, isn't it keen?"

Jared took the egg, very gently and carefully, holding it in the palm of his hand. "Yes," he agreed noncommittally, "keen." He handed it back and did not look at Maggie Royal.

She turned quickly away, a hurt look in her blue-violet eyes.

Constance's little brother Harry, known as the Horror, went up to Gramma to thank her for his present. "But, Gramma," he said, holding a packet of letters tied with pink satin ribbon, "what am I to do with these?"

"Orville, these were meant for you," Gramma replied, addressing Uncle Oomlot. "They're dear Sarah's letters. I saved them all these years. I meant to give them to you before, but I could never find a box the right size. They just happened to fit into the model-automobile box I had for Harry. Orville," she appealed to him, "is it possible I'm losing my mind? Everyone in our family gets dotty in their seventies, and I'm seventy-four."

"Of course you're not crazy, my dear," the old gentleman replied. "Just becoming forgetful, like all of us. Now I know why I received a model automobile! Here, Harry, let's trade."

The incident recalled another involving "dear Sarah's ashes," which one of the cousins hastened to relate. Gramma maintained a large present closet in the attic. A typewritten list of members of the immediate family and the dates of their birthdays, weddings, and anniversaries was pinned to the door. There were compartments for birthday, Easter, St. Patrick's Day, wedding, anniversary, and Christmas.

Following the death of his last wife, Uncle Oomlot had brought the urn filled with her ashes with him from England for burial in the family cemetery. Somehow he had left the urn in his stateroom aboard ship. When the loss was made known, the ship's steward searched the cabin without finding it. The urn was thought to be lost. Years later, shortly before Christmas, it was found still aboard the ship and sent to Starksville by Railway Express.

Gramma stowed it in her closet for safekeeping until such time as it would be convenient to have a memorial service. Then in the confusion of Christmas she forgot it. Finally, coming across it inadvertently, she decided it was something that would suit the aunts for the Starksville house and labeled it "Meg and Amy."

"Mercy!" Gramma exclaimed as the urn was opened and the ashes spilled out. "There goes Sarah! Orville, I *am* so sorry. There just wasn't time to dispose of her before Christmas, and I wrapped her up by mistake."

Christmas dinner was at four o'clock. The table stretched the length of the dining room, lit with candles in the chandeliers, sconces, and silver holders. Island holly and greens, camellias and gardenias from the greenhouse, provided an exotic centerpiece.

Gramma took her place at the end of the long table. The Reverend Mr. Johnson, who looked more like a Southern sheriff with a large stomach and loud laugh than the rector of the Starksville church, sat on her right and said a blessing. Dr. Bartow, the family doctor, sat on her left.

Maggie Royal was on one side of Sparrow, her cousin Constance on the other. Their handsome cousin from New Orleans, Noble LeFevre, was on the other side of Maggie Royal. Her cousin Adele sat on his left.

Sparrow wanted to talk to Maggie Royal, but Constance engaged him in conversation about the girls from Boston she knew at Farmington and the dances and proms she'd been to.

There was an array of silver at his place, several forks he could not identify. He found his mind wandering as Constance chattered on. Absentmindedly he picked up one of the forks and began polishing it with his napkin as he had learned to do in the "Quick and Dirty" where he worked part-time and where the eating utensils were not always well washed.

Suddenly a warm brown hand plucked at his sleeve.

"Newt wants to pass the fish course," Maggie Royal said. "You'll need your fork for the oysters."

He dropped the fork and napkin as if his hand had been burned. He felt himself turning the color of the holly berries as she hurriedly whispered, "Don't worry. Gramma wasn't watching."

The oysters, Maggie Royal said, were fresh from one of the tidal creeks. They were followed by terrapin soup. Maggie Royal explained it was an island delicacy and told him an extraordinary story about her and Gramma's carrying live terrapins to President Hoover at the White House.

The rest of the meal was equally memorable. Maggie Royal identified the courses for him: wild turkey ("I can't eat it," she explained, and told him how Jared called out the wild turkeys), saddle of venison, plump island quail, and home-cured ham. There were at least half a dozen vegetables, all grown in the island garden, hot rolls, and cornbread.

131

Sparrow could understand why invitations to Stark Island were as prized as second helpings, and had seconds of everything.

"You don't eat like a sparrow!" Constance observed tartly.

Uncle Oomlot, in charge of the wine, provided pale sherry, decanters of madeira and burgundy, a special Château Lafite going back to God knows when, and imported champagne with the plum pudding. The feast was served by Newt, the butler, and an assortment of waiters and waitresses, all of whom wore white cotton gloves.

"Gramma can't stand black hands," Maggie Royal explained. "I think it has something to do with Grandfather, who could never get his nails clean. You know, he worked in a coal mine."

"Maggie Royal, why do you tell Sparrow about Grandpa?" Constance interrupted. "You know it isn't nice to talk to strangers about family."

Maggie Royal smiled at him. "Sparrow isn't a stranger," she told her cousin. "He's one of us now."

Sparrow turned his chair away from Constance and asked Maggie Royal to tell him more about the island, what it had been like to grow up on it.

He watched her as she talked. Her eyes were the deepest blue he had ever seen. Her lashes both above and below were very thick, as were her brows. He hoped she wouldn't ever pluck them into a thin line like Constance, or cut her long black hair. She was just fourteen, but the indications of the beauty she was to become were there, the slim body, flawless skin, and blue-black hair. In her scarlet wool Christmas dress she was like a flame from the fat wood burning in the huge fireplace.

Her cousin Noble, clearly a young man with a high opinion of himself, was also aware of her budding beauty. After dinner he regaled the men, who had been dispatched to what Gramma called the smoking room, with reports of his escapades with the ladies on Bourbon Street. He had a great deal to drink, including several glasses of Uncle Oomlot's rare port.

When the men started back to join the women in the big room for carol singing, Noble suddenly caught sight of Maggie Royal. Going up to her as she was about to enter the living room, he grabbed her and pulled her under the mistletoe. Bending down, he attempted to kiss her. The girl's narrow dark face went white with anger as she fought to free herself, pounding on his chest with both fists.

Jared yanked him backward. "Can't you tell, the lady doesn't like to be manhandled!"

Noble's hands doubled into fists, and then, at sight of Jared's set angry face, relaxed. "I beg your pardon." He gave Maggie Royal a deep mocking bow, then turned again to Jared. "It would be a shame to lay rude hands on this island nymph, wouldn't it, now?" He straightened his jacket and shrugged. "Eat your heart out, Maggie Royal."

As if enough hadn't already gone into the day, there were carols to sing and games to play. The younger children were dispatched to bed.

132

There was much whining and protest until Gramma put down her small satin-clad foot. "Enough . . . to bed, all of you under twelve."

Everybody over twelve clustered around the concert grand. Aunt Meg played and everyone sang lustily. Dogs barked. Gramma's pet pig collapsed with a grunt into the piles of tissue paper that hadn't been removed from underneath the tree. The fire, warding off the winter chill, shot embers onto the Aubusson carpet. Somebody pounded on the floor above, demanding "Quiet!" and through it all moved Newt, the seemingly tireless and patient butler, passing coffee, liqueurs, and tall frosted glasses of fresh orange juice.

Finally Gramma excused herself, asking the last to bed to put up the screen around the fire and blow out the candles. "Jared," she said on her way out the door, "I want you to help me round up some of the horses. Mr. Lewis is coming over to look at them. He usually offers a fair price, and God knows we need the money. The way things are in Washington with young Franklin, we'll all soon be bankrupt. Come over about nine, will you? Good night."

She put out her hand to Sparrow. "So glad you were here with us. Dear Howard hasn't been near the island in years. Be sure to tell him to come soon."

"He's not Howard's son," Jared interrupted. "His name is Sparrow McKinney."

"McKinney?" The old lady looked mystified. "Do we have any McKinney relatives? No matter," she added. "He's an island person now. Good night, all."

The pine-paneled library opened into a glass-enclosed conservatory where chairs were placed around a tinkling fountain and the walls were hung with live orchids grown in the greenhouses. It served as stage for the ritual round of charades. Aunt Meg chose Jared and Sparrow for her team. Maggie Royal was on Adele's father's team.

Sparrow was given "A bird in the hand is worth two in the bush." He held out his hand and peered nearsightedly at a gardenia bush, as though through field glasses. His team guessed it immediately.

Maggie Royal was given "The Rape of the Lock." She tried plucking a hair from her head. "Hair," somebody said. "Full, hurt, cut . . ." Maggie went to the door and pointed to the lock. This got everybody off on the wrong track. Finally her time was up.

She turned on Jared, eyes flashing. "You thought it up. You wanted to see me embarrassed."

Jared lifted an eyebrow and smiled. "I told you she had a foul temper." He grinned back at Maggie Royal. "Stubborn, balky, like Tabby, the stable goat. . ."

"I don't know if anybody could have acted it better," Sparrow said to Maggie Royal. "I think you carried it off very well."

They seemed not to have heard him.

"I am not," Maggie Royal flung at Jared. Her hair tossed. Her chin jutted out. "Rape of the Lock!" She kicked him in the shins.

"Ouch!" Jared grabbed her and threw her down onto the sofa and spanked her.

"Children! Children!" Aunt Amy remonstrated mildly. "No more roughhousing!"

"I am not a child," Maggie Royal cried furiously, sitting up and pushing back her hair, all of which had come loose from the restraining red ribbon.

"Then stop behaving like one," Jared said.

"You . . . you . . ." She glared at him for an instant, then spun on her heel and ran from the room.

Jared and Sparrow said their good-byes and set out to walk to Long Point.

Jared didn't speak until they were almost home. "That's Maggie Royal." He shook his head incredulously. "She'll be a handful for any man when she grows up." He went on as if speaking to himself. "All fire and ice, sunlight and moonlight and sudden storms."

Sparrow lay in bed too overstimulated to sleep. He thought about why the day had been so special. There was an excitement on the island, an atmosphere of accomplishment coupled with naturalness. The family had a marvelous aura, a wonderful spontaneity that showed in their talk and games. There was a competitive spirit and yet an enthusiasm for fun that gave him a feeling anything was possible.

The island was a kind of jungle gym where one was free to bird-watch, play tennis, putter in boats or on a golf green, ride, swim, play croquet or the island version of baseball they called stickball. This combination of luxurious exclusivity imposed on wilderness provided scope for every kind of physical and mental activity.

No question but that the Starks were too rich, too arrogant, too insulated from the reality of rent money and Hoovervilles, too fearful of becoming dizzy to look down and give those on the bottom a leg up. Yet their contribution, he realized, was important. Theirs was a grace, a style, and they enjoyed a deep inner security that encouraged originality and tolerated eccentricity.

Sparrow had never met a real racist until he encountered Bo Cullen, the farm manager at Great Oak, the next day. Maggie Royal, Adele, Jared, and he went for a ride. Jared, who took an interest in all that took place on the island, wanted to see the lower pasture, where Cullen was building a fence to replace the rails that had rotted away.

"Why does it have to be wire?" Maggie Royal asked as they rode on ahead of Adele and Sparrow. "The horses could be hurt."

"Your grandmother says she can't afford a new rail fence," Jared replied. "Dividends are down." He grinned. "That man in the White House."

"Come on," Maggie Royal cried as they came out into the open field. "Let's gallop!"

Her mare broke into a canter. Jared's stallion caught up. Maggie Royal leaned forward, laughing and urging the mare on as the pair sped on ahead, neck and neck.

"Hey, where you think you're goin'?" they heard Cullen shout. "Ruinin' my field!"

Sparrow saw Jared and Maggie Royal look back and laugh as the irate farmer stood glaring after them, flicking his whip, a look of murderous rage on his face.

Sparrow asked Jared's father about Cullen.

"He is the mind of the tenant farmer, the sharecropper, the cotton-mill owner, the unreconstructed South. You see him sitting with the courthouse gang on the bench under the Confederate monument, spitting tobacco juice and talking about the niggers. Or Saturday night, drunk and goddamning in the roadhouses or swaggering into the secret, steamy brothels. Sunday you'll find him wearing a starched shirt, repenting at the Church of God or the Holy Rollers."

Mr. Stark warmed to the subject. He spoke of the fears and hates, as closely intermingled as the moss was with the oaks, that sparked the Ku Klux Klan. Doubt and change, flux and violence, were replacing the old familiar world that was fixed and certain. Godlessness and revolution now ruled in Russia.

Fear was the result. The fear that is mixed with hatred for whatever is different from oneself and one's pattern. Thus the Cullens banded together against outsiders, and the Klan with its militant and intolerant propaganda against the Red Menace found receptive soil. From 1900 to 1929 there had been eight local cases of lynchings, involving some fifty-four whites. The criminals got off with minor penalties and, at the most, three months in jail.

"I want to make this point clear," Mr. Stark said. "The Cullens are not solely to blame. The South has fostered the belief that nigger-baiting and lynching is due to the redneck white trash. Up North I knew people who boasted they would like to hang up and roast Negroes themselves. The Klansmen were able to do this because their betters, or the ruling class, consented quietly and in many cases gave their outright approval."

Mr. Stark slowly filled his pipe, carefully tamping the tobacco down with his thumb.

"By their very silence the master class give sanction to torture and sadism. It's not unheard-of for a white man to walk up to a Negro on the main street of Starksville and, for no other reason than the black man's refusal to move aside, shoot to kill. Such cases rarely go to court. If they do, the murderer is promptly acquitted. Those who can be pointed out as having slain a number of Negroes walk about free and are spoken of as folk heroes, 'good ole boys' wedded to the glorious traditions of the South."

Mr. Stark shrugged. "The killing of a Negro by a white man ceases in some instances to even call for a legal inquiry. If it does get to court, the coroner or jury will term it self-defense or justifiable homicide, that it was necessary to smash a sassy Negro or kill him. In order to assert the white man's prerogative, keep the black man in his place, the same methods are used to smash the so-called white nigger-lover."

Sparrow was perplexed and intrigued. He felt as if he were in a foreign country, a country in which he had no knowledge of the culture or character of the people. He had always thought of Southerners as cultured and intelligent. Some, however, like the aunts at Great Oak, still spoke of ancient glories, of a superior culture, as if the institutions they clung to were not outmoded, impersonal, and cruel. They reminded him of the great-aunts' Starksville house, where Jared took him one day, a place full of strange, high empty rooms with their windows sealed behind heavy curtains, shutting out the light of reason.

Mr. Stark became more specific. The bad blood between Cullen and himself began when the farmer first came to Stark Island. One day Cullen encountered Joe-Ali on the street. When the tall Negro refused to move out of the way, Cullen slashed him with his whip. Joe-Ali grabbed the farmer and might have choked him to death if he himself hadn't heard the commotion and rushed from his house to separate them. Cullen brought charges, and if they—meaning he and Joe-Ali—had not succeeded in his defense, the black man would no doubt have languished in jail or been sent out on the chain gang.

Part of Lawyer Stark's success hinged on being able to teach his clients what he called "courtroom technique." He spoke of the time he freed a Gullah fisherman of a rape charge.

"It was during old Judge Cantwell's time. He knew the island and had a healthy respect for the Gullahs and their superstitions. Joe-Ali managed to catch a buzzard. He let it into the courtroom through an open window. By chance it flew straight to the judge's bench and circled it." Mr. Stark threw back his head and laughed his great booming laugh. "Judge Cantwell dropped the case.

"I cautioned Joe-Ali not to talk too well or too fast," he continued. " 'I know you know better,' I told him. 'I know you're more educated than the state's attorney or Judge Upton, but if I'm to get you acquitted, you're damn well going to have to drawl. Now, drawl, dammit,' I said. 'Furthermore, don't fuss with the judge! Never approach Judge Upton until the proper time. The proper time is after ten-thirty, when he's digested breakfast and had his first cigar.'

"The secret of success in a Southern courtroom is the 'good-ole-boy' technique," he explained. "The outcome depends on how well you know the sheriff, the opposing lawyers, and the judge. If you went to the university and were fraternity brothers or fishing or drinking companions, or if your wife's cousin married the brother of one of the judge's sisters' husbands or had some other connection, then you might qualify as a good ole boy. I don't. Harvard, anything Yankee, doesn't qualify you as a good ole boy. Nor is anybody who takes Negro clients going to win a popularity contest. But there have always been Starks in this county, and the name still carries some weight.

"All the defendants that day were Negroes," he continued, "accused of some kind of petty crime. There was a boy who had stolen shoes from the general store. He explained he did not own any shoes and his way to school was over an oyster-shell road. He displayed the cuts and abrasions on the soles of his feet. He was sentenced to three months. Another was an old man, so ancient and ruined it didn't seem possible he could stand in his own defense or that he could have carried away the pig he was accused of stealing.

"The spectators seemed to want to see the prisoners put away somewhere out of sight and mind, not because they were offended by the crimes but because they were offended that their society, their world, had produced an element whose only possible chance for advancement lay in a career of crime. The fact that the majority of criminals could be counted on to be black was reassuring. It was what they expected of the Negro race."

Lawyer Stark paused to relight his pipe and continued. " 'How did you arrest this man?' I asked the sheriff. 'Without a warrant? Against county law . . . against state law . . . against federal law?'

"For an instant Sheriff Harper looked abashed. Then he brightened. 'It's how we do things in this county!'

"Then I asked the sheriff if he would kindly read the Georgia law. When he stumbled over the words, I asked the judge if he would like me to read the law to the court. 'Nigger law!' the sheriff said. He winked at the spectators. 'Brother Stark here knows it better'n I do!' There was laughter in the courtroom."

Sparrow visualized the courtroom on that hot summer day when the women fanned themselves with palm fans from "Drop Kick" Keeler's undertaking establishment and the low monotone of the defendants was scarcely more audible than the drone of bees in the magnolia behind the statue of the Confederate soldier in the yard.

"But you won the case," he said.

"Oh, yes, we won the case." Mr. Stark's booming laugh rang out. "Joe-Ali is a Mason. Three of the jurors—they looked like hanging jurors, too—wore Masonic rings. The judge never did figure why I didn't disqualify them, but I gambled they wouldn't let a brother down, even if he was a Negro.

"But that wasn't the end of it." Mr. Stark frowned. "Cullen vowed to revenge himself against the nigger and the lawyer who defeated him in court, shamed him before the Klan and his friends.

"One night his 'catch dogs' treed Joe-Ali's pet coon, Aristotle. Joe-Ali had gone to the mainland for some reason. Cullen saw his chance to go coon hunting. The farmer shook the terrified animal down into the midst of his dogs and it was torn to pieces. I had to use all my powers of persuasion to keep Joe-Ali from going after Cullen. Right now we're all existing in a kind of armed neutrality."

Jared's father had given Sparrow the copy of "The Bear" to read. Walking through the woods that day, Sparrow had imagined himself to be the boy, hoping to find the bear. Instead, he had come upon wild turkeys, long-legged, agile, burnished bronze in the light shafting through the green palmettos, moving with a grace and freedom unknown to their domestic relatives. In the shadows, white-tailed deer had whirled and run deeper into the wood, flaunting their flags, defying him for invading their secret fastnesses.

On the morning after the Cullen account, he rode with Jared before breakfast, sending the animals skittering into the underbrush as they cantered past. They were on their way to see a particularly fine specimen of a red-cockaded woodpecker Jared's father mentioned seeing in the overcup oak just off Mule Run, near Old Ugly's pool, when they met Maggie Royal.

A few yards farther on was a small corral, or holding pen, where the wild pigs were kept before slaughter and shipment to the mainland.

"The pigs were supposed to go off the day after Christmas, but the boat is broken down," Jared said. "I bet Cullen forgot to turn them loose after he rounded them up."

Suddenly Old Red, supposedly the safest guest horse, threw up his head, swerving so abruptly that Sparrow nearly fell off. The other horses swerved too, nostrils dilated, snorting, their ears pricked in the direction of the corral from which agonized squeals and grunts came.

"They must be starving," Maggie Royal cried, dismounting and running to the pen.

Her scream sounded like the cry of the red-tailed hawk that circled over the Long Point settlement.

A dozen or more sows and boars were crammed in the pen, so crowded some were standing on top of others. They had cut themselves in their panic, and there was blood everywhere. One boar had a newborn piglet in its mouth. Partially eaten carcasses were scattered about. The sow that had given birth lay crushed against the fence, bleeding profusely.

"Get out of the way," Jared cried, flinging wide the gate.

It took a second or more for the dazed, starving, blood-maddened beasts to make their escape. Then they fled, squealing in panic-stricken confusion, dispersing in all directions, until only the sow was left.

Jared knelt beside her. "Poor old girl," he murmured as the pig gave a final moan and died.

"Jared, look!" Maggie Royal pointed to a tiny black head seeking to emerge from beneath the sow's body. "There. She's lying on it."

One small piglet was left. All black, almost suffocated.

Maggie Royal took it in her arms and carried it some distance away. She sank down onto the ground by the pool. Her dark head bent over it as she slowly rocked back and forth crooning, "Oh, you poor little love. Poor, poor little baby pig!" She leaned down and kissed it on its wet pink nose. Sparrow heard the sudden intake of Jared's breath. Then Jared leaned down and touched her cheek as softly, as gently as the brush of the yellow cabbage butterfly's wing that rose from her shoulder.

Maggie Royal looked up and saw his eyes. For a long moment their glances held, his green and piercing, hers soft and darkly violet.

The morning sun slanted down, long jagged streaks of lemon light through the green oak leaves. Sparrow heard the raucous call of a Caspian tern, which meant he might catch a glimpse of one if he hurried, but he too seemed caught within the magic circle, the green-gold whispering silence, the tenderness and loveliness of Maggie Royal's face.

Now there were only the two of them on the island, in the world. For in that moment in time and space, for Maggie Royal and Jared and the little newborn pig lying between them, nobody else existed.

In spite of the glory of the morning, Sparrow was filled with sadness. He knew then the end of hope, like the final realization he might never see a Stark snipe. Subconsciously he had dreamed that one day Maggie Royal would look at him as she had just looked at Jared. A foolish hope, he knew now. To Maggie Royal he was just Sparrow, fat and funny and absentminded, not to be taken seriously. Nothing could exist between them but the lasting friendship that grows from having been young together, having shared these special timeless, sun-splashed days.

Now that he saw it before him, he realized it was Jared who made her alive, free to ride along the beach like the wind, her black hair streaming behind her. Jared could calm her when she was upset, or incite her to fury if he chose to. A look in his eye, a touch from his hand, and he could chase away time and give her today.

Today, Sparrow thought. But what of tomorrow? Jared's eyes, unlike his sister Susan's, were forever fixed on distant horizons, like those of his stallion, King, when he stood with his head upthrust gazing at something only he could see. Trying to tame him would be like attempting to catch a wisp of cloud.

The forest shut behind him like a door. There was an empty space in his heart that no number of birds, not even the Stark snipe, could fill.

At Long Point, Jared's mother laid the piglet on one of her Indian blankets and fed it warm milk from a bottle.

After lunch Susan showed Sparrow an advance copy of Roger T. Peterson's *Field Guide to the Birds*. It was an autographed copy of the book which the noted ornithologist, a frequent visitor to the island, had recently written and had published.

She told him then about the cardinal that came to the feeder Jared set up outside her downstairs bedroom window—and what pleasure it had given her to watch it hop onto the sill as she lay in bed, how she had learned to communicate with it by answering its loud slurred whistles.

"Then one day the cat came," she said. Her eyes glistened with tears. "The bird was so tame it refused to be alarmed. The cat sprang. I saw the beautiful red wings thrash frantically. Then its beak stopped opening and closing and it fell still in the cat's mouth. The bird lay where the cat dropped it, its fabulous color dimming, its feathers turning all scruffy."

Sparrow took Susan's hand and held it tightly.

Susan's eyes were soft and brown as the wings of a marsh hen. "Oh, Sparrow," she said softly. "You do understand."

He remembered his childhood when he lay listening to strange and unfamiliar night sounds, and realized that although Susan was surrounded by a warm and loving family, she, too, knew what it was to be afraid of the dark.

On an island, one begins to see and hear things one never noticed before, to see the miracle of nature, not as a visitor but as a guardian.

A layer of orange-pink over cerulean blue reflected in the marsh water, turning the tall cord grass, "Moses weeds," to gold, as Sparrow set out alone from Long Point that afternoon. The beach was so thick with shore birds it looked as if there was no standing room. Gulls scuttled and quarreled. Terns eddied and rose in a carillon of wings. Sandpipers crouched and twinkled.

He turned onto the path through the woods. As he approached a particularly thick part, he saw a flash of an orange tail. It was flying in a rapid zigzag pattern.

My snipe, he thought excitedly. It could be my Stark snipe. His hands were trembling. He was afraid to breathe for fear his wonderful discovery would disappear, when suddenly Maggie Royal crashed out of the underbrush. "Have you seen the tackies?" she cried.

Sparrow saw a flash of brown, and that was the last of his snipe. "No," he answered sharply. "What species is it?"

"Oh, Sparrow, not birds, horses!" She sank down onto a log lying on the ground. She had on ragged shorts and a blue shirt, rent at the shoulder. Her bare feet were muddy and scratched. "I've looked everywhere!"

"They'll come back, won't they?"

She went on as if she hadn't heard him. "Jared will be furious. I only wanted to ride Azilia, but that bay gelding Gramma wants to sell Lewis pushed past me, and the others followed before I could shut the gate." Her eyes filled with distress, and he noticed a red scratch along one cheek.

"Why should Jared be angry?" he asked, thinking of his lost snipe.

"After Gramma saw how well Jared did with King, she put him in charge of selling off some of the tackies and mares in foal."

"Well?" Sparrow sighed and started to fold up his telescope. "What do you want me to do about it?"

"Not a damn thing!" Jared exploded out of the brush. "This is Maggie Royal's problem." His eyes gleamed the color of the palmettos after rain as he strode over to her and pulled her to her feet. "How many times have you been told not to ride alone unless you write on the blackboard where you're going?" He shook his head. "Stubborn, pig-headed, just like that mare."

Maggie Royal planted her feet apart. She looked very small, defiant. "Azilia's gone, too, Jared." Her lips trembled. "I'm sorry. I didn't mean to cause any trouble."

"Trouble? You're nothing *but* trouble!"

"Oh!" Her hand went to her mouth. She took a backward step and might have fallen over the log if Sparrow hadn't caught her.

"It doesn't seem to me you're solving anything by shouting at each other." Sparrow gazed regretfully at the warblers the Negroes called "Lord God." They'd been flitting in and out of the oaks, working in little bunches. He would have liked to observe them more closely. "Shouldn't we look for the horses?"

They ignored him.

"King's gone, too," Jared said. "Jumped out of his paddock. By now the horses we're trying to sell have probably run through Cullen's wire fence and hurt themselves." He glared at Maggie Royal. "Especially that mare. She hasn't any more sense than you have. Don't you know by now not to go around in your bare feet? Snakes, sand spurs, you name it."

"She has so got sense!" Maggie Royal shouted. "She has more sense than that stallion of yours!" She turned aside. Her eyes sparkled with tears, and Sparrow sensed she would rather die or step on a rattlesnake than let Jared see her weep. She rubbed the tears away with the backs of her grimy fists and plunged back into the underbrush.

Maggie Royal left word she would not be at Great Oak for dinner. She put on sneakers and her red sweater, and, joined by Adele and Thorny, started out, plunging and crashing through the thick growth, making enough noise to frighten away all the birds on Stark Island. As there wasn't a chance of seeing or hearing their evening songs, Sparrow concentrated on not falling on the rough terrain which the pigs had rooted into holes and furrows. Commandeered by Jared, they walked the new fence line and covered the south end of the island near the empty corrals. The sun sank behind the marshes and the moon did not rise. Soon it was so dark it would have been impossible to see an elephant, let alone a horse.

They were in the wildest part of the island, where the poachers came up the tidal creek in their bateaux, not far from the boneyard at High Point, where the bones of the Negroes who had been lynched mingled with those of the animals buried in the ravine. The Negroes spoke of the place with awe, saying it was full of hants and evil spirits like the terrible Plateye.

Jared extinguished his flashlight, plunging them into darkness. Sparrow's palms were clammy. Sweat broke out on his forehead as his childhood fear of the dark reasserted itself.

He stumbled into a swampy pool, got water up to his waist, and twisted an ankle. He thought about snakes and alligators and wondered if he could find his way back to Long Point, sit in that fine warm kitchen with its wonderful smells, and eat Jared's mother's crayfish cooked in cream while he told Susan about almost seeing a Stark snipe.

Every so often Jared or Maggie Royal said something nasty to each other. "All right," Maggie Royal said finally, "I'll go off on my own."

Adele complained about the sand flies. "I see why Gramma says the sand flies were put here by God to keep the damn Yankees from taking over the South."

"Shhh," Jared said, stopping so suddenly they all banged into one another on the narrow path, like the seven dwarfs.

"Nah, don't do it that way," a familiar voice said. "Do it thisaway!"

"Wait," a second voice said. "Don't use the whip. Try and gentle her. Now, stroke her. See, she's calming down. Now, see if you can . . ." There was the sound of a struggle. "Nope, didn't make it," the first voice said. "Once I git holdt a her, I'll tie her down."

"Cullen," Jared whispered. "Son of a bitch."

Sparrow had a wild illogical urge to laugh. The black night, the weird conversation, and Jared's extraordinary anger. Something bit him, and he jumped, breaking a stick underfoot.

Jared plunged through the heavy growth. Sparrow followed as well as he could with his ankle now starting to hurt.

They came out in a small clearing. Jared switched on the flashlight, disclosing two men holding a horse.

Jared's voice shook with fury. "Let the horse go, you bastard."

"Now, Mr. Jared . . ." A whining, unfamiliar voice. "We weren't fixin' to do nuthin' with her, just trying to catch her for you."

"Get going, Lewis," Jared ordered, "before I have my father get out a warrant for your arrest as a horse thief."

"Yes, sir, Mr. Jared," the dealer replied, dropping Azilia's lead rope and vanishing into the dark.

Jared turned to Cullen. "So you've taken up poaching on the side."

Before the farmer could reply, King burst from the shadows into the clearing. At sight of Cullen the stallion reared. In the dim light he resembled a carved horse on a Roman frieze, ears flattened and teeth bared, frozen in time in his primitive rage. His nostrils were red and distended as he struck out, trying to savage the terrified farmer.

"King!" Jared's voice rang out like a pistol shot. "No, King." He walked up to the horse, within range of the flailing hooves.

The horse hesitated. His front feet returned to the ground and he swiveled his head around to face his master.

"Get going," Jared commanded, catching hold of King's head, as Cullen ran into the shadows.

"Stark." The farmer spat out the name. "I'll see you and your dad in hell."

Maggie Royal emerged from the brush. Azilia nickered at sight of her. She took the lead rope from Thorny, who'd been holding the mare, and looked at Jared.

"Adele thought the men had a girl," Thorny began, and doubled over laughing.

Maggie Royal looked at Sparrow, with his trousers torn and covered with briars. She made a choking sound that grew into raucous laughter. Jared looked at them both and then at Adele, starting to giggle. Then he too joined in. Sparrow forgot about his sore ankle as all of them roared, shattering the silence of the black night, causing the horses to gaze at them in wonder.

They found the other horses grazing quietly in the park near the great oak. The tackies followed King and Azilia back to the stable, where Jared checked them over, pronouncing them sound before turning them out and making sure the gate was securely latched.

Adele and Thorny stayed at Great Oak. Maggie Royal left word she was going to spend the night with Susan and walked back to Long Point with Jared and Sparrow.

There was a driftwood fire in the fireplace when they got there. Jared's mother cut pieces of homemade bread and heated up chowder. The little pig lay on piled blankets by the hearth alongside the dogs. The firelight danced in Maggie Royal's eyes as she described the hunt through the woods. Jared told of finding the mare.

"Cullen had her," he told his father. "Cullen and Horseface Lewis. I've seen him skulking around the south end of the island. I think Cullen's responsible for the rustling that's going on. You know that herd that roams the east side of the island. I noticed the other day that several steers were missing. There don't seem to be as many horses this year, either."

Jared's father nodded thoughtfully. "In order to do anything, you have to catch him in the act."

Jared got up and walked over to the fire and stared down into the dancing flames. Then he took his fist and banged it against the pine mantel. "By God, I'll catch Cullen and make him pay!"

Maggie Royal forced back a yawn. "A long day."

"Of course," Mrs. Stark said. "You're in the room at the end of the hall. The one with the Charles Dana Gibson, the man proposing on his knees."

"As if any man would do that!" Jared scoffed.

Maggie Royal's eyes flashed. "It's nothing to me. I never intend to get married!"

"Oh, don't you, now?" Jared grinned.

"Oh, you . . ." She pivoted around. "Good night, all." She smiled around the room. There was blood on her cheek from the scratch.

"Think we can trust you not to get into trouble between here and the second floor?" Jared reached out his hand and traced the thin red line of the scratch on her cheek.

His voice was suddenly husky. "No going off alone again, hear!" His finger moved to the shark's tooth on the chain around her neck. The way she stood gazing up at Jared, with the soft trusting and strangely expectant expression he had seen the day they carried the surviving pig home from the corral, wrung Sparrow's heart.

Coming from the harshness of New England, Sparrow found the Southern physical world a kind of gauzy conspiracy against reality. It nurtured the taste for the extravagant. The mood that lingered in his memory was one of rich odors, the perfumes of wisteria, jessamine, and magnolia, of pine woods and pale blue fog, or yellow-gold sunlight and the soft sensuous languor in which nothing seemed impossible other than the bareness of truth.

One morning Sparrow went with Maggie Royal and Jared to visit Dah in her little tabby house in the settlement.

"Her real name is Meena," Mr. Stark had said, "but to generations of Great Oak children she's Dah—that's the Gullah word for 'nurse.' Nobody knows how old she is. She's the high priestess of Gullah mysticism on the island."

The old nurse was almost blind and bedridden. "Dat you, missy, tunka punka?" she called out, greeting Maggie Royal with the Gullah for "darling." "God bless you. Take this place right beside the bed so I can look into your face."

"She thinks Maggie Royal is Gramma," Jared whispered as Dah's face, all bones and wrinkled skin, mirrored her delight. Her white hair rose like the spun-sugar rosettes her daughter, Cook Ada, concocted to decorate her cakes. Beneath the intricately designed patchwork quilt her body seemed shrunken, infinitely frail.

" 'Bout time you come see your old Dah. Come closer, tunka punka. Seem like it's gettin' dark and I can hardly see. Dat de master with you? Come." She extended her hand to Jared. "Yawl take this place beside my little tunka punka. Take her hand." She released Maggie Royal's hand and placed it in Jared's. "God bless you, child. Dat's perishable!"

"Perishable?" Maggie Royal asked softly.

"I done tole you, child, 'bout de old Gullah ooman. She so tired she jus a-settin' and a-rockin'. Come a knock at de door!" Dah reached up and knocked twice against the bed's headboard. "'Who dat?' she call out. 'Henry.' 'Whatcha got, Henry?' 'Bushel of peaches.' 'Henry, jus set 'em down by de door, for I'm too tired to get up and fetch 'em.' That's for true." She sighed and plucked at the quilt with her long bony fingers. "Pretty soon come another knock. Knock. Knock." Again Dah rapped against the headboard. " 'Who dat out there?' 'William.' 'Whatcha got, William?' 'Bushel of yams.' 'Jus set 'em down by de door, William, for I'm too tired to rise and fetch 'em inside.'

"Pretty soon comes another knock! 'Who dat?' " Dah asked once again.

" 'Sam.' 'Sam, whatcha got?' 'I ain't got nuthin',' Sam says. 'Nuthin' but a bushel of love!'

" 'Sam, yawl come right in!' de old ooman call out. 'Dat thing is perishable!' "

Dah turned her eyes toward Jared. "Somebody get de lantern for me. Ah'm ready now for de boat. Tunka punka, I ain't been lazy. Dat's for true. But de chilluns is grown and I'm weary ob de fight. Lord, I got for walk down that lonesome road without my man, without dat thing!" She stretched out her hand and touched Jared's. "Take care of my darling tunka punka." Her voice trailed off. "Dat thing is perishable!"

Slowly Jared and Maggie Royal rose. Still holding hands, they stood gazing down at Dah. The old woman's face against the white pillow was as still as the carved oaken bed her first husband had built for her and in which all of her children had been born.

Sparrow felt his throat tighten as Jared put his arm around Maggie Royal's waist and gently drew her away.

Two days later Sparrow was awakened by the sound of drums. Mr. Stark said the drums were announcing the "setting-up" to be held that evening for Dah, who had died during the night.

After supper they went to the little tabby church, "the praise house," behind which, beneath the bearded oaks, the setting-up was taking place.

"Death is a vital part of Gullah culture," Jared explained. "In the days of slavery it was the only freedom, the only release. The 'separatin' line' is the mystical line that separates heaven from earth. Crossing the separatin' line is celebrated by a night-long wake, a setting-up with shouts and ring dances and food set out. To the Gullah the ultimate tragedy is not death, but a death watch without the traditional coffee and bread to sustain the deceased on the journey across the separatin' line to eternity. Without the proper observance of the funeral ceremony, the spirit will never rest in the grave. The deceased becomes a wanderer on earth, haunting houses and burial grounds."

The little church cemetery was a rough field surrounded by barbed wire. The graves with their faded wreaths of paper flowers, broken crockery, bottles, and rough crosses, on which the names of the dead were written in a labored scrawl, were guarded by primitive wooden heads of men and animals glinting blindly through glass eyes.

The Great Oak mourners were already there: Gramma in black hat and veil; Maggie Royal in a tweed skirt and felt riding hat; Uncle Oomlot in his Sherlock Holmes hat, flowing cape, and carpet slippers; the aunts, whom Dah had brought up; and her well-dressed relatives from the mainland, children, grandchildren, great-grandchildren, and five small great-great-grandchildren. They all sat in a circle on the ground, rocking backward and forward, chanting, a strange and eerie humming made all the stranger by the weird primitive wooden heads with their eyes glittering in the shadows.

"Oh, pray right on, oh, pray right on, I don' need this world no more, for when I cross dat separatin' line, I can leave this world behind. Oh, sing right on, jus' sing right on . . ."

Oysters were roasted on iron bedsprings serving as a grill. Then children and grown-ups hopped shrieking and giggling as they swooped and knelt, doing the buzzard lope.

Cook Ada, her hands and arms ringed in silver against her "arthritis," stood in the center of the circle of dancers waving a tambourine made of Coca-Cola bottle tops. The bearded oaks swayed with them, making strange shadows in the eerie light of the fire and flambeaux as the mourners chanted:

> *Throw me anywhere in dat ole field*
> *I don't care where you throw me in dat ole field*
> *Throw me over hills and mountains, in dat ole field*
> *But still my soul is heaven-bound in dat ole field.*

"The ring dances, the shouts, go back to ancient times," Mr. Stark said. "Then the people made up songs, as Cook Ada puts it, 'To pacify thy own self.'

"In those days," he continued, "there were no caskets. The dead were buried anywhere in 'dat ole field.' They called it the boneyard, and the buzzards circling overhead for their prey were the principal witnesses."

Coffee and coarse homemade bread were passed to all. Then the corpse in a coffin Gramma had ordered from the mainland and insisted Dah be laid out in, was anointed with morsels of bread and three drops of water. The mourners were instructed to pour coffee into the casket for sustenance on Dah's way to eternity.

The grave was what the butler Newt called "un stylish grabe," well decorated with the deceased's effects.

Dah's porcelain pitcher and washbowl were smashed and scattered to symbolize the brokenness of life. The alarm clock she had used to awaken countless Great Oak children for nursery breakfast was set to awaken her on Judgment Day. The flashlight Gramma had given her was placed in her hand in order to light her way along the dark path to heaven, and the last objects she used—a bottle of aspirin, Vicks VapoRub, a mustard plaster, and a bottle of the cough syrup she'd administered to generations of children for croup. Beside the carefully carved marker her grandson Newt had made her lay the clay pipe she had smoked and an empty bottle of Uncle Oomlot's best Kentucky bourbon, which he had provided her in order to ease her "dropped palate" (sore throat).

146

"In olden times," Jared's father told them as they walked home, "animals were slaughtered to help speed the deceased on their way. A white chicken or a pig, and once one of Cullen's ferocious, evil-looking hog hounds was killed and left hanging on the barbed-wire fence to bleed on the grave of one of the field hands the farmer had beaten with his long-thonged whip."

The days, Sparrow suddenly realized, had passed too quickly. It was a magic time, as golden as the light shafting through the rich forest green, as bright and shining as the early mornings and the late afternoons when they sometimes went fishing for mullet with Joe-Ali.

He remembered one clear, cold afternoon. Joe-Ali had a fire going in the bucket in the bottom of his bateau. While they huddled around it, the giant Negro paddled along the creek.

"Never wish an island fisherman luck," Jared advised as Joe-Ali began arranging his net. "In Gullah it's a sign it will be bad. Island fishermen spit on their bait for luck. They throw away the thirteenth shrimp or crab and start out with the same rig used for their last big catch."

Taking one edge of his cast net in his teeth, another in one hand, and a restraining line in the other, Joe-Ali sailed the net out, letting it fall in a graceful circle onto the water.

When they pulled it in, it was full of wriggling mullet and the tiny translucent shrimp that grew in the marsh before becoming large enough to go to sea.

It was coming on toward what Joe-Ali called "sun-lay-down" time when they headed for home.

Jared sat with his back against the gunwale, gazing up at the sky. He was watching a Ford Tri-Motor from the airfield. He shaded his eyes with one hand, squinting upward with the same knowing expression Sparrow had seen on Al Daniel's face one day when Jared took him to the airport to meet his instructor.

The Long Point hawk was making his first circle of the evening flight. He soared higher, hardly moving his wings as he passed overhead. Sparrow could see his red tail feathers, like fire against the soft colors of his belly.

Suddenly the hawk went up and up. His circles widened as he drifted toward Great Oak, a dark speck with wings, like the plane. For a moment he hung motionless, outlined against a cumulus cloud. Then suddenly he was falling fast, in rhythm with the plane, swooping down, down, down. Faster, faster they dived, until it seemed both would hit the ground. Suddenly the plane spiraled upward again, but the hawk was gone.

"After one of Cook Ada's frizzled chickens," Jared said lazily.

The clouds were orange now, the color of canned apricots. Slowly the orange turned pink, then purple.

"Isn't the sunset beautiful?" Maggie Royal said.

"I've seen better," Jared answered. "Compared to some island sunsets, that's what Uncle Oomlot would call a sunset ordinaire!"

"I reckon the sky's worth looking at," Joe-Ali mused. "I have an idea it's a right nice place, but I don't want to go there until I have to."

"I'll take you up one of these days," Jared said. "And you'll change your mind."

"Man meant to fly," Joe-Ali said, "he'd been born with wings, like that hawk."

They drifted along the narrow creek in the dimming light. Walls of marsh grass pressed against the sides of the bateau as Joe-Ali recited the fable of the tortoise and the eagle. There was, he said, in Gullah dialect, a terrapin sunning by the seashore. "Seagull float right over him in the element. The cooter, he want to ride that sky like a bird. Please, suh, he say to the seagull, help me fly! But the seagull laugh at him.

"The cooter beg the seagull so hard to teach him to fly that the seagull call to the eagle floating around in the element. 'How much you gonna give me,' the eagle asked, 'to float you about in the element?' 'All the rich things in the Red sea,' replied the terrapin. Now, you know very well, suh, a cooter ain't got nuthin' that came out of the Red sea, not even de swamp. But the eagle don't say that. He catch de cooter in his claw, and off they go, up and up till they ain't but a speck high in the sky. They fly over the sea and over a mountain. The eagle open his claw and the cooter drops down, down. Before he smash his shell on a rock, he says to himself, serves me right. Poor fool! Can't even move about the earth, let alone fly. God made some men for creep, some for walk, some for run. Jackass for dance, foot will trip up. Snake try for sing, have frog in his throat."

There was a crunching sound as an oar wedged itself between oysters growing on a bar. "Plateye grab it," Joe-Ali said, wrenching the oar free.

"Plateye?" Sparrow asked.

"Plateye causes a lot of trouble," Jared replied. "Right, Joe-Ali? Far as I know, it's not known to have any recognizable form. Nor does anyone know the derivation of the name. Nonetheless, Plateye inspires real fear."

Sparrow gazed at Joe-Ali. In the dying light his proud, regal features could have been carved on an Egyptian frieze.

"Did you vote for President Roosevelt?" he asked.

"I don't vote," Joe-Ali said succinctly, "because I'm not permitted to vote."

"I'm not either," Maggie Royal said. "Not until I'm twenty-one."

"I'll be looking at fifty soon."

"Then why can't you vote?" Maggie Royal persisted.

"Black people aren't supposed to. Most of my people can't read or write. White people want to keep it that way."

"That's wrong," Maggie Royal said indignantly. "Everyone's supposed to be equal."

148

Joe-Ali nodded. "Men see only the color of my skin. They are unable to see that the rows of corn I plant are straight and true. Or how I can hollow out a tree, build a bateau fit for most any weather. It matters not to them that I have never done any man or woman wrong, that I owe no man or woman and am beholden only to myself and that which is mine."

He swung the tiller to avoid a log floating in the channel. "I pay no mind, for I am rich and the men I speak of are poor!"

"Rich, Joe-Ali?" Jared asked.

"Rich!" Joe-Ali repeated. "I have my bateau and the fish in the sea, the oysters in the creeks and the rainwater to wash them down. I can look at the day crack and hear the music in the wind. I can see the birds in the sky and the sun lay down." Sparrow looked at the proud, sculptured face of Joe-Ali. It seemed to him that the strong, straight features and finely shaped head spoke of bitter racial history. The longer he was on the island, the more he felt that sinister and contrary forces were at work. He felt it in the soft air, the silence, the secretiveness, and the great bearded trees. In the nights, languid and sensual, silent but for the mournful hoot of an owl or the melancholy sound of a foghorn. Somehow they unleashed passion, made any carnal act seem possible, almost natural, in that remote landscape where nobody would know.

Three days before New Year's, Jared sat on the steps of the Long Point house sketching the head of Maggie Royal's mare Azilia from a photograph Sparrow had taken. Sparrow was going over his life list, wishing that in the few days he had left on the island he could add a Stark snipe to it. Maggie Royal and Susan sat on the porch.

Jared's parents had taken the boat to the mainland. Jazzbo had come in the night, saying his son Jimmy had been accused of stealing a ham from the Starksville restaurant where he worked as a waiter, and had been jailed. Jared's father had gone to the mainland to see about his release. His mother, who needed food supplies and wool for her weaving, had accompanied him.

Suddenly Jared's dogs began to growl. Cullen and his hounds were approaching along the street. Cullen had a bottle of pop from the corner store. Now, as he walked along, he concentrated on dropping peanuts into the mouth of the bottle, shaking it up and then taking a swallow. Taking the bottle from his mouth, he wiped it with a swipe of his hand. His rolling, swaggering shuffle and his face, the color of Susan's cardinal, indicated he had been drinking something stronger than pop. He paused at the gate. "Hey boy," he called to Jared. "Come here, boy."

Jared put out a hand to restrain his dog Rufus. "Were you speaking to me?"

"Yes, sir, boy. It's 'Yes, sir,' when you address a white man. But I reckon people passin', like you and that Affey, wouldn't know that."

Sparrow could hardly believe his ears. Obviously Gramma knew nothing of the farmer's swaggering insults or she would not have tolerated them. He saw the color drain from Jared's face.

"I'll spell it out for you," the farmer said, opening the gate and starting up the walk. "Pretending you've got Indian blood." He spat into the border of narcissus. "Everyone knows most all the niggers on Stark Island are related to Starks. Stark mad, they say."

There was a deathly silence. Sparrow felt his hands growing cold and his forehead starting to break out in sweat. Both girls were sitting bolt upright, rooted to their seats.

Slowly Jared started walking, moving with that indefinable woodsman's grace, toward the heavyset farmer. Something in his face must have caused Cullen to realize he had gone too far, for unconsciously he took a backward step.

"Get out," Jared said, confronting him. His face was white with fury. "Get off this property."

With lightning speed the whip snaked out, catching Jared across the forehead. "Take that, you nigger-lovin' son of . . ."

As Jared staggered, the pointers lunged at the leopard dogs. Cullen turned to order them out of the yard, but Jared grabbed the big man by the shoulder, spun him around, and hit him across the mouth.

Cullen dropped the whip, lowered his head, and charged into Jared the way his "git 'im" dog charged a boar.

Their bodies locked together as they wrestled, their panting like that of the wild stallions Sparrow had seen fighting on the beach.

"Jared!" Maggie Royal screamed. "Oh, Jared." She leaped down off the porch and came at a run. Grabbing the whip, she lashed out at the farmer, hitting him across the back and shoulders.

There was a sudden deathly silence. All the figures seemed to stop, stay motionless for an instant. Susan sat rigid in her wheelchair, her hands gripping its sides, her eyes wide with shock. Cullen's arms dropped to his sides and he swayed with his head down, mumbling unintelligible oaths. Jared stood glaring, his fists doubled up, his eyes black with rage as blood dripped down from the cut on his forehead.

"Get out," he repeated. His voice lashed out like the whip, which he snatched from Maggie Royal and thrust at the farmer.

They watched as Cullen took his leave, sobering now. Possibly he was aware he had gone too far, for at the gate he paused and looked back. He started to say something that might have been a kind of apology, but Jared's expression stopped him. With a shrug he coiled his whip, whistled to the dogs, and started back along the street.

"You would have to get into this," Jared cried, turning on Maggie Royal. "Just once, couldn't you have minded your own business?"

The red line of the cut on his forehead stood out lividly in his dark violent face as he grabbed the astonished girl and began shaking her.

"Stop it," Susan shrieked. "Jared, have you gone mad?"

"Maggie Royal was just trying to help," Sparrow injected.

"That's the trouble!" Jared continued shaking her wildly. "She's always just trying to help. Well, this time she's gone too far."

Sparrow was angry now. "Jared, let her go," he ordered, walking up to him. "What the hell has gotten into you?"

Jared let her go so abruptly she staggered and fell against Sparrow. For an instant he held her, feeling her breath against his cheek. The pounding of her heart was soft and pulsating, like that of the terrified mourning dove with a broken wing he had found one morning in the seeded field near Middle Point.

Jared turned and stormed off to the house.

"Everything I do is wrong." Maggie Royal pressed her fist against her mouth. "I was afraid. Cullen's so big, so heavy. . ." She backed off, her eyes huge and helpless. "Why?" she whispered. "Why is he so angry at me, always angry, like the other night when I let the horses get away . . ."

Sparrow thought of Jared's face as he had stood touching the scratch on her cheek the previous evening. He thought he knew why, but somehow he couldn't tell her, not then.

"Don't you think you should tell Gramma?" Susan asked when Maggie Royal had gone.

"No." Jared was adamant. "This is between Cullen and me."

"But how can he stay on here?" Sparrow asked.

"Gramma's getting old, and she's worried about the island and about money. Every time something comes up, she insists Cullen is the first farmer she's had in years who knows how to make the farm pay."

The farmer's days, however, were numbered.

On New Year's Eve the traditional party was held at Great Oak.

Jazzbo and his Long-Point band had set up their instruments in the front room, where the rugs had been rolled back and the floor waxed. Guests from the mainland and neighboring islands were already dancing.

They came in an assortment of vessels ranging from motorboats to their parents' yachts. The boys drank corn "likker" from flasks in the bathroom or out in the garden. They talked about poontang and laughed uproariously at their racist jokes.

The girls wore filmy, floating dresses with puff sleeves and small waists and stood in clumps, giggling throughout the evening. They reminded Sparrow of the flocks of parakeets that twittered and screeched over the islands of Honduras, where he'd spent a summer crewing on a boat. Sparrow tried to talk to them but found their conversation virtually another language consisting of drawn-out cries and finishing-school chirping sounds not unlike the sounds Jared made calling out the wild-turkey gobblers during the mating season.

Sparrow found Maggie Royal in another room, playing Monopoly with the children.

"May I join you?" he asked, noticing the long slender curve of her neck and shoulder.

"Are you sure you want to?" she answered quickly, looking past him to see if Jared was with him. "Look!" She indicated the board. "I'm being murdered. I can't get past jail!"

"I always end up paying a luxury tax," Sparrow said, sitting down between her and Harry the Horror, who had a huge pile of Monopoly money in front of him. "Somehow I never get to Boardwalk!"

They played quietly for an hour or more. From the big room, they could hear the band.

"It's almost New Year's," Maggie Royal said, standing up. "Let's go see what's happening." Suddenly there was a fanfare of drums. Horns began to blow. "Come on," she said, and they ran to the big room just as the lights went out.

Sparrow found himself being pushed and shoved in the midst of a lot of strangers kissing, giggling, and wishing one another the season's greetings. He had always tried to avoid such occasions, and wished he was back at the Long Point house playing chess with Susan.

Thorny pulled Maggie Royal under the mistletoe and kissed her cheek.

"My turn," Jared said as Thorny turned away. In the dim light from the remaining candles, Sparrow could see Jared bend down. He thought he was going to kiss her, but he did not. Jared was never demonstrative. (Susan had explained it: "Jared hates to be touched. He squirms when I hug him. Maybe he gets it from Mother. She doesn't like Father to touch her in public. It must be the Indian in her.") The gesture he made was more meaningful than any kiss. He tipped her chin up and slowly, very gently touched the corner of her mouth where there was a tiny dimple.

The band had stopped, but somebody put on a record of "More Than You Know" on the wind-up Victrola.

Slowly Maggie Royal and Jared began dancing, moving together as if they had always danced together. Fire and ice. Light and darkness. The pulsing melody, the piano chords, filled the secure, high-ceilinged rooms, where it seemed trouble could never enter. Sparrow wanted to hold the moment, sustain it like the rippling, long, drawn-out notes, as if time itself could be slowed down and they could always remain as they were then.

At one o'clock the guests began leaving. Jared and Sparrow were at the door, saying their good-byes, when Noble LeFevre came in.

"Big doings at Cullen's house," he said, addressing Jared. "You ought to take your friend. Part of his education in Southern culture." He rolled his eyes mysteriously and lit one of his cheroots. "Better than Bourbon Street."

"Sorry, not interested." Jared brushed past him and went out into the night.

Not wanting to be impolite, Sparrow mumbled an excuse about rising early to go to the egret rookery and hurried out after him.

It was a foggy night. The great house, throwing pools of light into the darkness, looked immense. The trees in the park, some of their parts obscured by floating mist, seemed alive, as though moving in a wild dance themselves.

Jared walked silently ahead. He seemed in a hurry to get home. When they reached Mule Way, he turned off onto the shortcut that led past Cullen's house.

The house was well off the main track running through the center of the island, in a remote wooded area. The overseer who lived there before the Civil War was said to have murdered a number of slaves by hanging them from the branch of the "hanging tree" in the yard. The Negroes insisted they heard cries in the night and considered the place haunted.

This suited Cullen, allowing him to entertain his courthouse and Klan friends at wild parties which the Negroes spoke of in whispers.

Jared's dogs bounded ahead. Jared called to them, but the pointers, scenting Cullen's hounds, had already jumped onto the porch, growling and sniffing.

All the windows were open, and one could see into the house. A table was piled high with bottles. Jared told his father later he recognized some of the most influential men in the county—Matt Harper, the sheriff, Harold Haskins, the Klan lawyer, Judge LeRoy Upton, Mutton-head Malone, who owned the market, Horseface Lewis, and the pastor of one of Starksville's churches. Little Willie Rigsby sat apart in a corner, half-hidden by the fringed shade of a Kewpie Doll lamp won at the annual fair. The light caught the lenses of the bagman's glasses and the drops of perspiration on his forehead.

The women from the mainland ranged from light cream to black. They were sprawled on sofas and chairs and in the men's laps, in various stages of disrobement and drunken abandon. In the center of the room one danced alone, naked.

Sparrow felt a sudden irrational fear mixed with guilt. Gooseflesh prickled his skin as he stared, mesmerized. Her powdered face and red fixed smiling lips could have been a tribal mask. The eyes were hollow and dull, totally impersonal, as she moved mechanically through the obscene motions of her number.

"The dancer from the fair," Jared murmured disgustedly.

Sparrow was unaware that Jared and the dogs had retreated into the shadows and that he was alone. He could not take his eyes away from the slow, sensuous figure undulating to the tinny strains of the Victrola. The woman seemed oblivious of the men watching her, their lips loose and wet, like Cullen's "catch" dogs when they caught their quarry. The diamond that Sheriff Harper wore on his little finger glittered as he extended his arms, twisting his ample paunch in a slow grind. Little Willie Rigsby's maimed foot, in its high black-laced shoe with the built-up sole, beat a tattoo on the floor as he kept time to the tinny music.

Sparrow was torn between horror and fascination. This, then, was the double standard, the hedonistic behind-the-scenes sexuality, disguised by servility, the Sunday-go-to-meeting conformity. He shivered. The safety, the security of Stark Island, had suddenly become a dark, alien, brooding country, a savage land shaping people to its own image, a place where violence lay beneath the exterior coating of gentility as slivers of thin ice disguised the turbulent rushing current of the sound on a cold morning.

He was about to turn away when Cullen entered the room dragging the girl Affey, the maid he had seen in the hallway at Great Oak on Christmas Day. She was wearing the Japanese silk Gramma had given her and which she had made into a handsome dress. It was torn off one shoulder and her legs were scratched.

"Got me a virgin!" Cullen announced loudly. His beefy fingers sank into the girl's soft, creamy flesh. "Found her walking in the woods. Put a twitch on her and brought her here!"

The men forgot the naked dancer, who seized the opportunity to escape. They moved toward Affey, reaching out to touch her.

Sheriff Harper began unbuttoning his trousers.

"Nope." Cullen pulled her away. "Willie's first. Willie worked hisself into a decline gettin' you all those votes last election." He winked at the sheriff. "Might take the name of that dog that voted off the rolls. Buckeye Luttrell's name, too. Figured out he's been dead some ten years. Willie had him cast a dozen or more votes! Come on, boy," he called to the bagman. "Get going 'fore I change my mind."

"No!" Little Willie cried. "Leave me alone." He fought to free himself from the men laughing and crying out and trying to haul him from his chair to the cringing girl.

"S'matter?" Cullen jeered. "Cantcha get it up?" He turned to the others. "Told you he worked hisself most to death. Now he can't even find it! Come on, son." He glanced around at the company, some of whom, unable to control their erections, were clutching at their trousers. "Shucks," he said to the men holding Little Willie. "Let 'im go. We ain't gonna wait all night."

Little Willie let out a stifled sob and crumpled back into his chair. His face twitched and broke into ripples, like the surfaces of the island ponds. He threw a wild glance at Cullen. For an instant his eyes burned with a raw hatred, overriding his shame.

Cullen reached for his whip as Affey frantically tried to escape. Her beautiful dress ripped all the way down the front as she broke loose. The girls were screaming now, and the men cursing and yelling. Bottles and furniture crashed as Cullen chased the terrified girl around the table.

154

They caught her as she reached the door. Cullen and the sheriff lifted her from the floor and began tossing her in the air. Her limbs flailed like a rag doll's, wildly and without direction. Her hair whipped around her face, frozen into a mask of fear and disgust.

"Lookahere, boys," Judge Upton said, suddenly sober. "If Mrs. McDermott should hear . . ."

"*You* lookahere!" Cullen shouted furiously, pausing to wipe sweat from his face. "Just because this one thinks she's Stark gentry don't make her no different." He grabbed Affey's arm and pulled her from the sheriff. "Why, you ain't white. You ain't black. Girl, you ain't nuthin'!"

"Jesus!" Jared said, materializing out of the shadows. "I took the dogs away so Cullen's hounds wouldn't kill them. Sparrow, how long has this been going on? Never mind. Christ!" he gasped as Cullen slapped Affey across the face, attempting to subdue her. "We've got to get her out of there."

Sparrow felt sick. Briefly he was afraid he might vomit. He saw the avid red faces fastened on the half-naked girl, could almost hear the rapid breathing, smell the stale sweat. For one terrible second Affey's despairing, hopeless gaze seemed to meet his. Then he heard Jared shout. "Cullen, let her go!"

The farmer whirled at the sound of his voice. As he did so, Affey managed to twist from his grasp, dart between the men and out the door. Cullen gave a bellow of rage and lunged after her.

"Let her go," the judge shouted. "We don't want any trouble!"

Cullen pushed him aside. "Catch her. Hold her!" he commanded his hounds.

Although Affey was as fleet as one of the island deer, the dogs were faster. They surrounded her, pinning her against the yard fence.

"Jesus!" Jared cried out again. The still-unhealed wound on his forehead from Cullen's bullwhip stood out, a jagged uneven welt in the dim light, as he leaped down from the porch.

The rush of people pouring from the house overtook him. The sheriff wrapped his arms around him, hauling him back.

"Let me go!" Jared roared. He wrenched free and took off after Cullen.

Sparrow tried to follow, but tripped on an uneven board at the edge of the porch and fell. His bad ankle turned, and he crumpled in pain.

Jared caught Cullen and whirled him around. Sparrow heard the thud of blows, gasps, and a muffled groan as Jared landed a glancing blow on Cullen's head.

The big man staggered backward. "Git 'im!" he screamed.

While the other dogs held Affey prisoner the "git 'im" dog lunged at Jared. The attack from behind knocked him off balance. He staggered and fell, hitting the side of his head on one of the jagged whelk shells bordering the path. The dog stood over him growling and slavering.

"Lookahere, boys," the judge cried. "Time we were off."

With a courtly gesture he called to the women already collecting their belongings, "Come along, ladies. If Mrs. McDermott . . ."

The men needed no further urging. Before he finished the sentence they faded silently into the shadows, hurrying along the path to the hidden cove where the boats were moored.

Sparrow hobbled over to Jared, who was trying to pull himself upright. Blood oozed from the side of his head where he had struck the shell with such force that he was temporarily dazed.

"Got to find her," he muttered.

Jared recovered in minutes, but the forest was already silent. Cullen and Affey, the rest of the party, had vanished. Only a few broken bottles and the reek of spilled liquor remained as evidence.

"We've got to find her," Jared repeated desperately. "I keep thinking it might have been Maggie Royal."

"I'm afraid I can't help," Sparrow said abjectly. "I've sprained my ankle."

They did not find Affey. The boats were gone by the time the search party reached them. Old Ugly's pond and the tidal creeks were dragged. Every inch of Stark Island was gone over. When two weeks had passed, it was assumed that Affey was dead.

"In this state, *corpus delicti* has to be established before a man can be tried for murder," Mr. Stark said worriedly. "We've got to find the body before we can prosecute."

Gramma dispatched Captain Ben to the mainland with a message for the sheriff. She told him that if the farmer was not caught and convicted she would call on her good friend Franklin Delano Roosevelt to stop all relief payments to the state of Georgia. Furthermore, she threatened to get in touch with one of the Pritchards who was an editor of *Time* and give him the entire story, including tales of corruption in the courthouse, how the Klan had burned a cross in front of her relative Jared Stark's house and dragged the lawyer from the platform when he spoke in Starksville on behalf of Negro sharecroppers.

She also offered a substantial reward for any information concerning Affey.

Then she shut herself away in her room.

MAGGIE ROYAL

1935

· 7 ·

The morning before Maggie Royal was to return to school, Gramma called her into her bedroom. Gramma's favorite white camellias veined with pink, which grew in the greenhouse from the original Michaux bush, had not been arranged as usual in the silver vases. Annie Itch, the pet pig, and Marcel, the spaniel, had not been combed and the fire in the fireplace in front of which they rested had not been lit. The mono-grammed silver, velvet-lined Tiffany jewelry box "Mr. McDermott" had made for her when they were married no longer overflowed with the multicolored gems Maggie Royal had played with as a child. Instead, it stood on the dressing table closed, its contents locked inside.

The faint distinctive scent Maggie Royal always associated with her grandmother remained, a unique blend of camphor, witch hazel, calamine lotion, lavender, and attar of roses. Only, fainter, lighter, and fragile, like memory.

Gramma motioned her to her bedside. She no longer looked formi-dable as she lay back against her lacy pillows. Maggie Royal had never thought of her as old before. She had seemed indestructible. Now she seemed diminished, drained of the courage she lived by. She looked as Maggie Royal imagined she would when she was dead, with only the Stark bones unchanged.

"Maggie Royal, I should have spoken long ago." For an awful mo-ment Gramma looked as if she might weep. It struck Maggie Royal that seeing her grandmother cry would be like watching the great oak topple. "Your dear father." She shook her head helplessly. "They say I spoiled him. I reckon I did. He was my only son. Mr. McDermott wanted a son so badly." She took hold of Maggie Royal's hand. Hers felt dry, brittle, like the dead vines on the settlement fences at the end of summer.

"When your father was born, it was wonderful," she continued. "He was such a handsome, loving little boy. Everybody adored him. Child, hand me my water glass." She took a sip, and went on. "Joe-Ali was his best friend. Joe-Ali and his younger sister, Mary." She paused and stared out the window at the moss on the great oak swinging to and fro, and the warblers darting in and out. She drew a deep breath. "They went riding and fishing, did all those things together. I thought nothing of it. But there were nights that spring before your father went away to Harvard . . . nights when his bed wasn't slept in. Joe-Ali came to me. You see, your father . . ." Her hand tightened on Maggie Royal's. "Your father had gotten his sister in a family way!"

"Oh, Gramma . . ." Maggie Royal said. Her throat felt dry. It was hard to speak.

"I didn't know what to do. Mary was beautiful, light-skinned, almost white. She had that regal walk and manner Joe-Ali has, and the same features, too. Still, there wasn't any overlooking the fact she was colored. I sent your father north to college."

"Gramma, what happened to Mary?"

"She died giving birth to Affey." She spoke slowly, staring fixedly at the oak outside her window. "People did in those days, and Mary's pelvis was too small—she was so young . . . barely fourteen. There wasn't a doctor available, only Dah, as midwife."

"Oh, Gramma . . ." Maggie Royal repeated, and then stopped. It was a while before either spoke again. Gramma held on to her hand and gazed out the window as if she'd never seen the great oak before. Maggie Royal listened to Cook Ada calling to the chickens outside the kitchen door.

"Gramma," Maggie Royal managed finally, "I always knew Affey was different, but I didn't know why. I wish I'd known she was family."

"What would you have done if you'd known?" Gramma asked, bringing her eyes back and giving Maggie Royal one of her penetrating "see-through-you" looks.

"I don't know," Maggie Royal answered miserably.

"I didn't know either. I truly believed it was better for Affey if people didn't know. The awful thing was that there was no place for her, no place at all. Oh, my God . . ." Gramma turned her face against the pillow. She let go of Maggie Royal's hand. "Now, leave me, Maggie Royal."

Maggie Royal rose and slowly went to the door, half-expecting to see Affey silently waiting there, her strange, knowing look unchanged.

"Maggie Royal . . ." It was Gramma's old peremptory voice again. "You are not to speak to anybody about this, hear? Not anybody, ever. I've spoken to Joe-Ali and he agrees it's best. Nobody is to know."

As she went out the door, Maggie Royal heard her grandmother say to herself, "It was her eyes . . . the way she looked at me. . . ."

Maggie Royal told no one what Gramma had said. But Joe-Ali knew, and she sensed others knew too. She tried to pretend everything was the way it had been before, but she knew as she and the others left to return to school that it never would be again. From then on, whenever she looked into a black face, she saw Affey's eyes, saw her gazing at her as she had when she thought Maggie Royal wasn't looking, watching her with that curious expression on her face that was like a blackboard wiped clean, saying nothing and yet leaving Maggie Royal with a lifelong burden of guilt.

The next day, Maggie Royal said good-bye to Gramma and the aunts and all the servants and gave Azilia a double ration of carrots. "I wish I could take you with me," she told the mare, kissing her soft nose. "But you wouldn't like the North. You wouldn't be happy, away from King and the island." She left Azilia munching carrots and went to catch the island boat to return to Miss Mayo's.

Gramma and Susan wrote to her. From their letters Maggie Royal was able to piece together what was taking place on Stark Island.

By March there was still no trace of Affey. No body, no witnesses to what might have happened to her.

This was the situation on St. Patrick's Day, when Mr. Stark received a handwritten note asking him to be in the alley behind the aunts' Starksville house after the annual parade.

Jared's father waited in vain under a lamppost while the local Irish celebrated at the Hall House, Starksville's historic hotel.

The next day, while he was walking along the beach, Little Willie Rigsby popped out from behind a dune and limped up to him.

"Lawyer Stark, remember the note about meeting in the alley?"

Mr. Stark nodded. "I waited. Nobody came."

"I was there, all right." Little Willie dug the rounded toe of his specially built shoe into the sand. "Cullen and them, they was drinkin' at the Hall House. I left to meet you, but the sheriff came cruising around in his car. I got scared and ran." He paused and gazed out at the ocean. "You remember the time Big Boy Tarrington tried to take my land away. My ma been in the hospital with pneumonia and I couldn't make the mortgage payment."

"I remember," Mr. Stark said.

"You fixed it up at the bank for me to get a loan." The bagman gazed up at Mr. Stark. "I ain't forgot what you did." He glanced around fearfully. Convinced the beach was deserted, he continued. "If I tell you sump'n, you guarantee you won't tell nobody it's me that told?"

"I promise."

Little Willie took a deep breath. "Well, you ain't never gonna find no body."

"What?" Jared's father drew in his breath.

Little Willie paused and stared down at his feet. "They was all the time funning me, shaming me. I ran away. Back to the boats. Next thing I know, Cullen's got the girl, carrying her, and she's dead. He put her in a sack. Then he took the boat out to sea past the sandbar, and dropped off the body."

"Thank you," Mr. Stark said after a pause. "I wish you'd told me before."

"I wanted to." Little Willie gave a sigh of relief. "But I figured anybody found out I talked, Cullen might get me next." He glanced up. "You promise nobody will know I done tole you?"

"You have my word," Mr. Stark said.

Little Willie was wrong about not finding the body.

Cullen was not a seafaring man and reckoned without the tide.

It seemed a terrible irony that Joe-Ali should be the one to find the sack containing the bloated, decaying corpse, washed up on the bank of the tidal creek where he was fishing. It was all Jared's father could do to restrain him from going to the mainland, calling out Cullen, and killing him.

Sheriff Harper was one of the "good old boys," a Klan member and drinking companion of Bo Cullen. He was a soft, pudgy man with a hankering for grits and redeye gravy, the way his wife, Essie, prepared them for his noonday dinner. The lid of his left eye was torn. It gave him the faintly Oriental look of a fat Chinese brigand. The damaged eye, which he had almost lost, was a memento from the Klan, members of which had "roughed him up" for being so ignorant and flagrantly "illegal" as to arrest a Klansman for killing a Negro in retaliation for his stealing a cow. To be sure, the jury had freed the killer, calling it "justifiable homicide," even though the Negro had been ambushed and shot in the back. Nonetheless the sheriff was still considered slightly suspect. Every so often someone at the Plantation Bar or around the courthouse would bring the matter up, reminding him that as long as he kept on doing what he was told, he'd live to eat plenty more grits. Otherwise . . . well, just no way to tell what might happen!

Whenever he was agitated, he rubbed his torn eyelid. It was a reminder not to go against the Klan.

Jared's father found him at his desk in the county jail. "I want you to arrest Bo Cullen for murder," he said without preliminaries.

"Bo Cullen?" The sheriff pretended surprise. He leaned his chair back against the wall, beneath the plaque Gramma had ordered put up when she redid the jail after Maggie Royal's father was held there.

"You mean 'count of that nigger girl you been looking for on Stark Island." The sheriff stopped polishing his ring and stared at his fingernails.

"Yes. I want to talk to Bo Cullen." Mr. Stark spoke in his soft, even drawl. The more concerned he was, the lower, the calmer his voice.

"Let's see, now." Sheriff Harper squinted up at the white plaster ceiling, across which a fly was making a slow, erratic journey. "New Year's Eve, wasn't it? Just so happens Bo spent the night in town. Told me he missed the island boat. Came around to the house to talk about poachers. Reckon it was 'round midnight when he went up to the Plantation Bar. Said he was going to see some of the boys, have a drink or two to celebrate the new year."

"You and I know that's a lie, Harper," Jared's father interrupted. "We have witnesses who saw both of you on the island that night. Just bring Cullen in. Then we'll talk."

The sheriff looked at his diamond ring. Slowly he began polishing it, rubbing it against the sleeve of his khaki shirt. "I do recall sump'n 'bout that night. Seems to me your son assaulted an officer of the law. 'Course, I wouldn't dream of pressin' charges. You being Starks and all. No sheriff in his right mind would think of pressin' charges against people of your prominence."

Mr. Stark shook his head. "Won't work, Harper." He turned to leave. "Arrest Bo Cullen for murder."

The sheriff brought his chair back down to the floor with a crash. "Bo's got a lot of friends hereabouts. You don't just go bringing him in, like you would a nigger." He gazed slyly at Mr. Stark. " 'Sides, you ain't got no body!"

"Either you bring him in or we're going to bring in the FBI. Notify the press. *Time* magazine."

Sheriff Harper sighed. He began rubbing his drooping eyelid with the knuckle of his index finger. "I can't arrest him for murder. Not without *corpus delicti.* Anyway, he's gone out of town."

"I suggest you find him fast," Mr. Stark said. He paused at the door. Turning back, he added, "Try to act like a sheriff for once, even if you are a damn sorry excuse for one!"

Case No. 332: the *State versus William "Bo" Cullen,* charged with murder, was the most exciting within memory of the people of Starksville and the county. The trial was reported in all the Southern dailies and many Northern newspapers. Maggie Royal was at Miss Mayo's and read about it in *Time.*

Jared came down from Harvard to testify for the prosecution, describing in detail what he saw at Cullen's house.

Muttonhead Malone—Cullen owed him money for a year's supply of groceries and had refused to pay—also agreed to be a witness. Now that Cullen was behind bars, others came forward, including Jimmy, Jazzbo's oldest son, who came to see Lawyer Stark in his Starksville office.

"You got me out of jail, time for New Year's Day," he said, twisting his baseball cap in his hands.

"I did? I'd forgotten."

"I ain't," Jimmy replied. "Nor has Pa. Ma gave him the money for buy a ham for New Year's Day dinner. Pa lost it shooting crap at the corner store. I took that ham. I meant for give one back when I got my pay. But they put me in jail."

Mr. Stark remembered now. He'd gone to the mainland to post bail for the boy the day Cullen and Jared fought.

"Miss Maria baked a ham," Jimmy continued. "She had Pa bring it home for Ma, and Ma never did find out 'bout Pa losing the money."

"All right, Jimmy." Mr. Stark looked at the papers piled on his desk. "Good of you to tell me."

"I ain't finished," Jimmy said stubbornly. He swallowed and then proceeded doggedly to tell his story.

He had been walking out New Year's Eve with Charlene, Cook Ada's granddaughter. Before they reached the settlement, they saw the lights and heard voices. Jimmy could tell the men had been drinking. Knowing them to be nigger-hazers, he realized that if they found him, he'd be in trouble. He grabbed Charlene and pulled her down beside him behind the palmettos bordering the path.

Jimmy paused, not sure how to continue.

"Go on, Jimmy," Mr. Stark urged.

"Don' rightly know if I can," Jimmy murmured, looking away, and moving from one foot to the other.

It took a while to cut through his embarrassment and pin down his story. In spite of his mumbled shameful testimony, it was soon all too clear. When the other members of the party hurried ahead to their boats, Cullen remained behind with Affey. Enraged by Jared's attack and the liquor he had drunk, the farmer began beating the helpless girl with his whip. Then, fully aroused, he had his way with her.

When he was finished, Affey lay still, unmoving. Then Cullen lifted Affey's head by her long black hair. He drew the thong of his whip around her neck, fashioning a noose. Then, using both hands, he tightened the noose. When he was sure Affey was strangled, he removed the thong, recoiled his whip, and threw the girl's bloody, brutalized, lifeless body over his shoulder.

With Jimmy's testimony added to the information obtained from Willie Rigsby, there was little doubt about the outcome of the trial. Jimmy was spirited away to an undisclosed destination as protection from Cullen's friends. His halting yet moving and undoubtedly truthful disclosures of the events leading up to Affey's rape and murder had put his life in jeopardy. From then on until the trial ended and the sentencing took place, he was heavily guarded.

As the days passed and the case against Cullen became more airtight, the farmer's jovial mood of arrogant superiority changed. The laughing and joking subsided. Cullen's attitude became one of sullen anger.

Everyone agreed that Lawyer Stark's examination of the accused was masterful. There was no doubt but that his line of questioning caused Cullen to convict himself. "You're taking the word of a nigger against that of a white man," he shouted, enraged, after Jimmy's testimony was gone over point by point. His final statement was that because it was New Year's Eve, he had consumed a considerable amount of whiskey. Therefore he could not be held accountable for anything that might have happened during the evening.

Lawyer Stark's impassioned plea to the jury failed to bring the verdict he had hoped for. "Cullen should have been sentenced to the electric chair or at least put away for life," he told the Atlanta *Journal* and the Atlanta *Constitution*. "Instead, an appeal to the Pardon and Parole Board commuted the original sentence of twenty years to ten with the possibility of parole for good behavior."

Susan reported that Cullen passed Jared as he was led from the courtroom.

"Well, Cullen, it's over," Jared said grimly.

The farmer spat at his feet. "Ain't never gonna be over. Not till one of us is dead!"

Maggie Royal was what Aunt Lucy Howard, Adele's mother, called, in racetrack parlance, a late starter. Now she began to change.

She took her grandmother's advice and tried to forget the tragedy of Affey by plunging into school activities, by immersing herself in the school's social life, however intimidating and unreal. It didn't occur to her to rebel, to challenge her grandmother's authority. Nor, if it had, would she have chosen to follow the example of her mother, who at a time when divorce was still considered a stigma had chosen to divorce, not once, but twice. Maggie Royal was determined to marry once, for better or worse, have many children, and give them the love she lacked.

She found it did not take much of an effort to be popular. The secret was in conformity, talking with the same languid drawl as the rest, wearing the same clothes, baggy tweed skirts, Brooks Brothers sweaters, bobby socks, and dirty white "Wimbledon" tennis shoes or heavy Abercrombies with fringed tongues. It was a matter of knowing the "right" people, girls who went to Foxcroft, Farmington, Westover, or Miss Walker's; boys who went to Yale, Harvard, and Princeton, the small world of the suburbs, Sewickley and Lake Forest, Far Hills, Westbury, Greenwich, and the North Shore, of small horizons and large incomes, of shying away from anybody or anything that could be disrupting and not fit the intangible golden circle called Society.

That spring at the annual school horse show Maggie Royal won the Mosby trophy, awarded to the best rider in the school. The cup, named after the famed Civil War guerrilla leader, was given for the Confederate class. The girls wore peaked Confederate caps and only members of the Confederate Club were allowed to enter the class.

Adele's older brother Jere brought his roommate, Taylor Frederick DuPree III, from the University of Virginia for Easter. Adele, home from Farmington, said, "Wait until you meet him. He's divine and ever so rich. His great-grandfather built railroads and owned steamboats. He's a star racquets player and made the finals of the racquet championships at Tuxedo."

Jere introduced him to Maggie Royal. "This is Taylor DuPree. Scourge of women and foxes. Taylor, meet my little cousin Maggie

Royal McDermott, straight out of the wilds of Jawja."

Taylor was the popular founder of a group called the Roisterers. The Roisterers had members at all the Ivy League colleges.

To Roister seemed the only verb in their vocabularies, and the most serious thoughts in their sleek, well-shaped heads were the practical jokes they could dream up, and where to go after dinner, Eddie Condon's, La Rue's, the St. Regis, the Stork Club Sunday nights, or, if feeling flush, the Plaza to hear Hildegarde or Jack and Charlie's 21 for a late-night snack.

Taylor was good-looking in a faintly dissipated way, with bourbon-brown eyes, often slightly bloodshot from being out in the wind on the back of a horse or at the wheel of his maroon Chrysler convertible that he drove with the top down all year round. He had the slightly apologetic air of one who lives "high on the hog," as Aunt Lucy said, on money several generations removed from its source. Like many of the very rich, he rarely had any money in his pocket. "Pay you back next week," he'd say when the check for an evening of roistering was handed to him, and the other members of the party would have to come up with funds for the huge bill.

Maggie Royal's style, the way she rode and danced and her seeming indifference to him, intrigued Taylor. Instead of going home to New York for vacation after Easter, he shipped Tomboy, his point-to-point horse, from his Charlottesville stable to Middleburg for the remainder of the hunting season and the spring race meets. Magic days followed, days of hunting and riding home in the twilight to hot tea and leaping fires and dinner in the Howards' lovely old candlelit dining room with the ancestors gazing down.

Jared had told her to go away and grow up. With Taylor, she was doing it.

Still, there were times when she was desperately homesick for Stark Island. Each day she crossed out the date on her calendar, counting the days until summer vacation.

· 8 ·

Summer. Great Oak. Home. Gramma at the dock to meet her and smelling of lavender. The great oaks and the moss blowing in the wind. Gramma throwing firecrackers at the long-horned cattle to move them out of the path of the Packard. The wild pigs snorting and skittering at the car's approach. The dogs pouring from the house, barking, and Azilia with her head over the pasture fence watching. The light through the stained-glass windows and the polished door knocker. The smell of flowers and wax, of bread baking. The sound of voices. Cook Ada calling to newcomer Ada. Newt saying, "Howdy, Missy Maggie Royal, welcome home to Great Oak." Home from her first year at Miss Mayo's School.

Jared leaped off the afternoon boat, taller, darker, thinner, but with that same grace, moving all of a piece without wasted motion. He wore a Harvard blazer, white flannels, and tennis shoes.

Sparrow was with him, looking more owlish and absentminded than ever. He forgot his tripod, which Jared retrieved from the boat, and dropped his loose-leaf notebook in the sound. But he gave Maggie Royal a warm hug, told her she looked great, and asked her if she'd seen a something-or-other falcon he said was due any day from Mexico.

Jared and Maggie Royal shook hands formally, and there was a strangeness between them.

That night she had trouble sleeping. She thought of how Jared looked when they went clamming. She remembered the way the sun struck his long bare back, lean and brown, the muscles rippling beneath the skin as he bent over, crisscrossing the sand with his knife, then scooping up the clams he uncovered and dropping them with a metallic clang into the bucket. She touched the shark's tooth she wore on the chain around her neck and remembered the unfamiliar feeling she'd experienced as she looked at him, the almost irresistible urge to run her hand along his back, touch the veins and muscles and the warm soft skin.

She did not understand herself. During past island summers life had been filled with simple pleasures, doing things they had always done. Now tangled through this misty time were raw new emotions. Passions learned in books suddenly became real. She had trouble hiding her feelings. Everything seemed close to the surface, like the water bugs darting over the inland pools.

The winds of war were no more than faint warning zephyrs overheard on Uncle Oomlot's battery-charged radio. At Great Oak the days were spent as they had always been, doing the island things they had always done.

Into this element Jared had always fitted as easily and naturally as the wild horses, the deer and turkeys, and the wide white beach. But from the moment she saw him jump down off the island boat, the easy bantering camaraderie they had shared was replaced by something strange, almost fearsome that made her vault onto Azilia and ride like someone mad or haunted until the mood was replaced by tiredness that would allow her to sleep.

It seemed to her that they stood on the brink of something new, were being pushed toward it, not by their own desires but by time alone, by the forces of change gathering strength in their bodies, the chemistry of growth that caused Jared to suddenly become several inches taller, acquire a deeper voice and broader shoulders and a new adult certainty to his step, whereas she was aware of sudden passions in herself, like summer squalls, and a despairing sense of seeking to hold on to things she felt were receding from her with the relentlessness of the waves receding from the beach.

Jolly Olly Irving, one of the Roisterers; a Carnegie connection from Cumberland Island; and several members of the Torrey family from Ossabaw came by boat for some of the famous beach picnics. Thorny and the boy cousins had friends from school and college. One was a heavyset entering freshman at the University of Virginia named Tyger Trimble. Tyger had been a star halfback on the football team at Woodberry Forest and had fallen head over heels for Adele, who seemed equally crazy about him.

In the pool house somebody always had a Bluebird or Decca record on the old wind-up Victrola. Maggie Royal learned to dip and bend and spin and shift, stamp and weave marvelous new patterns, invent new twists and turns and steps. It was easier to follow Jared than it was Thorny, who pumped her arm up and down, or even Noble, who was supposed to be the best and most polished dancer of them all. With Jared she could really move out, sensing his every change—shut her eyes and float, following each subtle variation of the music with the mesmeric magic of that time and place, seeming to pack into each piano chord, each soaring trombone note, each drum solo, the sweetly sentimental sound of the thirties.

On the beach and behind the dunes the college crowd went to neck. They drank beer and bourbon and Coke from their flasks or straight out of the bottles that, following the old tradition, Newt left on their bureaus each day. They had petting parties, and once Maggie Royal stumbled over a couple writhing and gasping, in the throes of what Constance called a "dry fuck."

Mornings there were bottles and rubbers littering the beach. The first time Maggie Royal found a condom, she didn't know what it was. She decided it would be a fine thing in which to carry the little ghost crabs she planned to put in Constance's bed. She was carrying them home when Adele stopped her.

"For Pete's sake, don't let Gramma see you with that!"

"Why on earth not?"

"Don't you know what it is?"

"A little bag."

"You are a dope!" Adele said, shaking her head and giving Maggie Royal one of her long-suffering looks. "I honestly don't know how anybody as smart as you are about horses can be so dumb about other things."

"Well, then, if you're so smart, what is it?"

"Boys wear it," Adele said succinctly. "So girls won't get pregnant when they go the limit!"

"Ugh!" Maggie Royal dropped the object, and the crabs scuttled away.

As they were walking home, she asked Adele if she had . . . gone the limit.

"I don't go in for petting like Constance," she answered evasively, "or those Starksville girls like Cindy Lou Tarrington. They're teasers. They let boys do things until the boys get carried away and want to go . . . all the way. Then they stop 'em."

"Well, have you?" Maggie Royal persisted, hoping for some first-hand information.

"Ummm." Adele gave her one of her mysterious looks. "It's hard . . . with Tyger, not to be accommodatin'. Sometimes, well, it's hard to stop. But I don't want to get pregnant. I'd be disgraced. Why, Maggie Royal, I wouldn't be able to come out. Anyway . . ." She tossed her brown curls. ". . . men like girls to play hard-to-get. Treat 'em mean and keep 'em keen."

In July the great turtles come out of the sea, lurching inland across the shimmering brilliance of sands lit by the turtle moon. Veering from side to side, the great ponderous antediluvian monsters crawl, leaving a wide double track, to vanish finally among the shadows at the foot of the dunes. They dig deep holes. Lights, noise, any distractions disturb them, until, finally, they go into a kind of trance. Then nothing distracts them, as they lay hundreds of rubbery Ping-Pong-ball-like eggs.

The night of the turtle moon was the first time Cindy Lou Tarrington came to Stark Island. She was the daughter of Big Boy Tarrington. Gramma called him a Southern carpetbagger, descended from the "poor white trash" who went to work for Yankees after the "War of Northern Aggression." He had made a fortune out of the foul-smelling paper mill now starting to pollute the coastal waterway. He was also president of the Starksville Bank and was now building a resort on Gwinnett, one of the islands off Savannah. Big Boy had breached the charmed circle of Starksville society, the narrow, private, poor-but-proud ruling class, by marrying Minnie Cantwell, the judge's daughter. Now he was seeking to achieve further respectability via his daughter's popularity, promoted by a press agent.

Cindy Lou was already something of a legend, one of those girls that because of a bold nonconformity are whispered to be "fast." Her fragile blue-eyed beauty and audacious manner hinted at worldliness far beyond her sixteen years—and made her the envy of her female peers, who followed her wherever she went, laughing when she laughed, copying her gestures and way of speaking, delightedly repeating her jokes and witticisms, generally at the expense of others. She had been expelled from a number of expensive boarding schools along the East Coast. An only child, adored by her father, she was rewarded for *not* doing things.

When she managed *not* to be expelled from Miss Porter's for climbing down the fire escape and having a late date, her father bought her a yellow Buick roadster. When she ran it into a tree, she was compensated for not being injured by being given an imported English hunter, presumed to be safer.

The boys called her the Starksville sexpot. They whispered that she rode side saddle, not because it was the proper way for young ladies to ride, but because it was improper. The friction provided by the pommel produced a pleasantly erotic sensation.

Noble had been making numerous trips to the mainland to see Cindy Lou. It was natural for him to invite her to the beach picnic the night of the turtle moon. From that fateful day when Cindy Lou first came to Stark Island and, as Adele said, "batted her baby blues at Jared," nothing was to be quite the same again.

Cindy Lou came ashore like a young princess. Her shoulder-length hair was almost the color of silver. She wore boy's jeans with copper rivets, slung low on her imperceptible hips. However, no boy ever looked like Cindy Lou. Constance told the girls later that Cindy Lou immersed herself, wearing the jeans, in the swimming pool, in order to get them to fit her curves like skin.

Noble stepped forward to help her along the rough, uneven dock, but she brushed past him as if he were one of the oak trees. Widening her blue eyes in a way Adele described as sickening, she directed them at Jared, saying in an accent as thick as her eyelashes, "Jaredy Stark. Ah jus' cahn't wait to see every bit of your li'l ole island!" Her voice had a sharp, shrill sound that shattered the illusion created by her face. She glanced around at the shaggy, mossy trees and enormous chimneyed house in the distance. "Ah think it's jus' darlin', so rustic and all!"

"The New South rising," Thorny said cynically.

"Hush," Adele cautioned. "I declare, just look at Jaredy!"

Maggie Royal only half-heard her. She sat rigidly on Azilia, aware of a sudden sour taste in her mouth. Jared stood staring at Cindy as though hypnotized, like one of the island deer when a poacher's light was shone in its face at night.

Finally he rallied, offering her his arm and steering her over the dock's uneven boards as she continued to chatter, flashing her eyes at him, her pale hair swinging as she tossed her head backward and forward, like Azilia when she was overbitted.

"What a lovely horse!" she exclaimed, stopping in front of Azilia. "Jaredy, you must show me every bit of your island." She gave him a long, slow, sliding glance and ran the tip of her tongue over her full coral-tinted lips. "Jaredy, I'd just love to ride this mare. Ah'm sure I could . . ." She looked up at Maggie Royal, bareback in her raveled shorts. ". . . if children ride her!"

Maggie Royal was nonplussed. Jared knew that she never let anyone else ride Azilia. Now she heard him saying, "Well, if Maggie Royal doesn't mind."

"It so happens . . ." Maggie Royal began, and then saw the pleading expression on Jared's face.

"Thanks, Maggie Royal," he said gratefully. "Guests have the other horses, and I'd like to show Cindy Lou the island. That is, if Noble—"

"Noble doesn't like to ride," Cindy Lou said quickly before Noble could reply.

"Quite right. Horses don't like me, and I don't like them!" Noble answered flatly, turning on his heel and walking away.

"Here." Maggie Royal flung the reins at Jared and followed Noble. "I thought she was your girl," she said, catching up to him.

"She's not my girl," Noble retorted vehemently.

"But, Noble, you liked her . . ."

Noble stopped and faced her. "Does a hound dog like possum?" He spoke so loud some of the guests walking up from the pier paused to glance at him.

"Jaredy, you know Ah can't ride any way but side," Cindy Lou was saying. "Ah'm sure to fall off ridin' astride. Besides . . ." She looked over at Maggie Royal. ". . . Pa says it ain't ladylike."

"Maggie Royal," Jared called to where she stood looking at Noble's retreating back, "would you mind taking Azilia back to the barn and putting one of the side saddles on her?"

Maggie Royal started to protest that Azilia had almost thrown her off the time she rode her side saddle in the Starksville Horse Show. Then she thought better of it. They could take their chances.

Thorny, Jazzbo, and Jasper were shooting crap in the tack room when she went in to get the side saddle.

"You lettin' another lady ride Azilia?" Jasper asked wonderingly as he helped her hoist up the heavy, awkward saddle. "You know dat mare ain' a-gonna like it!"

"That's what I'm hoping!" Maggie Royal said, and they smiled understandingly at each other.

Cindy Lou had changed into field boots and a light tan linen habit.

On her head was a straw boater with a brown ribbon tied around it. Jared gave her a leg up. She lifted her right knee over the top of the pommel and slid her left foot into the iron. Jared slipped the elastic around her right foot and smoothed down the linen side-saddle skirt. Then he tested the girth and pulled the balance girth up another hole.

"Jaredy, my stirrup is too short. Dammit, stand still," she said angrily as Azilia began to fidget.

Jared let the stirrup down a hole.

Cindy Lou put her weight on the iron and stood up. "That's too long."

Jared shortened it again.

"I reckon it'll just have to do," she said resignedly.

She picked up her reins, settled her hat firmly on her head, and asked Jared to hand her her crop.

"Azilia isn't used to a whip," Maggie Royal said.

"Well, she'll have to get used to it," Cindy Lou replied airily. "I never ride without one."

Cindy Lou's hold on the reins was too tight, and she was tossing her head as she talked, as much as Azilia was tossing hers.

Jared, on King, trotted alongside. He reached out and brushed away a leaf that had fallen on the shoulder of Cindy Lou's elegant tan coat.

"Seems to me Cousin Jaredy is overmounted," observed Thorny dryly, emerging from the tack room.

The cousins were playing stickball on the lawn when Cindy Lou and Jared returned on foot, leading King. Cindy Lou's hand tightened and then loosened as she held onto Jared's arm. She had lost her hat, and her long pale hair hung down her back. When they reached the great oak, Maggie Royal saw there was mud on the dimpled cheek and one sleeve of the fine linen habit was torn.

"Looks as if she was ridden hard and put away hot!" Thorny whispered. Maggie Royal realized it was for her benefit. For Cindy Lou, her eyes shining and with color in her ivory cheeks, was beautiful.

"Some pigs came out of the palmettos and the mare shied," Cindy Lou announced in a tone of accusation. "I punished her with my whip, and she whirled and threw me." She looked up at Jared. "I hardly know what I'd have done if Jaredy hadn't been there to scoop me up. He carried me a ways until I could walk. He's soooo strong!"

"Where is Azilia now?" Maggie Royal asked.

"She ran back to the stable," Jared said. There was an edge to his voice as he added, "Cindy Lou might have been hurt badly."

"If that mare belonged to me," Cindy Lou added pointedly, "she wouldn't be allowed to get away with all that nonsense."

"Well, she doesn't belong to you," Maggie Royal said shortly.

Cindy Lou's mouth twisted downward in an expression of contempt. "I wouldn't have her. No manners, like some people I know!" She tossed her head, and the long white-gold hair swirled across her face.

With a gesture of annoyance she pushed it back. "Ah declare, Ah'm a sight! My hair drives me mad. I wish to goodness ah could cut it all off, but Papa won't let me."

Male grunts and exclamations served as the anticipated protests.

"They make me sick," Adele whispered disgustedly. "Any woman looks sexy with hair hanging down her back!"

"I'll just never get it to look right by tonight." Cindy Lou turned to the girls. "Maybe some of you have a hair pin."

" 'Fraid not." Adele patted her short bobbed frizz.

"I have some bobby pins," Constance said, and Maggie Royal could have hit her.

"Thank you, dear." Cindy Lou took the proffered pins and made an effort to raise her arm. "Oh, my goodness," she cried. "Jaredy, my arm. I must have hurt it when I fell. Ah declare, I just can't raise it. Jaredy, you'll just have to pin up my hair."

Jared gazed around desperately, aware of the snickers from the cousins. Then with a determined gesture he took Cindy Lou's hair in one hand and began coiling it, as though it was a line on a boat.

"Ouch!" Cindy Lou shrieked as he anchored it to her scalp.

"What's this about a fall?" Noble drawled, coming from the house.

"I'm all right." She gave him a wan smile. "If Jaredy hadn't picked me up, I might have been a whole lot hurt."

"She doesn't look hurt to me," Maggie Royal said grimly.

"You couldn't hurt her with a hammer!" Noble replied.

It was feeding time at the stable. The horses stamped and nickered as Jasper opened each door and dumped oats and bran into their bins.

"Hawss came back by herself," the groom said happily. "They has an acksident fuh true. Mister Jared come walkin' back with da ooman, full of sweetmout. Palabuffrin," he muttered disgustedly, using the Gullah term for "sweet talk."

Maggie Royal felt better until it dawned on her that Jared would spend the evening consoling Cindy Lou for her bruises.

A big driftwood fire was shooting sparks into the night, which was blue velvet, so dark and soft you could feel it closing around you.

Jazzbo and his Long Point band were playing. Their rich, full-throated voices filled the air with the old island songs and spirituals, reaching high to heaven over the sound of the waves.

> *I look to the eas'—and I look to de wes'*
> *An' I see de chariot a-comin'*
> *Fo' gray horses all in de lead*
> *to lan' you on de udder side o' Jordan!*
> *Moses in de bulrushes fas' asleep*
> *Playin' possum in de two-bushel basket*
> *Ebery hair on e head was a penny wort of candle*
> *To light you on de udder side of Jordan!*

Maggie Royal sat on the beach apart from the others, her arms around her knees, staring at the swirling flocks of peeps and pipers and gulls crouching and twinkling in the sea. A number of the visiting boys made an effort to talk and be polite, but she did not encourage them. She seemed frozen in a kind of cold inner tension. She was like the mare Azilia. When the other horses nickered and sought her out to be friendly, she laid back her ears and kicked out at them. Maggie Royal wanted terribly to be accepted, but only on her own terms. She did not want to be a part of the herd.

Adele was making hamburger patties from a bowl and setting them on a rack over the fire. She had washed her short bobbed hair and it stood out from her head, shaggy and brown and uneven. She wore a dirndl skirt busy with vivid squares of Tyrolean peasant figures that made her ample hips seem heavier than they were.

Constance's beau, Jolly Olly Irving, came from Sewickley. He was big and easygoing, with reddish hair and a booming laugh. He talked about the Allegheny Country Club and Rolling Rock and wore a green Tyrolean hat with ski and racing pins on it. He had just returned from touring Europe with the Yale Glee Club. He said that Hitler had come to a concert in Munich and had liked their rendition of "The Whiffen-poof Song."

"Too bad you didn't gang up on him when you had a chance," Thorny commented.

Jolly Olly drank from his can of beer and wiped the foam from his mouth. "Why would I do that? He seemed like a pleasant fellow."

"Pleasant!" Thorny cried. "Do you know what's happening to the Jews in Germany? Just the other day—"

"Thorny." Constance looked up from tossing the salad. "No politics, hear."

Noble stood watching. He was drinking from a paper cup of Gramma's very heady punch, which he'd made headier with the addition of some rum he'd bought at the Plantation Bar. Every so often he threw a bitter glance at Cindy Lou, sitting with Jared, her fair head close to his.

"Shit," Noble said, draining the last of his drink.

Jared sat with his back against a dune, sketching Jazzbo's face in the firelight. Cindy Lou peered over his shoulder. Slowly, lingeringly, she drew her hand along the back of his neck. "Oh, Jaredy, you're sooo creative!"

While most wore shorts or blue jeans, she had changed to a low-cut blue dress with tiny buttons down the front that showed off her breasts. A full skirt flared out from her small waist. Aside from a touch of pale lipstick that made her mouth seem full and moist, she wore none of the rouge or vivid red lipstick favored by the other girls. Her hair swirled and bubbled as she moved her head back and forth, or fell like a pale silken screen as she listened to Jared with a rapt expression. Her lips, slightly parted, displayed a slight gap between her two front teeth. She had taken off her high-heeled sandals, and her toenails were painted a bright red to match her fingernails.

She smoked incessantly, her long restless fingers darting back and forth, the charm bracelets she wore—Constance said each charm had been given to her by a different boy—jangling as they slid up and down her arms. When she inhaled, a dimple appeared in her left cheek.

Sparrow and Thorny sat on the sand by Susan's wheelchair. Sparrow held up a rat snake. "Won't hurt you. Hasn't any teeth!"

"Ugh!" Cindy Lou cried, shying away. "It smells horrid. Where did you find it?"

"In the chicken coop. It's eaten so many eggs it practically fell into my arms." He ran his hands along the snake's skin. "Bumpety, bump. Nothing but eggs."

"Let me." Harry the Horror patted the snake. He was ten now, all knobby knees and elbows.

"Not on your life," Maggie Royal answered quickly with visions of the awful-smelling creature turning up in her bed. "You'd probably flush it down the toilet like the alligator."

Cindy Lou looked confused, and Jared told the story. He had found a baby alligator, which he gave to Harry on his birthday. The Horror had taken it home to New York and kept it in his toilet bowl, until it was accidentally flushed into the sewer. In order to console the boy, Harry's father had said that the New York sewers were full of baby alligators that had been flushed down toilets and lived in the sewers happily ever after, growing to enormous size. Since then, Harry had been flushing bits of hamburger and other food down the toilet of the apartment for the 'gators to devour.

"Well, what are you going to do with the snake?" Harry asked Sparrow.

"Study it awhile and then turn it loose."

"Well, do it fast," Cindy Lou said. "The smell is so awful it's taking away my appetite!"

Jared began opening oysters.

"There's a shark," he said, pointing with his knife. "I noticed him the other day." They all looked and saw the ominous black fin glide along the horizon. Jared looked around. "Remember, no swimming alone! Island rules. That goes for you, too," he called to Harry the Horror, who was wading out toward the sandbar. "You come back here, now, you hear!"

They ate the oysters with abandon. Adele with her bright, eager, alert, always cheerful face, was laughing at her Tyger as he tried to suck the flesh off the half-shell without dribbling. Jared finished his own and began talking about flying.

"I wish you wouldn't, Jaredy," Cindy Lou entreated. "It's so dangerous."

"Al says the greatest danger is starving to death."

"What happens if your parachute doesn't open?" asked Tyger.

"Jared doesn't believe in parachutes," Noble replied. "You put your head between your legs and kiss your sweet ass good-bye!"

"Noble, really," Adele said. "If Gramma could hear you!"

"I think I'm going to leave college and go to Spain," Jared said, suddenly serious.

"Nobody with any ambition goes in the Army," Thorny put in. "It's bourgeois!"

Cindy Lou's head snapped back. "Leave Harvard? Volunteer? Jaredy, you all jus' funnin'. All you Southern boys are jus' dripping with ideals and honor. Why, one of those tough Yankees"—she smiled up at Jolly Olly and winked—"could take you and chew you up into little pieces."

"We'll have to stop Germany somewhere."

"Jaredy, I do believe you're serious! Papa says we learned our lesson in the last war. He says even Roosevelt"—she pronounced it Rooosevelt instead of Rosevelt—"wouldn't be dumb enough to get involved."

"Sometimes you get involved in things whether you want to or not," Jared said, looking into the fire.

"Well, I think we'd be crazy to get mixed up in an old war." Cindy Lou tossed her head. "Why, it isn't even here. It's way over there." Her bracelets clanked as she extended her arms dramatically toward the sea.

"Jared's right," Thorny said seriously. "The Popular Front is our last chance against fascism!"

"Hitler's right about the Jews," Noble declared, drinking still another cup of Gramma's very heady punch. "It's the Jews who want to take over the world!" His face was flushed, and a lock of hair fell over one eye.

"That's crazy, Noble," Jared remonstrated. "You sound like Father Coughlin."

"Noble, don't be so bourgeois!" Thorny put in.

"What are you, a damn Com-mune-ist?"

"That's enough, Noble." Jared's only indication of anger was the scar that stood out lividly on his forehead.

Noble had been drinking when nobody was looking, and the effects of the rum-and-brandy-and-tea mixture were starting to show. That and his resentment toward Jared for monopolizing Cindy Lou.

"Nothing for you to be so high and mighty about." He lit a fresh cheroot and slowly exhaled the smoke. "Everybody knows your dad was out trying to get niggers registered so as to vote for the Jew Deal." With an elaborate gesture he placed the cheroot back in his mouth.

Jared's hand shot out and grabbed it. "You better apologize!"

"No need for you to lose your temper," Noble said sulkily. "I was just kidding."

174

"Ah'm sure Ah don' know what everybody's runnin' on about," Cindy Lou said. "Jaredy, come back here and sit down and give me a ciggy-butt."

Noble stared at her for an instant. Then he stuck out his chest in its loose silk shirt, striking the kind of pose that a matador does when facing a bull. His long, slender body and sculptured head looked handsome and elegant in the firelight, as, with characteristic deliberation, he extracted another cheroot from his silver case and lit it with the gold lighter that had belonged to his father. Slowly taking it from his mouth, he flicked an invisible ash from its end and shrugged. "Eat your heart out, Cindy Lou."

"Everyone up for supper," Adele said briskly, breaking the tension.

During supper the talk turned to turtles. Sparrow explained in his dry, professional way that in spite of their enormous size and ponderous nature, the sea turtles had managed to survive since Triassic times by being very careful in choosing a site.

"Instrumental beings," Thorny, who had been reading Marx, commented dryly. "Marine projectiles, designed to accomplish intrinsic ends for the Socialist State of Jawja!"

"You're so smart!" Harry the Horror cried, sticking out his tongue at Thorny. "Why ain't you rich?"

"Jaredy, give me another cig," Cindy Lou said.

Jared's face wore an expression of hunger and desire as he lit Cindy Lou's cigarette. Maggie Royal shivered, struck by a premonition of something wrong, out of place. It was as if behind her smiling face, Cindy Lou hated them, carrying within her the seeds of their destruction.

Jared slowly stood up. "Time we went to see the turtles."

The boys had drunk a lot of beer and started to sing. Jared cautioned them to be quiet as they followed the tracks from the sea to the dunes.

They didn't find any turtles—Sparrow said they were too late, the turtles had finished laying and returned to the sea—and pretty soon people began to pair off. Adele and Tyger vanished into the troughs behind the dunes. Constance and Jolly Olly wandered off along the beach. Others returned to the pool house to dance or play poker. Maggie Royal found herself alone, feeling the cold wet sand squishing between her toes and the night wind whipping her hair.

It's not that I wanted to go with the others or that I'm jealous of the Starksville sexpot, she told herself passionately. It's because I let them do this to me. Make me feel this lack, this emptiness. Her eyes felt gritty, as though sand was blowing in them. She shut them, fighting to hold back the tears sliding from under her lids.

Cindy Lou's voice came to her as clearly as the whining wind. "Ah declare, Jaredy, Ah've just never seen dark like this. Ah can hardly make out a thing. Jaredy, honey, hold my hand. I'm afraid of the hants!"

They were very very close, behind one of the dunes, and Maggie Royal didn't dare move.

"Can't see nuthin' in the dark but truth," Jared said, quoting Joe-Ali.

"Honey, Cindy Lou's skairt of the dark, ever since mah mammy shut me away in a closet once when ma-mah and pa-pah were out socializin'. Mean ole nigger! Pa-pah ran her plum' off the place, soon as I told 'im. Honey, you all don't think there're any snakes here?"

"Don't worry," Jared said dryly. "I'll protect you."

Suddenly the moon came from behind a cloud and Maggie Royal saw them clearly. Cindy Lou looking small and helpless alongside Jared's height and gazing up at him with her wide-eyed "come-hither" look. Maggie Royal jumped behind one of the tall yuccas, growing like sentinels among the dunes.

"Jaredy, honey," Cindy Lou pouted, "Ah declare my finger's so sore from stabbing it against that thing, that plant."

"Spanish bayonet," Jared said. "Very important. Keeps the sand from blowing away."

"Jaredy, honey, you're so serious. Don't you ever have any fun? Here, kiss it, baby. Make it well."

Jared took Cindy Lou's hand in his and bent down and kissed the finger she had pricked. Taking it away, Cindy Lou slid her arms around the back of his neck and pulled his head down to meet her upturned face.

Maggie Royal could not move, and there was a strange dull ache between her legs.

"Jaredy, Jaredy!" Cindy Lou whispered as they sank down onto the sand. "That feels so good." Her voice was like thick honey as she pulled his face against her chest, pressing his lips against her small, perfectly shaped breasts. Jared gave a kind of groan as he held her close. His white shirt glimmered in the moonlight. Beyond them the sea kept up its low roar and the fragrance from the creamy white flowers blooming on the yuccas mingled with the strange musky scent of Cindy Lou's perfume.

Jared unbuttoned her dress. He began to caress one of her breasts, gently kneading the nipple. "Oh, Jaredy," Cindy Lou gasped, "do that . . ."

"My God!" Jared said, and pulled her roughly against him, bending her body back. His mouth moved over her as she strained against him and his hand reached for her legs.

Then he was no longer gentle. With a sudden rough gesture he clasped one of the exposed breasts while the other hand pressed against Cindy Lou's crotch.

"Oh," Cindy Lou breathed. Her eyes were shut tight and her face wore a glazed, slack look as she began to moan and twist her body against his.

"Oh!" Cindy Lou cried again, and her writhing motions increased.

176

"Oh, Jaredy, harder, harder, don't stop, pul-ese don't stop. Oh, Jaredy, oh."

Maggie Royal wanted desperately to run until she could run no farther, then fall down on the hard-packed sand, press against it . . .

"Jaredy, what are you doing?" Cindy Lou said abruptly. She pulled away from him and began to button her dress. "No, Jaredy, no." She made a slapping gesture at his hand as he reached to draw her back into his arms.

"What the hell do you mean?" he asked gruffly. "Jesus, Cindy Lou."

"Honey, that's enough pettin'." Cindy Lou began brushing sand from her dress.

Jared's voice was a harsh croak. "Cindy Lou, you've got to let me . . ."

"Now, Jaredy, you know you're not like those youngsters out there. Honey, you're a man. You've got control." She shivered suddenly. "Ah'm as cold as a spook!" She stood up and began to run down the beach.

"Goddamn bitch," Jared muttered. "Goddamn tease." He used some words Maggie had overheard during the stable crap games. And banged his fist viciously against the sand. "Goddamn her to hell!"

Maggie Royal ran back to Great Oak. When she reached her room, she quickly undressed. She got into the huge claw-footed bathtub and scrubbed herself as hard as she could. Still the same sensation remained. Before she knew what she was doing, her hand stole between her legs, and there in the bathtub the aching, almost unbearable ecstasy was finally temporarily stilled.

The previous summer Jared had found the remains of a Curtiss JN 4 "Jenny" at the Starksville airport. He had bought it on the installment plan and spent every free moment rebuilding the ungainly wood-and-fabric biplane, which he planned to fly with Al Daniels' newly organized barnstorming group called the Devils from Hell. Now that it was completed, he spent all his free time flying. Occasionally he flew over the island, coming in low over the beach, waggling his wings at those who were on it, pulling up just in time to avoid hitting the trees.

"You gonna kill you'self, boy," Cook Ada warned Jared. "Who you think you is, Lindbergh, slippin' and slidin' around in the sky?"

Gramma, his mother and father, even the cousins tried to keep Jared from joining the aerobatic team and taking part in air races.

But Jared was not to be dissuaded. When the Jenny was finished, he laboriously painted the picture of a devil with flaming wings on the side of the fuselage and above it his name, with "Stark Island" written beneath it.

Since he'd been flying, Jared had acquired an additional aura of glamour as well as a certain swagger. He had taken up smoking and grown a mustache. A pair of wings sprouted from the lapel of his leather jacket, and he wore a large wristwatch, consulting it with the same frequency with which he gazed up at the sky, breaking off in the middle of a sentence to watch a plane overhead. His conversation was larded with words like "prop-wash" and "P-factor," "dihedral" and "angle of incidence." He advised Jazzbo that when driving the Packard he should "keep speed up and nose down in the turns," and told Noble he had a "negative stagger" when he emerged from one of his drinking sessions at the Plantation Bar.

On the rare occasions when he returned to the island, he spoke obsessively of his barnstorming experiences. Eyes blazing with excitement, he talked of the towns he'd been to, landing in pastures on a Friday, the rush to put up posters for the weekend air show, of collecting money for tickets and then taking up as many people as he could in order to make enough money to get to the next town. "Sometimes there'd be so many kids aboard the plane we could hardly take off. No matter. People just wanted to say they'd flown!" He spoke of landing on highways and refueling with auto gas into which he added a pint of denatured alcohol and a teaspoon of iodine. He had become adept at looping and flying upside down, and he perfected the "devil dive"—diving vertically from about five thousand feet, pulling out at the last second, and landing directly in front of the grandstand.

Maggie Royal saw past his words to flying clouds and windswept places, of limitless opportunity and indomitable youth. More than anything she longed to fly with him in the cockpit of the little plane that had replaced King and home, even Stark Island, in his affections.

On a hot July day he appeared unexpectedly, riding King along the beach. Maggie Royal was sitting with her back against her favorite dune, writing in her journal. Jared got off the horse and came up to her. She had to stretch her neck back to look up at him.

"I see you flying up there." She pointed to the sky. "I wish I could go with you. I've never flown in a plane."

Something in her voice caught him. He smiled his sudden brilliant smile.

"Come with me!"

They went over to Starksville on the afternoon boat. Jared drove her from the dock to the airport in the secondhand Ford roadster he had bought that summer with his barnstorming proceeds.

The Starksville airport was a rough pasture adjoining the fairgrounds. It was festooned with power lines which Jared said unnerved even the most experienced pilots. The dilapidated hangar was converted from an old barn, and the terminal was an unpainted shack from which drooped a torn windsock. Planes were drawn up on the apron, some abandoned and derelict following crashes, as dead as the deer carcasses hanging upside down outside the Great Oak kitchen in the fall. Others were unbonneted, their entrails exposed while people in coveralls worked over and under them. Jared jerked his thumb in the direction of a lanky scarecrow of a man bending over a plane engine with a wrench. "Barney Ellis, one of the Devils. Was third in the Bendix Trophy last year. The man under the old wartime Sopwith Pup over there is the Reverend Pollock. Flies every minute he's not preaching."

Al Daniels was working on the engine of his Lincoln Standard bi-plane. He had flown the mail with Lindbergh and barnstormed in Jennys. He was tall, over six feet, and as thin as a wing strut. His face had a bleak handsomeness, the features regular, lacking sensitivity but filled with a certain dogged courage. There were smudges of dissipation under his eyes and a narrow black mustache on his upper lip.

The aura of glamour that surrounded him belonged to those who attempt the outer limits, riding harder, flying faster, defying the bound-aries ordinary mortals set up for themselves.

"Al flew with the Fighting Ninety-fifth Pursuit Squadron," Jared told Maggie Royal proudly. "He knew your father. Called him Mad-man McDermott."

Daniels wiped a greasy hand on the trousers of his coveralls and of-fered it to her. "Your father was a fine flier." He punched Jared in the ribs. "Not like some I know." He winked at Maggie Royal. "Here we try to make pilots out of them who aren't and help those who are."

Jared grinned. "Al says I'm the living proof it doesn't pay to be smart."

"Yeah. I tell 'em to do what I say in the air and keep out of trouble on the ground. This is what keeps you alive and eating." He broke off to watch one of his students land. The trainer hit the ground, bounced once into the air, and then leveled off. "I tell 'em I don't care if they kill themselves," he continued, "but it'll be bad for business if they kill any of their passengers."

Jared told Al they were going to fly over Stark Island.

"Better wear your snake boots if you're putting her through the aer-obatics!" Al said, winking at Maggie Royal. " 'Case you come down in one of them swamps."

Jared's plane was drawn up on the apron, its garish flaming devil standing out against its red-white-and-blue sides.

Maggie Royal watched him inspect it. He went over the struts and the propeller and tested the amount of fuel with his dipstick. The plane looked very small and she felt her stomach roil as her fear of heights as-serted itself.

Jared handed her a leather helmet and a pair of goggles. He showed her how to secure the helmet and helped her into the front cockpit.

"Okay?"

She nodded. Her mouth felt dry and she was almost afraid to speak.

Jared climbed into the cockpit behind her and called to the line boy to prop the plane.

"Switch off!"

"Switch off," Jared repeated.

"Clear prop . . . Contact!"

The engine began to pop and sputter.

Maggie Royal gripped the edge of the cockpit in front of her and shut her eyes as the plane began to move.

At the end of the airstrip, Jared spun it around, revving up the engine until the noise was almost deafening. He glanced around her and grinned. The goggles hiding the upper part of his face gave him a strange, unfamiliar look, as if already he was airborne, part of another world. He waved, and then the plane suddenly leaped forward. There was the odor of exhaust fumes and its fragile sides vibrated as the plane gathered speed. Maggie Royal looked over the side. She saw the ground receding as the plane began its dazzling climb toward the sun.

The plane rose over the power lines, and the airport fell behind. Below lay a cornfield. Nearby a red barn. Cattle were huddled in the farmyard. Slowly the plane turned away from the lowering sun, heading east. Ahead rose the alligator shape of Stark Island, thick and black with trees in the center, tapering off to a thin, pointed tail at Long Point. Slivers of light struck the sound as it wound through the marshes, turning the waterways to silver bands.

The sense of being a part of the roaring and the wind and the brilliant light was unlike anything she had known before—a feeling of magic and power, of omnipotence, as if she were somehow godly, separate and superior from the antlike creatures below.

This, then, was what Jared felt, only more intensely, for in him was the power to direct this unearthly creation of canvas and wood, to cause it to zoom and bank and roll.

They were over Great Oak now, looking down on its many chimneys and Uncle Oomlot's tower. There was the wind on her face and the hum of flying wires as the plane dived. Maggie Royal felt her stomach pressing against her spine. Jared pulled out of his "devil dive" just as it seemed to her they were about to strike the top of the highest chimney.

Cook Ada came out of the kitchen door. Maggie Royal could almost see the whites of her eyes as she waved her arms at them. They flew on over the stable and the paddocks. The horses lifted their tails over their backs and snorted as the plane zoomed by.

Over Long Point Jared did aerobatics—barrel rolls, loops, Immelmanns, and "a hundred things you never dreamed of." Maggie Royal could identify the children watching from their yards and Jazzbo's "traveling" mule tied in front of the village store where the crap games took place in the back room.

The sun was sinking behind the marshes to the west when the field slowly came back into focus, the hangar, the planes on the ground becoming larger as they descended. They hit the uneven runway with a thump. The plane bounded once, back into the air. Then it settled and taxied slowly to its parking place on the apron.

The propeller gave a final slow turn and was still. Jared pushed himself up with a deft, agile motion and jumped down from the cockpit. His face, as he undid his helmet and pushed up his goggles, wore a look of completeness and ecstasy. "How did you like it?" he asked, taking out a pack of cigarettes. "Not too breezy?"

"It was wonderful, Jared. Truly."

"Better not let Gramma know about the aerobatics. She'll cut you out of her will."

"I don't care." Those moments in the sky had released her tension, made her unafraid once again, independent. Feeling unbearably happy, she tossed her head and did a dance step.

Jared forced his eyes away from her glowing face. "I'll take you back to the boat." He looked at his big watch. "It'll be in, time we get to the dock."

"You're not coming back?" She paused in the middle of a twirl.

"No. I have a date tonight."

There in the plane, hearing the strumming of the wires, she had experienced the closeness, the way it had once been when they raced along the beach together. High among the clouds she had felt caught up in the immensity of living, in warm tenderness and wonder.

Now he would not look at her. He glanced at his watch.

"Come on, Maggie Royal." He began walking swiftly to the car. "I'm late."

On the last Saturday in August the Devils from Hell put on their air show at the Starksville fairgrounds. There were to be balloon-bursting and ribbon-cutting, wing-walking, mail pickup, and parachute jumping. An air race was to climax the day.

The cousins and the Starksville sillies waited breathlessly for Jared. They saw him finally, walking across the field to his plane, followed by a crowd of small boys begging for autographs and a ride in his plane. He wore riding breeches, well-polished boots, a leather jacket, and the silk scarf Cindy Lou had given him. There was an air about him that caused the children to run after him and the eyes of the crowd to turn toward him, a mystique setting him apart from the earthbound mortals who came to experience for one squinting, gaping moment, as they stared at the tiny, death-defying machines silhouetted against the sky, a sense of immortality.

Jared's plane took off with the others in a whirring of propellers, snarling engines, and strumming of flying wires. Briefly the planes flew overhead in perfect formation, then came screaming down out of the clouds, one following another in the balloon-bursting event. It was like an airborne jousting match as each plane leveled off and headed for the balloons drifting down from the sky, seeking to break them with their propellers.

The announcer they called "Cotton Mouth" described it as a lesson in frustration. "How any pilot can pop a balloon with his prop has to be seen to be believed. Hard enough to keep one's eye on the balloon, let alone bust it!"

"They should meet Harry the Horror!" Maggie Royal said.

Then came the ribbon-cutting. The crowd let out a collective gasp as Jared's red-white-and-blue Jenny dived. "Too close!" the announcer gasped. "Rack that plane around and clip off little pieces in passing."

Maggie Royal looked in the other direction as her heart kept pace with the rising and falling roar of aircraft.

"Wait, wait," cried the announcer. "Pull up! Pull up! Level off, wise guy! He's going to go into the trees. Nose is too high! You can't fly that plane sideways. He's going into a stall. A stall? Into a spin." The announcer sighed. "This could just ruin your whole afternoon!" Another cry from the crowd, and then a sigh like raw ocean receding from the beach. This was followed by a roar of approval as the plane swooped low over the field and then began to rise. "Whew!" breathed the announcer. "That was close!"

The mail pickup came next. Each pilot was supposed to drop one bag and pick up another, set between two poles, with a grappling hook.

This was accomplished without incident, and Jared began to land.

"He's coming in low," the announcer said. "Ah, a perfect landing. Right into the sun! A daring figure he presents indeed!"

Jared cut his engine, pushed himself up from the cockpit, and jumped to the ground. The announcer clapped him on the back. "That was pretty close."

"I was at least five feet off the ground," Jared said, smiling.

The crowd laughed and clapped, and Jared grinned and waved. Then he was gone, leaving behind him a certain envy for his devil-may-care attitude and a feeling among the earthbound mortals behind the wire that the men who flew the tiny planes were somehow gods.

Cook Ada had provided a huge hamper of food. Jared bought Cokes, and he and the cousins picnicked together under the trees. Cindy Lou came, picking her way through the crowd. The Starksville sillies followed.

"Jaredy you were wonderful," Cindy Lou said, clasping his arm and drawing her hand with the jangling charm bracelets slowly along its length. "Soooo brave!"

It was two o'clock when the sound of planes could be heard revving up again.

Jared stopped humming the theme from the movie *Lilac Time*.

"Time for the parachute jump," he said, squinting skyward.

"Jaredy, I thought you were taking somebody up to jump."

Jared shook his head. "Mabel Cody, she's the famous wing-walker and parachutist, couldn't make it! That's a joke," Jared said. "But I wish I had somebody to jump! I could use that twenty bucks!"

"I'd be scared witless to jump out of a plane," Cindy Lou said, pushing her hair back from her face and squinting up at the parachutes falling like blossoms from the sky.

"I wouldn't," Maggie Royal heard herself say.

"I just bet you would be," Cindy Lou retorted.

"I would not!"

"You'd be a cowardy cat," Cindy Lou taunted.

"I'm not scared," Maggie Royal repeated through clenched teeth.

She found Jared checking the fuel in his tank. "Jared, I want to jump."

"Jump?" he asked vaguely, staring at his dipstick. "Jump where?"

"Out of your plane."

"You're out of your mind." He stared at her.

"Jared, please take me up and let me jump. It's important. I have to prove something to myself."

"Not if you kill yourself doing it."

"Jared, please." She faced him. Her legs and arms were brown against her boy's white shirt with the rolled-up sleeves and shorts. Her hair was damp from the heat, and little tendrils curled around her face like feathers. Her eyes were dark with pleading and that certain implacable determination he had seen when she rode Azilia in the flat race.

"You really mean it, don't you?"

She nodded. "You'll be paid twenty dollars, too."

"Okay, but if anything happens . . ." He did not complete the sentence. "Come on. We've work to do."

He showed her how to climb out onto the wing and drop off. "Try not to step on the cotton fabric. People break through all the time," he warned, indicating where the wing had been patched. "Push öff the wing feet-first. Be sure you slowly count to ten, like this—one-one-thousand, two-two-thousand—so you don't do it too fast. Then pull the rip cord! Try for a stand-up landing. Whatever you do, don't land stiff-legged. You'll break every bone in your body."

"What is a stand-up landing?" Maggie Royal asked in a small voice.

"One that isn't sitting down. Then you must spill the chute. Pull the shroud lines on the bottom to collapse it. Otherwise the wind can pull you into trees or a wire fence." He wet his finger and held it up. "Lucky, almost no wind. Maggie Royal, sure you still want to do this?"

She nodded, not daring to speak for fear her voice would show how very frightened she was.

"Okay." He clapped her on her back. "Really nothing to it. All you do is yell Tomochichi and bail out! Just like getting out of bed in the morning. By the way," he added, "don't forget to pull the rip cord."

He held the parachute harness while she backed into it. Then he bent over and buckled the straps about her loins. She held herself rigid, feeling the chill of fear rising from her ankles upward. Her heart was beating so hard she was afraid it might jump out of her chest, and her mouth was parchment dry. She longed to touch the cowlick over his left temple as he fussed about the buckles and straps. She wished he would look at her and smile or squeeze her hand for reassurance.

"You can still change your mind," Jared said, gazing at her in the bulky harness from which her long, thin brown legs protruded like those from a fat stork.

Maggie Royal shook her head.

Adele came running up. "Maggie Royal, you mustn't. You might be maimed! Oh, Maggie Royal . . ." She threw her arms around her cousin's neck.

Maggie Royal backed away, awkward in the parachute paraphernalia. "Don't worry, Adele. Nothing to it. You just pull this cord . . ."

"Maggie Royal, don't be ridic . . ." Constance said behind her.

"Are you sure, Maggie Royal?" Sparrow looked very concerned.

"Cousin Maggie Royal, let me come too," Harry the Horror pleaded.

"Go with Adele," Jared told him, "and wait for us."

The plane looked very small and insignificant. The shadows were lengthening and the varnished propeller blades caught the light from the lowering sun. Jared helped her climb into the front cockpit. The checker came and wrote their names on a pad along with the number of the airplane.

"Any landing preference?" Jared asked.

She clenched her fists to control their trembling. "I don't care. Long as I land."

Jared laughed. "If you see you're going into the trees, back up and start all over again."

"Hey, girl," a man called out. "You gonna jump out of that parachute?"

"Not until she lands back here," Jared said dryly.

Then the amplified voice of the announcer: "You will see a living woman hurl herself into space, falling through space for two miles at the rate of one hundred and twenty miles per hour . . ."

Jared tapped her on the shoulder. "You can still back out."

"Out of this?" She turned and indicated the harness. Somehow she managed a smile, although her face felt frozen.

"Okay, Maggie Royal?" His wide white grin was as dazzling as the sun splitting the tendrils of fleecy cirrus clouds. "Just flop out. Only, don't forget your parachute!" He pulled the goggles down over his eyes and gave her a jaunty wave. "Happy landings!"

She was aware of quail rising from the brush at the edge of the field, gliding and then disappearing into the tall corn on the left of the runway. Some horses grazed unconcernedly in a nearby pasture.

"Contact!"

The plane waddled out onto the runway, turned, and stopped. Then the sound of the starting bomb, and again the plane moved, gathering speed, the roar of the engine becoming deafening as the Jenny began its long climb.

It was suddenly cold. Wisps of clouds rippled around the cockpit. In the distance, the island, bushy with trees, looked like a field of parsley. Briefly she wondered if she would ever see it again.

Jared circled and throttled back, holding the plane in position over the field. He smiled and raised his right hand, pointing to the wing.

She gazed down at the tiny square below, and the fear struck her full force. Her face burned, her heart pounded, and she could hardly breathe. There was a deadweight in her stomach, and she was rigid with cold. She was afraid she would be sick and the wind would blow the particles of vomit back onto Jared.

Jared throttled the engine back for slow flight. He waggled his fingers, motioning to her to move.

She never knew how she managed to clamber out of the cockpit. The wind struck her like a blow as she clung to the flying wires.

Jared held the wing steady under her weight and gestured her out toward the wing tip. Beneath her feet she felt the aluminum strips protecting the cotton fabric. She dared not look down. She was terrified but would rather jump from the plane than show it.

Slowly she inched her way toward the wing tip. Suddenly her foot slipped, between the ribs, breaking through the fabric. Instinctively she jerked it back. It would not come. She had to look down to see what was holding it. It was wedged sideways. She straightened it and withdrew it easily. It was then that she noticed the tiny field mouse. It had been calmly eating the wax on the thread that stitched the fabric when the plane took off. Now that it was airborne, it was as frightened as she was.

The sight of the little creature seemed to her so extraordinary that, momentarily, she forgot her fear.

The plane dipped as she reached the end of the wing. When Jared righted the plane, she was gone.

Afterward she remembered nothing other than the blind tearing wind, pulling her hair from her head, buffeting her body, flinging her into space, like a shot bird falling as she counted and then pulled the rip cord.

Her eyes were tight shut when the life-saving jerk came. When she opened them, there was the earth below as she had last seen it, a checkerboard of woods and fields, greens and yellows, as if painted on one of Jared's canvases. For what seemed a long time she seemed to hang motionless, slowly oscillating downward, afraid to believe it was true, that she was alive. Then came a moment of total and complete euphoria, of a sense of power and exhilaration and well-being such as she had never known before. She had done it. She had mastered her fear, her sense of loss and bereavement and hopelessness. She had risked all and come out ahead.

She was filled with a feeling of peace and serenity that was like her newfound vision of the earth below. No longer a dark place where people hurt and hated, sickened and died. As the ground slowly swam into focus, the pinhead figures, the hangar with "AIRPORT" in big white letters on the roof, and the tiny beetlelike planes clustered around it signified life, hope.

Suddenly the ground seemed to be rushing upward to meet her.

When Jared came running across the field to where she had landed, he had to pry her fingers loose from the rip cord. The parachute had dragged her along the ground before she could collapse it. Her knees were scraped, and one cheek wore a long scratch.

"Hey, Maggie Royal," Jared cried, "you came down pretty good!"

His smile was so warm, so approving, that the clamoring of her heart was replaced with a leaping happiness.

"Jared," she said, "I think I'd like a cigarette."

"But, Maggie Royal, you don't smoke!"

"No, I don't," she answered, sighing contentedly. "I just think I'd like to try one now!"

The air race, the last event of the afternoon, was the climax of the show. The fairgrounds were filled with people. The aunts, Judge Cantwell, Mayor Lovewell, and other relatives and friends crowded into Gramma's box. Maggie Royal and Adele had garnered a place against the fences near the scattering pylon.

The sillies were gathered around Cindy Lou's roadster, parked by the apron where the planes were drawn up. Jared, wearing his full flying regalia, stood by the car, smoking a cigarette.

Maggie Royal gripped the fence in front of her until her knuckles showed white.

"Cindy Lou'll shuck him the way she did me." Noble spat out a piece of his cheroot that had stuck to his lower lip. "Like an ole snakeskin!"

There were five in the race. The pilots ran through their final checks. Then the planes were moved slowly, like creeping wasps, their tails resting on the shoulders of their crews as they pushed them toward the starting line. The band was playing and the skyline filled with banners flying from the wooden stands.

The helmeted pilots clambered into their open cockpits, adjusted their chin straps, and settled their goggles. Maggie Royal saw Jared's hand raised from the red-white-and-blue plane and the white flash of his scarf as it blew back in the breeze.

Propellers began to spin. Then she heard a sudden abrupt snarl as the wasps began speaking to one another, their mechanical high-pitched voices calling out in harsh exclamations.

As the snarl faded into the distance, the announcer's voice could be heard. "Speed relay. Four times around the field. Here's the way the experts around the apron figure they'll come in. The winner will be Al

Daniels, flying the Lincoln Standard biplane. Al won the Tarheel Trophy at Orlando last year. Runner-up, Reverend Pollock, who flies as good as he preaches. The others, Jim Peters and Jackie Bonnor, are good pilots, but they haven't got the ships. Jared Stark is a green unknown. Now they're coming into the first pylon. It's Al Daniels and the Rev in front!"

Sparrow and Harry the Horror, a Popsicle clutched in his hand, joined them.

"Where is Jared?" Adele asked, shading her eyes with her hand.

"Sun's in my eyes," Maggie Royal answered. "I can't see."

Sparrow raised his bird-watching binoculars. "Look," he cried. "Jared's passing the yellow plane."

The announcer's voice suddenly lost its professional evenness of tone. "Folks, here's a race developing as wasn't expected. That plane with the red-white-and-blue rudder stripes moving into third place at the pylon is the dark horse. Jared Stark in his little homemade exhibition ship. Very racy it is, too. I'm told Jared made it hisself from war-surplus machines. He's one of the Devils from Hell. Oh, my, look at him goooo! See him take that pylon! If he can just hold Al, coz Al has the ship. Wait. Stark's trying to catch the Rev now. He gained two hundred feet on him at that turn. Now he's going for Al at the next pylon." The roar of the planes flashing low over the field drowned out the announcer's voice. The sun was behind them as they came on flashing like beads circling the neck of the field. Now the announcer could be heard again as the snarl faded. "There, there. Watch young Stark. He's beating them around the pylons. Now he's going to pass Al Daniels' green-painted plane unless his wings come off. Man, can he fly. Watch him, ladies and gents, watch young Stark . . ."

Again the advancing roar followed by the swiveling of heads turning as they followed the planes.

"He's in. Jared's got it made. He's taking Al, and Al's giving him room!"

The green-painted plane and Jared's machine hovered for an instant side by side. Suddenly the green plane dropped, spiraling downward as several thousand voices made a strangled "Ahhhh!" Harry the Horror's Popsicle slid from his fingers. His cherry-smeared mouth formed a horrified "Oh!" as the plane hit the ground with terrible force, exploding into a ball of flame.

One by one the other planes landed and taxied to a stop. Jared jumped down from his cockpit. With an impatient gesture he flung his white scarf back over his shoulder and brushed past the people crowding around him. There was no change in his face as he made his way to Cindy Lou's car. Only in his green eyes, emptied of all expression.

Later it was as if Jared somehow blamed himself for Al Daniels' death. He became more reckless than ever. "Those were crazy days!" he said when he spoke of that period. "I didn't give a goddamn if school kept or not."

He took over the Devils from Hell, putting on thrill shows throughout the state.

"When I'm not up there," he told the cousins, pointing up at the sky, "I'm under the cowling of some goddamn plane working on the engine."

"Dat boy askin' for it," Cook Ada muttered darkly one day after Jared dived down over the house, not pulling out of his dive until her frizzled chickens were scattered and cackling wildly. "Like Mama used to say, 'Never take any more trouble in your heart than you can kick off with your toes.' Dat boy kickin' off sump'n with more'n toes!"

· 6 ·
STARK ISLAND AND WASHINGTON
1936–1939

· 9 ·

A combined coming-out party for Constance, Adele, and Maggie Royal was given at Great Oak over the Christmas holidays in 1936, when Maggie Royal was sixteen. It was the epitome of island entertaining, with satellite house parties on the other islands. At Great Oak everyone joined in the preparations.

Around the glass-domed indoor swimming pool, tables were set up amid exotic plants and wicker chairs in imitation of a nineteenth-century tea pavilion. The old square steam-bath cubicles opening onto the poolside were decorated to serve as bars and buffets. The squash court was filled with cots to provide a dormitory for visiting collegians. A pressing room, barber shop, and shoe-shine parlor were set up.

The furniture was removed from the great front room and a gazebo erected in front of the fireplace, where the orchestra, led by Meyer Davis, was to play. From the walls the dark oils in their heavy gilt frames gazed down on the empty floor, which had been swept and waxed by some of the dozens of Negroes hired to help for the occasion.

The week before the party, reporters telegraphed from several Eastern cities and Savannah, Atlanta, and Jacksonville. *Life* magazine was sending a crew to do a *"Life* Goes to a Party" feature. The island boat made so many trips to the mainland for supplies, Captain Ben warned that the engine would burn out.

Cook Ada baked and grumbled and announced she really was retiring after the party. Cases of liquor and soft drinks were delivered and stacked where the bars were to be set up. The aunts arranged flowers until Aunt Amy said she was as blue in the face as a delphinium. Two days before the party, Gramma ordered camellias cut from those blooming out of season in the greenhouses.

"What are we to do with them?" Maggie Royal asked her.

"Tie them onto the bushes by the house and in the gardens."

"But, Gramma, there are hundreds of camellia bushes."

"Well, don't stand there," she replied. "Get to work."

The cousins worked all one day and the next. They ran out of wire and ribbon and string and had to send to the mainland for more.

"We can't have a party without more camellias," Gramma said. "Some bushes are blank."

The florist on the mainland sent what amounted to a small boat-load.

"Unload them," Gramma ordered. "Get them hung up."

"But we have pink ones mixed up with white, and red mixed with pink and white." Maggie Royal pointed to a bush blooming with myriad-colored blossoms.

"Pooh," Gramma retorted. "Nobody will know the difference."

The boys blew up balloons to hang in clusters from the ballroom ceiling. After Harry the Horror broke a number of them, he was forbidden to come to the ball unless he replaced the ones he had destroyed.

A few days before the party, Gramma called Maggie Royal into her room. Her small commanding figure seemed lost in the great bed, and the face that had been painted by Augustus John was seamed and lined, like the ancestral paintings that needed to be restored.

She stretched out her hand on which her husband's diamond blazed like an island sunset. "My dear, sit down." She held Maggie Royal's hand as they talked, and Maggie Royal thought of the day she had been told about Affey. "You are my namesake. I've been harder on you, demanded more. Young Franklin ..." she sighed. "No point in going into it now, what he's done to the country. And Eleanor. I hardly know what to think about Eleanor, all that running around. . . . Where was I?" Her hand let go of Maggie Royal's. "My dear, I'm very tired. I've missed Mr. McDermott more than I can say." Her voice faded and then gathered strength for a final effort. "I've made some bad investments. I'm in temporary straits. Your party will be the last great party on Stark Island." Her eyes closed.

Maggie Royal bent down and kissed her cheek. "Gramma, I love you."

She never knew if Gramma heard her or not.

Maggie Royal's mother arrived two weeks before the party. Her new husband came with her. He had been one of Mairin's most persistent suitors before her marriage to Maggie Royal's father. Recently widowed, he had renewed his courtship and prevailed.

He bore one of the great titles of the British Empire. Mairin called him Binkie. The servants called him "Mister Lord, suh." He wore an Eton tie and had served in the Coldstream Guards. His complexion was the color of the port Gramma served after dinner. He was, as Uncle Oomlot said, very pukka sahib. Thorny said it was people like him that had caused the American Revolution. They all had the feeling he looked down on them as provincial colonials, somewhat barbaric in their island ways.

What he had in common with Mairin is hard to say. Presumably she was dazzled by his title, his great house in Leicestershire, and his castle in Ireland. Undoubtedly, like many of his conservative and unimaginative ilk, he was bewitched by her selfish sensuality and superficial beauty.

The play in which she was starring that fall had closed. She was very tired. Her first week on the island was spent in bed in her room at the end of the long upstairs hall, where her maid, Naomi, brought her meals on a tray, gave her back rubs, and glared at his lordship and Maggie Royal when they knocked timidly at her door.

Maggie Royal visited her afternoons, after she had had her rest. Mairin wore silk nightgowns, and white paste covered her face from collarbone to hairline. She reminded Maggie Royal of pictures of young Masai warriors in Kenya being initiated into manhood. She shook her hair, tinted auburn that year, with a helpless gesture known to theatergoers on both sides of the Atlantic.

"It's absolute martyrdom to dye your hair," she said, patting it. "Maggie Royal, I really don't know how you can be a child of mine! You're like your father, all Stark. Your hands are grubby and your face is a fright! You're old enough now to use makeup. Your cousins Adele and Constance do. Naomi can show you. And your hair! You really must do something about your hair! It's as straight and limp as cooked spaghetti. You may use my curling iron. And those awful patched shorts and sweater buttoned all cockeyed, what your grandmother calls 'kattywampus,' and that mouth, as long as a butler's apron!"

Maggie Royal's hand went to her mouth as she sat tensely, waiting for her mother to finish enumerating her shortcomings, the list of which seemed as long as Sparrow's checklist of island birds.

"And you should eat more." Mairin gazed down at her bosom, barely disguised by a froth of lace. "You have no breasts at all!" Placing both palms beneath hers, she held them up, as though they were something served on a plate. Then she lay back against her pillows with a satisfied smile, and her eyes took on a dreamy expression as she stroked them lovingly, lingeringly.

Maggie Royal's breasts, such as they were, began to tingle as she watched. Her mother gave the impression of being what Adele called sexy, but Maggie Royal had the intuitive feeling that the only love she knew was self-love.

As Mairin lay back against her pillows, caressing her breasts, Maggie Royal knew her mother had forgotten her.

Binkie, Mairin's "belted earl," had killed lions in Africa and tigers in India and hunted with the Duke of Chatfield's foxhounds, one of the great packs in Leicestershire. He had never hunted in America, and Gramma suggested he have a day with the Starksville Hunt. Jim Bob Beasley said he would put on a special bye day and lend his lordship a horse. Maggie Royal and Jared were to accompany him.

Jim Bob Beasley, the master and huntsman, was something of a legend throughout the South. His father, Will Beasley, had bred the "lemony"-colored Stark hounds at the turn of the century. Old man Beasley had been killed jumping out of a barnyard. He had been so intent on his hounds ahead he had not seen the mule sitting by the fence. Just as the horse was about to jump, the mule decided to rise, upending the horse, in a crash that broke old man Beasley's neck. Great-Aunt Meg said that when they took him to the churchyard to be buried, they should have tied him onto his horse and sent him over the wall. For never in his life had old man Beasley gone through a gate.

Jim Bob Beasley was a tall, lean young man with a narrow face, sharp eyes and a long, narrow nose. "Varminty" was the way Aunt Meg described him, explaining that he had never married because he could not afford both a wife and his foxhounds and he had yet to find a woman who would share his bed with a bitch about to whelp.

Gramma said he looked like a groom among the gentry and a gentleman among stable hands, belonging as he did to one of those Southern families that are represented in every level of society, from Judge Cantwell, who was a cousin of his grandmother's, to "Drop Kick" Keeler, the mortician, who had married one of the Beasley girls.

Jim Bob boasted that his hounds would run anything. Jared, who acted as honorary whipper-in whenever he was able to hunt, inevitably returned to the island with tales of incredibly long runs, of gray foxes that ran like hares, rather than circling and climbing trees, or an occasional bobcat that headed for the hill country.

The hounds were free to roam and forage for food, on the theory that this would make them keener and more eager to hunt. All their ribs showed. Yet their coats gleamed with health and fitness and they were as fast as greyhounds, as active as terriers, and as lawless as African wild dogs. When they caught a fox, they were liable to eat it down to the nub of its brush.

As most of the country they rode over was owned or controlled by Beasley kin, a large number of whom made their living by operating stills, Jim Bob was able to hunt all year around. Much of the hunting was done through the pine woods, where Jim Bob, whooping like an Indian, galloped along narrow logging trails, skidding around corners, ducking branches.

The fields of peanuts, soybeans, and cotton surrounding the small homesteads of the Negroes and sharecroppers that studded the flat sandy land were enclosed by snake fences. They had stood since time immemorial and Jim Bob sailed over them on his famous wise, ugly gray mare, Miss Venus, with ease.

Maggie Royal would always remember the excitement of loading the horses onto the barge to travel to the mainland in the dark, then unloading them on the dock at Starksville and riding along the empty streets to the outskirts of town, where the ramshackle hunt stables and kennels were located near the fairgrounds.

In honor of the visiting lord, Jim Bob provided his special stirrup cup of home-brewed "corn likker" ("finest in Stark County!") and beaten biscuits filled with ham smoked in the fireplace of the crumbling ancestral mansion where he lived mostly in two rooms.

"Come in, come in. For God's sake come in and have a libation," he called from the doorway. "Warm the cockles on a cold morning," he added, giving his standard greeting, although the temperature of the Georgia morning already hovered around sixty in the predawn darkness.

The kitchen was a huge room with a stone fireplace surrounded by hanging iron pots. Saddles and bridles and old boots were piled in the corners, and a large cooking pot was full of bills. Some were so old the paper had turned yellow. Jim Bob boasted that once every month he drew a bill from the pot and borrowed the money from the bank to pay it. Creditors who complained were told that if they persisted, their bills would not even be put in the pot.

A clothesline stretched the length of the room, to which hats of all makes and categories were attached with clothespins. Most of the chairs were broken or else occupied by hounds, so that when you visited Jim Bob, you drank and ate standing up.

Hounds were everywhere, on the hearth, under the table, and on the chairs, while those thrust outside to hunt that day yelped and clawed and fought to regain their inner sanctum.

"Ain't gonna be much scent today," Jim Bob announced gloomily, shooing a hound from a chair and offering it to Binkie. "But we'll try to give you some kind of a chase!"

"He always says that," Jared explained. "Might be the greatest hunt in history, and Jim Bob would still apologize for not having a good day."

Jim Bob ignored him. "Getting late in the year," he said, riding his own conversational line. "I mind the old codger who was asked as he lay dying if he had any regrets. 'Yessum,' he said. 'I regret I didn't hunt more before Christmas!'"

"Why did he say that?" Binkie asked.

"Come to think of it, I don't rightly know," Jim Bob replied. "Reckon he was a Yankee. Yankees can't hunt much after Christmas. Ground freezes up. Here we hunt all year round."

Whereas his lordship was attired in his height-of-the-season ("It is the season, is it not?" he had asked, and been told that "Jim Bob's season lasts all year round!") Leicestershire appointments, high silk hat, immaculate white stock and waistcoat, black shadbelly coat, white breeches, and shining black boots, Jim Bob wore his usual garb, battered velvet hunting cap, brown with age, plaid open-necked workshirt, cowboy boots, and leather chaps. A pistol was tucked into its holster on his hip, " 'case we meet a rattlesnake," he told his lordship with a wink at Jared. He also carried a hunting crop.

Outside, he waded through the sea of goats and stable dogs, nodding and speaking to the riders assembled in the stable yard, and called

to his whipper-in and inseparable hunting companion, George Washington Roosevelt, known as "My Boy George," to bring out Ebenezer
Baptist Church for his lordship. "George done broke 'im and named him
after his church," Jim Bob explained. "Most all horses George broke are
named after churches. My Boy George thinks it'll keep 'im from going to
hell, coz he goes fox-chasing Sundays 'stead of churching. Horse he's riding . . ." He indicated a short-coupled chestnut with a long unpulled
mane. "That's Mount Sinai!"

At sight of Ebenezer Baptist Church, his lordship looked anything
but reassured. The horse's nose was more Roman than Caesar's and his
back sagged like Jim Bob's sofa.

"Safe as a church, he is," My Boy George said, aware of Binkie's
expression as it settled on Ebenezer's knobby legs and ewe neck. "Don'
you worry none, Mr. Lord, suh. Ole Ebenezer see to it you get there and
back!"

His lordship was introduced to the red-faced farmers in baggy
breeches and rubber boots, who replied, "Howdy, Mr. Lord; glad to
have you with us," in response to Binkie's "Howjado."

Jim Bob mounted Miss Venus, who had a smear of manure on her
white rump. "Jared," he commanded, pointing his whip at a couple that
had treed the stable cat, "go fetch those poodles and bring 'em here!"
The hounds ignored him, baying with bloodthirsty concentration. "I
love that bitch," Jim Bob interjected, pointing to a very long lean hound
coming from the hen house with an egg in its mouth. "She looks kind of
peculiar, but I tell you, she can flat run a fox!"

"And jus' 'bout anything else," muttered My Boy George darkly.

Jim Bob blew impatient toots on his dented hunting horn. "Time
they settled," he announced to the field at large.

"Time these hounds settle down be July," My Boy George said
under his breath.

After a great deal of horn blowing and whip cracking, eight or nine
couple ceased their individual pursuits and the huntsman led off along
the rippled clay road, the light-colored hounds swirling around his
horse's feet like the wake from a boat.

The field followed. It consisted of a number of local farmers on
horses equally suited to pulling a plow. Horseface Lewis, the dealer, told
Maggie Royal how well Azilia looked and asked if she would consider
selling the mare. "Mind you, miss," he said, eyeing Azilia speculatively,
"I can get you a good price!" A clutch of young people riding a variety
of horseflesh—the country-club set smartly turned out in jodhpurs and
velvet caps on well-groomed ponies and horses, others in dungarees on
ponies with long straggly manes and tails with burs in them—brought
up the rear.

They left the purple meadows adjoining the Beasley farm and the
fairgrounds and entered a thick woods. Suddenly a hound gave tongue.
Almost immediately the cry of hounds became deafening. Jim Bob let

out an ear-splitting holler. "Your Lordship," he shouted. "Ride on up with me. Mind you keep your legs close together, now."

Without waiting to see if Binkie followed his instructions, he gave Miss Venus a great kick and tore off along the woods path, so twisting and narrow that one's instinct was to press one's knees as closely as possible to the horse in order not to be swept off by the trees.

Maggie Royal shut her eyes and held on to Azilia's mane as the mare slid on the slippery clay, down into steep ravines, scrambling up out of dry creekbeds.

They seemed to stay in the woods for a long time. At intervals, people along the way pointed and yelled as the fox doubled and dodged in and out of brush and briars. Occasionally Jim Bob, My Boy George, or Jared about-faced, causing the field to back off the path into the bushes as they galloped past, wearing ecstatic expressions of concentration and exhilaration.

Maggie Royal's sense of direction and eye for terrain that came from the long hours in the island woods was tested. Her mind was a blur of fields, drops of dew on the cobwebs shining diamondlike against the gauzy white, as she tried to guide Azilia around them, not wanting the mare to destroy the fragile webs by stepping on them.

Jim Bob's hounds were together and in front, making a riotous cry like the chimes of all the churches the horses were named after.

His lordship rode in Jim Bob's pocket, and why he did not come off at each fence was due entirely to Ebenezer's expertise at throwing his overly long head up in the air and thus returning Binkie to his saddle. At one point he careened off Jim Bob on landing over a coop and cut in at top speed in front of Maggie Royal as they were scrambling up out of a creekbed.

Some of the children had come to grief over a high snake fence, and Horseface Lewis had pulled out, not wanting to injure the horse he hoped to sell. Jared and King galloped easily along.

Maggie Royal was ecstatic. This was the way it used to be. Jared and King galloping ahead. Nothing but the wind, the motion of the horse, and the countryside slipping past without any of the emotional complexities of growing up, of jealousy and hurt.

Hounds lost and then found again. The riders jumped boards leaning up against the wire fences surrounding the shacks and farmyards, makeshift chicken coops, barways, and leaning gates. Once they fetched up in a farmyard where an old mule gazed at the riders from beneath a slanting shed and an equally ancient Negro was hoeing in his garden. Children peered from the cabin windows, their eyes white in their black faces.

"Ah believes I seen some of dem dawgs running south a bit back," the old man said. "They was yowling real loud-like."

"More likely killing!" My Boy George said, neglecting to say killing what.

"See how free-ranging?" Jim Bob gazed down at a hound that had paused beside his horse to stare up at him questioningly. "My dawgs hunt on their own, but they always return to Papa!" He leaned down and spoke to the hound. "Go get 'im, baby!"

An exclamation of dismay interrupted the amenities of the check, causing Jim Bob almost to drop the flask of home-brewed bourbon he was passing around. The "free-ranging" hound, in response to Jim Bob's command, had flushed a couple who had been making love in the tall grass practically under Jim Bob's horse's feet.

"My word!" his lordship exclaimed. "Whatever was that?"

"Couple fornicatin'," Jim Bob answered laconically, his eyes on his hounds.

"Sure is a right nice day for it, Mister Lord, suh," My Boy George remarked cheerfully. "Ain't it, now?"

A hulloa from Jared at the edge of a field of peanuts sent Jim Bob and the hounds that had "returned to Papa" tearing around the edge of the planting. Jim Bob's hounds rushed to join those that had remained in the woods. The riders followed.

"Ain't no gray, running straight like that!" Jim Bob said, jamming his cap down hard on his head. "Let's go!"

They were out of their own hunting country now, in new and unknown territory. Briars tore at their clothes as they slid and clattered around corners on the greasy path, skated up and down hills and over an assortment of fences nobody could describe as civilized, brush piled against wire, spindly narrow barways, and in one instance a brass bedstead serving as a gate.

They emerged from the tunnellike paths in the pine woods to bright sunlight. Glancing around, Maggie Royal realized there was nobody left other than Jim Bob, Binkie, My Boy George, and Jared, who had all paused beside five strands of barbed wire decorated with a frieze of honeysuckle.

"Damn!" Jim Bob said disgustedly. "George, my boy, throw your coat over that wire!" After My Boy George had divested himself of his rusty long-skirted black coat handed down from old Will Beasley, and laid it on top of the awful-looking fence, Jim Bob turned Miss Venus around and drove her at it. Miss Venus was aged now and tended to go lame after a long hunt. She was also blown. She started to take off, decided she was unable to clear the fence, and stopped dead, her long bony head hanging dolefully down on the far side of the wire.

"Give me a lead," Jim Bob cried urgently, gazing longingly after his hounds.

"Miss Venus some lame," My Boy George commented. "Looks like her foot 'bout to drop off. That's the one got cut last year."

"I'll give it a try," Binkie volunteered bravely. But Ebenezer was not as optimistic. Wheezing like a scratched Victrola record, he was not about to go another yard. He dug his hooves into the ground in front of the obstacle, dropped his shoulder and likewise his distinguished rider, whose top hat went flying off and vanished into a briar patch.

"May have to go round by the road," My Boy George commented as his lordship scrambled upright out of the berry bushes. "Looks like they's heading for Hunting Hill!"

"Means losing the hunt," Jim Bob replied in the same tone of voice with which he might have announced the death of a favorite foxhound.

"I'll have a try," Jared said. He swung King around and headed him at the fence. Now, as Jared urged him on, the horse cleared the wire with inches to spare.

"Would you mind moving out of the way?" Maggie Royal called to Jim Bob, who was maneuvering Miss Venus around for another go at the obstacle.

"Now, look, Maggie Royal," Jim Bob began. "You know that mare's too small to jump a big fence like this. I don't want to have to tell your Gramma . . ."

"Maggie Royal, stop!" Jared's shout reached her as Azilia rose into the air like a cock pheasant bursting upward from the underbrush, soaring straight and true over the coat disguising the wire and landing lightly in the brush on the far side.

"Oh, you love!" Maggie Royal leaned forward, patting her, feeling the wonderful sense of achievement that comes from the challenge of clearing a big fence.

"Go on," she heard Jim Bob cry needlessly. "Stay with hounds."

"That was a terrible place," Jared said as she pulled up beside him. His eyes flashed happily. "Hey, we're alone with hounds. Maggie Royal, come on. Let's go!"

Hounds had long ago run out of familiar country, and there was little chance to give their horses a breather, for it was necessary to keep galloping in order to stay in sight of hounds. Young, fearless, they rode in a straight line toward the distant rise of Hunting Hill.

Hounds ran on in such a way that Jim Bob would have cheered ecstatically had he been there. As it was, they were gaining on the sinking fox heading for the rocks on the ridge.

The lead hounds were almost upon him when the exhausted fox reached a small Negro shack on the side of Hunting Hill. At the sound of hounds, children began pouring from it. To everyone's astonishment, the fox ran past their mother, hanging clothes on a line, and into the cabin. The frenzied hounds followed. The mother screamed, and two of the smaller children fell down in their hurry to escape the onslaught.

From inside the cabin came the frantic sounds of a scuffle. Jared leaped off his horse, threw the reins to Maggie Royal, and ran into the cabin. Hounds were whining at the hearth, some standing on one another, as they attempted to climb up the chimney, where the fox was lodged between some loose bricks. Chairs were upset. A pan of milk had fallen onto the floor, and several hounds were powdered with yellow cornmeal from a sack that had erupted, spewing its contents around the room.

Some of the hounds were lapping up the milk on the clay floor. Others were sniffing around the cupboard and stove. At sight of Jared and his hunting whip, a hound leaped from the table, scattering bowls and plates, and fled out the open door. The others followed, crashing through the obstacles in their path, yelping frantically in anticipation of the whip thong they expected to connect with them.

"I'm terribly sorry," Jared said to the family clustered defensively in the yard. He waved his arm in the direction of the devastated room. "I'll get the fox out of the chimney in a minute and see that Mr. Beasley reimburses you." He took hounds some distance away and then returned to the cabin, from which he shortly emerged holding the fox upside down by its brush. He dropped it beyond the yard, and the terrified animal was last seen headed for a den among the rocks high on the hill.

"How'd you dislodge him?" Maggie Royal asked.

"I just reached up and grabbed the blunt end," Jared answered, grinning.

Maggie Royal slid off Azilia and buried her forehead against the mare's steaming shoulder. "Thank you for letting the fox go free."

Binkie, Jim Bob, and My Boy George were in the stable yard when they returned. Ebenezer, Miss Venus, and Mount Sinai gazed curiously at them over the open half of their stall doors. Sacks serving as coolers were thrown over their backs, and chickens rooted along the aisle of the carriage shed that had been converted into the hunt stable.

Maggie Royal and Jared surrendered the now docile hounds. Jim Bob stood in their midst, calling congratulations and accounting for each hound by name. Then he lifted his head and laughed. "Sure took a miracle to pull a fox run today."

They went into the kitchen, and Jim Bob brought out a bottle of ice-cold French champagne from his icebox, which contained six bottles of beer, eight eggs, a pat of butter, and half a ham.

The cork zoomed out and he poured the foaming wine into cloudy crystal glasses that rested on the shelf alongside masses of jam and jelly jars.

"Champagne!" Maggie Royal exulted.

"Certainly," Jim Bob replied. "Always celebrate with bubbly after a good hunt." He nodded to her and held up his glass. "Here's to you, Maggie Royal. A fine foxhunter, like your Gramma. A real live flower of the Southland!"

My Boy George cooked scrambled eggs and fried ham, which they washed down with champagne, and as the afternoon waned, Binkie and Jim Bob talked endlessly of hounds and hunting, his lordship speaking his clipped English and Jim Bob talking his country jargon, yet communicating perfectly. Jim Bob described a famous hunt during which a bobcat sought refuge in a sharecropper's shack, followed by the hounds, "scarifying the family most to death. They came pouring out of that cabin's though Satan was after 'em!" Binkie countered with the tale of a fox that the Duke of Chatfield's hounds found in a copper pot. It climbed out onto the roof of a thatched cottage and clung there, defying the hounds until the huntsman drew them away in order to free the fox to run another day. And so it went through the long afternoon. Every so often Jim Bob would turn to Maggie Royal and smile and ask what she thought of the horse that had been champion at the Starksville show and had been sold up north by Mr. Lewis for a big price, or the stallion hound imported from the Duke of Chatfield the previous year.

Maggie Royal wanted only one thing in order to be filled with complete happiness: to have Jared look at her once with that same longing and hunger she had seen him show toward Cindy Lou—that private, unmistakable, all-consuming look she had learned to cherish and dread. But he sat by the fire silent and apart. After the excitement and exhilaration of the run, the closeness they had shared as they galloped over that vast lonely countryside, he had retreated to that island in his mind where there was no room for her.

Guests began to arrive for the shoot preceding the party. Engraved invitations with the Stark crest of the white horse tied to the great oak had been sent to people in Starksville, Savannah, Atlanta, Birmingham, Jacksonville, and the surrounding islands, Torreys from Ossabaw, Coffins from Sapelo, Carnegies from Cumberland, Morgans, Vanderbilts, Armours, Goodyears, Pulitzers, Rockefellers, and others from the Jekyll Island Club. Some came by train to the Starksville siding, others by boat, tying up at the Great Oak dock or anchoring in the sound, until it looked as if a regatta were in progress.

The Roisterers, the band of sports Maggie Royal had gotten to know at Miss Mayo's, came in Taylor DuPree's father's yacht from Jekyll. They had been drinking and came off the boat howling with laughter as if shot from a cannon. They pounded the boy cousins on the back and kissed the girls.

"You look great," Taylor told Maggie Royal. He ignored Cindy Lou, who, Adele reported, had been making a play for him ever since she had met him at Callie Hempstead's coming-out party at the Plaza in New York.

To the surprise of some, Big Boy Tarrington's boat also appeared.

"How could you ask that vulgarian to Stark Island?" Uncle Oomlot demanded when Gramma admitted the Tarringtons were invited.

"Miss Minnie's an old friend," she explained defensively.

She did not tell him the real truth, that against the advice of the "John Doe" uncles, she had refused to abandon the farm after the failure of the soybean crop. When the new farm manager, an "up-to-date" graduate of the Virginia Polytechnic Institute put everything in corn, subsequently destroyed by the earworm, Gramma piled more mortgages on Great Oak. Big Boy Tarrington's bank offered lower interest rates than any of the other banks. During the course of the negotiations the bank president boasted he had been shooting in Scotland and that he'd heard Stark Island was a wonderful place for game. Because of her indebtedness to him, Gramma felt she had no choice but to invite the Tarringtons to the Christmas shoot and the ball.

Tarrington's yacht, the *Cindy Lou,* was a cruising houseboat, with a huge smokestack in the center, gilt scrollwork, varnished mahogany, a great deal of brightwork, and a uniformed crew. There was a paid captain, a cook, two crew members, a hairdresser, and a man in a short white coat to serve drinks and empty ashtrays.

Uncle Thorndike Pritchard, who sailed his schooner single-handed and brought her up the narrow channel, all the way to the dock, before dropping his sails, termed the *Cindy Lou* a stinkpot. He said he'd never seen anything as vulgar as the lamps with fringes and the bead curtains subdividing the compartments, instead of doors. "Just like a whorehouse!"

"Yeah," agreed Noble, who'd been aboard the *Cindy Lou* on a fishing trip. "He has the steward bait his hook and cast for him, then hand him the rod when he hooks a fish!"

As Jared approached the landing to tie up the vessel, Big Boy Tarrington joined the captain on the bridge. He was a short man, beefy and heavyset, in white flannels and dark blue blazer. His gold-braided yachting cap was tipped toward the back of his head, and a dead cigar slanted from the corner of his mouth as he directed the captain on docking procedures.

The captain wore a long-suffering expression and kept his lips clamped tightly shut. Despite enough shouted instructions to confuse the most experienced sailor, the enormous power boat was somehow eased alongside the pier, nudging a piling as the strong current pushed the boat against it.

"Goddammit," Tarrington roared, holding his right hand up and snapping his fingers. "Get out the fenders!"

"Yassah," replied one of the crewmen. "Yassah, boss."

After the boat was secured, Tarrington lowered himself onto the dock and asked where to plug in for electricity.

Jared explained that the Delco generator did not supply dockside power.

Tarrington faced him, feet apart, broad shoulders thrown back. "What? No electricity! How will mother and baby dry their hair if they can't use the dryer? Well, might as well show me where the phone is. Have a call to make to the office."

Jared told him there wasn't a telephone on Stark Island.

"Christ!" Tarrington exploded. "I thought you Starks were civilized. How do you know what the stock market is doing?"

"This is a wilderness island, sir," Jared said, helping Mrs. Tarrington down the gangway.

"Miss Minnie" Tarrington looked years older than her husband. She was a big-boned woman, yet her flesh hung loosely about her, like her shapeless, unfashionable clothes. ("I don't know why it is," Gramma said, "that well-bred people consider it common to dress well.") Mrs. Tarrington had large blue eyes and a mass of faded brownish hair pulled back in a big untidy bun laced with tortoiseshell hairpins. Her skin, like the skin of Southern women kept from the sun, had gone from white to a dry yellow. As a concession to what her husband and daughter expected from her, she had dabbed rouge on her cheeks and rubbed vivid purplish lipstick across her disappointed mouth. She rarely spoke, preferring to listen to the conversation around her with lowered, unattentive eyes.

When everyone was assembled in front of Great Oak for the shoot, Joe-Ali drove up the first mule-drawn wagon. The dogs occupied the back part, several lean pointers and two spaniels. They were light and active, and any one could outwork the "lumpy" pig dogs Cullen had set such store by. The spaniels were short-legged, liver-and-white-colored. Their noses were thrust one atop another as they peered with joyous anticipation through the railings of their boxes.

Jasper was in charge of the mule wagon laden with guns. Hercules was driving the ox cart that was to carry Judge Cantwell, Big Boy Tarrington, the uncles, and some of the other visitors. (Binkie, bedridden with a sprained back from his fall foxhunting with Jim Bob, was devastated at missing the shoot.) Cook Ada, Newt, and the food and wines to be set out on the long table in the clearing at Middle Point were in another wagon. The aunts were in the surrey. Gramma said she would bring Mrs. Tarrington and some of the other nonshooters in the Packard in time for lunch.

"Mind you don't toss out any firecrackers at the cattle," Aunt Meg warned. "You'll scare away the game."

Adele grabbed Maggie Royal's arm. "Look at Mr. Tarrington!"

"He shore looks girthed up in his tailored shooting suit," Jasper said, "don't he, now?"

Big Boy Tarrington resembled a caricature of those British sportsmen pictured in *The Field*. His clothes and equipment all seemed to be brand-new. His short rotund figure was encased in a checked tweed knicker suit. He wore a shirt and crimson necktie, with pointers pointing on it, and stiff new chukka boots. The day promised to be warm, and it was obvious that in a very short time he would be overheated and uncomfortable, with leaves and sticks in his shoes.

The white-jacketed steward from the *Cindy Lou* walked behind. He wore a pith helmet of the kind known as a Jungle Jim and carried an elaborate leather trunk case with brass ends and leather straps. Gold initials were inscribed over the lock.

"Bring it here, boy," Tarrington commanded, snapping his fingers.

201

He turned to Uncle Oomlot, who had slipped easily into his shooting gear—worn plus-fours; broad-soled, flat-heeled "rattlesnake" knee boots; a sweater that had unraveled at the neck; and his old canvas coat, its mess of pockets held together by strips of dirty canvas described by Gramma as a "horror unspeakable"—saying he wouldn't miss this expedition for all the port in Portugal.

"Had myself measured for a matched pair of Purdeys," Big Boy Tarrington said. He eyed Uncle Oomlot's scarred Winchester pump gun as if it were something Tomochichi might have carried. "Took me a whole year, and cost a pretty penny, I can tell you." He paused for this information to sink in, and went on, "Double-barreled, with a cast-off stock. Got a Holland & Holland 12-gauge, too. Boy, open up the case. Like to show 'em to Mr. Stark, here!"

The "boy" opened the elaborate gun case. It was lined with green velvet and held a vast assortment of cleaning rods, patches, oil bottles, and solvents, as well as the beautiful guns.

"Bless my soul!" Uncle Oomlot exclaimed, staring at the antlered head inlaid on the polished stock of one of the Purdeys.

"Had a friend do it," Tarrington said proudly, holding up the gun in order to let Uncle Oomlot view the crude, vividly colored decoration. "Cost a pretty penny, too. Twenty pieces of wood. The nostrils are ebony. The nose and eyes holly. The head itself is curly walnut."

"Never saw such a thing," Uncle Oomlot said afterward. "It was as though he'd taken a Whippy and added all those scrolls and ornaments and things they put on saddles out West."

Cindy Lou wore a suede shooting jacket and a wide-brimmed hat decorated with a long pheasant feather. "I wouldn't dream of killing a little old bird." She smiled up at Jim Bob Beasley, who had come over with the Starksville contingent. "I'm just going along with Jaredy for the fun of it." She gave Jared one of her long, slow, sliding glances and brushed past Noble and the other cousins as though they were footmen.

Sparrow took hold of Maggie Royal's hand, noticing that it was growing colder and colder as he held it.

"Bet I know what you're thinking," Adele said to her. "You're wishing you could take her up into the tower and push her out!"

"You're not far wrong," Maggie Royal admitted.

Finally the cavalcade started off, the wagons followed by the cars. A number of children from the settlement ran alongside. Jared and Cindy Lou went in the wagon with the Starksville visitors.

Maggie Royal, Adele, Tyger, Sparrow, Noble, and some of the young people from the mainland squeezed into the wagon with the dogs. The dogs wagged their tails and whined, frantic to be loosed from their boxes.

"Hope Jazzbo brought some cider sperrits," Noble commented. "Nothing like that apple whiskey. Five minutes after drinking it, you're still shaking your head from side to side like Cindy Lou."

"Makes me think of the Bonus Marchers," Sparrow commented as the wagons lurched along the sandy track.

"Hardly," Thorny answered cynically. "More like the bourgeois imperatives of an imperialistic society being thrust on the masses. Get a load of Big Boy Tarrington smoking his big cigar while his boy, his slavey, runs behind."

"You didn't have to come," Adele said. "You could have stayed at the house, reading all those books."

"Wouldn't miss it for the world," Thorny answered. "Reminds me of those places in France where the kings went to screw and shoot."

"Thorny!" Adele cried, shocked. "You know you shouldn't use such words. Just because you spend your time in that awful Plantation Bar throwing dice in the stable."

Maggie Royal sat frozen and still, only half-hearing them. Ahead, Cindy Lou's fair head was next to Jared's. She could see the pale hair swinging back and forth as Cindy Lou chattered on with her usual animation.

At the crossroads beyond the Long Point settlement, small groups and dogs dispersed to different parts of the island.

"Good thing the island is big enough so everybody isn't in shooting distance of one another," Noble said, glancing meaningfully at Maggie Royal. "Or there'd be a lot of dead bodies."

They followed the lumbering ox cart carrying Big Boy Tarrington, the uncles, and other "gentlemens." The track zigzagged through the woods, past the pig-holding pens Cullen had built, and came out in the dove field.

Joe-Ali let loose the dogs. "Away, boys, away."

The ecstatic dogs took off like foxhounds on the line of a fox. At the first note from Joe-Ali's whistle they altered course and quartered the field.

"Looks like there aren't any birds here," Joe-Ali said after a while.

"I understood there were birds everywhere," Tarrington said peevishly. From one of his numerous pockets he extracted a silver flask, unscrewed the top, and offered it to his companions. "Prime corn. Friend of mine makes it, up in Windy Holler, back of Starksville." The men in the wagon shook their heads. "Well, don't mind if I do," Tarrington said, tipping the flask up to meet his mouth. He took a long swallow, wiped his lips with a brown silk handkerchief decorated with raised guns and falling birds, capped the flask, and returned it and the handkerchief to his pocket. From another pocket he extracted his cigar case. Ignoring the dark looks from the wagon, he took out a cigar and lit it with a matching platinum lighter. Then he clicked the lighter shut and said, "I mind the time I was shooting in Scotland. My loader says to me, 'Sir, you have a lord on either side of you.' I told him I hoped there was one above, too." He paused, waiting in vain for the expected laughter. He moved the cigar to the other side of his mouth. "One of them lords says to me he'd shore like to have a Purdey like mine. I told him a Purdey's more like a jail sentence than buying a gun. Two to four years to get delivery."

A gray cloud suddenly rose overhead. The doves came on fast. Shots rang out, and birds began falling. As the dogs retrieved them, those that were wounded were handed to Joe-Ali, who, while the guests averted their eyes, dispatched them swiftly and efficiently, the same way he did fish and in a manner Gramma described as "quite revolting." Seizing each bird firmly, regardless of its flopping, he proceeded to bite down on its skull, cracking it with his teeth. When the bird stopped moving, he flung it into his game bag.

"I hate it, I hate it," Maggie Royal burst out suddenly. She clenched her fists and banged one against the side of the wagon. "I hate seeing the birds and animals killed!"

"Typically bourgeois!" Thorny muttered. "A kind of socially acceptable slaughter!"

Along the fence Cullen had built, they came to a thick belt of oaks with a few young maples interspersed. If you followed it, you reached the high point of the island. In the middle lay the low swampy area, about five acres of dense thicket matted with briars and vines, bushes and shrubs—Blackbeard's territory.

"I'd give most anything to get me a big tom," Tarrington said, waving his gun at Joe-Ali. "I'm told there's a place where there's an old gobbler with a beard fourteen inches long."

"Ain't no turkeys gobbling round here," Joe-Ali replied, maintaining the tradition of all good turkey hunters, who like to keep the good spots a secret. He gazed apprehensively at Tarrington's gun. " 'Scuse me, sir, best not to wave that gun around!"

"Never shot anybody yet," Big Boy Tarrington retorted, still smarting from his failure to bring down a dove.

Joe-Ali called the dogs. In a minute they were out of sight, wiggling and fighting their way through the underbrush.

"Plenty of birds in there," Uncle Thorndike said.

"How do you flush 'em out?" Tarrington asked.

"You have to go through the thick of it."

Tarrington wiped his face with his silk handkerchief. The sun was hot now, and he was obviously uncomfortable.

Suddenly a woodcock exploded from behind a bush.

"A Stark Island woodcock," Sparrow cried excitedly. "First I've seen."

Tarrington pitched his gun up and pulled the trigger. Nothing happened.

"Maybe you should take the safety off, sir," Joe-Ali murmured as the bird vanished.

"Goddammit," Big Boy Tarrington cried. "I don't need no damn nigger telling me what to do!"

"Mark again!" Joe-Ali shouted, and there was the woodcock once more, darting over the brush to find sanctuary in the swamp.

Tarrington rallied, firing into the bushes. In the silence that followed, a bold fox squirrel peered from a branch above and several deer bounded from the palmettos. Then came the distinctive *putt* noise of alarm that a wild turkey makes.

Blackbeard, his feathers flashing in the slanting sunlight, emerged from the bushes. Confused by the dogs, he began flying toward them.

Big Boy Tarrington's gun went off. The turkey bobbled. It dropped to the ground but continued running.

Maggie Royal let out an anguished cry. "Blackbeard. He's shot Blackbeard."

Joe-Ali found the wounded turkey and killed it.

The dead turkey was delivered to the yacht where Big Boy Tarrington lay snoring in his cabin following Cook Ada's lavish lunch spread out under the oaks. In due course, Blackbeard's head and beard appeared on a wooden plaque in Big Boy's den in the new Gwinnett mansion.

The toasts had been drunk and Ada's island delicacies cleared away from the tables on the veranda and along the sides of the big room. Meyer Davis struck up the band, bouncing up and down as he led his red-coated musicians. There was a wide smile on his face as he greeted the debs and postdebs, the visitors from New York and Long Island and Pennsylvania at whose parties he had played and for whose daughters' debuts he would play decades later.

Gramma, the aunts, Adele, Constance, and Maggie Royal formed a receiving line flanked with tubs of gardenias and the florist's camellias. Maggie Royal wore her grandmother's white satin Worth gown that had been made for her in 1924 when she made her last trip abroad. It was cut so elegantly and simply that only those who knew clothes could have guessed at its original cost. Luckily few alterations had been necessary and its fine lines remained intact. Jared's shark's tooth, on the gold chain around her neck, was hidden by Gramma's pearls, given her as a coming-out present. She carried the gardenia bouquet that Sparrow had sent her.

Maggie Royal shook hands with what seemed to be hundreds of people. The relatives hugged her and told her she looked beautiful. The outside people said how fine it was to be at Stark Island once again, and what a pretty dress!

Mairin swept through the line. She wore a crimson dress that made her look more Spanish than Irish and made Maggie Royal feel drab and virginal.

Then Cindy Lou and Jared approached. Cindy Lou wore black lace over a pink satin slip that shone through the lace. "At least she wore a slip," Adele whispered as the matrons on the sidelines goggled and the stag line eyed her appreciatively. The *Life* photographer, whose name was Mac Malloy, festooned with cameras and equipment the way the dock was festooned with barnacles, angled in for a shot.

"Really too tacky!" Aunt Meg sniffed. "Doesn't she know that young girls don't wear black!"

Cindy Lou appraised Maggie Royal as if she were a slave girl on the auction block. Cindy Lou's eyes shone with the hard glint of Gramma's star sapphires. Then her lips curved into a triumphant catlike smile. "What a sweet little frock!"

"Why, thank you." Maggie Royal returned her smile. "Worth '24."

"Dollars?" Cindy Lou's curving catlike smile seemed glued to her face. "My dear, how quaint!"

"Come on, Cindy Lou." Jared put his hand under her elbow. "We're holding up the line."

Maggie Royal didn't know whether to laugh at Cindy Lou's reaction or cry because of Jared's refusal to meet her eyes.

Jared, she wanted to cry out, look at me. But his eyes did not rise beyond the pearls at her neck. It was then that she noticed the blotches at the corner of his mouth and that his hair was not lying quite flat.

Noble had recovered from his brief passion for Cindy Lou. He was now enamored of a very pretty girl named Debby May Marston from Magnolia, Mississippi. Debby May thought that everything was just too divine for words, and that included Noble. Maggie Royal thought him very good-looking in his white tie and tails, tall, debonair, with a rosebud in his buttonhole and a mischievous gleam in his eye that made her think of Robert Montgomery. Thorny had refused to wear tails. He had on a rumpled white linen coat that someone had left in an upstairs closet. His girl, Hester Archer, had come to the island to be with him for the party.

She was a supercilious girl with glasses, without makeup, and a patronizing attitude toward anyone who talked about anything that wasn't "serious." She wore a rusty black evening gown and dirty white sneakers.

The receiving line broke up and Gramma returned to her chair at the end of the room, looking as regal as a queen holding court, chatting with the guests who clustered around her.

Mairin danced a tango with Noble. The other dancers stopped to watch and applaud as Noble whirled her about so fast that her skirt billowed out, displaying her famous legs.

"A bit too, too . . ." Aunt Emily commented to Aunt Meg.

Adele and Tyger moved onto the dance floor for the next number. Maggie Royal thought how well and how happy Adele looked in her new white coming-out dress with puffed sleeves and full skirt. She had been dieting and was much thinner. Maggie Royal envied her the ease and confidence with which she danced and laughed as she gazed up at Tyger and put her cheek against his.

Constance looked well in pale blue that went with her eyes and fair complexion. Jolly Olly was giving her a tremendous rush.

The aunts, unable to resist the music, took to the floor, floating like balloons with strings tied around their middles, surprisingly light on their feet as they waltzed with their husbands, whose faces were flushed and perspiring.

Big Boy Tarrington danced with his wife. Beside his bulky figure, encased in evening clothes, white teeth flashing, his wife looked faded, shrunken. Her flowered chiffon fluttered against her bony limbs as if a gust of wind had picked her up and was blowing her across the room.

A number of boys stood in the corner of the room where Cindy Lou was dancing, taking turns cutting in.

"It really was better when we had dance cards," Gramma said. "Look at poor Sarah Sue Bartow, the doctor's daughter. She keeps going to the ladies' room. Maggie Royal, tell Thorny or Noble to dance with her."

Maggie Royal found herself having a rush. Jim Bob Beasley, resplendent in his scarlet evening coat, despite the warm island night, kept cutting in. Following his lead, some of the older men from the mainland and neighboring islands began whirling her about to a set of fast tunes. At one point, the floor cleared in order to watch her waltz with Jim Bob, who whirled her faster and faster, his scarlet tails flying out behind him. He complimented her breathlessly, as he lifted her off her feet.

"Making an exhibition of herself! Like her mother," Aunt Emily sniffed as Maggie Royal spun past her, her skirt flying up around her knees.

Taylor DuPree, as he cut back for the fourth time, invited her to the university for Easter week. Thorny held her close, taking great gliding steps the way the Choate School men did. Noble kept moving his hand up and down her back as he stared past her shoulder at Debby May; his breath smelled of whiskey. Sparrow danced the way he pursued birds, with complete concentration.

"Are you having fun?" Maggie Royal asked him.

"You bet," he replied. "One, two, three, four, glide. . . ."

"Sparrow, have you tried the punch?"

"Don't talk, Maggie Royal," he said. "I'm counting."

Jim Bob Beasley approached to cut in. Sparrow took her arm and led her off the dance floor. "Only way to get you away from the wolves." He brought her a glass of champagne and sat down opposite her. "You couldn't care less, could you?"

"Sparrow," Maggie Royal heard herself say, "I care terribly about lots of things."

"But I'm not one of them," he answered sadly, without bitterness. "You're like the lightning bugs I kept in a Mason jar when I was a kid. Now I see you. Now I don't. I felt then as I do now. A feeling of almost. Almost catching you. Then, just when I think I have your attention, you slip away."

"Sparrow, dear," she said gently. "You are a dear friend. You always will be."

Maybe she was a little giddy from the champagne, but as she watched, the dancers seemed to whirl faster and faster, blurring in and out of focus, becoming one with the great ball in the scrapbook given before the Starksville volunteers marched off to the War Between the States. Then the girls in their full-skirted gowns were as romantic as Jared's great-grandmother, who eloped from the island with a dashing Yankee officer who came ashore from a gunboat anchored in the sound. This Stark ancestor was said to have died of a broken heart after her husband was killed in the battle of Mobile Bay. The Negroes believed she was one of the hants of Great Oak, haunting the lower garden, floating along the winding path to meet her lover in the gazebo in her gauzy white dress, like a hand passing before the face of the moon.

At this imaginary ball the men were all tall, dark, and dashing, wearing their Confederate gray, carrying their faith like sabers.

In Maggie Royal's mind's eye, they looked like Jared.

She saw him then, his white shirt contrasting with his brown skin as he walked across the floor to cut in on Cindy Lou. His dark head bent over Cindy Lou's fair one. Her cheek rested against his heart, and as the music slowed, switching to a blues song, his arm tightened around her.

At midnight, Gramma excused herself and went to bed. She refused Maggie Royal's offer to see her to her room, saying that Molly, Affey's replacement, would bring her her Ovaltine and get her settled.

"Good night, child." She gave Maggie Royal her cheek in an uncharacteristic gesture. "Have a good time. This is a night you should remember."

The party was at its peak. Mrs. Johnson, the reverend's wife, slipped on the waxed staircase and sprained an ankle, and Inside Dick, having partaken of a bottle of port Uncle Oomlot had neglected to hide in his coffin, crashed down the stairs from the landing carrying the four bottles of Dom Perignon Uncle Oomlot had intended to serve at his table during midnight supper.

Then Jared came down the stairs. He walked past Noble, who had approached to ask Maggie Royal to dance, and wordlessly took her in his arms. The orchestra swung into "It Was Just One of Those Things."

Neither spoke as he held her closer. She could feel his trembling as her cheek touched his sun-dried shirt, the smell of which mingled with shaving soap and cigarettes.

Faster, faster. The balloons and people, the massed flowers and musicians, all becoming a blur of color.

Closer, closer, until she could scarcely breathe. The room began to clear and the music to change tempo, slowly to "Mood Indigo" and then accelerating to "Beer Barrel Polka."

Now there was no one left on the floor, and still around and around they went, Maggie Royal's feet following where Jared led, with the same magic ease with which she had followed him across country the day of the Starksville hunt.

She had a fleeting glimpse of her mother standing on the sidelines, a hard, disapproving expression on her face.

Then she saw Cindy Lou, her mouth narrowed into a thin line, that hard blue light in her eyes as she stared from the sidelines at Jared.

Abruptly the music ended. Jared stopped. As if in a trance he walked Maggie Royal over to where Sparrow stood by the doorway. Without a word or backward glance, he handed her over to his friend and went over to cut in on Cindy Lou.

"Sparrow, excuse me," Maggie Royal apologized. "There's something I must do."

She turned and ran down the steps, along the pathway between the magnolias and camellias with blossoms tied to their branches, to the lower garden and the gazebo, where Grandfather had kept his arboretum journal and smoked his pipe.

The night had a whispering, haunted quality, a scented sensual softness, as strange and ghostly as the shadows made by the moving moss dripping from the trees. Spirits seemed to walk, whisper, and make love, as softly and silently as the rustling of silk or the sound of petals falling. The fireflies made flashing lights like drops of green water. The music from the big house became faint, as dreamlike as the daguerreotypes of the dancers moving again in the orange-pink candlelight behind the windows.

She took off her high-heeled slippers and silk stockings and stowed them under the bench in the gazebo. Slowly she began to dance, faster and then faster, the white skirt swirling like foam around her knees. She did not know how long she danced before she saw him silhouetted in the doorway.

"Maggie Royal!" Jared took a step toward her and held out his arms. Slowly he drew her into them.

Time stood still. There was the sense of spinning, of turning faster and faster, of floating, flying, of a melting sensation as if her bones were becoming fluid as water.

Jared stopped so suddenly she missed a step and almost fell. For a moment they stood staring at one another. Maggie Royal noticed that his necktie was askew and a lock of hair fell onto his forehead. In the dim misted light his face was strange and unfamiliar.

"Maggie Royal!" He caught his breath.

Her hand went to her mouth.

He reached up and drew it down again. "Don't hide it. It's a beautiful mouth."

She swayed toward him, as if drawn by an irresistible force. He put out both hands, grasping her by the shoulders as though to keep her from falling. Her nose bumped against his chest, and she felt its warmth. For an instant he held her against him and she could feel his arms trembling. Then, abruptly, he released her.

"Maggie Royal!" There was a break in his voice. "Maggie Royal, I can't dance with you anymore. I don't want to hurt you. I can't explain."

He turned, lowering his head in order to go through the doorway, and began walking quickly to the house.

The music started up again, bittersweet, nostalgic, clichéd and sentimental, carried on the night breeze like the sweet smell of a gardenia corsage. She was glad it was dark so her hurt and bewilderment would not show.

The music paused for an intermission. She hid behind a gardenia bush on the veranda. She saw Jared sitting with Cindy Lou inside. Their heads were close together. Cindy Lou sipped from her glass and gazed up at him over its rim. She smiled, and even from a distance Maggie Royal could see the dimples at either side of her lipsticked cupid's bow, which made her skin and amazing platinum hair seem even paler.

The music began again. Jared took the glass from Cindy Lou's hand and pulled her to her feet. Deliberately she seemed to lose her balance, and her full breasts brushed his white shirtfront. Slowly they moved out onto the floor.

Maggie Royal felt her heart congeal, as if the wind blowing in from the sea was turning it colder and colder.

Long after that summer, she would hear the music, smell the gardenias, and feel the wind in her hair, and she would wonder why we are sent warnings and prophecies, given signs we cannot or will not listen to.

Mist came through the park, swirling, drifting through the hanging moss. Overhead, black shredded clouds moved across the face of the moon. Before the night ended, there would be rain.

There was that indefinable island scent, salt spray mingled with the bouquet of flowers, the overripe decaying stench of the marsh, and the faint dry musty smell of moss.

Holding up her skirt, she ran along the path to the beach, trying not to think of snakes that might be lurking. Trailing moss brushed against her like the fingers of a hand. Branches tore at her fragile dress. The music was submerged by the sound of surf pounding against the hard-packed sand. Several times she tripped in pig holes and over fallen branches.

The path widened. The dunes rose before her, huge hills of powder sand, shaped and reshaped by the wind, and the blue-white light after the dark woods was like coming from a long black tunnel into sunlight.

She climbed on top of a high dune. The beach was empty. She stood with the night wind whipping her dress around her, seeing the matching lips of the waves rolling up onto the beach, then receding, leaving but an instant glitter in the night.

Wildness filled her. She began to run, down the side of the dune, almost tripping over a couple nestled on a blanket laid in the hollow.

She stopped at the water's edge. She saw no one. Quickly she stepped out of her dress and unhooked the hated bra she'd been wearing.

Her breasts were hard and firm and uptilted. Not like Adele's or Cindy Lou's, which bulged from under their open-neck shirts. Hers hardly bulged at all. Yet when she ran the palms of her hands over them, they tingled and began to ache.

Clouds raced overhead, and the water with its ribbon of white foamed around her bare feet. Every area of skin and bone and hair seemed suddenly alive and shimmering like the phosphorescent water, as if her body was starting to flower, about to burst open like the buds on the camellias waiting to blossom.

The remembered feel of Jared's cheek, the palms of his hands flat against the hollow of her back, holding her against the long hardness of him, was almost unbearable. The tide was out and she had a long way to wade before the icy water, reaching to her shoulders, drowned the agony of wanting.

She swam with long even strokes. Her hair slapped the waves as she moved her head from side to side. When she looked up, she could not see the shore. The moon had gone behind a cloud and she felt a raindrop on her face.

She had broken a cardinal island rule. She had not meant to swim for so long or so far out. Nor had she told anyone where she was going. Gramma would be furious if she discovered that she had left her own party.

She turned and headed for shore, but found she was not making any headway against the current. She tried swimming harder but only succeeded in staying in the same place. She remembered all the things she had heard about drowning and the sharks sometimes seen off the beach.

Then she was no longer cold. The water seemed warm, comforting. She gave up trying to swim and let herself float.

"What the hell did you think you were doing?" Jared stood glowering over her. "You're island. You know about the tides. If I hadn't come looking for you, you'd have been a goner."

She crossed her arms over her chest, aware she was naked other than the pearls and shark's tooth on the chain around her neck. Her teeth began to chatter. The white shirt Jared had worn at the dance lay sodden and crumpled on the sand.

He picked it up and began rubbing her shoulders. "Idiot child. You're freezing. We'll go to the beach house. I'll build you a fire."

He pulled her to her feet, looking wild and romantic and angry. His skin against hers was damp and cold with a layer of warmth beneath it, like water below the surface of the sea.

The rain quickened, as did her heart. "I must go home," she said with an effort. "Gramma will be angry."

It didn't occur to her to wonder if her mother would be concerned. She had even forgotten she was on the island.

"Gramma won't miss you," Jared said, putting his dinner jacket over her shoulders. "The music stopped ages ago. The grown-ups have gone to bed. The diehards are in the pool house dancing, eating, drinking, and swinging on the rings. Jolly Olly greased the rings and everyone fell into the water in their evening clothes."

"Why aren't you there?"

"Let's just say I wanted to get away. Rufus found your dress lying on the sand. I figured only you would be crazy enough to swim out past the sandbar alone."

"My dress," she cried, picking it up. "It's ruined. What will I do? I can't wear it back to the house."

"Worth twenty-four dollars!" He began to laugh. "You were never one for dresses. I like you better this way."

"What if people start looking for us?"

"Let them," Jared said. He started to run, pulling her along. They ran along the beach to the old gray-shingled cottage Grandfather McDermott had built as a refuge from the big house when it was overrun with children and guests.

The years had taken their toll. The glass was gone from one window. Canvas chairs were ragged and torn. Several of her father's old polo mallets hung from a hook on the wall. Two carved wooden curlews sat on the mantel. A few pieces of driftwood and some cedar logs were stacked against the stone fireplace and a worn Indian blanket lay on the floor.

Expertly Jared laid a fire. He lit it and sat back on his heels, blowing on the beginning flames.

She sat cross-legged on the blanket, Jared's coat hiding her nakedness.

"Here." He handed her a silver flask from his pocket.

She took a sip. The liquor set up a burning inside, while the logs, bursting into flame, warmed her outside.

"Why did you swim out there alone?" Jared asked, sitting down beside her.

She took another sip and began to cough. "Let's just say I felt like a swim."

"Dammit, Maggie Royal, it's not like you to play games."

She sighed. "Cindy Lou . . ."

"Forget Cindy Lou," he said roughly.

She could hear his heart beating, and his hand was like the flames from the fire against her skin. The liquor eased tension, took fear away. Her trust lay in Jared. He had taught her how a mare foals, how the great turtles lay their eggs, how piglets are born, and where the best clams are to be found. Now at last she knew where the restless rides, the dreaming and sleepless nights, had been taking her. As if in a dream, she shut her eyes.

His words hit her like a blast of freezing wave. "Maggie Royal, I can't."

"Why?" She was appalled.

"You're so damn young!"

"Jared, I'm a debutante. Only three years younger than you are."

His face looked stony, closed, apart now. She suddenly felt exhausted. The wine, the whiskey, the long swim.

He was staring at her. "When you grow up, I'll paint you."

"Dammit, Jared. How grown-up does one have to be!"

"You think you know me, Maggie Royal, but you don't. You see me as you've always seen me, as I am on the island. There are other places, other things."

He lit a cigarette and threw the match into the fire.

"We're too much alike. What was it that nurse of yours used to say? Children of nature. The salt from the sea is the seasoning in our blood. Why did you swim out there tonight? Because it's where you feel closest to yourself." He drew on his cigarette and the hollows in his cheeks deepened. "It'll be a different world from now on. Maggie Royal, there's going to be a war. People will no longer own islands."

"Rubbish!" she exclaimed, using Gramma's word. "It will be here, an island to come back to!"

He touched the shark's tooth at her throat. "Maggie Royal, life can be very different from what you expect, what you think you want." His eyes darkened until they were almost black. "My God, there's so much out there!"

He rose and began walking back and forth. "I want it all," he said as if to himself.

Maggie Royal's head suddenly felt too heavy to hold. It was filled with fragments of thoughts, mixed with feelings, flashing on and off like Fourth of July sparklers shooting in different directions. She wanted to reach out to Jared and hold him as he had held her when they were dancing. At the same time she knew somehow she never could, and this instinctive knowledge caught her in a cold, frozen sense of apprehension that was like the morning's gray rain-filled dullness creeping in on them through the broken window.

It was still raining and the wind came down the chimney and blew the dying ashes into the room. They heard the sound of voices outside, on the beach. It was suddenly very cold in the little cabin, and although the voices faded away, the moment was gone.

Jared grinned his crooked grin. "Something tells me heaven's going to fall if we don't get the hell out of here." He glanced at his watch. "No point in sleeping. Why don't we have breakfast and then take a ride?"

They made sure the fire was out, straightened the rug, and swept up the sand and ashes. Then they put on their sodden clothes. Slowly they started back along the beach.

Jared bent down and picked up a pear whelk. "Nice?" He handed it to her. "Not chipped or broken."

She gazed at the shell in her hand. It was glimmering white outside, dusty pink inside. She thought of Cindy Lou Tarrington's pink-and-white complexion. She tried to imagine her walking along a beach at dawn in a ruined, sodden evening gown, barefoot, her perfectly waved hair tangled and blowing in the wind and rain.

They were almost at Great Oak when they heard a noise in the underbrush.

"Oh, thank God," Maggie Royal cried, recognizing Sparrow as he parted the palmettos and came toward them. "Sparrow, you do creep up on one. Surely you're not bird-watching in this weather?"

"I was looking for you." His face was very solemn. "Maid Marian and Robin Hood! Time to get out of the forest, pronto! Maggie Royal, you better get back to the house fast. There's a posse out looking for you!"

Jared was right about heaven. It fell in on them like one of his mother's pottery bowls, crashing against the hearth, breaking beyond repair.

The Long Point Negroes, under the direction of Newt, were sweeping the veranda and setting things to rights in the big front room.

"Your mother wants to see you," Newt said tactfully, managing not to look at her bedraggled dress.

"I'll see you at the stable," Jared said. He squeezed her hand. "It's a date."

"Not bloody likely," Mairin said from the doorway. On her face, as her glance traveled over them, was a terrible unreasoning anger. She pushed Maggie Royal inside and slammed the door shut before she could call back to Jared.

Gramma lay back against her lacy pillows looking old and frail.

"Mairin . . ." she began. Her voice dwindled off into a whisper. "I'm very tired, and today will be a long day. So many guests . . . Maggie Royal should change before she catches pneumonia. Can't this wait? . . ."

"No," Mairin answered flatly. "It's got to be stopped . . . now." Her famous eyes narrowed, wearing the expression of high indignation sometimes seen in her photographs taken onstage.

"The idea, the night of your own party. Staying out with . . . with that boy. Doing . . . Words fail me."

"I'm sure they were just roughhousing," Gramma said faintly.

"Roughhousing!" Mairin cried. Her eyes wore a hard blue light. "Like hell they were! Roughhousing all night!"

"Mother," Maggie Royal cried out desperately. "Jared wouldn't dream—"

Her mother never let her finish. "You're a worse fool than I thought." She lit one of her Turkish cigarettes and snapped her silver lighter shut. "All any man wants is sex. Love? What do you know about love? You're a child."

"I'm tired of being told I'm a child," Maggie Royal yelled. "Once and for all, I am not a child. I just came out."

"Be quiet," Gramma spoke up. "Both of you, hush. Mairin, I asked you not to smoke in my room. Now, I think we must postpone this . . . discussion . . . until later."

"You're hysterical," Mairin said to Maggie Royal. "Don't make more of a fool of yourself than you already have with this . . . this peasant."

"Enough!" Gramma said, managing to push herself upright. "Mairin, I won't have any more. Put out that cigarette now. Maggie Royal, go to your room and change. Maggie Royal?" Her voice was stern, but Maggie Royal thought she detected a twinkle in her eyes. "I trust this performance will not be repeated!"

"Gramma!" Maggie Royal ran to her bedside. She flung herself down on her knees and burrowed her head against her grandmother as she had so often in the past. "Gramma, please understand. It isn't what you think."

"Maggie Royal." Her grandmother's frail blue-veined hand bearing the great diamond was like the touch of a moth, as brief and ephemeral. "Mr. McDermott said once that a lie may seem the nearest exit out of an adolescent dilemma, but the truth is a more direct path to maturity. Go, now . . . we'll talk later."

At the door, Maggie Royal heard Gramma say with some of her old spirit, "Well, Mairin, I hope we're not going to have any more performances like that!"

"Magdalena!" Mairin came into her room without knocking and shut the door behind her. The hard blue light Maggie Royal had seen when her mother argued with a producer over her salary or a director over her lines shone in her eyes. She lit another one of her cigarettes and took a long drag and began to speak. Maggie Royal had the sense of unreality she always felt around her, as if Mairin didn't really believe what she was saying herself but was acting out the part she'd been told to play.

"I have brought you up to marry well. Money and a name."

Maggie Royal started to point out that Gramma had brought her up, but her mother cut her short. "Castles crumble, dung heaps rise, as they say in Ireland. The Starks have crumbled. The money's all but gone. As for those other Starks, a down-at-the-heel radical and his half-caste wife . . ."

"Mother," Maggie Royal said sadly, "why are you this way?" She felt a great regret, a sense of loss, and the waste of a human relationship that should have been meaningful and valuable and life-sustaining.

"I didn't bring up my daughter to throw herself away on a Georgia cracker with a ne'r-do-well for a father, a black woman for a mother."

Maggie Royal was beyond rage. "Jared's mother is not a Negro; she's an Indian princess."

"Hah!" Mairin answered. "And I'm the Queen of England." She began pacing up and down, taking quick, short puffs on her sickly sweet-smelling cigarette, which she smoked in a long carved ivory holder.

She turned suddenly, moving quickly across the room to where Maggie Royal had hung the towels she had taken from the linen closet. Maggie Royal had been in a hurry and had not noticed whether they matched or not.

"I've told you," Mairin cried, yanking the towels from the rack above the bedroom washbasin. "Towels should match and be hung properly." She dumped them one by one on the floor. She started toward the door. Halfway there she paused and said, "Magdalena, I forbid you to see your cousin Jared again. Now, change your clothes and pack. We're leaving this god-forsaken place by the next boat!"

Maggie Royal hopped from the bed and ran to the door.

"You are not to see that boy," her mother repeated. "You will not leave your room."

Maggie Royal stood dead-still. Outside the window the rain had begun again and was raising goose pimples on the leaden sound.

Slowly, carefully, Mairin ground out her cigarette. "He won't marry you. Why should he?" she asked contemptuously. "He's had what he wants."

The whelk shell Maggie Royal had been clutching in her hand crashed to the floor. Very carefully she picked it up and placed it on the mantel, noticing it was no longer unmarked. The fall had broken off the spiraled end.

It was raining again as Maggie Royal walked down to the dock to take the boat to the mainland. Newt told her he had not seen Jared since morning but had heard Miss Cindy Lou say she was meeting him to go riding. Nor had Jared left a message.

Mairin wanted Maggie Royal to go abroad to a Swiss boarding school, but because of the possibility of war—Maggie Royal secretly believed that her mother didn't want the responsibility of an almost-grown-up daughter—she agreed to let her return to Miss Mayo's and graduate in June.

Mairin had no need to worry about Maggie Royal's relationship with Jared. Both Jared and Thorny left Harvard after the Christmas vacation to serve in the Lincoln Brigade in the Civil War in Spain.

"Gramma pretended she didn't want him to go," Adele told Maggie Royal when she had a weekend off from school and the cousins were reunited at Pierre's in Washington for lunch. "She said the idea of a relation involved in anything concerning Mr. Lincoln made her blood run cold, but I think she was secretly pleased. She admitted it was what your father would have done, Maggie Royal. The rest of the family feels he should not have left Harvard before graduating. Uncle Thorndike was horrified. He called Jared and Thorny Bolsheviks. Thorny explained they were Republicans, fighting on the Republican side!"

Jared's father, Adele continued, was handling cases involving the civil liberties of Negroes at the Army base being built outside Starksville. "Some Klan people came over and burned a cross at Long Point. They got away before anyone could catch them."

Adele reached for a roll and began buttering it. "When I finished school and got engaged to Tyger, I saw no reason to diet anymore." She patted her stomach, around which her plaid skirt strained at its fastenings. "You're so lucky. You never have to diet. You eat like one of those birds Sparrow was always watching.

"By the way." Adele stared fixedly at her cousin. "Why ever did you steal away, after the party, like a thief in the night, without telling anyone?"

"Let's say it was a matter of smoke without fire."

"You do tend to talk in riddles," Adele said crossly, picking up the menu. "I think I'll have a chocolate éclair. I need energy if I'm going job-hunting." She eyed Maggie Royal over the top of the menu. "Nothing for you? I thought maybe your sudden departure from the island had something to do with Jared and Cindy Lou."

When Maggie Royal remained silently smoking, Adele continued. "I forgot to tell you. Before Jared and Thorny left for Spain, the Roisterers threw a stag dinner for them at the Starksville Country Club. Gaboons of champie and gin. Jolly Olly Irving and Piers Shaw tried to see who could drink the most, and both passed out. Noble fell out the window of the men's room into a rosebush and scratched himself to bits. But the big moment came when they brought in the cake.

"Two waiters came in carrying an enormous round cake laden with candles. They set it on the table in front of Jared. He blew out the candles and tried to cut the cake, but he couldn't, because it was cardboard." Adele paused, observing her cousin. "Then out popped Cindy Lou Tarrington, without a stitch on!"

"You're kidding," Maggie Royal gasped. "Naked!"

"As a jaybird," Adele continued. " 'Happy birthday, Jaredy!' she cried, and leaped from the table into his lap. Tyger said Jared's face got redder and redder as Cindy Lou kept hugging him. Then Cindy Lou got up, blew everybody kisses, and ran out of the room. A few minutes later she came back in a black satin evening gown that Tyger said was cut so low she might as well have been naked all over again."

"Let's have a brandy," Maggie Royal suggested.

"Why, Maggie Royal," Adele replied. "Ah declare, what's come over you? Brandy in the middle of the day. Better not let Miss Mayo smell your breath!"

Graduation came finally. Great-Aunt Amy wrote that Gramma was too ill to come. She had never completely recovered from Affey's death, and the coming-out party seemed to have drained her of her remaining strength. She became, in her words, "a little unwell."

"I knew she shouldn't have exerted herself, spent all that money," Aunt Emily sniffed. "I told her it was poor taste, with the depression and all. She argued that she was providing employment for many people. She wanted to finish in style, have one last party, *fare una bella figura,* as the Italians say."

Although Dr. Bartow came weekly from the mainland to see her, nobody knew about the cancer. "I was forbidden to speak of it to anyone," Dr. Bartow reported. "She always considered it poor taste to discuss one's illness."

Maggie Royal determined to travel to Stark Island as soon as the graduation ceremony was over.

Aunt Lucy came from Dunwoody to represent the family. She watched Maggie Royal receive her diploma from Miss Mayo, who cautioned her always to behave like a Mayo girl, "with style and discretion."

Maggie Royal was packing to leave school when the telegram came saying that Gramma had died.

Adele and many of the relatives were on the train to Starksville. "I suppose you've heard that Jared is coming home from Spain to marry Cindy Lou," Adele announced without preliminaries. "Good thing Gramma doesn't know. She'd have a fit. She always thought it would be Jared and you, Maggie Royal."

Maggie Royal stared at Cuffee. Wearing a dark armband sewn onto the sleeve of the white jacket, the steward was pouring drinks for the "John Doe" uncles.

"God damn you, Jared," she said under her breath. "God damn you to hell!" She tossed her head and reached for one of the drinks Cuffee was dispensing.

It's inconvenient to die on an island. In order to be embalmed it was necessary for Gramma's body to travel to "Drop Kick" Keeler's funeral parlor in Starksville, where the undertaker was unable to persuade the family to buy a "fitting" casket. "Don't you dare put me in one of those hideous boxes with plush and fancy handles!" Gramma had insisted. "I want to go simple!"

On the island, she was laid out in the living room in the pine box she had ordered made years before and which had resided in the cellar storeroom where Cook Ada's "frizzled" hens laid eggs in it. She was dressed in the gown she had worn at the coming-out party. Molly, Jasper's wife, arranged her lovely white hair, waving it back from her forehead and pinning it in a chignon. She had lain thus for a day and night while Annie Itch, the white pig, and Marcel, her old spaniel, stood guard, refusing to go outdoors unless they were dragged.

To Maggie Royal, the shrunken figure lying there was as shapeless and characterless as one of the crude voodoo dolls with which old Dah had cast spells. The carefully coiffed hair, rouged cheeks, and painted lips, the piercing "see-through-you" eyes sealed forever, was not Gramma.

Gramma had been the regal figure in the lion's-head chair, directing, cajoling, sympathizing, running the huge establishment with an iron hand in a velvet muff, cantering along the island trails, or patiently holding the lead line until the children learned to ride by themselves. She was the handsome, autocratic mistress of Great Oak, serving tea from the tea set now being fought over by the aunts and in-laws or sitting in the candlelight at the end of the long dining-room table set with the silver place plates and crystal wine goblets.

She had brought the children up to do things one doesn't want to do, brush teeth, read books, study, eat oatmeal and prunes. Young girls were taught how to pour tea and use a fish fork, to judge the correct amount of time to spend at dinner parties talking to one partner before "swinging with the cutlets" to converse with the other.

Certain topics were taboo. Divorce for one. Nobody "nice" got divorced. If it was somebody you knew it was obviously the other partner's fault and the matter was promptly buried under the Aubusson.

Maggie Royal and the cousins learned the intricacies of correctly tying a hunting stock and to bone boots but almost nothing about their physical selves or what happens in the dark between a man and a woman. These things were learned below stairs, from conversations overheard and by osmosis, in the warmth and earthiness and lack of pretense of the Negro community.

Gramma had taught Maggie Royal that you can't live without self-respect, for without it there could be no survival. "If you live long enough," she said once, "everything will happen to you. You learn to overcome, to survive." Self-respect without self-pity. If you make mistakes, she had told her, you don't go around asking for absolution or complaining of unfairness or embarrassment if you're caught out.

As she rode Azilia along the beach in the rain that morning, Maggie Royal thought of Gramma's words: Survive, Maggie Royal, survive. If you can do that and be useful at the same time, you'll have kept the faith.

She went to Long Point to see Jared's parents. It was the way it had always been. Jared's mother made sassafras tea and his father talked about the coming war. Susan told her Sparrow had proposed.

"That's keen, copacetic," Maggie Royal cried, hugging her. "I'm so happy for you both."

Nobody mentioned Jared or his coming marriage to Cindy Lou Tarrington.

She found Uncle Oomlot frail and shrunken, huddled beneath a mound of blankets. Inside Dick told her that since Gramma's death he had eaten very little and had not even shouted at him to bring the port. He did not care any longer if his shirts were not sent off to England in the wicker laundry basket. Nor did he listen to the radio. The hand that took hers was white and blue-veined and he failed to show any interest when she told him she had been foxhunting in Virginia.

She left him lying very still, gazing out the window at the gray water of the sound.

The island boat was busy all day bringing friends and relatives from the mainland. The dogs ran from one door to another, barking frantically at their approach—Mayor Lovewell, the Reverend Mr. Johnson and Dr. Bartow, old Judge Cantwell with roses, Mr. Perrin, the butcher, Mr. Tavis, the solicitor, and little Jenny Carson, bringing a batch of candles. Big Boy Tarrington came over in his speedboat. Mrs. Tarrington, he said, was feeling "poorly" but would attend the funeral. The aunts directed Newt to tell him they were "resting," and after leaving an ornate calling card in the silver salver by the front door, he roared away again.

The Long Point people came to pay their respects to Miss Maggie

Royal Gramma. All day long there was somebody or other at the back door with a basket or a plate covered with a napkin—a dozen eggs, a cake, rolls, fried chicken or a ham.

Flowers filled buckets and tubs. The aunts were busy arranging them.

"Whatever shall we do with this?" Aunt Lucy asked, removing tissue from a long florist's box to disclose an ornate cross made of lilies and eucalyptus and tied with wide purple satin ribbon. "From the Tarringtons. I declare, I never saw anything so tacky. Gramma loathed eucalyptus."

The great-aunts, Amy and Meg, were jointly running the house and fighting like the cats and dogs which were everywhere. They had been at Great Oak since Gramma had begun to fail.

That night dinner was late. Cook Ada, crippled by rheumatism, had retired, and her replacement, newcomer Ada, had cooked the roast too long and the potatoes too little.

Gramma had never permitted animals in the dining room. Now dogs lay all over the floor, making it necessary to detour or step over them.

"Watch out for dearest darling Reveler," Aunt Meg warned as one of the lemony hounds Jim Bob Beasley had given her growled at Aunt Amy, who had stepped on its tail. "Amy, you know Reveler doesn't like to be disturbed."

Aunt Meg rested her hunting whip beside her chair as she took her place at the head of the table. She lowered her head and asked the Reverend Mr. Johnson, who would officiate at the funeral in the morning, to say the blessing. While he did so, she began buttering bread for the dogs, who rose and clustered around her.

Newt brought in the roast beef, carved into thick, unwieldy slices, and, instead of passing it, placed the platter in front of Aunt Meg. He had hardly turned away when one of the hounds lunged at it.

Aunt Meg turned to Aunt Amy. "It's one of yours. Drive it away."

"No," Aunt Amy replied firmly. "It's yours, Meg. That's Starkie, the dog found on the beach. He's fattened up so you'd hardly recognize him."

While they argued, the dog in question surreptitiously snatched a thick slice of beef off the platter, splashing gravy onto the white cloth.

Aunt Meg reached for her whip and brought it crashing down, missing the dog and hitting the table. Two crystal wineglasses overturned and a Tiffany plate crashed to the floor. The dog carried the dripping meat over the carpet to a corner, where he promptly devoured it.

"Reh-ley," Aunt Emily said, wrinkling her nose in distaste. "Rehley, Meg."

Maggie Royal could hear Gramma: "Well, I do hope we are not going to have any more performances like that!"

After dinner some of the aunts began staking out claims on the articles they wanted to take from the house. There was a terrible argument over the place plates. Aunt Emily insisted Gramma had promised them to her for her Greenwich house. Aunt Leonie agreed to relinquish them only if she could have the Venetian mirror in the hall. Aunt Amy said that wasn't fair; the place plates were more valuable, family heirlooms.

Finally Great-Aunt Meg banged her whip down on the coffee table and announced it was poor taste to bicker over things in front of the rector, especially as Gramma wasn't even buried yet.

"What do we know about Gramma's will?" Aunt Emily asked the company at large.

"We have to wait for Mr. Tavis, the solicitor, to read it," Uncle Thorndike said reasonably.

"Yes," Maggie Royal whispered to Adele. "And another will will be found in Gramma's jewelry box and we'll have a million dollars and live forever, like turtles. Do you want to make book on whether or not Aunt Emily gets the place plates?"

It was raining the next day. The inside Negroes waited patiently in the park, beneath the great oak, their hats in their hands. Many were weeping as they bowed their heads and murmured the old-time sayings of sadness and mourning. "Oh, missus, our backs is broke" and "Oh, Lord, she's gone . . . she's gone, oh, Lord."

Mayor Lovewell, Dr. Bartow, Mr. Perrin, the butcher, the Tarringtons, and countless others from Starksville, as well as from neighboring islands, lined the avenue as Gramma's coffin was carried down the steps and put into the ox cart. Old Sapelo had polished the landau and the hackneys' harness for the great-aunts to ride in. Jasper had brought up old Darien, now in his mid-twenties, and placed Gramma's sidesaddle on the old horse.

The rest walked. Moss grew in patches on the drive. The oaks stood like an honor guard on either side. Their dead, sodden leaves carpeted the roadway. Overhead, bright green "new" leaves drew life from the old twisted "live" oaks, giving hope like the resurrection ferns slowly reviving in the rain. Daffodils held up their heads proudly. The camellias Gramma loved were in all their crimson, pink, and white glory. The air was filled with the fresh aromatic scent of the yellow jessamine clinging to the trees. A shy doe peered around the trunk of one and then vanished. A family of pigs rooting on the lawn paused to watch the funeral procession go by. From somewhere came the clear round notes of a cardinal calling to its mate.

As the ox cart trundled down the street, the men and women living in the settlement came out to stand silently with bowed heads.

Old Ada knelt beside the road, her almost blind eyes closed, and held out her clasped hands. "Tunka punka," she chanted, using the Gullah words. "My darling little missy. Miss Maggie Royal Gramma. Steal away! May the good Lord take a likin' to you . . ."

The cart carrying the coffin stopped at the entrance to the ancient burial ground where Jeremy Stark had been laid to rest after helping defeat the Spaniards in 1742. The "John Doe" uncles-in-law carried the coffin through the spiked iron gateway with the big ornate S in the center and the family motto across the top, "Keep Tryst."

The pine box was placed in the hole that had been dug next to Grandfather's grave. Flowers were massed around it—red roses from President and Mrs. Roosevelt, camellias in mounds, wreaths and sprays from the great and near-great she had entertained at Great Oak.

Maggie Royal stood with her head bowed next to Aunt Meg. She wished the Reverend Mr. Johnson weren't so long-winded. The Negroes were the only ones who seemed unafraid to show emotion. The white people restrained their grief, holding it in check by what they and their religion considered taste and decorum.

She thought of the world Gramma had left. Jared's father called it a world where faith had become a military motto, where religious and racial persecution masqueraded under the guise of loyalty and love of country, where personal relations were considered weaknesses to be done away with for the greater good of the state. The ends were justification for the means, he had explained, but nobody said what the "ends" were.

His words came to her with the same numbing dreariness as the rain. Perhaps civilization could only be born, he had said, as a child is born, with blood and violence and pain. But then it was up to the individual to put down, shackle, the monster that lives in us all, and bring up our children decently, teach them tolerance, compassion, and sympathy.

People needed an island of the mind, he had said, room to express themselves, to discover, read, and think—the right to create and live as one chooses within the bounds of decency, to criticize and accept criticism, in short, to be useful and survive. Democracy with all its faults permitted this. A totalitarian state did not.

"The grace of our Lord Jesus and the love of God and the fellowship of the Holy Ghost be with us all evermore . . ."

"*Un bel enterrement,*" Aunt Leonie LeFevre murmured as they made their way slowly back to the great house.

"I'm exhausted," Aunt Emily said, sinking into the sofa in the big living room, where the family had gathered with Mr. Tavis. "Standing out in that rain! Then feeding all those people! I really think it's much more civilized to be cremated."

"I thought Gramma's funeral was beautiful," Maggie Royal said. "She would have been happy so many of her friends came."

"Friends?" asked Aunt Leonie. "You mean like the butcher, the baker?"

"Yes, they were her friends," Maggie Royal insisted. "Like the Long Point people."

Mr. Tavis cleared his throat. "I'm afraid the will is vague in some respects. Mrs. McDermott mentions only a few specific personal effects. Now, if you are ready . . ."

"We're ready," Aunt Emily said. "We've already decided how the property should be disposed."

Mr. Tavis gazed at her in silence, and Maggie Royal thought she detected a faint malicious twinkle in his eyes.

"I'm afraid that Mrs. McDermott's fortune has been greatly depleted," he began. He looked around him over the tops of his spectacles. "For the past decade Stark Island has been run on sentiment rather than on a sensible and economic basis. I tried to keep Mrs. McDermott from dipping into capital." His dry voice sounded as if he had just reported a murder. "When I remonstrated with her about it, she explained she intended to finish in style!" He cleared his throat. "Those were her words."

"She spent the last of her capital on the party," said Aunt Leonie, who, not having a daughter to come out, had been against the expense. "She even sold her sapphires."

"We all tried to make her see the light," Uncle George said, "but she wouldn't listen. She refused to sell off any property."

"I could have doubled her income," Uncle Thorndike said.

"She was hopeless about money," Aunt Emily said. "She carried everything in that reticule of hers."

Mr. Tavis cleared his throat. "If I may continue."

He read the simple bequests first, money and personal gifts to the inside and outside employees. Jewelry and personal possessions were to be divided among the aunts, as they saw fit. The Stark pearls and mink coat had been left to Maggie Royal.

"What happened to the rest of the jewelry?" Aunt Hope interrupted. "Her engagement diamond?"

"Gone," Mr. Tavis replied tersely. "Sold to cover the party expenses. I believe the diamonds went in order to pay the orchestra."

"Her diamond engagement ring," Aunt Leonie breathed, "that father gave her! Incredible! I knew she should never have given that party."

"Only the pearls are left," Mr. Tavis said, gazing at Maggie Royal. "She thought they'd be more appropriate than diamonds for a young girl.

"Now we come to the difficult part." The solicitor cleared his throat again. "You are wondering what is to happen to Stark Island?"

Everyone nodded, and the solicitor continued.

"Here is what Mrs. McDermott wrote: 'Stark Island is one of the last virgin seashores. As Stark Island goes, so goes the coastline!' " He paused for effect and then continued to read: " 'I leave Great Oak house and all its furnishings, the stable and farm, to the last male Stark, Jared Stark of Long Point, on condition that he maintain it as a place for members of the family always to come home to.' "

There was a moment of shocked silence. Aunt Emily and Aunt

Leonie were both staring at the great stone fireplace with the model of the sailing ship over it, and Maggie Royal realized they were seeing their hopes of owning the silver place plates, Venetian mirror, and Tiffany lamps vanishing.

"Wow," Constance whispered to her. "If she'd known about Cindy Lou, I'll bet she wouldn't have left Great Oak to Jared. Not for a minute. Gramma had it all figured out that you and Jared . . ."

Maggie Royal pretended not to hear her. She felt as if her heart was being slowly squeezed, drawn from her body.

"I don't believe it," Aunt Emily said finally. "She must have been much more ill than we knew."

"A black Stark!" Aunt Leonie exclaimed. "One has only to visit that house, hear the talk, to know they're improvident, dreamers!"

"Gramma once said that those brought up on this island, so close to the wind and the ocean, were a little odd," Aunt Lucy put in.

"I'm sure we can demonstrate that *she* was not of sound mind," Uncle George said.

"She thought you might wish to do this," Mr. Tavis said. "She had Dr. Bartow witness this, her last will, and certify her sanity. And now, if I may, I will summarize the remaining contents of the will.

"Mrs. McDermott wrote that she was sure that Jared Stark would have the will and ability to keep and maintain Great Oak and to see that the island was not split up or sold out of the family." The solicitor glanced around once again at the group assembled in the room. "Mrs. McDermott was, as I have said, a romantic!"

The remainder of the island was to be divided into tracts among the aunts, to be inherited by their children. Maggie Royal was the one exception. The tract containing the egret pond was to go directly to her.

Mr. Tavis put aside the page he had been reading. "I'm afraid there are many debts. Mrs. McDermott's creditors did not want to dun her while she was so ill."

"What will Jared do? How will he maintain Great Oak?" Adele asked.

"Big Boy Tarrington will take care of that," Aunt Emily said bitterly.

"Gramma said the nice thing about living on an island was that you never needed any money," Maggie Royal said.

"You're a romantic," Constance said sharply, "just as she was. She was living in a dream world."

"It was a lovely one," Maggie Royal said, afraid the tears she still had not shed would betray her.

The great-aunts, Meg and Amy, agreed to stay on until Jared's return from Spain. Funeral expenses and current debts were to be paid with money from the sale of the Starksville house, a third of which had belonged to Gramma.

Mr. Jenkins was the latest of a series of farmers who had come following Bo Cullen's departure. He wore bib overalls, chewed tobacco, and was a devout Methodist. He was inclined to be lazy, and the farm did not produce as it had in Cullen's day. But he did not beat Negroes or horses or chase the children away when they forgot and rode too close to newly seeded fields. He agreed to round up the island horses and red island cattle, which would bring in money and keep the farm working at a minimum. "Might get a fair price for that chestnut mare," he said laconically.

"Absolutely not," Maggie Royal replied firmly. "I want you to try breeding her to King again. She can stay in the field with Darien, Gramma's retired hunter. These horses must not be sold under any circumstances."

The next day, Maggie Royal left. She gave Azilia a carrot, kissed her soft nose a final time, and went to catch the island boat. She did not look back.

Maggie Royal planned to live with Adele in Washington and find a job. Adele worked in a small bookstore in Georgetown, which suited her perfectly, as most of the business consisted of chatting with the customers.

Sparrow, who had one more year at Harvard, had gotten a summer job at Time Inc. At his suggestion, Maggie Royal began putting together the anecdotes and episodes she had jotted down in her island journal.

"It would make a fine book," Sparrow said.

"But I don't know how to write a book," Maggie Royal retorted.

"You learn to write the way you learn to cook, ride, or anything else," Sparrow said. "By doing."

"I don't know how to cook." Maggie Royal grinned. "I put the turkey in upside down Thanksgiving Day."

"Get a job on a newspaper," Sparrow said. "Best experience there is. You'll have to write, whether you like it or not."

Maggie Royal applied for a job at the *Times-Herald.* She was given a form to fill out listing college degrees and previous jobs. She had no choice but to leave the space blank. Under the heading of skills, she wrote, "horses, port, Southern dialects, dancing, typping," which she misspelled. Uncle Oomlot had given her his ancient Underwood portable when she had begun her Great Oak journal, and she had learned to hunt and peck.

"What specific port do you mean?" the city editor asked, looking over her application. "Marseilles—now, there's a port. I remember once during my college days . . ." He went on to describe a wild night with some French sailors.

"Port," Maggie Royal said, when he paused. She crossed her legs at the ankles and pulled her skirt down. "It's wine, but you never say port wine. Always just port."

226

He stared at her dark blue crepe dress with the round white collar, the Lily Daché hat with the veil and one pink rose that she had splurged on, the white gloves. "Society!" He snapped his fingers. "That's where you belong. Here." He handed her a piece of paper. "Go see Betty, over there." He pointed to a door at the end of the long city room marked "Society" in faded letters.

Society interested her not at all, but as her application form pointed out, she was singularly uneducated for any other kind of job. She was lucky to have been hired at all.

One day the city editor stuck his head in the door, asking if anyone was available to interview the mother of a murdered prostitute on 14th Street. Every reporter was out on assignment and the city editor wanted a short interview for the afternoon edition. Maggie Royal was the only person in Society at that moment. She immediately volunteered. Grabbing a notebook, her hat, and gloves, she took a taxi to the address that had been given her.

The piece, under the heading "Mother Says Her Dead Daughter Was a Good Girl," ran on the third page of the second section. It wasn't Pulitzer-prize material, but, with her ear for dialect, her quotes were colorful as well as accurate.

After that she was called on to cover minor police assignments. Many were in the worst sections of the city, as if she were being tested. Instinct warned her not to complain. Not even when she arrived at the scene of a knifing in a bar in one of the worst slum areas and managed to keep the victim from bleeding to death before the rescue people arrived. She remembered Doc Proxmire applying the tourniquet to King's leg at the Starksville fair and helped to save the man's life.

Slowly she worked into features. Most of the features were fun and good practice for the book she was writing nights when she did not have a date, and from five until seven mornings before going to work.

As they were finished she mailed the chapters to Sparrow. He wrote back that they were fine and to continue the good work. Slowly *Dancing Wax* began to take shape. Maggie Royal wrote what she remembered of Gramma's stories of her days after the War Between the States when she ran the plantation alone, of her meeting with Mr. McDermott, of Great Oak and Uncle Oomlot and the Gullahs.

Maggie Royal's salary from the newspaper enabled her to go to parties and do the things her contemporaries did. There was one exception. She did not like to be touched. Something about necking and petting seemed somehow soiling, as if the hands on her body violated something deep and personal inside her. She became adept at fending off passes. Her sense of revulsion, of physical withdrawal, stemming from some deep-seated old-fashioned feeling that whatever she had to give was being saved for a special time and place, won out over her sense of guilt about hurting feelings.

Her reticence seemed to act as a challenge. Secretly the men she went out with commented to one another that she was frigid. Still, they kept trying.

The following spring, Maggie Royal went to New York to stay with Callie Hempstead, her Miss Mayo's roommate, and celebrate Taylor DuPree's coming-of-age birthday at a dinner especially for the Roisterers and their dates in a private dining room on the second floor of 21. The menu was engraved with pictures of Taylor winning the Virginia Gold Cup, playing polo, and driving his convertible. The table was decorated in the DuPree racing colors. There were five courses, and 21's best champagne flowed freely.

Sparrow, now a fledgling writer on *Life* magazine, came to the party. He said he was on his way to Starksville for Jared's wedding.

"I thought he was in Spain," Maggie Royal said.

"He's back. I gather it's kind of a hurry-up deal."

"I didn't get an invitation," Maggie Royal said, and the light went out of her eyes. She felt the way she had climbing out along the wing of Jared's plane, as if her stomach was a block of ice.

After dinner several Roisterers had to be helped downstairs; Constance was furious when her date, Jolly Olly Irving, passed out on a sofa in the foyer.

"Hey, it's the Stork tonight," Taylor cried, and so a group went on to the club on East Fifty-third Street. Maggie Royal drank a lot of champagne and danced with all the Roisterers, jitterbugging wildly and, at one point, doing a modernized, improvised version of the Charleston, while the other dancers stopped to watch.

Taylor never took his eyes from her. On the pretext of a late date, he took her home to Callie's fourth-floor apartment.

"My birthday treat," he said, pushing her down onto Callie's sofa.

"Taylor, please." She fought against him, but he held her tighter. His breath smelled of liquor and tobacco, and his hands were hot and dry. His lips pressed against hers. He moved his tongue into her mouth.

"Look . . ." she protested.

"Don't talk," he said, forcing her head back farther.

"Taylor!"

"I said, don't talk, dammit." He pulled her black dress down over her shoulders, tearing it at the seam.

"Taylor, my pearls . . ."

"Shut up, dammit." He took one of her breasts in his mouth. He brought her hand down and put it between his legs. She felt the thing harden and was suddenly terrified.

The door opened then and Callie came in and turned on the lights.

In June, Maggie Royal met Sparrow for lunch at the restaurant adjoining the skating rink in Rockefeller Center, a block from the Time-Life Building.

She asked him to tell her about Jared's wedding.

Sparrow told her that after the ceremony Jared had gotten drunk with his Lincoln Brigade friends and gone to the Plantation Bar, where Big Boy Tarrington found him and dragged him home to Cindy Lou, sick and bleary-eyed, early the following morning. The gossips insisted Cindy Lou was pregnant and that her father had sent an ultimatum to Jared in Spain that he must return and marry her immediately. "Did everything but fire his Purdey at me!" Jared had said.

Maggie Royal stared out at the skaters. A tall thin man with a mustache and dark blue ski pants kept circling the other skaters, crossing one skate in front of the other at the corners, all in perfect rhythm. A woman with hennaed hair and wearing a short ballerina skirt with a spangled top was taking lessons in the center of the rink. Every so often she paused, teetering on the toes of her skates, smiling coquettishly over her shoulder at the instructor. Maggie Royal turned her head away, gazing down at her uneaten chef's salad. Her body ached like the collarbone she had broken hunting on one of the Howards' horses in Virginia.

Later that month Maggie Royal finished her book. Sparrow took the manuscript to an agent Mac Malloy, his writer-photographer friend on *Life,* recommended. The agent read the book and agreed to represent her—and sold *Dancing Wax* to the first publisher who saw it.

The sale of the book seemed to her to be miraculous. Adele's bookstore gave her an autograph party. She celebrated with Taylor at 21 and with Sparrow at the Versailles, on East Fiftieth Street, which was close to his office.

Summer 1939. The summer of nonintervention, of cities burning in eastern Europe, Czechs destroyed, Chinese being killed by Japanese, and crematoriums being fired up in German concentration camps. At Great Oak the fight over possessions remained unresolved. Jared was working for Big Boy Tarrington and living on the mainland. He had refused to accept Tyger's invitation to be an usher at his wedding, saying that he was unable to get away from his job.

The play Mairin was in came to the National Theater.

Maggie Royal had not seen or heard from her mother since their hurried departure from Stark Island three years earlier. Mairin had apparently decided to bury the past. She came to tea on a weekday when she did not have a rehearsal or matinee.

She brought Maggie Royal a package of Porthault underclothes, which she said she had ordered made in Paris. They were so sheer, so lovely, Maggie Royal wondered if she'd ever have the nerve to wear them.

"Now you're grown-up, you should have decent lingerie," Mairin said. "Always remember, you might be run over or in a hunting accident." She glanced around the room at the apartment's yellowed-horse-teeth walls and the faded chintz. "My dear Magdalena, surely you could find more suitable digs than these."

"It's all we could afford. Anyway, we're giving it up, as soon as Adele gets married."

"What are your plans?" Mairin asked.

"I want to come to England," Maggie Royal suddenly said.

"Whatever for? Binkie is sure we're going to have another war."

"That's one of the reasons I want to be there," Maggie Royal said. "Maybe I can write about it."

Adele's wedding to Tyger was planned for Labor Day weekend at Dunwoody.

"With all this war talk, we've decided to hurry it up." Adele sighed. "I wish it could be tomorrow. It's getting harder and harder every time we see each other to stop before going the limit."

They were having Sunday lunch the day before the wedding when the news came over the radio that Germany had invaded Poland.

"We should have known when Czechoslovakia fell to the Nazis," Uncle Thorndike Pritchard said.

"How dreadful," Great-Aunt Meg, who had come up for the wedding, intoned. "I went to Czechoslavia. Sailed along the Adriatic coast. You remember, Thorndike. You chartered a boat."

"You mean Yugoslavia," Uncle Thorndike corrected.

"No." Aunt Meg shook her head positively. "It was Yugoslavakia."

"They are two separate countries," Uncle Thorndike continued patiently. "Czechoslovakia and Yugoslavia!"

"Well, they're both over there somewhere," Aunt Meg said vaguely. "I never could keep all those little ole countries straight in my mind."

Uncle George said it was the warmongering elements that had gotten England up in arms and that the matter could certainly be settled without United States intervention.

"The Maginot Line will hold off the Germans," Aunt Leonie Le-Fevre from New Orleans said.

"We fought one war over there," Aunt Emily added. "That's enough. What Hitler does is none of our business."

Mr. Trimble, a political-science professor at the university who had come from Charlottesville for his son's wedding, disagreed. "England must acknowledge that Chamberlain was wrong. If the country had gone to war in 1937, she might have avoided what promises to be the biggest war in Europe's history."

Taylor DuPree planned to join the cavalry at Fort Riley. "There's good polo, and I think there's a hunt."

Tyger said he'd like to go there too.

"Oh, no," Adele wailed. "Not right after we're married."

Tyger put his arm around her. "Won't be right away, unless I'm drafted."

230

Some of the Roisterers said they'd go into the Air Corps. Jolly Olly Irving and Peabo Van Riker planned to volunteer for the Naval Reserve.

"I'll have no part of any imperialistic war," Thorny said. "Spain taught me that. I'm a conscientious objector."

"Won't they put you in jail?" Maggie Royal asked.

"I don't care if they do," Thorny replied. "War is no longer necessary except for emotional reasons. Laugh if you will, but I intend to devote my life to working for peace."

Jere gave his sister away in the old brick church on the main street of Middleburg. Maggie Royal was maid of honor. Constance and Callie Hempstead were bridesmaids. Taylor DuPree was best man. Thorny and Jolly Olly Irving, who was engaged to Constance, were ushers. Between the visiting relatives, the Trimble contingent from Charlottesville and the Howards' local friends, all the pews were full. Late-afternoon light came through the red-and-blue stained-glass window over the altar, bathing the bride in her ancestral satin and lace in a vague gold mist. Aunt Lucy's wedding dress had been shortened and let out at the waist. Still, Adele had been forced to diet strenuously in order to fit into it. Her new slimness was as becoming as the lovely old-fashioned dress with its full skirt and seed pearls sewn around the neck. She had never looked as pretty or as happy as when she came back down the aisle on Tyger's arm.

Maggie Royal followed, wearing lavender silk that matched her eyes, and carrying a bouquet of violets.

"Why don't you marry me?" Taylor whispered as they smiled and nodded at the people in the pews.

It was a gorgeous September day, warm enough for the reception to be held in the shaggy, overgrown, but still-beautiful garden. The wedding party stood at the end of the walkway lined with box, in front of the fountain, in the center of which a marble fish spouted water. Behind them the rolling Virginia foxhunting country stretched to the distant blue mountains, a tweedlike tapestry of green fields and reddish plowed land.

The bridal table was set up in the shape of a horseshoe. Many candid pictures were taken and toasts drunk. Then there was dancing on the veranda. Taylor took Maggie Royal in his arms and they whirled faster and faster as night fell and the sky began to fill with stars. The sense of war reaching from across the seas seemed to make the music and stars brighter, sharper.

She almost loved Taylor then. He was big and solid, comfortable, and she would never have to worry about money. Yet when she thought of him making love to her, she shuddered.

Adele was standing on the stairs about to throw her bouquet.

Taylor squeezed her hand. "Should you ever change your mind . . ."

Maggie Royal snatched her hand away in time to catch the bouquet.

"Maybe you better change your mind," Taylor persisted.

She gave him a brilliant smile. Then, standing on tiptoe, she reached up and kissed his cheek.

"You'll be the first to know," she promised, and ran toward the house.

Adele and Tyger drove away in a closed buggy with everyone pelting them with oats. ("For the birds to eat later," Aunt Lucy said.) They were smiling and looked wonderfully happy. There was a lump in Maggie Royal's throat as she watched their two heads come together in the back window.

A sudden bewildering variety of uniforms began appearing in the Mayflower lobby and the smart restaurants like Pierre's. The men thought only of when they could leave their newly won wives or jobs and put on a uniform, longing to be involved in something larger than themselves that freed them from excuses and responsibilities.

The days were mere preliminaries to the nights. The nights of beginning fall, a sharpening and quickening in the blood after the humidity of summer. Somebody was always in town to see somebody in the Navy Department about joining the ninety-day wonders at Church Street or going to Fort Riley, where you could take your horse and play polo. "We're getting in on the ground floor," they announced happily when their commissions came through and they could be fitted for their uniforms at Brooks Brothers.

Night after night they moved from somebody or other's house in Georgetown or on Foxhall Road or one of the embassies along Massachusetts Avenue, where groups formed and then reformed, to go on to dinner and then dancing at the Sulgrave Club or the Shoreham, with a frenetic mindlessness, the pleasure of which was accentuated by the sharp excitement of being on the edge of danger, close enough to savor the sensation without physical fear.

The Monday after Adele's wedding Maggie Royal went to see the man Uncle Thorndike Pritchard referred her to in the State Department. He did all he could to discourage her. When he saw she was serious, he agreed to call in a colleague, who knew somebody who knew somebody else and so on, enveloping her deeper and deeper in the deviousness the Roosevelt administration had begun practicing since the beginning of the war in Europe.

Weeks passed. Maggie Royal finished her Red Cross course in first aid and volunteered to roll bandages for Britain. Adele wrote tearfully that Tyger was going to Parris Island in the Marines. She went on to report that Jared had volunteered for training as a Navy flier. He was having difficulty being accepted at Pensacola. "Something about the fact he fought in Spain on the side of the Communists. Big Boy Tarrington handled the contract to build the Army base at Starksville, and I guess he carries a lot of weight. Anyway, he got the Senator from Georgia to pull some strings and Jared was accepted."

It was mid-October when the man in the State Department telephoned to tell Maggie Royal she had passage on a ship. The name was hush-hush, as were the sailing date, time, and destination.

They gave her a farewell party at the paper. They drank bourbon in Lily cups, and Wally, the foreign editor, made an unwelcome pass behind the filing cabinets in the Sunday editor's office where he lured her on the pretext of giving her some secret information about Roosevelt's plans for entering the war in Europe. "No harm in trying," he said when she managed to elude him by pushing a chair between them. "You have a fine glaze, Maggie, but at heart you're a Philistine." With the bleary wisdom of the semidrunk, he continued. "Guys like me will always be knocking on the gates and finding ourselves outside, but someday the right guy will come along and you'll give your all, like Catherine Barkley in *A Farewell to Arms.*" He nodded slowly, knowingly. "The perfect lady on the outside, all white gloves and correct posture, but deep down inside . . ." They parted friends, with the understanding that she would send a weekly article to the paper about life in wartime London. "Human-interest stuff," the editor said. "About the man in the street."

The State Department man told her she was to go to New York and be at a certain pier on a certain river at a certain time on a certain day the following week.

In New York Maggie Royal went to Klein's Reject Shop. In the basement she bought a red silk dress with a matching coat for fourteen dollars.

Sparrow took her to an early dinner at the restaurant across the street from the Time-Life Building on Forty-ninth Street.

"I wish I were going to England with you," he said wistfully, "but I'm 4F. I hope to get overseas by writing about it." He gave her a book on European birds and asked her to keep a checklist. "In Cornwall the cliffs are alive with guillemots. And choughs!" he continued enthusiastically. "Marvelous birds. Somewhere I read that King Arthur's soul resides in a chough."

When they reached the ship, Sparrow paid a dock worker to help carry Maggie Royal's paraphernalia down ladders and along companionways to the tiny cabin she was to share with a middle-aged housewife from Kent who had been visiting her sister in St. Louis when war broke out, and was just now managing to return home.

"If you have to man the lifeboats, be sure to wear that hat," Sparrow said, admiring her Lily Daché.

Mairin had sent a list of what she called gaieties. It included several kinds of makeup and lipsticks; hot-water bottles, "hotties"; a girdle, small size; a dozen pairs of stockings; and as many cartons of the Camel cigarettes her Binkie was addicted to as Maggie Royal could carry.

Maggie Royal had her portable typewriter, bicycle, bottles of whiskey, chocolate bars, cigarettes, and Cavanagh hatbox with the leather straps holding her derby. Her hunting clothes and evening clothes were packed in Gramma's Vuitton trunk with the brass handles. Although it was Indian summer, she was wearing her tweed suit and the wildly impractical Lily Daché hat and carrying the mink coat inherited from Gramma.

After all her gear had been stowed—the trunk and bicycle in an adjoining cabin that turned out to be empty—Maggie Royal went back on deck with Sparrow.

He paused at the gangway. "You don't really have to take this boat. You could miss it and marry me instead."

She laughed. "What would Susan say?"

"I'm serious," Sparrow said.

"Darling Sparrow. I've always loved you. I'm just not in love with you."

"I know." His voice was husky. "Maggie Royal, take care of yourself."

He was gone before she could reply.

Maggie Royal went below. There was a long, drawn-out haunting whistle that reminded her of the owls on Stark Island. Then the boat began to move away from the pier. She was on her own. Traveling to a distant war-torn land she had not seen since childhood.

Slowly she took off the frivolous hat and veil and set it on her bunk. Then, remembering that it was bad luck to put a hat on the bed, she removed it. Jared had broken their date, she thought, turning the hat around in her hand. He had taken Cindy Lou riding instead of herself and had let her go without even a good-bye. By doing so he had broken something inside her, and in its place had come independence and maturity.

BOOK TWO

·7·

ENGLAND
1939–1944

· II ·

The ship was a British freighter. There were only seven passengers, including Maggie Royal, and a cargo that turned out to be munitions.

During the sixteen-day voyage, in which the ship zigged and zagged across the North Atlantic to avoid enemy submarines and icebergs, crew and passengers never fully undressed. Maggie Royal wore the lovely lacy French lingerie, the Porthault underclothes her mother had ordered made for her in Paris. At the frequent lifeboat drills she speculated that if she was washed up on some foreign shore in the men's flannel pants and heavy sweater that she wore under her life jacket, the underwear would at least identify her as female when her outer clothes were peeled off.

As the other passengers were seasick—she was delighted not to have to hear more about her cabin mate's cattle and pigs and dairy cows in Kent—she spent most of her time on deck, in a chair behind one of the lifeboats, out of the wind. She began the journal she was to keep during the years she lived in England, jotting down descriptions and random thoughts.

In spite of the cold and rough weather, the days went almost too fast. She loved the ship and its crew. From her base behind the lifeboat, she could see the gray water stretching to the horizon, the same water that washed onto the beach at Stark Island.

The ship berthed in the blackout. It was November, foggy and very cold. After the tension and sleeplessness of the voyage, she suddenly felt tired and very much alone.

Her bags, bicycle, and typewriter were piled on the dock. No porters were available, and she wondered how to manage them all. She wished she hadn't loaded the heavy duffel with quite so many *gaieties*. The bicycle also posed a problem. Maybe she would have to ride it to London.

"You must be Magdalena McDermott," an American voice said. "I'm Warren Chadwick from the embassy. Sorry to be late. I keep forgetting how slowly one must drive in the blackout. These yours? I'll carry the duffel." He nodded to a uniformed chauffeur who materialized out of the black. "Thomas will bring the rest."

His broad shoulders and purposeful manner were reassuring, and she was delighted to follow him through customs. She had thought there might be trouble about the food and liquor, but as soon as Warren muttered the magic words "American embassy," the officials waved them past without opening any of her bags.

"Come along," Warren said when they reached the street. "The car's over there. Watch your step," he warned as she caught her heel. "Hard to see until your eyes become accustomed to the dark. There hasn't been a raid yet, but I don't like to use my flashlight here by the docks."

The driver stowed the luggage in the trunk and held the door of the Rolls for her to enter. After she was seated, Warren climbed in. There was room for the bicycle, with the jump seats folded up.

"Mind it doesn't scratch the woodwork," the chauffeur said, eyeing it dourly.

"We call him Doubting Thomas," Warren explained as the car started up. "I've yet to see him smile or be anything but doubting. However, he keeps the car in perfect condition and is an excellent driver." He spread a gray fur-lined rug over her knees. "It's too late to go down to the country. I rang up your mother to let her know when you'd arrive. She suggested you use her flat tonight. You can go down to Wickwold tomorrow. By the way . . ." He reached into the pocket of his coat. "She sent you this letter."

Maggie Royal leaned back on the wide comfortable seat, as luxurious as that of a chaise longue, and gave a sigh of contentment. She burrowed down further in her mink and with the lap robe drawn up to her waist felt as warm and safe as she had in the landau with Gramma.

"Now we can talk," Warren said, offering her a cigarette from a flat silver case.

He lit her cigarette and then his own. In the flickering light she had a glimpse of his profile. High cheekbones and forehead, and heavy, almost bushy eyebrows.

"Thanks for meeting me," she said gratefully. "I don't know what I'd have done if you hadn't turned up. I was wondering how to ride my bicycle through the blackout to London. By the way, how did you happen to meet me?"

"My pleasure," he answered. "Gave me an excuse to duck out of a deadly dull dinner party and away from the deadly dull wife of a rather seedy MP from the Midlands who was explaining the important contributions Sir Oswald Mosley's blackshirts have made to racial harmony."

"But how did you know where and when to meet me?"

"Ambassador Pritchard cabled the embassy that you were to have VIP treatment. I called a friend in the Admiralty and he told me when the ship was due. But tell me, why did you decide to come to England in wartime? All our countrymen are busy traveling in the opposite direction."

"Suddenly I felt I had to get out of Washington, that I had to be here. Something I can't quite explain."

"I think I understand," he said quietly. "The English are quite fantastic. Without heroics or help from the New World, they are standing up to Hitler."

The dark closed-in car and the cigarettes provided a sense of intimacy that made it easy to talk. She liked his voice. He had no noticeable regional accent and his diction was clear and concise. Her mother would have called it mid-Atlantic. He told her he was from the North Shore. His father had been in Uncle Thorndike's class at Harvard and he had been Porcellian with several of the family's New England connections. After graduation he'd gone to tutoring school in Georgetown and been one of four that year who passed the foreign-service examinations. He'd been posted to the Court of St. James's when war was declared. Although due for a transfer, he'd persuaded the Ambassador to let him stay.

"I have a slipped disc from football," he said apologetically. "Damn nuisance. I manage to play a little tennis and golf, but I can't ride or ski." He ground out his cigarette in the Spode ashtray balanced on the seat beside him. "Thomas doesn't approve of smoking in 'his Rolls,'" he explained, gazing through the glass partition at the chauffeur's rigid back. "So I empty my own ashtray! Tell me, however did you get passage?"

"It helps having a British mother and stepfather. Also, I was born in London."

"The Ambassador told me your father is the Marquess of Wickwold and your mother is Mairin O'Connor. Good grief!" His voice was awed. "I saw her in a Cochran musical. She was sensational!"

Maggie Royal laughed. "That's what they all say!"

"I didn't mean . . ." He broke off, embarrassed. "So you'll be living in the country?" he asked, sounding disappointed.

"I hope to live in London if I can find a flat. Do volunteer work. I plan to write some articles for an American newspaper."

The car lurched suddenly and Maggie Royal was thrown against him. He smelled of good tobacco and expensive cologne, and the velvet collar of his black topcoat was soft against her cheek.

"A bit dicey moving about." He reached into his pocket for his cigarette case as she righted herself. "But Thomas is a cockney. He knows London like the palm of his driving gloves and sees better in the dark than most of us in the daytime." He laughed. "He always doubts that he can make it. But he always does."

Maggie Royal hadn't realized they were already in London. Instead of the blaze of lights from the buildings and cinemas, only their vague outlines could be seen, and here and there a yellow streak of light from beneath a curtain or doorway. A few official cars crawled through the fog with one headlight on, the other hooded. Maggie Royal didn't know how the driver managed to drive the big car in the dark, but for some reason she had complete confidence in his ability, just as she was confident that Britain would win the war.

"Except for the blackout, you wouldn't know there's a war on," Warren said. "However, I have the feeling it will hit the fan soon. Well, Thomas has done it again. We're here."

They pulled up in front of the building where her mother had her "pied-à-terre." Binkie's old flat, she had written. "A place to rough it when we come up to London. It may be latish when you arrive, so Mrs. Finnigan, the caretaker, will let you in. You can come down to the country the next day. There's a 10-o'clock and a 2-o'clock train. If you feel like it, bring that nice young man I spoke to on the telephone with you."

Mrs. Finnigan was thin and angular, with white wispy hair and a mole on her right cheek with a long black hair growing out of it. She was thrilled to meet her ladyship's daughter. She'd never known she had one until her ladyship rang up to ask her to let Maggie Royal in. "But you're not 'alf like her ladyship," she announced, gazing at her critically.

Thomas deposited her "cases" in the hallway and gave her non-English bicycle a disparaging glance as he left it propped against the wall.

Maggie Royal scanned her mother's note and turned to face Warren. "Thank you again. I was wondering whether to sink from exhaustion or swim back aboard the boat when you rescued me."

"My pleasure," he replied, smiling. "Are you free for lunch tomorrow?"

"I wondered . . . that is, my mother suggests you might like to come down to Wickwold for the weekend—that is, if you're not busy."

Warren's face lit up. "Wickwold Hall! I'd be delighted. I believe there's a two-o'clock train. We could have an early lunch beforehand."

Maggie Royal felt a twinge of disappointment. It's not because of me, she thought. It's mother. Always the glamorous Mairin O'Connor.

Mrs. Finnigan preceded her into the flat. "It's gawjus," she said proudly, ushering her into the sitting room. "Her ladyship has made it just gawjus." She began opening doors. "The kitchen, the bedroom, and here's the toilet."

The six huge rooms with the heavy, massive furniture and dark curtains that had been Binkie's bachelor flat had been "feminized." The enormous bed had sheets and pillow covers of pink satin with an ornate Venetian mirror facing it. Maggie Royal could see her reflection in it as she lay against the pink pillows, bathed in the pink night light. She stared at herself for a long time, studying the wide-spaced blue-violet eyes, more violet than blue in the dim light. Except for the eyes, she was all Stark. Not at all like Mairin, whose small perfect heart-shaped face was so familiar to millions.

Dammit, I'm me, she thought, and I'm here in London. In London, on my own.

Warren called for her at noon sharp.

"We have time for a quick bite at Claridge's. The Buttery is quite good." His glance was admiring. "You look radiant this morning."

"I wallowed in Binkie's bed. Rah-ley," she continued, imitating her mother's drawing-room-comedy accent, "all I need is something small, over an air shaft. Instead I find myself in an enormous flat. And you should see the loo, large enough for one of Binkie's hunters to be stabled in."

Warren laughed. Walking on her left side, he tucked his hand—its doeskin glove turned back at the wrist into a cuff—under her arm.

Chars were polishing brass knockers on the tall, narrow elegant houses along the street. A man was picking rubbish from the gutter. Some children were playing in a small square, rolling hoops and laughing.

"Doesn't seem like wartime," she said.

Warren shortened his stride to avoid a man in a bowler walking a spaniel on a leash. "I have the feeling it won't be long now. The phony war won't last much longer. We'll be for it soon."

"You really believe that."

He nodded solemnly. "Most certainly. But let's not talk about the war."

Claridge's was dim and elegant. The Buttery was filled with characters who could have been taken from one of Mairin's plays, well-turned-out Londoners and uniformed Guards officers whom the headwaiter occasionally greeted as Lord or Sir and Lady. The headwaiter smiled at the sight of Warren and came at once. The calm authority with which Warren greeted him and gave their order for drinks—whiskey for himself, sherry for her—was impressive.

They had an omelet, wine, and fruit tarts from the oval table buffet.

"Who is that woman you nodded to as we came in?" Maggie Royal asked him. "She's positively gorgeous."

Warren turned to look at the ravishing blond with the patrician profile wearing a black silk suit and draped in sables sitting at a nearby table. A small hat hid her hair, done up in a French knot, and her half-veil came almost to the tip of her straight nose that crinkled slightly when she laughed. She was talking animatedly to a languid-looking young man with a cameo complexion, all pink and white and fine-grained, wearing the service dress with the insignia of the Royal Horse Guards.

"That's Lady Brenda, the Marchioness of Oakington. She's married to Ian, the only son of the Duke of Chatfield." A couple paused to speak to Lady Brenda on their way out of the restaurant. "Everyone knows Ian and Brenda," Warren said. "Surely you've read of the Chatfield set. I'm told Chatfield is a dandy castle to stay in!"

"The Duke of Chatfield!" Maggie Royal exclaimed. "The most famous hunt in England. Is that her husband?"

Warren shook his head. "Ian's in France with the Grenadier Guards. That's one of Brenda's beaux. Bertie something-or-other."

While Maggie Royal ate, she kept glancing around to look at the blond woman. There was about her that elegance, that absolute certainty of position, of her place in the world, that Maggie Royal had always envied. It lay in the tilt of her head, her gestures, and the way the people in the room and the waiters followed her with their eyes. The maître d' bowed her out and then stood for an instant in the doorway, watching her walk away.

After phoning ahead, they took the train to Wickwold. A gleaming estate car with a uniformed chauffeur was waiting at the tiny station. The elderly driver, who introduced himself as Yates, explained that her ladyship was terribly sorry but some magazine people had turned up unexpectedly to take pictures of her St. John's Ambulance Brigade volunteers and she'd been detained at the hall.

They drove through a green countryside with the exaggerated luxuriance of a Constable oil. Cattle grazed beside clear, winding rivers; dogs and small boys with sticks were herding sheep.

At length they turned in between tall wrought-iron gates topped with round brass balls and proceeded through a carefully manicured forest where roe deer switched their tails and gazed at them from beneath ancient trees. The pale sunlight, making shafts of gold between the huge old oaks, reminded Maggie Royal of Stark Island, and she felt a sudden pang of homesickness.

They emerged from the parkland into the open, acres of lawn centered on a lake, where swans rested on an island reached by an arched stone bridge.

Ahead rose a vast sprawling Palladian mansion. Long colonnaded wings extended from either side of the main structure, and peacocks flaunted their green-and-gold-bronze tails on the lawn, dragging them behind like ladies being presented at court.

"The front door is wide enough for a regiment to ride through it," Maggie Royal said, gazing with awe at the enormous oaken doorway with studs pounded into the wood.

"One did," Warren answered. "Literally. One of the Marquess's ancestors was in charge of a dragoon regiment at Waterloo. He liked to invite his officers home. It was traditional for them to ride their horses up the steps and into the dining hall, and whoever was brave or drunk enough would jump his horse over the banquet table."

"You must be joking!"

"No." Warren was serious. "When I found out I was coming down here, I looked up Wickwold Hall in *Historic Houses,* along with the train schedule."

"At least it keeps the rain off!" Maggie Royal switched to her Georgia accent. "Ah declare if her ladyship don' beat all. Ah reckon you cahn't fault her for fallin' directly into a tub of buttah."

A ferrety-looking footman took charge of their cases.

A very old white-haired butler ("My name is Cummings, miss"), whose territory did not extend beyond the front door, greeted them with the message that her ladyship was finishing up with the photographers and would meet them for tea in the small sitting room.

The door to a side room opened and a wolfhound came bounding out, growling. Mairin, wearing a nurse's uniform—Maggie Royal could tell it was custom-made—followed. The famous voice trilled, "Magdalena, my pet. You're here. Finally here at Wickwold Hall. Binkie will be ecstatic. And this is the young man I spoke to on the telephone." She extended both her hands and leaned back, cocking her head slightly to one side in a gesture familiar to numberless fans. "How divine of you to meet Magdalena and bring my baby to me after all this time!" Her eyes raked Maggie Royal up and down, and the old sense of inadequacy came hurrying back, causing Maggie Royal to stand with her hands twisting nervously in her gloves.

"I did want to be at the station to meet you," Mairin continued, "but I was at the hospital, rolling a cart of books through the wards. I rushed back just in time to meet the photographers. Thank God they've gone." Maggie Royal recalled how excited her mother had always been when newspapers and magazines asked for interviews. "Of course, I'd never let them on the premises if it weren't for this horrid war. Binkie deplores publicity. But we must all do our part!" She smiled brilliantly at Warren, and Maggie Royal saw that he had already succumbed, the way practically all men succumbed to Mairin's special brand of sexuality.

Cummings brought tea into the small sitting room. "This was Binkie's study," Mairin explained. "It was full of dusty old books and musty antiques, cracked leather furniture, and mothy fox brushes. I feminized it." She indicated the sofas and chairs, covered with peacocks and balustrades against glazed chintz, and the tables, holding snuffboxes, paperweights, and porcelain birds set off on little wooden stands. A long table held fashion magazines, copies of *Country Life, The Field,* and *Tatler,* so evenly spaced they looked as if it would be a crime to destroy their symmetry.

A cheerful fire burned in the fireplace, flanked by cushioned benches on either side.

"I insisted Binkie put in a new furnace," Mairin said, pointing to a radiator in the corner that was making a loud gurgling noise. "It's so tiresome to always be cold!"

Her starched skirt rustled as she sat down in front of the table spread with the ornate, intricately carved tea service. A tea trolley stood beside it, holding plates of biscuits, cucumber sandwiches, and delicate jam tarts.

"So tiresome, this war," Mairin rattled on as she poured the tea. "What with sugar rationing, we can only have the simplest things." She indicated the plates of sweets. "And the domestic problems are hideous. Binkie's valet and the second and third footmen have been called up. There's only the new man. Binkie caught him poaching in the pheasant brake and agreed not to prosecute if he would come and replace the former footman, go straight, as they say in the States." She smiled devastatingly at Warren, who hadn't taken his eyes off her since they had met. "The new man—Jenkins—doesn't know beans about boning boots or furling Binkie's umbrella. There's old Mrs. Dodson in the kitchen, and a helter-skelter girl from the village. Naomi does what she can, but she's getting on." She turned to Maggie Royal. "Of course, in America you wouldn't know about these things. The land of plenty. Oh, here's Binkie now."

Binkie looked older and more stooped than Maggie Royal remembered him from his visit to Stark Island. Her mother had written that he had suffered a terrible fall the past season and that he had given up fox-hunting. His long face, not unlike that of the basset hound that entered with him and sank down by the fireplace, lightened at sight of Maggie Royal.

"My dear girl," he said, shaking her hand. "What a pleasure to have you here. I hope you'll stay. Good to have some young people around to brighten up the old place."

"Darling," Mairin interrupted, passing him a porcelain cup and saucer. "This is Magdalena's friend. Warren . . . Warren . . ."

"Chadwick," Warren said.

"Of course," Mairin continued. "Binkie, this is Mr. Chatsworth from Chicago."

"Boston," Warren corrected.

Mairin sounded disappointed. "Boston? Isn't that the town the Irish settled? People like the Kennedys. I'm told the Ambassador is frightfully anti-British!" Her hand went to her mouth. "I am sorry. I forgot you're in the diplomatic."

"Do you hunt?" Binkie asked politely.

"No," Warren replied.

"Shoot, then?"

Warren shook his head.

"Pity." Binkie turned his attention to filling a plate with an assortment from the tea trolley.

"Was the train crowded?" Mairin asked, directing her attention momentarily to Maggie Royal.

"It was, a bit," Maggie Royal acknowledged. "Soldiers and quite a number of children, crying and looking scared."

"The evacuees," Mairin said disparagingly. "I'm told Brenda Oakington has practically turned Chatfield over to the slum children. Some have scabies. Others don't know any better than to spend a penny on the floor." She shuddered. "Warren, do have some more tea and some cakes, not bad really, considering our sugar ration." She pushed aside the dachshund lying on the sofa and picked up some knitting bundled in a silk handkerchief on the table beside her.

Maggie Royal watched her mother with suppressed amusement. This running a huge country house, overtaxing herself so cruelly with first-aid courses, and rolling books through the wards of the local hospital, was a new role. From the time of her earliest memories of the cold, damp, evil-smelling cottage in Ireland where she had been born, Mairin had played a part. (She had survived her childhood, she said once, by daydreaming. "The Irish are very good at it," she said. "We're such a poor people. Dreams and potatoes are all we have to live on.") She had always imagined herself landed gentry, like the Anglo-Irish landlords riding to hounds in their scarlet coats. When Binkie's wife died after a long illness, she acquired the part she had always aspired to.

As she watched her mother determinedly ignoring the dropped stitches that would make the heavy woolen sweater unwearable, Maggie Royal wondered how long she would be content to play this part.

Mairin rang for Cummings to remove the tea things. She moved to the peacock sofa. Putting down her knitting, she patted the seat next to hers. "Mr. Chatsworth, do come and sit. You were so kind to meet my headstrong child. She really shouldn't be here. All of us tried to dissuade her. But then, a mother must learn not to expect her children to be thoughtful or considerate. Not that Magdalena isn't!" She fluttered her long lashes and smiled her beguiling ingenue smile. "It's just that she's grown up on that wild island. An *enfant de nature.*" She broke off, turning to Maggie Royal with pretended astonishment.

"I believe you mentioned a job writing for a paper. How clever of you, darling. As I told Binkie, you inherited my love of culture. Not a bit like your father. By the way, Magdalena, where did you get that suit?" She stared at Maggie Royal's Bergdorf suit, the most expensive she had ever bought, costing a month's salary. "It's far too short. I'll have Naomi let the hem down." She glanced at Warren and gave a resigned shrug. "Such a tomboy, *une petite sauvage,* Mademoiselle used to say. I could never get her to pay the slightest attention to her clothes or her hair. Darling, I don't know who's been doing it for you, but it looks as if you've been using horse clippers."

"I think it looks rather well," Warren said surprisingly, looking at her for the first time since they had arrived. "I happen to fancy that natural look."

"If you don't mind," Maggie Royal said, standing up, "I think I'll go up and change."

"Darling, how thoughtless of me," Mairin said. "You must be exhausted, coming down from London with all those scruffy children. I'm sure you'd like a tub before dinner. We'll meet for cocktails in the long gallery at seven."

The helter-skelter maid—"My name is Polly, miss"—led her along an echoing marble hall hung with huge gilt-framed and gloomy oils to a staircase curving upward. Warren, waiting below to be shown to his room, stood gazing up at her, as if waiting for her to toss a bouquet. She had a wild illogical urge to giggle.

Polly paused opposite an enormous painting of a Wickwold addressing his regiment at Waterloo and opened a heavy door. "The rose room, miss."

Again it was obvious that Mairin had done her "feminizing." The dark oak paneling that was probably priceless had been painted shocking pink, and she had gone mad for roses, roses on the curtains, the skirt of the dressing table, the bedspread, chairs, and chaise longue, all covered with glazed chintz decorated with roses the size of cabbages.

In some miraculous way, in spite of the lack of adequate help— "the war, my dear"—Maggie Royal's luggage had already been unpacked. A persistent search yielded her underwear in neat piles in a drawer of the mahogany chest of drawers, her shoes on racks inside the wardrobe. Her boots and hunting clothes had been put away in a separate wardrobe, her dresses and Gramma's mink hung up. She went to the window and pulled aside the cabbage-rose curtains. It was almost dark, but still possible to see Leicestershire stretching away in the distance, a series of pale green enclosures bounded by hedges and ditches, the country Uncle Oomlot had described as the fairest hunting country this side of heaven.

Binkie was vigorously shaking a silver cocktail shaker when Maggie Royal came downstairs. "Martinis," he said. "Very dry, like the way you Yanks serve them!" He acted surprised when Maggie Royal declined, accepting sherry instead.

The declaration of war had obviously given Binkie a new lease on life. After years of filling in time between wars, he found himself in command of the local home guard, battalions of battered old wing commanders, colonels, and brigadiers in World War I who had come out of the herbaceous borders to help put the Jerries in their place and get the job done.

During dinner he spoke animatedly of drills and new procedures and defenses. After a five-course meal—clear soup; trout from the stocked lake; pheasant shot at home and served with bread sauce; lettuces; and fresh peaches from the orchard—during which Mairin apologized for the shortage of meat, Binkie had fallen asleep in his chair in front of the fire.

"Poor dear," his wife said as he emitted a faint snore. "He works so hard. Right now he's instructing the villagers how to make homemade bombs to throw at German tanks."

"Isn't the Chatfield hunt nearby?" Maggie Royal asked as Cummings took away the coffee tray.

"The old Duke has retired. His oldest son, Ian, is off to war, but I believe Lady Brenda is carrying on." Mairin then launched into one of the genealogical "who-she-married" explanations she prided herself on.

"She was Brenda Farr, the most publicized deb of the year, staggeringly lovely. Her father was the Earl of Swandale, frightfully rich. All those coal mines in the Midlands. The Duke was only too glad to have Brenda marry Ian in order to restore the castle and save the hounds from being sold. Of course, Ian was mad for her. No man can resist her." She looked over at her husband, whose head had sunk down onto his chest. "Not even Binkie!"

"Do you think she'd let me hunt with her?" Maggie Royal persisted. "I brought my hunting clothes."

Her mother gave her one of her disparaging looks familiar since earliest memory, appraising her too-thin body and distinctive Stark features. "That would be quite impossible," she said flatly. "It's the smartest hunt in England. Dress to the nines. The staff is turned out in the Chatfield livery. Hunting is by invitation only. Even Binkie wouldn't have the nerve to ring up and ask. The old Duke loathes Americans. I'm told he once refused to let Jennie Churchill hunt with him because she was from New York instead of Yorkshire."

That night Maggie Royal lay awake in the vast four-poster Queen Victoria was said to have slept in. The scent of late-blooming roses and grass came through the open window, and in the still of the night she heard a nightingale sing. I'm here, she thought, in the shires. The country of Hugo Meynell and Squire Osbaldeston, of Surtees and the Duke of Chatfield.

She got up and went to the window. In the distance a dog barked and a cow lowed. Country sounds that made her think of the island and home. She felt alien and adrift, far from friends and countrymen. A sense of duty had brought her to her mother's house, but there was nothing here to hold her. She would leave as soon as she could and find work and a flat in London.

But not until she had hunted over the country she had read and heard so much about. Names that rang in her imagination like bars of music. The Quorn and Cottesmore and the Belvoir (pronounced "Beaver"), and the legendary Duke of Chatfield, the pack Uncle Oomlot had spoken of with such reverence.

Warren left the next morning. "The Ambassador wants me back," he said, setting his homburg firmly at the correct angle on his head. "Magdalena, I'll see you in London. I hope it's soon," he added shyly as he went down the steps to the waiting car.

"So do I," Maggie Royal answered, meaning it. "Warren, you've been so kind."

"It's been great," he said almost boyishly, and she realized that his manner was much older than his actual age. He squeezed her hand. "It was a thrill to meet your mother, but frankly, I like you better."

Then he was gone, a strangely serious old-young man, overly responsible, with the weight of a complex world on his shoulders encased in his black chesterfield.

When Yates returned from the station, Maggie Royal asked him how to get to Chatfield. He told her there was a train to Melton Mowbray that would arrive in time for the eleven-o'clock meet. "We used to take it when his lordship and myself hunted with the old Duke." His faded eyes took on a distant expression. "I mind as how the Duke had to be lifted onto his horse, that crippled he was from all his falls. Yet there wasn't a man could touch him across a country. Hounds once ran through Melton town and fetched up close to Thorpe Trussell. There was his lordship and Lady Brenda. A real goer, that one!" Yates ran on, inspired by her interest, speaking of longer and faster runs that Binkie and he had experienced together before the godawful stake-and-bound fence with the hidden ditch in the Chatfield country that caused the broken vertebra, ending Binkie's career as a foxhunter. "You haven't hunted, miss," Yates concluded positively, "until you've followed the Duke of Chatfield's hounds!"

"I'd give anything to do it," Maggie Royal said wistfully.

"Pity his lordship is no longer riding," Yates said. "The young horses have been sold and the old ones put out to pasture. Horses hard to come by. The war and all." He snapped his fingers. "I have it. Hanson. He owes me a favor for persuading his lordship to buy that big brown King Arthur horse from him back in the twenties, 'stead of dealing with that crooked horse coper at Melton Mowbray. I could ring him up. Could be you could hire Lancelot. The horse is old now, but there not be a finer lepper in all Leicestershire."

That afternoon Mairin and Binkie went up to London. Mairin was tired of rolling bandages and dropping stitches. "What do you say in the States? Stir-crazy." They planned to see the new revues at the Palladium and Prince of Wales. "I'm going to talk to my old friend Noël about a play. Darling"—Mairin gave Maggie Royal a quick kiss—"forgive me for running off like this when you've only just come, but I do feel I should get back in harness. It's really my duty to perform before the troops. There is a war on, you know."

"We'll be home in time for tea Sunday," Binkie said, following Mairin to the car. "Mustn't take too long a leave, you know. My men wouldn't like it."

Maggie Royal was on her own. After a walk along the narrow country byways and through the gardens, she had tea, which Cummings brought to her in the library. In *Historic Houses,* a large ponderous tome on the shelf with *Gardens of England* and *British Songbirds,* she looked up Chatfield Castle.

> The history of the castle of Chatfield reaches back to the time of Queen Elizabeth I. The first Lord Chatfield was a Silver Stick. His duties were to "guard the very person of the Queen from actual bodily injury, against personal attack, and to do so with his own hands and body!" His descendants were created Earls of Chatfield in 1603 and Dukes in 1790. The present holder is the 6th Duke.
>
> The first Lord was a man of varied and outstanding talent and is believed to have designed much of the great house himself, taking some twenty years to complete it. The result is one of the most important examples of Elizabethan architecture existing today.
>
> Alterations in the late 1700's included the insertion of sash windows, the orangery, and vast formal gardens laid out by Capability Brown. They are the pride of the present Duke, an ardent farmer, foxhunter and horticulturist, whose Chatfield rose garden, featuring the Gloire de Chatfield, is world-famous.

There were seven pages of photographs of the interiors and of some of the castle's treasures. Carvings by Grinling Gibbons, tapestries by Gobelin, Soho, and Mortlake. There were two outstanding Rembrandts; a Rubens; a Brueghel; a host of ancestors by Gainsborough, Lawrence, and Reynolds; and four Stubbses.

On the shelves devoted to British field sports Maggie Royal found Binkie's *Hunting Diary and Guide 1937–38.* She looked up "Chatfield's, Duke of."

> CHATFIELD'S, DUKE OF (75 couple)
>   Four days a week
> *Master:* Marquess of Oakington, Chatfield Castle, Leicestershire
> *Huntsman:* Robert Piper (2 days), Marquess of Oakington (2 days)
> *Whippers-in:* George Brown, Fred Cox, Jack Fayers.
> *Secretary:* Mrs. Patricia Weston, Rose Cottage, Chatfield Village, Leic.
> *Kennels:* Chatfield Castle, Leicestershire.

Maggie Royal was having coffee that evening when Cummings announced that Yates would like to speak to her. He came in clutching his chauffeur's cap and reported that he had spoken to his friend Hanson. "It took a bit of persuading. Hanson said first off he hadn't a horse fit to 'unt, what with the war on and all. Only old Lancelot. What with petrol rationed, he was being used to pull the cart. I may have overstepped, miss, but I took the liberty of informing him you were a fine horse-woman. The meet's at Chatfield Village. That's the best of the Saturday country. Hanson will meet you at the station and drive you there."

Maggie Royal put aside her misgivings about riding a strange horse in a strange country with a strange hunt, to which she had not been invited, and set about giving her black boots the additional shine that Binkie's new valet had neglected.

That night she lay awake jumping the hedges and ditches and bar-ways she had seen from the train to Wickwold in her imagination.

A cold relentless rain was falling as she crept out of the house in her hunting clothes the next morning. Yates had enough gasoline to drive her to the station in the Morris Seven that had replaced the Rolls, now up on blocks in the carriage shed.

"Good luck, miss," he said as he saw her onto the train. He doffed his chauffeur's cap. "I'll meet the eight-o'clock. I'll be anxious to hear about the hunt."

She found a seat in the third-class carriage opposite two women in ATS uniform. They gazed at her curiously, noting her derby and black boots and Uncle Oomlot's hunting whip clutched in her string-gloved hand.

The ticket inspector told her there were two stops before Melton Mowbray. She thanked him and sat rigidly in her seat, conscious of looks of disapproval prompted in part by her American accent.

"You'd think people would have better to do than chase foxes," one of the women opposite said to her neighbor. "Time the Yanks came over and chased Nazis!"

Maggie Royal clutched her whip harder and stared out the window, her cheeks flaming.

A waiter came by. Breakfast was being served in the forward car. It offered an excuse to get away from the grim-faced women.

She was too nervous and excited to eat. Qualms began to assail her, like the rain against the window glass. She thought of the story Uncle Oomlot had told about the Duke's ordering one of his neighbors hunting with him to go home because he had come without a proper hunting whip. She glanced down at her well-fitting boots. "Fine boot legs, miss," the man from Peal's had said admiringly when he measured her for them during his annual trip to Middleburg. She had polished them until she could almost see the reflection of the soldier who sat across the aisle drinking tea and reading the *Times*. Her breeches and coat were the best that could be made by Mr. Gordon, the tailor in Middleburg. Her stock was flawlessly tied, thanks to Gramma's training. Her string gloves were immaculate. At least her appointments would be correct.

As the train lurched along, the pictures Uncle Oomlot had painted took shape in her mind—the lads in the Munnings paintings who took the horses to the meets, hacking long distances, making sure their arrival was at least a half-hour before the designated time of departure. During that period before the meet they cleaned the steel bits, went over the saddle and the horses with cloths and dandy brushes, making sure that when the Duke arrived and ran his yellow gloves over the horses and their tack there would not be a speck of dust or dirt. She recalled the incident when the Duke mounted his horse and found one stirrup leather had been changed, causing his iron to be a hole too long, and how the lad who made the mistake of not readjusting the leather to the proper length after it was cleaned was given notice on the spot. And the battalions of second horses ridden by grooms like Yates—wearing high silk hats with cockades the color of each owner's racing silks—who followed the roads, miraculously finding the hunt in time to relieve their employers of their tired horses, supplying them with fresh ones for the remainder of the day's sport.

She finished her tea and stared out at the misted countryside. Soft green enclosures, separated one from another by great rounded hedges, some with drainage ditches on both the takeoff and the landing side. Stone farmhouses nestling in hollows alongside pewter-colored rivers. Children playing in a field, and a swan swimming in a lake. Words from Uncle Oomlot's book about Leicestershire and its hunts ran through her mind. "I lived for the day when I would step off the train, sight the tower of Melton Church, take the road to Kirby Sellars, and canter home along the grass by its edge."

"Melton Mowbray." The ticket inspector interrupted her reverie. The train slowed to a stop. She walked along the platform to the street. She could see little through the rain and fog other than a gray, greasy pavement on which stood a battered truck. A horse's long bony brown head protruded over the rear gate.

"Miss McDermott? You are Miss McDermott from Wickwold?" She found herself facing a short, stocky man with the rosy, rubicund, cheerful face of the drivers of coaches on Christmas cards. He wore a stained, cracked mackintosh that came to the ankles of his muddy Wellingtons and a checked tweed cap slanted over an alert blue eye.

She put out her hand. "You must be Mr. Hanson."

"Yes, miss. We best get started," he said, leading her to the truck. "Bit dicey on the roads. Lorries full of troops and bicycles."

The horse box was a very old farm truck that had obviously been used to haul sheep, cattle, pigs, whatever. Wide-set intelligent horse eyes set in the ugliest head she had ever seen studied her from over the top of the wooden partition.

"Lancelot," the farmer announced proudly. "Finest lepper in all of Leicestershire."

At the sound of his name, Leicestershire's finest lay back his ears, bared his teeth, and let out a fart.

Maggie Royal clambered into the cab and sat huddled in her formal black coat. She wished she had the presence of mind to wear her riding raincoat on top of it.

"A fine flippant jumper," Hanson said, putting the vehicle in gear and pulling away from the curb with a sudden lurch that sent the horse crashing against the boards. "You may be sure he'll take you wherever you have a mind to go!"

And maybe where I haven't a mind to go, she thought, wishing she had a double bridle and martingale instead of the rusted ineffectual snaffle the horse was wearing.

They honked their way through the glistening streets, passing the George Hotel. "Many a whiskey mac I've had there," Uncle Oomlot once said. "They used to boast in the pub that if the distance traveled by the Chatfield hounds was to be measured by the yard, it would exceed the circumference of the globe!"

The farmer drove with casual abandon, slithering around corners, and passing slower vehicles, his hand on the horn, his foot on the accelerator flat against the floor. Maggie Royal could hear Leicestershire's finest crashing against the cab as he fought to keep his footing.

Across the bridge, on the Oakham road, was the red-brick, unpretentious "hunting club," Craven Lodge, where the Prince of Wales and Uncle Oomlot had played poker after long days in the hunting field.

Then they were on a narrow wet road with hedges and ditches on either side.

"Fine fences and ditches in the Chatfield country," Hanson volunteered. "Stiffest in the shires." Reassuringly he added, "You slide down four feet and fall the rest!"

The meet was at Chatfield Village. Thatched cottages with gardens lined the cobbled street outside the castle grounds. Hounds huddled against the wall of the Rose and Crown pub, seeking protection from the cold wind and rain. The old huntsman, Robert Piper, the same that Uncle Oomlot had hunted behind, presided over them. Instead of the livery Maggie Royal had read about, he was wearing brown boots, a gray coat, and matching bowler. The young whipper-in wore the same.

A thin elegant woman on a side saddle was talking to the huntsman. Maggie Royal saw with a sinking sensation that she, too, was turned out in ratcatcher rather than one of the dark formal habits worn during the official season, which, now that it was November, had just begun.

"Lady Brenda Oakington," Hanson said, his voice tinged with awe. The sound of crashing and scuffling came from the rear of the lorry as it came to an abrupt stop in front of the pub.

All eyes turned on Maggie Royal as she descended from the cab, feeling as if she had slid down four feet and fallen the rest.

The noise increased as Lancelot, in a fever of impatience to be freed from the evil-smelling manure-banked horse box, began leaping up and down, snorting and pawing.

"Loves to 'unt, 'e does!" Hanson said, by way of explanation. "Not a fence he can't jump. Weren't for his wind problem, he could have been a National horse."

Leicestershire's finest didn't bother to walk down the ramp. He made a flying leap, landing with a shattering impact and snort that caused the earth to tremble.

Of utterly plebeian conformation, he was over seventeen hands and so tall and leggy that Yates could have walked under him wearing his high cockaded silk hat. His back was as long as a Leicestershire ditch, his legs as gnarled as tree boles and so furry they resembled champagne bottles wearing wool socks. His coat was decorated with dried blobs of manure and there were areas where his hair had been worn off by harness, giving him the appearance of a worn plush sofa. His rusted snaffle bit was tied to his bridle with twine. The flat Whippy saddle was old and cracked, and one stirrup iron was missing. In its place was a loop made from a rope and tied to the worn leather.

" 'E's in a fever to go 'unting, and no mistake!" Hanson explained cheerfully as Lancelot gave an ecstatic bound into the air and came down on the farmer's foot. Holding back a terse expletive, Hanson found himself being towed along the street as if he were a locket around the horse's neck. " 'E 'asn't been out all season, d'ya see," Hanson called back as he sought to halt the horse's forward motion. " 'E's been pullin' a cart, gettin' the crops in!"

"Will he be fit enough?" Maggie Royal asked doubtfully, gazing at the horse's lathered coat.

"Aye, miss, that he is. Excitement's got 'im all of a sweat. 'E loves to 'unt, and no mistake! Mind, miss. Just follow my boy Ernie 'ere on the colt. 'E'll show the way." He beckoned to a small boy who had ridden up bareback in rubber boots, his cap back to front, on a chestnut with burs in its tail. A second boy, riding a bicycle, pedaled alongside, waving a hunting whip. The pair were arguing furiously about who had the right to ride the colt. "I caught 'im," said the bareback Ernie. "Had to go way down in the west field, I did. While you were asleep in your bed. Ain't that right, Paw?"

"My boys," Hanson said. "Ernie and Eddie. The wife names them all something begins with E. Mind, now," he cautioned them, "watch out for Miss McDermott here."

"Why, Hanson." It was Lady Brenda, gazing down from the top of her tall beautifully turned-out chestnut horse. "How nice to see you. I've missed having you hunt with us. And Ernie and Eddie. Keen as mustard, I see." She smiled at the boys and directed her attention at Lancelot. "Lancelot, is it not? Airy-fairy as ever!"

"That he is, milady," the farmer replied, struggling to hold the horse and simultaneously take off his cap. "Your Ladyship, this is Miss McDermott, come from America to 'unt with us."

Lady Brenda Oakington had looked marvelous at Claridge's, but

253

she looked even better on a horse. In her manner and bearing was that strange coalescence of the feminine and masculine that is curiously sexual. She sat her side saddle, controlling the big strong thoroughbred with a light deft hand. In her other hand she held a hunting whip balanced casually on the lap of her side saddle skirt.

Lady Brenda studied Maggie Royal with frosty blue eyes, taking in her formal habit with the yellow Starksville hunt colors on her collar that was in such contrast to her own smart tweeds.

"We don't have many visitors in wartime," she said coldly. "Those we do have generally ring up the hunt secretary for permission."

"I'm sorry—" Maggie Royal began.

Lady Brenda cut her short. "Why are you here? Why not home in America where it's safe and warm and there's plenty to eat?"

Maggie Royal's head came up, her eyes flashed. "Why, people are jus' as friendly and nice here as they are back in Jawja," she said, putting on her broadest Georgia drawl.

Lady Brenda's eyes narrowed, and Hanson looked more pained than when Lancelot stepped on his foot.

"I don't suppose you have much hunting where you come from," Lady Brenda said disdainfully.

"Jus' alligators, ma'am, and Injuns!"

Lady Brenda's mouth trembled and for an instant it looked as if she might laugh. "Well, Lancelot will take care of you. He's a sit-there horse. Anybody"—she emphasized the "anybody"—"can ride him. Right, Hanson?"

"Indeed so, milady," Hanson agreed. "Anybody can ride Lancelot."

Lady Brenda turned her horse away and nodded to the huntsman. "All right, Robert. Time we moved off."

"Yes, milady."

The huntsman put his finger to the visor of his cap, and motioned to the young whip to round up one of the hounds lifting its leg on the wheel of Hanson's lorry.

Hanson called to some bystanders to help him as Lancelot sidled and snorted, refusing to stand long enough to allow Maggie Royal to mount. While a man held each side of his head, Hanson gave her a leg up. Before she could gather up her reins—rather, one slippery wet snaffle rein ("They're from 'is 'arness, miss. A bit long, but you can knot 'em") tied together with twine in place of a broken buckle—the horse was off in a series of joyous crow hops. Her right stirrup was too long, and her left, the coiled rope, too short and lacking in purchase. Never in her life had she ever felt more insecure or uncomfortable than at that moment, when Lancelot, as if sensing her nervousness, let out another fart.

At sight of hounds moving off, the horse became hysterical with delight. Maggie Royal felt as if she was inside Binkie's cocktail shaker as

254

Lancelot pranced and pawed, frothed and foamed like draft beer. She was aware of glacial stares from several exquisitely turned-out women on elegant thoroughbred horses.

"What damned cheek coming hunting without an invitation," a small girl with vivid lipstick and penciled eyebrows commented as she rode past. "You'd think even an American would know that only rat-catcher is worn in wartime."

"Come now, Angela," her friend, who was very thin, with sharp pointed features and long elegant bootlegs, replied in a voice guaranteed to carry to Maggie Royal. "Whadaja expect of a colonial?"

A large man in a bowler with a Guard's mustache, on a handsome bay horse, rode alongside a short, heavyset woman astride a gray as large as a lorry. Her eyes, a bright inquiring blue, matched the wisps of blue-gray hair escaping from beneath the brim of her derby. She gave Maggie Royal a friendly smile and called out encouragingly, "A bit of a handful when you start out, Lancelot is, but he'll settle, once hounds start running."

A fat man with a red Jorrocksonian face on a chunky cob was accompanied by a thin woman on a smallish mare.

"Len, mind you ride careful, now!" she cautioned. "You'll not be taking the egg money again to buy drinks at the pub!"

Several farmers on horses with hair rubbed from their sides, indicating they'd recently been between shafts, and a clutch of children on ponies completed the turnout.

"A big jumped 'orse!" Hanson called after her as she clung to Lancelot's bur-clotted mane. "You'll be at the top of the 'unt, miss, and no mistake."

As though in reply, Lancelot rose into the air with a leap that would have done credit to Nijinsky.

Maggie Royal was caught up in the crowd of foxhunters, carts, and foot people like a herring in a net. Lancelot was already pulling her arms from their sockets as they jogged along the road. His mouth was as hard as the tarmac, and she had visions of herself overrunning hounds. Obviously, too, he had a wind problem. His snorts and head shakings were accompanied by a noise as deafening as the marching band at Buckingham Palace.

After trotting in a cavalcade past the castle walls and deer park, the hunt turned into a pasture. The rain had soaked through Maggie Royal's hunting coat and shirt. The wet reins, or rein, slipped through her soaked gloves. Cold and nervousness increased her need to find a convenient tree to hide behind, but she knew that if she ever got off Lancelot to go to the bathroom she would never again be able to get back up on him.

The huntsman rode across the field to the edge of the forest and stopped. His hounds massed obediently around his feet, waiting for their instructions. With a wave of his hand, he released them. Accompanied

255

by encouraging cries, they swept into the covert, an exultant sea of black-and-white waving sterns.

Lady Brenda sat on her horse, gazing intently in the direction in which hounds had gone. Her chestnut stood like a statue, his ears pricked, listening for the first encouraging whimper.

The other members of the field took their stations.

The rain was harder now. The raw wind whipped Maggie Royal's coattails around and threatened to blow off her derby. The delay and suspense were almost more than Lancelot could bear. His neck was white from the chafing reins. If the ground under his hooves had been red-hot coals, he couldn't have disported himself more uncontrollably.

" 'Ware heels," warned the cold-eyed Angela, "or my horse will give you a real whanger!"

" 'E's a silly billy, Ole Lancelot," Ernie said, "but there isn't a finer lepper—"

"I know," Maggie Royal answered grimly, "in all of Leicestershire."

"Watch out, Ernie," Angela's friend on the nervous brown mare cautioned. "You might get a terrible bang."

"I'd rather not be emptied into the water today," the farmer on the cob said to the tall, thin mustachioed man on the bay. "Last two hunts I've been on the floor and had to buy a round at the Rose."

"I'm Maggie Royal McDermott," Maggie Royal said, smiling at them, making her manners as she'd been taught in the hunting fields at home.

The tall man on the bay turned. There was a second of awful stillness while he looked her over, gazing at her with that peculiarly English putting-down look that speaks of bad form. "I'm sure that's no concern of mine," he said finally. Then, picking up his reins, he rode over to the woman with the mauve-tinted hair on the gray.

"Why do you suppose she spoke to me?" he asked, jerking his head in Maggie Royal's direction. "Shouldn't she have waited until I spoke to her?"

"My dear Twitchy," the woman replied, "she might have waited forever.

"Mustn't mind Lord Twatley," she said kindly after he had ridden away. "He's very toffee-nosed, Twitchy is. I think you call it stuck-up. Just turn a Nelson. A blind eye!"

"I merely wanted to find out whom to give my cap fee to," Maggie Royal said defensively.

"You may give it to me. My name is Pat Weston. I'm hunt secretary. We British are always thrilled to meet Americans," she added, "but then we behave in such an odd manner."

Maggie Royal turned helplessly to the kindly older woman. "I'm so sorry, but I must find a tree and . . ."

"Spend a penny." Pat's blue eyes were understanding. "Come," she said quietly. "I'll hold Lancelot."

Maggie Royal followed her into the woods, along a narrow path. Pat stopped by a large tree overlooking a small clearing. Maggie Royal flung herself off her horse and handed Pat the reins; she did not wait to see how Pat was going to manage the irrepressible Lancelot.

Her relief was so great that for an instant she leaned against the tree, letting the rain drip down from the brim of her hat onto her face. She was pulling up her soggy breeches when Lancelot's thrashings caused her to glance back into the clearing. A holly tree was growing beside the path, its scarlet berries giving color to the green-gray brush. It was a second more before she realized what it was that had attracted her attention. Then she saw it: a very large red fox with a long bushy brush with a white tip at its end was walking furtively across the clearing.

Pat's sudden blood-curdling "View hulloa!" like the sound an Apache might make when scalping an enemy, split the silence. "It's himself! The Chatfield fox! Hurry up, hurry up," she cried as Maggie Royal ran back to the horses. "Here. Take your horse and be quick or you'll lose the hunt."

Simultaneously a hound emerged from the underbrush and began working his way toward the line the fox had taken. There was a sudden joyous yelp of discovery as its nose picked up the scent. This was followed by a mad sound of cracking branches as what seemed to be seventy-five couple of "Chatfield's, Duke of" hounds crashed from the underbrush, like a black-and-white tidal wave.

"Gone away," came the urgent toots from the huntsman's horn. "Forrad, forrad, forrad . . ." as hounds poured around her, between Lancelot's legs, and tore along the path. Hard in the wake of the flying pack rode the huntsman and the young whip. Behind them came Lady Brenda, followed by the field. Maggie Royal could hardly hold Lancelot as he leaped up and down, almost pulling her off her feet. Unable to persuade the horse to move out of the way, she had to let the other riders detour around her. No one looked at her or offered to stop and aid her. Instead they pretended that the horse was merely an obstacle in their way, like a barway or fallen tree across the path.

Desperately Maggie Royal tried to make Lancelot stand beside a stump she found alongside the pathway, but each time she managed to get her left foot into the loop that served as a stirrup iron, he moved out from under her. It seemed an eternity before she managed to spring up on top of him. Then, before she could get her other foot in the stirrup, Lancelot was off, in a bounding leap that yanked the slippery reins from her hands and left her struggling to get back into the soaked saddle.

Maggie Royal found herself hurtling from the forest into the open. The riders were stick figures in the distance, racing toward a fence. Lancelot took off after them, and all she could do was cling to his mane and try to remain on his back.

Luck or her prayers helped her restore her foot in the right stirrup and gather up her reins before they reached the fence. Lancelot's mad rush carried her past the strung-out field and she found herself abreast of

Lady Brenda. She saw Lady Brenda lean forward and take hold of her horse as the fence loomed closer. She tried to do likewise. Instead, shaking his head impatiently as if to rid himself of an offending fly, Lancelot took hold of her. Maggie Royal's hands had no more purchase on the reins, made slippery from rain and the horse's lather, than did her foot in the resilient coil of rope that doubled as a stirrup. There was nothing whatever she could do to thwart the horse's determination to be at the top of the hunt.

The huntsman rose into the air and vanished on the far side of the intricately designed rails and stakes discernible within a very high hedge, the famous stake-and-bound fences indigenous to Leicestershire. Lady Brenda, riding her own line, jumped to one side, sitting as smoothly and easily in her side saddle as if in a rocking chair.

Lancelot came at the black-green wall, got his hind legs under him, and sailed upward, seeming to hang in the air—then Leicestershire's finest landed a healthy stride beyond the unsuspected bramble-disguised ditch on the far side. With a shake of his head, as if to say, "I told you so," he hit his stride again and continued at the same steeplechase pace.

Maggie Royal leaned down and patted his foaming neck. As if aware that they were now in greater accord and that she no longer intended to frustrate him from his overwhelming desire to be with hounds, his great bounding leaps slowed to a more controlled gallop and he stopped leaning on the bit, fighting her.

Fields of cattle and sheep rushed past. Fences flashed by. Hounds ran ahead, charging breakers tipped with white, pouring across that fabled land.

Maggie Royal forgot her former embarrassment, forgot everything but the soaring delight of rain-filled wind slashing at her face as for twenty minutes they traversed the cream of the shires, centuries-old pastureland, each enclosure separated by the legendary fences of the Lionel Edwards prints.

People fell. The farmer on the cob was the first to come to grief in a ditch. As he lay catching his breath, his wife, on the bay mare, caught up and began upbraiding him. "Didn't I tell you to turn a Nelson when hounds found? Instead, you bash on and come a cropper! Now the egg money is gone for sure. Into the hands of that villain Jennings at the Rose."

Pat, the blue-eyed woman on the big gray, who had befriended Maggie Royal, was swept off by a low-hanging branch. Maggie Royal tried to pull up in order to assist her, but she shouted at her to go on and not lose the hunt. One of the ponies left its rider back at a gate and ran loose in a field.

Lancelot never bobbled, changing stride only as he set himself for each fence, roaring like a steam engine as they labored up a long hill. Hounds checked at the top.

The rain had slackened. With amazing suddenness the black clouds lifted, pierced with light like pockets of gold. Below, all England seemed displayed before them. Chatfield vale, green and misted, crisscrossed with long green fences, sloped to the village, folded into the valley along the edge of a winding road. Against the far horizon rose the towers and turrets and battlements of Chatfield Castle, as medieval and unchanging as the spire of the village church cutting into the busy cloud-filled sky.

"Yonder he goes," cried Lady Brenda, pointing. Pat, who had retrieved her horse and was up with them again, put her finger in her ear and let out her holler, guaranteed to awaken the dead in the graveyard.

Maggie Royal looked and saw a small burnished-orange object moving easily and without seeming hurry over the green, heading toward the road.

Hounds resumed the chase. The remaining members of the field took their own line. The huntsman's horse jumped short, landing head-first in a ditch and pitching its rider over its head, whereupon the huntsman grabbed the reins, pulled the horse out, and remounted in a flash.

The bareback boy, Ernie, was still with them, his face flushed with the exertion of staying on the colt's round back, his eyes sparkling with delight. His brother had stayed up also, navigating the bicycle along cart tracks and lifting it up and over the fences.

Hounds checked at Chatfield road. Hanson's horse box was parked on the side along with several traps and bicycles belonging to foot followers.

"Did you see the fox?" cried the huntsman.

"Aye," they chorused. "He crossed here. The Chatfield fox. Know him anywhere," Hanson added. " 'E's as big as Ernie's chestnut colt."

Maggie Royal managed to stop Lancelot short of stepping on a hound sniffing about the hedgerow. The horse was white with foam and making a noise suggestive of Hanson's horse box. Still he had the energy to toss his head.

"Didn't I tell you you couldn't throw 'im if you tried?" Hanson inquired, beaming from ear to ear.

In that mysterious fashion that happens whenever the hunt goes by, children and farm laborers wielding pitchforks and shovels began materializing from the adjoining fields. Meanwhile hounds worked the hedgerows, scouring conscientiously for the lost line.

"I believe Mick has it," Lady Brenda said, indicating a Jack Russell terrier hunting with the pack. Hounds converged on the terrier at the spot in the hedge the crowd pointed to. The huntsman swung around, gave his horse three strides, cleared the three iron bars of the barway, and dropped down onto the highway. Lady Brenda followed, as easily and gracefully as the rooks circling overhead.

On landing, she collected her reins with one hand, waving with the other as she called out greetings to the people who had gathered to watch the hunt.

Lancelot appeared to take off ten feet before the fence. The reins slid through Maggie Royal's fingers and she lost her rope stirrup.

"Hold on, miss," she heard Hanson shout. Then, as she struggled to refind her rope-stirrup iron and gather up the long harness reins, she heard him cry proudly, " 'E could carry a sack, 'e could, and still be first across Leicestershire!"

They jumped out of a road into a seeded field. The farmer who had been digging potatoes in his garden shouted at Lady Brenda not to trample his crop.

"I'm so sorry, Mr. Thorpe," she apologized, pulling up and riding over to him. "I didn't realize your field was planted. Hounds haven't run through here in donkey's years. How is Mrs. Thorpe?"

"Well, thank you, milady," replied the farmer, mollified. The master turned to her field.

"Thorpe is one of our best farmers. Do spread out now and don't muck up his plantings."

"Never was any plow in Leicestershire before the war," grumbled the toffee-nosed Lord Twatley. "Nothing but grass!"

They cantered around the edges of the field and over a low hedge into the adjoining pasture. Suddenly there came a view hulloa and they saw the fox, "as big as a chestnut colt," heading for the castle grounds. Hounds came together, and picking up the line, raced ahead, followed by the old huntsman and the young whip. In their wake rode the field master, sitting her big thoroughbred with the ease and grace of one who at that moment in time is wholly and completely at one with her country, her horse, and herself.

After the check by the highway, Lancelot had regained his wind and original enthusiasm. What had gone before seemed but a pipe-opener. Pinning his ears back and shaking his head, he bounded forward as if determined to catch the hunted fox in his teeth. Maggie Royal tried to circle him in order not to pass the master and the riders flanking her, but the horse's neck was as straight and strong as the iron bars in the fence surrounding the deer park. Lady Brenda and Maggie Royal jumped it side by side, scattering the deer in their path.

Ahead rose the long line of the castle wall. The staff swung left toward a gate. Lady Brenda waved to the riders to follow. Maggie Royal tugged with all her remaining strength, but Lancelot was not to be turned away from hounds.

Lopsided, unable to apply brakes without the missing stirrup iron, she had as much effect on the horse's implacable stride as did the rusted bit in his mouth.

Lady Brenda glanced back and shouted something Maggie Royal took to be a reprimand, but Lancelot was making such a noise she was unable to hear the words.

There was no time for fear. Maggie Royal was committed. The fence rose higher as she and the horse came closer. She was unable to move or turn Lancelot away. Instead, she was aware of a wildness, an exultation that came with a sense of power and speed, the same feeling she'd experienced that long-ago day at the fair when she rode Azilia to win the flat race.

There was a streak of tan and the flash of a white flag as a deer dashed out of their way, and she remembered thinking that if she failed to survive the wall, she had at least realized her dream, riding one of Leicestershire's finest over the Duke of Chatfield's Saturday country.

Lancelot set himself. Standing well away from the high, vine-covered wall over which the hounds had scrambled before him, he rose like one of the stags in the park. The sensation was like the sudden upward swing of the Ferris wheel starting up at the Starksville fair. As he did so, the obstacle in front of the wall revealed itself as the remains of a deep moat, half-filled with green stagnant water. Lancelot's great thrust shot them over the moat to the top of the wall, where for a split second they seemed to hang before descending a very long way to land in Capability Brown's formal garden.

Hounds had stopped running. They were crowded around a rosebush, digging with their front paws and whining.

Finding himself suddenly alone without hounds or horses to lure him on, Lancelot came to a grinding halt, soup-plate hooves straddling a row of rosebushes.

Maggie Royal was mud-spattered from the top of her bowler to the toes of her boots. The net holding her hair in place had been torn by the thorns in the hedges through which they had jumped, allowing tufts of hair to escape, like the gray padding coming from the widening crack in the pommel of Farmer Hanson's saddle. With an effort, she detached her cramped foot from its rope sling and let it dangle.

"Young woman," a peremptory voice said, "you're standing on a Gloire de Chatfield!"

A very old man, wearing an ancient tweed jacket and Wellingtons, was leaning on a hoe and surveying her with the brightest, brownest eyes she had seen in years.

"I'm so sorry." It seemed to her that all she'd done all day was apologize. "I hope we haven't hurt it."

" 'Tis the castle fox," he said as she made Lancelot move into the path, away from the bushes. "He's to ground over there, beneath the Queen Elizabeth. That's one of the oldest of the roses, planted back in the fifteen hundreds. Fox knows he's safe there. Nobody would dig up Queen Elizabeth. One of the men found him in the hen house the other night. Wanted to shoot him. Hard as it is to find help in wartime, he was given the sack on the spot. Told to go and shoot Boches instead of foxes!" He chuckled gleefully. "Bless my soul. Haven't seen anyone fly the wall since the oldest son came down from Oxford. Did it on a bet, but the horse hit the top of the wall and landed upside down in Circus. That's Circus there." He pointed to the bushes behind her. "Lovely smell." He cocked his head to one side and continued. "Bless my soul, I do believe that's Lancelot. However did you come to be here, riding the finest lepper in Leicestershire, amidst the Chatfield roses?"

"I found somebody who knew Mr. Hanson. He agreed to let me hire his horse." She patted Lancelot's lathered neck and felt a wild illogical urge to confide in this old man. With the exception of Hanson and the nice white-haired woman named Pat, he was the only person who had spoken pleasantly to her all day. Considering the fact that she had been run away with, narrowly missed overriding hounds, and wound up amid the ducal roses, it was doubtful if she would ever see the hunt establishment of "Chatfield's, Duke of," again. Consequently it didn't matter much what she said or did. "I dreamed of hunting with the Chatfield hounds," she said. "I had read about all the great meets and coverts in the Monday, Friday, and Saturday countries. I knew that when hounds met at Turnpost Hall that second horses were to go to Frisby Pastures. I knew about the great Burrough-on-the-hill run and Twyford Vale." She broke off. He was gazing at her in the most curious way, as if suddenly seeing beyond her muddied, windblown appearance to what she was feeling inside. "It was so wonderful, so beautiful. I shall never forget hounds racing down that long slope to the road and the sun coming through the clouds to shine on the fox's coat."

She didn't know where the conversation would have taken them if the melodious sound of the huntsman's horn had not come wafting into the garden from some distant place. The hounds that had been sniffing around the Queen Elizabeth started in the direction of the horn. At sight of them, some of Lancelot's early vigor asserted itself and he shook his head, anxious to follow.

"As fine a lepper as ever looked through a bridle," the old man said, gazing at the horse admiringly. "King Arthur breeding out of a Percheron mare. Must be close to eighteen now. Follow the path around the rosebushes and you'll come to the avenue."

"Good-bye," Maggie Royal said, "and thank you. I hope we didn't damage the garden!" He must have been one of the castle grooms, she thought, to know so much about Lancelot. Too old to go to war, and put out to pasture among the roses.

The sun that had forced its way through the clouds following the rain was lowering as she rode into the village street, surrounded by the now docile hounds. Suddenly it was full of people emerging from houses and shops and the pub with its ornate gilt-edged sign of a full-blown rose beneath a gold crown. She saw Hanson at the wheel of the horse box. His expression was part astonishment, part apprehension, as he saw the huntsman, followed by Lady Brenda and the remaining members of the hunt, ride toward her.

She slid her foot back into the coiled-rope-stirrup iron and made an attempt at pushing back her hair. She straightened her stock and her shoulders and rode on to face them.

The huntsman's very old, lined face wore a look of amazed wonder as he asked politely, "Where did you find them, miss?"

She gestured back in the direction from which she had come. "The castle fox went to ground under Queen Elizabeth."

"Aye," he nodded soberly, "the earth in the garden."

"Yes. And thank you for a wonderful hunt. I won't ever forget it."

Lady Brenda's big horse had hardly any mud on him, and she looked as cool and untouched by the rain and mud and exertion as the cucumbers in Mairin's tea sandwiches. Beneath her velvet cap not a blond hair was out of place and the linked cuffs protruding from the sleeves of her beautifully cut tweed coat were as crisp and white as they had been at the meet.

"I'm very sorry," Maggie Royal apologized, more nervous than at any time during the hunt. "I didn't mean to crowd you—"

"Sorry!" Lady Brenda interrupted. "Did you say sorry?" She let out a peal of laughter as gay and clear as the song of a meadowlark. "My dear, you shouldn't be sorry. Not for going like a bomb and pounding the hunt!" She gazed fondly at Lancelot. "Wasn't he splendid when he leaped the wall?" She turned to the genial woman on the gray horse, who was also smiling. "Why, Pat, did you ever see such a leap? Didn't the Yank ride like an Indian, now?"

They were all smiling at Maggie Royal, even the toffee-nosed Twitchy.

"Didn't I say, miss, that Lancelot'd keep a jock on his back where another'd give him a nasty toss!" It was Hanson. He was out of his lorry and beaming with pride, now that he saw it was all right with her lady-ship.

"Thank you, Lady Brenda," Maggie Royal managed finally. "And you, Mr. Hanson, for letting me ride this wonderful horse. It's been one of the happiest days of my life." She glanced at her watch. "And now I must hurry to catch my train."

"Train!" Lady Brenda exclaimed. "It's early. Generally we're not in from hunting until dark. We call it a day sooner, now that it's wartime and we have no second horses. Len here"—she indicated the red-faced, mud-daubed farmer who had fallen in the ditch—"has invited us for a round. Haven't you, Len?"

The farmer forced a smile. "Yes, milady."

"It's his grounds fee," Lady Brenda explained. "The first to fall during the day treats us to drinks at the pub."

"I really can't," Maggie Royal answered. "I must see to my horse, and then Mr. Hanson has promised to drive me to the train."

"But Mr. Hanson is invited, too," Lady Brenda broke in. "Both Mr. and Mrs. Hanson. Mr. and Mrs. Boggs over there. Twitchy. And you, Robert. Everyone is invited."

"If your ladyship will let me," the huntsman answered politely, touching his cap, "I'll see to the hounds and horses and tell the missus."

As Brenda began inviting more and more people, the farmer Len looked increasingly agonized. Mrs. Len was glaring at him furiously. "I warned you," she hissed, "but you would bash on, like one of the young chaps."

An elderly groom in high button shoes, leather leggings, a jacket, tie, and cloth cap took hold of Lady Brenda's horse's head as she freed her right leg from the pommel of her side saddle. She shook her left foot from her stirrup iron, put a hand on the groom's shoulder, and dropped lightly to the ground.

"A good day, Williams. A spirited chase!" She reached up and patted the chestnut. "See that Highwayman gets a hot mash."

She turned to the people massed in the street.

"Come along, everybody."

Then, picking up her side saddle skirt and holding it as if it were a ball gown, she swept up the walkway into the Rose and Crown.

The Hansons were as ecstatic at being invited by "her ladyship herself" to join her party at the pub as Lancelot had been at the prospect of hunting. "Like being invited to tea with royalty," the farmer said proudly as he and Maggie Royal bounced over the rutted lane to his cottage. When they reached the cobbled stable yard, she had almost forcibly to detain him in order to see that Lancelot was cooled out and rugged up—his blankets consisted of flour sacks held in place with bits of twine—against the raw November evening. Maggie Royal gave Lancelot a final pat as he was put away in the grubby odoriferous stall in the stone shed he shared with Ernie's chestnut colt, a milk cow, and the chickens.

Owing to the excitement and exercise of the past five hours, she'd had no further need to go to the bathroom. Now the need was pressing. Hanson showed her to what he called the "thunder-box," an ancient toilet with a chain flushing arrangement, adjoining the kitchen.

The kitchen was full of children. Evacuees, Hanson told her. She counted eight under twelve years. "My daughter Effie," Hanson said, shoving a round-faced girl of about eighteen with a head full of curlers into her path. "Effie works at the castle for her ladyship." Effie gazed down at her slippered feet, wrung the grimy skirt of her blue gingham with reddened hands and mumbled, "Pleasedtomeetcha, miss."

"Mind you watch the children, now," Hanson admonished, "while we go to her ladyship's party. Excuse me, miss. I'll just go freshen up and tell the missus."

The children, ranged in various parts of the room, stared at Maggie Royal curiously. Three boys were playing a game with torn cards on a broken-down settee. Two infants with sticky faces were tied into high chairs. They were being fed bits of bread and jam by two older girls.

The boy Ernie, who'd been hunting, was cleaning his bridle with a sponge.

"Mr. Williams—that's her ladyship's head lad—told me I should clean it soon as I come in from 'unting," he explained. "Otherwise the leather won't last. Mr. Williams lets me help out in his yard." He paused and his eyes were bright with anticipation. "I'm going to be champion jockey someday."

"In a pig's eye!" scoffed his brother Eddie, who had been drinking tea in a corner.

"I will so," Ernie answered violently. "Mr. Williams says now that the lads that used to break the yearlings are all gone to the war, that come the spring he'll let me start riding the young horses."

"Boys, boys, stop your gabbing, now." Mrs. Hanson bustled into the room. "Pleased to meet you, Miss McDermott," she said, smiling. "You must excuse me boys, always arguing, the pair of them. Mr. Hanson told me you looked quite the thing," she added admiringly, "and pounded the hunt!" She was a huge woman, wonderfully attired in something resembling an orange bathrobe with a wide tasseled sash. Her flaming red hair was arranged in a kind of blowsy pompadour secured with amber hairpins. An amber chain bumped gently against her knees, and bracelets jangled on her arms. A lavish topping of white powder and crimson lipstick that clashed violently with the orange of her dress gave her face the look of a friendly Halloween mask.

The children crowded around her. Pulling at her tasseled sash, leaving drops of raspberry jam on her skirt, they asked if she would bring them biscuits and sweets and if they could wait up until her return to hear about the party.

Mrs. Hanson turned the matter over to Effie, who shrugged, saying it didn't matter to her what the children did. Tom, her boyfriend, on leave from the RAF, was coming for a full fortnight, and all her thoughts were occupied with that delightful prospect.

The smaller children ran around clapping their hands, upsetting the two dogs lying by the stove, and a rocking chair.

"Silence," thundered Hanson, coming from the other part of the house. He wore a tight brown suit, somewhat shiny, a stiff collar, and a lurid crimson tie. "Enough of that," he cried as the children danced and howled around him. "Miss McDermott will think we're a band of savages! Tuck yourselves up well, now!"

They left Effie ineffectually attempting to restore order in the kitchen and went out into the dusk.

"They're good children," Mrs. Hanson said contentedly as they rocketed back to Chatfield in the horse box. "I wouldn't mind taking in more, but Hanson says we haven't the room. Did get a bit thick when Ernie had the measles; then Eddie, Willy, and Bobby got them. Then the girls. Then it was mumps."

The recitation of the number of diseases that had beset the household was generous in detail and occupied the time required to drive back to the village.

The pub was dark and smelled of cabbage and tobacco. Through the mist of smoke Maggie Royal made out people standing at the high wooden bar and sitting at tables and benches along the wood-paneled walls, hung with portraits of Dukes of Chatfield with hounds grouped around their horses' feet. Bottles and glasses and the bald head of the publican behind the bar shone in the glow of the old-fashioned lamps swinging from the ceiling.

Lady Brenda detached herself from a group of farmers and uniformed men—"some of the locals on leave"—and came to welcome her. She had taken off her hunting cap and net. Daffodil-colored hair, smooth as corn silk and as fine, framed her face and what Jared would have called cerulean-blue eyes.

"My Indian!" she cried delightedly. "Here's Freddy's sister. All the way from America! Tell me, how did you leave Freddy, Bones, and Billy?"

Maggie Royal stared, mystified.

"I'm afraid I don't know any Freddy, Bones, or Billy."

"Pooh!" Lady Brenda wrinkled her nose. "Everybody knows Freddy. What a devil with women and foxes. Isn't that right, Angela?" she asked the girl with the penciled eyebrows. "You had quite a crush on him. Not that I blame you. Freddy went like a bomb. He dressed so well . . ."

"Yes," Angela put in, "and so quickly!"

"You should know," Lady Brenda retorted, laughing. She turned back to Maggie Royal. "Freddy didn't tell us he had such a smashing sister!"

"I'm not his sister," Maggie Royal protested weakly.

Lady Brenda paid no attention. "Twitchy, come meet Freddy's sister. You remember Freddy. He was so drunk we had to take off his trousers and shoes to keep him aboard when we put him on the train. This is Lord Twatley, known as Twitchy."

With visible effort the tall thin man with the mustache to whom Maggie Royal had tried to introduce herself outside the covert shifted his attention from a young girl with an elaborate upswept hairdo and mumbled, "Howjado."

"Mustn't mind Twitchy," Lady Brenda warned *sotto voce*. "The old boy thinks he's a siphon. He spits at everybody. That piece of fluff with him is his latest popsy. Miss Hayride of 1936, I believe. And this tarty-looking female is Angela Brewster-Collins. Angela, darling," she cried, raising her voice, "you mustn't mind if I tease you. And this is Pat." She indicated the older woman with the wonderful high coloring and mauve-tinted hair. "Pat here is good value, even if she is a bit large for the platter. Pat is Queen of the Chatfield. This is her fiftieth season."

"Good to have you with us," the Queen of the Chatfield said with her fine warm smile. "Freddy came to tea at my house the first time he hunted with us."

"But I'm not Freddy's sister," Maggie Royal said somewhat desperately.

"Pooh!" Lady Brenda exclaimed again, giving her a wink. "Incog or no incog, as an Indian you're superb. All Indians ride bareback," she explained to the room at large. "No wonder she could ride Lancelot without a proper stirrup iron, over that repulsive wall." She proceeded to tell everyone about Lancelot's leap. "Why, the moat itself is at least four feet wide and the wall is five feet high or my name is not Brenda. . . . Flew it like a bird, Lancelot did. The Indian hanging on like sticking plaster, but that's Freddy's sister for you!"

Maggie Royal decided it was simpler not to argue and to be escorted proudly to the bar and introduced to Mr. Jennings, the publican, who handed her the drink Brenda ordered "for my Indian."

"What is it?" Maggie Royal asked.

"Ginger beer and whiskey," the publican explained. "Only two drinks per person," he added apologetically. "The war, you know."

At that moment the "war, you know" seemed very far away. Lady Brenda and the Hansons saw to it that Maggie Royal met everyone from a Lord "You-Know-Who," who had something to do with films and owned a huge estate in the Monday country, to Jack, the earth-stopper who lived in a hut in Chatfield forest and knew every fox from Chatfield to Melton Mowbray.

Most were elderly, working on farms or at the castle. "The young ones are off to war," Mr. Whitely, the chemist now serving as air-raid warden, told her.

The jollity increased. Hunting clothes steamed and dried. Outside, it was raining again. At intervals the door swung open and new arrivals entered. Maggie Royal was introduced to them as the Indian or as Freddy's sister.

At one point a man came in with a horse. Room was made for the horse by the open fire, where it stood, steam rising from its coat. The publican's wife came around with a dustpan and cleaned up after it. The organist from the church began playing the piano. Mr. Hanson took Mrs. Hanson in his arms and whirled her around. Like many big women, she was very light on her feet. Maggie Royal was reminded of the aunts dancing at her coming-out party.

One of the young territorials asked the lipsticked Angela to dance, and the nice blue-eyed woman named Pat did a kind of Irish jig with Lord You-Know-Who.

Len, the farmer who had bought the drinks, asked Maggie Royal for a turn. He was very tiddly and made a whistling noise like Lancelot laboring up the long hill. His wife, who had tried vainly to restrain him when he offered to buy a second round of drinks, gazed at them grimly as they jitterbugged.

"Not to worry, Rosie," Brenda called to her. "He mercy sought, and mercy found, between the stirrup and the ground. In this instance between the stirrup cup and the ground! Aw, Rosie," she added, "we're having such a gas! Surely it's all well worth the candle!"

Now almost everyone was dancing, all but the horse patiently drying out at the fireside.

"A proper singsong!" Lady Brenda said happily as she swung past in the arms of a proud and beaming Hanson. The farmer had traded off his wife to the languid Twitchy, roused from his torpor by Miss Hayride, who had plunged him into executing a jig, then abandoned him when the music stopped, to go to the loo.

"Be nice to my Indian," Lady Brenda cautioned as Hanson relinquished her to the red-faced Len and then proceeded to tow Maggie Royal across the floor, much as Lancelot had pulled her along the village street.

The dance, more of a scrimmage actually, ended. Maggie Royal excused herself and went and sat down beside Pat. "I don't understand," she said. "You were the only person who spoke to me all day. Now everybody wants to speak to me."

"But, my dear, nobody speaks to strangers in the hunting field," the older woman said. "I once hunted with the Quorn, and nobody spoke until the end of the day. I had paused to fix my girth. I thought I was lost when suddenly I found myself back in the hunt, alone with hounds. Everyone including the huntsman had gone the wrong way. I was a heroine. In Leicestershire it's not who you are but how you ride across a country."

To Maggie Royal everything was beginning to seem dreamlike and unreal. Here she was at a proper British pub after her first hunt in England. She glanced at the faces around her, shining in the light from the brass lamps. At Lady Brenda, sitting with a group of farmers, her fine patrician head bent close to that of the farmer Thorpe who had angrily called out to her that morning. Now he was beaming fatuously as she said seriously, "We, the members of the hunt, are your guests. It's up to you whether or not foxhunting continues."

Mrs. Hanson was giggling and giving Twitchy coquettish glances over the top of her glass of ale. Pat, the Queen of the Chatfield, was laughing in a corner with Mr. Hanson. It was a juxtaposition of what Uncle Oomlot had called the gentle and the simple. Maggie Royal thought how strange it was that the English, so class-conscious, could at the same time be more honestly democratic than the most democratic politician running for office in the States. She decided the reason lay in the British sense of history and tradition, of being secure in the knowledge of one's place in the world, just as Lady Brenda had seemed totally at ease as she rode across country. Foxhunting was the catalyst. Nowhere was this coming together in a homogeneous fashion better demonstrated than in the hunting field.

She went over to thank Lady Brenda.

"Do meet my Indian friend," Lady Brenda said to her admiring audience. She turned to Maggie Royal. "Do you know, I don't even know your name."

"Maggie Royal McDermott from Jawja, the U-nited States of America. At your service, ma'am." She made a kind of curtsy and added, "Lady Brenda, I must go. I believe the last train leaves in half an hour."

"I wouldn't dream of letting Freddy's sister leave now." She stood up. Mick, her Jack Russell, which had hunted with the pack and followed her into the pub, rose from under her chair and looked up at her expectantly. "It's almost closing time. We're all going up to the castle. You must join us. Everyone's invited. Oakington brought me kippers with heads and tails—not in tins—and masses of whiskey the last time he was home. By the way you must call me Brenda."

"But, Brenda, the last train leaves . . ."

"You can ring up from the castle. You must stay the night. We're about the same size. I'll lend you a nightie and a hottie. Come along now, Maggie—is it all right if I call you Maggie? Not to worry." She added as Maggie Royal hesitated, "I'll see that you get home."

If the Hansons had been thrilled at being invited to the pub as Brenda's guests, they were ecstatic about going to the castle. Maggie Royal told Brenda that she would ride with them in the horse box. The farmer had made this day possible. She did not intend to desert him now.

At the castle Brenda directed her to a telephone, an ancient affair in a frigid stone alcove off the great hall. After a dozen or more rings a sleepy Cummings answered. Maggie Royal asked him to please tell Yates all was well and she would let him know on the morrow what train to meet.

She made her way back along the hall. The walls were paneled with dark oak. Suits of armor stood against them. A gallery ran around three sides of it from which flew multicolored battle flags. The banisters of the wide staircase were heavily carved. Blackened portraits stared dourly down at her. It was bitterly cold and she was glad to find her way to the drawing room, where there was a fire.

From somewhere food and drink appeared and the red-haired young man who had been dancing with Angela at the pub was playing a fiddle. Maggie Royal had taken off her coat, but still wore her waistcoat and muddy hunting boots. They clanged against the floor as she danced with an assortment of partners. Twitchy sang "John Peel" in a high quavering voice. Len, the farmer who had started it all, was carted home by his irate Rosie, who insisted they could no longer afford to hunt as long as he kept falling off. "You'll just have to give it up," she insisted sharply. "But, my dear, I can't do that!" replied her husband. "You'd never be invited to the castle again."

The kippers and whiskey had been consumed and the fire had burned down when the evening ended. The Hansons were the last to leave.

"You be sure to let me know, miss, when you want to hunt Lancelot again," the farmer said, going out the door.

"Your Ladyship." Mrs. Hanson caught hold of Brenda's arm to steady herself. "If you don't mind my saying so, you and Mrs. Pat Weston are the last ladies left in the countryside."

"Why, thank you, Mrs. Hanson." Brenda detached her arm. "So kind. So glad you could come."

" 'Pon my honor," Mrs. Hanson continued feelingly. " 'Twould be better for us to be tenants. His grace was a fine landlord. Now it's the government. We're beggared, bothered—"

"Good night, Mrs. Hanson," Brenda interrupted. "It's been lovely to see you." She edged the large woman slowly out the door. "Take care of all the children and be sure to look out for Lancelot. Whew!" She shut the door behind her and leaned against it for a moment. "The orange lady lashed into the tiddles! A proper bash, what? My dear Maggie, you must be exhausted. I'll just look in on the pater. He's gone to ground in the library. Then I'll find you a bed."

There he was, the man from the garden that afternoon. Only now, when he stood up, he leaned on a silver-handled mahogany walking stick. In place of the frayed tweed and muddy Wellingtons, he wore a velvet smoking jacket. Although a lot of the velvet had turned a rusty brown color and the cuffs were frayed, its original cut and elegance were apparent. A maroon foulard scarf was knotted around his neck, and he wore needlepoint slippers with fox heads on them. He was very spare and tall, with distinctive, aristocratic features, and Maggie Royal wondered how she could have mistaken him for an ordinary laborer. When Brenda showed her a photograph of her husband, Ian, the resemblance was startling.

"Let's have a nightcap and some of the Stilton I bought at Fortnum's," Brenda said brightly. "I'm sure my Indian would like some of your port."

"Never knew an American that did," the Duke answered grumpily. "Port's an Englishman's wine. Just as foxhunting is a British sport."

Brenda poured the liquid from a glass decanter with a silver nameplate around its neck. The Duke watched as Maggie Royal put the glass to her lips. His expression told her he begrudged her every ruby-colored drop of what she immediately recognized as an almost priceless vintage.

"Umm," she murmured appreciatively, holding the wine under her tongue. "Quinta do Noval 1931, I believe."

Brenda's glass stopped halfway to her mouth. "What did you say?"

Maggie Royal repeated the name of the wine. "One of the most-talked-about ports of this century."

Brenda leaned over her father-in-law's chair and said loudly, "Did you hear what my Indian said? Sometimes he doesn't hear very well," she added. "You'll have to shout."

"A most excellent port," Maggie Royal said, raising her voice. "Either Quinta do Noval 1931 or the 1927 Croft. Both were great vintages. I think, however, it's the Quinta."

"Bless my soul!" the Duke exclaimed, aware now who he was talking to. "A Yank who knows vintage port! My dear girl. No wonder you could ride Lancelot without a stirrup, fly the wall, and land in my prized Gloire de Chatfield. But pray tell me. How do you happen to know that this is Quinta do Noval 1931?"

Maggie Royal sat down on the leather-covered bench around the hearth that was covered with sleeping dogs, a very old foxhound, and two black Labradors. Brenda sat in the wing chair opposite and unbuttoned the top button of her yellow waistcoat. Mick jumped up into her lap and went to sleep as Maggie Royal began telling about Uncle Oomlot. She found herself talking about the old pine casket beneath his bed where he stored his wine in order to keep Inside Dick from imbibing. She told him about the time Cousin Noble swiped the bottle of Croft 1927 Uncle Oomlot was saving for after Christmas dinner. "The thing that made him so furious was not that his great-nephew had stolen the port, but that he'd drunk it with fish!"

"Bless my soul!" the Duke said, shocked. "As well he might!"

Maggie Royal related the names of the firms that made fine port— Croft, Fonseca, Graham, Sandeman, Quinta do Noval, and Cockburn (pronounced "Coeburn"), and many others that Uncle Oomlot had made her memorize, along with the famous meets and coverts in the Chatfield country.

"You say your uncle hunted here?" the Duke asked.

"Yes. His name was Orville Stark."

"Orville Stark!" the old gentleman exclaimed. "The only Yank I ever knew could ride across our country like an Englishman, as fine and brave a horseman as Bay Middleton or the great Meynell. And you're his daughter? Bless my soul! I might have guessed when I found you in my roses!"

Maggie Royal shook her head violently. "Not my father. My great-uncle!"

"No use, love," Brenda put in. "Orville's daughter and my Indian. What dif does it make? You're one of us now!"

· 13 ·

Maggie Royal awoke the next morning to find Brenda with Mick at her heels standing beside her bed, holding a tea tray.

"Thought I'd knock you up, love. Almost time for elevenses. Here's your morning tea. Sugar or milk or both?"

"Both, please." Maggie Royal stretched luxuriously. "I don't remember ever sleeping so well."

The muslin curtains ballooned inward from the open windows. Beyond them she had a glimpse of a silver ribbon of river. A cow lowed, and somewhere below, a child called out.

"The Sprat. The son and heir. He's a yearling. Not hunting quite yet." She glanced at her gold wristwatch. "I must leave you, love. Church with the pater. He demands it. Then I must see what is happening in the wing where the evacuees are. The most frightful squabbles go on between the village women in charge and Nanny, who believes the slum children are teaching Sprat all kinds of horrible habits. She's a veritable tartar." Brenda shrugged eloquently. "But then, what can I do? The war, you know. And she does take marvelous care of the young master. Then I must see to the kennels and stable, the farm, and give Mrs. Walton her orders for the week, before popping off to London."

Maggie Royal sat up guiltily. "And I really must get back to Wickwold."

"I'll drive you. It's on the way. The trains are dodgy on Sunday, even without a war on. It's the day they repair the tracks."

"You're sure it's convenient? Good form?"

Brenda smiled her dazzling smile. "It wasn't good form to come hunting without ringing up the hunt secretary, but then, you're my Indian and I forgive you."

"You cahn't expect us colonials to know bettah," Maggie Royal answered, imitating her accent. "I say, what about petrol? There is a wahr on, you know!"

"Honey chile, we has gracious plenty," Brenda replied, giving her back her own. "The ole Duke now, he's a National Hunt official. He has

272

extra. Oh, dear." She picked up the tray. "I must dash! Come to my room and I'll lend you something to put on."

Maggie Royal slipped into the dressing gown Brenda handed her and followed her down a long blue hall. Pillars held up the famous Antonio Verrio ceiling where angels in trailing nightgowns lay on or floated between clouds. Cherubs played with cornucopias spilling out fruit, and a young man with a visored helmet and Romanesque profile not unlike Warren's drove a chariot across the overblue sky.

Hunting prints and ancestors vied for wall space. Maggie Royal recognized several superb oils by Henry Alken as the originals of the prints Uncle Oomlot had had hanging on the walls of his tower bedroom. In Brenda's sitting room there were studies for some of Sir Alfred Munnings' most famous paintings. "He used me as model," Brenda said. "He lived on Exmoor. I was a frightful tomboy in those days. I was so long and leggy and thin I could double for the stable lads in his Downs and his Newmarket paintings. I rode astride until I married Ian. He said it wasn't ladylike and made me ride side saddle."

She laid out a tweed skirt, sweater, shoes, and knee socks. Miraculously, they fit.

"Holmes will give you breakfast," Brenda said. "You mustn't mind if he doesn't answer you. He's said to have served as a footman in the czar's palace, spied for the Allies in World War I, and been an extra in Korda films. Nobody knows really," Brenda added, "for Holmes never speaks."

Brenda's green MG sped across the countryside like a water beetle. "Mind if I let it out a bit?" she asked, driving with much the same dash with which she rode her big chestnut horse.

Mick, the Jack Russell, stood in her lap, his head over the car door, as they barreled through the misty green countryside, passing placid rivers and fields dappled with fat grazing cattle. Maggie Royal delighted in the picture-postcard villages of thatched cottages and gardens full of late-blooming roses.

Brenda asked why she had chosen wartime to come to England. Maggie Royal told her about wanting to move to the city, write, and do war work. "I must find an apartment," she said.

"But you can live in town with me," Brenda said simply. "Monica Bourne-Smith was going to stay with me, but she's joined the Wrens and moved back to Eaton Place."

Maggie Royal turned sideways to look at her lovely profile. "Are you serious? I never heard anything so kind. You hardly know me."

"Of course I know you," Brenda exclaimed. "You're Freddy's sister. My Indian, if you will. You can ride a horse, and I'll bet you're splendid when it comes to ordering the right wine. What more do I need to know?" She turned her head and gave Maggie Royal a flash of her brilliant smile. "Truthfully, I need somebody I can trust. Somebody to help run the place, keep the evacuees in line, the accounts straight. Somebody to hold the fort—in this case, castle—if I decide to bolt!"

Maggie Royal was at a loss. She didn't know what to say or how to answer this long-legged, beautiful girl who had been cold and patronizing and who now seemed to be confiding in her as if she were her dearest friend. It was her first inkling of how the English can freeze one to the core, wrapping themselves in tradition and confusing rituals, then quickly change, becoming the kindest, the warmest of friends.

"Where shall I drop you?" Brenda asked as they reached Wickwold village.

"My mother lives at Wickwold Hall," Maggie Royal answered.

The MG swerved. "But that's where Mairin O'Connor lives."

"That's my mum!"

The MG wobbled. A lorry came around a corner, almost sideswiping them as Brenda stared at her in amazement.

"You mean your mother is Mairin O'Connor. Well, bless my soul. Why on earth didn't you say so?"

"Would it have mattered?"

"Well," Brenda temporized, "you're already Freddy's sister, Orville's daughter, and my Indian. You might as well be Mairin O'Connor's daughter!"

"I really am," Maggie Royal said.

"You mean you really, really are?"

"Yes. Brenda, where is your flat?"

"It's a house, really. In Belgravia. Is your mother as beautiful as they say?"

"You can judge for yourself," Maggie Royal said dryly. "She should be back from London by now. Brenda, when may I move in?"

"I saw her at the Prince of Wales, in that musical in which she sang 'You're in the Guards Now.' She wore a military hat and carried a flag."

"Brenda, do you think I can do volunteer work in a hospital, or should I try the Red Cross?"

"Mairin O'Connor!" Brenda said again. "When I was a little girl my nanny took me to see her in one of those classy musical shows that Ivor Novello produced. She had on a very short spangled skirt and a feather headdress."

Mairin and Binkie were in the small sitting room having tea. Tara, the wolfhound, lay on his velvet pallet before the fire. Hans, the dachshund, was curled in Mairin's lap.

"So you're back!" Mairin said without getting up as Cummings showed them into the room. "Binkie and I couldn't imagine where you'd vanished to. Yates gave us a wild tale about your going to visit friends."

"Well, I did rather," Maggie Royal answered calmly. "I'd like you to meet Lady Brenda Oakington."

Binkie put down the *Horse and Hound* he'd been reading and stood

274

up, his usually doleful eyes filled with astonishment. Mairin's perfectly made-up mouth dropped, and she stared openly at Brenda.

"Lady Oakington." The famous voice was barely a croak. "But how ... I mean, Magdalena never mentioned ..."

"I've discovered there are a lot of things Maggie doesn't mention," Brenda said dryly.

"I went hunting," Maggie Royal explained. "Brenda very kindly invited me to stay the night."

"Stay the night, at Chatfield Castle?"

"Why, yes. The Duke was very kind. We discussed port."

"Sport," Binkie intoned. "Nothing like the sport of hunting. I'll never forget—"

"Port," Mairin interrupted. "Magdalena said 'port.'"

"Port?" Binkie looked astonished. "But Americans don't drink port." He gave Brenda a conspiratorial smile. "Only Englishmen, after the ladies retire! I still have twelve pipes. I prefer Graham. The Grahams are Irish, I believe. Even so, their port has a fine full fruity flavor. A bit sweet, perhaps, but possesses more finesse."

"Binkie," Mairin said tersely, "shut up!" Then, pulling herself together, she was suddenly as overly sweet as the Graham, "Lady Brenda, do sit down. Would you like some tea?" Her famous voice oozed charm. "Lemon or milk? And do have one of our little tarts."

Maggie Royal planned to move in with Brenda the following Monday. It was a strange week at Wickwold. She took long walks with Tara. Hans, the dachshund, toddled along behind, suddenly racing with great leaps across fields and through hedges in optimistic pursuit of rabbits. The mornings were cold and foggy, followed by bleak sunshine in the afternoons. One afternoon she walked with Binkie, who knew a surprising amount about birds. She jotted down the ones they saw in the book Sparrow had given her. There was a gorgeous woodpecker, and a thrush sang its sweet song from the leafless bough of an elm. When they returned for tea, Binkie showed her a fine stuffed specimen of a night-jar which he had trapped on Dartmoor.

One morning there was a sharp white frost. She drove to the village with her mother in the pony cart. Hans shivered uninterruptedly, his nose against Mairin's ankle. The trees looked stark and dead, like telephone poles. The fields lay rigid, as though under a shroud. The whistle of the morning train sounded thin and ghostly. Everything seemed silent and half-alive. All but the pony, which, filled with the delight that dangerous slippery ground and chill air often impart to equines, shied and pranced. Maggie Royal had no idea her mother was such an accomplished driver.

"A lot you don't know about me," Mairin said when Maggie Royal mentioned how well she handled the pony. "Maybe now that you're grown-up, we can be friends."

It was the first time she had ever made such an overture. Maggie Royal couldn't help but wonder if her change of attitude was because of her sudden friendship with Brenda. She decided to give her mother the benefit of the doubt. "I'd like that," she said, finding that she meant it.

Mairin told her about the part she'd been offered. "A musical. I would like to do a serious play about the war, but my agent says people want something light, something to laugh about. Anyway, the part's not bad. I sing and dance a bit."

Later that day Warren called. Maggie Royal asked him if he'd like to come down to the country Sunday. He said he would and that he might be able to borrow Thomas and the embassy car in order to drive her up to London.

Warren arrived in time for lunch. Now that Mairin had decided to return to the theater, she had switched roles again. Her old and known part, that of an accomplished professional returning to the world she knew and understood, was far more real and relaxed than the chatelaine-of-the-castle role. She quite enchanted Warren, telling him stories of the great and near-great, about Laurence Olivier and Vivien Leigh and Alexander Korda, who had directed her in an epic Ruritanian melodrama, how the great filmmaker had come out of Hungary with a roll of salami in his pocket and a loaf of bread and that even after he was famous and was entertained at Buckingham Palace he never forgot his humble origins.

Binkie talked about big-game hunting in Kenya, and Warren spoke knowledgeably about U.S. policy and the country's relationship to Africa, prophesying that after the war many nations would seek independence under black rule.

After lunch Warren and Maggie Royal walked. The sun was shining as they proceeded briskly along the lanes. It lit up the fronds of bracken among the undergrowth and the few remaining leaves on the oaks. Warren walked well, not too slow and not too fast. Maggie Royal found herself liking being with him.

He spoke feelingly about his work. He felt strongly that the days of isolationism were over. The United States must soon enter the war—the sooner the better, he said. Europe could not withstand two wars in one generation. The continent would be devastated. The United States would have to take over world leadership and put the world back together again. He wanted to play a part in this, help shape the course of history, if only in a small way as a foreign-service officer in some distant and upcoming country.

"I'm glad to be here, at this time." Warren scratched the side of his nose with his gloved index finger. "England and the English take knowing. But the system works." He paused to listen to the long sweet note of a thrush. "I wonder about America. What's going to happen. We have the most varied and beautiful country, the biggest and richest, and we seem hell-bent on destroying our forests and rivers and countryside. Look at our cities. Factories belching smoke. Ghettos breeding corrup-

276

tion and violence. Here"—he took a deep breath, breathing in the crisp autumn air—"they've managed to keep the country green, free of neon and billboards." He broke off, embarrassed. "It's too nice a day to talk about serious things," he said, smiling his slow grave smile.

He paused to light his pipe. A flock of yellow hammers fed busily in wheat stubble beside the lane. Sheep bleated from a gray-green hillside. Maggie Royal felt she already knew him well. He emanated sanity, solidarity. If she hadn't known he was a Bostonian, she might have taken him for a tweedy, pipe-smoking Britisher. His face fitted his speech and fine clothes. It was one of those classic New England faces with a strong, determined chin, a prominent nose, and direct gray eyes. He had the kind of *good* face and manner of those who lived by an inherited code, rights and privileges coupled with a sense of responsibility to one's fellowman that is passed on from one generation to another.

She tried to draw him out, but he was reticent about his background. From the little she could persuade him to say, she acquired a picture of a small lonely only child growing up in a dark gloomy town house on Beacon Street. His father was a banker and yachtsman. His mother was devoted to good works and served on numerous committees.

"I used to wait for her," Warren said, "watching from behind the living-room curtains for her to come home. But when she did, I was sent upstairs to the nursery in the attic while she made endless telephone calls. Funny," he said. "We spent the summers at Manchester. Our house overlooked the sea. I used to envy the other children, whose parents built sand castles with them. I was always sent to the beach with my governess. She never built sand castles!"

"Oh, Warren." She didn't know whether to laugh or cry. "Didn't you ever rebel?"

He furrowed his brow in thought. "I don't think I ever did."

"Not even a little bit?"

"Well, there was a time when I refused to buckle my galoshes."

She burst into laughter. "Oh, Warren, you are funny. Did you have any girls?"

He thought a moment. "There was a girl named Amanda Bundy. She used to walk along Beacon Street in front of our house carrying a cello. My mother was always trying to get me to go out and carry the cello for her. My mother called her wholesome." He grimaced. "That was the kiss of death!"

"I mean girl girls. Ones you were in love with."

"Not really," he answered seriously. There was a shy, wistful expression on his face as he added, "You see, I never found anyone who would build sand castles with me."

Brenda opened the door of the house in Belgravia with such a "View hulloa" it brought an air-raid warden on the run, calling, "The light, milady. Please shut the door."

"Oh, all right." Brenda stooped, hugging Maggie Royal. "But come in, Mr. Potts. Have a wee drop of his grace's Scotch to warm you up. Such a beastly night. Not even an air-raid warden should be out on a night like this. Mr. Potts, meet my Indian friend from the Good Old U.S. of A. Warren, don't stand there in the beastly wet. Bring the cases in."

"The bicycle, milady?" Thomas asked doubtfully.

"By all means roll in the bicycle," Brenda answered impatiently. "Lean it against the grand piano in the drawing room. Mind, now, you don't fall over the bucket of sand." She turned to the air-raid warden. "You see, Mr. Potts, I really am prepared. The water buckets are upstairs. My God, I forgot!"

Gathering the floor-length sable coat she was wearing around her, she tossed back her long blond hair and ran to the telephone.

"Quag's at eight tomorrow? Lovely. My Indian friend just arrived. No, silly. American. Freddy's sister. Didn't I tell you? Madly attractive. I'll be insanely jealous when you see her. Warren will come too, won't you, love?" She threw him a melting smile, and without waiting for an answer, turned back to the telephone. "Warren looks smitten already. Ring me back, lovey. Ta-ta for now!"

"Your husband?" Warren asked. "I thought he was out of the country."

"He is." Brenda wrapped the fabulous coat more closely about her. "Darling, Maggie. You'll get used to the cold. No central heating. Almost no coal. That was Bertie Fitch-Hammond. Warren, you remember Bertie? The weekend we met at Monica's. We played croquet. You sent my ball into the flowerbed. That wasn't at all kind. You mean you don't remember Bertie? Well, he was married to Pansy Harrison, but she did a bunk. Left him for Toby Hume, master of the Hume Harriers. He got her with pup and she made him marry her, although I don't honestly think he meant to go that far. Anyway, Bertie needs cheering. He's with the Blues, about to be sent to some ghastly place. Warren, do you mind lugging those bags up the stairs? I couldn't bear living in this mausoleum alone, so I did up a cozy flat on the top floor and closed down the rest of the house."

Thomas left the bicycle propped against the piano inside the door of the frigid drawing room, its furniture shrouded in white muslin for the duration. With as gloomy a demeanor as if he were going to a funeral, he joined the air-raid warden in the deserted pantry for a wee drop from the large brown bottle that Brenda had provided.

Warren, lugging Maggie Royal's gear, and Maggie Royal followed Brenda up three flights of wide crimson-carpeted stairs, past rooms hung with gilt-framed portraits, and the vast empty ballroom with its great chandelier and gold-painted chairs ranged neatly around the walls.

Brenda opened the door into a room that in the dim light was all pink and gold and magenta. Other than a vast canopied bed, a magenta-skirted dressing table, and a long table under which the telephone was housed ("In case the bombs fall," Brenda explained, "I want to be sure to be able to ring up my friends"), there was no other furniture, merely masses of tasseled cushions piled on the floor.

Brenda reached into a silver box on the floor and fitted a cigarette into a long ebony holder. "I thought it would be fun to have it look like a harem," she said. "Monica Bourne-Smith has this madly chic decorator. He had me cart away all the Chatfield heirlooms and do it up like the inside of a box of sweets. Nanny thinks it's positively sinful, and Ian hates it, but I love it."

"I know how Ian feels," Warren said dryly, looking uncomfortable.

"Damn that bloody phone," Brenda said as the persistent burr-burr of the British phone system erupted again. "Probably Monica about that beastly benefit. We're giving a ball. Maggie, you arrived just in time for it." She turned with characteristic suddenness. The coat fell open, disclosing a black lace nightgown worn over long-sleeved hunting underwear. "Darling Maggie," she called out, "do keep your coat on. The coal I ordered last week still hasn't come." She slid under the table and picked up the receiver. "Yes, love," she said into the mouthpiece. Then, putting her hand over it, she called out, " 'Bye, Warren, thank you for delivering my Indian."

"Your Warren's sweet," Brenda said when he'd gone.

"Brenda, he's not *my* Warren!"

Brenda continued as if she hadn't heard her. "He doesn't like horses, but he's a whiz at croquet." She flung her arms around Maggie Royal. "Maggie, my Indian. We're going to have such fun! What yawl say down suth, a bawl, honey chile? Sooner or later everyone comes up to London. Every night's a party. Heavens, it's late. I have to be at the factory for the early shift. Darling, you take the hottie. You'll freeze without it. Either that or let Warren keep you warm."

"Brenda, honestly . . ."

"In the morning, sleep in. I'll have Mrs. Potts knock you up and bring morning tea whenever you want. You'll need insurance cards, a ration book, clothing coupons, an identity card, and to be fitted for a gas mask. There's a place in Oxford Street. Mrs. Potts will direct you."

"I must find work, and I have to file for the paper as soon as possible."

"No problem," Brenda said. "Everyone's volunteered for something. You'll look smashing as Hemingway's Miss Catherine Barkley. St. George's is the nearest hospital. The matron was a friend of Ian's mother. I'll ring her up and tell her you're coming."

The next morning Mrs. Potts brought tea in a brown pot. Brenda rang up a half-hour later. "Remember we're dining at Quaglino's with Bertie and Warren," she reminded her. "Warren is picking you up at eight."

"You're not coming home?"

"I have to give my blood for the war," Brenda said. "I'll meet you there."

Maggie Royal went out into the bright autumn morning. "I'm in London," she said to herself, gazing around her with delight. The sky was a pale frosty color, patrolled only by clouds and barrage balloons bobbing like strange bulbous elephants against the blue.

Old men were sailing boats on the round pond in Kensington Gardens, but no children or nannies were to be seen.

She strolled along Bond Street. Many of the luxury shops were boarded up. Sandbags and strips of paper were gummed over windows. Some had been painted to match the paint on their buildings. Sidewalks were crowded with men and women in uniform, and there were a number of horse-drawn wagons and vans. Scott's, the hatters, varnished turnout boasted a coachman and footman wearing tin hats.

Maggie Royal wanted to see Trafalgar Square, where as a child she had climbed up onto the backs of the great carved lions. People were going into the National Gallery, and she found herself sitting on the floor at the first of many lunchtime concerts. She bought a cheese sandwich and listened happily to Chopin and Mozart. Afterward she joined the stream of people hurrying out onto the square, carrying their gas masks.

She found the place on Oxford Street and was fitted for one of her own. A bobby directed her to the hospital, where the matron, a worn-looking woman with an austere aristocratic face, interviewed her between directing orderlies and nurses who paused to ask questions about various patients and required medications. The interview consisted of a few perfunctory questions as to Maggie Royal's training (the Red Cross first-aid course in Washington), temperament (adequately calm), and reason for being there.

"I want to help Britain win the war," Maggie Royal said.

This seemed to please the matron, for her frosty visage broke into a semblance of a smile and Maggie Royal was taken on as a VAD (Voluntary Aid Detachment). A gray cotton dress with a white apron to be pinned in front and tied in back, along with a white cap to cover her hair, was issued to her and she was told to come to work the following morning.

Warren arrived at 7:45 on the dot. Maggie Royal wore her red silk, pearls, and Gramma's mink, and he told her she looked very well.

Thomas greeted her with uncharacteristic warmth, tipping his hat and saying, "Good evening, miss."

"You're spoiling me," Maggie Royal said as Warren helped her into the car. "You must be important to be able to commandeer Thomas and the Rolls."

"Not really." He smiled modestly. "I only have the use of it when the Ambassador doesn't need it."

It was like driving in a black tunnel. Changing green and red crosses of the masked traffic signals and the fireflylike flashes of pedestrian torches were the only lights in the sepulchral blackout.

Bertie Fitch-Hammond and Brenda were sitting at a table for four, their heads close together. They did not look up until Warren and Maggie Royal were standing beside them. Bertie, Brenda had told Maggie Royal the night before as they prepared for bed, was one of Ian's closest friends. They had gone up to Magdalen together, hunted and ridden against one another in point-to-points. Before the war Bertie had published two slim volumes of poetry. "The critics say he may well be this war's Rupert Brooke," Brenda said proudly after she introduced them. Maggie Royal saw that he was very good-looking, with that languid, somewhat effeminate handsomeness characteristic of many of the products of British public schools.

"So you've come to help us win the war," he said when they were seated. "Do you like sada?"

Maggie Royal looked at him blankly. "I beg your pardon. What's sada? A person or an African country?"

"Whiskey and sada, d'ye see?" he replied, lifting an eyebrow.

Maggie Royal stared back at him. "I prefer sherry."

He turned to Brenda. "Your usual?"

She smiled and nodded.

"Whiskey for me," Warren said shortly.

"Eh say, waiter." Bertie snapped his fingers. "Eh gless of wate wane fah her ladyship. Two whiskeys and sadas. One sherry, with ice, d'ye see?"

"But I don't like ice in sherry."

He looked at Maggie Royal in amazement. "All Americans like ice in their drinks, d'ye see?"

"Not all. Nothing's all anything!"

His eyelashes were long and golden in the candlelight. "Strange. You don't speak like one."

"Like one what?" Maggie Royal asked.

"An American, of course."

"And just how do you think an American speaks?"

Brenda and Warren were watching, Brenda with an amused expression, Warren with one that was wary.

"Why, they say 'dees' and 'doze' and 'get your gat'! D'ye see?"

Maggie Royal was becoming angry. "There's only a handful of gangsters in the whole forty-eight states. You've been seeing too many movies."

Bertie looked faintly abashed. "My word," he answered. "You Yanks are chippy." He glanced at Warren in his white Brooks Brothers shirt and dark pinstriped suit. "I suppose it's your sense of guilt about not coming into the war."

"That wasn't good form," Brenda admonished him. "Bertie, I'm quite cross with you."

"I admit it wasn't kind. Sorry. It just popped out." He smiled an enchanting boyish smile, oozing charm that reminded Maggie Royal of Errol Flynn about to seduce Maureen O'Hara. "Shall we order?"

While the rest of them ate Dover sole, Bertie wangled a steak, which he slathered in mustard and devoured with gusto. Maggie Royal could not understand Brenda's fascination with him. Although he couched his beliefs in different terms, they weren't so different from Mosley's: Mussolini and Hitler weren't all bad. Mussolini had made the trains run on time and Hitler had pulled the German economy together and gotten industry ticking again, whereas England was going down the drain, heading toward welfare-state status. Coal miners striking and railway workers asking for higher wages. Things were becoming too easy. People were getting soft. He hated to admit it, but maybe the war had come along at the right time. People would have to tighten their belts, toughen up.

Ray Noble was playing in the Savoy ballroom, and after dinner they drove through the blackout, passing hilarious couples, soldiers and sailors and their girlfriends, holding hands or kissing in doorways.

The ballroom was packed. The famous blind orchestra leader was conducting "The Very Thought of You." It brought back memories of parties on the island and nights in Washington. A dark-haired RAF officer with wings over his heart danced by. His hair grew into a spiral at the back of his neck, and Maggie Royal thought of Jared. Where was he now?

Warren danced stiffly, but very well, holding her firmly at exactly the right distance to execute a fast fox-trot. They danced well together and she found herself enjoying the excitement in the air, the achingly familiar music and the sense of being a part of something very big.

Bertie and Brenda danced past. His blond head was bent over her fair one resting against his chest. His eyes were partially closed, and there was a self-indulgent half-smile on his face as the music changed to the slow sweet strains of "I'll Be Seeing You."

"I can't see what Brenda sees in him," Warren said.

"I think he's a pain in the neck," Maggie Royal said.

"I have an even lower opinion," Warren replied.

Eric Benson wrote in his avidly read column that the Oakingtons' ball for Finnish relief was the last great London ball in the prewar tradition.

Brenda hired a jazz band. They set up round tables and the gilt chairs formerly used for her mother-in-law's concerts. Brenda took down the fine crystal wineglasses and the best china from the top shelves in the pantry. "They'll want to remember something lovely," she said, fixing masses of marigolds, asters, and chrysanthemums brought in from the country. Jack, the earth-stopper, doubling as gamekeeper, provided rabbits and pheasant for the midnight buffet. They pooled their sugar ration and Cook made fruit tarts.

Invitations were greatly sought after.

"Pity," Maggie Royal heard Brenda saying over the telephone before the party. "I'm making his book and you're not in it!" She slammed down the receiver. "Sybil Carruthers, oiling in, wants to come to the big hooli to meet Aly Khan. Bitch of the first litter. In school she used to trap spiders and grind them under the heels of her boots."

The life-size ancestral portraits that lined the walls were illuminated by the candles Brenda found in the pantry to fill the chandeliers and sconces. There was the Chatfield, wearing his magnificent Dragoon uniform, who had fought with Wellington at Waterloo, and one of a dark hawklike individual with a black patch over one eye. "Great-Grandfather was a slave trader," Brenda said. "A native spear put out his eye." The old Duke, clad in Highland dress, with his piper who served with him in the Scots Guards in World War I. The first Duchess of Chatfield and the late Dowager Duchess, Ian's Scottish mother. Brenda in her white lace Molyneux, in which she'd been presented at court, was wedged in between masters of foxhounds and cabinet ministers who for centuries had helped to rule England.

Brenda had on the same dress now. "My ordinary," she called it with classical understatement. "Unobtrusive, with good lines!" Instead of plumes in her hair she was wearing her late mother-in-law's tiara. "It has a certain dreary distinction!" she said, adjusting it. With her lovely hair, parted in the center and pulled back from her cameolike face into a smooth pageboy, Brenda was the envy of many of the women who gazed at her as coldly as the air in the gaunt, gusty, unheated town house.

Ian had been granted leave from the Grenadiers, his Guards Regiment, and stood with Brenda at the top of the red-carpeted stairs, greeting the guests at the entrance to the ballroom.

The warden replacing Mr. Potts (who was helping his wife with the midnight supper) banged on the door, demanding that the candles be extinguished, as light was coming from beneath the heavy blackout curtains. Brenda invited him in and gave him a crystal glass of her father-in-law's vintage champagne, which he almost dropped at sight of King George and Queen Elizabeth, putting in an appearance on behalf of Finnish Relief.

So much magnificence, the Queen in pale blue satin, the King in his evening clothes, both with wide blue sashes across their chests, the footmen in their gray-and-yellow Chatfield livery, the brilliance of the Guards officers in their glorious gold-and-scarlet mess kits, causing them to resemble overbred masters of foxhounds, provided a *Night Before Waterloo* sense of unreality.

Brenda's Ian came up and said, "You're Maggie. I've heard so much about you. May I have this dance?"

She liked him at once. He seemed the embodiment of all she had read or thought about the best of the British. It was not only his looks—he was tall, long-legged. His wide shoulders and slender waist were made for a scarlet hunting coat. His reddish hair was prematurely streaked with gray. He had blue eyes, a prominent nose, and a clear country English complexion that spoke of days on a horse or carrying a gun over the moors. There was an air of true-blue staunchness about him, in his steady eyes and fine warm smile. She had the feeling he would fight to the death for the old English values, a fox in the morning against a green vale, swans on a lake, and the right to call General Montgomery or anyone else a bloody fool!

His air of effortless composure was as distinctive as his looks. His manner indicated that he enjoyed life, and because he was so easy within himself, he made others feel at ease. With his air of unmistakable masculinity, he was markedly different from Bertie Fitch-Hammond and some of his friends. Maggie Royal envied Brenda the love he so obviously felt for her—his eyes rarely left his wife as she danced a rumba with Bertie—and thought how careless she was to jeopardize it.

Warren cut in. Ian thanked Maggie Royal and went off to find Brenda. Maggie Royal decided that Ian and Warren were much alike. Both were what Brenda called "good value." As they began to dance, she wished suddenly she could know the same leaping, fearful excitement, the dry mouth and pounding heart, like galloping fast behind a flying pack of hounds, that seeing the back of a dark head in a crowd caused her to feel.

Instead she touched the shark's tooth on its simple gold chain, hidden behind the strings of Gramma's pearls, and smiled up at Warren. That night he was her anchor in an alien sea, her bulwark against rows and rows of British strangers.

Ian's friends and Chatfield regulars were Terence Ratcliff, whose father was M.P. for a Leicestershire constituency —Terence was dark and dashing and a pilot in the RAF —Hugh St. John and Richard Hollis, members of the highly touted 7th Hussars. They danced energetically, their vivid red trousers flashing like banners amid the more conservative dancers. Derek Ainsworth had volunteered for a ski battalion being formed to serve in Finland. At the present time he was skidding down Scottish slopes on a thin coating of snow before going to a French ski resort—its name was top-secret—to learn ski soldiering on mountains and glaciers. Christopher Sargent, the Queen's jockey, had gone to Edinburgh to enlist in the Scots Greys, only to find that the regiment was replacing its horses with tanks.

There were many others in what was known that first year of the war as the Chatfield set. They were mostly Eton and Harrow, Oxford and Cambridge. Titled or with hyphenated names, they spoke like Evelyn Waugh characters. "Hello, Bertie, old chap. Haven't seen you since you were sent down from Oxford," or "That was the night Tony was caught climbing into New College after midnight, shinnying up to the window, over the broken bottles and barbed wire. Thought you were in Malaya, or Inja, or Kenya . . ."

284

be the godmother. Uncle Oomlot had died in his sleep, and was buried in the family burial ground.

The obituary from the Starksville *Herald,* which Adele enclosed with her letter, reported that the aunts had his tombstone engraved with one of his favorite quotations: "The Horseman's Grave Is Always Open." They had found island living too difficult and had moved to a nursing home in Starksville. Jared's father was deeply involved in getting Negroes registered to vote for Roosevelt in the upcoming national election. Susan and Sparrow had been married in a small private ceremony in Starksville and were now living in a New York apartment. Taylor DuPree and Callie Hempstead had eloped before going to Fort Riley. Jared was at Pensacola. Cindy Lou and their two-year-old son were living in Starksville. Cindy Lou was said to be "playing around." Adele added that an attempt had been made to breed Azilia to King, but the mare had turned out to be barren.

Friday afternoons, Brenda left her assembly-line job in a munitions factory to go down to the country. She usually asked a number of friends to make up a house party. Brenda's girlfriends with their fashionable, spidery good looks, elegant "boot" legs, and long, aristocratic necks were the English version of Miss Mayo's girls. They were the daughters of the aristocracy, old and new, ancient houses, robber barons, and politicians. They shared a similar upbringing and were named Rosamond and Amanda, Caroline, Jane and Davinia, Monica and Angela. They pitied that year's debs, who, because of the war, would not be photographed eating sandwiches in their Rollses or Daimlers outside Buckingham Palace as they waited in a queue to be presented at court. Nor would they trip over their trailing gowns and be able to wear gorgeous hats at Ascot—or see the King and Queen arriving in the royal carriage, for both the Derby and Ascot Gold Cup had been scrubbed from the list of race meetings.

Those most frequently referred to in the gossip columns as members of the Chatfield set included Monica Bourne-Smith, whose father-in-law, Sir Thomas Bourne-Smith, was the rich and powerful owner of several of the country's largest newspapers. Monica was tall and languorous, model-thin, with long, straight champagne-colored hair, and wore beautiful custom-made Paris clothes. She gave the impression of swimming languidly through her days in her own individual fishbowl. "I can't imagine how they'll cope with her in the Wrens," Brenda said. "She's never lifted one of those long elegant fingers except to file her nails!"

Angela was a small, dark, horsey girl whose conversation was almost entirely about horses. She had grown up on a hill station in India. Her voice was raw from cigarettes before breakfast. Her face, with its penciled brows and thin lipsticked lips, used as a windshield for years, was cobwebbed with the lines of time, wind, and weather, which she sought to disguise with layers of white powder. Her bobbed hair was a not-quite-believable black. Her husband had been a gentleman rider. He died in a car crash while speeding to Cheltenham to ride in the Gold Cup. Angela, Brenda said, was a good-time girl with a taste for brawny Irish stable lads. "She says the new lad in her yard is a wizard in bed, but she's having trouble teaching him how to use a pitchfork!" Brenda went on to say that Angela knew more strange ceilings than there are stars in the sky. "She covers her nipples with adhesive tape so she doesn't need to wear a bra. I can't imagine why she bothers," Brenda continued. "Last year she had a ghastly fall and was concussed. When they loosened her stock, they found she didn't have a stitch on underneath. Not that there was anything to see. All she has are two raspberries that look as if they'd been set on an ironing board!"

Terence Ratcliff, Bertie, Maggie Royal, and Warren were regulars. Sometimes Warren drove them in an embassy car. When none was available, they took the train.

Chatfield Village lay at the entrance to the long winding drive that followed the course of the wide gray river. Over the huge old trees rose the gold-tipped towers and turrets of the Disney-like castle. In daylight it wasn't at all like the guidebook. From every angle it resembled the worst of what Baedeker called a massive pile of domes, towers, buttresses, and thick stone arches forming a kind of medieval catacomb. Brenda recalled that when she first saw it leering at her from its grove of oaks, she burst out laughing.

The castle had been very run-down. She had changed the peeling wallpaper and loose covers, lightened the paint, and redone the bedrooms in fresh gay colors, providing the ancient building with a new atmosphere of gaiety and lightness.

When war was declared, one wing was delegated to evacuees, the other reserved for the family. The rest of the eighty rooms, including the long gallery filled with ancestral portraits, were closed off. After the death of his wife, the Duke secluded himself in the tower suite built by an ancestor to watch the hunt go by. There he worked on a massive history of foxhunting from the time of Charlemagne to modern times, emerging only to prune his famous roses or officiate on gala occasions: Christmas, Boxing Day, the Harvest Festival, and Opening Meet.

Over the centuries a profusion of outbuildings had grown up around the castle. The stable yard—twenty box stalls on each of the three sides opened onto the cobblestones—had once been filled with hunters and steeplechasers bearing the gray-and-yellow Chatfield colors. A handful of horses remained, tended by Williams, the old stud groom, and Robert Piper, the huntsman, now in his sixties, assisted by his fourteen-year-old grandson, Billy, acting as kennel huntsman and whipper-in. The adjoining kennels housed the famous Chatfield foxhounds, one of the first organized packs in Britain, dating back to the days of Hugo

Meynell. The Duke hunted them himself until Ian came down from Oxford.

Brenda told her that although the Duke was in his mid-seventies, he would doubtless still be hunting his hounds were it not for his bladder. "Must be all that port!" she said. "He's had the problem for years. When he was young, he was able to get on and off during the course of the hunt. When he could no longer remount, he was forced to give it up!"

After Ian married Brenda, they'd had but one season before he went off to war. People spoke of what a dashing couple they made. There were photographs in silver frames taken in the hunting field, and a Munnings painting of Brenda and Ian in front of the castle with hounds, Brenda on her chestnut Highwayman, Ian riding Stalker, the winner of two Cheltenham Gold Cups and third in the last Grand National before the war. Both wore the Chatfield livery, gray coat and lemon-yellow collar, which only members of the family and special members of the field designated by the master were permitted to wear. Uncle Oomlot and Ambrose Clark, who had spent several seasons hunting in the shires, were two of a handful of members of the field to whom the master had given the Chatfield buttons and colors.

When Ian's regiment was called up, it fell to Brenda to carry on the traditions and the sport that had made the pack famous. Management of the estate and farm—the wooded coverts where foxes were found in the fall and pheasants stalked arrogantly; the pigs, poultry, and dairy; the century-old turf, the famous "grass" of the shires that had been turned into plow; plus the huge echoing castle with a skeleton staff of retainers who had come out of retirement to replace the young housemaids who had gone to work in factories and the footmen and butlers who had joined up—had fallen on Brenda's slender shoulders. Yet she moved through her busy days with marvelous aplomb, seemingly unhurried, never complaining when Ian's heir, her infant son, fell ill with croup or Nanny insisted she come down from London to straighten out the never-ending domestic squabbles.

Brenda admitted to being terrified of the tall dour woman who presided over the nursery, guarding Sprat in the manner of a tigress defending her young.

At least once a month, following the inevitable clashes with Cook, she planned to give Nanny notice, send her to the home where retired nannies go, or wish her on one of her friends, armed with glowing references written on her best crested notepaper. "I try to give satisfaction, milady, as you might say!" Nanny sniffed with a martyred air whenever Brenda reprimanded her, and Brenda inevitably lost her nerve, saying in self-justification, "After all, she is totally responsible, and I'm away so much of the time."

In spite of shortages and domestic squabbles, weekends at Chatfield were blissful—music and laughter, stags' heads and suits of armor that

Brenda named after her friends (Warren was the one that stood stiffly, implacably erect, guarding the entrance to the long gallery, feet apart, a pike in one hand), hunting prints, and the silent butler, Holmes, who knew which guests belonged to which umbrellas.

The winter of 1940 was frigid. The Thames froze over. Villages were snowbound, trains late. Maggie Royal wore her long johns under her nurse's uniform and mink coat. Brenda used Mick, her Jack Russell, to warm her bed at night and wore her hunting underwear under her black lace nighties.

In April the phony war ended. The Wehrmacht invaded Denmark and Norway and Hitler began his campaign in the west. The BBC spoke of panzer thrusts far behind Allied lines and the slaughter of civilian refugees by Stuka dive bombers. Terence Ratcliff, flying a reconnaissance plane, reported endless lines of German troops advancing into the Lowlands.

Spring came like a slow smile. Flat racing opened at Hurst Park instead of Lincoln, breaking tradition. On Hampstead Heath soldiers and their girls rode swings at the Easter Bank Holiday fair and knocked Hitler's block off "three shies for a penny."

Sexuality was in the air, like the barrage balloons overhead and the daffodils in the parks, where soldiers and their girls lay on the ground entwined, oblivious of passersby. On weekends Chatfield teemed with people who slid in and out of each other's beds as easily as a knife through home-churned butter.

Everyone knew of Monica's predilection for handsome Guards officers and Angela's preference for virile stable lads. At night the blacked-out hallways were as well-traveled as the wood rides in the home covert during the foxhunting season.

Warren blushed furiously when Brenda told him to "creep hopefully into the right room behind closed doors," and guaranteed him a bed partner. "I know you'd prefer Maggie," she teased, "but she belongs to the Elsie Dinsmore era. She actually thinks that in order to spawn, you have to swim upstream, like salmon. Dear Warren, I promise you someone bedworthy. It's all the same in the dark!"

Once Maggie Royal was groping her way along to the bathroom when a hand reached out and pinched her breast. She tried to pull away. Instead she found herself caught in an embrace as a mustache moved over her face.

"Let me go," she hissed furiously.

"Oh, my God," cried the Right Honorable Something-or-other. "I thought you were Monica. Luck of the game, you know." And he vanished through a bedroom door.

One afternoon Warren and Maggie Royal were "having a walk through the forest," recording observations for Sparrow's notebook, when they came on a couple in a secluded glade. The girl and boy were so engrossed they did not hear the dogs or their approach.

Maggie Royal recognized the young man as Tom Lacey, the red-headed stable lad home on leave. He was undressing the pudding-faced housemaid, the voluptuous Effie Hanson, who worked at the castle.

The young man's head rose. His lips moved upward to Effie's breasts, caressing them gently at first, then more fiercely. Then he pulled her closer and they began to move together as one body, quickening, then slackening until the plunging motion became more violent. The girl cried out, then gave a final long shudder that ended in a sigh like the breeze in the trees.

Warren and Maggie Royal walked slowly back to the castle, not daring to speak or look at one another.

The following weekend Brenda went down to the country on Friday afternoon. As Maggie Royal was on duty at the hospital, Warren brought her in his Morgan two-seater Saturday morning. They found Brenda, pale and sniffling, lying back on her chaise longue nursing what she called a streamer.

Nanny stood stiffly in the center of the bedroom, as though at attention. Her face and body registered rigid disapproval.

"Now, Nanny, you mustn't get into a frizz," Brenda was saying. "Bad for the acids."

"I try to give satisfaction, milady," Nanny sniffed, "as you might say!"

"Of course you do. We couldn't get along without you."

"Well, milady, it's just that I don't want the young master to have a bad example," Nanny replied, faintly mollified. "But that Effie, now. She looks as if she needed a good scrubbing . . . pushes the dirt under the carpet and the beds . . ."

"Nanny, Nanny," Brenda said wearily. "There's a war on! Effie at least is better than nothing."

"Hardly, milady!" Nanny was off and running. "Who knows what she picks up, off in the woods, dillydallying with every Tom, Dick, and Harry, while I do the trays. Trays!" she added vehemently. "Nothing puts a house out so!"

Brenda began to cough.

"Well, milady," Nanny said, savoring her news until Brenda's coughing subsided. "You'll have to call Dr. Lessing. Effie has spots all over her. We don't want the young master catching some dread disease, do we, now?"

"Oh, dear," Brenda said, "and the castle chockablock over the weekend!"

"I'll do what I can, milady." Nanny turned to go. "I try to give satisfaction, as you might say."

"If Effie wants to have a boozle with the stable boy in the covert, it's her business," Brenda said when Nanny had departed. "Effie's reputation for casual dalliance with the local lads has been common knowledge since she was twelve."

She had hardly finished blowing her nose again when there was an urgent knocking on the door.

"Come in," Brenda choked. "What in God's name is it now?"

It was Effie, a barely recognizable Effie with spots all over, like an early Matisse. Her face was crimson from weeping or from her unidentified disease. "Milady," she cried in great distress. "My legs are covered with running sores."

"My God," Brenda exclaimed. "Syphilis! Go to bed. Whatever you do, keep away from the son and heir. I'll call Dr. Lessing.

"I think I'll go quietly bonkers!" she said after Effie ran from the room. "I keep thinking how lovely it would be to be Mrs. Hanson."

"Mrs. Hanson!" Maggie Royal was used to Brenda's flights of fancy, but the idea of Brenda in the orange lady's run-over-at-the-heel slippers was something hard for her to imagine.

"Yes," Brenda continued. "She leaves a furor behind her, but she's oblivious of the tiresome, overcivilized ethics we impose on ourselves."

"Fascinating." Maggie Royal looked at the original Munnings sketch of Brenda riding out at Newmarket that was hung over her desk. "What made you think of Mrs. Hanson?"

Brenda started to light one of her strong Turkish cigarettes and then decided not to. Instead she blew her nose again. "She has a cozy vegetable existence with her children growing up around her. She has no domestic worries as to whether the food is clean or the children fed the right vitamins on schedule. Hanson may come home squiffed from the pub and there may not be enough fry-ups to go around, but she doesn't need to worry about her figure or new loose covers for the furniture or whom Nanny is squabbling with. Her life will proceed along its course with far more serenity than yours or mine."

Dr. Lessing came that afternoon, driving up in the dogcart in which he now made his rounds. They waited apprehensively for his report.

When he finally emerged from the servants' wing he was shaking with laughter. "It's not what we fear, Lady Brenda," he said when he could speak. "Your girl has lain on an anthill!"

At the hospital Maggie Royal listened to the BBC whenever possible. Europe was obscured behind conflicting reports. New leaders tried to rally Allied troops. In London, Chamberlain was replaced by Churchill, whose thundering prose began to rally the whole of England.

On May 14 Holland, after a gallant fight, surrendered. On May 17 Belgium collapsed. Warren, acting as a spokesman for the U.S. embassy, advised the four thousand Americans still in Britain to leave.

"You must be joking," Maggie Royal scoffed when he telephoned the hospital suggesting she return to America. She gazed around the ward, where the patients were being shunted aside to make room for the waves of wounded expected soon to be pouring into London. "I'm rather busy, just now."

By that weekend it was clear the British Expeditionary Force in

France was cut off. The British Army began its desperate evacuation from Dunkirk. The hospital was unusually quiet. People talked to one another in low voices. Even the children were subdued and the noise of the rocking horse rocking was stilled.

Maggie Royal worked around the clock. The paper in Washington cabled her to send as many on-the-spot reports as possible. When not changing sheets, emptying bedpans, and assisting the desperately short-handed staff, she scribbled notes on whatever paper she could find—prescription forms and toilet paper and paper bags.

Ian returned from Dunkirk with the youth and gaiety gone from his eyes forever. He had seen his friends from Eton and Oxford gunned down by Nazi planes during the retreat along the roads of Normandy. Hugh St. John and Richard Hollis would never again wear the dashing maroon trousers of the "cherry pickers" and dance madly at one of Brenda's balls. Hugh had a leg blown off and Richard was paralyzed from a bullet in the spine.

For several days Ian paced the town house or the streets, unable to sleep or settle to anything. He did not visit White's or the Guards Club or go to Kensington barracks. Nor did he place any bets at the fashionable gambling clubs. He still laughed and joked and teased Brenda, but his eyes were dark and still.

Brenda took time off from her work and they went home to Chatfield. They had a week together before it was necessary for Ian to rejoin his regiment. Brenda rang up after he'd gone. "You and Warren must hurry down," she told Maggie Royal. "I'm perishing with loneliness."

The following weekend Maggie Royal and Warren went down by train.

St. Pancras was a madhouse. People with anxious faces searched the hospital trains, crying out at sight of a husband or son being carried on a stretcher. Children who had somehow escaped earlier evacuation were being towed along by harassed mothers or patient nannies.

A small curly-haired boy was being given a farewell kiss by a tall soldier. The child was trying hard not to cry.

"Now, then," his father said. "Stiff upper lip. We'll be better able to fight the Nazis without worrying about our tots. Be a big boy, now. Off you go."

A lump formed in Maggie Royal's throat as the little boy, clutching his authorized bundle containing a toothbrush, towel, and change of clothing, gave his father a final agonized glance before plunging through the crowd of wounded men on litters and weeping parents and boarding the outgoing train.

"You like children, don't you?" Warren asked, watching her.

"Oh, yes." She tried to smile. "I don't think any marriage should be without them. How could anybody not want to take in a little boy like that?"

"A lot won't," Warren replied, and quoted from a saying going the rounds. " 'Inspired by Britain's glorious cause / With seven maids to do the chores / Gather round at country teas / And grouse about evacuees.' "

They walked from the Chatfield station. One of the earlier dukes had installed a long walkway from the station to the castle so that when hounds and hunters traveled by train to a distant meet, it would be possible to keep one's boots clean and out of the wet.

"Brenda mentioned she invited Bertie down," Maggie Royal said.

"If she had any sense, she'd shove one of her spurs through his heart and bury him beneath the cabbages in the kitchen garden," Warren put in hotly.

"I love Brenda and Ian," Maggie Royal continued as they entered the courtyard. "But discretion is not her long suit. And Ian is too easy led."

"She's one of those women born without moral fiber."

"Nonsense," Maggie Royal cried defensively. "She just looks at things differently."

Brenda came running from the garden, her face alive and welcoming. She had on a blue muslin dress with a tight bodice and wide skirt, and her arms were full of flowers. Bertie followed, wearing white flannels and an open-neck shirt.

"Darlings," Brenda cried. "How marvelous to see you." She held the great bunch of sweet peas up to her face. "I've just got back from the Hansons' about Effie. She didn't turn up for work again. After the cottage, the stench of fry-ups, and all those children, there's nothing as pleasurable as burrowing one's nose in sweet peas. Darling Maggie, do have a smell."

"You're not unlike them, darling," Bertie said. "All soft bluey, pinky, lavender colors, and you smell good!"

In that one lightning moment, time stopped. That instant Maggie Royal felt that they were bound together in growing intimacy, a closeness that even included Bertie, because he so obviously worshiped Brenda—Brenda, temperamentally more suited to the ripe beauty of roses and complexities of vice than to sweet peas and the simplicity of virtue.

Maggie Royal found Warren studying the Duke's Alken paintings and took him to visit Sprat and Nanny.

Sprat was sitting in a nursery-sized chair at a round nursery-sized table. He was wearing a blue jumper suit with a blue linen bib tied around his neck and was covered with gooseberry jam from his square chin, which resembled his father's, to the roots of his fair hair, so much like Brenda's.

Nanny, who'd been to the village, was in an informative mood. Eddie, Ernie's older brother, had been hit by a lorry on the road to the airdrome and rushed to the hospital with a broken arm.

"What happened to his bicycle?" Warren asked.

"Smashed to smithereens," Nanny replied happily. "The traffic is turrible, as you might say. The soldiers have no road sense at all. All they seem to want to do is drive as fast as possible."

"I came to see if I could take the Sprat for a walk," Maggie Royal managed to say before Nanny took off on another tangent.

"Oh, may I," cried the little boy. "Please, Nanny."

Nanny thought a moment and then decided it might be permissible "if her ladyship agrees."

"She said fine," Maggie Royal said. "She's resting now."

Nanny's lips pursed into a thin line. "Her ladyship does rather overdo," she said severely.

Sprat, freed from the nursery, pranced gaily ahead as they walked through the village. They passed the Rose and Crown with its neat borders and white-painted yard fence and the carefully kept gardens and neat fronts of the stone cottages along the paved street.

After the butcher shop, the street dwindled into the Hansons' potholed lane. The heady scent of honeysuckle lining the hedgerows came to them. The sun was warm on their backs. Cushions of emerald moss shone between the cobbles of the stable yard. The brown-orange walls and steep roofs of the outbuildings were amber in the late-afternoon light. The old trees were silvery as the wind turned their leaves, disclosing their hanging gifts of small gnarled fruit.

Maggie Royal gave Lancelot and Ernie's colt carrots from the Chatfield garden. Lancelot crunched with hearty enjoyment, wrinkling his nose and rewarding her with a slobbery horse kiss.

A path led from the gate between flowerbeds that were a tangled mass of rosemary, currant, and gooseberry bushes, all incongruously intertwined. The house's walls were whitewashed, and the uneven roof of tiles, the color of burnt umber, was patched with golden lichen. There were no straight lines, and despite the appearance of age and general untidiness, no feeling of poverty or decay. The square cottage looked a part of the land, as strong as the oaks shading it, friendly and warm.

They were welcomed with joyous cries.

"My children," Mrs. Hanson said, beaming from the doorway. "You've come to see my children. Here." She indicated the ones clinging to her legs, disguised by muddy rubber boots. "Jenny and Jill, Tommy, Bobby and Billy . . . But you'll be coming in and having some tea!"

She ushered them into the live-in kitchen with its whitewashed walls and beams and oil lamp hanging from a center beam. A fire was burning in the wide fireplace and a kettle singing on the hearth. Potted plants and bottles—"Me wines!" Mrs. Hanson said. "Elderberry and cowslip and sloe gin; keeps Mr. Hanson out of the pub"—lined the wide sills of the two windows. One looked out over the pasture where Lancelot lived, the other to the ribbon of river in the distance.

Orange curtains fluttered from the frames. There was a highboy and several rush-bottomed ladder-back chairs. Effie's love child was tied to its high chair. A number of children sat around the wide oak table having their cooked tea. The table was covered by a blue-checked cloth and blue china.

"This is nice," Warren said appreciatively. He brought out his pipe. "Mind if I smoke?"

"Do light your pipe, sir," Mrs. Hanson put in quickly. Mr. Hanson, she explained, had gone in the lorry to fetch Eddie back from the hospital. "That Eddie! No more idea about getting out of the way than a babe unborn! Could 'ave been kilt."

"I'm so glad it wasn't worse," Maggie Royal said. "And how is Ernie?"

"Ernie's gone to Lord Twatley's. The older lads 'as gone to war. His lordship's letting Ernie ride out with the racehorses."

"He'll get to be champion jockey yet," Maggie Royal said.

Mrs. Hanson pushed several children to one side and set places for them. Her cheeks were like the wizened apples that grew in the old orchard in the fall. Her blazing mop of amber hair was coming loose from its pins. She was marvelously attired in an orange pinafore dress, a green velvet blouse, and Wellingtons. Aware of no necessity to prove herself better than anyone else, she was content to preside over her family and the evacuees, providing them with loving and zestful safety and contentment. With the same calm, unhurried dignity as the swans' on the castle lake, she poured out their tea from a large brown earthenware pot, which, when not in motion, was ensconced in a crimson knitted cozy.

"It tastes so much better poured from an earthenware pot," Maggie Royal said, watching the Orange Lady spoon dollops of cream into the strong, almost black brew.

"Cream!" Warren cried appreciatively. "Thick, fresh cream!"

"When the children first came, they wouldn't drink milk," Mrs. Hanson explained. " 'We can't drink milk like that,' they said. 'We have our milk out of bottles!' "

"Has it been difficult, having so many children to care for?" Warren asked.

"My word, no." Mrs. Hanson beamed at the children ranged around the room. "Now, there's some up to the castle'd make you think the world's coming to an end if you open your doors to the little tykes. But Mr. Hanson and me, we've had no trouble, not after the first." She went on to explain that when the city children originally came, they were unable to sleep. " 'It's the 'orrid quiet!' they said."

Warren brought out chocolate bars and the children climbed all over him, smearing jam on his clothing as Mrs. Hanson admonished, "Children, don't make a nuisance of yourselves."

Sprat and one of the evacuees, a short stocky little cockney called Billy, were wrestling in a corner. "Cowardy, cowardy custard!" cried Billy as his fist connected with Sprat's nose. Sprat retaliated with a punch that knocked Billy sideways. The boy grabbed Ernie's riding crop from the corner and belted his lordship across the chest. Sprat, blood streaming from his nose, fought back his tears and tore at Billy, fists flailing.

"That's enough!" Warren's feet grated on the grit on the floor. He picked up Sprat and threw him over his shoulder.

They thanked Mrs. Hanson and said good-bye to the children.

"This is a wonderful house," Warren said, giving the warm, light-filled room a final glance.

They walked slowly back through the park. The deer grazing under the great trees raised their heads as they approached, and then lowered them. The swans continued their dignified circles on the lake.

Maggie Royal held the little boy's hand and told him a story about Ugly, the alligator. "And his ancestors came out of the primeval ooze millions of years ago . . ." She went on to describe Ugly and his pool and his descendants who lived in the sewers of New York City because they were mistakenly flushed down toilets. "I know a little boy who leaves pieces of meat in his loo so that the alligators will have something to eat," she said, and launched into a tale about a sea turtle named Hortense who had a dress-up shell for dinner parties.

That afternoon they were watching the weekly cricket match on the village green—the Duke required guests at Chatfield to attend, saying it was the form—when Mr. Jennings, the publican, announced he'd heard over the wireless that the Germans had marched into Paris. Warren immediately called the embassy and discovered the report was true. During tea they huddled around the smoking library fire, listening to the wireless.

"We're in for it now!" Warren said solemnly, unconsciously aligning the Americans with the British.

Dinner was a solemn affair. Holmes moved silently around the table as they ate pheasant from the home covert that Ian had shot and fresh vegetables from the castle garden and drank fine French wine.

Afterward they returned to the library. The high-ceilinged cavernous room never became really warm. Even though it was June, the four-foot-thick walls remained damp with mildew. In spite of Brenda's bright chintzes, it was as cold and gloomy as the news pouring from the wireless.

Queen Elizabeth's broadcast to the women of France, rendered in precise "La Plume de Ma Tante" French, was followed by the "Marseillaise" and "God Save the King." Brenda wept unashamedly while the men busily got out cigarettes and stared at the brocade curtains lined with blackout material.

The old Duke sat motionless, staring into the fire. "Hard pounding, this," he said, quoting Wellington at Waterloo. "Let's see who will pound the longest!"

Maggie Royal's turn to cry came after midnight on Monday, when she huddled in the twin bed in Brenda's flat on the top of the house in

Belgravia and heard President Roosevelt's familiar voice promising guns and planes and hope.

A new French government was set up at Vichy under Marshal Pétain and Pierre Laval. From abroad, Charles de Gaulle broadcast pleas to the French people not to give in. Mr. Churchill spoke of the time when "the new world, with all its power and might, would come to the rescue and liberation of the old."

Bertie became notably silent on the subject of Mussolini after the news that Il Duce had joined forces with Hitler and sent troops across the French frontier. Attendance at the spaghetti places in Soho fell off. Quaglino's closed, and although its owners posted notices that they were 100 percent behind the war effort, some of the restaurant's windows were broken.

By the beginning of July the shock following France's acceptance of the crushing armistice terms imposed by the Nazis wore off and people went back to business as usual.

On July 10, 1940, the first wave of German bombers filled the skies. Clashes between the Luftwaffe and the RAF intensified over the Channel. The Germans had been honing their skills as fighter pilots since the Spanish Civil War. "They come down on you out of the sky like ruddy lightning!" Terence Ratcliff, now an RAF group captain, reported. "All I saw was the Channel," he added ruefully, "and I never learned to swim!"

On August 8, Hitler's all-out assault on Britain began. Air Marshal Dowding issued an Order of the Day to members of the Fighter Command: "The Battle of Britain is about to begin. Members of the Royal Air Force, the fate of generations lies in your hands."

The sky was full of planes, like bees. Stukas made continuous onslaughts on convoys in the Channel, and dogfights raged over the countryside.

August 12 was the day the grouse season opened. Terry Ratcliff told Brenda when he saw her next that his plane had been one of the Spits that had gone to work on a covey of Stukas and shot down nine. "Best shooting I ever had," he said.

On September 7 the first of the round-the-clock raids on London began. Although thousands had been evacuated to the United States and to the countryside, almost three thousand died in the rubble. More than ten thousand were wounded.

Wooden facades were thrown up to conceal ruined buildings. Workmen were so quick at clearing away wreckage after each bombardment, the city somehow managed to seem intact.

People settled in shelters, staking out their territory in the tubes, where some were to live for the duration, while overhead houses split apart, fires raged, and people died.

As the bombing continued, space on the platforms was given over to more and more families, who bragged about the size of the craters the bombs made when their dwellings and all their belongings were destroyed. The atmosphere was that of an informal picnic. Beds, cooking utensils, and sleeping bodies were stacked alongside the tracks. People made dates to meet in the nearest shelter, where they drank tea and chatted as if in their sitting rooms. The ventilation was bad at the best of times. Now, although smoking was banned, the humanity jamming the platforms made them unbearably foul. Yet one rarely heard a cross word spoken. Most felt like Mr. Potts, the air-raid warden, who said when his house was blown to bits, "There's them as has it worse."

Brenda considered it cowardly to "go to the tubes." She made a will and put it in the fridge. "If the house burns down, it will be safe," she said. "So will I. I intend to live to be an old lady wielding a walking stick and opinions."

Nights Maggie Royal journeyed home in the tubes, before the hour when the trains stopped running. The trains had wide mesh netting in the windows, with only a small diamond-shaped hole to see out. There were little verses like "I trust you'll pardon my correction, that stuff is there for your protection," then a cartoon showing somebody peeling it off the window. This led to penciled comments like "I thank you for your recitation, but I can't see the blinkin' station."

Maggie Royal became used to clambering over the bodies on the platform, sleeping, talking, reading, playing games, putting hair up in the awkward tin curlers the British called "dinkies," and making love.

The hospital, the bedpans, and pus and gangrene became routine. Maggie Royal was too busy and too tired to be frightened. She adopted Brenda's fatalistic attitude that if she was going to get it, then that's the way it would be.

Days and nights blended one into the other, punctuated by the sound of sirens and running feet and cries in the blackout. The paper in Washington asked for additional columns, and when she returned from the hospital she was sometimes so tired she fell asleep over the type-writer.

She lost weight and had to take a tuck in her uniform and tie her Red Cross apron tighter.

Warren cautioned, "You must eat more and get more sleep."

"Since the blitz, my day is your night," she told him. "I can't see you after eight. I go on duty at the hospital."

"Magdalena, you can't work both day and night. Besides, what in God's name can anybody do before eight in the evening?"

"Tea?"

"Tea!" he snorted. "Even though I've been here almost two years, I still prefer coffee. Well, all right; the Ritz at five. Still, the hour is *most* uncivilized."

And so they went to the Ritz, which, in spite of the bombs raining around it, remained unchanged, its gilt-and-marble elegance intact throughout the war, managing always to be one of the most civilized places in London.

They sat at their beautifully appointed table in the winter garden.

The old white-haired waiter who had known Brenda from the time she was a child having tea with her grandmother hovered discreetly in the background. The fountain in the alcove tinkled, and in spite of the wartime shortages, there was the delicious smell of rich women and food.

The Battle of Britain continued to rage. At Chatfield the approach of the planes was first heralded by pheasants rising from the covert behind the village and from the barnyard guineas, whose shrill warning cries were soon followed by the nightly thunder of motors, ack-ack, and vivid flashes like Fourth of July fireworks. The weak, tinny village siren sent the villagers, some wearing pots on their heads as helmets, scurrying to the shelter in the basement of the church.

Once a plane returning to a German base disposed of its bombs in a field of kale where Brenda and Maggie Royal had seen a litter of fox cubs when they were riding out. The next morning Jack, the earth-stopper, found them dead.

In the village, pots and pans were collected to be turned into planes. Brenda had a benefit garden party to raise money for the Chatfield Spitfire. Terry Ratcliff, who had just shot down his fourth Messerschmitt over the Channel, came and talked to the villagers, "rallying the home front." Afterward, when he was offered a drink, he replied he was too tired even to get drunk. He was, he said, exhausted by tiredness. He spent the time before it was necessary to return to his base walking through the rose garden. "It smells so good," he said. "I want to remember the scent."

In the village the innate British dislike of strangers was put aside, along with cherished knickknacks, favored mementos and breakables, in deference to evacuees. East End children sang, "Yah, yah, yah, Hitler, what a funny little man you are" as Lord Haw Haw's threats were transmitted by the BBC, which also issued instructions about what to do in air raids. The women knitted miles of stockings and scarves, and when hanging out their wash, boasted they were "gonna hang out the washing on the Siegfried Line."

The Duke came out of seclusion to preside at the tribunal in the schoolhouse, where meetings were held to take care of complaints.

The Duke and Maggie Royal had become great friends. They often had tea in the rose garden. She followed him as he ranged along the rows of rosebushes. "What is that rose?" she asked, pointing to a bush of pink blooms with a brownish-cream tinge.

"Aw, the Ophelia." He sounded pleased. "Not unlike your complexion, my dear. Not many Ophelias left, you know. They belong to another century, another time."

She taught him how to shoot crap, "rolling dem bones," using Negro jargon. They sat facing one another on a stone bench, rolling the dice between them, and the Duke was delighted when he made his point, winning a shilling from her.

Other times they discussed foxhunting. His words took her back to afternoons in Uncle Oomlot's tower room.

"It's the excitement of the land, you know. Knowing your hounds, your horse, and your country. I like the feel of the land." Leaning down, he picked up a handful of the rich English earth. In the "Great War" his sense of the land had enabled him to make numerous escapes from German patrols. "I could sense their coming, feel them in the offing."

He looked up at the sky, where a plane from the airdrome beyond the village was on its way to the coast. "It's all changing now. Nobody bothers with summer hunting. We'd drive the hunters in a trap to the far corners of the country and the staff would hack over with hounds. We put up at different farms. The farmers and their relations would come hunting with us.

"Then you knew everyone," he continued. "You could knock on any door and ask if you could come in. Hunting a pack of hounds in the shires was the grandest thing a man could do. Those days we had sixty horses in the yard. We mounted the staff four days a week, counting second horses. The second horsemen rode the roads. They wore high silk toppers with cockades, our stable colors, to distinguish them from Lord Lonsdale or the Marquess of Wickwold. Nobody smoked in the field. The women rode side saddle, and the only time we dined out during the season was Saturday. Before the Great War, four hundred people could ride across Leicestershire without ever meeting wire. The big estates all had agents. You met a bit of wire and rang up the agent and asked him to get it down. There were clauses in tenants' leases banning wire. We made sure the country was kept in grass by voting into office those we knew, people with hyphenated names or titles, as opposed to Smith or Jones." His face took on a distant expression. "Because of the plow-up, we're losing our best grazing land." He paused and then concluded sadly, "All changed now. This is the sadness, don't y'know? Change!"

In September Brenda and Maggie Royal rode out with hounds. Brenda rode her chestnut, Highwayman. Maggie Royal was mounted on Ian's steeplechaser, Stalker. He was a big bay horse and Maggie Royal soon learned that across country and over fences he was "patent safety," as bold and strong as Lancelot had proven to be.

Every few yards Brenda and the staff paused to speak to the villagers hanging up clothes in their yards or tending their allotments. "And how is your Ladyship?" they inquired, bobbing their heads. "Did you hear the ack-ack last night? Did you know, milady, that Dick Knot, the butcher's son, bought it last week in the North Sea?"

While Brenda nodded and commiserated and offered words of consolation or cheer, the hounds sniffed in the hedgerows and the young whip was kept busy seeing that the puppies did not chase cats or root in gardens. Beyond the village the mist was "thick out over" the lower valleys and the wooded coverts lay warm in the sun. They rode along the verges. Buses and lorries passed, the soldiers waving at the land girls in the fields and singing "Tipperary." The air was filled with the scent of late roses. Sweet Repose, which smelled like strawberry ice cream, Queen Anne's lace, and plumy lavender fireweed grew on the wide greensward where in former times old people and young children had tended sheep and cattle, paying to "tent," graze their animals beside the road.

Brenda called out to the people berrying, picking blackberries from bushes along the way. "Our people," she said protectively. "Now that Ian's gone, my responsibility!"

After the first frost, "when the dahlias died" in Mr. Jorrock's parlance, cubhunting began. Mostly they hunted in the kale. "I do like to see hounds hunting in the kale," Brenda said, as the bobbing black-and-white sterns, partially hidden by the green leafy plants, exploded into activity when a cub was found.

In November, when the official hunting season began, the woods were beautiful. Periwinkles, dog mercury, celandines, and pale primroses bloomed out of season, a gift of nature like the Christmas roses in the garden, the kingfisher flashing against the silver river. It was easy to forget the blitz then, the savage nocturnal bombings reducing great chunks of London to rubble. Brenda's spine-tingling holler, the huntsman's cheers, and the cry of hounds drowned out the drone of planes rising from the nearby airfield that had now come to seem as natural as breathing.

"It's England!" Brenda said. "As long as there's foxhunting, there will always be an England."

As the shortage of fuel increased, Maggie Royal slept in her mink, wrapping it around her in the freezing bed which she was unable to warm with the hot-water bottle, as it had developed a leak and could not be replaced. Brenda wore her "sinless sables." ("You have no idea how many ghastly hours of cricket and croquet I had to endure with the old Duke stranded in the shires when I longed to be dining at Quag's or dancing at the 400. Then the old boy presents me with my late mother-in-law's sables! Dear Maggie, believe me. I'd have settled for a polo coat if I could have escaped watching endless games of polo!")

Brenda had more petrol than most because Ian was issued pink petrol as an official of the National Hunts. Once when he got leave and wanted to go somewhere other than racing, Bertie suggested he put mothballs in the tank of the MG. This would eliminate telltale color in case they were arrested. Ian refused, saying it would be against the honor of the land.

Christmas came and went and still the German bombers came. After the awful December 29 bombing, in which fifteen hundred fires swept the East End alone, the weather turned bad and the Luftwaffe was forced to let up on its attacks. During January and February there was a respite. Paradoxically, the letup caused morale to sag. Without the air raids as a distraction, people became aware of the increasing scarcity of food. There was just enough meat for the average family to eat once a week.

Almost everything was rationed now. The only thing there seemed to be a plenty of was cabbage and brussels sprouts. Maggie Royal vowed that if she lived through the war, she would never eat either vegetable again.

While Brenda saw to the farm and coped with the problems of the estate, Maggie Royal gave the harassed village women and substitute nannies time off by taking the children. She read them *Sunny Stories*, told them tales of Stark Island, took them for walks, and taught them games—hide and seek, fox and geese, ring around the rosy, and rounders for the older ones.

Sometimes she joined the Hansons around the kitchen table for a cooked tea or one of Mrs. Hanson's fry-ups. Despite the confusion and haphazard housekeeping, the children looked happy and well-fed. There was a feeling of warmth and contentment many an affluent household could envy.

Adele remained a faithful correspondent.

> Your last letter came in pieces. Either that or your type-writer is missing some letters. We read your articles about the blitz. Maggie, I worry about you being maimed.
>
> Big news. Constance is having a baby. She is all worried about her figure and now plays only nine holes instead of her usual eighteen at Rolling Rock.
>
> Aunt Emily went down to the island but Cindy Lou wouldn't let her have the place plates. Apparently Cindy Lou has been behaving very badly, as to be expected. She tried living at Great Oak when the aunts moved out but soon took her child back to the mainland.
>
> The horses are fine, although one of the ponies got colic from too much grass but is all right now. Jiggs, the Lab, got a chicken bone caught in his throat, but the vet got it out. Mother has sold Dunwoody to some rich Yankees, who are moving the trees and box bushes to different spots and painting the library white.
>
> I almost forgot. I heard that Jared got his wings.

The last great raid of the Battle of Britain took place Saturday, May 10, 1941. Maggie Royal had just gone on duty when the sirens sounded. As the first bombs began to fall, the yellow action-station lights were turned on. The staff began putting patients under beds with their mattresses on top of them. Those on the upper floors able to move were evacuated to the lower floors. Those who could not be moved had to be left where they were.

A bomb blew a hole in one of the wards, and pandemonium reigned. There were sparks, flying cinders, the rumble of falling stone, and the sounds of screams as a never-ending stream of bombs fell. At one point, while trying to restrain a woman in convulsions, Maggie Royal happened to glance outside. Incendiaries glowed like fireflies on a summer night.

That night Maggie Royal learned what hell must be like. She saw things so awful that afterward she was never able to talk about them. She went from one burned, broken body to the next, fighting back her horror and nausea, struggling to keep her hands and voice steady as the city slowly turned red with flames and blood.

The children broke her heart. A little boy, two years old, with the blue eyes and golden hair of the cherubs on the ceilings at Chatfield, in shock. His mother had been killed. His father had lost a leg. An infant girl, horribly burned, saved and wrapped in a sack after her parents were burned to death. A boy about eight, ashen-faced, tearless, holding his arm, almost severed above the elbow, pleading to have it reattached. "Please, sir, might you put it back? Please, sir, can y' please put it back?"

One of the pump crews was hit. Blue-clad, fire-seared bodies were brought into the hospital lobby, where Maggie Royal was assisting the matron to sort the dead from the wounded. "Stay with me, auntie," one begged, grabbing her hand. "I'm pressed for time, lad," the matron said gently, disengaging it from his terrified grasp. But the smile she gave him from her wrinkled, exhausted face was that of an angel.

The dead were hastily piled in corners so that the space could be used for those still alive. A young woman lay amid the dying and wounded. She was in labor. At that moment a bomb fell, shaking the walls and bringing plaster down from the ceiling. The woman cried out in pain and terror. Her blood ran onto the floor.

"Quick," Maggie Royal cried to one of the nurses hurrying past. "Get the doctor." She grabbed the girl's hand and held it until the old doctor came.

He had been crippled at Château Thierry and had come out of retirement to ease the shortage of physicians. His hair was as white as the sheet covering the pregnant girl, and his face was grimed with sweat and traces of blood. He turned to Maggie Royal. "A breech birth," he said grimly, indicating the blood. "Hold her hand. Now, push," he told the girl. "Push hard!"

Bombs continued to fall, their blasts mingling with the anguished cries and moans of the wounded. Maggie Royal wiped the sweat away from the doctor's face as he probed gently at the child inside. Suddenly the legs appeared. The doctor extended his hands for Maggie Royal to clean the blood from them. He took a deep breath and grasped the baby's legs.

Inch by inch the baby started to emerge. It was not breathing, and slowly turning purple.

"Quick!" the doctor cried. "Cotton to clear the mouth and nostrils."

There was none.

Maggie Royal reached under her uniform and ripped apart her slip. A strip of French lace came off and she handed it to the doctor. Gently he wiped the mucus from the tiny nostrils.

304

Maggie Royal had forgotten the bombs falling outside. "Dear Father," she prayed, "guard with tenderness small things that have no words!"

There was a sudden intake of breath, then a cry.

The doctor's gray, soot-grimed face broke into a triumphant smile as he held up the squalling infant.

A cheer came from those lying nearby. The young mother, who had given birth without chloroform or hot water, amid the awful stench of blood and smoke and excrement, took the baby in her arms and with a small smile and look of utter peace went quietly to sleep.

Maggie Royal thought of the resurrection fern. Her faintness and nausea and fatigue were suddenly replaced by hope, coupled with a vast anger against the men in the death-dealing planes overhead.

She remembered hearing Big Ben's chimes breaking the dawn silence as the clock marked the end of the last mass bomber raid on London in World War II. Then somebody was holding smelling salts under her nose. The old doctor was patting her on the shoulder, and the matron was saying, "Well done. Go home now and get some sleep."

When she got into bed, she could not sleep. She was, like the RAF pilots, exhausted by tiredness. She arose and pulled aside the blackout curtains. Fires burned as far as she could see. Rescue workers picked their way through fallen buildings, rubble, and cratered streets. Across the way a railing was being pulled down for scrap and a man in a black coat and striped trousers was carrying a chair through the blown-out doorway of a house.

She looked at herself in the mirror, trying to see if any of the horror showed. She was paler, thinner, but that was all.

News of Pearl Harbor the following December had a stunning effect. "A
new species, saved from occupied France and sent to America when
Paris was taken, is being developed in California," the Duke said as they
walked among his rosebushes. "That's a good omen. Now the Yanks are
bound to come in!"

Yet it wasn't until June 1942 that the first American units arrived.
Maggie Royal stood on a corner in Piccadilly and saw the first GI's
march by. She made no attempt to fight back the tears that poured
down her face as the people of London, who had survived fifty-seven
consecutive nights of remorseless bombing, cheered and called out,
"Welcome, Yanks. We'll soon be hanging out the washing on the Siegfried Line."

Once the U.S. was committed, the American war effort moved with
incredible speed. England, only slightly larger than Colorado, prepared
to absorb two million Americans and provide them with the necessary
facilities for the great invasion. Motor buses of troops raced through the
countryside, while their passengers, in high good humor, waved, whistled, and sang.

The airfield and its facilities outside Chatfield was expanded to ac-
commodate one thousand men who descended on the village, consum-
ing all the liquor in the Rose and Crown and precipitating a great many
unplanned pregnancies.

The shortage of food, fuel, and other supplies was to be strained further. Nonetheless, it was considered bad form to discuss losses or complain.

In London the U.S. Army took over a large apartment building on
Grosvenor Square, which became known as Eisenhowerplatz, and began
laying the groundwork for the greatest war effort in history.

London's streets were full of American servicemen.

Maggie Royal was waiting to cross the street in Piccadilly Circus
one morning when she noticed a familiar-looking man in the uniform of
a Navy commander. He turned around and she saw him laugh and

point and realized with a thrill that it was Robert Montgomery, the movie star who reminded her of Noble LeFevre. Occasionally she saw a Navy uniform moving along the walkways with long, effortless grace and caught her breath. But it was never Jared.

Adele wrote that Tyger and Noble had been in battle. Taylor, Jolly Olly, Peabo Van Riker, and Piers Shaw had discovered that the cavalry had been mechanized and had joined OSS, the Office of Strategic Services, becoming known as the "O So Social, O So Secret." There was no news of Jared. Gas rationing and rolling bandages were boring and she wished the war would hurry up and end.

"I almost forgot," she added in typical Adele fashion. "Cullen's been paroled for good behavior. I know what you're thinking, but you know the Georgia prison system. Jared's father has been trying for years to reform it. He's always said that the Atlanta pen is one of the worst in the federal system. No way to keep out shanks [prison-made knives, used to murder and terrorize prisoners] unless everyone walks around naked. There've never been enough guards. Cullen was made a convict trusty. They said he was good at discipline!"

Maggie Royal sat holding the V-mail letter in her hand. In her mind's eye she saw Cullen walking along "the street," his dogs at his heels, his whip coiled around his body.

With a quick furious gesture she crumpled the letter into a ball and hurled it into the wastebasket.

Still the second front didn't materialize. Fatigue, years of interrupted sleep, and short rations began to wear people down.

One morning in May, Warren rang Maggie Royal up at the hospital to tell her that word had been received at the embassy of the death of Noble LeFevre. The destroyer on which he was serving had been sunk in the Battle of the Coral Sea.

"One of our correspondents was with him when he died," Warren said. "Apparently he was badly wounded and knew he couldn't survive long enough to be rescued. Noble was known in all the bars from Pearl to Sydney. He carried a green parrot on his shoulder that he had taught to ask for bourbon and branch water. He had a girl in every port and the last thing he said before he slipped away from the life raft was, 'If you ever get to a little old town called Starksville in Georgia, go to the Plantation Bar and have a drink on me!' Nobody saw him again."

"Noble couldn't swim," Maggie Royal whispered.

Slowly she put down the telephone. As she went about her rounds, she remembered how amused and superior and condescending she had been because Noble rejected the Army and accepted a commission in the more socially acceptable Naval Reserve. He had been all the things she had learned to disapprove of—racially intolerant, conceited, smug, snobbish, and isolationist. Yet he had died in a faraway war fighting for things he pretended not to believe in.

After Ian's departure, Brenda's affair with Bertie became notorious. The Duke warned her he did not want a scandal. "Divorce is something that happens to others," he said, "not to us. I remember when old Freeman-Westwood's wife bolted with his huntsman and there was a to-do in the press. The old boy said it made him uncomfortable in the Guards Club. He felt people were laughing at him behind his back when he left the bridge table."

Maggie Royal tried to reason with Brenda. "You shouldn't be seen in public with Bertie."

"We don't want to be in public," Brenda answered. "We just want to be alone." She turned her head away. "Darling Maggie, are you going to bully me, too?"

"Brenda, surely you don't love him. He's so effeminate."

Brenda gave Maggie Royal her direct blue-eyed stare. "Speak as you find! Bertie may not be your type, but he amuses me and he needs me. It's never been a secret that handsome young Guards officers stationed in London are prey to homosexuals. The pay is practically nothing and Bertie's poor as a church mouse. It's a way of supplementing his income." She lit a cigarette. "Bertie wanted to find out if he could do it again with a woman. You knew he was married before he turned to boys." She smiled brightly. "I've been helping him to regain his amateur standing. Maggie, don't look so shocked."

"But Ian—"

"Ian's as set in his ways as a fried egg," Brenda interrupted. "The only time he needs me is when he sends me through the brambles after a running cock! Darling Maggie, don't look so scandalized. A running cock pheasant, love. After Christmas, we only hunt cocks! His mum displayed him naked on a Georgian silver platter when he was an infant. Insisted he was heaven-sent, which is about as close to the Royals as you can be outside of heaven! He's totally self-sufficient, you see. Bertie needs me!"

"But, Brenda, Ian's so kind."

"Yes." Brenda nodded. "Always helping people over stiles and giving away hunt buttons and crested cufflinks." She turned to Maggie Royal helplessly. "To be sure, I've had one or two swing-rounds—I had a walk out with Chris Sargent the year he was the leading G.R., but that packed up fairly quickly. And a fling with Rex St. Claire before he rushed off to Kenya with the mulatto nursemaid his wife brought back from Jamaica, but they weren't like this. Maggie darling." She gazed at her imploringly. "Believe me. I've fought and fought, but I can't help it. I really am mad about Bertie."

She lit a cigarette and stared at the blacked-out window. "I hadn't broken my maiden when I married Ian. Barely out of the nursery. And Ian . . ." She shrugged and began buffing her nails. "Ian was great at cricket and in the hunting field, but in bed . . . what is it you Yanks say? 'Slam bam, thank you, ma'am.' It's quite impossible for him to mention the word 'love.' The only thing he's ever said to me is, 'Jolly good, old girl,' before rolling over onto his side of the bed and starting to snore."

Maggie Royal made a final effort. "Brenda, Bertie's politics—"

"Pooh!" Brenda blew out a cloud of smoke. "I don't give a hoot about his politics. It's his penis that's my concern. The peerless penis . . . we could write a poem, now, couldn't we?"

"Brenda, be careful," Maggie Royal warned. "I have a feeling Ian's one of those people you can push so far. Once they get the wind under their tail. Pow! They breathe fire and the earth trembles."

Brenda picked up her buffer and began working on her nails as if she hadn't heard her.

"Maggie darling," she said suddenly. "You've lost your Southern accent. Why haven't you lost your virginity? Our friends think you're divine, but you never give them a tumble. Warren is mad for you." She ground out her cigarette and stared at it soberly. "Just you wait, Maggie, m'love. Someday a certain man will come along and you'll be lost in the stars!"

September 1943. Numbers of Roisterers turned up, delighted to take Brenda and Maggie Royal to all the smart places. The only news they had of Jared was that he was "flying boats," on Atlantic patrol duty.

Maggie Royal had been given the evening off in order to go to an American-embassy party. It was part of Warren's job to talk to the officers newly arrived from Oregon and Oshkosh, Sioux City and St. Louis. She felt it her duty to make an effort also.

Some of the officers appeared to be all the British said they were, overpaid, oversexed, and over here. Compared to those guests who had been on British rations for almost three years, they did appear overweight and overly concerned about where to go for amusement.

Maggie Royal marveled at the new Ambassador, who had replaced Joseph Kennedy, standing for many hours, his face white and drawn after each whispered consultation with an aide, and subsequent disappearance to the telephone, then returning afterward, looking more anxious than ever, but forcing the same smile and simulated calm. "Now we've come in, things are bound to be better soon. . . . The war can't last much longer. No, I'm afraid I don't know what General Eisenhower has in mind. No, I don't have any information about the invasion. . . ."

Maggie Royal had hoped to see General Eisenhower at the party, but Warren told her the Commander-in-Chief of the European Theater of Operations had gone to an airfield to visit U.S. bomber crews prior to takeoff. The targets were German airdromes in occupied Holland and France. American planes were included as part of a larger British formation.

Maggie Royal really didn't want to go dancing with Warren after the party. She yearned for a bath and bed without the sound of sirens howling in the night, or ack-ack. But Warren was tense and wanted to relax. Since Pearl Harbor and the arrival of the American forces he had been working very hard. "I just want to go somewhere with you and have a quiet drink," he said, chewing on the stem of his pipe. "Forget the war."

The fog was so thick Warren's torch gave the cratered streets and piles of rubble a ghostly quality, as if they were walking through a London finished and dead. The nights of interrupted sleep and interminable work at the hospital, and the drinks at the embassy, had made Maggie Royal light-headed. She felt as if moving in a dream, without any will of her own. She was grateful to Warren for his reassuring bulk, his firm grasp on her arm, guiding her through the blackout with his usual calm certainty.

The 400 was probably the smartest of the nightclubs. Intellectuals like Brenda's friend Nancy Mitford and county English would not have been caught dead there, if the club had suffered a direct hit. But people like the Duke of Kent, killed in an air accident the summer of 1942, King Zog and Billy Fiske, the first American to die in the war, and officers in the Guards and Rifle Brigades had made it famous by congregating there whenever they came up to London on leave.

Inside, it was very dark. After passing through the double curtains at the doorway that shut out the light, it took a while for their eyes to grow accustomed to the candlelight.

The maître d' greeted Warren with his usual "Glad to see you back, sir. I'm afraid we haven't a table right now."

Warren smiled and called him by name. His diplomatic training had schooled him to remember people's names. Accordingly, he was generally able to get a table.

"Just a minute, sir," the maître d' replied. "I'll see what I can do. By the way, if you'd like a bite, there's a bit of game. When the season opened in Scotland, we were able to get some grouse."

Brenda was at a table against the wall with Bertie. She waved to come and join them. "I'd rather not," Warren said. "I want to be alone with you." He glanced around the crowded room. "I guess we have no choice."

The maître d' looked relieved. "Two more chairs at Lady Oakington's table," he ordered, snapping his fingers at a waiter.

"One drink and then home," Maggie Royal said, suddenly feeling very tired.

Chairs were brought. They stowed their gas masks under them, and because it was an American holiday, Labor Day, Warren ordered champagne. The waiter warned him that the few bottles left were very dear. "That's all right," Warren said, reaching for his wallet. "This is a celebration."

The waiter brought the wine and glasses.

"Bubbly, I love it!" Brenda buried her nose in the glass and let the bubbles tickle it. "Warren, you are a dear."

310

"Careful, darling," Bertie admonished fondly. "Don't drink it too fast."

"He nannies me," Brenda said happily, smiling at them.

The band was playing "I Can't Get Started" and the floor was jammed. People waved at them. "There's Mickey Bourne-Smith, Monica's brother-in-law. Somebody told me he's in Hertfordshire, scrounging for a general," Brenda said. "And that must be Lady Sybil over there in the shadows with her boyfriend."

"Her husband, now, a wormy bird if there ever was one," Bertie said. "He must have the patience of a Sioux Indian to be married to her!"

"Is she the one you say is a bitch?" Maggie Royal asked Brenda.

"I don't think she's a bitch," Brenda retorted flatly. "I just don't like her. The whole family's frightfully weird. They say her mum, the old Duchess, went to Buckingham Palace wearing her false teeth as a brooch." She broke off suddenly. "It's so dark in here I can hardly see my glass in front of me, but I do believe that is Terry Ratcliff who just came in." Brenda narrowed her eyes. "There's a chap with him."

Maggie Royal followed the direction of her glance, and her heart came up into her throat. She would have known that walk anywhere.

They were looking around for a table. Brenda waved to them. "Terry, love, over here."

Maggie Royal sat rigid, her heart pounding. She was aware of a mixture of longing and anxiety, as if all the anticipation of the long, long nights was about to dwindle to a reality that could not match all she had imagined during the weeks and months and years without him. It was the way she felt about riding Azilia, facing a big fence when she was unprepared. Then Terry was saying, "This is Leftenant Stark, United States Navy. We've had a few dust-ups together!"

"Why, Jared." Maggie Royal managed somehow to speak without a tremor in her voice. "Fancy meeting you here!"

Jared shook his head incredulously. "Maggie Royal," he said in that special lilting way.

They were all staring at her. Maggie Royal forgot she had been tired. She felt a growing, leaping excitement not unmixed with fear, as if the careful foundations she had built for herself were shifting.

The introductions were completed. Thanks to Warren, more chairs were brought and drinks were ordered all around.

Brenda was eyeing Jared's bright wings. "I'd be frightened to death up in one of those planes with those awful Nazis on my back!"

"Just doing a job!" Jared said offhandedly, not taking his eyes off Maggie Royal.

"Not bloody likely they'd be on your back!" Bertie murmured aside.

"Oh, you!" Brenda dug him in the ribs and turned back to Jared with a brilliant smile. "Tell me, Leftenant, how do you find Britain?"

"Fine." Jared smiled his flashing smile. "When I can find it. It's always night and raining and the weather knocks out the range, so we fly along the coast until we get lucky and a native lights a candle!"

"Jared's known on every front as the wild turkey," Terence said. "Whenever he spots a Jerry he makes a sound on the radio with what he calls his turkey caller. Either that or he's singing all the time."

Jared pushed his chair back. "Would you like to dance?" he asked Maggie Royal. Warren's expression led him to amend, "That is, if you don't mind, sir."

Maggie Royal saw Warren's lips tighten at the "sir." Then his expression righted itself and he smiled. "Of course not."

Maggie Royal was aware of the eyes following them. Jared was as handsome as ever. Handsomer, in fact. He still had the clean-cut hollow-cheeked look of the patrician, the strong chin and fine straight Stark nose. But there was a new look of maturity that matched the strands of gray in his thick hair. The helmet and goggles, the cow-pasture landings and rolls over the Sunday crowds; the whirring of propellers, the snarling of engines and strumming of flying wires had been replaced by the scramble signal, the call to challenge the Luftwaffe, the greatest air force ever assembled. The calm certainty with which he moved and spoke had replaced the bravado of the young barnstorming pilot, just as the old leather jacket and scarf had been exchanged for the beribboned magic of his uniform.

The band was playing "I'll Be Seeing You." The lights seemed to be dimming, the music louder, drowning out the beat of her heart. Time or Cindy Lou or the war had deepened the lines in the corners of his mouth.

"Maggie Royal!" he said happily, gazing down at her. She saw that his eyes were the same piercing green and the old familiar lights flickered in them like the flashlights people carried when they walked in the blackout.

The tension ran out of her. She was glad she had worn her red silk, her "Communist" dress bought in Klein's basement before she left the States. She knew she looked well, though why such chameleonlike changes came over her, why the attraction she had for others came to her at some times and not at others, she didn't know. As they began to dance, his every move was as familiar to her as her own body.

"Tell me, Leftenant," she said, "what took you so long getting here?"

"I thought a ticket to Pensacola would help me to check out faster. Turned out they wanted to hang on to us old boat pilots. Ambassador Pritchard finally called the Secretary of the Navy. Said I was going to go AWOL unless they sprang me." He held her tighter and did a spin. "Anyway, love, here I am."

"Come on, Jared," she said boldly. "Let's show our allies how to cut a rug so the floor shows!"

His hand held her firmly in the small of her back and they were moving together as one, the way it used to be on the island. It was a slow

"Body and Soul," and as he pressed her closer against him, his body seemed to her as familiar as her own skin.

Somebody cried "Lindy Hop," and they were closing, breaking, swinging, swaying. Maggie Royal's red skirt whipped in and out like a matador's cape. She shut her eyes and let herself be led, faster, faster. The room and the people in it began to run together in a spangled blur. There was only the dipping and semisplits and Jared, spinning and smiling.

Slowly the floor cleared. The beat changed to conga.

"Bash on!" she heard Bertie cry as they swept past their table.

The floor emptied and people stood around shouting and clapping and calling out, "Go to it, Yank."

The brass in the orchestra was on its feet, horns swinging in unison to "Stompin' at the Savoy," and they were dancing as they had never danced before.

The driving rhythm washed over them like a bombardment. There was a final crashing climax of rumbling drums and the music swung into "These Foolish Things." They moved without effort, bathed suddenly in the past, turning, gliding, the words bringing back memories.

Couples drifted back onto the floor and they became one with the uniformed men and their girls, holding each other.

Maggie Royal's face was flushed. In the dim light her eyes sparkled.

"I always knew you'd be beautiful," Jared said as if to himself. "Your beauty, Maggie Royal, has never been ordinary. Now your looks are your own." He reached up and touched the corner of her mouth. "You still have that little thing, that dimple." His hand fell to his side and his eyes slipped past her, to Warren sitting stiffly at the table, his eyes following them. The music came to a sudden halt. "I'm sorry I didn't keep our date to go riding," he said clearly. "I got married instead."

"So I understand." Maggie Royal's laugh sounded brittle. Silly thing to say. She would never understand, not really.

He put his hand under her elbow and began to pilot her through the dancers. "Your elderly friend is watching."

"Not so elderly," she answered defensively. "Harvard '34."

"Well, he doesn't look happy. Maggie Royal, we must meet again. Where can I call you tomorrow?"

The music was playing "Just One of Those Things." She remembered Meyer Davis out in front of the band at her party, bouncing up and down on the balls of his feet, holding the orchestra together in exuberant controlled style.

And Jared and Cindy Lou dancing. Cindy Lou smiling up at him, and the look on his face that wrung Maggie Royal's heart.

"Jared . . ." she said as they broke from the surge of dancers. "You're married, remember?"

He shook his head wonderingly. "Haven't you heard? There's a war on! Nobody knows what tomorrow will bring. Presuming tomorrow comes. Listen . . ." His grip on her arm tightened. "I must know where to reach you."

"Jared, I was not born yesterday. You yourself just admitted that I'd grown up!"

He grinned, and his eyes took on their old mischievous twinkle. "Delightfully."

She took a step away from him, toward the table where Warren and safety waited.

"Maggie Royal, wait."

She shook her head. "I waited once, Jared."

The table was in an uproar.

"Maggie, you constantly amaze," Brenda exclaimed. "You never told me you could dance like that."

"You never asked."

Brenda turned to Bertie. "Did I ever tell you about the port, when Maggie told the Duke . . ."

Bertie nodded. His patronizing smile was gone and he gazed at Maggie Royal as if seeing her for the first time. "You were top-hole, old girl."

"Wizard!" Terry cried, pounding Jared on the back. "You two looked as if you'd danced together always."

"In a manner of speaking, we have," Jared said dryly. "To be frank, Maggie Royal's jitterbug is a bit ragged, but nothing that can't be remedied with practice."

Warren was the only one who didn't offer congratulations. He stood quietly, holding Maggie Royal's chair for her, looking large and awkward in his dark diplomatic suit amid the uniforms.

The following afternoon Maggie Royal was sitting at the matron's desk while she went for a cup of tea when the telephone rang. It was Warren. "How do you feel?" he asked without preliminaries.

"Ackcherly, ghawstly, puffeckly ghawstlay."

"Some of the hair of the dog." Warren sounded happy. "Claridge's at six? It's about the last place left in London where you can still get whiskey."

"All right, Claridge's at six."

She heard it then, the unmistakable "nesty, broody" sound of a hen turkey calling out a gobbler. Then a brown hand ending in a blue sleeve with the two gold stripes of a navy lieutenant took the telephone from her hand and replaced it in its cradle.

"You're not meeting him at six." Jared put away his wing-bone caller, shoved the medical reports on the desk aside, and sat down. "You're coming with me."

"Yes, Leftenant, do take Maggie with you." The matron had returned and was smiling at him the way women old and young always smiled at Jared. "She needs some time off."

Jared leaped to his feet and bowed low over her hand. "Ma'am, you are the cream of British womanhood!" He turned to Maggie Royal. "Maggie Royal, an order is an order."

It seemed the most natural thing in the world to pick up her pocketbook, flashlight, and gas mask and follow him from the hospital. She had always followed him, whether it was across the island to Old Ugly's pond or along the beach to the clam flats. Only now it was bomb-shattered London at dusk.

They went into the first pub they came to and sat down at a small table wedged against the wall. The room was filled with smoke and soldiers standing three deep at the bar, behind which heavy-breasted women bartenders filled foaming tankards of beer and shoved them along the smooth waxed surface.

Girls in the uniform of the ATS and WRNS, blondes, brunettes, and redheads, good-time girls with upswept hair and cockney accents, padded shoulders, and plump calves teetering in suede high heels, laughed and clung to their men's arms.

Jared ordered sherry for Maggie Royal, beer for himself.

He looked wonderfully fit. His body was hard, muscular, with a reality, a rugged maleness lacking in Warren and the beautiful young men in Brenda's set. He told her he had been serving on South Atlantic patrol duty when he was transferred to England, where, under the British Coastal Command, he was now flying missions in conjunction with the RAF.

A warning bell rang in her mind. Leave now, Maggie Royal, before it's too late. She searched under her chair for her gas mask. "I just remembered another engagement."

"No, you don't." He put out his hand and pushed her back down onto her chair. "Thank God you haven't plucked your eyebrows, and your hair has grown out."

"Jared, the fact remains you are married. You have a child."

"Yes." A shadow crossed his face. "A son." He smiled crookedly. "Jared III. We call him Tertius. Almost six now. Full of the devil. Loves to ride." He broke off. "Maggie Royal, stay."

Nobody, she thought, ever said her name the way Jared did, slowly, softly rolling out the Roya-al. Suddenly she felt giddy, reckless. Who knew what would happen tomorrow? Monica's husband, killed in the attack against Oran, and Christopher Sargent, never again to be champion jockey, his head blown off by a gunner in the tank behind him at El Alamein. The butcher's parents wiped out when their house received a direct hit.

Jared paid for their drinks and they went out into the London drizzle. It was almost dark now. The early theaters had opened. *The Beggars' Opera* that Bertie called "The Buggers' Uproar" and a revival of *The Last of Mrs. Cheyney,* as well as Mairin's musical.

A crowd of drunken uniforms barged into them, pushing her

against Jared. She heard his quick intake of breath. His grasp on her arm tightened.

His arms slid over her shoulders, down to her waist. Her arms rose and went around his neck.

A light flashed in their faces and a voice said, "Naw, naw, what's all this?"

She broke away. "Not here, Jared. Not like this."

There are some things wars, blitzkriegs, famines, and food rationing cannot change. One is *coup de foudre,* that lightninglike flash of awareness that takes place between a man and a woman. Another is the Ritz.

Once they were inside the grand gallery with its chandeliers, heavy curtains, potted plants, and writing desks with their matching chairs upholstered in pink, the war was as remote as a pair of black silk stockings.

Lady Astor was in the lobby commenting to the desk clerk that the streets were full of drunken soldiers who should be lectured on temperance. Maggie Royal hid behind Jared, praying that Great-Aunt Meg's old foxhunting companion would not see her as they got into the elevator.

"Terence and I took this together," Jared said, opening the bedroom door. "But he's off to Suffolk with a girlfriend and told me he wouldn't be using the room tonight."

He closed the door and went to a table where there was a tray holding a bottle of Kentucky bourbon. "A libation?" he asked. "I stocked up at the officers' club."

Maggie Royal shook her head. She watched him pour himself a stiff drink and remembered that on the island she had seen him drink only an occasional beer or glass of wine at Gramma's ceremonial dinners.

The heavy curtains were drawn. The beds, their polished brass shining like the door knockers in Belgravia, had been turned down, the pink silk covers neatly folded and the sheets invitingly turned back into V's. The walls were cream white and the fireplace a mottled marble.

"The Ritz really is the most splendid place!" she said, setting down her gloves and gas mask. "All this gilt and gold and hushed luxury!"

"In many ways the British *are* the most civilized people in the world." He put down his drink and came toward her. "But we're not here to talk about our allies."

"What are we here to talk about?" She looked away from the turned-down beds.

He put his hands on her shoulders. "Maggie Royal, you're trembling."

"Yes. I mean, no."

"What do you mean, no?" He put his thumb under her chin to lift it up.

She shrugged out of his grasp and walked to the fireplace. She thought of Angela, who carried a diaphragm with her gas mask and boasted of being able to describe the ceilings in most of England's great country houses. Or Monica, who announced languidly, "I'll lie on my back and pray for England!" Lust rather than love. Curiosity instead of affection. "Having at it," Brenda said.

Somehow she couldn't "have at it" with Jared. There had to be more.

She picked up her gloves and gas mask and gazed once more around the room. "Let's not rush our fences."

His face was bony and closed. "You should be mature by now! You've always wanted all the pieces put together. Colors flat. No half-tones." Gone was all the teasing gaiety of last night's meeting.

Self-consciousness bound her like a straitjacket. "I'm no good at this game, Jared," she said stiffly. "I'm lousy at lying and I get upset when people get hurt. I doubt if I'll ever grow up to be a callous, conniving, cheating other woman. I don't want to fritter away my all, just because there's a war on. So, Jared, so long."

She went blindly out the door, down the hall, and into the elevator. Lady Astor was still haranguing the desk clerk as she hurried past.

"Tell me about this Jared," Brenda said as she walked into the house. "A connection, you say?"

"A distant cousin," Maggie Royal said, and told her about growing up on Stark Island, about early-morning rides on the beach, fishing, turkey hunting, and galloping through the woods like the wind, about a single blue heron flying over the sound and a wild horse rearing. Things irrevocably associated with Jared. Then that final fateful summer when she learned to dance with the cousins and Jared until Cindy Lou came. "You don't shack up with somebody unless you plan to marry him," she concluded. "At least, I can't. And Jared's married!"

Brenda put the milk on the burner in the tiny anteroom she called a kitchen. "You're a fool," she said, handing Maggie Royal a mug of cocoa. "Now he's here and you're here and the two of you . . ." She reached for a cigarette and fitted it into her holder. "I will simply never understand Yanks."

Maggie Royal didn't understand, herself. She knew only that some-where she had struck a bargain with Gramma. Commitments and con-sequences. That's what life is. It silenced her when she should have shouted "To hell with the consequences." It immobilized her when she should have grabbed the chance to enjoy. And yet without this inborn emotional check, the small inside voice that stopped her short of tossing her Lily Daché over the windmill, she would have been like Brenda, like Angela, like Monica . . .

There must be something more, she told God that night when she said her prayers, hands clasped, kneeling on the freezing floor as Miss Speers had taught her.

"Ian just got in," Brenda said as Maggie Royal was making morn-ing tea. It was Friday, two weeks after she'd seen Jared. Brenda was wearing her herringbone suit and gloves. "He's gone to Hamley's to get a teddy bear for Sprat and some wool at Harrods for Nanny. There's a lot of estate business to take care of, so we're taking an early train. By the way," she added, going out the door, "that divine connection of yours rang up when you were out. I invited him down for the weekend. Cub-hunting starts Saturday. He said he'd adore to come. I trust you don't mind. I told him to meet you at the station for the noon train. Angela has her eyes on him. If I were you, I'd put a twitch on him. Ta-ta for now!"

Jared came through the station crowd like a young conqueror in his Navy khaki with the wings over his heart.

"Miss Maggie Royal, honey, how's your war today?" he said, kissing her on the cheek.

Keep it light, she told herself. Play it cool! "It's being so cheerful as keeps me going," she answered, mimicking Mona Lott in "ITMA," the popular radio show. "And you, Leftenant, how's it going for you?"

"The better for finding you again." He picked up her case and his bag. "I'm looking forward to my first country weekend. Is it true what they say about bed partners guaranteed?"

"There's them as believes it's important to have friendly relations with our allies," Maggie Royal said in imitation of Mr. Potts. She gave him a sideways glance. "I doubt if you'll have any trouble finding somebody to warm your bed."

"I'm fairly particular," Jared said, looking at her.

They were lucky to find two empty seats. Outside the train there was rain and war, and inside the compartment enlisted men traveling back to the airdrome and uniformed women and a small boy who had missed being evacuated. They talked about the island and Tyger's farm and Constance's new house at Ligonier and did not mention Gramma or Cindy Lou or anything complicated.

Thorny's girl, Hester, the serious, sensible-shoe-wearing intellectual from Radcliffe, had thrown him over for a card-carrying Communist she had met in Paris.

"It was quite a blow," Jared said.

"Did he care so much?" Maggie Royal asked.

"He was glad to be rid of her. No, it was the Russian-German non-aggression pact. The great Red father crossed him up. Like losing your religion. He tried to pretend that Stalin had something up his peasant shirt sleeve, but he's starting to doubt. Last I heard he'd joined the American Field Service and was driving an ambulance."

Williams met them at the station in the pony cart and they drove through the golden gates onto the long avenue between the century-old trees. The white flags of the park deer flashed like waving flowers.

"It looks very old," Jared said as the golden towers and turrets of Chatfield came into view.

"Don't let it fool you," Maggie Royal answered. "They heard you were coming and assembled it. It came in parts, you know. Made in Providence, Rhode Island!"

"Maggie, love, Jared, hello darlings!" Brenda clattered down the stairs. Her hair was tied with a blue ribbon. She had on beautifully boned field boots with leather laces tightly tied at her ankles, canary-colored breeches, and a green-and-rust-colored tweed riding coat. Her face was free of makeup and her blue eyes clear and guileless. "Darling Maggie, you're to have the orange room this time. It's a little like being inside an egg, but it's really quite comfortable." She winked at Jared. "You'll need a mounting block to get into bed, so you better take Jared to give you a leg up."

"Brenda, you are bad!" Maggie Royal said, not daring to look at Jared.

"Well, I wish you were." Brenda grinned and tossed her head. "Jared agrees, don't you, love?"

They followed Brenda past the suits of armor. "We all got tiddly one night," she explained to Jared, "and gave each one a name. We put a kilt on Rory here. Angela spent the evening bringing people to peer under it, to see, as she put it, 'the tilt of the kilt.' "

As they went upstairs she outlined the weekend's gaieties. "Cubhunting in the morning. Cricket in the afternoon—madly boring, but the pater insists, especially when Ian's home. A little Saturday-night whoopee with the neighbors. Sunday tennis. Maybe shooting for the pot. It's the cock season. Here we are!"

Brenda flung open the door to the orange room. From the enormous four-poster two startled faces stared back at them. Bertie, his fair hair in disarray, and Angela, penciled brows lifting in a startled V. Bertie's flowered drawers were draped over a pillow and Angela's riding underwear had been dropped onto the floor.

With a howl of rage, Brenda marched over to the bed and ripped back the covers, exposing two naked forms, white as the linen, wearing identical expressions of stunned surprise.

"The very idea!" Brenda cried indignantly, starting methodically to strip the bed. "Dirtying up my very best sheets from my trousseau!"

If Bertie and Angela had had tails, they would have been between their bare legs as they fled for cover in the bathroom.

Bertie paused at the door. "My regiment's been ordered out!" he cried dramatically, clutching the orange puff to him. "Brenda, love, be merciful. I was merely saying my good-byes."

He ducked as Brenda picked up the flowered drawers and threw them at him, crying, "You really are too, too absolutely bogus!"

Bertie dropped the orange puff and caught the drawers. "Oh, how shy-making," he cried with pretended horror, covering his peerless penis with the shorts, then vanishing into the bathroom.

Brenda dropped the bedclothes in a heap on the floor. Maggie Royal could see she was having difficulty restraining laughter. "That pig of a girl! I wish she'd stayed on that bloody hill station in India, having a roll in the hay with all those randy subalterns, instead of mucking up my beds. Maggie, love, go to the wardrobe in the hall and bring me some fresh linen."

Jared leaned against the wall, convulsed with laughter.

"You're down at the end of the hall," Maggie Royal told him, returning with an armload of sheets. She laid a sheet on the bed and began making hospital corners.

"It's all part of the game," Jared said.

"How do you know?" Maggie Royal pulled the sheet taut. "I thought you were busy flying."

"Occasionally there's an all-clear." He started toward the door. "As the song goes, I'll be seeing you . . ."

"That's what you think!"

"Maggie Royal, what would the hunt be without the fox, the tail?"

She threw a pillow at him. He threw it back. Then they were wrestling on the bed, howling with laughter.

"Oh, my God," Brenda groaned. "Don't tell me I have to make the bed all over again?"

Ian was off on estate business. Jared was looking at the paintings in the gallery. Maggie Royal went to the pantry to help Brenda fix flowers.

"Effie's in tears again," Brenda said, putting the Duke's Damascus roses in a silver bowl. "Her baby's sick, and if you ask me, I think she's preggers again. Nanny told her she should wear her chemise. 'Not 'arf nice without it, as you might say.' " She rubbed her forehead with the back of her hand. "I think I might have a rest before Ian comes back for tea."

She was very pale and there were rings under her eyes. The factory where she worked had been hit, the roof destroyed. Work continued under tarpaulins in a cavelike atmosphere, damp and dangerous.

"Go have a nice lie-down, as Nanny says." Maggie Royal gave her friend a hug. "You do far too much. I'll cope."

"Bless you," Brenda answered. "See you at cocktails. We'll have an early night. Cubhunting at seven in the morning."

The meet was at Pat Weston's cottage at the north end of the village street. Ian was unable to go out. "I just have a few days' leave," he explained. "I have to straighten out the farm accounts and see about the plow-up—"

"Oh, darling, no," Brenda interrupted. "Do have a go with us."

Ian, however, was adamant. "Plenty of time when this war is over." He flicked a leaf from the shoulder of her tweed coat. "Anyway, I can't improve on the job you're doing!"

Bertie and a number of former point-to-point riders home on leave were in their battle dress. Angela and the other Chatfield ladies looked elegant as always. Angela's brows were as narrow as ever. There were tiny goose pimples beneath them where the hairs had been plucked out. Her lips were vivid, her face bland and free of embarrassment as she smiled and flirted openly with Jared.

Maggie Royal introduced Jared, thin and handsome in his borrowed ratcatcher, to her newfound friends. Even Twitchy managed to thaw long enough to murmur, "How ja do?"

"Don't he make a smart appearance, though?" whispered Miss Hayride of 1936 to Angela as Maggie Royal led Jared over to meet Pat, the Queen of the Chatfield.

"Righto," Angela replied. "I'd like to stand him at stud!"

"I do hope we'll be able to show you some sport," Pat said graciously, blue eyes twinkling.

"I've seen quite a bit already," Jared replied with a meaningful glance at Maggie Royal.

Williams cupped his hands and gave Brenda a leg up. "Mind, milady, you don't overdo," he warned as she adjusted her side-saddle skirt. "The horses aren't fit, you know."

"I won't," she told the old groom. "What a lovely morning. Come along, everybody."

"Williams is very nanny," she said as they rode off. "He worries about me." She lifted her hunting veil and lit a cigarette. "Really pesty of the pater to keep Ian from hunting when he's home for so short a time. Anyway, when he's not out, I can smoke. Ian loathes women smoking in the hunting field."

They rode along the lane, past the Hansons' cottage. Lancelot galloped up to the hedgerow, interlaced with bedsprings, that served as a fence. Then, filled with the exultation that foxhunting sparked in him, he whirled and went tearing across the pasture, snorting.

The trees stood motionless and black against the pure pearl-gray sky as they rode to the first covert. Mist lay in the hollows of the quiet fields, and the faint clean smell of wet grass mingled with that of clean horse.

Dawn came, a golden dawn of infinite promise without a plane in the sky. Mist lifted and the grass was so vivid a green it seemed to shimmer like glass. Banks were studded with jewels of moss and lichen and the wet hedges shone with sunshot slivers of gold.

Hounds found almost at once. Instead of confining them to the covert as customary until the official season in November, Brenda impulsively decided to "let hounds go!" Her voice rose above their music. "Gone away. Gone away!" Pat's face glowed with delight as she put her finger to her ear and hollered hounds away.

"You'll have to teach me to holler like that," Jared told her. "It'll electrify my squadron when we meet the Jerries. Better than singing 'Dixie,' any day!"

The black-and-white river of hounds foamed out over a nasty barway. Maggie Royal let Stalker run on down to his fences without a qualm. After Aintree, they were as hurdles to the big horse.

With Jared galloping alongside there was no past or future, only the now of speed and challenge and the beauty of the morning.

"Oh, isn't it lovely?" she cried as they paused on a hillside.

Jared's face was flushed and the golden lights danced in his eyes. "Look at hounds! Running under a blanket."

"Your hounds in America may run under a blanket," Brenda corrected. "Chatfield hounds run under a pocket handkerchief. Oh, I wish Ian were here to see them!" she cried as they set off once again.

It was as wild a scamper as hunting with Jim Bob Beasley. Some of the Yanks from the airdrome whom Brenda invited to come hunting were on farmhorses, jobbed from the locals. They wore their trousers tucked into the tops of their GI lace-up boots and short khaki jackets. "I'm glad the Duke isn't here to see this," said Brenda, shuddering at sight of a young soldier with binder twine tied around his knees in place of jodhpur straps. "Aren't your legs chafed?" she asked kindly. "Wouldn't you like my garters?"

The lad looked horrified. "Oh, no, thank you, ma'am."

"Oh, God," Brenda exclaimed, riding away. "He thinks I meant what you people call garters to hold up stockings. I meant my leather boot garters!"

Criticism gave way to congratulations when she saw that the soldiers somehow managed to stay up with the hunt. "God, they're brave!" she commented wonderingly, "or else quite mad! Most can't ride in an ass cart with a net thrown over them. Yet once they get tuned up, they'll ride at anything!" Some had only ridden western. Others hardly at all. Yet here they were hunting with one of the fastest, most famous packs in Britain, riding borrowed horses, a few straight from the shafts of a cart, soaring over some of the most awesome obstacles in the land, made doubly treacherous by the fact that the fences had yet to be cleared of their summer accumulation of briars and brush.

Hounds checked finally, losing the line amid a herd of cattle.

"My God, we've been running thirty minutes," Brenda said, glancing at her watch. "We'll kill off our horses before the season begins."

"Huntsmen don't carry watches," she said, hunching forward in her saddle to watch hounds work. "My father-in-law forbade it. 'Take his mind off his job,' he warned. 'First thing you know, he'll be thinking of getting home to tea instead of his work.' "

Brenda rode over to where the old huntsman sat on his bony horse. As huntsman for "Chatfield's, Duke of" for forty years, he carried each hound in his mind, in his heart, and in his dreams. And this responsibility had caused the lines in his face, the body hunched in thought, and the eyes which looked off into the distance where 25 couple of the finest foxhounds that could be bred stretched forever, running under a pocket handkerchief.

"The ground is hardy," Brenda said.

"Yes, milady." He did not glance up from his hounds. "Hup now, Bouncer, have at 'im, Barber."

Brenda tried again. "It's rather warm."

" 'Tis that, milady. I think Bouncer may have it."

"His grace won't like it if the horses are broken down."

"Quite right, milady," the old huntsman replied abstractedly. "I think Bouncer's got it. Worrreeee."

"We can't replace the horses, you know."

"I quite agree, your Ladyship."

Brenda took a deep breath. "I think we really must take hounds in. You know there is a war on."

"Without a doubt, milady. Ayyyy." His voice rose exultantly. "Bouncer has it."

Before Brenda could utter another word, the old huntsman was off, hulloaing away his hounds, galloping down to a five-bar gate. Aware of it only as an obstruction in his path, keeping him from his cherished pack, he hardly glanced at it as his horse soared over it.

Hounds were flying now, over hedges and blind ditches and rails. The war was forgotten in the rush of wind and speed, the pure physical exertion of staying in the saddle. The blind fences claimed numerous followers among the Yanks from the airfield, who vanished headfirst into briars and watery ditches, to reappear hatless and covered with mud, in high good humor.

The locals were also having a go. Len rolled off into a pile of briars, but as he was not the first to fall, his wife on her cob did not upbraid him. Angela's young horse turned over in a ditch. A number of Bertie's chums pulled up, forming a protective phalanx around her, yearning to unbutton her waistcoat to see whether or not the rumor that she did not wear a brassiere was true.

Jared, on one of the hunt horses, was well up. "Pulls like a train," he confided as he tore past.

Stalker caught up to him, and together they galloped down the long green slope of hillocky turf. Farmers tending their fields of wheat and barley and land girls spreading manure from carts paused in their work to watch and cheer them on. People left the roads to run across the fields and stand on hillsides to follow the course of the hunt. Ahead, the fox crossed a tufted green pasture dotted with puffballs of black-faced sheep.

The wind laughed, and the touch of it against Maggie Royal's cheek was like the touch of Jared's hand. Her mind was wiped clean of everything but the fox, the river winding slowly past willows and under an arched stone bridge, the ramparts of Chatfield Castle on a high hill, and in the distance the slender spire of the village church.

Brenda cried "Hold hard" as hounds, momentarily confused by the sheep, halted. The sun and wind and sky, the green grass and winding gray river, and the fox with his glimmering russet coat were no longer impersonal, but friends, like Ernie on his lathered unclipped colt, the florid-faced farmers, the muddy yet unbowed GI's in their baggy pants and lace-up boots. Even Twitchy and his popsy, her hair falling down beneath her derby, her lipstick smeared, belonged to this special moment in time and space.

Hitler, Maggie Royal decided, would never understand.

It seemed as if they'd been running for hours. The early-morning cool was giving way to the heat of midday. Sweat dripped from the horses' grass-fed bellies and their sides heaved with exertion.

She saw the expression on Jared's face and realized they shared the same contentment, as if the air, the green land, the cloud-filled sky had set them down in an unclouded peaceful land of the elements.

They reached the village. The fox ran through the graveyard past the church and onto the green, where a soccer match was in progress, between some of the enlisted men from the airdrome and villagers. Hounds poured onto the field, disrupting the game and causing a number of the American players to glare at the riders.

"So sorry." Brenda gave them a brilliant smile. "We'll be on our way shortly."

"Haven't you chaps anything better to do?" Twitchy asked in his usual peremptory fashion as the ball rolled in front of his horse, causing it to shy and almost unseat him. "There's a war on, donchaknow!"

Then Brenda's terrier Mick refound the line and they were off once again.

Over the cry of hounds they heard the planes approaching. Neither the old huntsman intent on his hounds ahead nor the young whipper-in in his wake glanced up. Nor did Brenda.

Suddenly there was a series of violent shocks. The pack ran on, concentrating on the line of the fox as German pilots, seeking to jettison their remaining ammunition on their way home, dropped their bombs on the distant countryside.

Brenda dismounted and stood amid her hounds at the entrance to the fox den, fondling them and crooning "lalalala" and calling them her little darlings as they leaped up against her. Mick growled jealously at the attention bestowed on them. The old huntsman stood beaming with pride while the young whipper-in led the horses around, attempting to look as if hounds' unswerving loyalty to the line was all in the day's work.

Jared walked his blown horse in a circle. "A great day. Beats being shot at," he said with a wide, happy grin.

"They can't take this away from us," Brenda said as the noise of the bombs continued intermittently.

It was the usual Chatfield weekend, chockablock with activity. Lunch was no sooner over than Brenda suggested tennis. "Let's have a knock-up!"

The rackets needed to be restrung. Brenda insisted that keeping the balls in the fridge preserved them. They bounced out whenever anybody opened the door, and Cook complained that one ended up in the shepherd's pie she made for the Duke. Nonetheless, they were as dead as the kippers Brenda acquired from her friends at the airdrome. The old clay court with the roses climbing the surrounding wire took Maggie Royal back to her island summers. The court was rough and untended and the net was torn. Yet, while the big allied bombers flew overhead, moving in precise formations on their way to their enemy targets, they had hilarious games with the warped rackets and frozen balls that bounced soggily over the cracks on the court.

Later there was a cricket match on the green. "A fine day," the Duke said, gazing up at the sky. "Dry at intervals."

Ian was the hero of the village game. In his flannels, he was tall and lean with an easy masterful manner, the picture of public-school unconcern as, in classic style, he drove four balls to the boundary lines for six runs apiece. He made five more graceful swipes and then began to take risks that brought about his removal from the innings. "The son of the house should put on a good show," the Duke said proudly. "Then retire and let the village team do the rest!"

Brenda left soon after the first overs, saying she had to see about dinner. Maggie Royal found her in the dining room. She had on her bath cap.

"Hunting hair!" she sighed. "I have it up in pin curls." Her arms were full of boot trees. "There's nobody left to carry the coals. I found piles and piles in an old dressing room. We can burn them in the fireplaces until we get some men to chop wood." She sighed.

"I've had the most frightful row with Nanny. I've spent an hour polishing silver and trying to placate her. Effie's preggers and Nanny called her a slut to her face. Nanny makes the most revolting and unnecessary sacrifices. I found her emptying all the ashtrays and picking up glasses from last night. She sniffed and said that the late Duchess of Norfolk never went to bed without first emptying the ashtrays, as you might say!"

They had not dressed for dinner since Dunkirk. Changing generally consisted of wearing a new shirtwaist and pearls or a different skirt. That night, in honor of Ian's homecoming Maggie Royal wore her red silk. Brenda, with her blond hair and pink-and-white Meissen skin, was meltingly lovely in prewar blue chiffon. She was as vivacious as ever, but her Wedgwood-blue eyes were shadowed and there were tiny lines of tension around her mouth. She reminded Maggie Royal of a quote she had seen in *The Field,* that "a clean-lined neck and set of the head bespoke a thoroughbred in a woman, a horse, or a racing pigeon."

Angela, with her short bobbed hair and turned-up nose, looked particularly piquant and sexy in a green sleeveless organdy. She wore her hunting underwear beneath it, and an inch or so of white wool emerged from beneath the sleeves of her dress when she waved her cigarette about. Monica was in rose satin with a very low back. The Duke wore his green velvet smoking jacket, a ruffled white shirt, gold foxhead studs, Chatfield-hunt-button cufflinks, and his petit-point evening slippers.

Ian's face was sun-blackened and his hair quite gray. He had received the Distinguished Service Order for his part in the rearguard action during the Dunkirk evacuation. ("He doesn't believe in swanking around," Brenda explained. "He hates wearing that cabbage on his chest.") He had been made a major and put on General Montgomery's staff, shuttling back and forth with secret dispatches. ("All frightfully hush-hush!" Brenda said.)

The dining table was set with the heavy carved Georgian silver Brenda had polished that afternoon. At its center was a great bowl of chrysanthemums flanked by two silver sleeping foxes and candelabra, their entwining arms reaching upward like the espaliered fruit trees on the stable walls. The Labradors and Mick sprawled asleep in front of the fire. The burning boot trees cast a ruddy glow on the dark-paneled walls.

Holmes and Effie, her lace cap at a faintly rakish angle and her frilled apron tied tightly around her burgeoning waist, passed the various courses. It was unusual to see so much food. There was Mrs. Walton's specialty, home-shot jugged hare, as well as grouse, woodcock, and pheasant and several different kinds of fresh vegetables.

Nobody spoke of the war. The Duke talked of hounds and hunting, point-to-points won and lost, of the time he served in India. In his tall, spare figure and leonine head it was easy to imagine the heyday of the Empire, pig sticking and pukka sahib. Polo and the posh life. *Port Out and Starboard Home.*

He had been gored by a wild boar near Luchow. It had been a painful, difficult wound, and he had not been able to ride for months. The worst thing about it, he insisted, was that he had been forced to ruin a pair of Peal boots.

"Better than losing a leg," Brenda said.

"I'm not so sure," the Duke replied seriously. "Almost impossible to get well fitting boots today."

For dessert there were the bottled fruits Brenda and Maggie Royal had put up the previous summer, peaches, plums, and raspberries, with thick Guernsey cream scooped up with a spoon. There was some of the "stenchy" Camembert Ian had brought from France, for a savory.

Coffee was served in the drawing room, which even with the boot-tree fire was as cold as the dungeon at the foot of the tower with the grating over it through which scraps of food were once thrown to the prisoners. Brenda poured it from a silver Georgian pot into fragile eggshell-colored cups in silver holders.

Angela leaned forward, listening intently to a story Jared was recounting about his barnstorming days. With her penciled brows and carefully made-up face, Maggie Royal thought, she looked like an Easter egg.

Abstinence, Maggie Royal had read, is the best aphrodisiac. She sensed it was this quality, a quality of strength and selectivity, that made Jared attractive to women. He did not practice the casual intimacies of Brenda's set, the women who kissed one another and called each other "darling," the men who patted and stroked them in public, lessening the sexual tension that feeds on restraint.

At length the Duke excused himself to return to his rooms and listen to the news on the BBC.

"There's no need for you to come to church tomorrow," he said to Ian, "when you have such a short time at home."

"I would like to go with you, Father," Ian said dutifully. "So would Brenda." He looked at her meaningfully. "Wouldn't you, dear?"

Brenda gazed down at her hands, nails shortened from factory work and cleaning silver. "Of course. We'll all go. It will give the vicar a gas. Poor old bod has a time keeping his flock together these days." She gazed pointedly at Angela. "It will be good for our souls."

The old gentleman looked pleased as he said his good-nights and departed.

People began drifting in. Pat Weston arrived in her Bentley with her cairn terrier, who joined Mick and the gun dogs in front of the fire. Twitchy had his "piece of fluff." Lady Sybil Carruthers arrived in a sputtering Rolls ("With black-market petrol," Brenda commented nastily) accompanied by a languid pink-and-white young man Brenda called "Droopy Drawers" because his breeches always slid down in the hunting field.

"Come in, come in," Brenda called out. "Have a French Seventy-five."

"Whatever do you mean?" Ian asked, mystified.

"Darling," she answered, "don't ask. I hope it tastes all right," she whispered, ladling out the brown liquid from the silver punch bowl one of the horses had won. "I used your Scotch for the champie. The Pimms Number One cup somebody left for the brandy."

"But the Pimms has a gin base," Ian interrupted. "Everyone will be plastered."

"So much the better, my pet," Brenda said, filling the silver cups with punch.

"My God," Jared cried, taking a swig. "Tastes worse than Jazzbo's apple whiskey or Gramma's spirited punch."

The gramophone played on and on. Some of the Americans got drunk and were driven back to the airdrome in jeeps, with much laughter. Others danced or lay about on sofas or sat at Brenda's feet. One long exquisite leg was tucked up under her as she lolled in the deep chair in the casual manner of one to whom lolling was natural and graceful. Mick clambered up into her lap.

She was teasing Bertie. "Do you remember when we pinned the rose—Gloire de Chatfield, I think it was, or one of those old cottagy types with a lovely smell—on the back of your morning coat just before you went into the Royal Enclosure to meet the King and Queen?"

The crowd thinned out. Brenda danced with Bertie. Apparently she had forgiven him his assignation with Angela, for she was laughing up at him, crinkling her nose. Ian, who disliked dancing, stood to one side, surveying them, a thoughtful expression on his face.

When the record was changed to "The Lambeth Walk," everyone linked arms and began to sing. Maggie Royal noticed that Brenda and Bertie were no longer in the room.

The music switched to "I'll Be Seeing You." Over the heads of the dancers Maggie Royal found herself looking at Jared. Ignoring Twitchy, who was standing beside her, Jared approached and put his arm around her. They began to dance.

Maggie Royal seemed to be moving in a dream, floating free and unattached, like an escaped balloon in Hyde Park. The slow sweet notes fell around them like silver slivers of light. She could feel the hardness of his body, his strength. The old pull of him was a dense surging in her blood. She was back on Stark Island with the wind in her hair, the rain in her face, galloping along the white beach.

The room was retreating, the candles dimming. The record ended.

"Let's walk," Jared said.

They moved like sleepwalkers toward the hall. Jared helped her into her coat and they walked down the wide stone steps to the box-lined gravel path that led to the movable summerhouse, where, when it was windy, the family sometimes had tea. They continued past the Spanish chestnut to the Duke's rose garden. A white moon rode across hurrying clouds.

"A Jerry moon," Jared said, gazing up at a fighter plane that hung for an instant, silhouetted like a toy cut-out against the face of the moon. "I wonder how many make it back. The flak's so bad over the sub pens at Kiel it burns the seat of your pants."

He lit a cigarette, blew out the match, and put it in his pocket. "Maggie Royal," he said quietly, "I have a week's leave. Will you go away with me?"

Over the lake, mist writhed like spirits. In Chatfield covert a fox barked.

"You're married, Jared," she said.

"It's no good, Maggie Royal."

"Then why . . . ?"

"I did it for the child."

"That afternoon," Maggie Royal continued, "when you didn't come . . ."

"Your mother said you wouldn't see me."

"You let my mother frighten you off!" She tried to move away, but his grip on her arm tightened.

"You were young. So damn young. I thought in Spain I'd forget."

"You didn't forget Cindy Lou!"

He let go of her arm and drew on his cigarette. A cloud moved across the moon, and she couldn't see his face.

"She was an obsession. Like those vines in the woods, wrapping herself around me. I was caught up in it. It was something I had to go through. Like war. Like growing up. Something you can't escape. You don't want it but it's stronger than you are." He paused and then added softly, "I always knew it wouldn't work. She wasn't the kind of girl I could take turkey hunting. All those clanking bracelets!" He dropped his cigarette with an abrupt gesture and began grinding it into the ground with his foot.

"But, Jared . . ."

"I have never kissed you," he said. "There were many times when I wanted to . . ." His voice was husky. "It wasn't the right time. Now time is running out." His arms tightened around her.

"Jared, things must be clear between us."

"Haven't they always been?"

She heard the planes, louder now, drowning out the beat of her heart. Then the outlines of the castle, its towers and turrets, stark against the night sky, vanished. The music faded away. There was only the sound of a dog barking in the distance and the roughness of Jared's chest where her cheek collided with his wings.

He was forcing her mouth up to meet his. She could feel the hardness of his body as her lips softened and parted under his kiss. When Taylor DuPree had kissed her she glued her lips shut, hating the feel of his moist mouth and wet tongue seeking to force its way between her teeth. Now she wanted to thrust herself as close to Jared as she could, and as she did so, the kiss that began as tender and gentle changed to something firm and hard and demanding.

"Darling," Jared whispered. "Oh, darling! Darling Maggie Royal!"

She noticed the way the hair grew back from his forehead and wanted to touch the tiny cowlick at the side by the part. She had the same feeling she'd had when she parachuted from the plane. Fear of the unknown followed by total delight, as if she'd been granted a brief glimpse of immortality.

• •

Brenda was waiting in the hall to go to church. She had on a gray suit with a frilly blouse and a minute felt hat with a finger veil. Her face was washed clean and she looked demure and ladylike, holding her prayer book in her gloved hand. The Duke wore a black suit with a stiff white collar and gray cravat held in place with a pearl stickpin.

"Hurry," Brenda whispered. "Now that there's a war on, the Duke insists we have to go to church earlier and earlier in order to keep the Yanks and other undesirables out of the family pew!"

The small square Norman church was very simple, very plain. They sat on wooden benches in the family pew. It was like a box stall with a hinged door. The elderly sidesman greeted the Duke warmly and shut it carefully once they were seated. In the corner there was a fireplace filled with ashes.

A very old white-haired vicar opened the service with a moment of silence for "our dear departed lads" and then read off the names of the butcher's son whose ship had been sunk in the North Sea; the baker's son, who had bought it in Burma; the chemist's son, who had died at El Alamein; the oldest Jennings boy, taken prisoner in the desert; and a dozen more who had died or been wounded on some far-flung battlefield fighting for the British Empire, in a parish that couldn't have numbered more than three hundred parishioners.

The Duke read the lessons with a trembling yet still beautiful voice. In the general thanksgiving, Maggie Royal gave thanks to the Hansons for letting her ride Lancelot, for Brenda's friendship that had begun then, and for finding Jared.

She glanced over at the Hansons and the children, filling two entire pews, and smiled, and then they all filed up to the altar for Communion.

Afterward they walked in the graveyard, looking at the crooked ancient stones while squadrons of bombers flew overhead.

Ian reached down and picked up a clod of earth and put it to his nose. He inhaled deeply. "There's nothing like the smell of English earth. And the horses," he said, watching several young horses gamboling in a pasture. "Nothing like our English horses!" His eyes followed them as they turned and raced across the field. "They bring moments of great elation as well as despondency." He glanced up and smiled. "No man ever wanted to die with an untried two-year-old in the barn!"

The postwoman pedaled past on her bicycle. "I left a telegram for the Major," she said as she continued along the avenue.

Ian picked up the message on the silver salver in the hall and ripped it open. He handed it to Brenda. "Leave canceled."

"Oh, no," Brenda cried. In an unexpected display of emotion, she threw her arms around his neck. Tears streamed down her face as she held her husband as if she would never let him go.

After Ian left, waving good-bye to them all from the pony cart in which Williams drove him to the station, Brenda went upstairs and went to bed with Bertie.

"Don't look so shocked, Maggie, love," she said later, reaching for a cigarette. "In the beginning I was helping Bertie get over his homosexual phase." She smiled her enchanting smile. "I bloody well succeeded. Now he wants the world to know!"

"I thought when I saw you with Ian everything had changed."

"Bertie wanted me to tell Ian. I intended to. Then he left so suddenly."

"But, Brenda, you found Bertie in bed with Angela!"

Brenda pulled on her cigarette, inhaling deeply. "That little boozle with Angela didn't mean a thing." She gave Maggie Royal a triumphant smile. "Bertie's proposed!"

"Did he get down on his knees?" Maggie Royal asked sarcastically.

"Why, no," Brenda replied, blowing smoke rings. "Just up on his elbows!"

"I see you're in cracking spirits and full of wickedness," Brenda commented the next morning as they prepared to go up to London.

"My new suit," Maggie Royal said. "Miss Jarvis' best. Took all my rations for the cloth at Harrods."

"It's not the suit, although it looks smashing. It's the stars in your eyes. The ice maiden's starting to thaw." She tucked her hand under Maggie Royal's arm and whispered, "Pack up your old kit bag and go with him. And don't forget your diaphragm!"

· 15 ·

Euston station was bedlam. A macabre scene, a little the way one imagines Dante's hell to be, the outer circle with all the lost souls fighting for passage. Trains arrived hours late and it was hard to find out when the train to Scotland would depart.

Soldiers' faces were eerie in the dim gray light. They had packs on their backs and girls clinging to their arms. There were women in Red Cross uniforms helping with the wounded and serving tea from canteens set up around the station. There were women not in uniform with painted faces and odd flowered hats and babies by the armload.

When they were finally able to board the London-Midlands-Scotland train, Maggie Royal found herself wedged alongside Jared in the packed corridor, pushed and jostled by soldiers with strained, anxious faces and drunken sailors on shore leave. And yet, leaning against Jared, the side of his leg touching hers, Maggie Royal had no desire to be anyplace else.

As if voicing her thoughts, Jared said, "A week with you and no interruptions." He looked out at the grayish piles of Midlands towns they were passing through, made more melancholy under a light drizzle. Abruptly he turned back to her. They stood looking at one another, saying nothing, aware of the intense intimacy brought on by the closeness of the corridor, the weird light, the constant motion, the train stopping and starting, people getting on and off.

A very young girl dressed in a gaudy plaid coat pushed up alongside them. In her arms was an infant who kept up an incessant weak whimpering as if it no longer had the strength to cry. The girl was white from exhaustion. She swayed as the train started up and would have fallen if Maggie Royal hadn't grabbed her arm.

Maggie Royal volunteered to hold the baby. The girl gazed at her gratefully and handed over the small bundle in its sour-smelling blanket.

"He's a mite dirty," she apologized. "We've been traveling since yesterday and I have no other clothes to put on him."

The baby was so small, so light, it did not seem real. The small puckered face was blue-gray. One tiny hand curled around Maggie Royal's finger.

Then the baby yawned and its eyes closed. Maggie Royal drew him close. She looked up at Jared and laughed with delight. "I've never seen a baby yawn, but then, I've never seen many babies."

"I don't think I have either." His green eyes held a strange soft light. Maggie Royal's heart started to swell. It suddenly seemed miraculous to find herself with Jared on a crowded train in wartime England on their way to find their Scottish heritage.

They reached Oban at four the following morning to find the Hebridean boat was leaving at six.

They took the steamer to Stornoway. It was loaded with herring fishermen, commercial travelers, soldiers on leave, sheep in nets, and shaggy Highland cattle in pens.

Maggie Royal was glad she had always been a good sailor, for the sea was very rough. The sky overhead was black with clouds moving through the mist like guilts and anxieties. She and Jared could hardly see the Isle of Skye as the fog thickened. The ship rolled and pitched as they made their halting way forward to where the miserable animals swayed from side to side, bleating and lowing painfully.

The rain came suddenly, sending those on deck below. Maggie Royal and Jared were flung together by the toss of a wave, then torn apart as the ship fell in the trough.

The rain seemed to gather in strength, and the seas to match the weather. Jared was thrown across her, pressing her back against the rail. His arms imprisoned her on both sides as the ship teetered and then fell. She felt the warmth and dampness of his Navy greatcoat, the smell of his tobacco and shaving soap, as the wind and water held them in an embrace.

They went below to the tiny cabin where they had stored their gear. Two seasick soldiers were sitting on the narrow bunk.

Jared reached into his bag and brought out a bottle of whiskey. "If you wouldn't mind," he said, handing it to them, "you'll feel better out in the air.

"Do you remember the day we met on the beach?" he asked her after the soldiers lurched off. "You were cold, forbidding, Englishy. Until we went to see Old Ugly. Then you weren't afraid." He cupped her chin in his hand. "Why are you now? Darling, stop trembling." He put his hand on her neck and slowly drew her upward. The boat rolled, and she swayed against him.

He took his hand away from her neck and put his arm around her. His body pressed against hers, softening it, like her lips under his kiss, as she felt herself melting, becoming lost, without a will of her own. The world rocked and hummed, the waves beating against the ship like the clamor of her heart, until she felt herself soaring upward, tossed by such a tumult of feeling that the sudden sharp pain became a part of her pleasure. It was as if the sea had set her free. She had labored upward, like Sisyphus and his rock, only to be overwhelmed by her grandmother's warnings and her mother's calculated restraints, until this now—a now of thundering waves, wildly pitching steamer, bleating animals, and seasick passengers; a now of wonder and exultation and sudden completion.

"Maggie Royal!" He stared at her in wonder. "My darling, I didn't know."

Maggie Royal put up a finger and touched his lips. She moved it to the cowlick and slowly circled it. "That last summer on the island. I read *A Farewell to Arms*. I imagined I was Catherine Barkley. I would be a nurse, give my all without regret. Of course, it had to be the right man."

He kissed the corner of her mouth. "Good for you."

"You're damn right it was." She threw him a wicked grin. "Worth waiting for!"

They were suddenly starving. Jared dug out another bottle of whiskey and some tins of herring. They shared them with two sailors they found in the lounge. One said he was the only survivor of a trawler that had gone down in the North Atlantic. He had been fished out of the sea by an American freighter in the convoy.

When the steamer berthed, he directed them to a small gray hotel overlooking the curving seawall, where they devoured high tea, boiled eggs, toast, and scones.

The ancient brass bedstead was in no way comparable to the one at the Ritz. There was a depression in the middle into which they rolled laughing and made love as hungrily as they had devoured the simple meal.

"I'm afraid I'm awfully ignorant," Maggie Royal said.

"You are fast becoming the most delightfully depraved woman I have ever known." He touched her breast. "I am here to see that you become more so."

"Oh, darling . . ."

"Hush." He ran his hand gently down her stomach. "Your all was worth waiting for!"

The bus left at 9:30. It was loaded with newspapers, bags of mail and oats. The driver said his name was MacDonald. He wore a Harris-tweed suit and tam-o'-shanter tilted at an angle as rakish as the turns he took. At each stop his "wee doggie" leaped down onto the ground to round up the passengers, who came from their black houses. When not stopping to deliver mail and receive parcels and passengers, the driver threw the newspapers out the window.

They seemed to have drifted back into the Stone Age—lakes and moonlike craters and tiny cottages of peat and straw anchored down with rocks, from which came puffs of black smoke. Black strips ran like scars between giant boulders where peat had been cut.

334

At Harris they toured the tweed factory, where Harris tweed, hand woven by women in cottages throughout the Hebrides, was exported in large quantities before the war. Hand in hand they walked through the village, smelling the bread baking and the sea. There was a total lack of interest in sales. Jared wanted to buy Maggie Royal a red-blue-and-green tam "so you'll have something to throw over the windmill." "I won't sell it to you," the ambassadorial-looking proprietor told him. "I cannot recommend it. It is too dear."

At Lochmaddy, on the island of North Uist, they boarded the Stark Island steamer. The royal mail was put aboard and sheep stowed in the hold. A very old man with a tam and checked knickers came on board, followed by a limping Labrador retriever. On shore, turf cutters were etched against the bleak gray skyline. A Highland bull stared at them fixedly from beneath his shaggy auburn locks as the vessel was cast off.

In late afternoon they reached Stark Island. The sun suddenly parted the mist, disclosing pyramidal ruins gleaming gray and gold against the shaggy splendor of the purpled hills.

"A man can take a breath in the moors," said the old Highlander, leaning on the rail.

Jared squeezed her hand. She knew they were both thinking the same thing, that from these ancient stones atop the sea-sundered headland their ancestors had sprung.

They walked up the single street. Gray-stone cottages clinging to the rocky hillside fought off the tireless wind bringing with it cold and mist and the capacity to stir the ocean to paroxysms of foaming anger.

The hotel crowned the hill.

A coal fire was burning in the green-tiled fireplace. The walls were red damask, and the chairs, with white antimacassars, were faded red plush. A grotesque mahogany bookcase with carved cupids, cross-eyed lions, a dragon, and two bosomy women—"Nothing you could live with," Jared said—held Scott's works and legal tomes with gilt bindings.

A few Swedish-modern coffee tables stood about, crowded with tin Martell ashtrays.

They had boiled eggs and tea in front of the fire.

The proprietor and his wife pointed out the thousand-year-old beams overhead and said it was a "funny old place." The proprietor was tall and spare, with a fine craggy face. He resembled a shepherd or a prime minister. His wife was gaunt with graying hair pulled back in a taut knot, and a dour, disapproving manner. Jared invited them to join him in a glass of whiskey. They refused, saying they were temperance, but as soon as his wife had departed to the kitchen, the proprietor winked at Jared, who poured him a portion, which the man drank neat.

"My God, a steak would taste good," Jared said.

"I prefer bed."

He laughed and squeezed her hand. "At this rate I'll soon need red meat."

Their room was frigid, unheated. The window looked out onto the stream gurgling past. "A magic casement opening on the foam" was painted on the windowsill. There was a small vase of dried heather on the bureau.

It seemed to take forever to reach the bathroom, which was at the far end of a long black hallway.

The room was dark when Maggie Royal returned. She let the mackintosh she was wearing as a wrapper fall to the floor. A thin strip of moonlight came through the window. It left a horizontal stripe from her shoulder down across her breasts.

Jared caught his breath in a kind of gasp. "Hurry," he said pulling back the covers.

Maggie Royal slid in beside him. "My feet are perishing cold."

"I'll warm them." He wrapped her in his arms and her body began slowly to warm, like blood becoming illuminated by light.

"We should do something different," she said after a while. "We mustn't reach a stalemate."

"You could never be that!" Jared said, closing her lips with his.

"Oh, darling." She buried her face in the hollow between his cheek and his shoulder, murmuring unintelligible endearments.

"Come again?" Jared asked.

"Oh, yes, please," Maggie Royal answered.

It rained and blew all night. The wind sound, like the sound of aircraft, intensified as it approached, diminishing with distance. They clung together under the one thin blanket, Jared's greatcoat, and her mackintosh.

She awoke suddenly and pulled herself upright, thinking she heard the proprietor's wife with tea. She felt Jared's hand moving along her back.

"What are you doing?"

"Kissing your beautiful back," he said as his lips found the hollow between her shoulder blades.

"Gramma taught us to sit up straight."

"I'm glad. Now, why don't you lie down straight?"

When they awoke again it was one of those lovely clear days that come on the heels of the worst weather. Maggie Royal parted the curtains to look out at the ruins on the hill. The sheep on the moor stood out like white puffs against the bracken and purple heather. The brook—"the burn," the proprietor called it—was filled with yellow leaves, like gold coins.

"Jared," she called. "Come quick. Look!" He knelt beside her as they watched the great stag come slowly, watchfully, to drink the crystal-clear rushing water.

The proprietor recalled there were once Starks in the village, but that had been long ago. He believed the ruins to the north had once been the Stark Castle. At sight of Jared's ten shillings his wife grudgingly furnished them with bread and cheese and hard-boiled eggs from her chickens. Jared put the food in his knapsack with the bottle of wine he had brought with him.

"Mind the witches' pool," she warned darkly as they left. She pointed across the moor. "It's where suspected women were given a choice of drowning to prove their innocence or floating to prove their guilt."

"My goodness," Maggie Royal said, "that's not much of a choice."

The proprietor's wife's reply was a visible tightening of the lips as she gazed coldly at Maggie Royal's ringless engagement finger.

"She makes me feel like a Red Cross package," Maggie Royal said as they walked up the hill past the great boulders. "One they'd have trouble mailing."

"That's what you get for being a kept woman. I once read my father's copy of Dr. Johnson's travels through the Outer Hebrides. Very proper, these people."

"I think I'm more unkept." Maggie Royal pushed back her wildly blowing hair.

Jared's eyes narrowed against the ever-changing light. He reached out and gently touched the top of her head. "When you're old you'll be even more beautiful, like Gramma."

"Old!" She shivered as though, like the Gullahs, she had seen a hant.

"Come close to me," Jared urged. "Closer," he whispered as she reached out to him.

The high land was ruled by heather. The hotelkeeper had told them it was fired every few years to permit the grass to grow and the sheep to graze. But after a while the heather crept back and the cycle began again. Light and shadow fell on the great boulders and pastures of sheep. Red Highland cattle, their "bangs" falling over their faces, stared at them stoically. Through the open doorways of whitewashed cottages they saw old men and women weaving the tweed that would go to the factory in Harris.

The road was narrow and rutted. It led to an ancient stone church on a high point of land facing the sea. Here they found the tomb of a patriarchal Stark who fought at Culloden, sired ten children, and died at ninety-two.

"You see, we're long-lived people," Jared said as they found other gravestones of Starks who had lived into their eighties and nineties.

They came to the cliff against which the sea frothed and foamed. Piled stones guarded the ruins, overrun with gorse and briars. It was a gaunt wraith of a castle, a romantic pile. It didn't matter if it was their castle or not. They adopted it as their own.

Sitting on the ruined wall, they ate to the music of the waves below and the cries of gulls overhead. One bolder than the rest grabbed a piece of bread from Maggie Royal's hand. His comrades were enraged. They fell on him screaming, seeking to wrest it from him. The wind ruffled her hair like a giant hand and blew back her skirt. Instinctively she pushed it back down over her knees.

"Don't." Jared took her hand away. "Stop being a proper Southern girl and let me look at your knees. They aren't knobby anymore. I remember the first time I saw you, sitting on the beach. All skinny bones. I wanted to reach out and grab you and touch the hollows at the sides of your kneecaps. Did you know that? That there were times I wanted to hold you and feel your bones jutting out?" He put his hand on her neck and slowly ran it upward, through the thick dark hair. "Funny. After a while it became difficult to touch you."

"You could have touched me," she said, talking to the wind.

"I know that now." He bent down and slowly, lingeringly kissed her on the lips.

Overhead the gull dropped the crust in its beak, and the birds dived on it.

Jared turned to watch. "See how he flies!" He took his sketchbook from his pack and began quickly drawing one of the swooping gulls. "Notice how he pounced on that unsuspecting bird below, the one with something in its beak. The first rule of air combat is to see your opponent first. The Germans learned that in Spain. One of the reasons Franco won."

She watched the birds shrieking and swirling over the sea. "Oh, Jared." She put her arms around his neck and rested her head on his shoulder. "I don't want anything to happen to you."

His hand traced the line of her cheek. "A plane is the safest place to be. You can always jump. In a ship you can be torpedoed. In a submarine you can't get out. In a tank you get blown up. As for the infantry . . . My God, all that mud!" He paused and drank from the wine bottle.

"But, Jared, the next time you might not be as lucky."

"Darling Maggie Royal, it's like falling off a horse. You have to get back on again." He threw eggshells at the circling gulls. "Come on. Let's walk." He reached to help her down off the wall.

Life is strange and wonderful, Maggie Royal thought. A moment catches you up, like that time in the garden at Chatfield. "I wish we could bottle memories," she said. "Like peaches or plums. I'd like to bury something of value here, then come back after the war and dig it up and relive this time."

"We'll dig a hole," Jared said.

"I know. The wine bottle. We'll put a note in it. Jared, write it on your sketchpad. On this September day of 1943, Jared Stark and Maggie Royal McDermott were here."

He raised his head, staring at her with a look she couldn't read. She waited for him to speak, but he turned away quickly and began digging the hole. Carefully he lowered the bottle with the note into it. Then he piled the dirt back. Maggie Royal took a sprig of heather and laid it on top.

She straightened up, gazing at Jared. His head was thrown back and his eyes were fixed on a plane high in the heavens above them. Slowly he turned his head, and his eyes met hers. She felt the familiar, joyful surge, desire deep inside her. Impulsively she started toward him and then stopped. She recognized the look in his eyes from the past. It was the same strange, feverish look she had seen when he wanted something —a horse, a house, a woman. Fear like the cold wind sweeping in from the sea caused her to shiver. It was as though already he had left her, moved on to some distant place of the mind where she could not follow.

On their way back to the hotel they stopped at a crofter's cottage. It was spotlessly clean and the owner's wife served them tea and scones, straight from the top of the iron stove where she had cooked the cakes on a griddle until they turned brown and their edges began to crumble.

Her husband was a prisoner of the Japanese, she said, captured in Burma. She took care of the children and worked at her loom, weaving the wool into tweed. "Harris lasts forever," she explained, "because it takes so long to make."

When they left, the woman whispered to Maggie Royal, "May God preserve you both."

The moor seemed all glistening and new, brilliant with color. Van Gogh colors, Jared said, as the sun zigzagged behind clouds, shedding patches of golden light like throw rugs on the hillsides. Then suddenly the rain returned, soaking them before they could retrace their steps back to the sanctuary of their casement room.

Maggie Royal peered at Jared's sleeping form in the half-light. She wondered if, should they live to old age together, the promise of physical ecstasy would diminish. Would a time come when habit and familiarity dulled magic?

Jared did not waste words or tenderness. His strength and power left no room for them. There was a primitive quality about his lovemaking that gave her a sense of fulfillment and caused her to exult in submission.

One fine long-fingered hand lay outside the blanket. She thought of how it felt when he touched her. Now, finally, she understood what Brenda meant when she said it was possible to give up everything for those secret things that can take place between a man and a woman in the night.

"What are you staring at?"

"You."

"Please don't. It's distracting and I'm busy."

"Busy?"

"Yes. I'm rescuing Harry the Horror from the jaws of Old Ugly! There isn't a second to lose. He already has one leg."

"But alligators don't eat people," Maggie Royal said. "Just croco-diles."

"Darling, you sound like the Horror. Now, do look out the window and count the sheep on the moor and let me pull Harry out before the alligator gets the other leg and starts creeping up his torso."

"Darling," Maggie Royal said, "the proprietor's wife will be in any moment with tea."

She started to get out of bed.

He grabbed her leg and pulled her back.

She tried to wriggle from his grasp. "Go back to your rescue. Harry must be half et by now. The proprietor's wife takes a dim view of us as it is. What will she think if she comes in and catches us roughhousing, as Gramma used to say?"

At that instant the door swung open and there was the proprietor's wife's disapproving face behind the tin tea tray. Pretending not to notice them, she placed the tray on the table in the far corner of the room. She went to the windows and drew back the heavy curtains, flooding the room with the gray light of a stormy Hebridean morning. Without looking in their direction, she left, closing the door behind her with a decisive bang.

"What a shame!" Jared sighed. "If she'd waited she could have had a real treat!"

The days went by, falling like pages from Jared's sketchbook. They spent hours on the moor. Sparrow would have loved the birds. Rock pipits soared and dived like fighter planes. The bark of corn crakes awakened them in the night.

Gorse turned the hillsides to gold, mixed with heather. The burns rushed, churning the water to foam.

On their last afternoon they climbed high on the heathered hill overlooking the sea. A shepherd rounding up sheep in the distance paused and gazed up at them. High above they saw a pair of golden eagles. They hoped the shepherd would not shoot them for preying on his lambs.

Maggie Royal began to run. Jared followed. They ran until they could run no farther. Maggie Royal fell into a clump of heather. It prickled her nose and scratched her legs through her stockings. She buried her face in it as if trying to absorb all of the damp Scottish earth. Jared lay with his arm across her back, catching his breath. Finally they were still.

"Darling Maggie Royal." Jared's voice was husky. "Do you remem-ber my father's book *Monsieur Nicolas?* One day while wandering with the family flock, Monsieur Nicolas came on a secret valley. It was won-derfully beautiful and filled with rare animals and birds. All marve-lously tame and gentle. In his mind it became his valley, his secret place. We all have our own valley somewhere. A place outside the ordinary world." He gazed at the sheep grazing below. "We'll go home to Stark

Island. You and I. There will be children. Black, white, yellow. We'll spend our days riding, looking for shark's teeth, fishing with Joe-Ali." The yellow lights danced in his eyes. "We'll live on love and peanut butter and hush puppies, grits and chocolate ice cream. Whoever sets foot on the island will undergo a transformation. People and animals will never be killed or die. Man will live a thousand years and lose the power to slay!"

Gently he turned her over. Her face was framed by the heather, the color of her eyes. She put up her arms and drew him down to her.

His lips were cold, then warm. She could feel him, every part of him as he held her closer and closer. And then, at the height of her happiness, of passion, came the distant flutter, the hint of darkness, like the long, rounded dark brown wings of the eagles that hovered over the island sheep, ever closer, bringing a kind of nameless dread she could not define or discount.

On the last night they lingered long at their table in the empty dining room. The proprietor's wife's attitude had become less forbidding. Jared had jollied her with chocolate and soap and had listened to her eerie tales of the moors, of coaches drawn by four horses running wild in the night, and of lost children. In honor of their last meal she let them burn a candle at their table, warning them to be chary with the light.

Along with allowing them a candle, she had killed and cooked one of her chickens, baked bread, and made a special fruit tart. The proprietor chanced his wife's disapproval by producing a hidden bottle of wine. Jared told him to save it, but the proprietor paid no attention.

"Almost nobody comes to Stark Island now," he said, indicating the empty dining room. "Never was exactly a vacation spot. Too bleak and cold for trippers." He smiled at them and lifted his glass in the old Scottish toast: "When the trouble is over, haste ye back!"

· 16 ·

D Day came finally. In the hospital there was a strange hushed unease. One sensed the wounded men were projecting themselves across the water to those dying on French beaches, in orchards and along mined roadways. Hawkers selling cornflowers and red and white peonies made little patriotic floral arrangements which Maggie Royal bought and put by the beds of her soldiers.

Six days later came the first V-1 pilotless plane. People came to identify the three sounds, like instruments in an orchestra. The first faint noise like a finger drawn across parchment, then an enormous fart, followed by a rumble like a carload of rocks being emptied, then all three merging into waves of noise. Maggie Royal wrote back to the paper that although Londoners loathed the unearthly missiles, they seemed more frightened of seeming to be frightened than they were of the flying bombs. People late for appointments apologized, saying they'd been held up, and it was only later revealed their houses had been leveled.

Pilots tucked their children into bed, kissed their wives good-bye, and drove to their airfields to face the murderous flak over Hamburg and Düsseldorf and Berlin. They spoke of flying as "just doing a job." Their cockpit was home, their flight bags their only possessions. Sleeplessness, cold tea, and the itching discomfort of oxygen masks were their norm.

They made Maggie Royal think of the barnstormers at the old thrill shows. There was a mystique about them, an exhilaration that came from being members of a well-disciplined unit. They were part of a new culture. They were without past or future, living and lusting for the moment, outside the range of ordinary respectability, some as incapable of true and long-lasting love as men who know instinctively they won't last very long.

Jared made sketches of his companions. Sparrow's friend Mac Malloy had them published in *Life,* and they created an impact on the home front. His singing on missions and turkey calls became famous.

342

"Loch Lomond" and "I've Been Working on the Railroad" sounded well, he said, when accompanied by the plane's powerful engines.

On the last weekend in June, Jared came up to London. After D Day he'd been on an almost never-ending alert. His squadron had suffered heavy casualties. His copilot, Chuck Sturgis, and his tail gunner had both been severely wounded during a fight over the Channel.

The members of the Guards Regiments Maggie Royal had met at Brenda's ball had all but disappeared from the streets and smart restaurants. Only Bertie remained on duty at the Palace. At the last minute his orders to go out of the country had been canceled.

"That guy sure pulls a lot of stateside duty," Jared commented when he heard the news.

On Saturday night Jared and Maggie Royal dined with Brenda and Bertie at the Savoy. Brenda had been in the country for a week recovering from another "streamer" and had come up to London that afternoon. She presented Hansen, the head porter, with a clutch of plovers' eggs wrapped in a chiffon handkerchief smelling of the last of her postwar Chanel Number 5, a paper bag holding her diamond tiara, her Purdey that she'd brought up to London as protection against the jewel thieves that had robbed several Belgravia houses, and a fruitcake Mrs. Walton, the cook at Chatfield, had baked for Mr. Potts's birthday.

"But, milady, I can't fit the shotgun into the safe," Hansen said, gazing at the gun as if it might go off at any moment. "Surely there's some other place you could leave these things!"

"I thought they'd be safest with you." Brenda smiled sweetly. "I like to keep them nearby. One never knows when a tiara, a gun, or a fruitcake may be useful."

Finally she charmed him into locking up the jewels and stacking the gun in a closet with the umbrellas.

"I don't think we should go dancing. I think we should scram," Bertie said when they finished dinner. "You haven't been getting enough sleep, love."

"My feet are swollen from standing on them all day and dancing all night," Brenda agreed. "I sometimes wish I were in the MTC like Kay What's-her-name who drives Eisenhower around. Other day I saw Davinia St. Clair change a tire in eight minutes in the Strand in the pouring rain." She made a face and put out her cigarette. "Must be that new tobacco. Tastes horrid. Or maybe it was the pigeon pie. Luigi, the maître d', catches the pigeons on window ledges." She pushed back her chair. "Maggie darling, I feel quite unwell. Come with me to the loo."

Maggie Royal gazed at her friend worriedly. She did look unwell, thinner than ever, with dark circles under the blue eyes.

In the ladies' room Brenda sat down in front of the mirror and stared at herself. "I'm so pale." She began dabbing rouge from the tip of her little finger onto her cheeks. "Bother!" She waved the stub of her lipstick. "Dried up like old bread, and you can't get any more." Her

343

hand dropped suddenly and she clutched the edge of the dressing table. "I feel throwing-up sick!"

Minutes later she emerged from the toilet. "There, I feel better." She turned to Maggie Royal. "Darling Maggie, does it show?"

"Does what show?" Maggie Royal asked in surprise.

"The baby. I'm preggers." Brenda cupped her breasts in her hands. "They're bigger. I always wanted bigger boses." The circles under her eyes made them seem huge in her white face.

Maggie Royal stared at her, speechless.

"Really, Maggie," Brenda said impatiently. "It occurs to me you have a very low threshold of shock. I've worried about your innocence ever since I found out you were twenty and still a virgin."

"It's just that I don't understand how you could sleep with Bertie when you have Ian!"

Brenda turned her blue eyes on Maggie Royal and crinkled her nose. "You Americans are so bourgeois! Does one eat boiled cabbage every day?"

"What if Ian finds out?" Maggie Royal asked.

"How will he find out? I have no intention of hanging over the cradle to dote. I'll simply get rid of it. Monica got ergot shots from a doctor friend. And used her perfume bottle. She filled it full of sterile water and salt and stuck the atomizer part up her uterus. Angela tried a hoof pick. I can always borrow one of Nanny's knitting needles. Fortunately I have time before hunting starts."

"Brenda, no," Maggie Royal cried, horrified. "That's out."

"So was my thingamajig," Brenda said regretfully. "It has a leak. A hole as large as the one in my umbrella. You can get diaphragms now only on the black market."

"Well, why haven't you gotten one?"

"Darling Maggie." Brenda fixed Maggie Royal with her guileless blue-eyed gaze. "Black market, purple market, I wouldn't dream of it. Maggie darling, it would be against the honor of the land!"

Maggie Royal and Jared were staying at the Ritz. They had just gone to bed when the whistles of wardens and fire guards and the sound of running feet penetrated the thick curtains.

Maggie Royal groaned and burrowed deeper beneath the blanket. She was more despairing of further dampness and the nauseating stagnant air of the tube than of taking her chances by staying in their room.

"Come on," Jared urged, pulling her upright.

"Jared, I must dress."

"Everybody out." It was the manager banging on the door. "Hurry, now."

"Brenda says she'd rather plug her ears and—"

"I don't give a damn what Brenda says." Jared swept up her black

344

lace slip from the floor and threw it at her. "Wear some of your spiffy, lacy, sexy underwear. Just the thing for a shelter," he added as she pulled the slip over her head. She found her shoes, grabbed her mackintosh, and followed him out the door.

Soldiers, sailors, and civilians were pouring out of newsreel theaters and cinemas and being directed to the nearest shelter.

They heard the spine-chilling buzz of the engine, the sudden awful stillness. Then the dull burr becoming a roar as it struck. Jared pulled her into the Underground station as a nearby building was hit.

She had tried to emulate Brenda's cheerful fatalism. Yet she found herself clinging to Jared, fighting against the desire to scratch like a dog burying a bone and dissolve into the floor.

The corridors and platforms were jammed with people. Packed like the herrings they'd eaten in Scotland. Haggard white-faced women nursed squalling babies. Old women drank tea and men played darts, slinging them over the heads of those huddled below. Children cried out in their sleep, and over all lay the stench and dirt of too much humanity.

They found a space on the Underground platform between an old prostitute wearing a skimpy fox fur and lavish makeup, and a frail carrot-haired boy of eight or nine. "Freedom is in Peril / Defend it with your Might" read the poster over his head. Someone began to sing: "A blackout warden passing yelled / 'Ma, pull down that blind / Just look at what you're showing' and we / shouted, 'Never mind, Oh! / Knees up, Mother Brown . . .'" Soon everyone was singing. Maggie Royal felt a wave of affection for these people, the plucky whore, the grubby boy. He had the pinched grayish pallor of the city child, blue eyes, and lusterless hair. He was clutching a damp odoriferous package of fish and trying hard not to cry.

Jared asked him his name.

"Jamie, sir. Jamie Bush."

Jared asked him where his parents lived and he replied they had been killed in the December 29 raid in the 1940 blitz when their house suffered a direct hit.

Maggie Royal asked why he hadn't been evacuated.

Biting his lip, holding back tears, he explained that he'd been billeted in a foster home. A farm family kept him a few weeks and then sent him back to London. "They said I used bad words," he explained. "They didn't want me around their little boy." Now he'd been turned over to an uncle and aunt already overburdened with small children. He had been on his way home with the fish when a warden shooed him into the shelter. "They'll give me a good wigging for spoiling the fish," he said sadly.

Jared drew a pair of dice from his pocket. He spread his Navy greatcoat on his knees and rolled the dice in such a way that they did not fall off his lap.

Jamie stopped sniffling to watch.

"Let's see who collects the most bees," Jared said. "Pretend the dice are sugar lumps. The dots on them are bees. With each roll count the bees that settle on them. If you get a higher number, you win."

People sitting nearby were soon engrossed, watching Jared throw the dice with the expertise of Jazzbo and the stable hands on Stark Island.

"Come on, Big Dick from Boston . . . cripes! Snake eyes!" Jared rubbed the dice between his palms. He kissed them and threw again. "Little Phoebe. Come to Mother, baby. Aha, seven come eleven!"

Maggie Royal leaned forward, forgetting the close fetid air and the smell of Jamie's fish. Her coat fell open, revealing her slip. She saw the prostitute's knowing smile and caught the look of envy that momentarily softened the harsh lines of her worn, aging countenance. Jared started to laugh as she pulled the mac back across her front.

The time passed quickly. When the all-clear sounded, they straggled back up the long flights of stairs to the street.

They took Jamie and his fish back to the basement where he shared two dank rooms with his aunt and uncle and their four children. It was obvious from what the child said that he was unloved, unwanted, and charged with the job of fetching food and caring for the younger children. Jared gave him a chocolate bar and they bade him a warm goodbye. They were a block away when Jamie caught up, grabbed Jared around one leg, and clung to it, weeping.

Jared swung him into his arms and held him. "When you hear the bombs buzzing like bees, keep counting until you get tens, twenties, hundreds . . ."

He set the child gently down on the boards that served as a sidewalk.

"But 'er ain't no bees!" Jamie choked.

"That's the point!" Jared handed him his dice. "Just remember the dots on the dice. Think of them as bees sitting on sugar lumps."

Jamie stared wonderingly at the dice. Then, clutching them in a filthy fist, he turned and marched resolutely back to the basement flat.

"I'm going to ask the Hansons to take Jamie," Maggie Royal said.

Jared paused by a lamppost. A fire was burning nearby. Firemen were manning pumps and shouting at one another. They could feel the heat from the flames. Jared bent his head to hers and kissed her. People coming out of the shelters surged around them as they clung together.

The next morning, shortly after Jared left to rejoin his squadron, the congregation at the Guards' Chapel at Wellington Barracks rose to sing. "We praise thee, O God: we acknowledge Thee to be our Lord." Overhead, the buzz became a roar, drowning out the voices of Guards officers and their relatives. As the engine cut out, the *Te Deum* broke the silence. This was followed by a terrible deafening noise. Seconds later, nothing was left of the Guards Chapel but bricks and mortar.

Some eighty Guards officers and their relatives were killed instantly. Another hundred and twenty were badly injured. Bertie had been standing by the door when the bomb hit and was able to escape. He returned to the building to help rescue a young woman with both legs blown off. He was trying to lift her when part of the remaining wall fell on him, burying him.

Brenda was in the country. She had not been well, and Dr. Lessing had advised her to stay home from work and rest. Maggie Royal found her feverishly polishing silver in the pantry.

"I know how you feel," she said helplessly.

"The hell you do!" Brenda's voice, normally low-pitched, was shrill. Picking up her cloth, she began rubbing a Queen Anne teapot with dogged attention. "They all die! And for what? The Empire! I say to hell with the Empire. To hell with . . ." Suddenly her body sagged. She put down the teapot and buried her face in her hands.

Maggie Royal put her arms around her friend. "Bertie is dead. Let your love die with him. Put it by, love. The days have been."

Brenda made an incoherent sound. She picked up the teapot and began rubbing it again. "Ian has a forty-eight. He wants me to go up to London and take Sprat. He says it's important. Nanny is in a frizz. The doodlebugs and all."

"For God's sake, Brenda. Let go! From now on, let it be Ian. Brenda, Ian is good. Brenda, Bertie wasn't."

Brenda banged the teapot down on the counter with a savage gesture. She faced Maggie Royal, her face distorted. "Just when did anyone ever fall in love with goodness?"

"You should have taken leave when you had a chance," Maggie Royal said the following Saturday as she was having tea with Jared at Claridge's.

"I couldn't. Something's come up. I can't tell you about it." He lit another cigarette from the butt of his old one. "Darling." He reached over and put his hand on hers. "Not to worry. Remember my 'crazy' days when planes didn't have sissy things like brakes or tail wheels. Now we have every kind of gadget. Anyway, the war will be over soon. Then we can all go home!"

"I'm convinced it'll never be over," Maggie Royal said bitterly. "When the lights come on again. When the nightingale sings in Berkeley Square, a new war will be beginning."

She took a deep breath, seeking to compose herself, and set down her teacup. "Brenda brought Sprat up to see Ian."

Jared looked surprised. "I thought he was in Normandy."

"He wangled a ride on an RAF plane. Brenda received word it was urgent."

"Sprat shouldn't be in London. The buzz bombs."

"Brenda believes that appointments in Samarra are kept only when you're trying to avoid them."

Jared looked at his watch. "We'll stay here. You can still order whiskey if you live here."

"London's chockablock," Maggie Royal said. "You may not be able to get a room."

"You should know my powers of persuasion by now," Jared said, grinning.

Maggie Royal couldn't hear what he said to the room clerk. She still felt prickles of embarrassment when they registered at a hotel together. She remembered the innkeeper's wife in the Hebrides, her talk about the witches' pool, and tried to hide behind a pillar as the receptionist glanced in her direction. The man they knew had been replaced by a suave mustachioed clerk with sleek hair and a shifty manner. He looked like a draft dodger or a magician. At sight of Jared's whiskey bottle he became a magician.

"I wonder who was evicted," Maggie Royal said as they went up in the lift.

"Don't worry about it. Probably a chicken colonel and his popsy whose war is right here."

A deferential bellhop, carrying her overnight case and typewriter, ushered them into an enormous suite. There were two bedrooms done in silver and blue, a dining room, conference room, and sunken tub.

"My God, Jared. This must have cost a packet."

"It's on the house." He grinned. "General Montgomery's suite."

"But how?"

"I merely told the receptionist the general was a friend."

"But you don't know—"

"Hush, now." He put his arm around her. "I did meet him once. He was coming out of Grosvenor House with Ike. Terence introduced us. Monty said, 'Howjado, Yank. Keep your wing tips up!' "

Maggie Royal threw her hat on the bed and did a dance around the silver-blue room. "First I'd like to have a bath!"

"Here." He tossed her a large American bar of soap from his bag. "Live dangerously. Forget the water-saving mark and fill the tub full."

She had forgotten the wonders of a proper bath. The water was tepid, but at least it wasn't cold. As she luxuriated in the enormous tub she thought of the women they had seen lying on the grass in the parks. Many in the shapeless khaki and sagging stockings of the Auxiliary Territorial Service and the other services. She wondered how they managed to clean away the sweat and the stink, the after effects of fornication, in filthy lavatories without hot water or soap. How many, living a life where sex was as easy, as open and banal as drinking tea, could know of longing, of tension and timing and build-up, a little at a time, like discarding layers of clothing piece by piece? Nor could the information on venereal disease and contraceptives the American forces had made available everywhere do other than destroy the magic, cause anticipation to dwindle to just so much clinical reality.

Maggie Royal sighed luxuriously. "I'm not leaving this luscious place tonight. War or no war. Bombs or no bombs! Bless General Mont-gomery!"

She uncovered her portable, took some copy paper from her over-night case and the notes made during the week.

"Sorry," she said, starting to work, "but I didn't have time before. It's been hectic at the hospital." For a moment she sat frowning, chew-ing on the end of her pencil, wondering which of the leads she had stored in her head would be best.

Jared leaned over her shoulder and tapped out "shirdlu." It came out "shi dlu."

"What do you do without an r?"

"It's been that way fo the past month. Unde wood needs his annual checkup, but the place whe e I used to take him got blown up. Haven't you hea d? The e's a wa on! By the way, whateve happened to old She man and the wa -is-hell theo y?"

"Da ling," he typed out, "I only have a sho t time left $%&'*#!'"

Suddenly it was no longer fun and games. Each letter stabbed her heart with the cold hardness of icicles. She felt herself sliding, slipping into a helpless rage, and could not stop herself.

"You can't wait to go back," she heard herself crying passionately. "To your bloody plane. To being a bloody hero." She made a sweeping gesture that sent her notes billowing to the floor. "I saw you when you first came, marching to 'Tipperary.' I leaned out my window and waved a flag and cried. I saw Brenda's friends, the Guards in their marvel-ous uniforms, bands playing, bugles blowing, girls throwing flowers at them, flinging themselves at them as they were about to charge into the cannon's mouth. I've bloody well seen where it ends, too. Long, bare, stinking rooms where the men from Dunkirk and Dieppe and Salerno lie in endless rows. Bandages soaked with blood. Bones sticking through their flesh. Groaning. Coughing up blood. Crying out in the dark."

Her nails were biting into the palms of her hands. She had never let herself go like this before.

"I've seen the 'body sniffers,' snuffling in the debris like dogs, stop-ping every so often to listen for signs of life. 'Blood here,' they call out. Then, after another sniff, 'Fresh blood . . . still flowing!' "

"Write it," Jared said quietly when she paused for breath. "There's your story." He cocked his left eyebrow. "Might leave out some of the 'bloodys.' "

She whirled around. "You bloody well wanted to go to Spain. You couldn't wait to get into this war. Like that piratical ancestor of yours. For the adventure!"

Suddenly he was no longer smiling. "Are you quite finished?" His hands on her arms were hurting. "Because if you are, I'll tell you what Spain was like." His voice was low, savage. "It was a village. No arms. No soldiers. Nothing but old people and children. You hear the planes.

The Germans. Flying low, directly over the square, spraying the people with gunfire. Back they come. One after another. The bombs start falling. The sound drowns out the screams as people begin running from their burning houses. A stork topples from its nest on the steeple of the church. I dive into a ditch. There's a little boy there, about the age of Jamie Bush."

Maggie Royal started to speak. Then at sight of his face she did not.

"Instead of a package of fish, he's holding his insides, trying to keep them from oozing out around his fingers and spilling onto the dirt. And the planes come back and back. Blood is running in the ditch from the dead and dying. Women, children, old people, and babies. Horses, donkeys, dogs, a canary lying dead in its overturned cage, and the stork, its beak open and its feet sticking up, like Susan's cardinal after the cat killed it.

"The little boy's screams begin to lessen. I have no medicine, no way to help. A gun, but no more ammunition to put the animals out of their misery. Pretty soon the little boy is quiet. I put my jacket over him. The vultures begin to circle. Lower and lower." He slammed his fist against the wall.

Later, after he'd gone, she'd be desperately sorry. Still, she couldn't stop. Fury and fatigue held her like the long high notes of Jazzbo's "gee-tar," holding tension as the groundswell of melody gathered strength beneath it.

"So you just happened to volunteer for a mission. A little extra. 'Lagniappe,' as Noble would say. 'Brawtus,' a final gift, as if you hadn't already given enough." She paused for breath and rushed on. "You should be riding King and carrying a lance, Jared Stark. You're so damned honorable you even marry a woman you don't love—"

The scar on his forehead stood out lividly in his dark high-boned face, pale now with anger. His green eyes were black. Once before she had seen them that way. The day he fought with Cullen.

The palm of his hand sounded like a shot against her cheek. She swayed backward and stood staring at him, tears welling in her eyes.

She put her fist against her mouth. Her teeth bit down on it. Rage and misery made her stammer. "D-d-damned waste! N-nothing b-b-ut waste! Death, devastation. For w-w-what?"

"I'll tell you for what," he snarled at her. "To get the goddamn war over with and go home!" He cleared his throat and then said quietly, "We had a chance to avoid all this, if we'd stood up and been counted in Spain. Now we have no choice but to fight like hell."

"What do you think I've been doing for the past four years?" she screamed at him. "Do you think I like emptying bedpans, binding up wounds that can't be binded?"

"Bound," he said.

"All right, bound. Oh, for God's sake! I was fine until you came back into my life."

"I'm sorry it was such a hardship. There're plenty of other girls. Take your friend Angela."

"You take her!" she lashed out, kicking him in the shin. She lost her balance and would have fallen if he hadn't grabbed her.

He pushed her back onto the bed. She struggled angrily. Then his full weight was on her and his tongue began forcing its way into her mouth. The pain shocked him as she bit down, and he could taste blood. Violently he pushed his knee between her legs. She relaxed suddenly. Her back arched, as though fighting against a gale, and she thrust herself against him, greedy with a passion she had never imagined.

Maggie Royal got up and took another bath. When she returned to bed Jared was lying on his back, staring at the ceiling. In the time they'd been together, she had become addicted to his body. She who had never liked to be touched wanted his hands on her continuously. His slow, sure fingers against her nipple could almost bring her to climax. She pressed his hand against it. The nerve ends stiffened at his touch, causing her nipples to become as hard, as tactile, as strong rubber.

His long hard body lay against her, pinning her to the soft bed. Claridge's fine linen sheets were cold. They felt the way the clothes taken out of the cold closet at Chatfield felt, frigid, icy, clammy. In spite of Jared's warmth, she shivered. She wondered if she could be catching the flu she'd avoided all winter.

Suddenly, uncontrollably, the hated tears were running down her cheeks again.

"It's over, Jared. I know it. Us. I can't stay here after you go. When I hear Big Ben, see the lions in Trafalgar Square. When the tulips are blooming like crazy. Mist lies in the hollows and there is the scent of roses and new-mown hay and I view a fox, its coat shining in the patches of sunlight as it runs down a long vale toward a steepled village."

"Don't, Maggie Royal," Jared whispered as she clung to him. "We're back in the hunt now. We'll finish soon, on top!"

"That's a lousy pun." The tears were running down the sides of her face onto the sheet. "I don't know why I'm crying. Dammit, I never cry!"

Jared began kissing the tears away. "Blow your nose," he said. "Dammit, you never have a handkerchief. I don't either."

She thought of Warren, who always had a clean handkerchief.

"Close," Jared whispered as the air-raid alert rent the night with its eerie keening notes. "Somewhere near Belgravia."

Jared kissed her forehead, her eyelids, and her nose. He kissed the place at the corner of her mouth, and then her mouth. His hands moved over her body, and she began to feel the unfolding, like one of the camellias at Great Oak, changing from winter's frozen buds to the warmth of sun and spring, as the blossoms began slowly to open, a petal at a time.

351

While the sirens howled and London burned, they made love, violently, with terrible urgency.

She lay awake while Jared slept. She'd learned not to listen to the bombs. Once you started, it was like a dog barking somewhere in the night. You lay tensely, waiting for the next bark. When she heard the bomb explode, she felt relief. God knows how many people had died, but she had survived. She thought of waking Jared, making love again. Somewhere she'd read the statistics on pregnancies in cities that were being bombarded. The more ferocious the bombings, the higher the rate.

She got out of bed and went to the window. Here and there fires burned, like candles flickering over the blacked-out city. She wondered if she was pregnant and then decided that if she was she would keep the baby. She would not do what Brenda intended as soon as Ian left.

She heard Jared turn in bed; then he began to thrash about. "Jerry, ten o'clock high," he cried out. "Get 'im for Chrissake. Jesus, there's another . . ."

"Jared." She went to him and took him in her arms. He made a noise that sounded like a sob. Then he was fully awake. "Just a dream," he said. "Didn't mean to wake you. There go the sirens again."

Outside, there was the sound of bombs and running feet. She heard none of it. Only the beating of their hearts as there, in the dark for a brief moment in time, only the present existed.

She awoke to find Jared had pulled back the blackout curtains and was gazing out at the rain-filled sky, bristling with barrage balloons.

"My God, it's dark out there. London seems to be lying under permanent fog. Sky's either filled with Germans or giants with weak kidneys. We're either being bombed or caught in a rainstorm!"

"My feet are cold again, Jared." She raised herself on an elbow. "Must you go?"

He swung around, facing her. "I'll meet you back here. We'll celebrate. Bath soap and champagne cocktails. I'll warm your feet!"

"And General Montgomery?"

"Monty won't mind." Jared grinned. "Not when I describe to him—"

She threw her pillow at him. Then her nose was against his chest and his face was buried in her hair and her laughter became tears.

"Honestly," she managed finally, "I don't know what has come over me. I never cry. Well, almost never. There was that time the pigs died!"

He held her tighter.

Big Ben began tolling the hour.

Jared grabbed his bag.

"Jared, please be careful."

He grinned his crooked grin. His eyes were a very bright green.

"Darling Maggie Royal. I'm the carefulest guy you'll ever meet. I'll live to be a thousand."

"Give 'em effing hell!" she called as the door slammed shut.

She heard his footsteps die out and sat down slowly on the bed. For a long time she stared at the notes in the corner she had forgotten to pick up.

•   •

At first glance it didn't register what was missing. Then the realization dawned on Maggie Royal that it was the inside of the house. Rescuers were digging about in the smoking ruins. She stumbled over a charred object. It was barely recognizable as the teddy bear Ian had given Sprat on his last leave. One of Brenda's high-heeled satin bedroom pumps with the fur pom-poms on the front had fallen sideways on the doorstep.

Mr. Potts stopped her. "You can't go in there, miss."

"Are they . . . ?" A glance at the warden's face gave her the answer.

"Her ladyship was well liked," he said sadly, shaking his head.

Ian sat motionless on a pile of rubble. He didn't move or look up as she approached. She put her arms around his shoulders, holding him as tightly as she could to keep him from shaking.

"The plane was delayed," he said dully. "I just arrived." He looked up. His eyes were glazed with pain and anguish. "I managed leave to tell her I knew about Bertie, Rex St. Clair, and the rest and that when the war was over I intended to divorce . . ." His voice broke and he lowered his face in his hands.

Rescuers were digging through the rubble. One called out, "Scrub this one! Blood's stale. It's a stiff!"

Warren was the only person she could think of to turn to. She had not seen him for weeks. Now she desperately wanted his reassuring presence. They agreed to meet at the Ritz.

She left the telephone kiosk and began walking blindly. The rain had stopped and a daffodil-colored sun fought to free itself from black clouds. A long-legged English girl came swinging by on the arm of a handsome Coldstreamer. She walked with Brenda's fluid grace, and when she turned, Maggie Royal saw that she had the same hyacinth-blue eyes, high cheekbones, and beautiful English skin. A cold sense of bereavement swept over her, like the wind making little wavelets in the round pond where the old men continued, despite the bombs, to sail their boats.

In her mind's eye she saw Brenda walking along Regent Street on Bertie's arm, laughing at something outrageous he had just said. Or as she had seen her on that unforgettable day when she rode her big chestnut across the shires, totally at one with her horse and her country.

Warren looked worn and grave when she met him at the entrance to the bar. The silver-haired waiter inside led them to a table in the corner.

"One of the wardens told me her ladyship bought it," he said sadly. "I'm very sorry, miss. We all liked her ladyship."

In spite of the wartime shortage, he somehow managed to produce two glasses of whiskey.

Instead of diluting it, making it last as long as possible, Warren drank his neat. Maggie Royal sipped hers, feeling suddenly ill. She told him about Ian. "I can't think of anything that will help him."

Warren reached across the table and took her hand in his. "Nobody ever really helps another. We can only help others to help themselves."

There was such sadness in his voice that she looked up at him, startled. She thought of what he had told her about the grim, austere house on Beacon Street, the lonely little boy sitting by the window, waiting for his mother to return from her endless committee meetings. Ordering him upstairs to the third-floor nursery because she had telephone calls to make about tomorrow's meeting . . .

Suddenly she clutched the edge of the table. "Dear God, Warren, I think I'm going to be sick. My God, I can't. Not at the Ritz!"

"Come along." He rose quickly and helped her out of her chair. "Fresh air will help."

He apologized to the old waiter and told him they would be back.

They walked to Green Park, found an empty bench, and sat down. A nanny wearing a blue cape with a red lining went past, pushing a sleeping baby in a pram with one hand, holding on to a small boy whose fair hair shone in the sunlight with the other.

"Sprat, also . . ." She wept onto his chest, great racking sobs that seemed to have broken forth from some dark buried place inside. Her nose was running and she no longer cared. Warren pulled out the large white, carefully pressed linen handkerchief that he always wore folded exactly right in his breast pocket, with only the tip showing. She thrust it away. "I'll get it dirty. Like guest towels. I'm always afraid to use them."

"I have an extra." He began gently wiping her face, and she thought how like him, always to have an extra!

"Sorry," she managed after a while. She blew her nose and pushed back her hair. "It's just that I feel diminished. John Donne and all that." She reached into her purse. "I have the article for the paper, if you wouldn't mind sending it off."

"You know I will."

She swallowed and blew her nose. "You're a dear, kind, good man, Warren. A girl can count on you."

His face softened. He stretched out his hand. "Magdalena, marry me."

"I can't Warren," she said quietly. "I'm pregnant."

They took the train to Chatfield for the memorial service. Twitchy was a pallbearer. "Ring me up," he said as he ushered them into a front

354

pew. "Shooting's top-hole just now. Cubhunting will begin soon. Glad to lend you a horse."

The Duke and Ian came in as the service was about to begin. The Duke looked very old and frail in his plain clothes, the dark pinstripe suit, like Ian's, made by the regimental tailor, stiff collar, Guards tie, and black armband. They sat alone in the family pew with the empty fireplace in the corner. Once during the service she saw Ian's shoulders shake almost imperceptibly. But the old Duke did not move. He sat as if he'd been arrranged on the hard wooden bench, set in position with an unseen iron bar placed behind him to keep him rigidly upright.

The little church was jammed, every seat taken and people standing outside in the graveyard. Farmers, foxhunters, villagers, and the staff. Nanny, Cook, and Effie had settled their differences and sat together with the silent Holmes, their heads bowed, handkerchiefs clasped in their hands. The Chatfield set. The long, leggy girls and beautiful young men, their number decimated by death on some far-flung battlefield.

Mr. and Mrs. Hanson and all the little Hansons and their evacuees sat in a rear pew. Mrs. Hanson wept openly, holding an orange rag that looked as if it had been cut from the skirt of her orange gown. "Her ladyship was a real true lady," she snuffled when Maggie Royal went up to speak to her.

Jamie Bush responded shyly when she hugged him, and asked when she could come to see him. He had been with the Hansons less than a month. Still, he had gained weight and there was color in his cheeks. He was riding now, he said happily, Sprat's pony, which the Duke had sent to the Hansons.

The family vault had been opened. It was not far from where Ian had picked up the "English earth" on that last weekend at Chatfield. Two caskets, one large and one small, contained the remains rescue workers had managed to find. Maggie Royal dropped the dog roses and honeysuckle and flowering thyme Brenda had loved when they rode out together on top of the caskets.

She thought of Brenda's hands, capable of holding the most difficult horses, of making munitions and cleaning silver, soft and creamed on top, like her face, tough and capable, yet sensitive enough that if the palm was turned over she could feel a petal drop. "Why didst thou promise such a beauteous day," she said to herself, "and make her travel forth without a cloak?" She could hear Brenda saying, as the old huntsman blew the long, haunting notes of "Gone to Ground": "Put it by. The days have been."

Warren stood with his head bowed, his hat in his hand. "Poor Brenda. Beautiful, brittle, doomed. Making munitions and making love. That combination of seeming frailty and strength, sensuous yet frigid. Patriotic and patrician and pleasure-loving. Frittering her life away as arbiter of domestic squabbles or on the back of a horse. And yet . . ."

355

He made a helpless gesture. "Without her the world won't be as much fun!"

Monica Bourne-Smith rented Maggie Royal a bed-sitter in the house on Eaton Place.

In mid-August Terence Ratcliff rang her up to tell her that the special mission Jared had volunteered for was almost finished and she was to meet him at Claridge's the following afternoon.

She had her hair done, and arranged with the matron at the hospital to trade shifts.

The next afternoon she dressed in the green silk and matching coat Miss Jarvis had made from the material bought with Nanny's coupons. As she adjusted the skirt she realized she had put on weight. Her breasts were fuller. She remembered how they felt when Jared touched them. How would he react when she told him about the baby? Surely he would be pleased.

She waited at Claridge's until midnight, rooted there like the potted plants. She must have dozed, for suddenly it was daylight. Rising, she wrapped her crumpled finery around her and crept furtively past the mustachioed room clerk and doorman out into the street.

She rang up the matron from her flat and told her she was ill. "That's quite all right," the matron replied. "I said to myself yesterday that you looked a bit under the weather."

When Big Ben struck noon there was still no word. Maggie Royal picked up the telephone to see if it was working. It was.

At teatime she forced herself to drink a cup and eat a piece of dry toast. Then she sat huddled in a chair, willing the telephone to ring. He'll call, she told herself, before Big Ben chimes again.

At midnight when the clock chimed there was still no word.

It was another gray-filled dawn. The green dress was wrinkled and there was a run in her last pair of stockings.

Jared noticed such details. Quickly she rubbed makeup on her smooth white legs and began drawing a "stocking seam" up the back of her calf with an eyebrow pencil. It reminded her of the times she had seen Brenda using this substitute for stockings, now so hard to come by. Now she longed for Brenda's breezy optimism. Even Warren's dry reassurance.

Finally she could stand it no longer. She rang up the embassy, only to be told Warren was not in London. His secretary said he was on an assignment with the Ambassador and she did not know when they would return.

She decided to walk to Grosvenor Square. There she was directed to a young foreign-service officer who told her anything pertaining to air operations was top-secret. After using every name she could think of, from the duke's friend Prime Minister Churchill to General Eisenhower, she persuaded the young man to call her if he received any news.

356

She returned to the flat, undressed, took a bath, and again sat down to wait.

The radio reported that an intense aerial campaign was being waged against the V-2, that both the RAF and American planes were bombing storage depots and launching sites.

The embassy man rang up at ten P.M. Word had been received that Lieutenant Stark's plane was down, somewhere in German-occupied France. He was sorry but all reports indicated little if any hope of survivors.

She remembered Gramma saying she regretted not making each moment of her life memorable. She had mistakenly thought there would be years of marriage, of bringing up children, of time to argue and quarrel, hurt one another and make up. "Maybe it's best to live as our ancestors did," she commented once, "in the daily awareness that death walks with us, hand in hand."

Brenda had said the way to live was from one fence to the next, one alert to the next, making the most of the moment.

Now the present was the past. Do not cry for Johnny in the sky/ Save your tears for him in later years/ Better far to keep your head/ And see his children fed!

Put it by. The days have been!

The features she had done on life in wartime London had been well received. The last article, the one she had written at Claridge's after Jared left, had been run on the front page and syndicated. A publisher wrote he would like to compile them into book form. He asked if she would do several more on the post–D-Day aspects of living and rebuilding. She did not feel like writing or seeing people. She was racked by morning sickness and a sense of hopelessness. It did no good to tell herself how lucky she was, that she had not lost her family or all her worldly possessions. She was convinced she was a failure. Finally she became so ill she was unable to work at the hospital.

Monica Bourne-Smith, who also was living in the house, had changed during the past year. She no longer wore beautiful clothes or slept most of the day. Because of her father's influence, she had an important job in the Operations Room at 10 Downing Street. She brought Maggie Royal hot Bovril on her way to work and begged her to "see that gorgeous hulk from the embassy who has been camping on the doorstep." She set the tray down beside Maggie Royal's bed, adding, "He's too good to waste, darling. If you don't want him, I'll set my cap for him." She winked and put her Wren officer's tricorn at a rakish angle.

"Okay." Maggie Royal managed a smile. "Send him up. And, Monica, thank you."

"Think nothing of it," Monica replied. Pausing in the doorway, she added, "You should have a hysterectomy. Then you wouldn't have to muck about with all that fuss. 'Bye, love. Ta-ta for now!"

Warren came up the two long flights of stairs, into the blacked-out room. He stood holding his homburg, looking tired and worried and uneasy. "I've made some inquiries," he said stiffly. "I've got the name of a man. He's supposed to be safe!"

Maggie Royal could tell that he had hated making the "inquiries," that only his highly developed sense of honor had forced him into such an embarrassing position.

"Dear Warren." She stretched out her hand. "Come. Sit on the bed. I know how difficult this is for you. Warren, how can I ever thank you! But I'm going to have this baby. I've thought it all out. Look, when you think of all the people who have died, right here in London, in Berlin, Leningrad, Bataan, and Guadalcanal. . . . Children in the cities. Blinded by glass splinters, burned by incendiaries, maimed for life if there's any life left." She stopped. She didn't mean to be melodramatic. "Warren, it wouldn't be right to . . . well, you know."

He sat down, looking oddly relieved. "Are you quite sure?"

She gave a short laugh. "Funny, isn't it? I was so superior. All those girls in the parks. Knocked up. I forgot—it has a different meaning at home than it does here. Turkey in the oven. Preggers. A bloody riot, Warren, a bloody—"

And all at once he was holding her, hard. She clung to him, rocking back and forth, holding on to him as if her life depended on it.

The next morning she got out of bed and dressed, determined to return to work. She reached the lower level of the tube when she felt a knifelike pain. She managed to stay on her feet until she found a lavatory.

An ancient char was mopping the tile floor. Maggie Royal rushed past her, spattering the freshly scrubbed tiles with blood. It seemed a terrible thing to lose Jared's child in this way. She felt empty, bereft, as she took off the lace underpants he had admired and stuffed them up inside of her.

"There, there, dearie," the lavatory attendant crooned. "Have a sit-down and a cuppa." From an electric kettle boiling in a tiny cubbyhole she produced a white tea. Maggie Royal sat on the bench, motionless, staring fixedly at a crack in the tiles where a "dinkie" hair curler had fallen. Her tea grew cold while she rubbed her hands together, subconsciously wondering if they would ever feel warm again.

"There, there, dearie," the woman repeated sympathetically, patting her shoulder. "I'll just get you a sanitary towel."

After what seemed a very long time, she helped Maggie Royal to the street and saw her into a taxi, before returning to her cavernous domain to mop up the floor.

In October all remaining hope died. Jared's copilot, a lanky Californian named Bus, who had replaced Chuck, had escaped via the

358

French underground. He came to see Maggie Royal and told her that the mission Jared had volunteered for was top-secret. Because of military security, he could not disclose details. All he could tell her was that the plane had crashed and exploded.

"No chance he might have jumped?"

Bus was adamant. "I barely made it myself."

Maggie Royal spent long hours at the hospital. She went to the theater with Warren and to Wickwold weekends. They took long walks and she learned to name some of the birds and recognize their calls. She dined with Warren at the little restaurants that he knew, where the headwaiters knew him. They drank wine and laughed together and she listened to him speak authoritatively on politics and foreign policy. He told her about the trips he had made with the Ambassador and amusing anecdotes about Prime Minister Churchill and President Roosevelt. Maggie Royal listened and admired his ease and articulateness and beautiful manners, but the deep secret personal part of her remained untouched.

It was only when she heard the words of a tune they had danced to, hurried past Claridge's or the Ritz, or saw a well-shaped dark head in a crowd that her reserve crumbled and she struggled to regain the frozen numbness that obliterated feeling.

She could have gone home to America, but something held her, made her feel she must see it through. She set up her battered typewriter on a table by the blacked-out window and wrote. At first she typed aimlessly, anecdotes, conversations, incidents. As time passed, the material began to achieve a kind of form. Trying to ease the pain of her patients at the hospital left no room for self-pity.

She listened to the men's ravings brought on by morphine. They told her they wished they'd been left for dead. They had no desire to leave the hospital and go home, and there was little she could do to keep them from staring all day at the ceiling, their eyes deadened and glazed from drugs.

She heard the final requests of those who were dying. Some were simple and loving and silly. There was a soldier from Sussex who was a lepidopterist. During the Normandy landings he had seen a rare specimen, usually found only in southern Spain and North Africa, perched on the top of a tank. He had forgotten about the war, the guns blazing around him, and gone to rescue it. A bomb had landed at the place where he had been standing, killing three of the tank crew. Although he was now dying of bone cancer, he had survived D Day to bring the dead butterfly home to England. It was a particularly beautiful specimen, and he wanted it sent to his father.

• • •

On a November weekend Warren and Maggie Royal revisited Chatfield. It was a warm day of bright sunshine. The brake fern on the hills was turning bronze and yellow. Some had been cut and left to dry on the hillsides where Brenda and Maggie Royal had cub-hunted in the fall. Juniper berries shone blue against the green along lanes where they had roaded hounds. By the tennis court, where they'd so often had tea, the fruit of the Spanish chestnut was in full flower.

In the rose garden the newly developed *Peace* rose, named in celebration of the end of the French occupation, that the Duke had ordered from America was still blooming, pale yellow petals veined with pink.

They found the Duke propped up against the pillows in his vast canopied bed. He looked very frail and spoke with labored breath. When Maggie Royal mentioned Brenda's and Sprat's names he turned his face to the wall.

The evacuees were gone. "Scabies!" Nanny sniffed. "A wonder the young master was never infected!" Holmes had died, presumably as silently as he had lived. There was nobody left of the staff other than Nanny and Cook.

Cook apologized for there not being any lunch. "Just trays for his grace." She sighed. "Chatfield's not what it used to be when her ladyship was alive."

"Cook was always easy upset," Nanny sniffed when they went up to the nursery to see her. "The late Duchess of Norfolk's cook was never easy upset. Even when the Duchess brought twenty or more unexpected. The Duchess could always count on a good dinner, as you might say."

Maggie Royal suspected that in spite of Nanny's words, her longtime animosity toward Cook had been buried in the wake of tragedy and they were now united by the very abrasiveness of their longtime power struggle. She remembered how frightened she had been of the formidable governess. Now there was nothing any longer to fear. Nanny was merely a tired old woman who had devoted her life to her young charges. Deprived of them to bully and fret and fuss over, she was as powerless as her crippled hands, gnarled and swollen with arthritis and no longer able to hold her knitting needles.

She brewed tea for them on her nursery stove and offered them biscuits. Maggie Royal sat in the little nursery chair with the duck painted on the back, where she had often sat having tea with Brenda, Nanny, and Sprat.

Nanny read her thoughts. "It does seem to bring it all home, as you might say! It might not have happened if her ladyship had listened to my advice and not gone up to London. Those buzz bombs didn't sound too nice. But then, her ladyship was that headstrong, as you might say. I mind the time she took his lordship to the Savoy so that she could go dancing." Her lips narrowed disapprovingly. "Put him in a bathtub! Now, a bathtub is hardly the place for a marquess's son, as you might say! And without his liberty bodice! Her ladyship always forgot to put on his liberty bodice." She picked up the glass dome filled with different-colored layers of sand on the table beside her. "Brought it back from the seaside for the young master, I did." Her eyes filled with tears. "'E never did see it! To think," she added, "I gave him a good wigging before he went up to London. He *would* flush all his dinner down the toilet, said it was for the alligators to eat!"

Warren interrupted to say they should be going.

"I want to see Jamie Bush at the Hansons'," Maggie Royal said.

"Cook tells me she stopped there last week," Nanny said with a touch of her old asperity. "The cottage was in a state that was deplorable. Cook says Mrs. Hanson is in hospital, something about miscarrying her latest. Effie was left in charge, as you might say." Nanny's eloquent sniff indicated her feelings about Effie had not changed. "Cook says she was putting her hair in dinkies while her brat played on the dirty floor. The sink was piled high with dirty dishes . . ."

Nanny would have gone on happily detailing the deplorable state of the Hansons' domicile, as you might say, if Warren hadn't interrupted again to point out they really had to be leaving.

"I think you made her day when you mentioned the Hansons," Warren said after Maggie Royal had hugged Nanny and said a final good-bye and they were on their way down the stairs.

They went into the silent drawing room. The heavy curtains were pulled shut and there were dust covers on the furniture.

"There was so much life here," Maggie Royal said, looking at the painting of Brenda and Ian over the fireplace. "All those nights when Brenda held court. There would be kippers 'with heads and tails' or beer from the base or Ian's Scotch or that ghastly punch Brenda made that got everyone tiddly. The gramophone would be playing 'I'll Be Seeing You.' Some people would dance. Others would be sprawled on sofas sitting at Brenda's feet. Brenda in one of her little dresses—'I've had it for donkey's years, love.' "

"I'll be seeing you . . ." The tinny rhythm of the worn, scratched record ran through her head. Whenever she heard it she would see Brenda, her lovely legs drawn up under her on the sofa, Mick tucked under one arm while she gesticulated with her other, waving a silver cup or mug of cocoa, laughing in the firelight, teasing Bertie: "Do you remember when we pinned the rose on the back of your morning coat just before you went into the Royal Enclosure to meet the King and Queen?"

Williams, the old head lad, hobbled out to greet them. The stable yards were empty. The young horses Ian had loved, "the untried two-year-olds" he had remarked on the last weekend he was home, had been sold. The staff horses had been put down. Only Brenda's chestnut, Highwayman, and Stalker remained in the orchard pasture, where in the fall they had picked the hardy green apples, filling bags for the horses.

The old huntsman told Maggie Royal he remembered the day she "pounded the hunt" and the time the bombs went off. "Not one of my lads lifted 'is 'ead!" He went on speaking of the hunts they'd had as "his lads" in the kennels leaped against the bars of their runs, an ecstasy of ears and tongues and teeth anxious for their wartime meal of maize and boiled potatoes, simmering on the kennel cook-stove.

Maggie Royal asked what would happen to the hunt. He told her Twitchy and Pat Weston were to take over until Ian returned from the war. Possibly Angela would be a field master. "Won't be the same, miss," he murmured sadly. "Never again the way it was in the great days. With her ladyship . . ." His voice caught. "And," he added politely, "yourself on old Stalker, miss." He turned to Warren. "Only one I ever saw outside of his lordship could ride the old horse, he being that strong!"

The potholed lane was sunk deep into the earth. Grassy banks crowned with ramparts of golden gorse lined either side. It was barely wide enough for the car, and at each bump Thomas' back went rigid with offense.

"Springs won't stand for it, sir," he commented after one particularly ominous crash into a water-filled trench.

Thomas piloted the reluctant Rolls between the remains of the vintage lorry and a wagon with a missing wheel and brought the car to a stop in front of the cottage gate, hanging on one hinge.

"This it, sir?" he inquired of Warren. His face registered intense disapproval.

Whereas the village gardens were wonders of neatness and floral design, the Hansons' yard held only untidy earth littered with equally untidy children digging in it.

At sight of the Rolls they rose in a body and ran into the house, crying, "Miss McDermott, Jamie's lady, is here!"

Jamie, who had somehow gotten the word, came galloping across the field bareback on Sprat's pony. In spite of the general feeling of contempt for Mrs. Hanson's housekeeping and dietary skills, the little slum child looked wonderfully healthy. His city pallor was gone. There was color in his cheeks and his eyes sparkled with the happiness of riding and seeing them. As he escorted them to the cottage, he told them about the pony, the dead mouse he'd found squashed by a wagon, the dog Pip that chased rabbits, and other thrilling country discoveries. He was also a junior salvage collector and had collected more than anyone else in the village. "Doesn't have to go far," Warren commented, gazing around the junk-filled premises.

Inside the house two of the older girls were feeding the infants, one of whom was Effie's latest love child, tied to their high chairs with bits of brown string. Their faces were smeared with what appeared to be several days' accumulation of an assortment of jams, ranging from light apricot to raspberry.

At sight of Warren and Maggie Royal, the hands holding the bread ceased in midair and Effie, whose hair was in paper bags in preparation for the Saturday-night dance at the airdrome, dropped a glob of margarine onto her pinafore. Only the mongrel, Pip, and a rooster continued their casual wandering, the dog eating bits of fallen bread while the rooster pecked at the debris by the stove.

Jamie pushed one of the children off a rush-bottomed chair from which most of the rushes had come loose, grabbed a pair of pink bloomers that had fallen behind it, wiped off some of the jam sticking to its seat, and offered it to Maggie Royal.

Warren sat down on the sagging settee, crossed his elegant silk-clad ankles as though he were in the Ambassador's office, and pulled out his pipe. He asked Effie if she minded if he smoked. The children found the question hilarious, bursting into wild giggles as he began carefully to fill his pipe.

"Where is your father?" Maggie Royal asked Effie. She replied that he was at the Rose and Crown and that her mother was returning from the hospital that afternoon. "Don't you think it would be nice to tidy up before she gets here?" Maggie Royal asked. "I'll help. So will Mr. Chadwick, won't you, Warren?"

Warren, who had just lit his pipe, began to cough.

"Fine," Maggie Royal exclaimed. "I knew you'd help. Now, all we have to do is send Thomas to the store for carbolic soap and Jeyes fluid."

Warren threw her a glance that told her he'd as soon tell the Ambassador to go jump in the Thames as transmit her request to Thomas outside, carefully guarding the Rolls from an expected invasion by the evacuees.

"First we'll wash the dishes," Maggie Royal said briskly.

She sent Jamie to fill the kettle and put it on the stove. The water was boiling when Warren returned carrying a broom, followed by the chauffeur with several bundles.

"Here's your shopping, miss." With a martyred air Thomas set washing soda, Vim scouring powder, soap flakes, a wire pot cleaner, and Jeyes fluid down on the table amid the tea debris and fled back to the car to protect it from the children clustered around it.

"Took a lot of coupons," Warren said, opening the box of Sylvan soap flakes.

Maggie Royal picked up what she thought was a smudged dish towel. It turned out to be a chemise. She threw it at Warren. With a resigned expression he set down his pipe and tied it around his waist.

"No, dear," she said, sliding an enormous pile of dishes into the boiling sudsy water. "You're to dry with it."

"Behind the ears?" Warren asked innocently, gazing at the filthy children crawling about the floor.

She understood why Brenda had chosen to shine silver. It was easier not to think when you had a pile of cutlery and greasy pots and pans to clean. Effie and an older evacuee, Rose, helped Warren to dry and stack. When the pile had been done away with, Maggie Royal set about scouring the sink and wiping off the stove. Not wanting to stop this mindless activity, she asked Effie to collect the clothes strewn around the room and began washing them on the scrub board that had been standing by the sink.

Warren picked up the broom and swept what Pip, the dog, and the rooster had left on the floor out into the yard.

"When is Leftenant Stark coming to see me?" Jamie asked. "Every time the planes go over, I count bees. I want to tell him about riding the pony."

It was the moment she had dreaded.

"He's not coming back, Jamie," she said finally, rubbing a pair of coveralls as hard as she could. "He was pranged. Somewhere in France."

Jamie's face crumpled, like tissue paper caught in a fist.

Maggie Royal knelt down on the grimy floor and put her soapy arms around the little boy. "I'm sorry, Jamie."

He dropped the dice that had been clenched in his fist. "Not the Leftenant!"

"I'm afraid so, Jamie." As he sobbed against her shoulder, she noticed something black crawling in his hair. It reminded her that work remained to be done. "You can carry the basket out, Jamie," she said. "Mr. Chadwick will help you hang the clothes on the line."

"Ain't no line," Jamie managed, fighting back tears.

"Well, use the fence."

More water was heated and Maggie Royal filled the tin tub that Effie unearthed in the dark hallway, along with half a rake, an old saddle, several mothy checked caps, Wellies, and an ancient mackintosh so dried and hardened it practically stood by itself.

The children were called in. Warren reached into his pockets and pulled out several packs of chewing gum, promising each a piece after their baths. To the children's delight he began singing the song currently going the rounds:

> Does your chewing gum lose its flavor
> On the bedpost overnight?
> When your mother says don't chew it
> Do you swallow it in spite?
> Do you stick it on your tonsils?
> Do you heave it left and right?
> Does your chewing gum lose its flavor
> On the bedpost overnight!

Several of the other children also had lice. "You wouldn't want the pony to get it," Maggie Royal told Jamie as she scrubbed his head with the Jeyes fluid she'd used to clean the garbage pail. "You'd have to shave off his nice mane and tail."

Jamie howled in anguish and ran from the room, rubbing his stinging scalp with Mrs. Hanson's orange petticoat he grabbed blindly from a chair. Maggie Royal wished that there was some outside pain she could inflict on herself that would help to do away with inside pain as easily as the disinfectant had managed to assuage Jamie's.

"There, that does it." She straightened up. The last child had been dunked and scrubbed. "Now Mrs. Hanson will find a nice clean house!"

"Are you sure you haven't forgotten anything?" Warren asked. His white shirt was grimy, his Porcellian tie askew, and there was a streak of soot across his cheek. "There are still the walls, the ceiling, the dog. Perhaps the horse needs a bath!"

His expression was so droll she couldn't help laughing. "I'll go say good-bye to Lancelot."

The old horse trotted up as she leaned over the fence. He thanked her for the dried apple she had brought from Chatfield by slobbering over the front of her suit. Then, with some of his old vigor he turned and kicked up his heels, let out a familiar farting sound, and set off across the field.

Thomas was almost in tears. The freshly laundered and deloused evacuees were playing ring around the Rolls, sitting like a shiny black olive in their midst. There were finger marks on the mudguards and long black bonnet.

Already Jamie's hurt seemed diminished. His tears had dried and he intimated that the Hansons' haphazard yet loving household was heaven. He said he would like to remain in the country when the war ended. Maybe he could get work as a lad, like Ernie, perhaps for a trainer, and ride out with the race horses.

Maggie Royal gave him a hug and another of Warren's chocolate bars and got into the car.

Warren rolled up the glass separating them from Thomas' rigid disapproving back, which visibly flinched each time the car was shaken by a rut or a pothole.

Warren sat smoking his pipe and staring out the window. "Well, my dear," he said after a while, "I had no idea you were such a good scrubber. Why don't you reconsider and marry me? I've been assigned as Deputy Chief of Mission in Portugal." He paused to relight his pipe. When it was burning to his satisfaction, he took it out of his mouth and said with slow deliberation, "I'd like you to go with me."

"Oh, Warren," she said helplessly. "Couldn't we just live together?"

"My intentions are strictly honorable." He brushed a sticky bread crumb from his trousers. She noticed it left a small grease spot. "I can never remember to send my suits to the cleaner's. I need somebody to remind me. Maggie Royal, I don't want to live in sin. It requires too much effort and subterfuge."

She gave his hand a quick affectionate squeeze. "You don't really need me. You'll be an Ambassador soon, and Ambassadors have valets to send their suits to the cleaner's."

At that moment the Rolls lurched and a particularly virulent bump threw her against him. Warren gave a kind of gasp. He set his pipe down in the Spode saucer that served as an ashtray and put his arms around her. "Magdalena, I love you. I need you. Say you'll marry me!"

She clung to him, finding him as strong and secure and somehow comforting as the rock on which his ancestors landed at Plymouth.

"All right, Warren," she answered, "if you're quite sure you're sure!"

BOOK THREE

· 8 ·
STARK ISLAND
1950

"An island always to come back to," Grandfather McDermott had said when he rebuilt Great Oak. Maggie Royal thought of Melville's lines that had been over the mantel in Jared's Long Point house: "Push not off from that isle; thou canst never return."

She had pushed off. Now she was returning. She told herself it was to buy the painting Warren wanted. But she knew that wasn't the true reason.

When there was no answer to her letter, she tried to call but was told there still wasn't a telephone on the island. As a last resort she telephoned the Plantation Bar, where they used to leave messages in the old days. Whoever answered the telephone said that the island boat would be at the Stark Island dock at four the following afternoon. She called Mr. Charles for a hair appointment and asked Warren's secretary to make reservations on a morning flight to Atlanta. The train had long since ceased to run. She would have to take the feeder plane to Starksville.

A wide concrete runway replaced the dirt strip where Jared had practiced takeoffs and landings, and a large modern terminal stood in place of the original Starksville flying school.

Advertisements in display cases lined the way to the baggage collection.

GWINNETT ISLAND

A championship golf course
A terrific tennis complex
Sailing and boating in deep-water sounds
Nine miles from the heart of Starksville
A Tarrington Community

She collected her bags and hired a taxi. The great oaks that had lined the road to Starksville had been cut down. The once open country where on that long-ago day the Starksville Hunt hounds had run a fox up the chimney of the little cabin was completely built up. Billboards lined the highway where Gramma had ordered Jazzbo to hack down the Burma-Shave signs with the ax they carried in the trunk of the Packard. Used-car dealers had contrived to make the approaches as garish as the colored pennants that floated over their canopies. They were interspersed with Negro shacks, "shotgun houses" that a bullet could travel through, emerging in the backyard after terrorizing the inmates. Sheets of crumpled tin served as their roofs. Children and dogs and an occasional pig rooted among rusted cans and refuse.

The railyards were overgrown and the siding where the *Maggie Royal* once stood in all its polished pristine grandeur was high in weeds.

Maggie Royal's eyes blurred. She was overcome with *saudade,* the Portuguese word for the remembrance of things past. She was on the *Maggie Royal* and it was slowing down. She was standing in the corridor with the luggage piled around her, stooping to see the shacks and cotton fields on the outskirts of Starksville. She was sixteen and it was the Christmas vacation of her coming-out party. "Brush you off, Miss Maggie Royal," Cuffee said as she waited for the door to open. Then with a wide white grin. "Last stop, Miss Maggie Royal!"

There was nothing she wanted to see in Starksville. The great-aunts had died while she was in Portugal. First Aunt Amy and then Aunt Meg. The old house of mellow brick and wrought iron, with its galloping veranda, draped in wisteria, had been stripped of furnishings (Maggie Royal wondered about the fleas) and was now open to the public as a historic house, part of Big Boy Tarrington's Starksville Square complex.

The town, once a quaint and picturesque, slow-paced Southern community, with its lovely old trees and languid sense of time, its green lawns and gardens of camellias, magnolias, and oleanders, had succumbed to twentieth-century commercialism. The new Golden Isles replaced the Hall House, the old hotel where Robert E. Lee had stayed when he came to organize the Southern command of the Confederacy. To kill time until the four-o'clock boat, Maggie Royal sampled the Colonial-style Buffet, Starksville she-crab soup flavored with sherry, a Lymon Hall hamburger with black-eyed peas and a tomato, served with the house specialty, brittlebread. In her mind's eye she saw Cook Ada laying the dough out on big flat baking sheets, baking until it was the color and texture of fine leather, then taking it off hot, rolling it into folds and layers.

She paid her bill and left quickly, leaving half the hamburger and all the brittlebread. A cabdriver took her to the private dock along the waterfront that was reserved for the Stark Island boat.

Once it had been kept painted and free of trash. Now the wooden benches were rotting and paintless. A rusted wire basket overflowed with cans, cartons, papers, and fish heads, which, combined with the evil-smelling fumes from the pulp mill, were nauseating.

The old brick warehouses overlooking the sound, where cotton commerce had flourished during the nineteenth century, stood gaunt and gutted, waiting to be pulled down to make room for office buildings and apartments. The Plantation Bar now had a blue-and-red neon sign over the swinging doors. As Maggie Royal watched, they swung open and three soldiers from the nearby base catapulted out onto the street, followed by shrill laughter and catcalls from within.

A shrimp boat, its rakish bow slicing through the bourbon-brown water as its captain gunned the powerful diesel, pulled away from the adjoining pier.

The big black woman fishing from it did not glance up. She wore a floppy wide-brimmed felt hat and a pink shift. Her feet, in broken black shoes, dangled down over the pier. She could have been Gullah, one of the Stark Island Negroes, but there was no recognition in her face as she stared sullenly at Maggie Royal.

Cartons of groceries and fuel drums lined the island dock. Maggie Royal sat down on one of the benches, pulled the skirt of her navy Chanel suit down over her knees, and pretended to ignore the crews of the shrimp trawlers mending nets and lounging on the public dock alongside.

She tried to concentrate on the foreign-affairs section of *Time* in order to make what Warren called intelligent conversation at their next dinner party. She often wondered if any new information was ever forthcoming at the innumerable "important" social events people in Washington felt duty-bound to attend. It seemed to her that the earth-shaking pronouncements imparted in seeming secrecy by high officials were but recycled *Time* and *Newsweek* columns so imbued in public consciousness it was no longer possible to know what was real and what was filtered.

She put down the magazine and gazed out across the marshes and silver sound to the brooding outline of the island rising against the sky.

Suddenly cold wind swept in from the water. It was the second week in March, the month of radical changes in the weather, of sun-filled eighty-degree days changing overnight to freezing, of sudden storms sometimes making the sea so rough it was difficult for the island boat to make its twice-weekly run.

The Negroes called it the uneasy time, when the wind whined through the oaks, causing the hanging moss to writhe and dance in eerie, monstrous shapes. It was the time of year when babies cried fretfully, horses got colic, and the mules came down with distemper, to be treated by the Gullah remedy of fumes of tar and burned feathers.

It was the season of sudden death and doom, of divorce and a curious mood that settled over the island like the odd yellow haze obscuring the sun.

She gazed at the gray, refuse-strewn water and was no longer eager, anticipatory. The island couldn't be the way she remembered it. The magic with which she had invested it in her mind would have been stripped away, like the swinging curtains of moss on the great oaks Big Boy Tarrington had felled for his "Tarrington Communities."

"Here comes the Stark Island boat," one of the shrimpers said, sending a jet of spittle onto a bollard. He was unshaven and heavyset. His feet were bare and he wore a fish knife attached to his leather belt. "That bastard Stark just missed putting a bullet through me the other night." He bent down and rubbed his calf. "Son-of-a-bitch dawg of his got me in the leg. One of these nights I'm gonna get that dawg."

"Why you keep going over there?" his friend, mending a net, asked. "You know how Stark feels about people comin' onto that island!"

"Well, I went over to drink some beer. Look around. Maybe get me a deer."

"I wouldn't go on that island. Bad things happen there. They say Stark'll shoot you dead if he finds you trespassin'."

The first shrimper patted his knife. "Who he think he is, anyhow?"

"He's a Stark. That's who. Time was, the Starks owned everything there was to own in these parts."

"Only thing I know, he's a bastard," the first shrimper said positively, and spat again.

The boat—*Great Oak V,* it said on the bow in faded blue letters—came alongside the dock. It was a shrimp trawler converted to cargo carrier. The back deck had been cleared of winch and nets to make space for island necessities, fuel drums, and food supplies. A large ferocious-looking hound with the yellow-and-black "leopard" markings of Cullen's old "pig dogs" stood on the bow.

Jared came out of the wheelhouse. He called to the shrimper mending the net to make the boat fast, and threw him a line. With difficulty he swung his stiff leg over the rail and onto the dock. He limped to a bollard and secured the stern line.

Maggie Royal started to rise and greet him, but he hurried past her, unseeing.

The dog remained on the bow, its front paws on the rail. One of its eyes was a milky blue color, the other brown and baleful as it fastened them on the shrimpers, growling.

There was something odd about Jared. His eyes! The green she could never forget looked black, like the still island pools. Black with a green glaze that did not move. His face was gaunt, white, with a yellow tinge, as though he was suffering from one of the fevers once prevalent on the island.

A cold sick feeling of apprehension swept over her, like the chill wind moving in from the sound.

She watched him come out of the bar. He was carrying a bag and walked more slowly now. She recognized the old tweed jacket with chamois patches at the elbows from his college days. He had on an open-neck blue button-down shirt, khakis, and sneakers. He was bare-headed, and his black hair was streaked with gray.

Gone was the easy grace. He moved awkwardly, thrusting his lame leg forward. Still, he was an impressive man. There was that old air of defiance, the quality of command that could not go unnoticed. She was aware of the heads of passersby turning, of the shrimpers' gaze following him.

His face was set, unsmiling and unshaven, the blue-black stubble like specks of gunpowder. He deposited the bag, cold beer, and several bottles of bourbon on the deck of the boat and started to load the cartons from the dock. The shrimper with the knife turned away and spat into the water. Jared straightened up and glanced around. His eyes fell on Maggie Royal. It was as though they were gazing into nothing.

She took off her sunglasses and stood up. "Jared. It's me. Maggie Royal."

They stood and looked at each other like strangers waiting to be introduced.

"Maggie Royal?" His voice seemed to come from a great distance.

"Well, Jared," she managed finally, "aren't you going to ask me aboard? Didn't you get my message?"

"Message?"

"Yes, at the Plantation Bar."

"I forgot to ask." He fumbled for a cigarette, and she saw that his hand was shaking. "You're coming to the island?"

"Yes, Jared. That's why I'm here. There are some things to talk over. What to do about Stark Island, for instance."

He was immediately defensive. "What about the island?"

"Why, nothing, really. Sparrow thought . . ."

"Just what did Sparrow think?"

"Oh, Jared." She was appalled. "Nothing, Jared. Honestly. I'll explain when we get to the island."

"You won't be comfortable. I live very simply."

"Jared, I don't mind. Truly." She was almost in tears.

"How long will you be staying?"

"Only until Friday."

"Forty-eight hours." He sounded relieved. "Okay. Let's get started."

He picked up her suitcase and the alligator-skin cosmetic case from Elizabeth Arden that Warren had given her at Christmas. His expression of distaste reminded her of his fondness for the island alligators and his hatred of the poachers who killed them for their hides.

The spotted dog also seemed to resent her. He stood guarding the gangway, eyeing her suspiciously.

Like a blind person reassuring herself that she was in the right place, she put out her hand to touch him. The dog cringed away. Baring his teeth, he emitted a low growl.

"It's all right, Poacher," Jared reassured him. At the sound of his voice, the dog relaxed. Placing his front paws back on the rail, he re-directed his attention to the watching shrimpers.

Jared eyed her high heels with the same expression he had worn when he picked up the alligator case. He did not offer to help her as she teetered aboard.

The diesel roared into life.

"Hey, you guys. Mind casting me off?"

When the shrimper with the knife failed to respond, his friend put down the net he was mending and rose slowly. Grudgingly he picked up the line that had been looped around the bollard and tossed it back onto the bow.

"Thanks," Jared called to him, but the man did not glance back or reply.

The boat moved away from the pier, churning the filthy water frothed with the acids and wastes from his father-in-law's mill. It circled and then headed east, toward the island, its roughened outline black against the leaden sheen of the stained water.

"It may be cold," Jared called above the engine's noise. "You'll be more comfortable in the cabin."

The dog's strange eyes followed her as she went inside, and the dis-appointment of this meeting was as though the shrimper's knife was twisting in her heart.

She sat on a hard wooden bench. Cartons of groceries, rolls of canvas, and a box of paints were piled on deck. Her elegant luggage looked as out-of-place as she felt. The boat gathered speed and the har-bor and paper mill fell behind it. She looked out at the lowering sun turning the marshes to gold. Wild ducks rose squawking as they passed. A blue heron stood delicately on one foot. It ignored them as it contin-ued its quest at the water's edge.

Through the glass partition separating the wheelhouse from the makeshift lounge she saw Jared sitting on a stool at the wheel. His back was to her. She remembered the silkiness of the hair growing in the hol-low of his neck, like that of a fine horse.

The palms of her hands twisted inside her white gloves.

As though aware that she was staring at him, Jared turned. Their eyes met, but in his there was no sign of warmth or welcome.

"Maybe you'd like to come up here." He spoke as he would to one traveling to the island for the first time. "You can see better."

She went out on deck, stumbled over a cleat in her unsuitable shoes, and forgot to lower her head as she entered the wheelhouse.

"You'd think I'd never been on a boat before," she said, chagrined, as she readjusted her hat.

"Take the damn thing off!" Jared said violently. He reached out and grabbed the brim and sent the Lily Daché she had worn in England planing out over the water.

"There," he added, observing her. "That's better. A little less Sea Island and more Stark Island. Here, sit on this." He shoved the stool to-

374

ward her and turned back to the helm. His smile fell away and she saw the lines around his mouth and the harshness of his cheekbones, like a rock ledge framing the sadness in his eyes.

She sat down obediently, hands clasped in her lap. She felt as though she was in the old schoolroom at Great Oak and being sent to Coventry.

The wind blew back her hair as the boat gathered speed, and she realized that Mr. Charles's best efforts would be ruined by the time they reached the Island.

Jared reached down into the cooler at his feet. "Want a beer?"

She shook her head.

"Cigarette?" He extended a crumpled pack. She started to refuse, remembering Warren's warnings, then recklessly accepted one. She bent her head to the flame from the match cupped in his hand. As soon as she inhaled, he drew back his hand, as if the lighted match had dropped onto it.

She began to cough. "I've almost stopped," she said when she could speak. "Warren, my husband, wants me to." She stumbled over the word "husband" as she had on the gangway in her high heels. Once again she was aware of his quick impersonal glance, as if they were strangers meeting for the first time. "You'll see him Friday," she added helplessly. "He's flying down to pick me up."

He opened a can of beer and drank thirstily. "Why did you come back?" he asked abruptly, setting the can down on the shelf in front of the wheel.

"I wanted to see . . ." She had been about to say "you." Quickly she amended it to "the island."

"Before the bulldozers move in!" He spoke with such vehemence she turned to stare at him. "Is that why you're here? To tell me you're selling out, like the rest?"

She started to speak, but he cut her off. Talking as if to himself, he continued. "My father-in-law won't rest until he gets Stark Island, adds it to his galaxy of resorts, turns it into another Gwinnett. Long lines of green-painted mailboxes, all identical, on streets with names like Palm Drive and Cabbage Way. Well, let me tell you this, Maggie Royal. The only way he'll set foot on Stark Island is over my dead body!"

A fishing boat was coming toward them. Jared swung the helm hard right to make room for it to pass.

On the port side lay the winding waterways and tidal creeks, twisting through the golden grass, where generations of Starks had waited in their flat-bottom boats for the wild ducks and geese to fly overhead. To starboard lay the island, the clam flats at the southern tip, their round pools mirroring the cloud-filled sky.

"Do you still dig clams?" she asked.

"Not often. Nobody to eat them." He tossed his cigarette out the wheelhouse door. She watched as the swift current spun it away.

The channel narrowed. Instead of smooth terraced lawns, a choked

375

wilderness of live oaks, palmetto, and marsh grass descended to the water's edge.

Suddenly she saw the familiar chimneys and the tower of Great Oak, riding over the tops of the trees.

Impulsively she reached out and grabbed Jared's arm. He looked down at her white-gloved hand and shrugged away from it.

"You won't find it the way it was in Gramma's day." The coldness in his voice was as though he had struck her.

The barnacled dock had lost a piling and sagged dangerously. The only thing that looked new was the freshly painted sign nailed to it.

PRIVATE ISLAND
POSITIVELY NO TRESPASSING

"Looks as if you mean it," she said.

"Damn right I mean it," he answered grimly. "Guys from the Army base drop down in helicopters at the north end of the island. They shine their searchlights in the animals' faces, blind them, and then shoot them. I've complained to the commanding officer, without results. Now if I catch people poaching I shoot them."

He put his hand on the dog that had come up beside him. "This is Poacher. Some bastard dropped him off onto the island from a boat. He lived off the land until he became so weak I was able to catch him. Newt and I fed him warm milk and whiskey for a week before he began to rally. Be careful until he gets to know you. He's not partial to humans."

"He looks like those fierce leopard dogs Cullen used to hunt the wild pigs."

Jared nodded. "Same breeding. I wouldn't be surprised if Cullen dropped him off."

"You mean he's still free? He wasn't convicted for burning your father's house?"

The scar on his forehead stood out and his knuckles were white as he clenched the wheel. "The good ole boys banded together to protect him. We could never break his alibi. Newt!" he bellowed. "Where are you?"

"You still have Newt," she said in amazement. "He must be close to eighty."

"Not quite," Jared replied as the black man emerged from the shadows, "but almost. He lives in the rooms off the kitchen with Cook Ada. She's in her nineties. The young ones have all left the settlement to work for Tarrington or the Army on the mainland. Maggie Royal . . ." His voice took on an urgency. "Don't pay any attention to what Newt or Cook Ada say. They're both a little teched. They tend to imagine things."

Jared secured the boat and helped her onto the dock, keeping her from falling when one of her heels caught in a rotting board. It was the way he would have unloaded a new horse he wasn't sure of.

376

"You come at your own risk," he warned, striding ahead.

As if echoing his words, a flock of boat-tailed grackles rose from an oak at the water's edge, yuk-yukking their shrill hoarse warning cry as they flew out over the marsh.

"Howdy, little missy. Lawdy, Lawdy. Little missy done come home." Newt gave her a wide toothless smile. His hair was as white as the dogwood starting to bud, and his skin was wrinkled and crepey, like that of the pelicans diving for fish in the sound. After Jared's coldness, the warmth of the old butler's welcome made her want to throw her arms around his ancient gnarled neck.

"I shore hope you gwine stay awhile." Newt glanced furtively at Jared's retreating back. "Maybe you can ease the trouble here at Great Oak!"

She didn't have a chance to ask him what he meant, for Jared was calling to her to hurry.

Her suitcase was heavy, but Jared picked it up as though it were made of cardboard and set it in the back of a battered topless jeep parked at the end of the pier.

"Hardly the same as the Packard with Jazzbo at the wheel," he said, holding the door, "but it'll have to do. I'll run you up to the house and come back for Newt and the supplies."

He threw his stiff leg over the closed door on the driver's side and slid down behind the wheel. Poacher leaped into the back. He gave Maggie Royal a resentful look, as though warning her to keep her distance, and then draped his head over Jared's shoulder. The jeep lurched, striking a pothole with a neck-breaking jolt. Pigs had rooted up the track, and the branches that had fallen across it had not been removed. Jared detoured around them, driving the scarred jeep through the brush and palmettos.

Gaunt bony horses mixed in with red island cattle and black-and-white pigs grazed on what had once been lawn. At sight of them she was almost afraid to ask the question foremost in her mind. "Are King and Azilia alive?" she shouted over the noise of the motor.

"King was dead when I got back. Nobody could tell me how he died. Maybe Cullen shot him." Again his smoldering anger reached her, and she shuddered.

"Azilia?" All these years she had thought of the mare running free, content and well-fed on her island home. It had never occurred to her that Jared would not maintain the condition of the island animals.

"She's alive," Jared replied tersely. "Stays with the other band at the egret pond." He sighed. "Too bad she never had a foal."

"Don't you keep any horses up to ride?"

"I turned them loose, let them go feral when Jenkins, the farmer, left."

"You don't ride anymore?"

"Can't." He patted his stiff leg. "I'm running on the rim! Anyway, there's too much to do." He swerved to avoid a scrawny black-and-white sow and her piglets. "I'm afraid you'll find the horses aren't much. Marsh tackies. Dwarfed and inbred."

At that moment the curtain of lichen-speckled oaks and hanging moss parted to disclose Great Oak.

The jeep jolted to a stop in front of the steps leading upward to the veranda. She waited for Jared to undo the wired-up door and release her.

She had been warned not to expect the house to look as it had in Gramma's day, but nothing had prepared her for the air of neglect that surrounded it. The grape arbor had fallen in. The acres of gardens and the arboretum were a wilderness through which peeked a few rare trees and exotic shrubs that had survived the onslaught of tropical growth. The faint outlines of the terraces that had stretched down to the sound, the peaked roof of the pool house, the broken statuary and crumbling steps, the camellias gone wild and as tall as cabbage palms, and pink, mauve, and white azaleas, untrimmed and growing higher than her head—they were all that remained of one of the most famous gardens in the South.

The replica of the Trevi Fountain Grandfather had ordered from Italy for the center of the courtyard was filled with rubble. Pigs had rooted up the park. Deer, cattle, and horses had gnawed the bark away from the trunk of the Great Oak. Jared told her vandals had stolen much of the statuary and some of the marble slabs leading up to the veranda had been removed for the patio of the new Golden Isles Hotel. The wrought-iron gas lamps were gone and the tongue was broken off one of the great roaring lions that guarded the steps.

As a child, she had considered Great Oak massive, magnificent, a castle where knights and their ladies came and went. Gramma was Queen Guinevere, and Uncle Oomlot, Merlin. But now the house, with its pepper-pot turrets overgrown with vines, looked forbidding, as grim and uncompromising as Jared.

But it was the condition of the animals that shocked her the most. The island cattle, used to drought and hardship, were thinner than she had ever seen them, their ribs showing beneath their rough red hides. The tackies, their tails matted into heavy balls by the swamp clay, looked starved. Even the pigs seemed poorly. The sow with the piglets that had crossed in front of the jeep trotted across the lawn, her empty teats hanging beneath her flabby sides, swinging loosely.

She stepped from the jeep into a pile of steaming fresh dung.

Jared's disapproval was almost tangible as she scraped the sole of her alligator pump against a stone.

When she finished cleaning off the shoe, she walked over to the great oak. She ran her hand over the soft patches of pink lichen that splashed its trunk like paint. It hadn't rained, because the resurrection ferns growing from the long branch, stretching along the ground like the arm of some prehistoric monster, had turned brown, withered, and crumbled, like marsh grass before it dies.

The sun was a crimson ball bathing the sound in fire. As she walked slowly up the familiar steps, she forgot the great house's ruined appearance. It seemed to reach out to her, reeling her back to a time and place when her heart was whole and her island world intact.

"I put your bags in your old room," Jared said. "I'm afraid it hasn't been aired. But then, I didn't know you were coming." The grandfather clock in the hall bonged five. "I'll meet you on the veranda for drinks in an hour. Unless you'd rather rest."

"That will be fine," she answered quickly. "I'm a fast dresser. You learn to be, in the diplomatic."

"I suppose you do. The hot water may take a while. I just got the heater fixed this morning. By the way," he added, "we dress for dinner."

She wondered, looking around the familiar hall, if he was clinging to this last civility as a prop against the reality of the circumstances. For the interior of the house was no more reassuring than the outside had been.

The hall smelled of dust and mildew and the sea. The six-branch brass chandelier was black with tarnish. The floors no longer gleamed with the Dancing Wax spread by Newt's minions on their hands and knees and polished by skating around on flannel cloths. The beautiful old carpets were faded and worn through in spots. The huge chest that had belonged to the same seafaring ancestor who had brought the tea set from Japan was piled high with coats and rain gear. Boots had been tossed into a corner along with walking sticks and part of an old bridle. Newspapers and unopened mail—her letter was probably there—stood on the dusty table where visitors had once left their calling cards on a silver tray.

Her room, the blue room that she had moved into her coming-out year, was at the end of the long second-floor hallway.

She passed Affey's room. She could see her now, her slender body curved as her head bent over her fine sewing, her dark hair hiding her delicate profile like a veil. Gramma's form stood in a corner. There Affey had cut and pinned together the lovely filmy dresses Gramma always wore. She thought of the time Harry the Horror had put pins in the dummy and how furious the old nurse, Dah, had been, saying it would bring on the bad luck she called "bad mouth."

The broom closet was next. A favorite hiding place. And the linen room with its cedar chests marked "Best Linen" for the important guests and "Second Best" for relatives and children.

She pushed open the door of the nursery. Toys lay about in profusion. The music box with its lovely inlaid top was still there. She opened the lid, cranked it up, and the old tinny twinkling strains of "Bohemian Girl" reached into memory through the dust of the years.

She recognized the doll that lay on the floor with one leg missing as the one Constance had thrown at her when she accused her of being a "fraidy cat" for not wanting to climb the great oak.

There was Jinx, the rocking horse with its mane pulled out, on which the cousins first learned to ride; the wind-up toys, a dancing bear and a Lipizzan horse from Vienna that walked on its hind legs; a red fire engine that had belonged to Noble.

Noble of the cheroots and debonair insouciance. Noble, who had tried to kiss her under the mistletoe that long-ago Christmas. Noble, who had left Debby May from Magnolia, Mississippi, and heaven only knew how many other girls eating their hearts out. . . . She continued down the long ghost-ridden hallway to her room.

The wooden shutters, painted with exotic birds perched incongruously on tasseled crimson bell pulls, were closed. She had trouble opening the windows to dispel the closed-in scent of dust and something that smelled faintly of her mother's old perfume, as if after so many years her presence still dominated her surroundings.

Late-afternoon light poured into the old room with its flaking blue walls bordered by pink tiles of primroses. Here, at least, nothing had changed. The terra-cotta parrot still swung on its perch over the desk. Her treasures remained on the mantel—sharks' teeth, tarnished silver loving cups, the bear won at the Starksville fair, and the shell of the pear whelk with part of its lip chipped off.

In the bathroom the marble in the claw-footed tub was black-streaked, like the vein in a shrimp. There was a brown stain beneath each faucet. Water trickled in slowly, leaving a residue of rust and the stench of sulfur. Yet the length of the tub, the gold faucets, and the wicker seat on the commode seemed, at a time when modern plumbing had become as sterile as frozen food, infinitely luxurious.

Warren was right, she thought, when he said that details made the difference between the civilized and the primitive. She had always taken the details at Great Oak for granted. Now she saw with what infinite care they had been attended to: the enamel hooks and painted doorknobs; the Tiffany light fixtures; thick carpets and ample chiffoniers; the upright hat stands, painted to match the rooms in which they stood; the glass-topped, brocade-lined boxes, with illustrations from *Godey's Lady's Book,* on the dressing tables. Details infinite and endless, which, like the total disregard for saving space that characterized the era when the great house was built, belonged to another time and place.

She put on the Pucci pajamas that she had bought in Rome and which were becoming fashionable. She brushed out her hair. The expensive wave was gone, so she put it up, twisting it into a French knot. She applied makeup carefully, and when she studied her reflection in the old flawed mirror, she saw the woman Jared had seen. Magdalena Chadwick, who belonged in Washington and world capitals. Not the Maggie Royal of predawn rides and stickball, of wading through marshes and sliding down banisters. Not the girl in the painting reaching out to an imaginary lover. Seductress or seductee?

Quickly she went through the clothes she had brought. At the bottom of the case she found the long-sleeved jersey dinner dress she planned to wear at the Greenes' on Sea Island. She took off all her jewelry, leaving only the thin gold chain on which the shark's tooth was hung. Then she wiped off her makeup and undid her hair, letting it fall to her shoulders. Once it had been as black as the boat-tail grackles at the dock. Now, on Mr. Charles's advice, it was streaked with his special silver-rinse preparation.

She thought of the night of her coming-out party. How young and gauche and unsure she had felt in the unadorned white Worth gown, how she had yearned for what Mademoiselle called *une grande robe de soir*, something sophisticated and off the shoulders, and Gramma had said: "You're too innocent, Maggie Royal, to follow the dictates of fashion. Follow your instincts. That way you heighten the mystery."

That had been the night Cindy Lou wore the black strapless ball gown from Bergdorf's that looked as if it had been pasted to her figure, and Jared—

"Maggie Royal!"

He stood in the hall below, looking up the stairs. He had shaved and put on evening clothes. In the dim light his white shirtfront gleamed against his dark tormented face. He had a glass in one hand, a cigarette in the other, and was holding himself as rigidly as the marble statue of Modesty on the pedestal in the wall niche at the landing.

She had a sudden sense of unreality. The dinner jacket, the careful pantomime they'd been enacting, seemed ridiculous.

She had one of those sudden impulses one shouldn't have after the age of ten. The skirt of the white jersey was full enough to allow her to throw a leg over the banister as she would have over a horse. In a flash she was sliding down, the skirt billowing around her waist. She intended to land upright. Instead, her heel caught in the hem of her skirt and she landed in a heap at Jared's feet.

For an instant he stood transfixed, staring down at her. Then the green eyes lightened. He bent down to help her up, and they both began to laugh.

"That was quite an entrance," he said finally, holding open the door onto the veranda. "Not exactly a stand-up landing! I bet you don't do that in Washington."

"If I did, I'd be more in practice," she retorted. "The last time was when you brought Sparrow to Great Oak, that first Christmas you were at Harvard. Do you remember?"

"I remember." He looked away. "May I fix you a drink?"

"Do you have any Scotch?"

He shook his head. "Sorry, just bourbon. I don't have many guests."

In Gramma's day the grown-ups sat on the veranda during their cocktail hour to watch the sun set. Now it was peopled with ghosts. It seemed to Maggie Royal she could see President Roosevelt sitting in the wicker chair with the fan-shaped back, the aunts on the hanging swing feeding hors d'oeuvres to Gramma's pet pig, and Gramma sitting so very erect in one of her filmy white dresses and pearls.

"Here you are." Jared handed her a glass. "You never used to drink anything but wine."

"I've changed."

"So I see."

He bent over the tray set on the old wicker tea trolley. Poacher pushed open the screen door, padded across the veranda, and sank down against the wall, resting his head on his paws.

Jared sat facing her. She wished she had a cigarette, and looked at the sun slowly sinking behind the golden grass into the sound.

There was so much to remember, to talk about. Yet conversation was as labored as Poacher's long, drawn-out snore. The ice that had cracked briefly began to harden again. Jared seemed tense, ill-at-ease. He had always been given to brooding silences, but now she sensed something more. Something she couldn't grasp lay behind the taut face, the nervous hands, and odd burned-out look in his green eyes.

The subtle aromatic scent of the yellow jessamine and the sweet heavy smell of wisteria hanging like mauve pendants from the vines encircling the balustrade failed to dissolve the image of decay, which she sensed was not only physical but also of the spirit.

As if reading her mind, Jared lashed out with a sudden violence that was like the thunder and lightning of the summer storms. "So you came to see what a mess I've made of things, to ask me to move out, so you can sell your share, like Susan and the others." He drained his glass and went to the bar tray to pour himself another.

"I came about the painting," she said reasonably. "I saw your exhibition in Washington. Jared, you're a success. A fine painter. People are talking about you. Warren wants to buy the one of me."

His face twisted suddenly. "Maggie Royal, you're very beautiful. You always were. But you're different now. You're not the girl I painted. That girl went away." His voice had the dry, rattling sound of palmetto fronds in the wind. "She's gone from this island and from me."

"Jared, that's hardly fair. We all thought you were dead."

He turned away. "The painting is not for sale."

The park was filled now with green-gold light. The dying sun shafted between the curtains of moss, turning the cabbage palms to what Jared once called Naples yellow. Then the sun vanished, swallowed up in the waters of the sound. The shapes of the animals tearing at the sour, sparse grass became shadowed. There was a sudden grunt as an old razorback boar ran past the remains of the fountain, his long tusks white in the dusk.

Jared downed three drinks to her one and chain-smoked, flicking the stubs over the balustrade.

"Aren't you afraid of fire?" she asked.

"The pigs eat them."

While he was speaking, the black-and-white sow began rooting up the cigarette butts and devouring them.

"My God, Jared," Maggie Royal exclaimed. "The animals are starving."

He rose and began pacing up and down, swinging his stiff leg out in front of him like a horse doing an extended trot.

"I suppose you'd rather see them killed or maimed by poachers." His voice was bitter, violent. "You consider me selfish because I want to keep the island, its animals in their natural state. You and the do-gooders, like Sparrow, believe I should let people come from the mainland, dirty up the island, kill the animals. 'Culling' is the term Sparrow used."

"Sparrow says a National Park is the best way to preserve the island."

"Bodies, beer cans, trash!" He drained the last of his drink and refilled his glass with straight bourbon. "The world's gone mad. Grown men blowing one another to bits. Millions tortured, destroyed. And we call ourselves civilized. We're the only creatures that learn nothing from experience."

She understood why Jared was so vehement about the poachers or anyone killing the island animals. But was his way humane or practical? In Gramma's day the natural predators had been replaced by human predators who came in the fall for the shoots. There had been the annual cattle and pig roundup, and Great Oak and the Long Point community had enjoyed all the beef and pork they could eat.

Private islands had gone out of style. Still, she hoped for a solution. Too many islands, too many old families and noble eccentrics, had already bowed to economic facts. While the slide-rule-and-computer types, the Big Boy Tarringtons who figured out how many acres were needed for apartments and ranch houses, for tennis courts and barbecues, pools and the other appendages of the developing postwar boom, destroyed the marshes and the oxygen necessary for life, people would be told it was the only way to save the islands.

Yet how long could Jared survive, stay stagnant like the island pools, remain static without stimulation, while the animals slowly starved?

"There's been enough killing," Jared said flatly. His face shocked her. It was white and strained, the face of someone suddenly old. He lit a cigarette and continued. "When I was ten, Dad gave me his old saddle gun."

"I remember. We used to practice knocking cans off the fence."

Jared began speaking jerkily, the way he was walking up and down. "The day I hit the silver dollar Joe-Ali tossed into the air, he told me I was ready to go with him to get the deer we killed every fall to be hung and eaten during the holidays.

"We rose in the dark. I remember how cold the floor felt on my bare feet, and how the mist lay over the marshes as it began to get light. In the woods near Ugly's pond we came across a big eight-point buck guarding two does. We crept up on them upwind. They didn't smell or hear us.

"The buck made an easy target. I did the things I'd been taught. I took aim and shot where the heart is. Here, have a drink." He took her glass and poured more bourbon into it. There was a compulsiveness about the way he refilled his own.

"The buck dropped instantly. The does paused, undecided. Then up went their white flags and they vanished into the woods. There was an awful silence. The animal that had been so glossy and proud lay crumpled, motionless. One front leg was bent back under it, and his head lay to one side. His eyes were half-shut, and blood dripped from his open mouth.

"Joe-Ali told me I'd done well. He hauled the deer around, handed me his knife, and told me to gut it. Handfuls of sticky, bloody, slippery intestines!"

His voice thickened. She couldn't tell whether it was from liquor or emotion. "We hauled the buck home. For a long time afterward it hung from a pole, upside down, its legs aspraddle. I told my father how I felt. He said it was necessary to kill in order to keep the deer population under control. But he never suggested I go again, and I think he understood why I didn't eat venison at Christmas."

"Jared—" she began, but he cut her off.

His eyes had a wild look about them. "In Spain, in England, it was the same. Like stalking deer. You didn't say, 'Please come over and let me kill you.' No. You go into the woods, or the bull ring, or up into the sky, and it becomes a slow subtle battle. Kill or be killed. Like sex. Not so much how you maneuver but how you feel."

She had never heard him sound this way before.

"You had to get yourself together," he continued, as if talking to himself. "In order to kill, you had to master your fear, wrap it up inside, so tightly it became a cold deadly rage. A rage to kill! That's when destiny takes over, controls your fate. Your soul becomes one with the soul of your quarry. Like that of the matador when he faces the bull. It's a profound battle of wills. On the ground, in the air. Invisible. When you're ready. When you're finally in range, it is your power to slay that carries the bullet or the knife home. The means with which you kill becomes a projection of the killer's fate. Your fate and that of the killed are intertwined."

He paused, and when he spoke again he sounded very tired. "I've seen deer, pigs, cattle, horses, and humans die. No matter who and what they are, the color of their blood is the same. Handfuls of sticky, bloody, slippery intestines. Hundreds here, thousands there, killed, like ducks or deer in the fall! Rows and rows of dead faces like Gramma's white camellias in the moonlight. The generals and politicians never saw the dogs in Spain eat the legs and arms that were tossed out the windows after amputations. They find no relationship between the bomb that fell on Hiroshima and the immediacy of a deer's mortality, between pulling the trigger and eternity."

The dinner gong sounded.

Jared drained his glass and turned back to the bar tray. She noticed that half of the bourbon bottle was already gone.

"Forgive me. I didn't mean to be rude or bore you. It's been a while since I've had anyone to talk to other than Newt and Poacher." He indicated his glass. "I'm going to take one with me. What about you?"

She shook her head. She'd never seen him drink like this. Not during the bombings or even that last night in London.

"Helps me to paint better," he said defensively as they went into the house.

She thought of Sparrow's comments about his present-day abstracts. "I'm anxious to see your work. Sparrow tells me your new paintings are very interesting."

"You're being diplomatic. Sparrow didn't like any part of them."

The enormous dining room was dark, cavernous. In the shadows the figures in the heavy gilt frames along the walls were faceless. Nobody had taken the leaves out of the long table, and it stretched almost the length of the room. In her mind's eye she saw it set for the ceremonial dinners, the damask and crystal and silver place plates for thirty or forty people.

Now there were two.

Jared formally held her chair and then sat down in what had been Gramma's place at the head of the table.

Almost immediately he stood up again. "Maggie Royal, this is where you should be sitting."

"No, Jared." She picked up one of Gramma's white damask napkins, yellowed with age and with the S monogram torn. "It's more your place than mine."

He seemed strangely relieved as he sat down once again.

Poacher took his place to one side and raised his head, anticipating a morsel.

She noticed that the Peale of the first Stark who had come to Georgia with Oglethorpe was missing.

"I sold it," Jared said, as if reading her thoughts. "It paid to patch the roof and repair the *Great Oak V* when vandals set fire to her at the dock."

"But what happened to Great-Great-Grandfather Jeremy Stark and Aunt Leonie LeFevre?"

"The frames fell apart. I carried them up to the attic." He pointed to the blank space opposite him at the far end of the room. "Your painting was there. I miss it. I didn't want to exhibit it, but the man from the gallery insisted. Now I want it back." His eyes were the green-black phosphorescent color of the grackles' wings as they flew out over the water. "It's the way I think of you."

"Miss Maggie Royal, darlin'. My darlin' little missy!" The door from the pantry flew open and she was engulfed in Cook Ada's arms. "I heered you'd come back. Tunka punka! My darlin' little missy!"

For such an old woman her arms were amazingly strong. Maggie Royal suddenly wanted to stay where she was, with her head pillowed against the gingham bosom smelling of soap and sun. Cook Ada lifted her head and Maggie Royal realized that she was blind. She began to sing, rocking slowly back and forth, as though in a trance. On her face lay the faith and fatality of the blackened idols in the Long Point burial ground.

"Precious Lord take my hand, down at the water's edge. My Darlin' little Missy. May God touch your body. Please, God, touch her body. Touch Great Oak. Take away bad mouth."

Her sightless eyes opened as if suddenly aware of where she was. Briefly a look of terror flashed across her face, as if she had seen Plateye, that most terrible of all evil spirits.

In her blind eyes as she turned away was the Gullah's ancient all-seeing foreknowledge of terror and death. "May God touch your body," she said, pushing open the pantry door.

There was a momentary silence. Into the room came the remembered nightly symphony of the tree frogs, the distant hoot of an owl, the sound of a dish breaking in the pantry.

"Her mind wanders," Jared said. "Newt must have said something. She thinks you're Gramma risen from the grave. Pass it by, as your friend Brenda used to say. She's an old woman, full of crazy superstitions."

Old Newt hobbled in, carrying the gold-rimmed Tiffany soup plates that used to sit on the top shelf of the butler's pantry, in his white-gloved hands. Now he put the plate with the chip in it before her as though it were a newborn baby. His ragged black alpaca was freshly pressed and his cracked black shoes gleamed with polish. As he padded in with the numerous courses that made the traditional evening meal at Great Oak, he maintained a running commentary, mumbling that the "tarrypin" soup needed more sherry and that the cuts of beef Jared bought on the mainland nowadays weren't fit to serve at the Great Oak dinner table.

Yet the wine that Jared poured out from the dusty bottle was a Margaux, mellow and exactly old enough.

"It's a heavenly wine," Maggie Royal commented, sipping it appreciatively.

"From Uncle Oomlot's cellar. One of the last bottles he laid down."

Newt removed the dessert plates and put the delicate Venetian finger bowls used in the past for presidents and special guests in front of them. He had even remembered to float pale pink camellia petals in the bowls.

This is all a crazy dream, she thought. Jared, Newt, Cook Ada, fine wine, chipped Tiffany plates, and petals in finger bowls.

"Did Aunt Emily get the place plates?" she asked finally.

"Somebody did." Jared sounded uninterested. "They weren't here when I got back."

"And Aunt Leonie the Venetian mirror?"

"Probably. Vultures. All of them vultures. All they want is to break up the Island, sell out to Tarrington." He ground out his cigarette and pushed back his chair. "If you're finished, we'll have coffee in the living room.

"Will you pour?" Jared asked formally, setting the coffee tray on the table in front of her. Maggie Royal filled one of the gold-embossed coffeecups. It was chipped and the inside was stained brown.

She passed it to Jared. "Cream or sugar?"

"Black, please." Jared sat down in the wing chair by the fireplace and made a visible attempt at polite conversation. "Maggie Royal, I see your photograph in magazines and newspapers. Your life must be exciting, eventful."

She wished he wouldn't try to keep up pretenses, and then realized with a shock that her life was built on pretense; that exciting, eventful life he spoke of was Warren's, Warren's pattern of living.

"Yes," she answered. "Very exciting, eventful."

"Tell me about it." He leaned forward and for a moment he was the old Jared, concentrated, making her feel that nobody else mattered.

She went into her act, relating anecdotes and experiences that she had stored up to amuse her dinner partners from London to Leningrad. She told him about her first dinner party in Portugal, how Maria went out and met the turkey man walking from Lisbon to Estoril, prodding his charges along the highway with a long stick.

"Maria brought the turkey into the kitchen and poured bourbon down its throat to relax it so that she could wring its neck."

She started to tell him about the White House dinner when the elastic in her slip broke as she was going in to dinner on the arm of the Senator from Georgia.

"Did you say the Senator from Georgia?" Jared broke in. "Son of a bitch had Cullen paroled."

"I didn't know," Maggie Royal whispered, remembering the dinner party, the Senator's remarks about Jared.

"Sure. He's one of the courthouse gang. How do you suppose he keeps on being reelected?"

Maggie Royal gazed around the room desperately, searching for a safe topic. "By the way, where is Gramma's chair, the one with the lions' heads carved on the arms?"

"In the attic."

"The attic must be getting pretty full."

Jared's lips tightened. "What would you have me do? Repair the furniture along with the rusted pipes, keep the horses up for visitors? I haven't noticed you or other members of the family showing much interest."

"Jared, I wasn't accusing you." She stopped helplessly. There didn't seem to be anything they could discuss rationally.

"I'm sorry," he apologized. "I realize it's hard for you to see Great Oak this way. For Christ's sake." His voice was bitter. "Don't think I like it any better than you do, seeing everything go to hell."

"Jared, I have some money. I could lend you some."

"No," he answered violently. "I'm not going to accept help from you. I'll sell some paintings."

She backtracked quickly. "You've become a fine painter, Jared."

His laugh was bitter. "Cindy Lou didn't think so. She hated the island, hated my painting. She called me a cracker Van Gogh." He stood up and walked over to the fireplace. "When the war ended, when I was able to return, I came directly to Stark Island. I planned to live here with Tertius, bring him up to know and love all the things that I did. I discovered that while I was off fighting the war, Big Boy Tarrington had himself appointed legal guardian. I tried every way I could think of to get the boy back. I even agreed to try to live with Cindy Lou again." He paused. She could see the thin line of the scar on his forehead as he went on tonelessly. "Big Boy and the Judge are in cahoots. Big Boy persuaded him that I'm an unfit father. I've appealed. I intend to get custody of my son." His face darkened with anger. "I'm going to have him here if it means going to his school and getting him out."

"Jared, you can't do that. You can't kidnap Tertius." She sighed. "Tarrington is the boy's grandfather. He did take care of him all those years you were away."

"So you're against me, too. You think I'm an unfit father!"

"Jared." She looked at him despairingly. She was suddenly too tired, too upset, to continue. She stood up. "I think I'll go to bed."

"I understand." He sounded relieved to have the evening over with. "That life you lead must be exhausting."

He walked her down the long shadowed hallway, past the closed doors holding their memories along with the broken toys, the linens, the dust-filled corners.

"Good night, Jared. I'll see you in the morning. We'll talk." She put her hand on his arm. Somehow she had to make things right between them. "Jared, it's good to be home."

"You never needed to lie to me before, Maggie Royal." He reached out his right hand. Just as he seemed about to touch the corner of her mouth with his index finger, he drew it back. In that sudden, abrupt way of his, he turned and began walking stiffly back along the hallway. She stood motionless until the strange thumping noise of his footsteps died away.

She knelt beside the bed and said her prayers, first in French as Mademoiselle had taught her, then in English.

Still her tension did not ease. There was something about Jared that was more than disturbing, almost deranged.

After a while she decided it was the quiet that was keeping her awake. The lack of any noise other than that which was natural. Still, she must have slept, for suddenly the sound of a dog barking disturbed her. Someone shouted. Then there was a shot followed by the noise of an engine. Gradually it died away, leaving only the whispering of the wind in the trees. For a long time she lay still, listening tensely—for what, she did not know.

It was still early when she awoke again. Through the window she could see a layer of mist hanging over the bright gold of the marshes. She lay still, waiting for the remembered anticipation of the new island day to begin, hoping for the old sense of silence and space to renew her.

When she came downstairs, Newt was setting the table for breakfast. He was singing one of the old-time songs.

> *Throw me anywhere in dat ole field*
> *I don't care where you throw me in dat ole field*
> *Throw me over hills and mountains in dat ole field*
> *But still my soul is heavenward in dat ole field*

She watched him shuffle around the table, carefully setting out the silver, forks to the left and knives to the right of each place. "Looks like brides and grooms," he used to say.

When he came to Jared's place at the head of the table, he took the knife and crossed it over the fork, leaving the silver utensils in the center of the mat where the plates would be placed. He shook his grizzled head, muttering. "De sperrit never res' in dat grave!"

She wanted to ask him what he meant, but she knew he would never tell her.

Jared did not appear for breakfast. Newt told her he had not slept at the big house. "He stays down at the beach house. Painting, not sleeping."

She asked who had come by boat in the night.

"Poachers, they come nights. Get drunk. Shoot up the animals and leave cans and bottles on the beach. Mr. Jared say he catch 'em, he shoot 'em all!"

"What about the law?"

"Mr. Jared, he de law on Stark Island!"

She asked when he thought Jared would return.

Newt shook his grizzled head, and his face was troubled. "No telling. Mr. Jared full of strange and wild ways. Miss Maggie Royal, 'tain't for me to say, but something goes on in Mr. Jared." He shook his head sadly. "Reckon you got to take the bitter with the sweet in this here life, but Mr. Jared, now, seems as if his been mostly bitter and sour." He paused dramatically and then said clearly, "Miss Maggie Royal, there's a curse on this hyar island, something so wild and strange like the eyes of man has never seen. Nights there's moanings and cries and carryings-on. Can't get help here nohow." He rolled his eyes heavenward. "De Lord's hand lies heavy on Stark Island!"

He returned to the kitchen, and when he carried in her breakfast, his ebony face was once again guarded and unreadable.

He brought juice, scrambled eggs, and grits. "Georgia ice cream!" she exclaimed delightedly. She hadn't tasted any in years.

She sat drinking coffee, watching the glitter of dust on the sideboard where the sun's rays struck the tarnished silver tea set. Through the window she saw the scrawny black-and-white sow and her black-and-white piglets rooting in the ground by the grape arbor.

She returned to her room. She took off the white linen she'd brought for lunch at the Cloister. She went through her things and wondered what had possessed her to bring so many unsuitable clothes, and then she realized she no longer had the kind of clothes suitable for Stark Island. She remembered the chest that used to be on the sleeping porch, the big sea chest where the articles forgotten and left over at summer's end were put away. She found it crammed with mothy sweaters, shorts, old-fashioned one-piece woolen bathing suits, disreputable hats and sneakers.

Suddenly she yearned to go back in time, to bare feet and ragged pants and hair flying in the wind. She recognized the jeans stained with blue paint that she'd worn the summer they painted the sides and hull of *Great Oak III.* She found a pair of sneakers and her old Nardi riding coat. She let her hair hang loose and did not put on any makeup.

"Why, Miss Maggie Royal," Newt exclaimed as she entered the kitchen, "you look the same as when you was a girl."

She asked about Cook Ada, but he warned her she was "feeling poorly." Later she'd feel more like "visiting."

She began filling the pockets of her coat with dried apples left over from the making of Newt's "cider sperrits."

"You gonna peruse?" Newt asked. "Don't you all get yourself lost, now."

"I could find my way blindfolded," Maggie Royal told him.

"Miss Maggie Royal, don' go near High Point." He rolled his eyes. "'Tain't safe nohow."

So Newt still believed in the hants that populated the hanging ground, and was warning her away from that haunted place where hangings and lynchings had taken place.

In the bright morning light his superstitions seemed foolish and unaccountable. The sun was burning through the mist. Intricate lacy spiderwebs clung tenaciously, like small hammocks, to the leaves of the oaks that patterned the ground. Carefully she avoided stepping on them. Dry, brittle brown leaves, pushed out by the new growth that gave the live oaks their name, rained down, crackling underfoot like potato chips.

The camellias that bloomed in February had shed their blooms, leaving mounds of the pale pink petals Gramma loved on the ground. Now it was the azaleas' turn, and they were blooming in all their glory. Those dating back to the first plantation gardens were as tall as the old wire fence surrounding the ruined tennis court. The salmon-pink bush she had always loved was ablaze with blossoms, like fire in sunlight. Over it hovered masses of lemon-yellow cabbage butterflies.

The avenue, now a dirt track, was lined with slanting abandoned outbuildings—the laundry and smokehouse and machine shop. The old Packard touring car and her father's rusted Hispano provided a roosting place for the chickens.

Instinctively she turned toward the stable. The stall doors hung drunkenly. The rows of brass balls that had once decorated the varnished wood paneling were gone. In the carriage room Gramma's landau, the dogcarts and breaking carts, shooting wagons, and the tally-ho stood in varying degrees of decay. Rotting, moldering harness and tack, Sapelo's pride, that he had kept as polished and supple as silk ribbons, lay about in cracked, hardened, mildewed piles. The padding was coming out of the side saddles. Stirrups and billets were missing. The leathers had been used as straps for steamer trunks in which steel bits had been stored in drawers full of sawdust to avoid rusting. One of the trunks bore her father's Cambridge address.

It was a relief to reach the woods. The bearded forest remained unchanged. The jessamine was blooming, filling the air with its delicate fragrance, shedding its blossoms joyously, like yellow confetti, on the pathway. Redbuds and swamp maples brightened the gray-green vista of oak and palmetto and dogwood, soon to blanket the forest in their lacy springtime network.

Her feet made no noise on the sandy track. A wild turkey walked regally ahead. At sight of her, it began to hurry, running awkwardly along the path, reminding her of the market women in Portugal, carrying panniers on either side. She wondered if Jared still called them out, using the wing bone of a hen.

Pigs were everywhere. Almost every inch of grainy, sandy terrain had been dug up in search of sustenance. Red island cattle, their bones jutting out like the hat rack in the hall at Great Oak, stood disconsolately amid the oaks. Even the deer, usually round and sleek, showed signs of malnutrition. She had thought Sparrow was exaggerating when he spoke of the condition of the animals and the sparseness of vegetation. But now she noticed that almost every bit of green had vanished. Even the palmetto fronds had been eaten down to the nub.

Nobody lived in the Long Point settlement now. She hurried along the street, past the graveyard with its broken crockery and carved images. No fresh graves had been dug, and many of the wooden markers had fallen down. The windows of the praise house were broken, as were those of the cabins along the street, their porches rotting away and the once neatly kept yards overgrown.

She came to the ruins of Jared's parents' house on the point at the end of the street. Such a flood of memories swept over her, she had to cling to the sagging gate for support. There was the oak where Susan's cardinal and the blue jay had disported themselves. The tabby walls, part of the porch, where they'd sat that day Jared and Cullen fought one another, and the chimney were all that remained of the house that had been so warm and welcoming.

A shadow fell across her path. A vulture. Glancing up, she noticed several circling High Point. Something must have died. One of the animals, dead from starvation. She shivered, thinking of Azilia. If the tackies were in the same condition as the other animals, she would have to destroy the mare.

Her steps slowed. She dreaded what she would find. Azilia was aged now, almost twenty years old. If it was necessary to put her down, Maggie Royal knew she would have to do it herself. After what Jared had said about killing, he would never shoot Azilia.

The jeep pulled up beside her.

"You didn't come by High Point?" he asked. He looked very tired and there was a smear of paint on his forehead below the scar.

"No." She wondered why everyone warned her away from High Point. "I was on my way to the egret pond to see Azilia."

"That's good." He sounded relieved. "There's a dead steer in the boneyard." He gazed up at the vultures. "Might not be too pleasant. Tell you what." His voice quickened and the green in his eyes lightened. "You can see Azilia tomorrow. Today belongs to us." He leaned over and opened the door of the jeep. "Get in. We'll go to the beach."

"By the way," he said as they drove off. "I was looking for Poacher. Did you see him, by any chance?"

"No. Just the usual animals."

"He's probably off hunting," Jared said. "He does that sometimes."

The great deserted beach blazed white in the sunlight. The sun struck her face and arms, warming, sustaining her.

"There's beer in the cooler, and a can of herring," he said, and his smile was the sudden quick, utterly charming smile of the past.

"You remembered I'm a beer-and-herring girl."

"I remember everything about you." He reached out and touched the shark's tooth on the chain around her neck. "Clams, for instance. You never learned to slurp them off the shell without dribbling."

They sat with their backs against the burning sand wall made by the dunes. The sky was cerulean blue, a "too-good-to-be-true color," Jared said, "like your eyes, Maggie Royal."

They drank cold beer from the cooler and ate the fish from the can with their fingers. She thought of the rain in Scotland, the sea swirling below the ruins of the ancient castle where they'd buried the bottle, their "crock of memories." Her face and hands were oily, her hair wild and tangled. She rubbed the fish flakes from her mouth and laughed. Her sense of strangeness was gone, and she felt as if, finally, she was home.

"What would official Washington say if they could see you now?" He touched her lips. "Sand and oil and good red herring! This is the way I think of you. Not the way you were on the dock. A hat, gloves! Artificial!"

For an instant he stared out across the water.

"Those weeks in hiding. I dreamed of you. We'd have children to inherit this. What else is a beach for, other than children? One that stretches to infinity. Come on." He pulled her to her feet. "Let's go to infinity!" The yellow lights flickered in his eyes, gold and brown on green. Now he was the old Jared, like the current in the sound which nobody could swim against.

She had shed the past along with the hat and gloves. There were only the dunes now, and rippled sand. Matthew Arnold's "shingles of the world," Jared said. It was strange to have to wait for him. Jared, who had once walked and danced so effortlessly, so freely.

He drove the jeep with one hand, holding hers with the other. Waves had pushed back the sand, uprooting the giant oaks in their path. The power of the sea had left a forest of strange, twisted shapes, an inferno of gray-white roots with branches intertwined and molded to them like tormented souls. The trees above the water line clung to the disintegrating earth, fighting desperately to survive the ocean's inexorable march, slowly undermining them, leaving their bone-white roots naked and exposed.

Occasionally Jared swerved the jeep to avoid a living shell or an animal that had wandered down to the water's edge. A thin red cow and her calf moved out of their way. Gulls rose from the water as they passed. There was not a human being in sight.

"'Gator tracks." Jared leaned out of the jeep, staring down at the sand. "Let's follow them."

This is what the world needed, she thought. To relearn faith in ordinary life. The caring about little things. A shell, an alligator track.

The wide flat track led up and over a dune, through palmettos and down a steep descent to the dark pool she recognized as Old Ugly's.

"He's hibernating," Jared said. "Probably won't come out until it's warmer, but we can try." He gave his harsh drawn-out 'gator call. They waited. Suddenly the great reptilian head emerged from the primeval ooze.

"Old Ugly." She was delighted. "I was afraid he'd be dead."

"'Gators are long-lived. I'm not sure how old he is. Been a while since I looked at his teeth." He smiled. "He has a mate." He pointed to a depression by the pool that had been filled in with vegetation. "Her nest is there."

She took a step forward.

He pulled her back. "Have you forgotten? The only time an alligator is dangerous is at mating time. The females set up territories. They won't allow anyone near. She may have eggs in there."

"When will they hatch?"

"In about sixty days."

Gently he turned her away from the pool. His hands began moving down her body. Yesterday all they had been to each other had seemed soiled, outraged. Now it was as she had dreamed it would be, the sun and the sea around them and Jared murmuring, "Maggie Royal. Darling. Tunka punka!"

Her mouth found the warm curve of his neck above the blue shirt collar that was frayed and needed to be turned, and she forgot everything except the ecstasy his body had always given her. It was the way it had been before, back on the island, before Cindy Lou, when the sky had seemed wider, bluer, the wild animals fat and glossy, moving joyously through the woods, and the birdsong louder than anywhere else on earth.

With sudden insight she knew there would never be anyone for her but Jared. At the same time she knew he would never belong to her, to any woman. That at the very moment he held her with violence that crushed and hurt, he was already gone from her. Back to the wild woods and golden marshes, the great oaks and singing birds.

"Let's pretend," she whispered, "that today is tomorrowless!"

Unaccountably she felt him stiffen, like a wild horse the first time a halter is put on its head. "Clams!" he said quickly. "We'll dig some for dinner."

Behind his smile she saw that the tension was back in his face.

On the way to the clam flats they found a small brown wood duck with an injured leg. She held it in her lap. Its soft feathered body was warm against her arm. When they reached the end of the island, she put it in the empty cooler that was in the back of the jeep with Jared's gun and sketchpad.

Jared took off his sneakers and rolled up his khakis. Submerging his bare feet in the gray mud, he bent over and began slashing at the sand with his clam knife. At intervals he reached down, picked up a clam, and slit it open.

"Jared, why don't you roll up your sleeves?" she asked, noting that they were caked with mud.

"I have an allergy," he said quickly. "Here." He handed her an opened clam. "Have you forgotten? Suck it off the shell, into your mouth, like spaghetti."

They washed the clams in the rivulets of water that divided the sand like the tidal creeks that cut through the marshes. When the bucket was full, Jared hoisted it to his shoulder. He steadied it with one hand and held hers with the other as they made their way back to the jeep.

The little duck was there, scrunched down in a corner of the cooler. The day was going, like the changing light. Jared shifted into four-wheel drive in order to navigate the heavy sand up and over and down the dunes to the sandy track that led into the sudden darkness of tangled trees.

A deer leaped across the path, and a mare with a spotted foal. She wondered how to get feed to the horses at the egret pond. She would order it, she decided, when she returned to the mainland. The mainland that suddenly seemed as distant as her other life.

They drove along the avenue beneath the branches bending like cupped hands. The house emerged from its backdrop of oaks and moss, like a face obscured by an unruly tangle of hair. Light struck its many windows with such brilliance that it seemed gold-lit from within.

Jared got out of the jeep and called to Poacher, but there was no sign of the dog. "He never stays away this long," he said worriedly.

He took the bucket of clams to the kitchen and then helped her with the injured duck, frowning in concentration as he splinted the injured leg. Now his hands were steady and sure, his long artist's fingers moving deftly as he secured a flat piece of wood to the tape.

They left the duck in the fountain, with a board to extricate itself from the water, and put chicken wire over it to keep the animals out.

"A hell of a lot of trouble for one small duck," Jared said when they finished, but he was smiling and his face had lost its drawn, tense look. "Time to get cleaned up and have a drink!"

Maggie Royal's skin burned from the sun. She could hardly draw a comb through her hair, matted from wind and the salt air. She thought of washing it, but there were no showers at Great Oak, or nurses, like old Dah, to hold one's head down in a basin and rub it with soap until the scalp tingled.

Jared was waiting. He wore clean khakis and another shirt, a tie, and the old tweed jacket. The opened clams, surrounded by wedges of lemon, lay on the blue-crested Lowestoft platter that had once belonged to a Portuguese king.

"No sign of Poacher?" she asked, sitting down.

He shook his head.

"Surely he'll turn up."

"We'll have drinks and the clams and watch the sunset. Then we'll go to the beach and build a fire. Steak and salad. Poacher will probably show by then."

"I want to see your paintings."

"Later," Jared said.

They watched the green-gold light change to pink-mauve as the animals began moving from the darkness of the forest into the park. The trees looked fake, unreal. The great coiled ropes of vines and curtains of moss hung like scrims on a stage, lit by the new moon that glimmered from above.

"We should have seen it rise over the ocean," Maggie Royal said. "Dah used to say it was bad luck to see a new moon through trees."

They sat cross-legged in front of the fire of fat wood and pine logs that Jared built on the beach. They ate the steaks he cooked and drank wine from a dusty bottle, another relic of Uncle Oomlot's cellar.

They talked and laughed and reminisced until the food and wine were gone. Then Jared rose, put the dishes away in the picnic basket, piled sand on the fire, and called to his dog. Still there was no Poacher.

They got into the jeep and drove the length of the beach and back, but without results.

"We'll go to the beach house," Jared said. "He knows I'm usually there at night."

The beach house had been swept out, the doors and window repaired. There was a drawing board, an easel, and a table piled high with painting paraphernalia. An old pine cupboard stood against one wall. There was a cracked leather sofa with a brown blanket thrown over it in front of the fireplace. A hatch-cover table stood in front of it.

There were shelves of books. She recognized the works of Edgar Allan Poe and John Donne and an assortment of art and nature books. Driftwood was stacked by the hearth. Jared handled the sea-sculptured pieces with care, turning them over, caressing the shimmering silver-gray wood.

"Poacher and I often spend the night here," he said as the fire blazed into life. "Sometimes I paint all night."

She looked at the paintings ranged around the wall and gasped, shocked at their violence, so unlike the island paintings she had seen on exhibition. The dark abstracts looked as if he had undergone a continuing battle with their contents. Color and form were a radical departure from the structured figures and soft romantic pastels of traditional painting. Their power manifested itself on the canvas, deep shades of gray and blue, like the ocean, the numerous greens encountered in the woods, hurting yellows, violent reds, stark whites, and chilling blacks.

"The paintings you saw in Washington were done before the war," he said. "Before I crashed. . . ."

"Can you tell me about it?" Maggie Royal asked.

"I don't like to think of that time. I lost faith in myself. I could stand fear and loneliness and pain for a short while, but not day after day when there seemed no hope of ever being free again." He stared at her, his eyes bleak. "I was willing to do anything to get away from the pain."

"Tell me all that happened after I saw you in London," she said when he hesitated. "Please, Jared. I want to understand."

He went over to the fireplace and stood staring into the flames. "Al Daniels used to tell us that aviation in itself is not inherently dangerous, but like the sea, it is unforgiving of carelessness or neglect. He taught me to leave nothing to chance. Before a mission I checked everything out myself. I was one of the most experienced pilots in our squadron." He paused and lit a cigarette. "I guess it's all right to talk about it now."

"Yes," she urged, "go on."

"England was catch-as-catch-can, a feel-and-touch business. Us old boat pilots were ordered to fly bombers in conjunction with the RAF. After D Day, volunteers were requested to knock out the rocket-launch-

396

ing sites." He drained his glass and continued jerkily. "My plane was crammed with several thousand pounds of high explosives to be dropped on target. We hit a lot of unexpected weather. A monstrous front. Rain you wouldn't believe. So heavy we had to keep climbing to stay level. Things got blacker and blacker. 'This ole bugger don' seem to wanna fly atall,' Bus, my copilot, said." He looked at Maggie Royal and smiled crookedly. "That's when you wonder why you got into this business!"

"What happened?" Maggie Royal whispered.

"We were blown off course. Lost. Somewhere, we hit flak. The plane was as full of holes as a doughnut, and losing altitude. I expected it to blow up any second. I yelled to Bus to jump." He got up and put another log on the fire. "Anything under a thousand feet is pretty dicey. My leg was smashed. I don't know how I managed to unharness my parachute. A woman came running from a nearby cottage, grabbed the chute, and ran back to the house."

"What did you do then?"

"I don't know what happened after that. I don't know how long I was unconscious, a few hours or days or weeks."

He picked up the bottle and poured more liquor into his glass. The wind rose, battering the bleached walls, screaming like the Gullahs' hants. Surf pounded as though beneath the floor.

"Reckon we're in for some weather," Jared said. "I wish Poacher would show up."

"Go on." Perhaps in the telling she could find what it was that had eluded her since returning to the island.

"When I came to, I was in an attic room, in bed. Later I learned why the peasant's wife had taken the parachute. She used it to make a wedding dress for her daughter." He laughed abruptly. "It had 'U.S. Navy' stenciled on it!"

The wind coming through the cracks in the walls blew the smoke from his cigarette into gossamer spirals.

"The woman and her husband were 'dans la combine,' in the underground. They were wonderful to me, those people. They could have been shot for what they did. I've often thought of going back and finding them, thanking them.

"The farm was very isolated and there wasn't a doctor near, or one that could be trusted. Blood poisoning set in. They did what they could for me. They got morphine from the village priest. I was afraid of morphine. I had seen what it did to some of my friends who'd been wounded." He lifted his glass and drank again. "I finally had to take it to keep from crying out with the pain when the house was being searched.

"I'd come down in an isolated part of Brittany. It was one of the last pockets of resistance. The Germans kept up a relentless search for downed fliers. Lots were hiding in the woods. Many died of wounds and exhaustion. The Germans hunted them as if they were foxes in a covert.

They surrounded it, slowly closing the circle. The password 'Cherchi Midi' meant danger. It meant the Gestapo—one in particular was straight from central casting, blond and blue-eyed with a leather jacket and boots—was at the door.

" 'Search for noon' was the signal for me to take the painkiller and remain silent.

"The Germans came almost daily. There'd be a pounding on the door and I could hear them threatening the family. Every so often you'd hear shots. It meant somebody had been stood up against a wall and killed.

"For months I lay in that attic room. I remember constant unremitting hunger and pain. I dreamed. Terrible dreams. Colors moved around in my head, smearing as though on a palette." He stiffened, listening. "Did you hear anything? I thought I heard a dog bark."

"No," she answered honestly. "I was absorbed in what you were saying."

He went to the door and opened it. The night wind rushed in from the sea, blowing ashes from the fire into the room. For a moment he stood calling, "Poacher," a tall, overly thin figure outlined against the night. When there was no response, he closed the door and returned to his seat.

"Poacher's never been gone this long before."

"I'm sure he'll come back. Maybe he's at Great Oak now. Jared, please go on. The dream."

"Yes, the dream. Always the same dream."

He poured himself more bourbon. "I was hallucinating. The colors became live things. A monster with the head and tusks of a razorback hog." He indicated one of the canvases against the wall she hadn't been able to decipher. "Feet of a turtle. Tail of an alligator with a big spiky ball on it, like the ones on the tackies' tails. Only not of clay. Iron spikes like those on the gate of the family cemetery. I knew that if I saw the new moon through the trees the 'gator would hit me with his spiky tail and I would die. If I could only call out! Then I could make the creature vanish. But I never knew when a search would take place, and I couldn't call out without endangering the lives of the people who had saved me. In the dream, I lie there. The new moon flickers and dies. The animal comes to kill me. He has the face of the central-casting German."

She thought of the wounded men she had cared for in London. Their sleep had been haunted by terrible shapes and awful fears that moved in from the dark, flickering over their nerve centers. How many times had she sought to comfort those lying with paralyzed limbs and broken bodies, men yearning for the anesthetic of sleep, at the same time dreading the deeper terror of their dreams.

"My leg wasn't healed," Jared was saying, "but the family became convinced that the central-casting German was suspicious. The village priest arranged for me to escape from the house under a load of grain. I

398

was taken to the town bordello. The girls were wonderful. Somehow they managed to get me morphine, usually by sleeping with the Germans."

He poured the last of the bourbon into his glass and sat down. "I took morphine and painted in my head. I saw the colors, the reds like blood, the vermilions and yellows as different shades of pain." He glanced at the canvas on his easel. "I've been trying to capture those colors, liken them to live things. Sometimes I work all night. But the colors are too sharp, the time too slow. In the morning I throw everything away."

She stared at what seemed to be black trees with the faces of women. Vines were coiled around them, twisting them into strange and tortured shapes not unlike the gray derelicts they had seen on the beach.

Jared narrowed his eyes, studying the painting. "Color's wrong. The color of yesterday changes today."

"Once you said black was a dead color."

"It is," Jared said flatly. "The color of death!"

For a while he'd been the Jared she had known. Now he had reverted to the stranger, as unknown to her as his paintings. In the years they'd been apart, he had changed. Or perhaps he had remained the same. Primitive, basic, and it was this quality bordering on violence that gave his painting its power, and that, she realized now, had given him his power over her. For at the time she was most fearful of his moods and violence, she longed most for his body.

His hand lay at his side, long-fingered, strong, sensitive to splinting a small duck's leg. All those intervening years she had only to shut her eyes to remember the feel of his hands, certain and sure in the knowing.

When he didn't speak, she leaned over and touched his arm. He started, and when he turned to face her, there was such a look of anguish, of despair, on his face that her heart seemed to stop within her.

"When the Americans came, I was sent home. I came back to the Island and saw what they'd done at Long Point. My father had been working to register Negroes to vote. The Klan began burning crosses, doing what they could to harass the black voters. A few nights after Roosevelt's election, some of the 'good ole boys' came to the island and set fire to the house." He paused to light a cigarette and then continued grimly, staring into the fireplace. "It hadn't rained, and everything was very dry. The few Negroes left in the settlement came to help, but they couldn't haul water fast enough. Joe-Ali got Mother out. By then the place was a holocaust. The Negroes tried to keep him from going back for Father. They said Joe-Ali was like a crazy man. He plunged back into the flames. The roof caved in . . . ." His voice broke and he buried his face in his hands.

"Jared," she said slowly. "Oh, Jared. I loved them, too."

He turned to her then. His hand moved slowly, cupping her breast, as gently, as carefully as it had held the wounded bird.

"Maggie Royal, darling . . ." His touch splintered the abstinence she had imposed on emotion, dissolving it into flashes of ecstasy, like the flames of rainbow-colored light from the fire.

Suddenly his grasp became hard and hurting. The strangeness returned, something black and self-destructive.

"Jared, you're hurting me!"

He dropped his hands as if she had struck him.

"I've become a hurter of things. Everything I touch is hurt or dies." His face wore a haunted look. "I need another drink."

He went to the cupboard and opened it. She saw a shelf lined with bottles and pills and syringes. First-aid supplies, she thought. How simple it would be if hurt could be bandaged and made well, longing alleviated by a pill.

He took out a fresh bottle of bourbon, opened it, and poured himself another drink. The harshness of the lines around his mouth deepened as he began to speak, rapidly, with a kind of wild desperation.

"There can't be love without possession, without wanting to be possessed by somebody who makes life less lonely, less black. 'To be no part of anybody is to be nobody,' John Donne said. It's like an abstract form. It must be part of you. The Germans call it *Einfuhling,* a connection between inner reality and the external, an active fusion of affinities." His eyes were like the fire, burned down now to ashes.

Realization struck her, like the wind hurling itself against the house. Possession to Jared meant hanging on to a world long gone, a place of broken dreams he could not let go of. It meant a relationship without a tomorrow. One that could only be destructive, allied with romantic irresponsibility. Always Jared had escaped, to war, to those horizons that lay in the imagination.

A sense of her own hopelessness overwhelmed her. She had been equally irresponsible, weaving dreams as unattainable as Jared's, as a wisp of cirrus cloud in the cockpit of his plane that summer afternoon when they flew high in the heavens, believing the sun would always shine on them, the stars always light their way at night.

"Jared, do you remember Dah's story about leaving the fruit, the yams, outside the door? But not love. 'Dat's perishable!' Jared, I loved you. I couldn't believe you didn't love me the same way. But I never reached you. Not even in Scotland." She faced him despairingly. "It was always as if you'd go away again. Vanish into yourself. Since I've been here, you haven't once asked me about myself. Oh, I know you pretended to listen when I told you those silly stories over coffee, but you weren't really hearing me." Her voice was low and sad. "You left my love outside, to perish."

The little house shook from the onslaught of wind and weather. It seemed to burrow deeper into the dunes, becoming colder and colder. She gazed around the room, wondering irrelevantly what had happened to her father's old polo mallets.

"All day we've been pretending there is no tomorrow. But, Jared, there's always tomorrow, and now tomorrow is today!" A gust of wind came through the cracks in the door and blew the ashes in the fire into a wild dance. "Well, I guess that's that," he said bitterly. "When there aren't any more alternatives, life becomes very simple." He went to the door and opened it. "Poacher," he called, but Poacher did not come. "I'll drive you back to the house and then go look for him."

She took one last glance around the room, at the dark haunting canvases stacked against the walls, the table of paints and brushes, the sand they had tracked onto the floor, the empty bourbon bottles, and the dead fire.

She remembered the night they spent there after her coming-out party, her mother's accusations, when nothing had happened between Jared and herself. She wished now that it had. I was so pitifully ignorant, she thought. Maybe if I'd thrown myself at him then, the way I yearned to. If I had fitted my head in that hollow between his chin and shoulder, shut out the world, things might not have worked out as they have. Life never moves in a straight line. Happiness and holding, blazing up and then dying, becoming gray dust.

Jared undid the wire that held the jeep door shut and helped her into the front seat. He turned distractedly. "I forgot something," he said. "Back in a minute."

When he returned, some of the lines in his face had smoothed. His hands on the wheel were steadier. But his eyes, dark and dilated, held a blackness, a hopelessness, drugs could not dispel.

He drove fast, shoulders hunched, head bent against the wind buffeting the topless vehicle. They left the beach, winding around beneath the oaks. She saw the tabby wall of the graveyard ahead. "I want to see Gramma's grave," she said.

Jared swung off the pine-needled track. Something was hanging on the gate. He jammed on the brakes. "Oh, my God," he said. "Poacher!"

Poacher's body was impaled on the iron spikes. The blood had dripped from it, staining the ground below. Jared carefully lifted the dog off the spikes. The strange blue and brown eyes were half-closed, sightless. Jared stood staring at the bullet hole between them.

"Bastards!" he whispered vehemently.

She took a step toward him, wanting to put her arms around him.

"Don't touch him," he cried out violently, clasping the mangled body to him.

Maggie Royal turned and ran blindly.

As Great Oak rose before her, a strange sense of peace came to her. She'd rolled the dice and lost. Or had she? She straightened her shoulders, aware suddenly of the relief that comes from the end of false hopes, of a divided self. Time now, she thought, to draw another card, keep trying to move ahead. Even if she failed to win the game, she could try to finish with style.

Uncle Oomlot's old Parker was still in the gun room. She found some shells, and, carrying the gun, broken over her arm, started for the egret pond. As she walked, she noticed the vultures circling over the boneyard at High Point. Their number seemed to have increased.

The horses huddled disconsolately beneath the trees of nesting birds. Azilia was almost unrecognizable. Her coat was long and rough and matted with mud, her mane ragged and uneven, her hooves, long and untended. The ball of gray swamp clay had hardened on her tail, almost sweeping the ground.

"Azilia. Oh, Azilia!"

The old mare lifted her head. The fine eyes, once like liquid chocolate, were filmed over with the milky white of opthalmia. The small curved ears and the flash of white on her forehead were all that remained to remind one of the once-beautiful brave head carried like a banner.

Maggie Royal ran to her and threw her arms around her neck. Azilia pushed her head against Maggie Royal's shoulder, nickering softly. The old familiar gesture unleashed Maggie Royal's tears. Now, when there was nobody to see, she was free to let them run slowly, scaldingly down her cheeks.

The walk to the edge of the ravine seemed endless. The rock-hard clay balled at the end of Azilia's long tail swung, hitting her hind legs with each halting step. The vultures seemed to be circling lower and lower as the starved, weakened mare paused to rest. There was the sound of pigs grunting and scuffling and a sickening odor. Maggie Royal was reminded of the ginkgo tree in front of the Washington house. She had forgotten to leave orders to have it cut down.

As they reached the edge of the ravine, the stench became almost unbearable.

It had been a long time since she had used a gun, but the motions came automatically. She loaded it, cocked it, and brought it to her shoulder. It took some seconds for her arm to stop wobbling. She aimed at the star in the center of Azilia's forehead and pulled the trigger.

The sound of the shot reverberated through the forest. The egrets rose, making hoarse high-pitched squawks of alarm. The pigs scattered as Azilia dropped into the ravine.

Maggie Royal choked back her nausea and looked down.

Instead of the dead steer Jared had mentioned, she saw the unmistakable remains of a human body. The thong of a long black whip was taut around the throat.

Maggie Royal backed away. She began to run. It was like running in a nightmare. Palmettos brushed against her. Branches caught at her hair. She stumbled over vines and roots, moving like an automaton.

She had thought the past could not touch her. Now it had converged upon her, overtaking her, blocking the way like the fallen branches that had not been removed from the roads and byways. She had to get away. Escape. The island had become an island of despair.

Just as Jared had destroyed it by attempting to possess it, the island had destroyed him. He had gone wild, become feral, like the starving animals. By isolating himself, blaming others, refusing the demands of other people, declining even to answer their letters, he had run from himself, run to Great Oak to refind himself, and found nobody home.

"Maggie Royal!" Jared clambered out of the jeep, carrying his carbine. "I heard a shot."

She stood paralyzed, watching him walk toward her. For an awful moment she thought he might be coming to kill her, as he had killed Cullen.

"Jared!" she cried. "You killed Cullen!"

"Yes," he answered calmly. "He came ashore and tried to ambush me." Matter-of-factly he went on. "He pulled his gun. I killed him before he could kill me. I thought nobody would find the body until I had time to get rid of it. The Negroes consider the place haunted. Even the poachers don't come here."

He took a step toward her. "Maggie Royal, it's over, finally finished."

The physical attraction he had always held for her still pulled at her. She yearned to throw herself against his chest, as she had against Azilia, and weep for all that had been and what might have been. She forced herself to face him.

The young chevalier with the hunting horn slung over his shoulder, the prince riding through a wood full of friendly animals, had vanished. Now the line of the jaw and the taut mouth suggested terrible bitterness, even a touch of madness. The bones showed through the skin of his face and temples. The eyes, once so green and piercing, had a strange glitter. In them she saw the "acquired sorrow" Gramma had spoken of that hung over the black Starks like mist over the marshes. A pig trotted past, carrying something in its mouth. The tackies stood beneath the trees by the pond, gaunt and starved, their coats as rough as uncarded wool. Over all lay the stench of death.

"Jared, don't you see? This island is doomed. It's a place without a future. Nothing is growing, producing. Do you remember Chatfield? No part of the estate was wasted. Do you remember Brenda's concern for her tenants? 'My people,' she called them. She truly cared. Their lives were part of that land. They mattered. Don't you understand? Affey was less an individual than a possession. Replaceable. Disposable." Desperately she hurried on. "Jared, there's no future in the past. You have a responsibility to this island, this land." She wondered if anything she was saying could reach him. "Jared. *Your* only desire is to possess it. Because you believe Big Boy Tarrington has robbed you of your wife and your son and wants to rob you of your island, you're determined to keep him from having it." Behind his stricken eyes she sensed cold anger.

"So you've sold out, along with the rest."

The bitterness in his voice singed her like a flame. She must escape before the flame enveloped her once again. "Jared," she said gently, "I don't want to be caught up for the rest of my life in this madness. In fire and bloodshed and killing. I have a husband who loves me, who needs me. It won't be as I have loved you, Jared, but I'll know peace of mind."

For an instant they faced each other. The vultures circling overhead cast a shadow across Jared's face, as, very gently, he reached up and touched the corner of her mouth. Then he turned away and began walking to the jeep, slashing at the palmettos with his gun. Silently he drove her back to the house.

Upstairs in her bedroom she looked at herself in the mirror. Warren would expect her to be "bandbox fresh" for Sea Island. Her face was windburned and her nose had begun to peel. She managed to draw enough hot water in the tub to wash off the mud and sand, but there wasn't enough for her to be able to wash her hair. Warren would be appalled when he saw it.

Finally she was dressed, Chanel suit and high-heeled alligator pumps. She closed her cases and looked around the room. The terra-cotta parrot swayed gently on its perch, and the old mirror, cracked and glazed, reflected the light from the rising sun. Her eyes fell on the whelk. She reached up and unhooked the gold chain around her neck. She took off the shark's tooth and laid it beside the shell.

She thought of the things Jared had meant to her, the way he had with horses, the look of his hands as he held a maimed animal, the things he had been reluctant to show anybody but that he had once been able to express in his sketches, the liking for books and the sound of music and rain, dancing together to the records on the Victrola, the scent of jessamine and the sweetness of wisteria, and caring enough about people to be hurt by them. She thought of all the growing-up things, the inside things, like playing Confederates and Yankees and racing each other along the beach, crabbing and clamming and fishing for mullet with Joe-Ali, a whelk shell and a shark's tooth on a gold chain.

There was much she left out, so many corners left dusty and unopened in the cupboard of memory. The green-gold light just before sunset and the dry rattling sound of palmettos rubbing against one another. Azilia's lovely head raised, listening. A white egret flying high over the marsh.

She gave herself a final glance in the mirror. The smile, the eagerness, and the expectancy were gone, like the young Maggie Royal. Somehow, she must relearn to laugh, for Warren's sake!

The plane came on fast, swooping low over Great Oak to alert them of its arrival.

Maggie Royal walked down the steps, holding herself as carefully as Newt carried the Tiffany plates. She was aware of a sense of unburdening, as if a door was slamming shut against the past. The end, or else a beginning. She would be humble. At the same time proud that she had once been a part of those days when the present had been so full it did not seem possible there could be a tomorrow.

She remembered to say good-bye to the great oak. She ran her hand along the corrugated bark, over the pink pockmarks of lichen that now seemed like wounds. The resurrection ferns had undergone their marvelous revival, from brittle dried-up lifelessness to vibrant, living green. As she walked away, she wondered if she could achieve a renewal of life through Warren's love, which she knew now had always been there, as steady and life-renewing as the night's rain.

Jared stowed her bags in the back of the jeep alongside the body of Poacher, which he had not yet buried. He had covered it with an old horse blanket, stained now with the dog's blood.

Maggie Royal clung to the dashboard as he drove recklessly to the airstrip, crashing through the uncleared brush, bouncing over ruts and pig holes.

"Jared," she shouted at his grim profile, "will they come and take you to jail?"

He spun the wheel to avoid a red cow standing in the roadway. "Honey chile, don' yawl worry 'bout me. I'll jus' be here a-settin' and a-scratchin'."

"Jared," she cried desperately, "be serious!"

"They won't prosecute. Cullen had enemies as well as friends. He was trespassing on my property." With a touch of his old confidence he added, "You forget, I'm a Stark!"

It was true, she thought, looking at his beautifully cut tweed jacket with the threads from its frayed lining hanging down and the chamois patches at the elbows. In spite of all that had happened, he still had that Stark quality, that intangible air of authority so often taken for arrogance.

The airstrip had been Grandfather McDermott's nine-hole golf course. Now all that distinguished it from the overgrazed fields was the raveled windsock, hanging disconsolately in the stillness that followed the violence of the night's storm.

Jared braked to a stop. He clambered out of the jeep and unloaded Maggie Royal's luggage and then opened the door for her. "I'll be off," he said. He glanced at the plane circling to land. "Maggie Royal, you may have the paintings. All of them. I'll notify the gallery in Washington."

"Jared . . ." She clutched his arm. "Nothing compels you to stay here, warding off poachers with your carbine. Jared, you can do anything you want. Go to New York and paint, or parachute on the Amazon. Oh, Jared," she concluded helplessly, "don't stay here. Don't stay on Stark Island."

She saw his jaw tense like that of a contrary horse that refuses to accept the bit in its mouth. Already he was gone from her. This wild

405

wood and marsh was his territory. Here on this island his convictions had been formed, taken from the sound of the sea, drawing inspiration from the golden marshes, the hidden pools, the wind and spray and animals, from quick sunlight and impenetrable darkness. And just as the female alligator turned mean when her nest was threatened, Jared would fight off predators, builders, and bulldozers as long as there was breath left in his body.

"I never cared about the things other people care about, Maggie Royal. Being famous. Making money. I was never a good ole boy. I don't want to be pushed into a place where I don't fit." He looked around at the trees, the animals grazing on the airstrip, the ocean stretching to a distant horizon. "This is where I want to be, where I will always want to be." He paused, and then added gravely, "I don't want to hang around the rest of my life and watch it disappear." He smiled then, and his smile was the sudden curiously sweet smile that came like sunlight after a night of storm and violence, melting her heart. "I love you, Maggie Royal. I always loved you. From that first day . . . on the beach."

She stared at him. All those years she had yearned to hear those words, had wanted Jared to want her, to love her in the way she had loved him. Now was the time to tell him about the baby, but something stopped her. "Jared, you never really knew how to love. Sparrow once said that heroes are incapable of caring. Jared, you were a hero." The plane was descending now. There was nothing more to say. She flung her head back. The long column of her neck arched as she stood on tiptoe and kissed him on his cheek.

"*Rien ne va plus!*" She smiled, wrinkling her nose, which was starting to itch. "Jared, the last bets are in." She held his gaze with hers. "It's time we both learned to face the present. You and I." She tossed her head, and her eyes flashed. "We owe it to Gramma to finish in style, to try . . ."

"You always try," he said gravely. "That's one of the good things about you." For an instant the gold flecks in his green eyes flickered, like the reflection from the fire that had blazed up so briefly and then died in the beach house. Then his face twisted into a wry, crooked grin. "Eat your heart out, Maggie Royal!"

He did not look back as he drove off.

The animals that had been grazing on the rutted runway scattered as the little chartered plane that carried passengers from the mainland to the islands taxied to a stop. She could hear Gramma's voice saying sternly, "Maggie Royal McDermott, stand up straight and button your sweater. It's . . . kattywampus." Automatically she straightened her shoulders, made sure her suit jacket was buttoned correctly, and began walking toward the plane.

"Whew!" The young pilot pushed aside the window of the cockpit. "Yawl call that an airfield!"

•   •

The little plane rose into the air.

The pilot wiped his brow with the back of his hand. "That's the last time I fly in there."

Warren was watching her with that tired, worried expression she realized had become habitual. His gray eyes were shadowed, sunken, as if he hadn't slept. In them lay the question to be answered.

Suddenly she felt almost carefree. "Have I told you, Warren, how terribly glad I am to see you? I don't know what I would have done if you hadn't turned up when you did." It occurred to her that she had said the same thing when the ship carrying her to England docked in the blackout. He had been there to meet her. He had always been there when she needed him.

She reached across the distance between them and took his hand. "Warren, we can build sand castles, you and I."

Some of the bleakness in his eyes faded. "Magdalena, I want to be sure that you are sure."

"Dear Warren." She pressed his hand against her cheek. "I was living in a romantic crazy past. You made it possible for me to grow up. Warren, I need you. I've always needed you."

He smiled suddenly, almost happily. It had been a long time since she had seen him look other than tired, worried.

Slowly he drew his hand away and touched her hair. "I like your hair the way it is, Maggie, but what happened to your hat? I always liked that hat."

"Forget my hat!" She reached up and pulled his face down to meet hers. "We'll have children to build sand castles with," she said, and kissed him full on the mouth.

They were starting to descend. Behind them lay Stark Island, a dark green alligator-shaped mass, bordered by a beach, wide and white and empty, stretching to infinity, a beach made for children to play on.

Warren leaned over and took her hand in his. "Darling." He swallowed and took a deep breath. "Darling, Maggie Royal!"

EPILOGUE

Great Oak is no more. Only the chimneys stand as a reminder of a time that will never come again.

Great Oak burned to the ground. Jared Stark died with it. Nobody believed Newt when he testified at the inquest that Jared had dispatched Cook Ada and himself to the mainland and then fired the house. It was assumed the poachers had accomplished their revenge, coming in the night and setting fire to the house while Jared slept.

Today Stark Island is a wildlife preserve. Thousands take part in programs funded by the Chadwick Foundation.

The Gullahs who live in the tin-roofed, blue-painted houses along the rivers and marshes of the Golden Isles will tell you there is a curse on Stark Island. To them the tragedy is not that Jared died but that he died without a proper "setting-up." His charred body was buried inside the tabby wall next to his father's grave. Newt carefully laid out the few articles he could find in the ruins of Great Oak. A silver-backed hairbrush, an empty bourbon bottle, several used-up tubes of paint, and a chipped whelk shell.

This was not sufficient to keep Jared from joining the band of restless spirits that haunts the island.

When there is a new moon the last Stark to live at Great Oak is said to ride an Appaloosa stallion along the avenue, beneath the great oaks that flaunt their hanging moss like funeral veils.

Begun Ossabaw Island, Georgia, 1976
Finished Middleburg, Virginia, 1980

· ACKNOWLEDGMENTS ·

So many people have helped with this book, it is impossible to mention them all. However, I must thank Peter Manigault of Charleston, South Carolina, and the Audubon Society, who checked me out on birds. Eleanor Torrey West, president of the Ossabaw Island Foundation, Georgia, and Albert Bradford, co-director of the Ossabaw Island Project, who provided me with sanctuary and background material; Mrs. Lucy Ferguson and her son O. Ricketson (Rick) Ferguson of Cumberland Island, who also provided invaluable information. The Virginia Center for the Creative Arts allowed me the time and peace of mind necessary to pull this book together.

Some of my Gullah tales and information are from *The Lost Legacy of Georgia's Golden Isles,* by Betsy Fancher, published by Doubleday in 1971.

Special thanks to Dick Reeves for his wonderful Gullah recordings, recorded by Leonard Fulghum's Lenwal Enterprises, Inc., 654 King Street, Charleston, South Carolina, and distributed by John Huguley Co., 263 King Street, Charleston, South Carolina.

(Please forgive me if various Gullah spellings seem incorrect to the reader. Nobody agrees on how certain words, *e.g.,* "kattywampus" and "Plateye," should be spelled.)

W. J. Cash's brilliant book *The Mind of the South* influenced my thinking.

Others who helped with the Stark Island section are Thornton (Doc) Saffer, Talbot (Toby) Talbot, and General Frank W. Norris.

Edward (Shirley) Turner, Colonel Cloyce J. Tippett, Lloyd Kelly, Augustus Watkins, and Ernest K. Gann clarified my memories of the barnstorming days in the thirties.

I could not have written the English section without the help of my friend Joan White Campbell, who lived through the blitz. Mrs. Pat Weldon's tales of wartime foxhunting were invaluable. The late Lady Daresbury, who as Lady Helena Hilton-Green—Boodley—acted as master of the Cottesmore while her husband, "Chatty" Hilton-Green, was at war, and Mrs. Ulrica Murray Smith, longtime joint-master of the Quorn, provided me with brilliant examples of how one should ride across the shires.

Dozens of people typed and retyped and made Xerox copies of large sections of almost illegible manuscript. Helen DeHart, Jane James, Linda Rupp, Sandra Horwege, Peggy Smedley, Joyce Griffith, and Tammie Rose of Middleburg Secretarial Services, Jean Head and Carol Wilson at Simon and Schuster.

Mairin O'Mahony, Gillian Kyles, and Joan Crane, along with their "reading dogs" Lily, Rory, and Dardanelle, read and corrected and bolstered my flagging confidence and energy.

Carroll Kem Shackelford, James O. Brown, Mary Jamieson, Ann Willets Boyd, and Ellin and Dick Roberts gave freely of their time and advice.

Mention must be made of my editors Michael Korda and John Cox as well as Rebecca Head who kept hers when all around her people were losing theirs.

Last and most important—my loving and supportive family, my husband, Nelson; my son Steve and his wife, Penelope; and my son Christopher, who all put this book first, sacrificing their own desires and ambitions and comforts over the years it took to write it.